D0457318

DISCARDED

THE BEST OF McSWEENEY'S

M^CSWEENEY'S
SAN FRANCISCO

www.mcsweeneys.net

Copyright © 2013

Cover art by Eric March
Interior art by Andrés Lozano

All rights reserved, including right of reproduction in whole or part in any form.

McSweeney's and colophon are registered trademarks of McSweeney's,
a privately held company with wildly fluctuating resources.

ISBN: 978-1-938073-59-5

JAN 2 8 2014

THE BEST OF
M^cSWEENEY'S

Edited by DAVE EGGERS and JORDAN BASS

YUMA COUNTY
LIBRARY DISTRICT
2951 S. 21st Dr. Yuma, AZ 85364
(928) 782-1871
www.yumalibrary.org

INTRODUCTION

by DAVE EGGERS

PUBLISHING OTHER PEOPLE'S work is a hell of a lot more enjoyable than publishing your own. Publishing your own work is fraught with complicated, even tortured, feelings. Invariably you believe that you've failed. That you could have done better. That if you were given another month or another year, you would have achieved what you set out to do.

Actually, it's not always that bad.

But usually it is.

Publishing someone else's work, though, is uncomplicated. You can be an unabashed champion of that work. You can finish reading it, or finish editing it, and know that it's done, that people will love it, and that you can't wait to print it. That feeling is strong, and it's simple, and it's pure.

That's what's driven McSweeney's for fifteen years now—far beyond the four or eight issues we originally thought this journal would run. We thought the fun of it would end after a year or so, but that feeling, of finding a new voice, or a new piece by an established voice, and setting it into type and printing it and sending it into the world, is still just as good as it was back when we started in 1998.

Back then, it was me opening submission envelopes in my kitchen, and being astonished that anyone would trust this new quarterly with their work. When I was the only one reading the submissions, I was an easy audience. I was so overwhelmed with the whole thing that I pretty much accepted every other story. And then I couldn't wait to get them into print. I would usually accept a story and lay it out the same day. If I couldn't get a digital version of it soon enough, I would just retype the whole story and lay it out that night. This is what I'm talking about: this simple and good feeling of knowing you'll be able to introduce a new writer to new readers.

Early on, most of the writers in McSweeney's were lesser known, or were starting out in their careers. After a few issues, we began getting work from some established authors—even without asking, which was startling—and since then, our goal has been to balance these known quantities with the newcomers, and balance both of them with an eye toward occasional experimentation—some of these experiments improbably successful. Sometimes these commissions were simple acts of matching a great writer to unusual subject matter. Thus we sent Andrew Sean Greer to a weekend NASCAR rally in Michigan. Sometimes these commissions were based on iffy notions that yielded great results—for example, when we asked dozens of writers to each write a short story in 20 minutes. In one issue we asked our writers to write stories based on the notebook jottings of F. Scott Fitzgerald. In another we asked them to help resurrect dead forms like the pantoum and biji.

But most of what we've published over the years has simply come through the mail. We still open every submission envelope, and each time we do, we want to be surprised, we want to be reawakened. I'm rarely the person opening these envelopes anymore, but the other day, while talking to the volunteer readers about the responsibility entrusted to them, I found myself using the word sacred. It was hyperbole, I'm sure, but here's what I meant: it takes a particular mix of madness and courage to write short stories—they do not pay the rent, they are not widely read—and it takes even greater courage to put them in the mail, submitting them for judgment by strangers. So thinking about these senders, batshit-crazy and full of hope and dread, and the fact that they would entrust our readers to judge their work, and for us to print their work, I used the word sacred. It still seems right in some way.

Art is made by anarchists and sorted by bureaucrats. Thus, over the years, there have been a few bureaucrats who, feeling the need to categorize and label, have posited that McSweeney's has some house style. But this is not the case. Even the earliest issues, which even I assumed did lean toward the experimental, always balanced these formal forays with more traditional storytelling. Issue Three, for example, included a story by David Foster Wallace that we ran on the spine, but it also featured a 25,000-word essay about a writer's correspondence with Ted Kascynski. This balance has held true ever since. We've sought to publish the best work we can, no matter its genre or approach or author. We've published everything from oral histories from Zimbabwe to experimental prose-poems from Norway. The only thing common to all in this collection, to the work in every one of our 45 issues so far, is that the work was good and told us something new.

Some years ago, I was in Galway, Ireland, and happened to meet a man named Timothy McSweeney. I got to know him and his wife, Maura, who also had the last name McSweeney. We talked about a writer she liked, and she said, "He writes like he's seeing the world for the first time." That's what we look for—writers who make us feel like they're seeing their world, whatever world that is, with fresh eyes, and who allow us to experience it through their words.

This collection is called Best of, and to some extent that's true—this volume includes some of the best writing we've put out—but there are many dozens of great stories missing from these pages. This anthology clocks in at over 600 pages, and getting it down to even that bloated number was tough. Though we could have filled 1,000 pages with great and more or less traditional short stories, we sought here to represent both those stories and also the range of special projects and commissions that we've published over the years. So you'll see samples from our genre-fiction issue, edited by Michael Chabon, from our comics issue, edited by Chris Ware, from our dead-forms issue, edited by two interns, Darren Franich and Graham Weatherly, and our South Sudanese fiction issue, put together by Nyuol Tong. Undergirding it all is plain great writing.

Some housekeeping items:

- This collection represents work published only in the McSweeney's quarterly, which has appeared, assiduously, three times a year since 1998. The website, which is a humor-based operation, is a very different entity, edited by unsavory people who work alone and without praise.

- Starting with Issue 2, the quarterly had part-time, unpaid help from Sean Wilsey, Todd Pruzan, Diane Vadino, and Lawrence Weschler. Later, given the generosity and faith of our subscribers, fulltime help was affordable, and so entered Eli Horowitz. He was the first paid editorial person at our company, and he edited a huge chunk of the best work we've published. Since Issue 23, the primary editor of the quarterly has been Jordan Bass. Mr. Bass has been the day-to-day workhorse and visionary who has guided the journal, and has endeared himself to many a writer with his great sensitivity in bringing their work into print. I want to thank Eli and Jordan for keeping the quarterly so good for so long.

When I think about fifteen years of McSweeney's, the overwhelming emotion I feel is gratitude. For the staff who has kept the machinery working, for the readers who have supported us, for the bookstores who have stocked us, for the writers who have given us their stories. It's a strange and improbable thing when a literary quarterly lives this long, and we don't take it for granted. Thank you kindly.

{Below find some of our favorite letters, commissioned and otherwise, from the first forty-five issues of the journal. They are no longer in chronological order.}

DEAR McSWEENEY'S,
Well, I've arrived here in Paris! *McSweeney's* first foreign correspondent! Haven't had a chance to leave the apartment yet, but I'm telling you, I simply cannot wait to tackle this amazing city! A dream come true! Very, very, VERY excited! Europe, here I come!
MIKE SACKS
PARIS, FRANCE

DEAR McSWEENEY'S,
The older I get, the more I realize how the breadth and depth of most human conversation is very limited. I mean, I meet my friends at coffee joints like everyone else, and we have the usual parley—"I can't go on; I'll go on," etc.—but there really isn't room in most daily interchanges for the important topics, the meaningful ones, that make life worth living.

You know something I think about that I can't say to my friends over coffee? I can't say, You know, I'm not sure I believe in the power of the written word anymore. I can't say, Look, there is only one good book that has ever been written and it's a hundred and fifty years old and its name is *Walden*. Do you know how good *Walden* is? It's so good that we should eat it. It's so good that it should be ground up and sprinkled on our food. It is so good that every letters-to-the-editor page in every printed-on-paper newspaper around the world should be replaced with quotes from *Walden*:

A slight sound at evening lifts me up by the ears, and makes life seem inexpressibly serene and grand. It may be in Uranus, or it may be in the shutter.

That is so good it is insane.
Here's what I think: I think we are coming into a new era, an era in which the written word won't matter much anymore. What will matter in the future is not what we say with words, or what we write with words, but what we do with words. And I have an idea about that: I think words should go on toast. I think one word in particular should go on toast, and then we should eat that word/toast every day and say that word all day long.

The word I have in mind is *peace*, but I don't know how to get that on my toast, so I am experimenting now, like Thoreau, with what I have at hand, with what is around me, with what is available. I have gone to my high-speed Internet connection, which has in turn directed me to the NFL online gift shop.

Now this is what you do, to create a peace-toast word-world, for yourself, in your home. First, go online to the NFL gift shop and purchase two toasters, each of which will emblazon your toast with the emblem of an NFL team. You must buy toasters with the emblems of two rival teams. If you pick two teams that never play each other, the experiment won't work. I myself have purchased one toaster for the NY Giants, and one for the NY Jets.

Each child in my house, each morning, sits down to a Jets–Giants Nutella-toast sandwich. I have three kids; that means at least six pieces of toast each morning. Sometimes ten.

I stand over them while they eat.
Taste the chocolatey, hazelnut goodness,
I say. Taste the sweetness between bitter
opponents. Taste the flavor of the pieces/
peaces of wheat bread that are also a book
that also offers you chocolate, a book that
is food, which is words, which are right
now connecting you and other people on
Earth in a fabulous, sticky, and slightly
incomprehensible way. Savor the ineffable,
Walden-esque, chocolate-toast bookword,
here at this Sharpie-scarred dining table
in New York City, and know, as you wipe
the crumbs off your mouth, your simultaneously big and small place in the task of
transforming this strange world.

Then I say, Now go and get ready for
school.

AMY FUSSELMAN
NEW YORK, NY

DEAR McSWEENEY'S,
I have a common name. According to some
estimates, nearly 40 percent of men are
named "Tom O'Donnell." I once shared
an airport limo with two other Tom
O'Donnells. In the time it took me to write
this sentence, chances are you named at least
one of your children "Tom O'Donnell."

This would all be fine if it were still
Bible times, but today it's a problem.
Why? Because it's basically impossible to
Google myself. I'm tired of searching for
"Tom O'Donnell" and coming up with
Irish politicians. It's like, "Okay, sure, you
were a member of Parliament, representing
West Kerry from 1900 to 1918, who
fought for agrarian reform. We get it."

At least the Irish politicians are famous.
What really bugs me are the legions of
anonymous Tom O'Donnells, with their
"law firms" and their "medieval studies,"
standing between me and the first page of
search results. You could argue that I am

not famous and haven't done anything
particularly notable with my life, either,
but I would counter that that's a really
mean way of putting it.

Ultimately, my name's popularity is
hurting my overall brand. It's served me
well for more than thirty years, but I've
decided to change it to something else.
I've narrowed down my list of potential
replacements to the following six:

Vladislav Fukuyama-Gomez: I love names
that combine several different ethnicities,
because they're used in movies to tell you
it's the future.

Tom O'Donne11: I've replaced some of the
letters with numbers, but look closely—it
still kind of spells "Tom O'Donnell." Do
you see it now?

Dennis Pulley: I can think of no better way
to honor my great-grandfather's memory
than by taking the name of the man he
killed.

Jimmy "The Hammer" Graziani: I like this
name because it makes it sound like I own
a hammer.

G'torthax of Saldur: This is my Dungeons
& Dragons character's name. In some ways,
it would be an easy transition, because
I already make everyone I know call me
this at all times.

QUIZNOS® Presents Todd DeMoss: Sure,
it's a mouthful—but so is the delicious
Chipotle Prime Rib sandwich, only
available at QUIZNOS®.

Please conduct some sort of poll or
contest or tournament to determine
which of these will be my new name,
and then devote the next issue of your

journal to presenting the results in the most dramatic way possible. In the event of a tie, I will rename myself "Dougie Delicious." Thanks,
TOM O'DONNELL
BROOKLYN, NY

DEAR McSWEENEY'S,
Out of here. Just didn't like it, truthfully. Will be back in Brooklyn day after tomorrow, if you need me for anything. Thanks for the chance.
MIKE SACKS
PARIS, FRANCE

DEAR PHOEBE,
You know that moment of resignation when you know you're just about to get hit in the face? Well, you don't. You're fifteen months old. But you will. I wish I could protect you from it. I'm sorry to have to tell you this. Anyway, I've been approaching life lately with this sort of useless, too-late flinch on my face—waiting for the inevitable punch. Since you and your beautiful, red-haired mother left, I've been in a bit of a lonely daze. Tired but sleepless. The house too quiet. At night I tried running up and down the stairs to make some noise, but that didn't work. All I'd wanted was some peace to finish a book that I will never finish, and there it was—and so of course I began going out of my skull. Four and a half Schlitzes at the Mill didn't help, either. So here I am. I arrived the day before yesterday. Brother Francis greeted me after Vespers. He sat me in his office and he explained how things work around here. He handed me a paper with the schedule:

VIGILS: 3:30 A.M.
LAUDS: 6:30 A.M.
MASS: 7:00 A.M.
READING/PRIVATE PRAYER: 8:00 A.M.
TERCE: 9:15 A.M.
WORK: 9:30 A.M.
SEXT: 11:45 A.M.
LUNCH: 12:00 P.M.
NONE: 1:45 P.M.
WORK: 2:00 P.M.
READING/PRIVATE PRAYER: 4:30 P.M.
VESPERS: 5:30 P.M.
READING/PRIVATE PRAYER: 6:00 P.M.
SUPPER: 7:00 P.M.

"Everything's optional," Brother Francis said. "But if you're going to skip a meal, let me know and I'll inform the cook."

"Everything optional?" I asked.

"For you. Not for us."

"I don't have to do anything, go to anything?"

"You sound disappointed."

"I was hoping—" I wasn't sure what I was hoping. "I was hoping you'd whip me into shape."

Brother Francis stared at me. Then he squinted at his watch. He's a kind man, used to lost souls wandering in here day after day, but he's also busy as hell.

"I'm Jewish," I apologized.

"Why should that matter? We welcome all creeds here. Last week we hosted three Hindus on retreat." He threw me a bone. "We do lock the door at ten."

"Awesome."

"But if you should find yourself locked out, you can always hit the bell outside the front door, and the night porter will—"

I didn't last long, not being locked up. I still needed to at least *pretend* to escape. So this morning, after Lauds, I drove to Dubuque to get a cup of coffee. Nothing against the coffee here. It's actually pretty good. And there's a coffee room where you can get it 24-7. Just like at the Comfort

Inn. Even so, I had to run from something. Spring has finally come to eastern Iowa and the fields are green, jungle green, the sort of carpetish green that makes you want to roll around out there with someone you don't know. Perhaps this is an inappropriate thing to say. (Shmoo, don't share this with anybody beautiful and red-haired.)

In Dubuque, looking for the Starbucks, I drove down Grandview Avenue where the bright yellow recycling boxes gleamed in the driveways of house after house. I tried to have a spiritual experience over those recycling boxes. It nearly worked. You should have seen them. The people of Dubuque never forget to put out the recycling and they always sort it very well, too—in very yellow boxes.

So, as I said, the lie is that I am here to finish a book I know I will never finish. At some point, I may actually work on it. In the meantime, I am sitting here in the monastery library reading François Mauriac's *Life of Jesus*. Mauriac says something interesting in the first chapter, which is as far as I have gotten since I keep putting the book down to think of you. Mauriac says that the Bible says nothing at all about those years that the carpenter Yeshua, son of Mary and Joseph, lived in the straggy village of Nazareth, of which there is no mention in history and which the Old Testament does not name.

> There he lived for thirty years—but not in a silence of adoration and love. Jesus dwelt in the thick of a clan, in the midst of the petty talk, the jealousies, the small dramas of numerous kin…

This doesn't sound so bad compared to being nailed to the Cross. Let's hear it for small dramas. Send a little my way, Jesus! But back then, of course, he wasn't the world-famous Son of God. No, wait, he *was* the Son of God, even then, it's just that nobody knew it. Did he know it? Or did he just feel that there might be something on the horizon besides carpentry? Mauriac also says Jesus was one of three carpenters in Nazareth, and he wasn't even considered the best. So maybe he felt he had to branch out into another line of work just for the sake of doing something different. You know, make his mark another way. So he started making miracles, and that was the start of it. Or the end of it, depending on how you look at it.

But before all that, Mauriac imagines what Jesus and Mary might have talked about for all those years over the dinner table after Joseph died. There she was, sitting with the future King of the World, "whose reign shall have no end," and she knew it. But Mauriac says there must have been times over those long years when she questioned the prophecy. All that time, she kept it to herself. He conjectures that they must have talked mostly about tools. I like that. It's probably right. When in doubt, talk about tools.

One last thing: The monks here at New Melleray are famous for their coffins. In the gift shop they sell jam, hymnals, used books—and coffins. They are beautiful coffins made of walnut.

PETER ORNER
PEOSTA, IA

DEAR McSWEENEY'S,
My New Year's resolution is usually to "get healthy" or "exercise more." But since the world is going to end in 2012, my resolutions are a little bit different this time around:

1) Gain one hundred pounds
2) Try every drug in the world

Now, I know what you're thinking: "Yes, the Mayans prophesied that the world would end in 2012. So your resolutions make a lot of sense. You are smart and those are good resolutions."

Thanks. Here are some more resolutions I'm going to do if I have time before the world explodes:

3) Try that KFC sandwich that has fried chicken instead of bread
4) Say the meanest things ever to my friends, things so shocking and hurtful I could never take them back
5) Gain fifty more pounds
6) Do the weirdest sex things I can think of, things so weird I won't even really want to do them, but it'll be like, "Well, this thing I'm about to do is really crazy and I kind of have to fight against my nature to do it, but the world's about to end and I might as well have all the sex experiences I can have while I'm still inside this human body."
7) See Paris

Again, I know what you're thinking: "Those resolutions are good. The sex one in particular makes a lot of sense. You shouldn't be ashamed about trying weird sex things, because we're all about to die and you might as well. You are still a good person, no matter what happens."

Thanks,
SIMON RICH
SAN FRANCISCO, CA

DEAR McSWEENEY'S,
I live in St. Paul, Minnesota. A nice place where God tries to ice-murder all inhabitants every year. If you survive, you have defeated God, so that gives you a nice boost of confidence heading into springtime.

On a recent spring day, I took two of my three kids to see a Minnesota Timberwolves basketball game. I encourage my kids to follow the exploits of the Timberwolves—they can be very instructive. The Timberwolves' players are not generally all that interested in playing basketball, and you get the sense that they are only playing the game to get a little exercise so that when they adjourn to play Xbox for the rest of the night, they won't feel so guilty. I tell my kids not to make the wrong choices in life or they could end up playing for the Timberwolves themselves. I did not take the third child to the game, because she is too young to be exposed to such things.

Prior to the game, we decided to stop for dinner at the Subway restaurant on Fairview and Grand Avenue in St. Paul. You know the one. It's by the movie theater and kitty-corner from Whole Foods. We like Subway. My son gets the meatball sub so he can drip sauce on his shirt and look like a slob all day. My daughter enjoys a turkey sandwich so bereft of additional ingredients that it's a crime to pay what I do for it.

After she ordered her turkey sandwich, I thought turkey sounded pretty good too. So here's what I did: I ordered a turkey sandwich with Havarti cheese. Turkey and Havarti. One of my favorite combinations. Can't go wrong. A surefire winner.

But the order did not fire sure. It was not a winner. "Turkey and *what*?" asked the incredulous sandwich artist.

"Turkey and… Havarti? You don't have Havarti, do you?"

"I don't even know what you're talking about!" she said with kind of a chuckle. "That's not a real thing, is it?"

"Of course it's a real thing," I stammered. "It's Havarti cheese. It's creamy and delicious and goes well with turkey."

"*Havarti?*" she asked, turning to her fellow sandwich artists, who offered only confused expressions and shakes of the head.

She thought this: I had entered a Subway with two young kids, decided to make up a complete nonsense word, and pretended that it was a form of cheese. This, deduced the sandwich artist, was a choice I had made.

McSweeney's, have you ever been in a situation where you're telling the truth but someone doesn't believe you? And the more you insist on the truth, the more it sounds like you're lying? This was me. I had to defend Havarti's existence. But it's as if I was defending a legitimately fictitious cheese. "Do you have any Blamptonshire cheese? How about Flogvers? Or a lovely slice of Greevenheimer?"

It was at this point that I thought about hauling the kids across the intersection to Whole Foods, where I'm sure Havarti could be had, and buying a slice just to bring back. I might have even done it. I'm kind of a jerk like that. But then I worried that maybe I was a snob. I never thought of Havarti as being an elite cheese, a cheese for the cheese cognoscenti—but did I truly understand what made a cheese elite, *McSweeney's?*

A Subway is a hell of a place to have an existential crisis. I told them fine, pepper jack. Whatevs, you know?

We went to the Timberwolves game and they lost badly to the Phoenix Suns as thousands of Minnesotans watched. It was a grim, self-flagellating exercise.

Okay then, *McSweeney's*. Bye. I love you.
JOHN MOE
ST. PAUL, MN

DEAR McSWEENEY'S,
Medical dramas are hot right now, there's no denying it. I've been pitching shows to one network after another, drawing up little sample posters for my presentations to show the execs how they'd be able to market them. Unfortunately, there haven't been any bites yet, and I'm running out of options. I know that television production isn't what you do, but you seem like you might have friends who can make things happen, so I figured it was worth the stamp.

Okay, so the first one is called *Doctor Baby*, and on the poster there's a picture of a baby dressed as a doctor. Cute, right? But here's the hook: the show is actually about a doctor named Frank Baby, and he's a charismatic neurosurgeon.

Another idea is for a show called *Dog Doctor*. That poster has a dog who is dressed up like a doctor, but the show is about a pediatrician who is actually a baby. I think it could be big.

The last idea I have is called *Dog Baby Doctor*. That poster is sort of a combination of the last two, with dogs and babies dressed like doctors all over the place. That one is exactly how it sounds. Hope to hear from you soon,
STEVE DELAHOYDE
CHICAGO, IL

DEAR McSWEENEY'S,
I used to think only poor people set fires. Two reasons for this: (1) I'd never known anyone whose house had burned down, and (2) when I worked for the Social Security Administration, "It burned up in a fire" was a common response to my request for documents. Marriage licenses, birth certificates, W-2s, DD-214s—they had all burned up in fires. And then I started setting fires, and the people around me

started setting fires, and I saw that it wasn't that hard: put a cigarette out in a worm farm; don't clean your stove; spill food while cooking.

The first one was the worst.

It was summer and my very sexy boyfriend and I were half-naked on my balcony, which was high up and decorative, and which housed my roommate's worm farm. I wasn't really a smoker, or I only smoked when I drank, which was something this boyfriend had me doing more and more of. I remember thinking that I was so high up no one could see how little I was wearing. It was the kind of night where all I'd remember in the morning was moving from room to room.

So we were up there on the little balcony we shouldn't have been standing on when I slipped my cigarette into a perfect cigarette-shaped slot in one corner of the worm farm, which looked a lot like an empty pot for a plant. I didn't know it was full of shredded newspaper and chemicals, which meant that it was basically an explosive device. We'd gone back inside and started making out on the floor when I saw the flames.

For a while after that I followed my boyfriend around screaming while he filled a trashcan in my shower and ran back and forth to the balcony. But the water pressure was bad, and he didn't seem to be doing much. Finally, because I was getting in his way, he gave me an assignment: "Find my pants." I made an attempt, but it proved to be beyond my capabilities, and he grabbed a towel and wrapped it around his waist. Then my landlord came bounding up the stairs in his boxer shorts with a fire extinguisher and then the firemen arrived. All the while the alarms were going off and the red lights were flashing.

One of the firemen said: "Who puts a cigarette out in a box of newspaper?"

A month later, my boyfriend got a bill for about ten thousand dollars. We broke up shortly thereafter.

When my roommate returned from India, she said, only half-jokingly, "One thousand souls lost." She wanted me to get her a new farm, and I said I would but I didn't and we don't live together anymore. There's no way I'm buying that bitch a worm farm now.

Sincerely,
MARY MILLER
JACKSON, MS

DEAR MCSWEENEY'S,

One question I get a lot is, *Ellie, how the hell are you such a genius at giving maid-of-honor wedding toasts?* Another question I get a lot is how to spell *Ellie.* To the first group I answer, *Well, I've had a lot of practice—and a lifetime of best friends.* To the second group I say, *Here's an idea: why don't you just start spelling and see what you come up with, Buddy?* I get pretty fed up with people pretty fast.

Was I born amazing at giving maid-of-honor toasts? Of course not. Was Mozart born amazing at composing symphonies? Yes. One thing you can say about both Mozart and me, however, is that both of us wore ponytails well into our twenties. Another thing about both Mozart and me? We both practiced the hell out of our respective crafts. You'd give Mozart a spare five minutes and you'd find him down in the palace basement, furiously scribbling some song or another. You give me a spare five minutes, and I will think about how many calories were probably in the portion of LUNA bar I just ate. Then, if I have any time left, I will try to remember whose wedding I am attending this upcoming weekend.

The formula for a solid maid-of-honor

wedding toast does not exist. Not unlike snowflakes, every one of my brides is unique, and—for the most part—white. Accordingly, every bride requires her own unique toast. Nevertheless, there are a few extremely general rules that I follow.

About four months before or on the airplane flight to the wedding, I will hunker down and reflect on the friend I'm writing about. The first thing I'll do is write down her name. Then I'll make a note in the corner reminding myself to find out her middle name. Next, I put on those big Bose noise-canceling headphones and close my eyes. I usually wake up about an hour or so later, feeling pretty refreshed and ready to hunker down and reflect on the friend I'm writing about.

At that point I try to think of some of the phenomenal times we've had together. This is the part of the process where my brow really furrows, and I ask the stewardess for a ginger ale, no ice. If any unforgettable moments spring to mind, I immediately write those down. I've never claimed to have the best memory in the world (at least, I don't think that I have), so often I have to furrow my brow for quite some time. Slowly but surely, though, some pretty amazing and unforgettable memories begin to saunter in: amazing times in Cabo San Lucas; phenomenal nights in Las Vegas; unbelievable conversations at the Theta dinner table; unforgettable lemon bomb shots at the Are You Out Or Inn; priceless hangovers in Palm Springs; insane nights in Miami; unforgettable evenings at the beer garden in Queens; phenomenal tofu we've ordered. By the time I've finished, I'm sitting in a pool of my own damn tears, and I have some pretty heavy explaining to do to the rest of the passengers in my row.

Following the delivery of my toast at the wedding reception, there is anywhere from one to fifteen minutes of silence. The fifteen-minute silence usually only occurs when the person who is supposed to give the next toast is in the bathroom (which happens more often than you'd think). As my audience slowly shakes itself out of its collective awe, one guest begins to clap. Then, his or her significant other begins to clap. Then the rest of that particular table begins to clap, followed by the table next to that table, and then the band or DJ, and then the table next to the band or DJ, and so on and so forth until the entire reception hall is nothing more than a big sloppy mess of applause. *I wish I could do what she does,* I can hear their silent thoughts thinking. *I'm going to go home and practice my speech in front of my mirror, like I used to do after Miss America, or CrossFire. I hope she can't hear me right now.*

But they can't do what I do. And, news flash, I *can* hear you right now. So hear me right back: Maybe in no fewer than ten thousand hours you could do what I do. However, that is a hell of a lot of hours, and you will probably be dead by then. Unfortunately for you, Ellie Kemper doesn't know the first thing about giving a eulogy.

Let us raise a glass!

ELLIE KEMPER
LOS ANGELES, CA

DEAR McSWEENEY'S,
I have recently become an expert on the subject of red wine.

Unfortunately, like many people, I was intimidated by red wine. It has so much complexity, history, and nuance that some people believe that it can only be enjoyed by scholars and wealthy narcissists.

But this is not true. For while red wine is noble, it is also humble. It is the simplest recipe in the world, requiring only grapes, yeast, human feet, and time, plus an enormous amount of pharmaceutical-grade pseudoephedrine. If you are going to make it at home, you should probably own a handgun and some really violent dogs. This is how the European peasantry has made and enjoyed wine since 6000 BC. In quaint mobile wine labs, with thatched roofs, that still evade capture today.

In Europe, red wine remains a part of life. While we in the U.S. have long demonized alcohol, most Europeans are always drunk, and will frequently enjoy a glass of red wine even in the middle of one of their many naps.

In France, children do not hide their drinking. They join their parents at the dinner table, where they are served red wine, because it is believed it will make the children more sexy.

So how can you learn to enjoy red wine like the sexy French children?

It is easy.

Of all the varieties of wine—white wine, red wine, box wine, prison-toilet wine, and sparkling "Champagne," or "French Thunderbird"—the best kind of wine is red wine.

Named for its color, red wine has the most healthful tannins and antioxidants. This is why the baby boomers love it. For doctors agree, if you drink red wine, you will become immortal. You will start to look prosperous and self-pleased and salt-and-pepper-bearded, and you will learn to tell long, pointless stories that go nowhere because you love the sound of your own voice. To your health, rich dad!

Red wine also offers the greatest depth of flavor, ranging from the bright berry, ozone, and burnt hair notes of a jammy Cabernaz Beausoleil, to the luxuriously pungent Argentine velociraptors, with their end of bitter chocolate and chewed-up aluminum foil and fried crickets. These wines have the viscosity of marmite and spit, and connoisseurs know to not pour them, but to rub them on the bare chest like a poultice.

Some famous people who famously drank red wine include Val Kilmer.

Finally, a note on choosing a wine. You may think it's enough to just read Val Kilmer's red wine blog and drink what he drinks. And for the most part, you'd do fine. But sometimes Val Kilmer gets confused and drinks Thousand Island dressing, and so it's important to develop your own taste, and your own palate.

Go to your reputable wine store and start exploring. Look at the labels. Does it have a kangaroo on it? That's probably a good wine.

Does it have a quirky picture of the winemaker's dog on it, and is it named for that crazy, funny, ugly dog? That's probably a good wine.

Make sure the font on the label is cool: no cursive, and easy on the serifs. And remember: no landscapes. If you buy a wine with a landscape on it, it means you are not intelligent.

And don't forget: some of the best red wine is synthesized right here in America. Try a tasting tour of the California's wine country, especially beautiful Lumlum and Subadadada counties. As you drink and drive and drink and drive from vineyard to vineyard, don't be afraid to ask questions.

Ask the salesperson: Is it a white wine? If it is, throw it on the ground. Is it red? Good, drink as much as you can, fast, and fall asleep in a field. Can the wine be colored red with blood? If so, then it is a rosé, and that is acceptable as well, especially if you are a Spaniard.

Thank you for your kind attention. To your health, rich dad!

That is all.

JOHN HODGMAN
BROOKLYN, NY

DEAR McSWEENEY'S,

There are two prisons at the edge of Lima, Peru: Castro Castro, a maximum-security penitentiary mostly for convicted terrorists; and another, larger complex for common delinquents, known simply as Lurigancho. While neither is very nice, this second prison is hellish. It is, by some estimates, the most overcrowded prison in Latin America. By comparison, the men who've done time there view Castro Castro as a reprieve, a place of calm and relaxation. A place to think.

It was in Castro Castro that I met Beto. He'd been a member of Los Destructores—the Destroyers—a band of armed robbers that terrorized Lima in the 1990s. When we met, he'd recently been transferred from Lurigancho, and was relieved to have left, though his new arrangement at Castro Castro was not exactly ideal. It did not, for example, include a bunk. Beto was sleeping on the floor of a cell he shared with two other men, but it didn't matter. He assured me he'd been in worse places, and I believed him.

Beto is tall and strong, with giant hands and a broad smile. The authorities had brought him to Castro Castro in the dead of night, with no warning, but before he'd left Lurigancho he had managed to gather his few belongings: some clothes, a handful of photographs, and his most prized possession, the manuscript he'd been writing by hand for the last six years. It was the story of his youth: his early days on the streets of Callao, his initiation into the life of a criminal. Beto had little hope of getting out, but when he was writing, the time seemed to pass painlessly. At Castro Castro, as he had at Lurigancho, he kept these pages wrapped in a burlap bag, tied with a string. It rested on the floor of his borrowed cell. Every morning after breakfast, he'd work on it. At lunch,

he'd put away the text and plan the next day's writing. He had a lot to tell. It was going to be a great book, he was sure. As it happened, the manuscript was sitting on the floor of his cell when, early one morning, a pipe burst and flooded the entire tier.

Beto left school around the time he started robbing people—age eleven. He has no education to speak of, but even when he was robbing banks and armored cars, he liked to write. No one in the Destroyers had much use for his hobby. They made fun of him, but Beto didn't care. The morning the pipe burst, Beto was sitting outside in the yard. Normally he would have been writing at that time, but that day, for some reason, he'd decided to take a break. When he heard the news, he ran up to his borrowed cell, frantic, to discover the ankle-deep water had pooled over his manuscript. He was devastated.

Each prison tier has a yard, an irregularly shaped patch of cement that must be shared by the four hundred inmates who live there. It's a prized space: in the mornings, it's an informal market, and most afternoons, the yard becomes a soccer pitch, or a place to sit, think blank thoughts, and look at the sky. The day the pipe burst, Beto took his soaked manuscript and could think of nothing but rescuing it. The yard was his only option, so he set his life story out to dry, page by page, on the floor of the prison yard. He placed a rock on each sheet of paper, and spent the day tending to the pages, turning them over when one side had dried, straightening out others if the wind shifted them. He sat there all afternoon on a pile of bricks as the sun passed overhead. The other inmates gathered to watch this enormous stranger among his papers, this newly arrived prisoner depriving them of their open space. Beto was no one in the established hierarchy of the prison. He had no allies. There were murmurs. There were glares. Who did he think he was?

Then an inmate dared to step out on the yard.

Beto wasn't having it. "If you fuck with my literature," he said, "you fuck with me." He stood up so the man could see what he was getting into.

How many of those who call themselves writers have ever defended their work like this?

It was a week later when we spoke, and the pages were dry now. Beto showed them to me. They were crinkled and smeared, scrawled with his crooked handwriting, full of phonetic spellings and words capitalized randomly for emphasis. With some effort you could read it. I started flipping through the pages, but Beto pulled them back.

"I'm not finished," he said. "When it's ready, I'll show you."

DANIEL ALARCÓN
LIMA, PERU

DEAR McSWEENEY'S,

Five years ago, I played an angry gay teenager in a small coming-of-age film. The angry gay teenager ends up finding true love with a shy girl from the high school. The other characters were my character's mom; a young guy from my class (initially the crush-object of the shy girl) who has a heavy-duty affair with the mom; and the young guy's sister, a fashion model who becomes an ice-skating showgirl in Las Vegas.

The movie's dialogue was idiosyncratic and, it must be said, not very much like the way young people talk, but there were some genuinely poignant scenes. The mother-daughter competition and the young characters' sexual discoveries were treated with disarming frankness.

I needed a job. But I was also really fond of my character. She was the closest character to myself I'd ever played. Also, though nobody would guess from watching the movie, the action was ostensibly set in Minnesota, where I grew up.

Toward the end of the shoot, we worked on a scene set "four years later" (when the characters are age 22). My character and her girlfriend were at the showgirl's house in Las Vegas. Visually, the scene was an homage to the charming scene in that old movie *That Touch of Mink*, where the two leading ladies chat while lying in single beds set at an L-shaped angle. Light streamed in from the windows of the showgirl's guest room, which was really in suburban Long Island. The beds were decked out in frilly white eyelet. A desolate Western magic-hour light streamed into the room, golden and sad, thanks to lavender filters, gigantic beige Japanese paper lanterns, and big silver bounce cards. In the scene, my girlfriend and I engaged in distracted small talk until I suddenly broke down and asked if she would list me as a beneficiary in her will. I quickly explained that my own mother had not listed me in her will, a fact I discovered in high school, when I had run an errand to this safety deposit box, only to discover the hurtful and bitter truth. The scene ultimately turns into this big profession of commitment and, by the end, winds up being touching, in spite of how arcane it sounds.

I was having a hard time connecting to the whole safety deposit box thing. I could understand the whole hurt/left out aspect, but I had a hard time getting to the extreme vulnerability that the character seemed to need there and then. I just couldn't get past the safety deposit box part of it. It seemed so clinical.

As actors, my girlfriend and I were friendly enough, but we weren't what anyone would call soulmates. So in order to do the scene I had to do some emotional substitution. I found this thing, rather randomly, that had come up in my mind a few times.

I thought about this time when I was around eleven. My two sisters and I were with my dad at a cabin in Wisconsin that my folks had rented for the summer. It was early October, and we had returned to bring home the last of our stuff, shut off the water, and close it up for the winter. It was Saturday morning, overcast, beyond brisk but just shy of cold. We were talking about what to eat for lunch. There were a couple of cans of Spaghetti-O's, which we wanted. My dad was concerned that there would either be too much or not enough—I can't remember which. My sister Ingrid and I got into a combative argument about which one of us could eat a whole can of Spaghetti-O's:

Ingrid: I can eat a whole can. I will.
Me: No you can't.
Ingrid: Yuh-huh, I CAN. I'm gonna.
Me: You never ate a whole can. No way.
Ingrid: I have so.
Me: WHEN?

My dad got up from where he was sitting, screamed, "God!" and lurched past us, letting the screen door slam behind him. Ingrid and I watched as he walked a few feet and stopped in front of the fence. He faced the fence and clenched his fists, his barrel chest heaving. He exhaled through his mouth, hissing, and shook his head. We glanced at each other, still mad, but mesmerized by Dad. He generally had a demeanor of gruff good-heartedness, but he was not to be messed with. He taught at a vo-tech school and had a lot of tough students—ex-cons, addicts, lost souls. His usual method of controlling other people's bad behavior was to wind his arm up like a pitcher and then pound his fist on the nearest available flat surface. He was intense and quick to anger, but this was the closest we'd ever seen him come to losing it.

After a few seconds I followed him out to the fence and stood behind him. He wouldn't acknowledge me. I kept saying, over and over, "Daddy, please, I'm sorry, I'm so sorry, I didn't mean it." And then, "Daddy, I didn't mean to make you mad, I'm sorry." But he wouldn't even look at me. He didn't wave me away or say a word. He just kept drawing in and expelling huge breaths. I freaked out. I was scared to go any closer to him, and began to cry. All I remember after that is somehow ending up in the tiny bathroom, sitting on the toilet seat, blankly staring at the crimp of the thin metal baseboard where it met the carpet. So I relived all of that while I did the big scene. It worked, but it was exhausting.

The coming-of-age film was screened for exactly one week at the Quad Cinema, a tiny art-house place on 13th Street, and was reviewed kindly by Steven Holden of the *New York Times*. I saw the movie once, at its small premiere in Los Angeles, with my then-manager, who hated it because he thought I looked fat in the love scenes. The movie was never sold for distribution or released on video. I don't even have a copy of it. All I have is a ten-minute sample I got during editing—just a rough-cut of the big scene and a couple of others. My then-manager refused to let me use the big scene in my reel because it was too sad, and also because in it, my nose is red from crying.

COLLEEN WERTHMANN
NEW YORK, NY

DEAR McSWEENEY'S,

There can be no more soul-searching experience than reading another writer's complete works in a systematic fashion. I recently accepted an assignment to contribute to a guidebook to contemporary fiction. I was in charge of four authors. Thus I spent nine straight action-drunk days last August devouring the entire oeuvre of a writer of legal thrillers; five frequent-flying weeks in which I read everything by a California science fictioner only in the air (which complemented his dreamy style by the by); a half week with the novels of an acclaimed essayist/ less-acclaimed novelist; and a lovely Thanksgiving weekend re-reading a quartet of small-town tragicomedies by one of America's quiet geniuses. What made my heart sink was each author's inadvertent repetition, their crutches, and odd little obsessions. The legal thriller author was guiltiest of all, not only because he resorted to the same trite phrases in book after book, but because of the insidious nature of his hackery. For instance, unable or unwilling to spend a couple of minutes thinking up another way to describe a beautiful woman, there is a hottie in almost every one of his books who isn't wearing makeup, but who "needed none." But mostly, the repetitions spoke to the way writers are both driven by their obsessions and/or trapped by the circumstances of biography. In my assigned authors this was either distracting or endearing. Like, I got the feeling that the thriller writer might be a secret alcoholic because of the overabundance of male characters with a love for "the taste of beer." That's how he puts it: "the taste of beer." The essayist/ novelist, a native of California, always manages to plant a "jacaranda tree" into her narratives. I, a dual native of dogwood and Douglas fir country, had never heard of

such flora. I looked it up: "Any of several trees of the genus *Jacaranda*, native to tropical America, having compound leaves and clusters of pale-purple flowers." The jacaranda's appearance (in four books) became a little madeleine of irritation, a jolt out of narrative action which is even more annoying when you're getting paid crap and thus fiscally rewarded for speed, speed, speed. The quiet genius, bless him, has a lovely habit of giving birth to a male character with a feeling for books; there's the boy from a broken home who finds solace in a corner of the public library, or the sexagenarian laborer whose disability sends him to community college where he secretly enjoys his first and last philosophy class.

I leave out those authors' names not to protect the innocent, but rather to appease my own incompetence. I mean, they're novelists, a job which thankfully limits their output. I read them as a journalist, horrified that anyone reading everything I ever wrote (dozens if not hundreds of pieces) all in a weekend would know me for the bumbler I am. And since I work mostly as a critic, a job with the inherent pitfall of coming up with fresh new ways to say "good" or "bad," I tremble at the thought that a Nexis search in my name would unearth something like 394 repetitions of the word "crummy" alone. Or that I have mentioned the canceled television drama *My So-Called Life* at least eighteen times in the last two years, in everything from a review of the new album by Slayer to last week's meditation on the legacy of World War II. And it wasn't even my favorite show! Or the Elvis obsession: Said one academic after we appeared together on a public radio talk show devoted to the admittedly lame topic "defining cool," "You have some good ideas." (Thanks!) "But you have got to get over Elvis." The truth is, I live in a cozy little world of pop music and TV shows and my writing will reflect this. Still, it could be worse. I switched to words after a teen fling with composing orchestral music. One reason I quit the symphonic life was the claustrophobia of being locked into the chromatic scale—twelve measly notes. I didn't want to spend the next fifty years beating the perfect fifth to death. Not that English is the most choice-happy language to get stuck with. (Though ending sentences in prepositions certainly expands one's options.) I'm reminded of the multilingual space aliens in Jonathan Lethem's novel *Girl in Landscape*—a book I actually paid cash money for. The Archbuilders, as they're called, come from a planet with around fifteen thousand native languages. Each Archbuilder speaks hundreds of tongues. They are said to be fascinated with English, however, because "Archbuilders describe English as a language of enchanting limitations… English words seem, to an Archbuilder, garishly overloaded with meaning." How generous! I feel better, don't you? Think I'll celebrate with the taste of beer. In the Archbuilder scenario, then, falling back on my old friend "crummy" might not be the failing of a lazybones on deadline, but rather a jacaranda in bloom, bursting with the pale-purple flowers of significance.

SARAH VOWELL
CHICAGO, IL

P.S. I am not wearing makeup, because I need none.

DEAR McSWEENEY'S,

This was when I was working at The Texas School for the Blind, back in 1997. I was given charge of an 11-year-old boy named Jarvis who was both blind and deaf. He would walk around with his head down and both his arms waving about in front of him. Sometimes he would just take off and run, zig-zagging around the room until he got tripped up or smacked into some object that his outstretched hands did not detect.

I had no idea how to communicate with Jarvis. During the day he attended classes with trained professionals who tried to teach him words by drawing letters onto his palms with their fingers. No one explained to me how this worked. My job was to get him some exercise, feed him dinner, and get him into bed.

I would often talk to Jarvis, though I understood, obviously, that he could not hear me. I'd say things like "Look out, Jarvis!" or "Come here."

An interesting thing about him was that he would identify people by the way they smelled. Each afternoon, when I picked him up at the school building, he would take my arm and sniff it. Even when we walked together he'd keep his head pointed down, like a hunchback. I tried to get him to hold his head up, but he didn't like that. It was understandable, I guess, why he would see no reason to hold his head up while he walked.

Jarvis and I never became good friends. He bit me the first time I tried to give him a shower—he didn't like water touching his skin. Sometimes he would grab onto me and squeeze very tightly and it was for this reason I made sure to keep his fingernails cut short. The residential staff had a set of fingernail clippers which we were supposed to use, but Jarvis had unusually thick fingernails and I couldn't get them to fit in between the pinchers. So I used a set of scissors from the office. They were sharp scissors and performed the task very well.

One evening I was getting Jarvis ready for bed and he grabbed my hair and wouldn't let go. When I finally pried his fingers loose I noticed his nails needed to be cut. I got the scissors and began to clip away. Then Jarvis grabbed my hair again with his other hand. I put down the scissors and tried to pry him off. He was pretty strong. I sat there trying to get him off for quite a while. I was thinking about picking him up and dunking him into a tub of water so that he'd be forced to either drown or let me go. Then I noticed there were streaks of red blood on the bedsheets and suddenly there was a thick damp spot underneath where I was sitting.

I thought, "Damn, Jarvis cut me."

But what actually happened was he had grabbed the scissors with the hand which wasn't holding my hair, and stabbed himself in the leg. This was a real mess. I'm not even sure Jarvis knew what had happened. I picked him up and wrapped him up in the sheet. We ran down the hallway until we got to the front desk, where I called an ambulance. Jarvis was still holding onto my hair and he took a whole fistful of it with him when I finally pulled his hand away. I used towels to soak up the blood, which was copious. Then the ambulance arrived.

Jarvis had punctured a large vein in his inner thigh, but he was okay. When we got back from the hospital the supervisor at the school made me fill out about fifty pages of forms and then I had to clean up the bed. I should not have brought scissors into Jarvis's room, explained the supervisor.

I was suspended from work for three weeks while they reviewed my conduct. When I returned to the job I was no longer working with Jarvis. In fact, I was transferred to another dormitory altogether. There I was given charge of two brothers from Mexico, Santos and Miguel. Their parents were farmworkers who had been exposed to some strong pesticides in South Texas. As a result, their two sons had been born without eyes. Where the eyes should

have been, they had these little flesh-colored balls of skin.

But Santos and Miguel could hear everything. Their ears worked well. They knew how to communicate. Everything with them would be fine.

ARTHUR BRADFORD
RURAL VIRGINIA

DEAR MCSWEENEY'S,
The birds are most beautiful in the morning. The whole thing is morning at this time of year, but my body clock keeps the beat like a palace guard. It's uncanny. I've never gone a half hour without looking at my watch when I was off the base, but here I am, watching the birds, marching out the days. I watch them climb the rocks for four hours every day. I boil an egg every 24 hours. I trim my beard twice a month. Not much, just so the icicles don't give me grief.

Ronald and I are taking notes. He's only been here two weeks, but he's got the hang of it. Great kid. Ask him anything you want to know about penguins. Go ahead, ask him. He'll keep you glued to your seat for an hour. I'm not kidding. He's a great storyteller.

It's 8:45 in the morning by my watch, 8:48 by my head, and the birds are out, marching. Ronald is taking photographs. I have a giant reel-to-reel going, and a big boom mike. I think the penguins like it. Then they start doing something I've never seen—they start *flying*. In distress, maybe. Ronald puts the Nikon down and watches them.

He doesn't hear a thing. I see it about two seconds too early, and far too late: the #36 Broadway bus, from Chicago, roaring over the ice, bearing down on Ronald with a hiss. He doesn't know what hits him, and if I could tell him—and, oh God, I wish

I could—I'm sure he'd just laugh at such a strange fate.

I can't believe I saw what I saw but I saw it, I swear I did. And then, just like that, the penguins were on the ground again, and the bus was gone.

TODD PRUZAN
MAPLEWOOD, NJ

DEAR McSWEENEY'S,
This letter—which, since it's sort of a story, probably should have been published ten or so pages hence, with a nice title and a little illustration below the title—is called:

DO YOU KNOW WHAT SEAWEED IS?

My aunt curates an astronaut museum near the Johnson Space Center, just outside Houston. Her (second) husband (if you don't count a brief marriage when she was a teenager, which would make him her third) is a chemical engineer for Monsanto.

She has no children. She is incredibly affectionate toward me. (I am the same way back.) She speaks in a drawl. On the Fourth of July she dresses up like the Statue of Liberty and her husband dresses up like Uncle Sam and they ride around town in a Cadillac convertible.

They're in love.

In tangential keeping with her fascination for manned space missions, she collects strange objects. Recently she acquired a stuffed bear, the design of which dated back to the 19th century. She'd spent months tracking it down. It cost $800. When I said that seemed like a lot of money, she told me that a friend "has $10,000 in bears."

She is 76 years old and not in the least senile—she still has an assassin's glare she uses when displeased—but she seems to have frozen me at age eight. When she addresses me she phases into a bedazzled, euphoric, baby-like, isn't-all-the-world-a-wonder, persona of great cheer. The last time I visited we were sitting in the kitchen when a neighbor lady called to say she was bringing over a custard for us. We waited in silence, and then my aunt asked, in the way you might ask a foreign visitor, "Have you ever had a custard?"

I said yes.

Somehow thrown off course—she evidently wanted to be the one to initiate me to custard—her cheerfulness faltered. She looked doubtful. A sadness passed over her face. But then she recovered, and in a wildly enthusiastic Texas square-dance MC's sing-songy voice, asked, "Have you ever had a pie?"

The next day, we were planning on going out somewhere. She told me she'd just been to Galveston, a nearby Gulf Coast town. "When I was last in Galveston there was seaweed all over the beach!" she said, then paused, and then triumphantly added, "Do you know what seaweed is?!"

My aunt only drives Cadillacs. Her husband compulsively buys them for her. He also names them after her, putting the word "Baby" before her name to make the car's name: "Baby Glendora." She wrecks one every five years. About the last wreck she explained, somewhat unconvincingly, "He ran a red light, but he says I ran a red light!" Describing the wreck before that, she said, "I took out 300 feet of NASA fence!"

Her husband's voice is clipped and loud. He uses colons for commas, breaking his sentences into isolated fragments. He calls my aunt "your little aunt," and calls whisky "the John Barleycorn," or "the sweet Lucy." He prefers three-word phrases like this. He exclaims them, proclamation-style, and chuckles. At dinner one night he got talking about about World War II, where he was a flight instructor and a gunner. He said, "The atomic bomb: was just the period: at the end of the sentence."

My widower uncle Charles, Glendora's brother, an old-world-handsome ex-Nazarene minister turned real estate mogul (at age 80, now in the early stages of Parkinson's) is a sort of de facto third member of my aunt's marriage. Since his wife died a couple years ago he's become fascinated with sex. He's become extremely roguish, though he is a visual ideal of rectitude. When the four of us went out to lunch last summer, he hoisted a shaky tea cup to his lips—it made its way there slowly, waving hypnotically, spastically, somehow beautifully, back and forth, like an out-of-control wrecking ball, past his perfectly tied tie, and then back down to the saucer—and told me about the hairdresser from whom he likes to get a weekly cut.

"She's my pimp," he said.

"She's got big bosoms," my aunt added.

"What?" I said.

"It's true," Uncle Charles said. His accent is scratchy, Johnsonian Texan. "She says to the girls that come into the shop, 'You wanna go over there tonight and have sex with this gentleman?'"

Aunt Glendora delivered her displeased look. And then a skeptical look. Then she turned away for a moment.

Uncle Charles leaned forward confidentially and said, "I'm doing a new thing in the community where I'm taking black folks and Mexicans into my real estate office to work with me. I've got a big painting behind my desk of all the races. When this Mexican fella came in the other day I pointed it out to him and I asked 'What do you see?'

"'I see a big black dude,' he said.

"'That means I'm not prejudiced. And you won't be prejudiced. We're humans. So let's agree that if one of us does anything stupid—and that's natural—the other one, in the spirit of brotherhood, will just look at him and say "Stupid."'"

My aunt and her husband went to get their Cadillac. I waited with my uncle. I asked if my aunt ran the red light. He said she maybe did.

On the phone tonight, with precision ("I remember what people had for dinner and the rugs on their floor—I'm detailish," she said), my aunt told me that her prior marriage ended in Junction, Texas, in her very first car wreck. This was in the mid-sixties, toward the end of a long trip back from California. She was driving while her husband slept in the back seat. An oncoming truck started drifting into their lane (or could they have started drifting into the truck's lane?—it was so fast). Her husband woke up for some reason, looked over the back seat, saw the truck just before the head-on collision, and pushed my aunt down.

"He was decapitated," she said. "I stayed off work for several weeks getting my soul together." Then she went back to work at Monsanto, near Galveston.

SEAN WILSEY
HOUSTON, TX

THE CEILING

by KEVIN BROCKMEIER

(fiction from Issue 7)

THERE WAS A sky that day, sun-rich and open and blue. A raft of silver clouds was floating along the horizon, and robins and sparrows were calling from the trees. It was my son Joshua's seventh birthday and we were celebrating in our back yard. He and the children were playing on the swing set, and Melissa and I were sitting on the deck with the parents. Earlier that afternoon, a balloon and gondola had risen from the field at the end of our block, sailing past us with an exhalation of fire. Joshua told his friends that he knew the pilot. "His name is Mister Clifton," he said, as they tilted their heads back and slowly revolved in place. "I met him at the park last year. He took me into the air with him and let me drop a soccer ball into a swimming pool. We almost hit a helicopter. He told me he'd come by on my birthday." Joshua shielded his eyes against the sun. "Did you see him wave?" he asked. "He just waved at me."

This was a story.

The balloon drifted lazily away, turning to expose each delta and crease of its fabric, and we listened to the children resuming their play. Mitch Nauman slipped his sunglasses into his shirt pocket. "Ever notice how kids their age will handle a toy?" he said. Mitch was our next-door neighbor. He was the single father of Bobby Nauman, Joshua's strange best friend. His other best friend, Chris Boschetti, came from a family of cosmetics executives. My wife had taken to calling them "Rich and Strange."

Mitch pinched the front of his shirt between his fingers and fanned himself with it. "The actual function of the toy is like some sort of obstacle," he said. "They'll dream up a new use for everything in the world."

I looked across the yard at the swing set: Joshua was trying to shinny up one of the A-poles; Taylor Tugwell and Sam Yoo were standing on the teeter swing; Adam Smithee was tossing fistfuls of pebbles onto the slide and watching them rattle to the ground.

My wife tipped one of her sandals onto the grass with the ball of her foot. "Playing as you should isn't Fun," she said: "it's Design." She parted her toes around the front leg of Mitch's lawn chair. He leaned back into the sunlight, and her calf muscles tautened.

My son was something of a disciple of flying things. On his bedroom wall were posters of fighter planes and wild birds. A model of a helicopter was chandeliered to his ceiling. His birthday cake, which sat before me on the picnic table, was decorated with a picture of a rocket ship—a silver white missile with discharging thrusters. I had been hoping that the baker would place a few stars in the frosting as well (the cake in the catalog was dotted with yellow candy sequins), but when I opened the box I found that they were missing. So this is what I did: as Joshua stood beneath the swing set, fishing for something in his pocket, I planted his birthday candles deep in the cake. I pushed them in until each wick was surrounded by only a shallow bracelet of wax. Then I called the children over from the swing set. They came tearing up divots in the grass.

We sang happy birthday as I held a match to the candles.

Joshua closed his eyes.

"Blow out the stars," I said, and his cheeks rounded with air.

That night, after the last of the children had gone home, my wife and I sat outside drinking, each of us wrapped in a separate silence. The city lights were burning, and Joshua was sleeping in his room. A nightjar gave one long trill after another from somewhere above us.

Melissa added an ice cube to her glass, shaking it against the others until it whistled and cracked. I watched a strand of cloud break apart in the sky. The moon that night was bright and full, but after a while it began to seem damaged to me, marked by some small inaccuracy. It took me a moment to realize why this was: against its blank white surface was a square of perfect darkness. The square was without blemish or flaw, no larger than a child's tooth, and I could not tell whether it rested on the moon itself or hovered above it like a cloud. It looked as if a window had been opened clean through the floor of the rock, presenting to view a stretch of empty space. I had never seen such a thing before.

"What is that?" I said.

Melissa made a sudden noise, a deep, defeated little oh.

"My life is a mess," she said.

Within a week, the object in the night sky had grown perceptibly larger. It would appear at sunset, when the air was dimming to purple, as a faint granular blur, a certain filminess at the high point of the sky, and would remain there through the night. It blotted out the light of passing stars and seemed to travel across the face of the moon, but it did not move. The people of my town were uncertain as to whether the object was spreading or approaching—we could see only that it was getting bigger—and this matter gave rise to much speculation. Gleason the butcher insisted that it wasn't there at all, that it was only an illusion. "It all has to do with the satellites," he said. "They're bending the light from that place like a lens. It just looks like something's there." But though his manner was relaxed and he spoke with conviction, he would not look up from his cutting board.

The object was not yet visible during the day, but we could feel it above us as we woke to the sunlight each morning: there was a tension and strain to the air, a shift in its customary balance. When we stepped from our houses to go to work, it was as if we were walking through a new sort of gravity, harder and stronger, not so yielding.

As for Melissa, she spent several weeks pacing the house from room to room. I watched her fall into a deep abstraction. She had cried into her pillow the night of Joshua's birthday, shrinking away from me beneath the blankets. "I just need to sleep," she said, as I sat above her and rested my hand on her side. "Please. Lie down. Stop hovering." I soaked a washcloth for her in the cold water of the bathroom sink, folding it into quarters and leaving it on her night stand in a porcelain bowl.

The next morning, when I found her in the kitchen, she was gathering a coffee filter into a little wet sachet. "Are you feeling better?" I asked.

"I'm fine." She pressed the foot lever of the trash can, and its lid popped open with a rustle of plastic.

"Is it Joshua?"

Melissa stopped short, holding the pouch of coffee in her outstretched hand. "What's wrong with Joshua?" she said. There was a note of concern in her voice.

"He's seven now," I told her. When she didn't respond, I continued with, "You don't look a day older than when we met, honey. You know that, don't you?"

She gave a puff of air through her nose—this was a laugh, but I couldn't tell what she meant to express by it, bitterness or judgment or some kind of easy cheer. "It's not Joshua," she said, and dumped the coffee into the trash can. "But thanks all the same."

It was the beginning of July before she began to ease back into the life of our family. By this time, the object in the sky was large enough to eclipse the full moon. Our friends insisted that they had never been able to see any change in my wife at all, that she had the same style of speaking, the same habits and twists and eccentricities as ever. This was, in a certain sense, true. I noticed the difference chiefly when we were alone together. After we had put Joshua to bed, we would sit with one another in the living room, and when I asked her a question, or when the telephone rang, there was always a certain brittleness to her, a hesitancy of manner that suggested she was hearing the world from across a divide. It was clear to me at such times that she had taken herself elsewhere, that she had constructed a shelter from the wood and clay and stone of her most intimate thoughts and stepped inside, shutting the door. The only question was whether the person I saw tinkering at the window was opening the latches or sealing the cracks.

One Saturday morning, Joshua asked me to take him to the library for a story reading. It was almost noon, and the sun was just beginning to darken at its zenith. Each day, the shadows of our bodies would shrink toward us from the west, vanish briefly in the midday soot, and stretch away into the east, falling off the edge of the world. I wondered sometimes if I would ever see my reflection pooled at my feet again. "Can Bobby come, too?" Joshua asked as I tightened my shoes.

I nodded, pulling the laces up in a series of butterfly loops. "Why don't you run over and get him," I said, and he sprinted off down the hallway.

Melissa was sitting on the front porch steps, and I knelt down beside her as I left. "I'm taking the boys into town," I said. I kissed her cheek and rubbed the base of her neck, felt the cirrus curls of hair there moving back and forth through my fingers.

"Shh." She held a hand out to silence me. "Listen."

The insects had begun to sing, the birds to fall quiet. The air gradually became filled with a peaceful chirring noise.

"What are we listening for?" I whispered.

Melissa bowed her head for a moment, as if she were trying to keep count of something. Then she looked up at me. In answer, and with a sort of weariness about her, she spread her arms open to the world.

Before I stood to leave, she asked me a question: "We're not all that much alike, are we?" she said.

The plaza outside the library was paved with red brick. Dogwood trees were planted in hollows along the perimeter, and benches of distressed metal stood here and there on concrete pads. A member of a local guerrilla theater troupe was delivering a recitation from beneath a streetlamp; she sat behind a wooden desk, her hands folded one atop the other, and spoke as if into a camera. "Where did this object come from?" she said. "What is it, and when will it stop its descent? How did we find ourselves in this place? Where do we go from here? Scientists are baffled. In an interview with this station, Dr. Stephen Mandruzzato, head of the prestigious Horton Institute of Astronomical Studies, had this to say: 'We don't know. We don't know. We just don't know.'" I led Joshua and Bobby Nauman through the heavy dark glass doors of the library, and we took our seats in the Children's Reading Room. The tables were set low to the ground so that my legs pressed flat against the underside, and the air carried that peculiar, sweetened-milk smell of public libraries and elementary schools. Bobby Nauman began to play the Where Am I? game with Joshua. "Where am I?" he would ask, and then he'd warm-and-cold Joshua around the room until Joshua had found him. First he was in a potted plant, then on my shirt collar, then beneath the baffles of an air vent.

After a time, the man who was to read to us moved into place. He said hello to the children, coughed his throat clear, and opened his book to the title page: "Chicken Little," he began.

As he read, the sky grew bright with afternoon. The sun came through the windows in a sheet of fire.

Joshua started the second grade in September. His new teacher mailed us a list of necessary school supplies, which we purchased the week before classes began—pencils and a utility box, glue and facial tissues, a ruler and a notebook and a tray of watercolor paints. On his first day, Melissa shot a photograph of Joshua waving to her from the front door, his backpack wreathed over his shoulder and a lunch sack in his right hand. He stood in the flash of hard white light, then kissed her good-bye and joined Rich and Strange in the car pool.

Autumn passed in its slow, sheltering way, and toward the end of November, Joshua's teacher asked the class to write a short essay describing a community of local animals. The paragraph Joshua wrote was captioned "What Happened to the Birds." We fastened it to the refrigerator with magnets.

> There were many birds here before, but now there gone. Nobody knows where they went. I used to see them in the trees. I fed one at the zoo when I was litle. It was big. The birds went away when no one was looking. The trees are quiet now. They do not move.

All of this was true. As the object in the sky became visible during the daylight—and as, in the tide of several months, it descended over our town—the birds and migrating insects disappeared. I did not notice they were gone, though, nor the muteness with which the sun rose in the morning, nor the stillness of the grass and trees, until I read Joshua's essay.

The world at this time was full of confusion and misgiving and unforeseen changes of heart. One incident that I recall clearly took place in the Main Street Barber Shop on a cold winter Tuesday. I was sitting in a pneumatic chair while Wesson the barber trimmed my hair. A nylon gown was draped over my body to catch the cuttings, and I could smell the peppermint of Wesson's chewing gum. "So how 'bout this weather?" he chuckled, working away at my crown.

Weather gags had been circulating through our offices and barrooms ever since the object—which was as smooth and reflective as obsidian glass, and which the newspapers had designated "the ceiling"—had descended to the level of the cloud base. I gave my usual response, "A little overcast today, wouldn't you say?" and Wesson barked an appreciative laugh.

Wesson was one of those men who had passed his days waiting for the rest of his life to come about. He busied himself with his work, never marrying, and doted on the children of his customers. "Something's bound to happen soon," he would often say at the end of a conversation, and there was a quickness to his eyes that demonstrated his implicit faith in the proposition. When his mother died, this faith seemed to abandon him. He went home each evening to the small house that they had shared, shuffling cards or paging through a magazine until he fell asleep. Though he never failed to laugh when a customer was at hand, the eyes he wore became empty and white, as if some essential fire in them had been spent. His enthusiasm began to seem like desperation. It was only a matter of time.

"How's the pretty lady?" he asked me.

I was watching him in the mirror, which was both parallel to and coextensive with a mirror on the opposite wall. "She hasn't been feeling too well," I said. "But I think she's coming out of it."

"Glad to hear it. Glad to hear it," he said. "And business at the hardware store?"

I told him that business was fine. I was on my lunch break.

The bell on the door handle gave a tink, and a current of cold air sent a little eddy of cuttings across the floor. A man we had never seen before leaned into the room. "Have you seen my umbrella?" he said. "I can't find my umbrella, have you seen it?" His voice was too loud—high and sharp, fluttery with worry—and his hands shook with a distinct tremor.

"Can't say that I have," said Wesson. He smiled emptily, showing his teeth, and his fingers tensed around the back of my chair.

There was a sudden feeling of weightlessness to the room.

"You wouldn't tell me anyway, would you?" said the man. "Jesus," he said. "You people."

Then he took up the ashtray stand and slammed it against the window.

A cloud of gray cinders shot out around him, but the window merely shuddered in its frame. He let the stand fall to the floor and it rolled into a magazine rack. Ash drizzled to the ground. The man brushed a cigarette butt from his jacket. "You people," he said again, and he left through the open glass door.

As I walked home later that afternoon, the scent of barbershop talcum blew from my skin in the winter wind. The plane of the ceiling was stretched across the firmament, covering my town from end to end, and I could see the lights of a thousand streetlamps caught like constellations in its smooth black polish. It occurred to me that if nothing were to change, if the ceiling were simply to hover where it was forever, we might come to forget that it was even there, charting for ourselves a new map of the night sky.

Mitch Nauman was leaving my house when I arrived. We passed on the lawn, and he held up Bobby's knapsack. "He leaves this thing everywhere," he said. "Buses. Your house. The schoolroom. Sometimes I think I should tie it to his belt." Then he cleared his throat. "New haircut? I like it."

"Yeah, it was getting a bit shaggy."

He nodded and made a clicking noise with his tongue. "See you next time," he said, and he vanished through his front door, calling to Bobby to climb down from something.

By the time the object had fallen as low as the tree spires, we had noticed the acceleration in the wind. In the thin strip of space between the ceiling and the pavement, it narrowed and kindled and collected speed. We could hear it buffeting the walls of our houses at night, and it produced a constant low sigh in the darkness of movie halls. People emerging from their doorways could be seen to brace themselves against the charge and pressure of it. It was as if our entire town were an alley between tall buildings.

I decided one Sunday morning to visit my parents' gravesite: the cemetery in which they were buried would spread with knotgrass every spring, and it was necessary to tend their plot before the weeds grew too thick. The house was still peaceful as I showered and dressed, and I stepped as quietly as I could across the bath mat and the tile floor. I watched the water in the toilet bowl rise and fall as gusts of wind channeled their way through the pipes. Joshua and Melissa were asleep, and the morning sun flashed at the horizon and disappeared.

At the graveyard, a small boy was tossing a tennis ball into the air as his mother swept the dirt from a memorial tablet. He was trying to touch the ceiling with it, and with each successive throw he drew a bit closer, until, at the height of its climb, the ball jarred to one side before it dropped. The cemetery was otherwise empty, its monuments and trees the only material presence.

My parents' graves were clean and spare. With such scarce sunlight, the knotgrass had failed to blossom, and there was little tending for me to do.

I combed the plot for leaves and stones and pulled the rose stems from the flower wells. I kneeled at the headstone they shared and unfastened a zipper of moss from it. Sitting there, I imagined for a moment that my parents were living together atop the ceiling: they were walking through a field of high yellow grass, beneath the sun and the sky and the tousled white clouds, and she was bending in her dress to examine a flower, and he was bending beside her, his hand on her waist, and they were unaware that the world beneath them was settling to the ground.

When I got home, Joshua was watching television on the living room sofa, eating a plump yellow doughnut from a paper towel. A dollop of jelly had fallen onto the back of his hand. "Mom left to run an errand," he said.

The television picture fluttered and curved for a moment, sending spits of rain across the screen, then it recrystallized. An aerial transmission tower had collapsed earlier that week—the first of many such fallings in our town—and the quality of our reception had been diminishing ever since.

"I had a dream last night," Joshua said. "I dreamed that I dropped my bear through one of the grates on the sidewalk." He owned a worn-down cotton teddy bear, its seams looped with clear plastic stitches, that he had been given as a toddler. "I tried to catch him, but I missed. Then I lay down on the ground and stretched out my arm for him. I was reaching through the grate, and when I looked beneath the sidewalk, I could see another part of the city. There were people moving around down there. There were cars and streets and bushes and lights. The sidewalk was some sort of bridge, and in my dream I thought, 'Oh yeah. Now why didn't I remember that?' Then I tried to climb through to get my bear, but I couldn't lift the grate up."

The morning weather forecaster was weeping on the television.

"Do you remember where this place was?" I asked.

"Yeah."

"Maybe down by the bakery?" I had noticed Melissa's car parked there a few times, and I remembered a kid tossing pebbles into the grate.

"That's probably it."

"Want to see if we can find it?"

Joshua pulled at the lobe of his ear for a second, staring into the middle distance. Then he shrugged his shoulders. "Okay," he decided.

I don't know what we expected to discover there. Perhaps I was simply seized by a whim—the desire to be spoken to, the wish to be instructed by a dream. When I was Joshua's age, I dreamed one night that I found a new door in my house, one that opened from my cellar onto the bright, aseptic aisles of a drugstore: I walked through it, and saw a flash of light, and found myself sitting up in bed. For several days after, I felt a quickening of possibility, like the touch of some other geography, whenever I passed by the cellar door. It was as if I'd opened my eyes to the true inward map of the world, projected according to our own beliefs and understandings.

On our way through the town center, Joshua and I waded past a cluster of people squinting into the horizon. There was a place between the post office and the library where the view to the west was occluded by neither hills nor buildings, and crowds often gathered there to watch the distant blue belt of the sky. We shouldered our way through and continued into town.

Joshua stopped outside the Kornblum Bakery, beside a trash basket and a newspaper carrel, where the light from two streetlamps lensed together on the ground. "This is it," he said, and made a gesture indicating the iron grate at our feet. Beneath it we could see the shallow basin of a drainage culvert. It was even and dry, and a few brittle leaves rested inside it.

"Well," I said. There was nothing there. "That's disappointing."

"Life's disappointing," said Joshua.

He was borrowing a phrase of his mother's, one that she had taken to using these last few months. Then, as if on cue, he glanced up and a light came into his eyes. "Hey," he said. "There's Mom."

Melissa was sitting behind the plate glass window of a restaurant on the opposite side of the street. I could see Mitch Nauman talking to her from across the table, his face soft and casual. Their hands were cupped together beside the pepper crib, and his shoes stood empty on the carpet. He was stroking her left leg with his right foot, its pad and arch curved around her calf. The image was as clear and exact as a melody.

I took Joshua by the shoulders. "What I want you to do," I said, "is knock on Mom's window. When she looks up, I want you to wave."

And he did exactly that—trotting across the asphalt, tapping a few times on the glass, and waving when Melissa started in her chair. Mitch

Nauman let his foot fall to the carpet. Melissa found Joshua through the window. She crooked her head and gave him a tentative little flutter of her fingers. Then she met my eyes. Her hand stilled in the air. Her face seemed to fill suddenly with movement, then just as suddenly to empty—it reminded me of nothing so much as a flock of birds scattering from a lawn. I felt a kick of pain in my chest and called to Joshua from across the street. "Come on, sport," I said. "Let's go home."

It was not long after—early the next morning, before we awoke—that the town water tower collapsed, blasting a river of fresh water down our empty streets. Hankins the grocer, who had witnessed the event, gathered an audience that day to his lunch booth in the coffee shop: "I was driving past the tower when it happened," he said. "Heading in early to work. First I heard a creaking noise, and then I saw the leg posts buckling. Wham!"— he smacked the table with his palms—"So much water! It surged into the side of my car, and I lost control of the wheel. The stream carried me right down the road. I felt like a tiny paper boat." He smiled and held up a finger, then pressed it to the side of a half-empty soda can, tipping it gingerly onto its side. Coca-Cola washed across the table with a hiss of carbonation. We hopped from our seats to avoid the spill.

The rest of the town seemed to follow in a matter of days, falling to the ground beneath the weight of the ceiling. Billboards and streetlamps, chimneys and statues. Church steeples, derricks, and telephone poles. Klaxon rods and restaurant signs. Apartment buildings and energy pylons. Trees released a steady sprinkle of leaves and pine cones, then came timbering to the earth—those that were broad and healthy cleaving straight down the heartwood, those that were thin and pliant bending until they cracked. Maintenance workers installed panels of light along the sidewalk, routing the electricity through underground cables. The ceiling itself proved unassailable. It bruised fists and knuckles. It stripped the teeth from power saws. It broke drill bits. It extinguished flames. One afternoon the television antenna tumbled from my rooftop, landing on the hedges in a zigzag of wire. A chunk of plaster fell across the kitchen table as I was eating dinner that night. I heard a board split in the living room wall the next morning, and then another in the hallway, and then another in the bedroom. It sounded like gunshots detonating in a closed room. Melissa and Joshua were already waiting on the front lawn when I got there. A boy was standing on a heap of rubble across the street playing Atlas, his upraked shoulders supporting the world. A man on a stepladder was pasting a sign to the ceiling: SHOP AT CARSON'S. Melissa pulled her jacket tighter. Joshua took my sleeve. A trough spread open beneath the shingles of our roof, and we watched our house collapse into a mass of brick and mortar.

I was lying on the ground, a tree root pressing into the small of my back, and I shifted slightly to the side. Melissa was lying beside me, and Mitch Nauman beside her. Joshua and Bobby, who had spent much of the day crawling aimlessly about the yard, were asleep now at our feet. The ceiling was no higher than a coffee table, and I could see each pore of my skin reflected in its surface. Above the keening of the wind there was a tiny edge of sound—the hum of the sidewalk lights, steady, electric, and warm.

"Do you ever get the feeling that you're supposed to be someplace else?" said Melissa. She paused for a moment, perfectly still. "It's a kind of sudden dread," she said.

Her voice seemed to hover in the air for a moment.

I had been observing my breath for the last few hours on the polished undersurface of the ceiling: every time I exhaled, a mushroom-shaped fog would cover my reflection, and I found that I could control the size of this fog by adjusting the force and the speed of my breathing. When Melissa asked her question, the first I had heard from her in many days, I gave a sudden puff of air through my nose and two icicle-shaped blossoms appeared. Mitch Nauman whispered something into her ear, but his voice was no more than a murmur, and I could not make out the words. In a surge of emotion that I barely recognized, some strange combination of rivalry and adoration, I took her hand in my own and squeezed it. When nothing happened, I squeezed it again. I brought it to my chest, and I brought it to my mouth, and I kissed it and kneaded it and held it tight.

I was waiting to feel her return my touch, and I felt at that moment, felt with all my heart, that I could wait the whole life of the world for such a thing, until the earth and the sky met and locked and the distance between them closed forever.

NEW BOY

by RODDY DOYLE

(fiction from Issue 18)

CHAPTER ONE
HE IS VERY LATE

H E SITS.

He sits in the classroom. It is his first day.

He is late.

He is five years late.

And that is very late, he thinks.

He is nine. The other boys and girls have been like this, together, since they were four. But he is new.

—We have a new boy with us today, says the teacher-lady.

—So what? says a boy who is behind him.

Other boys and some girls laugh. He does not know exactly why. He does not like this.

—Now now, says the teacher-lady.

She told him her name when he was brought here by the man but he does not now remember it. He did not hear it properly.

—Hands in the air, she says.

All around him, children lift their hands. He does this too. There is then, quite quickly, silence.

—Good, says the teacher-lady. —Now.

She smiles at him. He does not smile. Boys and girls will laugh. He thinks that this will happen if he smiles.

The teacher-lady says his name.

—Stand up, she says.

Again, she says his name. Again, she smiles. He stands. He looks only at the teacher-lady.

—Everybody, this is Joseph. Say Hello.

—Hello!

—HELLO!

—HELL-OHH!

—Hands in the air!

The children lift their hands. He also lifts his hands. There is silence. It is a clever trick, he thinks.

—Sit down, Joseph.

He sits down. His hands are still in the air.

—Now. Hands down.

Right behind him, dropped hands smack the desk. It is the so-what boy.

—Now, says the teacher-lady.

She says this word many times. It is certainly her favorite word.

—Now, I'm sure you'll all make Joseph very welcome. Take out your *Maths Matters*.

—Where's he from, Miss?

It is a girl who speaks. She sits in front of Joseph, two desks far.

—We'll talk about that later, says the teacher-lady. —But maths first.

That is the first part of her name. Miss.

—Miss, Seth Quinn threw me book out the window.

—Didn't!

—Yeh did.

—Now!

Joseph holds his new book very tightly. It is not a custom he had expected, throwing books out windows. Are people walking past outside warned that this is about to happen? He does not know. He has much to learn.

—Seth Quinn, go down and get that book.

—I didn't throw it.

—Go on.

—It's not fair.

—Now.

Joseph looks at Seth Quinn. He is not the so-what boy. He is a different boy.

—Now. Page 37.

No one tries to take Joseph's book. No more books go out the window. He opens his book at Page 37.

The teacher-lady talks at great speed. He understands the numbers she writes on the blackboard. He understands the words she writes. LONG DIVISION. But he does not understand what she says, especially when she faces the blackboard. He does not put his hand up. He watches the numbers on the blackboard. It is not so very difficult.

A finger pushes into his back. The so-what boy. Joseph does not turn.

—Hey. Live-Aid.

Joseph does not turn.

The so-what boy whispers.

—Live-Aid. Hey, Live-Aid. Do they know it's Christmas?

It is Monday, the tenth day of January. It is sixteen days after Christmas. This is a very stupid boy.

But Joseph knows that this is not to do with Christmas or the correct date. He knows he must be careful.

The finger prods his back again, harder, very hard.

—Christian Kelly!

—What?

It is the so-what boy. His name is Christian Kelly.

—Are you annoying Joseph there?

—No.

—Is he, Joseph?

Joseph shakes his head. He must speak. He knows this.

—No.

—I'm sure he's not, she says.

This is strange, he thinks. Her response. Is it another trick?

—Sit up straight so I can see you, Christian Kelly.

—He was poking Joseph's back, Miss.

—Shut up.

—He was.

—Fuck off.

—Now!

Miss the teacher-lady stares at a place above Joseph's head. There is silence in the classroom. The hands-in-the-air trick is certainly not necessary.

—God give me strength, she says.

But why? Joseph wonders. What is she about to do? There is nothing very heavy in the classroom.

She stares again. For six seconds, exactly. Then she taps the blackboard with a piece of chalk.

—Take it down.

He waits. He watches the other children. They take copy books from their school bags. They open the copy books. They draw the margin. They stare at the blackboard. They write. They stare again. They write. A girl in the desk beside him takes a pair of glasses from a small black box that clicks loudly when she opens it. She puts the glasses onto her face. She looks at him. Her eyes are big. She smiles.

—Specky fancies yeh.

It is Christian Kelly.

—You're dead.

CHAPTER TWO
THE FINGER

—You're dead, says Christian Kelly.

This is the dangerous boy who sits behind Joseph. This boy has just told Joseph that he is dead. Joseph must understand this statement, very quickly.

He does not turn, to look at Christian Kelly.

Miss, the teacher-lady, has wiped the figures from the blackboard. She writes new figures. Joseph sees: these are problems to be solved. There are ten problems. They are not difficult.

What did Christian Kelly mean? *You are dead.* Joseph thinks about these words and this too is not difficult. It is very clear that Joseph is not dead.

So, Christian Kelly's words must refer to the future. *You will be dead.* All boys must grow and eventually die—Joseph knows this; he has seen dead men and boys. Christian Kelly's words are clearly intended as a threat, or promise. *I will kill you.* But Christian Kelly will not murder Joseph just because the girl with the magnified eyes smiled at him. *I will hurt you.* This is what Christian Kelly means.

Joseph has not yet seen this Christian Kelly.

It is very strange. Joseph must protect himself from a boy he has not seen. Perhaps not so very strange. He did not see the men who killed his father.

The girl with the magnified eyes smiles again at Joseph. This time Christian Kelly does not speak. Joseph looks again at his copy book.

He completes the seventh problem. 751 divided by 15. He knows the answer many seconds before he writes it down. He already knows the answer to the ninth problem—761 divided by 15—but he starts to solve the eighth one first. He is quite satisfied with his progress. It is many months since Joseph sat in a classroom. It is warm here. January is certainly a cold month in this country.

Christian Kelly is going to hurt him. He has promised this. Joseph must be prepared.

—Finished?

It is the teacher-lady. The question is for everybody.

Joseph looks. Many of the boys and girls still lean over their copy books. Their faces almost touch the paper.

—Hurry up now. We haven't all day.

—Hey.

The voice comes from behind Joseph. It is not loud.

Joseph turns. He does this quickly. He sees this Christian Kelly.

—What's number 4?

Quickly, Joseph decides.

—17, he whispers.

He turns back, to face the blackboard and the teacher-lady.

—You're still dead. What's number 5?

—17.

—How can—

—Also 17.

—No talk.

Joseph looks at the blackboard.

—It better be.

—Christian Kelly.

It is the teacher-lady.

—What did I say? she asks.

—Don't know, says Christian Kelly.

—No talk.

—I wasn't—

—Just finish your sums. Finished, Joseph?

Joseph nods.

—Good lad. Now. One more minute.

Joseph counts the boys and girls. There are twenty-three children in the room. This sum includes Joseph. There are five desks without occupants.

—That's plenty of time. Now. Pencils down. Down.

One boy sits very near the door. Unlike Joseph, he wears the school sweater. Like Joseph, he is black. A girl sits behind Joseph, beside a big map of this country. She, also, is black. She sits beside the map. And is she Irish?

—Now. Who's first?

Miss, the teacher-lady, smiles.

Children lift their hands.

—Miss, Miss. Miss, Miss.

Joseph does not lift his hand.

—We'll get to the shy ones later, says the teacher-lady. —Hazel O'Hara.

Hands go down. Some children groan.

The girl with the magnified eyes removes her glasses. She put them into the box. It clicks. She stands up.

—Good girl.

She walks to the front of the room.

What do Irish children look like? Like this Hazel O'Hara? Joseph is not sure. Hazel's hair is almost white. Her skin is very pink right now; she is very satisfied. She is standing beside the teacher-lady and she is holding a piece of white chalk.

—Now, Hazel. Are you going to show us all how to do number one?

Hazel O'Hara nods.

—Off you go.

Christian Kelly does not resemble Hazel O'Hara.

—Hey.

Joseph watches Hazel O'Hara's progress.

—Hey.

Hazel O'Hara's demonstration is both swift and accurate.

Joseph turns, to look at Christian Kelly.

—Yes? he whispers.

—D'you want that?

Christian Kelly is holding up a finger, very close to Joseph's face. There is something on the finger's tip. Joseph hears another voice.

—Kelly's got snot on his finger.

Joseph turns, to face the blackboard. He feels the finger on his shoulder. He hears laughter—he feels the finger press his shoulder.

He grabs.

He pulls.

—What's going on there?

Christian Kelly is on the floor, beside Joseph. Joseph holds the finger. Christian Kelly makes much noise.

The teacher-lady now holds Joseph's wrist.

—Let go. Now. Hands in the air! Everybody!

Joseph releases Christian Kelly's finger. He looks at Hazel O'Hara's answer on the blackboard. It is correct.

CHAPTER THREE
YOU'RE DEFINITELY DEAD

Joseph looks at the blackboard. Miss still holds his wrist. There is much noise in the room.

He sees boys and girls stand out of their seats. Other children lean across their neighbors' desks. They all want to see Christian Kelly.

Christian Kelly remains on the floor. He also makes much noise.

—Me finger! He broke me finger!

—Sit down!

It is Miss.

—Hands in the air!

She no longer holds Joseph's wrist. Joseph watches children sit down. He sees hands in the air. He looks at his hands. He raises them.

—Joseph?

He looks at Miss. She kneels beside Christian Kelly. She holds the finger. She presses the knuckle. Christian Kelly screams.

—There's nothing broken, Christian, she says. —You'll be grand.

—It's sore!

—I'm sure it is, she says.

She stands. She almost falls back as she does this. She puts one hand behind her. She holds her skirt with the other hand.

Joseph hears a voice behind him. It is a whisper. Perhaps it is Seth Quinn.

—I seen her knickers.

She is now standing. So is Christian Kelly.

—What color?

Miss shouts.

—Now!

Christian Kelly rubs his nose with his sleeve. He looks at Joseph. Joseph looks at him. There is silence in the classroom.

—That's better, says Miss. —Now. Hands down. Good. Joseph.

Joseph hears the whisper-voice.

—Yellow.

Joseph looks up at Miss. She is looking at someone behind him. She says those words again.

—God give me strength.

She speaks very quietly. She turns to Christian Kelly. She puts her hand on his shoulder.

—Sit down, Christian.

Christian Kelly goes to his desk, behind Joseph. Joseph does not look at him.

—Now. Joseph. Stand up.

Joseph does this. He stands up.

—First. Christian is no angel. Are you, Christian?

—I didn't do anything.

She smiles at Christian. She looks at Joseph.

—You have to apologize to Christian, she says.

Joseph speaks.

—Why?

She looks surprised. She inhales, slowly.

—Because you hurt him.

This is fair, Joseph thinks.

—I apologize, he says.

A boy speaks.

—He's supposed to look at him when he's saying it.

Miss, the teacher-lady, laughs. This surprises Joseph.

—He's right, she says.

Joseph turns. He looks at Christian Kelly. Christian Kelly glances at Joseph. He then looks at his desk.

—I apologize, says Joseph.

—He didn't mean to hurt you, says Miss.

Joseph speaks.

—That is not correct, he says.

—Oh now, says Miss.

Many voices whisper.

—What did he say?

—He's in for it now.

—Look at her face.

—Now!

Joseph looks at Miss's face. It is extremely red.

She speaks.

—We'll have to see about this

Her meaning is not clear.

—Get your bag.

Joseph picks up his schoolbag. Into this bag he puts his new *Maths Matters* book and copy book and pencil.

—Come on now.

Is he being expelled from this room? He does not know. He hears excited voices.

—She's throwing him out.

—Is she throwing him out?

He follows Miss to the front of the room.

—Now, she says. —We'd better put some space between you and Christian.

Joseph is very happy. He is to stay. And Christian Kelly will no longer sit behind him.

But then there is Seth Quinn.

A girl speaks. She is a very big girl.

—He should sit beside Pamela.

Many girls laugh.

—No, says the black girl who sits beside the map.

Joseph understands. This is Pamela.

—Leave poor Pamela alone, says Miss. —There.

Miss points.

—Beside Hazel.

Joseph watches the girl called Hazel O'Hara. She moves her chair. She makes room for Joseph. She wears her glasses. Her eyes are very big. Her hair is very white. Her skin is very pink indeed.

—Look at Hazel, says the big girl. —She's blushing.

Hazel speaks.

—Fuck off you.

—Now!

Joseph sits beside Hazel O'Hara.

—Hands in the air!

Joseph raises his hand. He hears a voice he knows.

—You're definitely dead.

Joseph looks at the clock. It is round and it is placed on the wall, over the door.

—Don't listen to that dirtbag, says Hazel O'Hara.

It is five minutes after ten o'clock. It is an hour since Joseph was brought to this room by the man. It certainly has been very eventful.

—Joseph?

It is Miss.

—Yes? says Joseph.

—I'm not finished with you yet, says Miss. —Stay here at little break.

What is this little break? Joseph does not know. The other boys in the hostel did not tell him about a little break.

—Now, says Miss. —At last. The sums on the board. Who did the last one?

—Hazel.

—That's right. Who's next?

Hands are raised. Some of the children lift themselves off their seats.

—Miss!

—Miss!

—Seth Quinn, says Miss.

—Didn't have my hand up.

—Come on, Seth.

Joseph hears a chair being pushed. He does not turn.

CHAPTER FOUR
MILK

The boy called Seth Quinn walks to the front of the room. He is a small, angry boy. His head is shaved. His nose is red. He stands at the blackboard but he does not stand still.

—So, Seth, says Miss, the teacher-lady.

—What?

—Do number three for us.

She holds out a piece of chalk. Seth Quinn takes it but he does not move closer to the blackboard.

Beside Joseph, Hazel O'Hara whispers. —Bet he gets it wrong.

Joseph does not respond. He looks at Seth Quinn.

—Well, Seth? says Miss.

Joseph knows the answer. He would very much like to whisper it to Seth Quinn.

Miss holds out her hand. She takes back the chalk.

—Sit down now, Seth, she says.

—Told you, says Hazel O'Hara.

Joseph watches Seth Quinn. He walks past Joseph. He looks at the floor. He does not look at Joseph.

—Maybe we'll have less guff out of Seth for a while, says Miss.

Joseph decides to whisper.

—What is guff?

—It's a culchie word, Hazel O'Hara whispers back. — It means talking, if you don't like talking. She says it all the time.

—Thank you, says Joseph, very quietly.

—Jaysis, says Hazel O'Hara. —You're welcome.

—Now, says Miss. —Little break.

Some of the children stand up.

—Sit down, says Miss.

This, Joseph thinks, is very predictable.

Miss waits until all the children sit again.

—Now, she says. —We didn't get much work done yet today. So you'll want to pull up your socks when we get back. Now, stand.

Pull up your socks. This must mean *work harder*. Again, Joseph feels that he is learning. He does not stand up.

—Dead.

It is Christian Kelly, as he passes Joseph.

The room is soon empty. Joseph and Miss are alone. It is very quiet.

—Well, Joseph, she says. —What have you to say for yourself?

Joseph does not speak. She smiles.

—God, she says. —I wish they were all as quiet as you. How are you finding it?

Joseph thinks he knows what this means.

—I like school very much, he answers.

—Good, she says. —You'll get used to the accents.

—Please, says Joseph. —There is no difficulty.

—Good, she says. —Now.

She steps back from Joseph's desk. Does this mean that he is permitted to go? He does not stand.

She speaks.

—Look, Joseph. I know a little bit about why you're here. Why you left, your country.

She looks at Joseph.

—And if you don't want to talk about it, that's grand.

Joseph nods.

—I hope you have a great time here. I do.

She is, Joseph thinks, quite a nice lady. But why did she embarrass Seth Quinn?

—But, she says.

Still, she smiles.

—I can't have that behavior, with Christian, in the classroom. Or anywhere else.

—I apologize.

She laughs.

—I'm not laughing at you, she says. —It's lovely. You're so polite, Joseph.

She says nothing for some seconds. Joseph does not look at her.

—But no more fighting, she says. —Or pulling fingers, or whatever it was you did to Christian.

Joseph does not answer.

—You've a few minutes left, says Miss. —Off you go.

—Thank you, says Joseph.

He stands, although he would prefer to stay in the classroom.

He walks out, to the corridor.

He remembers the way to the schoolyard. It is not complicated. He goes down a very bright staircase. He passes a man. The man smiles at Joseph. Joseph reaches the bottom step. The door is in front of him. He sees children outside, through the window. The schoolyard is very crowded.

He is not afraid of Christian Kelly.

He reaches the door.

But he does not wish to be the center of attention.

He cannot see Christian Kelly in the schoolyard. He pushes the door. He is outside. It is quite cold.

Something bright flies past him. He feels it scrape his face as it passes. He hears a smack behind him, close to his ear. And his neck is suddenly wet, and his hair. And his sleeve.

He looks.

It is milk, a carton. There is milk on the glass and on the ground but there is also milk on Joseph. He is quite wet, and he is also the center of attention. He is surrounded.

—Kellier did it.

—Christian Kelly.

Even in the space between Joseph and the door, there are children. Joseph does not see Christian Kelly. He removes his sweatshirt, over his head, and feels the milk on his face. He must wash the sweatshirt before the milk starts to smell. He touches his shoulder. His shirt is also very wet. It too must be washed.

He is very cold.

There is movement, pushing. Children move aside. Christian Kelly stands in front of Joseph. And behind Christian Kelly, Joseph sees Seth Quinn.

CHAPTER FIVE
THE BELL

Christian Kelly stands in front of Joseph. Seth Quinn stands behind Christian Kelly.

All the children in the school, it seems, are watching. They stand behind Joseph, pressing. They are also beside him, left and right, and in front, behind Christian Kelly. Joseph knows: something must happen, even if the bell rings and announces the conclusion of this thing called little break. The bell will not bring rescue.

Joseph remembers another bell.

For one second there is silence.

Then Joseph hears a voice.

—Do him.

Joseph does not see who has spoken. It was not Christian Kelly and it was not Seth Quinn.

He hears other voices.

—Go on, Kellier.

—Go on.

—Chicken.

Then Joseph hears Christian Kelly. He sees his lips.

—I told you.

Joseph remembers the soldier.

The soldier walked out of the schoolhouse. He held the bell up high in the air. It was the bell that called them all to school, every morning. It was louder than any other sound in Joseph's village, louder than engines and cattle. Joseph loved its peal, its beautiful ding. He never had to be called to school. He was there every morning, there to watch the bell lifted and dropped, lifted to the teacher's shoulder, and dropped. Joseph's father was the teacher.

—I told you, says Christian Kelly.

Joseph does not respond. He knows: anything he says will be a provocation. He will not do this.

There is a surge of children, behind Christian Kelly. He is being pushed. Christian Kelly must do something. He must hit Joseph. Joseph understands this. Someone pulls at Joseph's sweatshirt. He has been holding the sweatshirt at his side. He does not look; he does not takes his eyes off Christian

Kelly, or Seth Quinn. Someone pulls again, but not too hard. He or she is offering to hold it. Joseph lets go of the sweatshirt. His hands are free. He is very cold. He looks at Christian Kelly. He knows. This is not what Christian Kelly wants. Christian Kelly is frightened.

The soldier held the bell up high. He let it drop; he lifted it. The bell rang out clearly. There were no car or truck engines in the air that morning. Just gunfire and, sometimes, the far sound of someone screaming or crying. The bell rang out but no children came running. Joseph hid behind the school wall. The soldier was grinning. More soldiers came out of the schoolhouse. They fired their guns into the air. The soldier dropped the bell. Another soldier aimed at it and fired.

Christian Kelly takes the step and pushes Joseph. Joseph feels the hand on his chest. He steps back. He stands on a foot, behind him. Christian Kelly's hand follows Joseph. Joseph grabs the hand, and one of the fingers.

This is a very stupid boy indeed.

Joseph watches Christian Kelly. He sees the sudden terror. Christian Kelly realizes that he has made an important mistake. Once again, he has delivered his finger to Joseph.

It is now Joseph's turn. He must do something.

The soldiers had gone. Joseph waited. He wanted to enter the schoolhouse; he wanted to find his father. But he was frightened. The bullet noise was still alive in his ears, and the laughing soldiers, his father's bell—Joseph was too frightened. He was ashamed, but he could not move. He wanted to call out to his father but his throat was blocked and too dry. He had dirtied himself, but he could not move.

Children shout but Joseph does not look or listen. He looks straight at Christian Kelly. He knows: he cannot release the finger. It will be weakness. Seth Quinn stands behind Christian Kelly. He stares at Joseph.

The school bell rings. It is a harsh electric bell.

No one moves.

The bell continues to ring. Joseph continues to look at Christian Kelly. The bell stops.

He found his father behind the schoolhouse. He knew it was his father, although he did not see the face. He did not go closer. He recognized his father's trousers. He recognized his father's shirt and shoes. He ran.

Christian Kelly tries to pull back his finger. Joseph tightens his hold.

He hears children.

—This is stupid.

—Are yis going to fight, or what?

There are fewer children surrounding them. The children stand in lines, in the schoolyard. They wait for the teachers to bring them back into the school. Joseph and Christian Kelly are alone now, with Seth Quinn.

—Let him go.

It is Seth Quinn. He has spoken to Joseph.

—Seth Quinn!

It is Miss, the teacher-lady. She is behind Joseph. Christian Kelly tries to rescue his finger.

—And Christian Kelly.

Miss sees Christian Kelly's finger in Joseph's fist.

—Again?

Joseph knows what she will say.

—God give me strength.

He is learning very quickly.

CHAPTER SIX
ROBBING A BANK

Miss the teacher-lady follows the other boys and girls into the classroom. She stops at the door and turns to Joseph, Christian Kelly, and Seth Quinn.

—Not a squeak out of you, she says. —Just stand there.

She is looking at Joseph. Does she think that he will run away?

She walks into the room. Joseph remains in the corridor.

—Now!

Joseph hears the noise of children sitting down, retrieving books from schoolbags. He hears Miss.

—Open up page 47 of *Totally Gaeilge*. Questions one to seven. I'll be right outside and listening out for any messing.

Joseph does not look at Christian Kelly or Seth Quinn. They do not speak. They face the classroom door but cannot see inside.

Miss has returned.

—Now, she says.

She stands in front of them.

—I didn't do anything, says Christian Kelly.

—Shut up, Christian, for God's sake.

Joseph looks at Miss. She does not look very angry.

—We have to sort this out, boys, she says.

—I didn't—

—Christian!

It is, perhaps, a time when she will say *God give me strength*.

But she doesn't. She looks at Seth Quinn.

—Seth, she says. —What happened?

—Nothing.

Christian Kelly is looking at the floor. Seth Quinn is looking at Miss.

—It was a funny sort of nothing I saw, says Miss. —Well, Joseph. Your turn. What happened?

—Nothing happened, says Joseph.

Miss says nothing, for three seconds. These seconds, Joseph thinks, are important. Because, in that time, the three boys become united. This is what Joseph thinks. They are united in their silence. They do not like one another but this does not matter. They stand there together, against Miss.

She looks at the three boys.

—You're great lads, she says.

Joseph does not think that she is sincere.

—What'll I do with you? she says.

Again, the boys say nothing.

Seth?

Seth Quinn shrugs.

—Joseph?

Joseph looks at her. He does not speak. He will not speak. He will be punished but he is not frightened or very concerned. He is, at this moment, quite happy.

—Nothing to say for yourself? says Miss.

Joseph shakes his head. He looks at the floor. There are many loud noises coming from the classroom. Joseph hopes that these will distract Miss. She does not speak. He hears her breathe. He looks at her feet. They do not move.

She speaks.

—Right, so. If that's the way you want it—

—Miss?

Joseph looks. It is Hazel O'Hara, the girl with the magnified eyes. She is at the door.

—Yes, Hazel? says Miss.

—I seen it.

—Now, Hazel—

—But I seen it. Christian Kelly pushed—

—Back inside, Hazel.

—But he—

—Hazel!

Hazel lifts her very big eyes and makes a clicking sound with her mouth. She turns and walks back into the classroom. They hear her.

—She's a bitch, that one. I was only telling her.

Miss follows Hazel. She rushes into the classroom.

—Hands in the air!

Seth Quinn speaks.

—She thinks she's robbing a fuckin' bank.

Christian Kelly laughs quietly. Seth Quinn laughs quietly. Joseph smiles. They listen to Miss. They cannot see.

—Hazel O'Hara!

—What?

Joseph laughs. It is like listening to a radio program.

—I heard you what you said, Hazel O'Hara!

—It was a private conversation.

He laughs because the other boys are also laughing. He hears them snort. He also snorts.

—Don't you *dare* talk to me like that!

—Like what?

Joseph looks at Christian Kelly. He looks at Seth Quinn. They laugh, with him. Their shoulders shake.

—Stand up! says Miss.

—I *am* standing.

—Hands in the air!

—She's an eejit, whispers Christian Kelly.

The three boys laugh together.

It is quiet in the classroom.

Seth Quinn whispers, —Now.

And—

—Now, says Miss, inside the room.

This is, perhaps, the funniest thing that Joseph has ever heard. He laughs so much, he cannot see. He wipes his eyes. The other boys also wipe their eyes. He tries to stop. He knows that Miss will soon reappear.

He stops.

Then he says it.

—Now.

He thinks suddenly of his father; a great weight drops through his chest. He cries now as he laughs. He feels the weight, the sadness, fall right through him. He wipes his eyes. He continues to laugh. Many times, Joseph made his father laugh. He remembers the sound of his father's laughter; he sees his father's face.

He laughs. He wipes his eyes. He looks at the other boys. They are looking at the classroom door.

Miss stands in front of Joseph.

He stops laughing. He waits.

He is surprised. She does not seem angry. She looks at Joseph for some long time.

—The three musketeers, she says. —In you go.

She stands aside.

Christian Kelly enters the room. Joseph follows Christian Kelly. Seth Quinn follows Joseph.

THE OPERATIVES BALL

a twenty-minute story by LAIRD HUNT

IT WAS PART of their Organization's policy that operatives must fill out an application before seeing each other in anything more than the most leisurely and amicable way. They duly traipsed down to the local applications office and asked for the appropriate form. The individual behind the counter coughed. We're all out, he said. And why aren't you wearing your sunglasses?

We didn't think, said the man.

It was necessary to do so, said the woman.

In our free time, said the man.

You're on Organization property, aren't you? You're taking up Organization time, aren't you? said the individual.

How very true, said the woman.

But never mind that, said the man, when will you have the forms?

They were told to try again the next day. That night the man assisted at a kidnapping and the woman led a small group into a trap. Neither engagement went off particularly smoothly. When they were finished, they happily honored the terms of a rendezvous at the bar they were in the habit of frequenting.

I'm tired, said the man.

Exhausted, said the woman.

Feeling sexy, though, said the man.

Entendu, said the woman.

They drank. Pretty soon they were drunk. Pretty soon they were in bed together. The next day they went back to the applications office and asked for a form.

No form, said the individual behind the counter.

But we have to have a form, said the man.

No, apparently you think you don't, said the individual.

That night the man was conked on the head and shipped off to another duty station, and the woman was tossed into a box. They both recovered. Ten years went by. They both did well, very respectably. By chance, they met up again. At an operatives ball.

You've grown so lovely and fat, she said, swooshing up to him.

As have you, he said.

They smiled and tittered and they looked at each other through their sunglasses.

I was actually under the impression you were dead, said the woman.

I was told that you definitely were.

Well I'm not, said the woman.

Nor am I, said the man.

They giggled, moved toward each other, tangled shoulder holsters, danced a couple numbers, then left. They had only been in the dark for a few delicious all but undressed moments when they heard a cough and the lights came on.

—April 7, 2002, 6:43 – 7:03 p.m., New York, NY

The idea started with an exchange I had with Dave Daley, then the books editor at the *Hartford Courant*. Daley asked me to write something, and I agreed, then dawdled and did nothing. On the last possible day, I told him, desperate and pleading, that I couldn't finish an actual story in the time left, but I could maybe write a bunch of stories, each in twenty minutes, thus illuminating the creative process, the working mind, the limits of space and time. This load of bullshit he swallowed. They weren't uniformly terrible, and the exercise went a long way to convincing me that sometimes speed is helpful. And so we began talking about asking other writers to do the same thing. —DAVE EGGERS, *from the introduction to "Twenty-Minute Stories," in Issue 12*

STATISTICAL ABSTRACT FOR MY HOMETOWN, SPOKANE, WASHINGTON

by JESS WALTER

(fiction from Issue 37)

1. The population of Spokane, Washington is 203,268. It is the 104th biggest city in the United States.

2. Even before the recession, in 2008, 36,000 people in Spokane lived below the poverty line—a little more than 18 percent of the population. That's about the same as it was in Washington, DC at the time. The poverty rate was 12.5 percent in Seattle.

3. Spokane is sometimes called the biggest city between Seattle and Minneapolis, but this is only true if you ignore everything below Wyoming, including Salt Lake City, Denver, Phoenix, and at least four cities in Texas.

4. This is really just another way of saying nobody much lives in Montana or the Dakotas.

5. My grandfather arrived in Spokane in the 1930s, on a freight train he'd jumped near Fargo. Even he didn't want to live in the Dakotas.

6. On any given day in Spokane, Washington, there are more adult men per capita riding children's BMX bikes than in any other city in the world.

7. I've never been sure where these guys are going on those little bikes, their knees up around their ears as they pedal. They all wear hats—ballcaps in summer, stocking caps in winter. I've never been sure, either, whether the bikes belong to their kids or if they've stolen them. It may be that they just prefer BMX bikes to ten-speeds. Many of them have lost their driver's licenses after too many DUIs.

8. I was born in Spokane in 1965. Beginning in about 1978, when I was thirteen, I wanted to leave.

9. I'm still here.

10. In 2000 and 2001, the years I most desperately wanted to move out of Spokane, 2,645 illegal aliens were deported by the Spokane office of the U.S. Border Patrol. They were throwing people out of Spokane and I *still* couldn't leave.

11. In 1978, I had a **BMX** bike. It didn't have a chain guard, and since I favored bellbottom jeans, my pant legs were constantly getting snagged. This would cause me to pitch over the handlebars and into the street. My cousin Len stole that bike once, but he pretended he'd just borrowed it without my permission and eventually he gave it back. Later on it was stolen for good by an older guy in my neighborhood named Pete. I was in my front yard afterward, being lectured by my father for leaving my bike out unprotected, when I saw Pete go tooling past our house on the bike he'd just stolen from me. Stocking cap on his head, knees up around his ears. I was too scared to say anything. Fear has often overtaken me during such situations. I hated myself for that. Far more than I hated Pete.

12. In 1978, Spokane's biggest employer was Kaiser Aluminum. My dad worked there. Kaiser went belly-up in the 1990s, and all of the retirees, my dad included, lost a chunk of their pensions.

13. Now all of the biggest employers in Spokane are government entities. Technically, I haven't held a job since 1994. This does not make me unique in my hometown.

14. The poorest elementary school in the state of Washington is in Spokane. In fact, it's right behind my house. 98 percent of its students get free and reduced-price lunch. I sometimes think about the 2 percent who don't get free lunch. When I was a kid, we lived for two years on a ranch near Springdale, on the border of the Spokane Indian Reservation. My dad commuted sixty miles each way to the aluminum plant. On the third day of school, in 1974, a kid leaned over to me on the bus and said, "What's the deal, Richie, you gonna wear different clothes to school *every day?*" Because of my dad's job, my siblings and I were the only kids in school who didn't get free lunch *and* free breakfast. At home, we had Cream of Wheat. At school they had Sugar Pops.

15. Sugar Pops tasted way better than Cream of Wheat. In 1974, my dad got laid off from the aluminum plant and we *still* didn't qualify for free breakfast. You must have had to be really poor to get Sugar Pops.

16. Now they're called Corn Pops. Who in their right mind would rather eat Corn Pops than Sugar Pops?

17. While it's true that I don't technically have a job and that I live in a poor neighborhood, I don't mean to make myself sound poor. I do pretty well.

18. In Spokane it doesn't matter where you live, or how big your house is—you're never more than three blocks from a bad neighborhood. I've grown to like this. In a lot of cities, especially in Spokane's more affluent neighbors, Seattle and Portland, it can be easier to insulate yourself from poverty; you can live miles away from any poor people and start to believe that everyone is as well-off as you are.

19. They are not.

20. The median family income in Spokane, Washington is $51,000 a year. In Seattle, the median family income is $88,000 a year. Point: Seattle.

21. In Seattle, though, the median house price is $308,000. In Spokane it is $181,000.

22. Drivers in Spokane spend a total of 1.8 million hours a year stuck in traffic on the freeway. This is an average of five hours a year per person in the metropolitan region. In Seattle, they spend 72 million hours stuck on the freeway, an average of twenty-five hours per person in the region. That's an entire day. Suck on that, Seattle.

23. What would it take for you to willingly surrender an entire day of your life?

24. This used to be my list of reasons why I didn't like Spokane:
    • It is too poor, too white, and too uneducated.
    • There is not enough ethnic food.
    • It has a boring downtown and no art-house theater and is too conservative.

25. In the past few years, though, the downtown has been revitalized, the art scene is thriving, and the food has gotten increasingly better. There are twenty-nine Thai and Vietnamese restaurants listed in the yellow pages. The art-house theater briefly reopened at a time when similar theaters were closing everywhere else. There are bike paths everywhere, and I keep meeting cool, progressive people. The city even went for Obama in '08—barely, but still.

26. For the most part, despite all that, Spokane is still poor, white, and uneducated.

27. My own neighborhood is among the poorest in the state. It has an inordinate number of halfway houses, shelters, group homes, and drug- and alcohol-rehab centers.

28. I remember back when I was a newspaper reporter, I covered a hearing filled with South Hill homeowners, men and women from old-money Spokane, vociferously complaining about a group home going into their neighborhood. They were worried about falling property values, rising crime, and "undesirables." An activist I spoke to called these people NIMBYs. It was the first time I'd heard the term. I thought he meant NAMBLA—the North American Man/Boy Love Association. That seemed a little harsh to me.

29. Bedraggled and beaten women, women carrying babies and followed by children, often walk past my house on their way to the shelters and group homes. Often they carry their belongings in ragged old suitcases. Sometimes in garbage sacks.

30. Poverty and crime are linked, of course. Spokane's crime rate is well above the national average, and ranks the city 114th among the four hundred largest American cities, just below Boston. There are about ten murders a year, and 1,100 violent crimes. There are almost 12,000 property crimes—theft and burglary, that sort of thing. One year, a police sergeant estimated that a thousand bikes had been reported stolen.

31. I believe it.

32. My wife looked out the window at two in the morning once and saw a guy riding a child's BMX bike while dragging another one behind him. He was having trouble doing this, and eventually he laid one bike down in the weeds. I called the police and crouched by the window all night, watching until they arrested him when he came back for the second bike. I felt great, like McGruff the Crime Dog.

33. Another time, before I was married, I had gone for a bike ride and was sitting on my stoop with my bike propped against the railing when a guy tried to steal it. He just climbed on and started riding away. With me sitting there. I chased him down the block and grabbed the frame and he hopped off. "Sorry," he said, "I thought it was mine." What could I say? "Well... it isn't."

34. Another time, we hired a tree trimmer who showed up with three day laborers in the back of his pickup truck. One of them disappeared after only an hour of work. The tree trimmer didn't seem concerned; he said workers often wandered off if the work was too hard. It wasn't until the next day that I realized the day laborer had made his escape on my unlocked mountain bike. I'd paid only $25 for that one, at a pawn shop where I was looking, in vain, for my previous bike, which had also been stolen. Since pawn-shop bikes have almost always been stolen from somewhere, it seemed somehow fitting that it would be stolen again.

35. A friend's rare and expensive bike once went missing and showed up for sale on Craigslist. I drove with him to meet the seller. We made this elaborate plan that involved the two of us stealing the bike back, or confronting the thieves, or something like that. I just remember I was supposed to wait in the car until he gave me a signal. When we arrived at their house we discovered that the bike thieves were huge, all tatted up and shirtless. They were sitting on a couch on their porch, drinking malt liquor and smoking. I waited for the signal. A few minutes later my friend got back in the car. It wasn't his bike. He was disappointed. I was tremendously relieved.

36. The largest number of people I ever saw walking to one of the shelters in my neighborhood was five: a crying woman and her four children, all behind her, like ducklings. I smiled encouragingly at them. It was a hot day. I had the sprinkler on in my front yard and the last duckling stepped into the oscillating water and smiled at me. I don't know why the whole thing made me feel so crappy, but it did.

37. Once, when I was watching sports on TV, a guy pounded on our front door and started yelling, "Tiffany! Goddamn it, Tiffany! Get your ass down here!"

38. I went to the door. The guy was wearing torn jeans and no shirt and a ballcap. He seemed sketchy and twitchy, like a meth user. I said there was no one inside named Tiffany. He said, "I know this is a shelter for women and I know she's here." I insisted that it wasn't a shelter, that

the place he was looking for was miles away, and that I was going to call the police if he didn't leave.

39. He said he was going to kick my ass. I tried to look tough, but I was terrified.

40. My lifetime record in fistfights is zero wins, four losses, and one draw. I used to claim the draw as a win, but my brother, who witnessed that fight, always made this face like, *Really?*

41. The shirtless guy looking for Tiffany swore colorfully at me. Then he climbed on a little kid's BMX bike and rode away, his knees hunched up around his ears.

42. Later, when I was sure he was gone, I went to the shelter and knocked on the front door. A woman's voice came from a nearby window. "Yes?" she said. I couldn't see her face. I told her what had happened. She thanked me. I left.

43. For days, I imagined the other things I could have said to that asshole. Or I imagined punching him. I felt like I'd not handled it well, although I can't imagine what I should have done differently.

44. After that I decided to volunteer at the shelter. I'd always seen kids playing behind the high fence, and I thought I could play with them or read to them. But I was told they only had a small number of male volunteers because having men around made so many of the women nervous.

45. Of the 36,000 people living in poverty in Spokane, most are children.

46. Right at the peak of my obnoxious and condescending loathing for my hometown, I rented a houseboat in Seattle for $900 a month so I could pretend I lived there. While staying on that boat, and hanging around Seattle, I had a conversation with someone about all that was wrong with Spokane. He said that it was too poor and too white and too uneducated

and too unsophisticated, and as he spoke, I realized something: this guy hated Spokane because of people like me. *I* grew up poor, white, and unsophisticated. I was the first in my family to graduate from college. And worse, I had made the same complaints. Did I hate Spokane because I hated people like me? Did I hate it for not letting me forget my own upbringing? Then I had this even more sobering thought: Was I the kind of snob who hates a place because it's poor?

47. I think there are only two things you can do with your hometown: look for ways to make it better, or look for another place to live.

48. Last year I volunteered at the low-income school behind my house, tutoring kids who needed help with reading. Most of the other tutors were retired, and it was sweet to watch the six-year-olds take these smiling seniors by the hands and drag them around the school, looking for a quiet place to read. One day I was helping this intense little eight-year-old, Dylan. We read a story together about a cave boy who was frightened by a wolf until the wolf saves his life and becomes his friend. Every time I showed up after that, Dylan had the wolf book out for me to read. I'd say, "You should get another book," and he'd say, "Why should I read another book when this one's so good?" Point: Dylan.

49. One day we talked about what scared us. After I told Dylan how I used to be afraid of the furnace in our basement, Dylan told me he was scared that his brother would kill him. I laughed at the commonalities of all people and told him that brothers just sometimes fight with each other, it wasn't anything to be afraid of, his brother loved him, and he said, "No, my brother really tried to kill me. He choked me and I passed out and my stepfather had to tear him off me. I was in the hospital. He still says he's gonna kill me one day." I reported this to the teacher, who said the boy's brother had indeed tried to kill him.

50. The Halloween before last, I glanced out the window and saw a woman making her way past the front of my house with a toddler in her arms. I grabbed the candy bowl, thinking they were trick-or-treating, and that's when I noticed a young man walking beside the woman. I noticed

him because out of nowhere, he punched her. She swerved sideways but kept limping down the street. I dropped the candy and ran outside. "Hey!" I yelled. "Leave her alone!" Now I could see the woman was crying, carrying crutches in one hand and a three-year-old boy in the other. Her boyfriend, or whoever he was, was red with anger. He ignored me and kept yelling at her. "Your mom told me you were coming here! Now stop! I just wanna talk to you! You can't do this!" I stepped between them. "Leave her alone!" I said again; then I said, "Get outta here!" He balled his hands into fists and said, "That ain't happenin'." But during all of this he refused to look at me, as if I weren't even there. His eyes were red and bleary. I was terrified. I told him he just needed to go home. He wouldn't acknowledge me. He kept stepping to the side to get an angle on his girlfriend, and I kept stepping in front of him. At some point the woman handed me her crutches so she could get a better hold of her child. She was limping heavily. We air-danced down the block this way, painfully slowly, silently: her, me, him. Eventually I said, "Look, I'm gonna call the cops and this is all gonna get worse." His face went white. Then he tensed up and took a short, compact swing. At himself. It sounded like a gunshot, the sound of his fist hitting his own face. It was loud enough that my neighbor, Mike, came outside. Mike is a big, strapping Vietnam veteran, about as tough and as reasonable a man as I know. The guy seemed worried by Mike, certainly more worried than he'd been by me. Mike and I stood on either side of the woman until her angry young boyfriend gave up and stalked off. Twice more he punched himself as he walked. He was sobbing. We waited until he was gone and then we escorted her to the shelter. All the way there, the little boy stared at me. I didn't know what to say. For some reason I asked if he was going trick-or-treating later that night. His mother looked at me like I was crazy.

51. At the shelter, I gave her back the crutches. The woman knocked on the door. It opened. Mike and I stayed on the street, because that's as close as we're supposed to get. Maybe as close as we want to get. A gentle hand took the woman's arm and she and her boy were led carefully inside.

CIRCUS

a pantoum by JENNIFER MICHAEL HECHT

My people were existential thugs.
At circus, monkeys in derbies rode us.
Muttering, Life, in a full-bodied shrug,
at circus we swept up the sawdust.

At circus, monkeys in derbies rode us,
while the great rode feathered horses.
At circus we swept up the sawdust,
the dove's debris and patrons' losses.

While the great rode feathered horses,
humming to Pegasus, Oh Peggy Sue,
we'd unglove, debrief, and pocket losses.
Tanneries are what my people knew.

Brushing Pegasus to strains of "Peggy Sue,"
catching acrobats. Shadow of a big top,
tailor's tales of what the ball gown knew.
Sequins and confetti on a rag mop.

Catch an acrobat's shadow on the big top
muttering, Life, with a bruise. Shrugged
sequins; drooped confetti like a rag mop.
My people were existential thugs.

A Western descendant of the Malay *pantun*, a pantoum is a poem composed in quatrains,
in which the second and fourth lines of each stanza reappear (with small alterations)
as the first and third lines of the next stanza, and the first and third lines of the first
stanza return as the last and second lines, respectively, of the final stanza. There is no set
length, rhyme scheme, or subject matter for a pantoum, and artful manipulation of the
repeated lines is encouraged. The three included in this anthology were commissioned
for Issue 31, dedicated to "Dead Forms"—the pantoum, the consuetudinary, the biji, the
Graustarkian romance, and more.

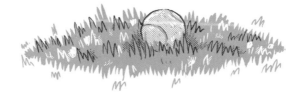

PHANTOMS

by STEVEN MILLHAUSER

(fiction from Issue 35)

THE PHENOMENON

THE PHANTOMS OF our town do not, as some think, appear only in the dark. Often we come upon them in full sunlight, when shadows lie sharp on the lawns and streets. The encounters take place for very short periods, ranging from two or three seconds to perhaps half a minute, though longer episodes are sometimes reported. So many of us have seen them that it's uncommon to meet someone who has not; of this minority, only a small number deny that phantoms exist. Sometimes an encounter occurs more than once in the course of a single day; sometimes six months pass, or a year. The phantoms, which some call Presences, are not easy to distinguish from ordinary citizens: they are not translucent, or smoke-like, or hazy, they do not ripple like heat waves, nor are they in any way unusual in figure or dress. Indeed they are so much like us that it sometimes happens we mistake them for someone we know. Such errors are rare, and never last for more than a moment. They themselves appear to be uneasy during an encounter and swiftly withdraw. They always look at us before turning away. They never speak. They are wary, elusive, secretive, haughty, unfriendly, remote.

EXPLANATION #1

One explanation has it that our phantoms are the auras, or visible traces, of earlier inhabitants of our town, which was settled in 1636. Our atmosphere, saturated with the energy of all those who have preceded us, preserves them and permits them, under certain conditions, to become visible to us. This explanation, often fitted out with a pseudoscientific vocabulary, strikes most of us as unconvincing. The phantoms always appear in contemporary dress, they never behave in ways that suggest earlier eras, and there is no evidence whatever to support the claim that the dead leave visible traces in the air.

HISTORY

As children we are told about the phantoms by our fathers and mothers. They in turn have been told by their own fathers and mothers, who can remember being told by their parents—our great-grandparents—when they were children. Thus the phantoms of our town are not new; they don't represent a sudden eruption into our lives, a recent change in our sense of things. We have no formal records that confirm the presence of phantoms throughout the diverse periods of our history, no scientific reports or transcripts of legal proceedings, but some of us are familiar with the second-floor Archive Room of our library, where in nineteenth-century diaries we find occasional references to "the others" or "them," without further details. Church records of the seventeenth century include several mentions of "the devil's children," which some view as evidence for the lineage of our phantoms; others argue that the phrase is so general that it cannot be cited as proof of anything. The official town history, published in 1936 on the three-hundredth anniversary of our incorporation, revised in 1986, and updated in 2006, makes no mention of the phantoms. An editorial note states that "the authors have confined themselves to ascertainable fact."

HOW WE KNOW

We know by a ripple along the skin of our forearms, accompanied by a tension of the inner body. We know because they look at us and withdraw immediately. We know because when we try to follow them, we find that they have vanished. We know because we know.

CASE STUDY #1

Richard Moore rises from beside the bed, where he has just finished the forty-second installment of a never-ending story that he tells each night to his four-year-old daughter, bends over her for a goodnight kiss, and walks quietly from the room. He loves having a daughter; he loves having a wife, a family; though he married late, at thirty-nine, he knows he wasn't ready when he was younger, not in his doped-up twenties, not in his stupid, wasted thirties, when he was still acting like some angry teenager who hated the grown-ups; and now he's grateful for it all, like someone who can hardly believe that he's allowed to live in his own house. He walks along the hall to the den, where his wife is sitting at one end of the couch, reading a book in the light of the table lamp, while the TV is on mute during an ad for vinyl siding. He loves that she won't watch the ads, that she refuses to waste those minutes, that she reads books, that she's sitting there waiting for him, that the light from the TV is flickering on her hand and upper arm. Something has begun to bother him, though he isn't sure what it is, but as he steps into the den he's got it, he's got it: the table in the side yard, the two folding chairs, the sunglasses on the tabletop. He was sitting out there with her after dinner, and he left his sunglasses. "Back in a sec," he says, and turns away, enters the kitchen, opens the door to the small screened porch at the back of the house, and walks from the porch down the steps to the back-yard, a narrow strip between the house and the cedar fence. It's nine-thirty on a summer night. The sky is dark blue, the fence lit by the light from the kitchen window, the grass black here and green over there. He turns the corner of the house and comes to the private place. It's the part of the yard bounded by the fence, the side-yard hedge, and the row of three Scotch pines, where he's set up two folding chairs and a white ironwork table with a glass top. On the table lie the sunglasses. The sight pleases him: the two chairs, turned a little toward each other, the forgotten glasses, the enclosed place set off from the rest of the world. He steps over to the table and picks up the glasses: a good pair, expensive lenses, nothing flashy, stylish in a quiet way. As he lifts them from the table he senses something in the skin of his arms and sees a figure standing beside the third Scotch pine. It's darker here than at the back of the house, and he can't see her all that well: a tall, erect woman, fortyish, long face, dark dress. Her expression, which he can barely make out, seems stern. She looks at him for a moment and turns away—not hastily, as if she were frightened, but decisively, like someone who wants to be alone. Behind the Scotch pine she's no longer visible. He hesitates, steps over to the tree, sees nothing. His first impulse is to scream at her, to tell her that he'll kill her if she comes near his daughter. Immediately he forces himself to calm down. Everything will be all right. There's no danger. He's seen them before. Even so, he returns quickly to the house, locks the porch door behind him, locks the kitchen door behind him, fastens the chain, and strides to the den, where on the TV a man in a dinner jacket is staring across the room at a woman with pulled-back hair who is seated at a piano. His wife is watching. As he steps toward her, he notices a pair of sunglasses in his hand.

THE LOOK

Most of us are familiar with the look they cast in our direction before they withdraw. The look has been variously described as proud, hostile, suspicious, mocking, disdainful, uncertain; never is it seen as welcoming. Some witnesses say that the phantoms show slight movements in our direction, before the decisive turning away. Others, disputing such claims, argue that we cannot bear to imagine their rejection of us and misread their movements in a way flattering to our self-esteem.

HIGHLY QUESTIONABLE

Now and then we hear reports of a more questionable kind. The phantoms, we are told, have grayish wings folded along their backs; the phantoms have swirling smoke for eyes; at the ends of their feet, claws curl against the grass. Such descriptions, though rare, are persistent, perhaps inevitable, and impossible to refute. They strike most of us as childish and irresponsible, the results of careless observation, hasty inference, and heightened imagination corrupted by conventional images drawn from movies and television. Whenever we hear such descriptions, we're quick to question them and to make the case for the accumulated evidence of trustworthy witnesses. A paradoxical effect of our vigilance is that the phantoms, rescued from the fantastic, for a moment seem to us normal, commonplace, as familiar as squirrels or dandelions.

CASE STUDY #2

Years ago, as a child of eight or nine, Karen Carsten experienced a single encounter. Her memory of the moment is both vivid and vague: she can't recall how many of them there were, or exactly what they looked like, but she recalls the precise moment in which she came upon them, one summer afternoon, as she stepped around to the back of the garage in search of a soccer ball and saw them sitting quietly in the grass. She still remembers her feeling of wonder as they turned to look at her, before they rose and went away. Now, at age fifty-six, Karen Carsten lives alone with her cat in a house filled with framed photographs of her parents, her nieces, and her late husband, who died in a car accident seventeen years ago. Karen is a high school librarian with many set routines: the TV programs, the weekend housecleaning, the twice-yearly visits in August and December to her sister's family in Youngstown, Ohio, the choir on Sunday, dinner every two weeks at the same restaurant with a friend who never calls to ask how she is. One Saturday afternoon she finishes organizing the linen closet on the second floor and starts up the attic stairs. She plans to sort through boxes of old clothes, some of which she'll give to Goodwill and some of which she'll save for her nieces, who will think of the collared blouses and floral-print dresses as hopelessly old-fashioned but who might come around to appreciating them someday, maybe. As she reaches the top of the stairs she stops so suddenly and completely that she has the sense of her own body as an object standing in her path. Ten feet away, two children are seated on the old couch near the dollhouse. A third child is sitting in the armchair with the loose leg. In the brownish light of the attic, with its one small window, she can see them clearly: two barefoot girls of about ten, in jeans and T-shirts, and a boy, slightly older, maybe twelve, blond-haired, in a dress shirt and khakis, who sits low in the chair with his neck bent up against the back. The three turn to look at her and at once rise and walk into the darker part of the attic, where they are no longer visible. Karen stands motionless at the top of the stairs, her hand clutching the rail. Her lips are dry, and she is filled with an excitement so intense that she thinks she might burst into tears. She does not follow the children into the shadows, partly because she doesn't want to upset them, and partly because she knows they are no longer there. She turns back down the stairs. In the living room she sits in the armchair until nightfall. Joy fills her heart. She can feel it shining from her face. That night she returns to the attic, straightens the pillows on the couch, smooths out the doilies on the chair arms, brings over a small wicker table, sets out three saucers and three teacups. She moves away some bulging boxes that sit beside the couch, carries off an old typewriter, sweeps the floor. Downstairs in the living room she turns on the TV, but she keeps the volume low; she's listening for sounds in the attic, even though she knows that her visitors don't make sounds. She imagines them up there, sitting silently together, enjoying the table, the teacups, the orderly surroundings. Now each day she climbs the stairs to the attic, where she sees the empty couch, the empty chair, the wicker table with the three teacups. Despite the pang of disappointment, she is happy. She is happy because she knows they come to visit her every day, she knows they like to be up there, sitting in the old furniture, around the wicker table; she knows; she knows.

EXPLANATION #2

One explanation is that the phantoms *are not there*, that those of us who see them are experiencing delusions or hallucinations brought about by beliefs instilled in us as young children. A small movement, an unexpected sound, is immediately converted into a visual presence that exists only in the mind of the perceiver. The flaws in this explanation are threefold. First, it assumes that the population of an entire town will interpret ambiguous signs in precisely the same way. Second, it ignores the fact that most of us, as we grow to adulthood, discard the stories and false beliefs of childhood but continue to see the phantoms. Third, it fails to account for innumerable instances in which multiple witnesses have seen the same phantom. Even if we were to agree that these objections are not decisive and that our phantoms are in fact not there, the explanation would tell us only that we are mad, without revealing the meaning of our madness.

OUR CHILDREN

What shall we say to our children? If, like most parents in our town, we decide to tell them at an early age about the phantoms, we worry that we have filled their nights with terror or perhaps have created in them a hope, a longing, for an encounter that might never take place. Those of us who conceal the existence of phantoms are no less worried, for we fear either that our children will be informed unreliably by other children or that they will be dangerously unprepared for an encounter should one occur. Even those of us who have prepared our children are worried about the first encounter, which sometimes disturbs a child in ways that some of us remember only too well. Although we assure our children that there's nothing to fear from the phantoms, who wish only to be left alone, we ourselves are fearful: we wonder whether the phantoms are as harmless as we say they are, we wonder whether they behave differently in the presence of an unaccompanied child, we wonder whether, under certain circumstances, they might become bolder than we know. Some say that a phantom, encountering an adult and a child, will look only at the child, will let its gaze linger in a way that never happens with an adult. When we put our children to sleep, leaning close to them and answering their questions about phantoms in gentle, soothing tones, until their eyes close in peace, we understand that we have been preparing in ourselves an anxiety that will grow stronger and more aggressive as the night advances.

CROSSING OVER

The question of "crossing over" refuses to disappear, despite a history of testimony that many of us feel ought to put it to rest. By "crossing over" is meant, in general, any form of intermingling between us and them; specifically, it refers to supposed instances in which one of them, or one of us, leaves the native community and joins the other. Now, not only is there no evidence of any such regrouping, of any such transference of loyalty, but the overwhelming testimony of witnesses shows that no phantom has ever remained for more than a few moments in the presence of an outsider or given any sign whatever of greeting or encouragement. Claims to the contrary have always been suspect: the insistence of an alcoholic husband that he saw his wife in bed with *one of them*, the assertion of a teenager suspended from high school that a group of phantoms had threatened to harm him if he failed to obey their commands. Apart from statements that purport to be factual, fantasies of crossing over persist in the form of phantom-tales that flourish among our children and are half-believed by naïve adults. It is not difficult to make the case that stories of this kind reveal a secret desire for contact, though no reliable record of contact exists. Those of us who try to maintain a strict objectivity in such matters are forced to admit that a crossing of the line is not impossible, however unlikely, so that even as we challenge dubious claims and smile at fairy tales we find ourselves imagining the sudden encounter at night, the heads turning toward us, the moment of hesitation, the arms rising gravely in welcome.

CASE STUDY #3

James Levin, twenty-six years old, has reached an impasse in his life. After college he took a year off, holding odd jobs and traveling all over the country before returning home to apply to grad school. He completed his course-work in two years, during which he taught one introductory section of American History, and then surprised everyone by taking a leave of absence in order to read for his dissertation (*The Influence of Popular Culture on High Culture in Post–Civil War America, 1865–1900*) and think more carefully about the direction of his life. He lives with his parents in his old room, dense with memories of grade school and high school. He worries that he's losing interest in his dissertation; he feels he should rethink his life, maybe go the med-school route and do something useful in the world instead of wasting his time wallowing in abstract speculations of no value to anyone; he speaks less and less to his girlfriend, a law student at the University of Michigan, nearly a thousand miles away. Where, he wonders, has he taken a wrong turn? What should he do with his life? What is the meaning of it all? These, he believes, are questions eminently suitable for an intelligent adolescent of sixteen, questions that he himself discussed passionately ten years ago with friends who are now married and paying mortgages. Because he's stalled in his life, because he is eaten up with guilt, and because he is unhappy, he has taken to getting up late and going for long walks all over town, first in the afternoon and again at night. One of his daytime walks leads to the picnic grounds of his childhood. Pine trees and scattered tables stand by the stream where he used to sail a little wooden tugboat—he's always bumping into his past like that—and across the stream is where he sees her, one afternoon in late September. She's standing alone, between two oak trees, looking down at the water. The sun shines on the lower part of her body, but her face and neck are in shadow. She becomes aware of him almost immediately, raises her eyes, and withdraws into the shade, where he can no longer see her. He has shattered her solitude. Each instant of the encounter enters him so sharply that his memory of her breaks into three parts, like a medieval triptych in a museum: the moment of awareness, the look, the turning away. In the first panel of the triptych, her shoulders are tense, her whole body unnaturally still, like someone who has heard a sound in the dark. Second panel: her eyes are raised and staring directly at him. It can't have lasted for more than a second. What stays with him is something severe in that look, as if he's disturbed her in a way that requires forgiveness. Third panel: the body is half turned away, not timidly but with a kind of dignity of withdrawal, which seems to rebuke him for an intrusion. James feels a sharp desire to cross the stream and find her, but two thoughts hold him back: his fear that the crossing will be unwelcome to her, and his knowledge that she has disappeared. He returns home but continues to see her standing by the stream. He has the sense that she's becoming more vivid in her absence, as if she's gaining life within him. The unnatural stillness, the dark look, the turning away—he feels he owes her an immense apology. He understands that the desire to apologize is only a mask for his desire to see her again. After two days of futile brooding he returns to the stream, to the exact place where he stood when he saw her the first time; four hours later he returns home, discouraged, restless, and irritable. He understands that something has happened to him, something that is probably harmful. He doesn't care. He returns to the stream day after day, without hope, without pleasure. What's he doing there, in that desolate place? He's twenty-six, but already he's an old man. The leaves have begun to turn; the air is growing cold. One day, on his way back from the stream, James takes a different way home. He passes his old high school, with its double row of tall windows, and comes to the hill where he used to go sledding. He needs to get away from this town, where his childhood and adolescence spring up to meet him at every turn; he ought to go somewhere, do something; his long, purposeless walks seem to him the outward expression of an inner confusion. He climbs the hill, passing through the bare oaks and beeches and the dark firs, and at the top looks down at the stand of pine at the back of Cullen's Auto Body. He walks down the slope, feeling the steering bar in his hands, the red runners biting into the snow, and when he comes to the pines he sees her sitting on the trunk of a fallen tree. She turns her head to look at him, rises, and walks out of sight. This time he doesn't hesitate. He runs into the thicket, beyond which he can see the whitewashed back of the body shop, a brilliant blue front fender lying up against a tire, and, farther away, a pickup truck driving along the street; pale sunlight slants through the pine branches. He searches for her but finds only a tangle of ferns, a beer can, the top of a pint of ice cream. At home he throws himself down on his boyhood bed, where he used to spend long afternoons reading stories about boys who grew up to become famous scientists and explorers. He summons her stare. The sternness devastates him, but draws him, too, since he feels it as a strength he himself lacks. He understands that he's in a bad way; that he's got to stop thinking about her; that he'll never stop thinking about her; that nothing can ever come of it; that his life will be harmed; that harm is attractive to him; that he'll never return to school; that he will disappoint his parents and lose his girlfriend; that none of this matters to him; that what matters is the hope of seeing once more the phantom lady who will look harshly at him and turn away; that he is weak, foolish, frivolous; that such words have no meaning for him; that he has entered a world of dark love, from which there is no way out.

MISSING CHILDREN

Once in a long while, a child goes missing. It happens in other towns, it happens in yours: the missing child who is discovered six hours later lost in the woods, the missing child who never returns, who disappears forever, perhaps in the company of a stranger in a baseball cap who was last seen parked in a van across from the elementary school. In our town there are always those who blame the phantoms. They steal our children, it is said, in order to bring them into the fold; they're always waiting for the right moment, when we have been careless, when our attention has relaxed. Those of us who defend the phantoms point out patiently that they always withdraw from us, that there is no evidence they can make physical contact with the things of our world, that no human child has ever been seen in their company. Such arguments never persuade an accuser. Even when the missing child is discovered in the woods, where he has wandered after a squirrel, even when the missing child is found buried in the yard of a troubled loner in a town two hundred miles away, the suspicion remains that the phantoms have had something to do with it. We who defend our phantoms against false accusations and wild inventions are forced to admit that we do not know what they may be thinking, alone among themselves, or in the moment when they turn to look at us, before moving away.

DISRUPTION

Sometimes a disruption comes: the phantom in the supermarket, the phantom in the bedroom. Then our sense of the behavior of phantoms suffers a shock: we cannot understand why creatures who withdraw from us should appear in places where encounters are unavoidable. Have we misunderstood something about our phantoms? It's true enough that when we encounter them in the aisle of a supermarket or clothing store, when we find them sitting on the edge of our beds or lying against a bed-pillow, they behave as they always do: they look at us and quickly withdraw. Even so, we feel that they have come too close, that they want something from us that we cannot understand, and only when we encounter them in a less-frequented place, at the back of the shut-down railroad station or on the far side of a field, do we relax a little.

EXPLANATION #3

One explanation asserts that we and the phantoms were once a single race, which at some point in the remote history of our town divided into two societies. According to a psychological offshoot of this explanation, the phantoms are the unwanted or unacknowledged portions of ourselves, which we try to evade but continually encounter; they make us uneasy because we know them; they are ourselves.

FEAR

Many of us, at one time or another, have felt the fear. For say you are coming home with your wife from an evening with friends. The porch light is on, the living room windows are dimly glowing before the closed blinds. As you walk across the front lawn from the driveway to the porch steps, you become aware of something, over there by the wild cherry tree. Then you half-see one of them, for an instant, withdrawing behind the dark branches, which catch only a little of the light from the porch. That is when the fear comes. You can feel it deep within you, like an infection that's about to spread. You can feel it in your wife's hand tightening on your arm. It's at that moment you turn to her and say, with a shrug of one shoulder and a little laugh that fools no one: "Oh, it's just one of them!"

PHOTOGRAPHIC EVIDENCE

Evidence from digital cameras, camcorders, iPhones, and old-fashioned film cameras divides into two categories: the fraudulent and the dubious. Fraudulent evidence always reveals signs of tampering. Methods of digital-imaging manipulation permit a wide range of effects, from computer-generated figures to digital clones; sometimes a slight blur is sought, to suggest the uncanny. Often the artist goes too far, and creates a hackneyed monster-phantom inspired by third-rate movies; more clever manipulators stay closer to the ordinary, but tend to give themselves away by an exaggeration of some feature, usually the ears or nose. In such matters, the temptation of the grotesque appears to be irresistible. Celluloid fraud assumes well-known forms that reach back to the era of fairy photographs: double exposures, chemical tampering with negatives, the insertion of gauze between the printing paper and the enlarger lens. The category of the dubious is harder to disprove. Here we find vague, shadowy shapes, wavering lines resembling ripples of heated air above a radiator, half-hidden forms concealed by branches or by windows filled with reflections. Most of these images can be explained as natural effects of light that have deceived the credulous person recording them. For those who crave visual proof of phantoms, evidence that a photograph is fraudulent or dubious is never entirely convincing.

CASE STUDY #4

One afternoon in late spring, Evelyn Wells, nine years old, is playing alone in her backyard. It's a sunny day; school is out, dinner's a long way off, and the warm afternoon has the feel of summer. Her best friend is sick with a sore throat and fever, but that's all right: Evvy likes to play alone in her yard, especially on a sunny day like this one, with time stretching out on all sides of her. What she's been practicing lately is roof-ball, a game she learned from a boy down the block. Her yard is bounded by the neighbor's garage and by thick spruces running along the back and side; the lowest spruce branches bend down to the grass and form a kind of wall. The idea is to throw the tennis ball, which is the color of lime Kool-Aid, onto the slanted garage roof and catch it when it comes down. If Evvy throws too hard, the ball will go over the roof and land in the yard next door, possibly in the vegetable garden surrounded by chicken wire. If she doesn't throw hard enough, it will come right back to her, with no speed. The thing to do is make the ball go almost to the top, so that it comes down faster and faster; then she's got to catch it before it hits the ground, though a one-bouncer isn't terrible. Evvy is pretty good at roof-ball— she can make the ball go way up the slope, and she can figure out where she needs to stand as it comes rushing or bouncing down. Her record is eight catches in a row, but now she's caught nine and is hoping for ten. The ball stops near the peak of the roof and begins coming down at a wide angle; she moves more and more to the right as it bounces lightly along and leaps into the air. This time she's made a mistake—the ball goes over her head. It rolls across the lawn toward the back and disappears under the low-hanging spruce branches not far from the garage. Evvy sometimes likes to play under there, where it's cool and dim. She pushes aside a branch and looks for the ball, which she sees beside a root. At the same time she sees two figures, a man and a woman, standing under the tree. They stare down at her, then turn their faces away and step out of sight. Evvy feels a ripple in her arms. Their eyes were like shadows on a lawn. She backs out into the sun. The yard does not comfort her. The blades of grass seem to be holding their breath. The white wooden shingles on the side of the garage are staring at her. Evvy walks across the strange lawn and up the back steps into the kitchen. Inside, it is very still. A faucet handle blazes with light. She hears her mother in the living room. Evvy does not want to speak to her mother. She does not want to speak to anyone. Upstairs, in her room, she draws the blinds and gets into bed. The windows are above the backyard and look down on the rows of spruce trees. At dinner she is silent. "Cat got your tongue?" her father says. His teeth are laughing. Her mother gives her a wrinkled look. At night she lies with her eyes open. She sees the man and woman standing under the tree, staring down at her. They turn their faces away. The next day, Saturday, Evvy refuses to go outside. Her mother brings orange juice, feels her forehead, takes her temperature. Outside, her father is mowing the lawn. That night she doesn't sleep. They are standing under the tree, looking at her with their shadow-eyes. She can't see their faces. She doesn't remember their clothes. On Sunday she stays in her room. Sounds startle her: a clank in the yard, a shout. At night she watches with closed eyes: the ball rolling under the branches, the two figures standing there, looking down at her. On Monday her mother takes her to the doctor. He presses the silver circle against her chest. The next day she returns to school, but after the last bell she comes straight home and goes to her room. Through the slats of the blinds she can see the garage, the roof, the dark green spruce branches bending to the grass. One afternoon Evvy is sitting at the piano in the living room. She's practicing her scales. The bell rings and her mother goes to the door. When Evvy turns to look, she sees a woman and a man. She leaves the piano and goes upstairs to her room. She sits on the throw rug next to her bed and stares at the door. After a while she hears her mother's footsteps on the stairs. Evvy stands up and goes into the closet. She crawls next to a box filled with old dolls and bears and elephants. She can hear her mother's footsteps in the room. Her mother is knocking on the closet door. "Please come out of there, Evvy. I know you're in there." She does not come out.

CAPTORS

Despite widespread disapproval, now and then an attempt is made to capture a phantom. The desire arises most often among groups of idle teenagers, especially during the warm nights of summer, but is also known among adults, usually but not invariably male, who feel menaced by the phantoms or who cannot tolerate the unknown. Traps are set, pits dug, cages built, all to no avail. The nonphysical nature of phantoms does not seem to discourage such efforts, which sometimes display great ingenuity. Walter

Hendricks, a mechanical engineer, lived for many years in a neighborhood of split-level ranch houses with backyard swing sets and barbecues; one day he began to transform his yard into a dense thicket of pine trees, in order to invite the visits of phantoms. Each tree was equipped with a mechanism that was able to release from the branches a series of closely woven steel-mesh nets, which dropped swiftly when anything passed below. In another part of town, Charles Reese rented an excavator and dug a basement-size cavity in his yard. He covered the pit, which became known as the Dungeon, with a sliding steel ceiling concealed by a layer of sod. One night, when a phantom appeared on his lawn, Reese pressed a switch that caused the false lawn to slide away; when he climbed down into the Dungeon with a high-beam flashlight, he discovered a frightened chipmunk. Others have used chemical sprays that cause temporary paralysis, empty sheds with sliding doors that automatically shut when a motion sensor is triggered, even a machine that produces flashes of lightning. People who dream of becoming captors fail to understand that the phantoms cannot be caught; to capture them would be to banish them from their own nature, to turn them into us.

EXPLANATION #4

One explanation is that the phantoms have always been here, long before the arrival of the Indians. We ourselves are the intruders. We seized their land, drove them into hiding, and have been careful ever since to maintain our advantage and force them into postures of submission. This explanation accounts for the hostility that many of us detect in the phantoms, as well as the fear they sometimes inspire in us. Its weakness, which some dismiss as negligible, is the absence of any evidence in support of it.

THE PHANTOM LORRAINE

As children we all hear the tale of the Phantom Lorraine, told to us by an aunt, or a babysitter, or someone on the playground, or perhaps by a care-less parent desperate for a bedtime story. Lorraine is a phantom child. One day she comes to a tall hedge at the back of a yard where a boy and girl are playing. The children are running through a sprinkler, or throwing a ball, or practicing with a hula hoop. Nearby, their mother is kneeling on a cushion before a row of hollyhock bushes, digging up weeds. The Phantom Lorraine is moved by this picture, in a way she doesn't understand. Day after day she returns to the hedge, to watch the children playing. One day, when the children are alone, she steps shyly out of her hiding place. The children invite her to join them. Even though she is different, even though she can't pick things up or hold them, the children invent running games that all three can play. Now every day the Phantom Lorraine joins them in the backyard, where she is happy. One afternoon the children invite her into their house. She looks with wonder at the sunny kitchen, at the carpeted stairway leading to the second floor, at the children's room with the two windows looking out over the backyard. The mother and father are kind to the Phantom Lorraine. One day they invite her to a sleepover. The little phantom girl spends more and more time with the human family, who love her as their own. At last the parents adopt her. They all live happily ever after.

ANALYSIS

As adults we look more skeptically at this tale, which once gave us so much pleasure. We understand that its purpose is to overcome a child's fear of the phantoms, by showing that what the phantoms really desire is to become one of us. This of course is wildly inaccurate, since the actual phantoms betray no signs of curiosity and rigorously withdraw from contact of any kind. But the tale seems to many of us to hold a deeper meaning. The story, we believe, reveals our own desire: to know the phantoms, to strip them of mystery. Fearful of their difference, unable to bear their otherness, we imagine, in the person of the Phantom Lorraine, their secret sameness. Some go further. The tale of the Phantom Lorraine, they say, is a thinly disguised story about our hatred of the phantoms, our wish to bring about their destruction. By joining a family, the Phantom Lorraine in effect ceases to be a phantom; she casts off her nature and is reborn as a human child. In this way, the story expresses our longing to annihilate the phantoms, to devour them, to turn them into us. Beneath its sentimental exterior, the tale of the Phantom Lorraine is a dream-tale of invasion and murder.

OTHER TOWNS

When we visit other towns, which have no phantoms, often we feel that a burden has lifted. Some of us make plans to move to such a town, a place that reminds us of tall picture books from childhood. There, you can walk at peace along the streets and in the public parks, without having to wonder whether a ripple will course through the skin of your forearms. We think of our children playing happily in green backyards, where sunflowers and honeysuckle bloom against white fences. But soon a restlessness comes. A town without phantoms seems to us a town without history, a town without shadows. The yards are empty, the streets stretch bleakly away. Back in our town, we wait impatiently for the ripple in our arms; we fear that our phantoms may no longer be there. When, sometimes after many weeks, we encounter one of them at last, in a corner of the yard or at the side of the car wash, where a look is flung at us before the phantom turns away, we think: Now things are as they should be, now we can rest awhile. It's a feeling almost like gratitude.

EXPLANATION #5

Some argue that all towns have phantoms, but that only we are able to see them. This way of thinking is especially attractive to those who cannot understand why our town should have phantoms and other towns none; why our town, in short, should be an exception. An objection to this explanation is that it accomplishes nothing but a shift of attention from the town itself to the people of our town: it's our ability to perceive phantoms that is now the riddle, instead of the phantoms themselves. A second objection, which some find decisive, is that the explanation relies entirely on an assumed world of invisible beings, whose existence can be neither proved nor disproved.

CASE STUDY #5

Every afternoon after lunch, before I return to work in the upstairs study, I like to take a stroll along the familiar sidewalks of my neighborhood. Thoughts rise up in me, take odd turns, vanish like bits of smoke. At the same time I'm wide open to striking impressions—that ladder leaning against the side of a house, with its shadow hard and clean against the white shingles, which project a little, so that the shingle-bottoms break the straight shadow-lines into slight zigzags; that brilliant red umbrella lying at an angle in the recycling container on a front porch next to the door; that jogger with shaved head, black nylon shorts, and an orange sweatshirt that reads, in three lines of black capital letters: EAT WELL / KEEP FIT / DIE ANYWAY. A single blade of grass sticks up from a crack in a driveway. I come to a sprawling old house at the corner, not far from the sidewalk. Its dark red paint could use a little touching up. Under the high front porch, on both sides of the steps, are those crisscross lattice panels, painted white. Through the diamond-shaped openings come pricker branches and the tips of ferns. From the sidewalk I can see the handle of an old hand mower, back there among the dark weeds. I can see something else: a slight movement. I step up to the porch, bend to peer through the lattice: I see three of them, seated on the ground. They turn their heads toward me and look away, begin to rise. In an instant they're gone. My arms are rippling as I return to the sidewalk and continue on my way. They interest me, these creatures who are always vanishing. This time I was able to glimpse a man of about fifty and two younger women. One woman wore her hair up; the other had a sprig of small blue wildflowers in her hair. The man had a long straight nose and a long mouth. They rose slowly but without hesitation and stepped back into the dark. Even as a child I accepted phantoms as part of things, like spiders and rainbows. I saw them in the vacant lot on the other side of the backyard hedge, or behind garages and toolsheds. Once I saw one in the kitchen. I observe them carefully whenever I can; I try to see their faces. I want nothing from them. It's a sunny day in early September. As I continue my walk, I look about me with interest. At the side of a driveway, next to a stucco house, the yellow nozzle of a hose rests on top of a dark green garbage can. Farther back, I can see part of a swing set. A cushion is sitting on the grass beside a three-pronged weeder with a red handle.

THE DISBELIEVERS

The disbelievers insist that every encounter is false. When I bend over and peer through the openings in the lattice, I see a slight movement, caused by a chipmunk or mouse in the dark weeds, and instantly my imagination is set in motion: I seem to see a man and two women, a long nose, the rising, the disappearance. The few details are suspiciously precise. How is it that the faces are difficult to remember, while the sprig of wildflowers stands out clearly? Such criticisms, even when delivered with a touch of disdain, never offend me. The reasoning is sound, the intention commendable: to establish the truth, to distinguish the real from the unreal. I try to experience it their way: the movement of a chipmunk behind the sunlit lattice, the dim figures conjured from the dark leaves. It isn't impossible. I exercise my full powers of imagination: I take their side against me. There is nothing there, behind the lattice. It's all an illusion. Excellent! I defeat myself. I abolish myself. I rejoice in such exercise.

YOU

You who have no phantoms in your town, you who mock or scorn our reports: are you not deluding yourselves? For say you are driving out to the mall, some pleasant afternoon. All of a sudden—it's always sudden—you remember your dead father, sitting in the living room in the house of your childhood. He's reading a newspaper in the armchair next to the lamp table. You can see his frown of concentration, the fold of the paper, the moccasin slipper half-hanging from his foot. The steering wheel is warm in the sun. Tomorrow you're going to dinner at a friend's house—you should bring a bottle of wine. You see your friend laughing at the table, his wife lifting something from the stove. The shadows of telephone wires lie in long curves on the street. Your mother lies in the nursing home, her eyes always closed. Her photograph on your bookcase: a young woman smiling under a tree. You are lying in bed with a cold, and she's reading to you from a book you know by heart. Now she herself is a child and you read to her while she lies there. Your sister will be coming up for a visit in two weeks. Your daughter playing in the backyard, your wife at the window. Phantoms of memory, phantoms of desire. You pass through a world so thick with phantoms that there is barely enough room for anything else. The sun shines on a hydrant, casting a long shadow.

EXPLANATION #6

One explanation says that we ourselves are phantoms. Arguments drawn from cognitive science claim that our bodies are nothing but artificial constructs of our brains: we are the dream-creations of electrically charged neurons. The world itself is a great seeming. One virtue of this explanation is that it accounts for the behavior of our phantoms: they turn from us because they cannot bear to witness our self-delusion.

FORGETFULNESS

There are times when we forget our phantoms. On summer afternoons, the telephone wires glow in the sun like fire. Shadows of tree branches lie against our white shingles. Children shout in the street. The air is warm, the grass is green, we will never die. Then an uneasiness comes, in the blue air. Between shouts, we hear a silence. It's as though something is about to happen, which we ought to know, if only we could remember.

HOW THINGS ARE

For most of us, the phantoms are simply there. We don't think about them continually, at times we forget them entirely, but when we encounter them we feel that something momentous has taken place, before we drift back into forgetfulness. Someone once said that our phantoms are like thoughts of death: they are always there, but appear only now and then. It's difficult to know exactly what we feel about our phantoms, but I think it is fair to say that in the moment we see them, before we're seized by a familiar emotion like fear, or anger, or curiosity, we are struck by a sense of strangeness, as if we've suddenly entered a room we have never seen before, a room that nevertheless feels familiar. Then the world shifts back into place and we continue on our way. For though we have our phantoms, our town is like your town: sun shines on the house fronts, we wake in the night with troubled hearts, cars back out of driveways and turn up the street. It's true that a question runs through our town, because of the phantoms, but we don't believe we are the only ones who live with unanswered questions. Most of us would say we're no different from anyone else. When you come to think about us, from time to time, you'll see we really are just like you.

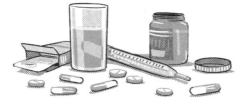

DO NOT DISTURB

by A.M. HOMES

(fiction from Issue 7)

M Y WIFE, THE doctor, is not well. In the end she could be dead. It started suddenly, on a country weekend, a movie with friends, a pizza, and then pain.

"I liked the part where he lunged at the woman with a knife," Eric says.

"She deserved it," Enid says.

"Excuse me," my wife says, getting up from the table.

A few minutes later I find her doubled over on the sidewalk. "Something is ripping me from the inside out."

"Should I get the check?" She looks at me like I am an idiot.

"My wife is not well," I announce, returning to the table. "We have to go."

"What do you mean—is she all right?"

Eric and Enid hurry out while I wait for the check. They drive us home. As I open the front door, my wife pushes past me and goes running for the bathroom. Eric, Enid, and I stand in the living room, waiting.

"Are you all right in there?" I call out.

"No," she says.

"Maybe she should go to the hospital," Enid says.

"Doctors don't go to the hospital," I say.

She is a specialist in emergency medicine. All day she is at the hospital putting the pieces back together and then she comes home to me. I am not the one who takes care. I am the one who is always on the verge.

"Call us if you need us," Eric and Enid say, leaving.

She lies on the bathroom floor, her cheek against the white tile. "I keep thinking it will pass."

I tuck the bath mat under her head and sneak away. From the kitchen I call a doctor friend. I stand in the dark, whispering, "She's just lying there on the floor, what do I do?"

"Don't do anything," the doctor says, half-insulted by the thought that there is something to do. "Observe her. Either it will go away, or something more will happen. You watch and you wait."

Watch and wait. I'm thinking about our relationship. We haven't been getting along. The situation has become oxygenless and addictive, a suffocating annihilation, each staying to see how far it will go.

I sit on the edge of the tub, looking at her. "I'm worried."

"Don't worry," she says. "And don't just sit there staring."

Earlier in the afternoon we were fighting, I don't remember about what. I only know—I called her a bitch.

"I was a bitch before I met you and I'll be a bitch long after you're gone. Surprise me," she said, "tell me something new."

I wanted to say I'm leaving. I wanted to say, I know you think I never will and that's why you treat me like you do. But I'm going. I wanted to get in the car, drive off and call it a day.

The fight ended with the clock. She glanced at it. "It's six thirty, we're meeting Eric and Enid at seven; put on a clean shirt."

She is lying on the bathroom floor, the print of the bath mat making an impression on her cheek. "Are you comfortable?" I ask.

She looks surprised, as though she's just realized she's on the floor.

"Help me," she says, struggling to get up.

Her lips are white and thin.

"Bring me a trash can, a plastic bag, a thermometer, some Tylenol, and a glass of water."

"Are you going to throw up?"

"I want to be prepared," she says.

We are always prepared. The ongoing potential for things to go wrong is our bond, a fascination with crisis, with control. We have flare guns and fire extinguishers, walkie talkies, a rubber raft, a small generator, a hundred batteries in assorted shapes and sizes, a thousand bucks in dollar bills, enough toilet paper and bottled water to get us through six months. When we travel we have smoke hoods in our carry-on bags, protein bars, water purification tablets, and a king-sized bag of M&M's.

She slips the digital thermometer under her tongue; the numbers move up the scale—each beep is a tenth of a degree.

"A hundred and one point four," I announce.

"I have a fever?" she says in disbelief.

"I wish things between us weren't so bad."

"It's not as bad as you think," she says. "Expect less and you won't be disappointed."

We try to sleep; she is hot, she is cold, she is mumbling something about having "a surgical belly," something about "guarding and rebound." I don't know if she's talking about herself or the NBA.

"This is incredible," she sits bolt upright and folds over again, writhing. "Something is struggling inside me. It's like one of those alien movies, like I'm going to burst open and something is going to spew out, like I'm erupting." She pauses, takes a breath. "And then it stops. Who would ever have thought this would happen to me—and on a Saturday night?"

"Is it your appendix?"

"That's the one thought I have, but I'm not sure. I don't have the classic symptoms. I don't have anorexia or diarrhea. When I was eating that pizza, I was hungry."

"Is it an ovary? Women have lots of ovaries."

"Women have two ovaries," she says. "It did occur to me that could be Mittelschmertz."

"Mittelschmertz?"

"The launching of the egg, the middle of the cycle."

At five in the morning her temperature is one hundred and three. She is alternately sweating and shivering.

"Should I drive you back to the city or to the hospital out here?"

"I don't want to be the doctor who goes to the ER with gas."

"Fine."

I'm dressing myself, packing, thinking of what I'll need: cell phone, notebook, pen, something to read, something to eat, wallet, insurance card.

We are in the car, hurrying. There's an urgency to the situation, the unmistakable sense that something bad is happening. I am driving seventy miles an hour.

"I think I'm dying," she says.

I pull up to the emergency entrance and half-carry her in, leaving the car doors open, the engine running; I have the impulse to drop her off and walk away.

The emergency room is empty. There is a bell on the check-in desk. I ring it twice.

A woman appears. "Can I help you?"

"My wife is not well," I say. "She's a doctor."

The woman sits at her computer. She takes my wife's name and number. She takes her insurance card and then her temperature and blood pressure. "Are you in a lot of pain?"

"Yes," my wife says.

Within minutes a doctor is there, pressing on my wife. "It's got to come out," he says.

"What?" I ask.

"Appendix. Do you want some Demerol?"

She shakes her head. "I'm working tomorrow and I'm on call."

"What kind of doctor are you?"

"Emergency medicine."

In the cubicle next to her, someone vomits.

The nurse comes to take blood. "They called Barry Manilow, he's a very good surgeon." She ties off my wife's arm. "We call him Barry Manilow because he looks like Barry Manilow."

"I want to do right by you," Barry Manilow says, as he's feeling my wife's belly. "I'm not sure it's your appendix, not sure it's your gall bladder either. I'm going to call the radiologist and let him scan it. How's that sound?"

She nods.

I take the surgeon aside. "Should she be staying here? Is this the place to do this?"

"It's not a kidney transplant," he says.

The nurse brings me a cold drink. She offers me a chair. I sit close to the gurney where my wife lies. "Do you want me to get you out of here? I could hire a car and have us driven to the city. I could have you med-evaced home."

"I don't want to go anywhere," she says.

Back in the cubicle, Barry Manilow is talking to her. "It's not your appendix. It's your ovary. It's a hemorrhagic cyst; you're bleeding and your hematocrit is falling. We have to operate. I've called a gynecologist and the anesthesiologist—I'm just waiting for them to arrive. We're going to take you upstairs very soon."

"Just do it," she says.

I stop Barry Manilow in the hall. "Can you try and save the ovary? She very much wants to have children. It's just something she hasn't gotten around to yet—first she had her career, then me, and now this."

"We'll do everything we can," he says, disappearing through the door marked AUTHORIZED PERSONNEL ONLY.

I am the only one in the surgical waiting room, flipping through copies of *Field and Stream*, *Highlights for Children*, a pamphlet on colon cancer. Less than an hour later, Barry Manilow comes to find me. "We saved the ovary. We took out something the size of a lemon."

"The size of a lemon?"

He makes a fist and holds it up. "A lemon," he says. "It looked a little funny. We sent it to Pathology." He shrugs.

A lemon, a bleeding lemon, like a blood orange, a lemon souring in her. Why is fruit used as the universal medical measurement?

"She should be upstairs in about an hour."

When I get to her room she is asleep. A tube poking out from under the covers drains urine into a bag. She is hooked up to oxygen and an IV.

I put my hand on her forehead. Her eyes open.

"A little fresh air," she says, pulling at the oxygen tube. "I always wondered what all this felt like."

She has a morphine drip, the kind she can control herself. She keeps the clicker in hand. She never pushes the button.

I feed her ice chips and climb into the bed next to her. In the middle of the night I go home. In the morning she calls, waking me up.

"Flowers have been arriving like crazy," she says. "From the hospital, from the ER, from the clinic."

Doctors are like firemen; when one of their own is down they go crazy.

"They took the catheter out, I'm sitting up in a chair. I already had some juice and took myself to the bathroom," she says, proudly. "They couldn't be nicer. But of course, I'm a very good patient."

I interrupt her. "Do you want anything from the house?"

"Clean socks, a pair of sweat pants, my hair brush, some toothpaste, my face soap, a radio, maybe a can of Diet Coke."

"You're only going to be there a couple of days."

"You asked if I needed anything. Don't forget to feed the dog."

Five minutes later she calls back—crying. "Guess what, I have ovarian cancer."

I run out the door. When I get there the room is empty. I'm expecting a big romantic crying scene, expecting her to cling to me, to tell me how much she loves me, how she's sorry we've been having such a hard time, how much she needs me, wants me, now more than ever. The bed is empty. For a moment I think she's died, jumped out the window, escaped.

In the bathroom, the toilet flushes. "I want to go home," she says, stepping out, fully dressed.

"Do you want to take the flowers?"

"They're mine, aren't they? Do you think all the nurses know I have cancer? I don't want anyone to know."

The nurse comes with a wheelchair; she takes us down to the lobby. "Good luck," she says, loading the flowers into the car.

"She knows," my wife says.

We're on the Long Island Expressway. I am dialing and driving. I call my wife's doctor in New York.

"She has to see Kibbowitz immediately," the doctor says.

"Do you think I'll lose my ovary?"

She will lose everything. Instinctively I know that.

We are home. She is on the bed with the dog on her lap. She peeks beneath the gauze; her incision is crooked, the lack of precision an incredible insult. "Do you think they can fix it?" she asks.

In the morning we go to Kibbowitz. She is again on a table, her feet in the stirrups, in launch position, waiting. Before the doctor arrives she is interviewed and examined by seven medical students. I hate them. I hate them for talking to her, for touching her, for wasting her time. I hate Kibbowitz for keeping her on the table for more than an hour, waiting.

She is angry with me for being annoyed. "They're just doing their job."

Kibbowitz arrives. He is enormous, like a hockey player, a brute and a bully. I can tell immediately that she likes him. She will do anything he says.

"Scootch down a little closer to me," he says, settling himself on a stool between her legs. She lifts her ass and slides down. He examines her. He peeks under the gauze. "Crooked," he says. "Get dressed and meet me in my office."

"I want a number," she says. "A survival rate."

"I don't deal in numbers," he says.

"I need a number."

He shrugs. "How's seventy percent."

"Seventy percent what?"

"Seventy percent live five years."

"And then what?" I ask.

"And then some don't," he says.

"What has to come out?" she asks.

"What do you want to keep?"

"I wanted to have a child."

This is a delicate negotiation; they talk parts. "I could take just the one ovary," he says. "And then after the chemo you could try and get pregnant and then after you had a child we could go in and get the rest."

"Can you really get pregnant after chemo?" I ask.

The doctor shrugs. "Miracles happen all the time," he says. "The problem is you can't raise a child if you're dead. You don't have to decide now, let me know in a day or two. Meanwhile I'm going to book the operating room for Friday morning. Nice meeting you," he says, shaking my hand.

"I want to have a baby," she says.

"I want to have you," I say.

Beyond that I say nothing. Whatever I say she will do the opposite. We are at that point—spite, blame, and fault. I don't want to be held responsible.

She opens the door of the consulting room. "Doctor," she shouts, hurrying down the hall after him, clutching her belly, her incision, her wound. "Take it," she screams. "Take it all the hell out."

He is standing outside another examining room, chart in hand.

He nods. "We'll take it though your vagina. We'll take the ovaries, the uterus, cervix, omentum, and your appendix if they didn't already get it in Southampton. And then we'll put a port in your neck and sign you up for chemotherapy, eight rounds should do it."

She nods.

"See you Friday."

We leave. I'm holding her hand, holding her pocketbook on my shoulder trying to be as good as anyone can be. She is growling and scratching; it's like taking a cat to the vet.

"Why don't they just say eviscerate? Why don't they just come out and say on Friday at nine we're going to eviscerate you—be ready."

"Do you want a little lunch?" I ask as we are walking down the street. "Some soup? There's a lovely restaurant near here."

She looks flushed. I put my hand to her forehead. She's burning up. "You have a fever. Did you mention that to the doctor?"

"It's not relevant."

Later when we are home, I ask, "Do you remember our third date? Do you remember asking me—how would you kill yourself if you had to do it with bare hands? I said I would break my nose and shove it up into my brain and you said you would reach up with your bare hands and rip your uterus out through your vagina and throw it across the room."

"What's your point?"

"No point, I just suddenly remembered it. Isn't Kibbowitz taking your uterus out through your vagina?"

"I doubt he's going to throw it across the room," she says. There is a pause. "You don't have to stay with me now that I have cancer. I don't need you. I don't need anyone. I don't need anything."

"If I left, I wouldn't be leaving because you have cancer. But I would look like an ass, everyone would think I couldn't take it."

"I would make sure they knew it was me, that I was a monster, a cold steely monster, that I drove you away."

"They wouldn't believe you."

She suddenly farts and runs embarrassed into the bathroom—as though this is the first time she's farted in her life. "My life is ruined," she yells, slamming the door.

"Farting is the least of it," I say.

When she comes out she is calmer. She crawls into bed next to me, wrung out, shivering.

I hold her. "Do you want to make love?"

"You mean one last time before I'm not a woman, before I'm a dried old husk?"

Instead of fucking we fight. It's the same sort of thing, dramatic, draining. When we're done, I roll over and sleep in a tight knot on my side of the bed.

"Surgical menopause," she says. "That sounds so final."

I turn toward her. She runs her hand over her pubic hair. "Do you think they'll shave me?"

I'm not going to be able to leave the woman with cancer. I'm not the kind of person who leaves the woman with cancer, but I don't know what you do when the woman with cancer is a bitch. Do you hope that the cancer prompts the woman to reevaluate herself, to take it as an opportunity, a signal for change? As far as she's concerned there is no such thing as the mind/body connection, there is science and there is law. There is fact and everything else is bullshit.

Friday morning, while she's in the hospital registration area waiting for her number to be called, she makes another list out loud: "My will is in the top left drawer of the dresser. If anything goes wrong pull the plug. No heroic measures. I want to be cremated. Donate my organs. Give it away, all of it, every last drop." She stops. "I guess no one will want me now that I'm contaminated." She says the word *contaminated* filled with disgust, disappointment, as though she has soiled herself.

It is nearly eight p.m. when Kibbowitz comes out to tell me he's done. "Everything was stuck together like macaroni and cheese. It took longer than I expected. I found some in the fallopian tube and some on the wall of her abdomen. We cleaned everything out."

She is wheeled back to her room, sad, agitated, angry.

"Why didn't you come and see me?" she asks, accusitorily.

"I was right there the whole time, on the other side of the door waiting for word."

She acts as though she doesn't believe me, as though I went off and screwed a secretary from the patient services office while she was on the table.

"How're you feeling?"

"As though I've taken a trip to another country and my suitcases are lost."

She is writhing. I adjust her pillow, the position of the bed.

"What hurts?"

"What doesn't hurt? Everything hurts. Breathing hurts."

Because she is a doctor, because she did her residency at this hospital, they give me a small folding cot to set up in the corner of the room. Bending to unfold it, something happens in my back, a hot searing pain spreads across and down. I lower myself to the floor, grabbing the blanket as I go.

Luckily, she is sleeping.

The nurse coming in to check her vital signs sees me. "Are you in trouble?" she asks.

"It's happened before," I say. "I'll just lie here and see what happens."

She brings me a pillow and covers me with the blanket.

Eric and Enid arrive. My wife is asleep and I am still on the floor. Eric stands over me.

"We're sorry," Eric whispers. "We didn't get your message until today. We were at Enid's parents—upstate."

"It's shocking, it's sudden, it's so out of the blue." Enid moves to look at my wife. "She looks like she's in a really bad mood, her brow is furrowed. Is she in pain?"

"I assume so."

"If there's anything we can do, let us know," Eric says.

"Actually, could you walk the dog?" I pull the keys out of my pocket and hold them in the air. "He's been home alone all day and all night."

"Walk the dog, I think we can do that," Eric says, looking at Enid for confirmation.

"We'll check on you in the morning," Enid says.

"Before you go; there's a bottle of Percocet in her purse—give me two."

During the night she wakes up. "Where are you?" she asks.

"I'm right here."

She is sufficiently drugged that she doesn't ask for details. At around six she opens her eyes and sees me on the floor.

"Your back?"

"Yep."

"Cancer beats back," she says and falls back to sleep.

When the cleaning man comes with the damp mop, I pry myself off the floor. I'm fine as long as I'm standing.

"You're walking like you have a rod up your ass," my wife says.

"Is there anything I can do for you?" I ask, trying to be solicitous.

"Can you have cancer for me?"

The pain management team arrives to check on my wife's level of comfort.

"On a scale of one to ten how do you feel?" the pain fellow asks.

"Five," my wife says.

"She lies," I say.

"Are you lying?"

"How can you tell?"

The specialist arrives. "I know you," he says, seeing my wife in the bed. "We went to school together."

My wife tries to smile.

"You were the smartest one in the class and now look," he reads my wife's chart. "Ovarian cancer and you, that's horrible."

My wife is sitting up high in her hospital bed, puking her guts into a metal bucket, like a poisoned pet monkey. She is throwing up bright green like an alien, like nothing anyone has seen before. Ted, her boss, stares at her, mesmerized.

The room is filled with people—people I don't know, medical people, people she went to school with, people she did her residency with, a man whose fingers she sewed back on, relatives I've not met. I don't understand why they don't excuse themselves, why they don't step out of the room. They're all watching her like they've never seen anyone throw up before—riveted.

She is not sleeping. She is not eating. She is not getting up and walking around. She is afraid to leave her bed, afraid to leave her bucket.

I make a sign for the door. I borrow a black magic marker from the charge nurse and print in large black letters: DO NOT DISTURB.

They push the door open. They come bearing gifts, flowers, food, books. "I saw the sign, I assumed it was for someone else."

I am wiping green spittle from her lips.

"Do you want me to get rid of everyone?" I ask.

I want to get rid of everyone. The idea that these people have some claim to her, some right to entertain, distract, bother her more than me, drives me up the wall. "Should I tell them to go?"

She shakes her head. "Just the flowers, the flowers nauseate me."

An hour later, I empty the bucket again. The room remains overcrowded. I am on my knees by the side of her hospital bed, whispering "I'm leaving."

"Are you coming back?" she whispers.

"No."

She looks at me strangely. "Where are you going?"

"Away."

"Bring me a Diet Coke."

She has missed the point.

It is heartbreaking seeing her in a stained gown, in the middle of a bed, unable to tell everyone to go home, unable to turn it off. Her pager is clipped to her hospital gown, several times it goes off. She returns the calls. She always returns the calls. I imagine her saying, "What the hell are you bothering me for—I'm busy, I'm having cancer."

Later, I'm on the edge of the bed, looking at her. She is increasingly beautiful, more vulnerable, female.

"Honey?"

"What?" Her intonation is like a pissy caged bird—*cawww*. "What? What are you looking at? What do you want?" *Cawww*.

"Nothing."

I am washing her with a cool washcloth.

"You're tickling me," she complains.

"Make sure you tell her you still find her attractive," a man in the hall tells me. "Husbands of women who have mastectomies need to keep reminding their wives that they are beautiful."

"She had a hysterectomy," I say.

"Same thing."

Two days later, they remove the packing. I am in the room when the resident comes with long tweezers like tongs and pulls yards of material from her vagina, wads of cotton, gauze, stained battlefield red. It's like a magic trick gone awry, one of those jokes about how many people you can fit in a telephone booth; more and more keeps coming out.

"Is there anything left in there?" she asks.

The resident shakes his head. "Your vagina now just comes to a stop, it's a stump, an unconnected sleeve. Don't be surprised if you bleed, if you pop a stitch of two." He checks her chart and signs her out. "Kibbowitz has you on pelvic rest for six weeks."

"Pelvic rest?" I ask.

"No fucking," she says.

Not a problem.

Home. She watches forty-eight hours of Holocaust films on cable TV. Although she claims to compartmentalize everything, suddenly she identifies with the bald, starving prisoners of war. She sees herself as a victim. She points to the naked corpse of a woman. "That's me," she says. "That's exactly how I feel."

"She's dead," I say.

"Exactly."

Her notorious vigilance is gone. As I'm fluffing her pillows, her billy club rolls out from under the bed. "Put it in the closet," she says.

"Why?" I ask, rolling it back under the bed.

"Why sleep with a billy club under the bed? Why do anything when you have cancer?"

During a break between *Schindler's List*, *Shoah*, and *The Sorrow and the Pity* she taps me. "I'm missing my parts," she says. "Maybe one of those lost eggs was someone special, someone who would have cured something, someone who would have invented something wonderful. You never know who was in there. They're my lost children."

"I'm sorry."

"For what?" she looks at me accusingly.

"Everything."

"Thirty-eight-year-olds don't get cancer, they get Lyme disease, maybe they have appendicitis, on rare occasions in some other parts of the world they have Siamese twins, but that's it."

In the middle of the night she wakes up, throws the covers off. "I can't breathe, I'm burning up. Open the window, I'm hot, I'm so hot."

"Do you know what's happening to you?"

"What are you talking about?"

"You're having hot flashes."

"I am not," she says as though I've insulted her. "They don't start so soon."

They do.

"Get away from me, get away," she yells. "Just being near you makes me uncomfortable, it makes my temperature unstable."

On Monday she starts chemotherapy.

"Will I go bald?" she asks the nurse.

"Most women buy a wig before it happens," the nurse says, plugging her into the magic potion.

I am afraid that when she's bald I won't love her anymore. I cannot imagine my wife bald.

One of the other women, her head wrapped in a red turban, leans over and whispers, "My husband says I look like a porno star." She winks. She has no eyebrows, no eyelashes, nothing.

We shop for a wig. She tries on every style, every shape and color. She looks like a man in drag, like it's all a horrible joke.

"Maybe my hair won't fall out?" she says.

"It's okay," the woman in the wig shop says. "Insurance covers it. Ask your doctor to write a prescription for a cranial prosthesis."

"I'm a doctor," my wife says.

The wig woman looks confused. "It's okay," she says, putting another wig on my wife's head.

She buys a wig. I never see it. She brings it home and immediately puts it in the closet. "It looks like Linda Evans, like someone on *Dynasty*. I just can't do it," she says.

Her scalp begins to tingle. Her hair hurts. "It's like someone grabbed my hair and is pulling as hard as they can."

"It's getting ready to go. It's like a time bomb. It ticks and then it blows."

"What are you, a doctor? Suddenly you know everything about cancer, about menopause, about everything?"

In the morning her hair is falling out. It's all over the pillow, all over the shower floor.

"Your hair's not really falling out," Enid says when we meet them for dinner. Enid reaches and touches her hair, sweeps her hand through it, as if to be comforting. She ends up with a handful of hair; she has pulled my wife's hair out. She tries to put it back, she furiously pats it back in place.

"Forget that I was worried about them shaving my pubic hair, how 'bout it all just went down the drain."

She looks like a rat, like something that's been chewed on and spit out, like something that someone tried to electrocute and failed. In four days she is 80 percent bald.

She stands before me naked. "Document me."

I take pictures. I take the film to one of those special stores that has a sign in the window—WE DON'T CENSOR.

I give her a baseball cap to wear to work. Every day she goes to work; she will not miss a day, no matter what.

I, on the other hand, can't work. Since this happened, my work has been nonexistent. I spend my day as the holder of the feelings, the keeper of sensation.

"It's not my fault," she says. "What the hell do you do all day while I'm at the hospital?"

Recuperate.

She wears the baseball cap for a week and then takes a razor, shaves the few scraggly hairs that remain and goes to work bald, without a hat, without a wig—starkers.

There's something aggressive about her baldness.

"How do you feel?" I ask at night when she comes home from the hospital.

"I feel nothing."

"How can you feel nothing? What are you made of?"

"I am made of steel and wood," she says, happily.

As we're falling asleep she tells me a story, "It's true, it happened as I was walking into the hospital. I accidentally bumped into someone on the sidewalk. 'Excuse me,' I said and continued on. He ran after me, 'Excuse me, Excuse me. You knocked my comb out of my hand and I want you to go back and pick it up.' 'What? We bumped into each other, I said excuse me, that will have to suffice.' 'You knocked it out of my hand on purpose. You're just a bald bitch. A fucking bald bitch.' I wheeled around and chased him. 'You fucking crazy ass,' I screamed. 'You fucking crazy ass,' I screamed it about four times. He's lucky I didn't fucking kill him," she says.

I am thinking she's lost her mind. I'm thinking she's lucky he didn't kill her.

She gets up and stands on the bed—naked. She strikes a pose like a bodybuilder. "Cancer Man," she says, flexing her muscles, creating a new super hero. "Cancer Man!"

Luckily she has good insurance. The bill for the surgery comes—it's itemized. They charge per part removed. Ovary $7,000, appendix $5,000.

The total is $72,000. "It's all in a day's work," she says.

We are lying in bed. I am lying next to her, reading the paper.

"I want to go to a desert island, alone. I don't want to come back until this is finished," she says and then looks at me. "It will never be finished—do you know that? I'm not going to have children and I'm going to die."

"Do you really think you're going to die?"

"Yes."

I reach for her.

"Don't," she says. "Don't go looking for trouble."

"I wasn't. I was trying to be loving."

"I don't feel loving," she says. "I don't feel physically bonded to anyone right now, including myself."

"Will we ever again?"

"I don't know."

"You're pushing me away."

"I'm recovering," she says.

"It's been eighteen weeks."

Her blood counts are low. Every night for five nights, I inject her with Nupagen to increase the white blood cells. She teaches me how to prepare the injection, how to push the needle into the muscle of her leg. Every time I inject her, I apologize.

"For what?" she asks.

"Hurting you."

"Forget it," she says, disposing of the needle.

She rolls far away from me in her sleep. She dreams of strange things.

"I dreamed I was with my former boyfriend and he turned into a black woman slave and she was on top of me, between my legs, a lesbian slave fantasy."

"Could I have a hug?" I ask.

She glares at me. "Why do you persist? Why do you keep asking me for things I can't do, things I can't give?"

"A hug?"

"I can't give you one."

"Anyone can give a hug. I can get a hug from the doorman."

"Then do," she says. "I need to be married to someone who is like a potted plant, someone who needs nothing."

"Water?"

"Very little, someone who's like a cactus or an orchid."

"It's like you're refusing to be human," I tell her.

"I have no interest in being human."

This is information I should be paying attention to. She is telling me something and I'm not listening. I don't believe what she is saying.

I go to dinner with Eric and Enid alone.

"It's strange," they say. "You'd think the cancer would soften her, make her more appreciative. You'd think it would make her stop and think about what she wants to do with the rest of her life. When you ask her, what does she say?" Eric and Enid want to know.

"Nothing. She says she wants nothing, she has no needs or desires. She says she has nothing to give."

Eric and Enid shake their heads. "What are you going to do?"

I shrug. None of this is new, none of this is just because she has cancer— that's important to keep in mind, this is exactly the way she always was, only more so.

A few days later a woman calls; she and her husband are people we see occasionally.

"Hi, how are you, how's Tom?" I ask.

"He's a fucking asshole," she says. "Haven't you heard? He left me."

"When?"

"About two weeks ago. I thought you would have known."

"I'm a little out of it."

"Anyway, I'm calling to see if you'd like to have lunch."

"Lunch, sure. Lunch would be good."

At lunch she is a little flirty, which is fine, it's nice actually, it's been a long time since someone flirted with me. In the end, when we're having coffee, she spills the beans. "So I guess you're wondering why I called you?"

"I guess," I say, although I'm perfectly pleased to be having lunch, to be listening to someone else's troubles.

"I heard your wife was sick, I figured you're not getting a lot of sex and I thought we could have an affair."

I don't know which part is worse, the complete lack of seduction, the fact that she mentions my wife not being well, the idea that my wife's illness would make me want to sleep with her, her stun-gun bluntness—it's all too much.

"What do you think? Am I repulsive? Thoroughly disgusting? Is it the craziest thing you ever heard?"

"I'm very busy," I say, not knowing what to say, not wanting to be offensive, or to seem to have taken offense. "I'm just very busy."

My wife comes home from work. "Someone came in today—he reminded me of you."

"What was his problem?"

"He jumped out the window."

"Dead?"

"Yes," she says, washing her hands in the kitchen sink.

"Was he dead when he got to you?" There's something in her tone that makes me wonder, did she kill him?

"Pretty much."

"What part reminded you of me?"

"He was having an argument with his wife."

"Oh?"

"Imagine her standing in the living room, in the middle of a sentence and out the window he goes. Imagine her not having a chance to finish her thought?"

Yes, imagine, not being able to have the last word?

"Did she try and stop him?" I ask.

"I don't know, " my wife says. "I didn't get to read the police report. I just thought you'd find it interesting."

"What do you want for dinner?"

"Nothing," she says. "I'm not hungry."

"You have to eat something."

"Why? I have cancer. I can do whatever I want."

Something has to happen.

I buy tickets to Paris. "We have to go." I invoke the magic word. "It's an emergency."

"It's not like I get a day off. It's not like I come home at the end of the day and I don't have cancer. It goes everywhere with me. It doesn't matter where I am, it's still me—it's me with cancer. In Paris I'll have cancer."

I dig out the maps, the guidebooks; everything we did on our last trip is marked with fluorescent highlighter. I am acting as though I believe that if we retrace our steps, if we return to a place where things were good, there will be an automatic correction, a psychic chiropractic event, which will put everything into alignment.

I gather provisions for the plane: smoke hoods, fresh water, fruit, M&M's, magazines.

"What's the point?" she says, throwing a few things into a suitcase. "You can do everything and think you're prepared, but you don't know what's going to happen. You don't see what's coming until it hits you in the face."

She points at someone outside. "See that idiot crossing the street in front of the truck, why doesn't he have cancer? He deserves to die."

She lifts her suitcase—too heavy. She takes things out. She leaves her smoke hood on the bed. "If the plane fills with smoke, I'm going to be so happy," she says. "I'm going to breathe deeply, I'm going to be the first to die."

I stuff the smoke hood into my suitcase, along with her raincoat, her extra shoes, Ace bandages for her bad ankle, reusable ice packs just in case, vitamin C drops. I lift the suitcases, feeling like a pack animal, a sherpa.

In France, the customs people are not used to seeing bald women. They call her "Sir."

"Sir, you're next, Sir. Sir, please step over here, Sir."

My wife is my husband. She loves it. She smiles. She catches my eye and strikes a subdued version of the superhero/bodybuilder pose, flexing. "Cancer Man," she says.

"And what is the purpose of your visit to France?" the inspector asks. "Business or pleasure?"

"Reconciliation," I say, watching her—Cancer Man.

"Business or pleasure?"

"Pleasure."

Paris is my fantasy, my last-ditch effort to reclaim my marriage, myself, my wife.

As we're checking into the hotel, I remind her of our previous visit—the chef cut himself, his hand was severed, she saved it and they were able to reattach it. "You made medical history. Remember the beautiful dinner they threw in your honor."

"It was supposed to be a vacation," she says.

The bellman takes us to our room—there's a big basket of fruit, bottles of Champagne and Evian with a note from the concierge welcoming us.

"It's not as nice as it used to be," she says, already disappointed. She opens the Evian and drinks. Her lips curl. "Even the water tastes bad."

"Maybe it's you. Maybe the water is fine. Is it possible you're wrong?"

"We see things differently," she says, meaning she's right, I'm wrong.

"Are you in an especially bad mood, or is it just the cancer?" I ask.

"Maybe it's you?" she says.

We go for a walk, across the river and down by the Louvre. There could be nothing better, nothing more perfect and yet I am suddenly hating Paris, hating it more than anything, the beauty, the fineness of it is dwarfed by her foul humor. I realize there is no saving it, no moment of reconciliation, redemption. Everything sucks. It is irredeemably awful and getting worse.

"If you're so unhappy, why don't you leave?" I ask her.

"I keep thinking you'll change."

"If I changed anymore I can't imagine who I'd be."

"Well if I'm such a bitch, why do you stay?"

"It's my job, it's my calling to stay with you, to soften you."

"I absolutely do not want to be softer, I don't want to give another inch."

"Well, I am not a leaver, I worked hard to get here, to be able to stay."

She trips on a cobblestone, I reach for her elbow, to steady her, and instead unbalance myself. She fails to catch me. I fall and recover quickly.

"Imagine how I feel," she says. "I'm a doctor and I can't fix it. I can't fix me, I can't fix you—what a lousy doctor."

"I'm losing you," I say.

"I've lost myself. Look at me—do I look like me?"

"You act like yourself."

"I act like myself because I have to, because people are counting on me."

"I'm counting on you."

"Stop counting."

All along the Tuileries there are Ferris wheels; the world's largest Ferris wheel is set up in the middle.

"Let's go," I say, taking her hand, pulling her toward them.

"I don't like rides."

"It's not much of a ride. It's like a carousel, only vertical. Live a little."

She gets on. There are no seat belts, no safety bars. I say nothing. I am hoping she won't notice.

"How is it going to end?" I ask while we're waiting for the wheel to spin.
"I die in the end."

The ride takes off, climbing, pulling us up and over. We are flying, soaring; the city unfolds. It is breathtaking and higher than I thought. And faster. There is always a moment on any ride where you think it is too fast, too high, too far, too wide, and that you will not survive.

"I have never been so unhappy in my life," my wife says when we're near the top. "It's not just the cancer, I was unhappy before the cancer. We were having a very hard time. We don't get along, we're a bad match. Do you believe me?"

"Yes," I say, "we're a really bad match. We're such a good bad match it seems impossible to let it go."

"We're stuck," she says.

"You bet," I say.

"No. I mean the ride, the ride isn't moving."

"It's not stuck, it's just stopped. It stops along the way."

She begins to cry. "It's all your fault. I hate you. And I still have to deal with you. Every day I have to look at you."

"No, you don't. You don't have to deal with me if you don't want to."

She stops crying and looks at me. "What are you going to do, jump?"

"The rest of your life, or my life, however long or short, should not be miserable. It can't go on this way."

"We could both kill ourselves," she says.

"How about we separate?"

I am being more grown up than I am capable of being. I am terrified of being without her but either way, it's death. The ride lurches forward.

I came to Paris wanting to pull things together and suddenly I am desperate to be away from her, to never have this conversation again. She will be dying and we will still be fighting. I begin to panic, to feel I can't breathe. I have to get away.

"Where does it end?"

"How about we say goodbye."

"And then what? We have opera tickets."

I can't tell her I'm going. I have to sneak away, to tiptoe out backward. I have to make my own arrangements.

We stop talking. We're hanging in mid-air, suspended. We have run out of things to say. When the ride circles down, the silence becomes more definitive.

I begin to make my plan. In truth, I have no idea what I am doing. All afternoon, everywhere we go, I cash traveler's checks, I get cash advances, I have about five thousand dollars' worth of francs stuffed in my pocket. I want to be able to leave without a trace, I want to be able to buy myself out of whatever trouble I get into. I am hysterical and giddy all at once.

We are having an early dinner on our way to the opera.

I time my break for just after the coffee comes. "Oops," I say, feeling my pockets, "I forgot my opera glasses."

"Really?" she says, "I thought you had them when we went out."

"They must be at the hotel. You go on ahead, I'll run back. You know I hate not being able to see."

She takes her ticket. "Hurry," she says. "I hate it when you're late."

This is the bravest thing I have ever done. I go back to the hotel and pack my bag. I'm going to get out. I'm going to fly away. I may never come back. I will begin again, as someone else, someone who wants to live, I will be unrecognizable.

I move to lift the bag off the bed, I pull it up and my knee goes out. I start to fall but catch myself. I pull at the bag and take a step—too heavy. I'll have to go without it. I'll have to leave everything behind. I drop the bag, but still I am falling, folding, collapsing. There is pain, spreading, pouring, hot and cold, like water down my back, down my legs.

I am lying on the floor, thinking that if I stay calm, if I can just find my breath, and follow my breath, it will pass. I lie there waiting for the paralysis to recede.

I am afraid of it being over and yet she has given me no choice, she has systematically withdrawn life support: sex and conversation. The problem is that despite this, she is the one I want.

There is a knock at the door. I know it is not her, it is too soon for it to be her.

"*Entrez*," I call out.

The maid opens the door, she holds the DO NOT DISTURB sign in her hand.

"Oooff," she says, seeing me on the floor. "Do you need the doctor?"

I am not sure if she means my wife or a doctor, a doctor other than my wife. "No."

She takes a towel from her cart and props it under my head, she takes a spare blanket from the closet and covers me with it. She opens the Champagne and pours me a glass, tilting my head up so I can sip. She goes to her cart and gets a stack of night chocolates and sits beside me, feeding me Champagne and chocolate, stroking my forehead.

The phone in the room rings; we ignore it. She refills my glass. She takes my socks off and rubs my feet. She unbuttons my shirt and rubs my chest. I am getting a little drunk. I am just beginning to relax and then there is another knock, a knock my body recognizes before I am fully awake. Everything tightens. My back pulls tighter still, any sensation below my knees drops off.

"I thought something horrible had happened to you. I've been calling and calling the room, why haven't you answered? I thought you'd killed yourself."

The maid excuses herself. She goes into the bathroom and refreshes my cool washcloth.

"What are you doing?" my wife asks.

There is nothing I can say.

"Knock off the mummy routine. What exactly are you doing? Were you trying to run away and then you chickened out? Say something."

To talk would be to continue; for the moment I am silenced. I am a potted plant and still that is not good enough for her.

"He is paralyzed," the maid says.

"He is not paralyzed, I am his wife, I am a doctor. I would know if there was something really wrong."

from the INTRODUCTION TO McSWEENEY'S 13
WHICH CONSISTED OF AN ASSORTED SAMPLER
OF NORTH AMERICAN COMIC DRAWINGS, STRIPS,
AND ILLUSTRATED STORIES

by CHRIS WARE

T HIS IS ONE of the hardest things I've ever done," said one contributor to this issue. "I started to write you a letter telling you why I couldn't do it," said another. "I can't do this," gave up a third. "It's just too hard."

Such pleas may come as a surprise to normal, non-cartoonist people who think of cartooning as a "fun," "dreamy," or a "gosh I'd love to do that more than the crappy job I have to go to every day" sort of a thing. Really, what *could* be more fun than sitting around all day drawing up imaginary worlds full of imaginary people? Doesn't a comic strip more or less approximate the way we first learn to make and tell stories without people telling us how: draw this here, then draw it again there, little doodles of memory or fantasy, as real as our skills allow us to make them? Out of nowhere, one can create a world that doesn't have to depend on eloquence or grammar—it all just appears, picture after picture, page after page. Even better, it's made with the same stuff it always has been: pencil and paper (or pen and ink, if one is feeling old-fashioned)—but nothing more than anyone's ever needed to write a letter. And cheaply printed? Why, they're almost junk. In fact, they *are* junk. Anyone can do it, right?

Thing is, drawing comics really isn't that easy. From the first moment you sit down to draw—after finding any excuse you can not to face the increasingly stupid-sounding idea you'd been nursing uneasily for the previous day or so—a host of unforeseen decisions and hurdles start to multiply and crop up. Let's take an example: your "idea" demands a scene which starts at night... someone sitting at a table, tired, drawing. Now unless you're dealing with a character you've already developed, you realize, once you start to think about it, you don't really know how to draw the person you thought you were imagining more or less clearly all this time. How old is he? What color is his hair? (What does hair color *mean*, anyway?) Also, should you show *all* of him sitting at that table, or should you just show his face? From the front, or side? If he's tired, is he resting his head on his hand, or should he be yawning?

Eventually, really having no other reason not to start, you just start sketching, maybe drawing the figure from the side, hoping for the best. Shortly, however, he looks sort of bent over, like maybe he's in pain, or bloated, or sick. *But he was just supposed to look sort of tired*, you think. *A normal guy, just sitting there.* Erase. You decide to turn him around, maybe show him from above, since that's easier to draw, the shoulders and the hips sort of moving away from the viewer at an angle... then you can draw what's on his table, or what's out the window, too, maybe, like the moon, that's easy—

But now he looks like an animal, squatting. And why from *above*, anyway? That seems weird, like something from a detective film. Erase. Better to just keep it simple—draw it from the side again. *Something sort of normal-seeming about that, anyway.*

Before long, you arrive at your first panel, and it doesn't look quite as bad as you thought it would, though you wasted a lot of time getting up from your table to check your e-mail and get a couple of snacks—and maybe you added too much detail to the drawing, too, though the detail is good, sort of, since it gives you some feeling of confidence. *Probably false*, you wonder.

Anyway, in that next panel, he's got to sort of look like he's considering what he's been drawing, sort of concerned a bit, for this to work. Maybe like he's squinting at it, or something.

But. *God—do I have to draw that whole stupid room completely all over again?*

Fuck that. I'll just draw a close-up of his face, furrowing his brow, hand on forehead, squinting... squinting... but—then he looks constipated, like he's noticing something, somewhere far away. Erase. *Maybe hand on chin? Universal thinking posture? I'll just add a quick scribble-around to sort of indicate it. Nope, no—looks like he's biting his fist, for some reason. Maybe I could just write "He was concerned, squinting..." over the drawing. Authorial Voice, or whatever that's called. Maybe good to introduce that now, too, as it could come in handy later, as a way of complementing/commenting on the action, like writers do. Maybe it'll go faster that way. God, I hate myself.*

Finally, you arrive at the conclusion that the only way the two drawings work next to each other without over-dramatizing the moment, or making the page into a mess, is to redraw the whole room from the same angle and same composition and just rotate the character's head a little bit sideways—which you discover by accident when you read an errant fleck of eraser on the paper as one of his eyes, fallen halfway around the side of his head. Happy mistake! You read the pictures back and forth. *Yep, he looks tired, then concerned.* Tired, concerned. Tiredconcerned. It works!

And only two or three hours have passed—on to panel three.

And so on.

Needless to say, comics aren't exactly the most efficient or buoying of creative languages. It's not something one can get "caught up in," like writing, or painting, or composing music. Compared to movies, however, setting up the previous "shot" would take days and thousands of dollars; in the hands of the capable cartoonist, it only wastes a couple of hours. And, even better, it's entirely the product of a single imagination, not a photograph or an approximation. And, despite the brittle, choppy process of its creation, when the accumulated three or four days of work speed through the mind in the eight to ten seconds it takes to read, it will all, hopefully, acquire a peculiar fluidity, seeming to come "alive," right there on the printed page.

In the past decade or so, comics appear to have gained some greater measure of respect and acceptance than ever before, due in no small part to the number of cartoonists who have begun to take the medium seriously, appearing in magazines as journalism, museums as art, and literary magazines as writing. Even so, many cartoonists gradually slow down, give up, and move on, the energy (or was it naïveté?) that drove them as youths dwindling away, the extraordinary amount of time it takes to simply finish a book offputtingly insurmountable, the remuneration meager. Even in light of the ever-ringing dinner bell of "comics not being just for kids anymore" (usually in review of some gallery show titled "Zap! Bang! Pow!"), the associations of childhood and puerility are still hard to shake; comics are the only art form that many "normal" people still arrive at expecting a specific emotional reaction (laughter) or a specific content (superheroes). Not that the art itself shouldn't be blamed; the accumulated world-dump of comics is piled high with nonsense (but, then again, so is Hollywood, and movies aren't exactly considered an innately childish form, despite their recent predilection for lifting plots and characters from said superhero comics). Simply put, drawing comics demands an incredible amount of time and devotion from the creator, a willingness to put up with being not only misunderstood, but also possibly disregarded—not to mention an understanding of so many different disciplines—that it ends up not being a terrible inviting or rewarding field.

Throughout the process of assembling this anthology, occasional metaphors would occur to me, poking at my resolve as to why it was, exactly, I was doing it: at one point, I felt as if I was treading water around a sinking barge, blowing up hundreds of balloons and attaching them, one by one, to its hull. Another time I felt a bit like the director of a talent show at an institution for developmentally disabled students, standing at the front of the auditorium, trying to encourage the parents to clap louder. Despite comics' slow acceptance, cartoonists frequently still have to explain and defend themselves, so I guess I'm just trying to articulate the most cogent example possible of a unique language that conflates the strengths of so many different art forms (design, drawing, writing, poetry, music, typography, etc.) from the work of many of the artists who inspired me to do it myself.

In art school, I was frequently criticized because many of my instructors simply didn't understand why I was drawing comics. It was hard to explain that no one was telling me to do it, that I wasn't fulfilling any editorial requirement, and that I wasn't doing it as a commercial "gig" (as one of them implied). Any artwork created for reproduction flirts with this sort of aesthetic dismissal; inherently valueless as an "object," a printed picture vibrates with no resonance of having been touched by the artist, except as a sort of cheap souvenir. Its surface is flat, mechanical. But cartooning isn't really drawing, any more than talking is singing. A cartoon drawing lives somewhere between the worlds of words and pictures, sort of where road signs and people waving their arms in the middle of lakes operate: you don't really spend a lot of time considering the aesthetic value of an arrow telling you not to crash, or the gestural grace of a person drowning; you just read the signs and act appropriately. Similarly, most cartoon drawings are pretty bad; the more detailed and refined a cartoon, the less it seems to "work," and the more resistant to reading it becomes. The possible vocabulary of comics is, by definition, unlimited, the tactility of an experience told in pictures outside the boundaries of words, and the *rhythm* of how these drawings "feel" when read is where the real art resides. All cartoonists have a signature "style" that exists beyond the look of their art or the quality of their writing—a sense of experience, a feeling of how they see the world—as expressed in how their characters move, how time is sculpted. Comics are an art of pure composition, carefully constructed like music, but structured into a whole architecture, a page-by-page pattern, brought to life and "performed" by the reader—a colorful piece of sheet music waiting to be read. Best of all, without the critical language of fine art to surround it, comics are also, I believe, perceived more clearly than any other art form; i.e., you don't blame yourself for not "getting" a comic strip—you usually blame the cartoonist. Conversely, if you don't "understand" a modern painting, you're much more likely to blame yourself and your ignorance of the history of art rather than the painter. Unlike prose writing, the strange process of writing with pictures encourages associations and recollections to accumulate literally *in front of the eyes*; people, places, and events appear out of nowhere. Doors open into rooms remembered from childhood, faces form into dead relatives, and distant loves appear, almost magically, on the page—all deceptively manageable, visceral, the combinations sometimes even revelatory. This odd, almost dreamlike characteristic may be rather unique to the medium; Rodolph Töpffer, the comic strip's "inventor," even realized it in 1845. Where real writing and reading includes a sort of temporary blindness, comics keep the eyes half-open, exchanging the ambiguity of words for the simulated certainty of pictures.

All of this flouncy nattering, however, doesn't change the fact that comics are also wonderfully vulgar and coarse, resistant to too much fluffing up or romanticization. They've always appealed to the desire to *see*, and to see really nasty things—some of the earliest examples of picture stories from the 1400s reenact public executions, and the "comics code" instituted in the 1950s was designed to protect children from pictures of things like half-naked women having their eyes gouged out. The selection of material for this anthology thus reflects a good slice of the visible spectrum of self-produced comics currently extant: fictional, biographical, autobiographical, and the uncategorizable. All of the artists have in some way reinvented the language to suit their own particular sensibilities, with no work done to fulfill any ancillary commercial obligation. Comics are not a genre, but a developing language, and despite the discipline's extraordinary difficulty, labor-intensiveness, and paltry recompense, the real reward of this bastard form of half art/half writing—a purely individual, musical vision that comes to life on paper—is hopefully hinted at by the selections presented herein.

122

127

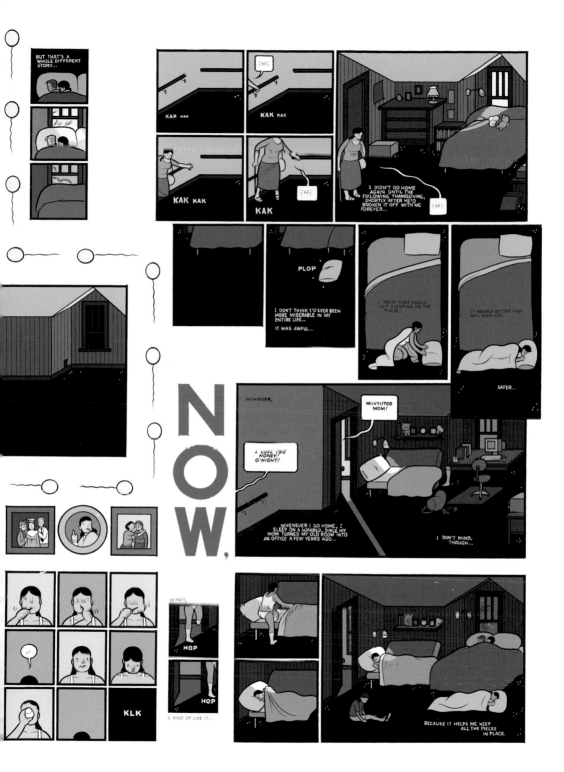

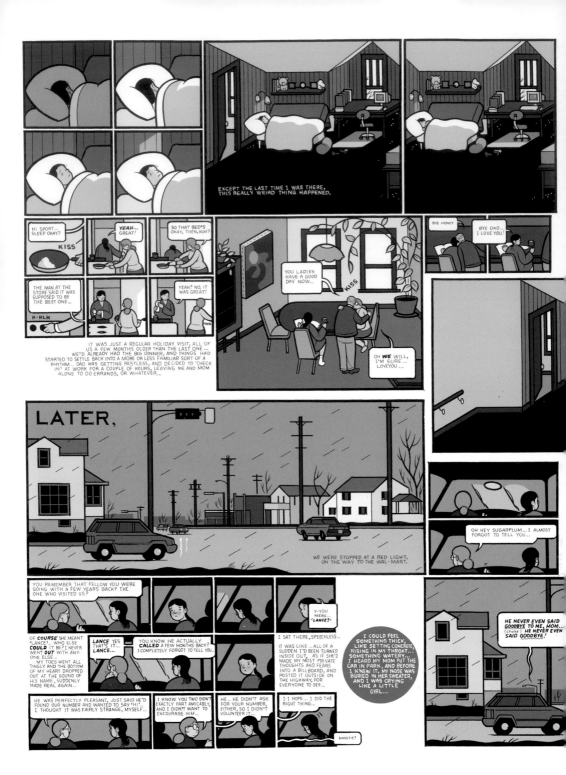

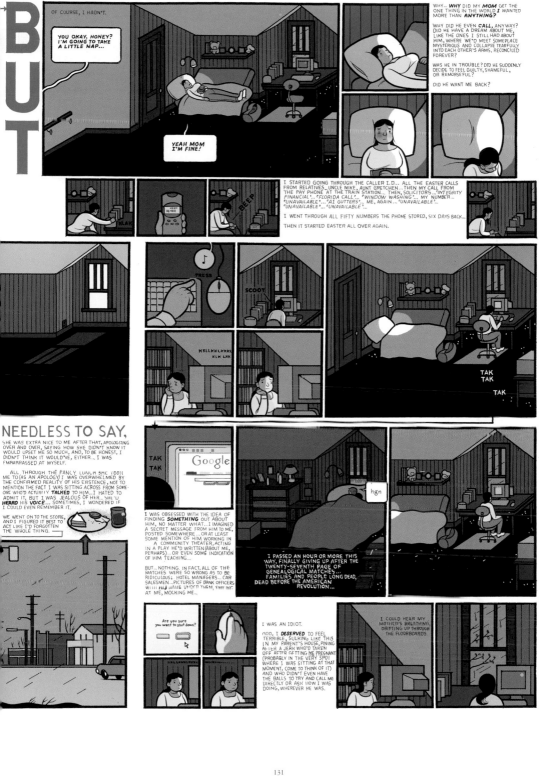

Neven knows about line-of-sight.

He knows about muzzle velocity, rate of fire, the effect of over-water air currents on the trajectory of a bullet.

If you're talking sniper rifles, and he often is, there's four great ones, he says.

1995

His personal favorite is a Winchester and Lee-Enfield hybrid with a night-vision scope that magnifies received light 50,000 times.

The scope needs one star, he says, just one, to illuminate its target.

So even now, with the cease-fire looming, with the war pushing back from the table, belching, and motioning lazily for the final bill, there's no need to make a spectacle of ourselves—

WOULD YOU MIND TURNING THAT THING OFF?

J. SACCO '02

But beyond the parity of such frothy exchanges, I must defer to Neven's preeminence in martial matters, for it is he, Neven, who has walked through the valley of the shadow of death and blown things up along the way.

So when he makes pronouncements about, say, the security arrangements at the Presidential Palace for a Visiting American Diplomat —

...WHY ALL THE FUSS? ALL YOU NEED IS THREE MEN STATIONED AT THE ENTRANCE...

— who am I to add corollaries?

And when he describes an extended metal baton wrapped in leather with which—

...YOU CAN CRACK SOMEONE'S SKULL OPEN WITH JUST A FLICK OF THE WRIST...

— I must admit that I haven't got a favorite hand-to-hand weapon.

138

A CHILD'S BOOK OF
SICKNESS AND DEATH

by CHRIS ADRIAN

(fiction from Issue 14)

MY ROOM, 616, is always waiting for me when I get back, unless it is the dead of winter, rotavirus season, when the floor is crowded with gray-faced toddlers rocketing down the halls on fantails of liquid shit. They are only transiently ill, and not distinguished. You earn something in a lifetime of hospitalizations that the rotavirus babies, the RSV wheezers, the accidental ingestions, the rare tonsillectomy, that these sub-sub-sickees could never touch or have. The least of it is the sign that the nurses have hung on my door, silver glitter on yellow poster board: *Chez Cindy.*

My father settles me in before he leaves. He likes to turn down the bed, to tear off the paper strap from across the toilet, and to unpack my clothes and put them in the little dresser. "You only brought halter tops and hot pants," he tells me.

"And pajamas," I say. "Halter tops make for good access. To my veins."
He says he'll bring me a robe when he comes back, though he'll likely not

be back. If you are the sort of child who only comes into the hospital once every ten years, then the whole world comes to visit, and your room is filled with flowers and chocolates and aluminum balloons. After the tenth or fifteenth admission the people and the flowers stop coming. Now I get flowers only if I'm septic, but my Uncle Ned makes a donation to the Short Gut Foundation of America every time I come in.

"Sorry I can't stay for the H and P," my father says. He would usually stay to answer all the questions the intern du jour will ask, but during this admission we are moving. The new house is only two miles from the old house, but is bigger, and has views. I don't care much for views. This side of the hospital looks out over the park and beyond that to the Golden Gate. On the nights my father stays he'll sit for an hour watching the bridge lights blinking while I watch television. Now he opens the curtains and puts his face to the glass, taking a single deep look before turning away, kissing me goodbye, and walking out.

After he's gone, I change into a lime-green top and bright white pants, then head down the hall. I like to peep into the other rooms as I walk. Most of the doors are open, but I see no one I know. There are some orthopedic-looking kids in traction; a couple wheezers smoking their albuterol bongs; a tall thin blonde girl sitting up very straight in bed and reading one of those fucking Narnia books. She has CF written all over her. She notices me looking and says hello. I walk on, past two big-headed syndromes and a nasty rash. Then I'm at the nurse's station, and the welcoming cry goes up, "Cindy! Cindy! Cindy!" Welcome back, they say, and where have you *been*, and Nancy, who always took care of me when I was little, makes a booby-squeezing motion at me and says, "My little baby is becoming a woman!"

"Hi everybody," I say.

See the cat? The cat has feline leukemic indecisiveness. He is losing his fur, and his cheeks are hurting him terribly, and he bleeds from out of his nose and his ears. His eyes are bad. He can hardly see you. He has put his face in his litter box because some-times that makes his cheeks feel better, but now his paws are hurting and his bladder is getting nervous and there is the feeling at the tip of his tail that comes every day at noon. It's like someone's put it in their mouth and they're chewing and chewing.

Suffer, cat, suffer!

*   *   *

I am a former twenty-six-week miracle preemie. These days you have to be a twenty-four-weeker to be a miracle preemie, but when I was born you were still pretty much dead if you emerged at twenty-six weeks. I did well except for a belly infection that took about a foot of my gut—nothing a big person would miss but it was a lot to one-kilo me. So I've got difficult bowels. I don't absorb well, and get this hideous pain, and barf like mad, and need tube feeds, and beyond that sometimes have to go on the sauce, TPN—total parenteral nutrition, where they skip my wimpy little gut and feed me through my veins. And I've never gotten a pony despite asking for one every birthday for the last eight years.

I am waiting for my PICC—you must have central access to go back on the sauce—when a Child Life person comes rapping at my door. You can always tell when it's them because they knock so politely, and because they call out so politely, "May I come in?" I am watching the meditation channel (twenty-four hours a day of string ensembles and trippy footage of waving flowers or shaking leaves, except late, late at night, when between two and three a.m. they show a bright field of stars and play a howling theremin) when she simpers into the room. Her name is Margaret. When I was much younger I thought the Child Life people were great because they brought me toys and took me to the playroom to sniff Play-Doh, but time has sapped their glamour and their fun. Now they are mostly annoying, but I am never cruel to them, because I know that being mean to a Child Life specialist is like kicking a puppy.

"We are collaborating with the children," she says, "in a collaboration of color, and shapes, and words! A collaboration of poetry and prose!" I want to say, People like you wear me out, honey. If you don't go away soon I know my heart will stop beating from weariness. But I let her go on. When she asks if I will make a submission to their hospital literary magazine I say, "Sure!" I won't, though. I am working on my own project, a child's book of sickness and death, and cannot spare thoughts or words for Margaret.

Ava, the IV nurse, comes while Margaret is paraphrasing a submission—the story of a talking IV pump written by a seven-year-old with only half a brain—and bringing herself nearly to tears at the recollection of it.

"And if he can do that with half a brain," I say, "imagine what I could do with my whole one!"

"Sweetie, you can do anything you want," she says, so kind and so encouraging. She offers to stay while I get my PICC but it would be more comforting to have my three-hundred-pound Aunt Mary sit on my face during the procedure than to have this lady at my side, so I say no thank you, and she finally leaves. "I will return for your submission," she says. It sounds much darker than she means it.

The PICC is the smoothest sailing. I get my morphine and a little Versed, and I float through the fields of the meditation channel while Ava threads the catheter into the crook of my arm. I am in the flowers but also riding the tip of the catheter, à la fantastic voyage, as it sneaks up into my heart. I don't like views, but I like looking down through the cataract of blood into the first chamber. The great valve opens. I fall through and land in daisies.

I am still happy-groggy from Ava's sedatives when I think I hear the cat, moaning and suffering, calling out my name. But it's the intern calling me. I wake in a darkening room with a tickle in my arm and look at Ava's handiwork before I look at him. A slim PICC disappears into me just below the antecubital fossa, and my whole lower arm is wrapped in a white mesh glove that looks almost like lace and would have been cool back in 1983, when I was negative two.

"Sorry to wake you," he says. "Do you have a moment to talk?" He is a tired-looking fellow. At first I think he must be fifty, but when he steps closer to the bed I can see he's just an ill-preserved younger man. He is thin, with strange hair that is not so much wild as just wrong somehow, beady eyes and big ears, and a little beard, the sort you scrawl on a face, along with devil horns, for purposes of denigration.

"Well, I'm late for cotillion," I say. He blinks at me and rubs at his throat.

"I'm Dr. Chandra," he says. I peer at his name tag: SIRIUS CHANDRA, MD.

"You don't look like a Chandra," I say, because he is as white as me.

"I'm adopted," he says simply.

"Me too," I say, lying. I sit up and pat the bed next to me, but he leans against the wall and takes out a notepad and pen from his pocket. He proceeds to flip the pen in the air with one hand, launching it off the tips of his fingers and catching it again with finger and thumb, but he never writes down a single thing that I say.

* * *

See the pony? She has dreadful hoof dismay. She gets a terrible pain every time she tries to walk, and yet she is very restless, and can hardly stand to sit still. Late at night her hooves whisper to her, asking, "Please, please, just make us into glue," or they strike at her as cruelly as anyone who ever hated her. She hardly knows how she feels about them anymore, her hooves, because they hurt her so much, yet they are still so very pretty—her best feature, everyone says—and biting them very hard is the only thing that makes her feel any better at all. There she is, walking over the hill, on her way to the horse fair, where she'll not get to ride on the Prairie Wind, or play in the Haunted Barn, or eat hot buttered morsels of cowboy from a stand, because wise carnival horses know better than to let in somebody with highly contagious dismay. She stands at the gate watching the fun, and she looks like she is dancing but she is not dancing.

Suffer, pony, suffer!

"What do you know about Dr. Chandra?" I ask Nancy, who is curling my hair at the nursing station. She has tremendous sausage curls and a variety of distinctive eyewear that she doesn't really need. I am wearing her rhinestone-encrusted granny glasses and can see Ella Thims, another short-gut girl, in all her glorious, gruesome detail where she sits in her little red wagon by the clerk's desk. Ella had some trouble finishing up her nether parts, and so was born without an anus, or vagina, or a colon, or most of her small intestine, and her kidneys are shaped like spirals. She's only two, but she is on the sauce, also. I've known her all her life.

"He hasn't rotated here much. He's pretty quiet. And pretty nice. I've never had a problem with him."

"Have you ever thought someone was interesting? Someone you barely knew, just interesting, in a way?"

"Do you like him? You like him, don't you?"

"Just interesting. Like a homeless person with really great shoes. Or a dog without a collar appearing in the middle of a graveyard."

"Sweetie, you're not his type. I know that much about him." She puts her hand out, flexing it swiftly at the wrist. I look blankly at her, so she does it again, and sort of sashays in place for a moment.

"Oh."

"Welcome to San Francisco." She sighs. "Anyway, you can do better than that. He's funny-looking, and he needs to pull his pants up. Somebody should tell him that. His mother should tell him that."

"Write this down under 'chief complaint,'" I had told him. "I am *sick* of love." He'd flipped his pen and looked at the floor. When we came to the social history I said my birth mother was a nun who committed indiscretions with the parish deaf-mute. And I told him about my book—the cat and the bunny and the peacock and the pony, each delightful creature afflicted with a uniquely horrible disease.

"Do you think anyone would buy that?" he asked.

"There's a book that's just about shit," I said. "Why not one that's just about sickness and death? Everybody poops. Everybody suffers. Everybody dies." I even read the pony page for him, and showed him the picture.

"It sounds a little scary," he said, after a long moment of pen-tossing and silence. "And you've drawn the intestines on the outside of the body."

"Clowns are scary," I told him. "And everybody loves them. And hoof dismay isn't pretty. I'm just telling it how it is."

"There," Nancy says. "You are *curled*!" She says it like, you are *healed*. Ella Thims has a mirror on her playset. I look at my hair and press the big purple button underneath the mirror. The playset honks, and Ella claps her hands. "Good luck," Nancy adds, as I scoot off on my IV pole, because I've got a date tonight.

One of the bad things about not absorbing very well and being chronically malnourished your whole life long is that you turn out to be four and a half feet tall when your father is six-four, your mother is five-ten, and your sister is six feet even. But one of the good things about being four and a half feet tall is that you are light enough to ride your own IV pole, and this is a blessing when you are chained to the sauce.

When I was five I could only ride in a straight line, and only at the pokiest speeds. Over the years I mastered the trick of steering with my feet, of turning and stopping, of moderating my speed by dragging a foot, and of spinning in tight spirals or wide loops. I take only short trips during the day, but at night I cruise as far as the research building that's attached to, but not part of, the hospital. At three a.m. even the eggiest heads are at home asleep, and I can fly down the long halls with no one to see me or stop me except the occasional security guard, always too fat and too slow to catch me, even if they understand what I am.

My date is with a CFer named Wayne. He is the best-fed CF kid I have ever laid eyes on. Usually they are blond, and thin, and pale, and look like they might cough blood on you as soon as smile at you. Wayne is tan, with dark brown hair and blue eyes, and big, with a high wide chest and arms I could not wrap my two hands around. He is pretty hairy for sixteen. I caught a glimpse of his big hairy belly as I scooted past his room. On my fourth pass (I slowed each time and looked back over my shoulder at him) he called me in. We played a karate video game. I kicked his ass, then I showed him the meditation channel.

He is here for a tune-up—every so often the cystic fibrosis kids will get more tired than usual, or cough more, or cough differently, or a routine test of their lung function will be precipitously sucky, and they will come in for two weeks of IV antibiotics and aggressive chest physiotherapy. He is halfway through his course of tobramycin, and bored to death. We go down to the cafeteria and I watch him eat three stale donuts. I have some water and a sip of his tea. I'm never hungry when I'm on the sauce, and I am absorbing so poorly now that if I ate a steak tonight a whole cow would come leaping from my ass in the morning.

I do a little history on him, not certain why I am asking the questions, and less afraid as we talk that he'll catch on that I'm playing intern. He doesn't notice, and fesses up to the particulars without protest or reservation as we review his systems.

"My snot is green," he says. "Green like that." He points to my green toenails. He tells me that he has twin cousins who also have CF, and when they are together at family gatherings he is required to wear a mask so as not to pass on his highly resistant mucoid strain of Pseudomonas. "That's why there's no camp for CF," he says. "Camps for diabetes, for HIV, for kidney failure, for liver failure, but no CF camp. Because we'd infect each other." He wiggles his eyebrows then, perhaps not intentionally. "Is there a camp for people like you?" he asks.

"Probably," I say, though I know that there is, and would have gone this past summer if I had not been banned the year before for organizing a game where we rolled a couple of syndromic kids down a hill into a soccer goal. Almost everybody loved it, and nobody got hurt.

Over Wayne's shoulder I see Dr. Chandra sit down two tables away. At the same time that Wayne lifts his last donut to his mouth, Dr. Chandra lifts a slice of pizza to his, but where Wayne nibbles like an invalid at his food, Dr. Chandra stuffs. He just pushes and pushes the pizza into his mouth. In less than a minute he's finished it. Then he gets up and shuffles past us, sucking on a bottle of water, with bits of cheese in his beard. He doesn't even notice me.

When Wayne has finished his donut I take him upstairs, past the sixth floor to the seventh. "I've never been up here," he says.

"Heme-Onc," I say.

"Are we going to visit someone?"

"I know a place." It's a call room. A couple of years back an intern left his code cards in my room, and there was a list of useful door combinations on one of them. Combinations change slowly in hospitals. "The intern's never here," I tell him as I open the door. "Heme-Onc kids have a lot of problems at night."

Inside are a single bed, a telephone, and a poster of a kitten in distress coupled with an encouraging motto. I think of my dream cat, moaning and crying.

"I've never been in a call room before," Wayne says nervously.

"Relax," I say, pushing him toward the bed. There's barely room for both our IV poles, but after some doing we get arranged on the bed. He lies on his side at the head with his feet propped on the nightstand. I am curled up at the foot. There's dim light from a little lamp on the bed stand, enough to make out the curve of his big lips and to read the sign above the door to the hall: LASCIATE OGNE SPERANZA, VOI CH'INTRATE.

"Can you read that?" he asks.

"It says, 'I believe that children are our future.'"

"That's pretty. It'd be nice if we had some candles." He scoots a little closer toward me. I stretch and yawn. "Are you sleepy?"

"No."

He's quiet for a moment. He looks down at the floor, across the thin, torn bedspread. My IV starts to beep. I reprogram it. "Air in the line," I say.

"Oh." I have shifted a little closer to him in the bed while fixing the IVs. "Do you want to do something?" he asks, staring into his lap. "Maybe," I say. I walk my hand around the bed, like a five-legged spider, in a circle, over my own arm, across my thighs, up my belly, up to the top of my head to leap off back onto the blanket. He watches, smiling less and less as it walks up the bed, up his leg, and down his pants.

See the zebra? She has atrocious pancreas oh! Her belly hurts her terribly—sometimes it's like frogs are crawling in her belly, and sometimes it's like snakes are biting her inside just below her belly button, and sometimes it's like centipedes dancing with cleats on every one of their little feet, and sometimes it's a pain she can't even describe, even though all she can do, on those days, is sit around and try to think of ways to describe the pain. She must rub her belly on very particular sorts of trees to make it feel better, though it never feels very much better. Big round scabs are growing on her tongue, and every time she sneezes another big piece of her mane falls out. Her stripes have begun to go all the wrong way, and sometimes her own poop follows her, crawling on the ground or floating in the air, and calls her cruel names.

Suffer, zebra, suffer!

Asleep in my own bed, I'm dreaming of the cat when I hear the team; the cat's moan frays and splits, and the tones unravel from each other and become their voices. I am fully awake with my eyes closed. He lifts a mangy paw, saying goodbye.

"Dr. Chandra," says a voice. I know it must belong to Dr. Fell, the GI attending. "Tell me the three classic findings on X-ray in necrotizing entero-colitis." They are rounding outside my room, six or seven of them, the whole GI team: Dr. Fell and my intern and the fellow and the nurse practitioners and the poor little med students. Soon they'll all come in and want to poke on my belly. Dr. Fell will talk for five minutes about shit: mine, and other people's, and sometimes just the idea of shit, a Platonic ideal not extant on this earth. I know he dreams of gorgeous, perfect shit the way I dream of the cat.

Chandra speaks. He answers *free peritoneal air* and *pneumatosis* in a snap but then he is silent. I can see him perfectly with my eyes still closed: his hair all ahoo; his beady eyes staring intently at his shoes; his stethoscope twisted crooked around his neck, crushing his collar. His feet turn in, so his toes are almost touching. Upstairs with Wayne I thought of him.

Dr. Fell, too supreme a fussbudget to settle for two out of three, begins to castigate him: a doctor at your level of training should know these things; children's lives are in your two hands; you couldn't diagnose your way out of a wet paper bag; your ignorance is deadly, your ignorance can *kill*. I get out of bed, propelled by rage, angry at haughty Dr. Fell, and at hapless Dr. Chandra, and angry at myself for being this angry. Clutching my IV pole like a staff I kick open the door and scream, scaring every one of them: "Portal fucking air! Portal fucking air!" They are all silent, and some of them are white-faced. I am panting, hanging now on my IV pole. I look over at Dr. Chandra. He is not panting, but his mouth has fallen open. Our eyes meet for three eternal seconds and then he looks away.

Later I take Ella Thims down to the playroom. The going is slow, because her sauce is running and my sauce is running, so it takes some coordination to push my pole and pull her wagon while keeping her own pole, which trails behind her wagon like a dinghy, from drifting too far left or right. She lies on her back with her legs in the air, grabbing and releasing her feet, and turning her head to say hello to everyone she sees. In the hall we pass nurses and med students and visitors and every species of doctor, attendings and fellows and residents and interns, but not my intern. Everyone smiles and waves at Ella, or stoops or squats to pet her or smile closer to her face. They nod at me, and don't look at all at my face. I look back at her, knowing her fate. "Enjoy it while you have it, honey," I say to her, because I know how quickly one exhausts one's cuteness in a place like this. Our cuteness has to work very hard here. It must extend itself to cover horrors—ostomies and scars and flipper-hands and harelips and agenesis of the eyeballs—and it rises to every miserable occasion of the sick body. Ella's strange puffy face is covered, her yellow eyes are covered, her bald spot is covered, her extra fingers are covered, her ostomies are covered, and the bitter, nose-tickling odor of urine that rises from her always is covered by the tremendous faculty of cuteness generated from some organ deep within her. Watching faces I can see how it's working for her, and how it's stopped working for me. Your organ fails, at some point—it fails for everybody, but for people like us it fails faster, having more to cover than just the natural ugliness of body and soul. One day you are more repulsive than attractive, and the good will of strangers is lost forever.

It's a small loss. Still, I miss it sometimes, like now, walking down the hall and remembering riding down this same hall ten years ago on my Big Wheel. Strangers would stop me for speeding and cite me with a hug. I can remember their faces, earnest and open and unassuming, and I wonder now if I ever met someone like that where I could go with them, after such a blank beginning. Something in the way that Dr. Chandra looks at me has that. And the Child Life people look at you that way, too. But they have all been trained in graduate school not to notice the extra head, or the smell, or the missing nose, or to love these things, professionally.

In the playroom I turn Ella over to Margaret and go sit on the floor in a patch of sun near the door to the deck. The morning activity, for those of us old enough or coordinated enough to manage it, is the weaving of gods' eyes. At home I have a trunkful of gods' eyes and potholders and terra-cotta sculptures the size of your hand, such a collection of crafts that you might think I'd spent my whole life in camp. I wind and unwind the yarn, making and then unmaking, because I don't want to add anything new to the collection. I watch Ella playing at a water trough, dipping a little red bucket and pouring it over the paddles of a waterwheel. It's a new toy. There are always new toys, every time I come, and the room is kept pretty and inviting, repainted and recarpeted in less time than some people wait to get a haircut, because some new wealthy person has taken an interest in it. The whole floor is like that, except where there are pockets of plain beige hospital nastiness here and there, places that have escaped the attentions of the rich. The nicest rooms are those that once were occupied by a privileged child with a fatal syndrome.

I pass almost a whole hour like this. Boredom can be a problem for anybody here, but I am never bored watching my gaunt yellow peers splashing in water or stacking blocks or singing along with Miss Margaret. Two wholesome Down's syndrome twins—Dolores and Delilah Cutty, who both have leukemia and are often in for chemo at the same time I am in for the sauce—are having a somersault race across the carpet. A boy named Arthur who has Crouzon's syndrome—the bones of his skull have fused together too early—is playing Chutes and Ladders with a girl afflicted with Panda syndrome. Every time he gets to make a move, he cackles wildly. It makes his eyes bulge out of his head. Sometimes they pop out—then you're supposed to catch them with a piece of sterile gauze and push them back in.

Margaret comes over, after three or four glances in my direction, noticing that my hands have been idle. Child Life specialists abhor idle hands, though there was one here a few years ago, named Eldora, who encouraged meditation and tried to teach us Yoga poses. She did not last long. Margaret crouches down—they are great crouchers, having learned that children like to be addressed at eye level—and, seeing my gods' eye half-finished and my yarn tangled and trailing, asks if I have any questions about the process.

In fact I do. How do your guts turn against you, and your insides become your enemy? How can Arthur have such a big head and not be a supergenius? How can he laugh so loud when tomorrow he'll go back to surgery again to have his face artfully broken by the clever hands of well-intentioned sadists? How can someone so unattractive, so unavailable, so shlumpy, so low-panted, so pitiable, keep rising up, a giant in my thoughts? All these questions and others run through my head, so it takes me a while to answer, but she is patient. Finally a question comes that seems safe to ask. "How do you make someone not gay?"

See the peacock? He has crispy lung surprise. He has got an aching in his chest, and every time he tries to say something nice to someone, he only coughs. His breath stinks so much it makes everyone run away, and he tries to run away from it himself, but of course no matter where he goes, he can still smell it. Sometimes he holds his breath, just to escape it, until he passes out, but he always wakes up, even when he would rather not, and there it is, like rotten chicken, or old, old crab, or hippopotamus butt. He only feels ashamed now when he spreads out his feathers, and the only thing that gives him any relief is licking a moving tire—a very difficult thing to do.

Suffer, peacock, suffer!

It's not safe to confide in people here. Even when they aren't prying—and they do pry—it's better to be silent or to lie than to confide. They'll ask when you had your first period, or your first sex, if you are happy at home, what drugs you've done, if you wish you were thinner and prettier, or that your hair was shiny. And you may tell them about your terrible cramps, or your distressing habit of having compulsive sex with homeless men and women in Golden Gate Park, or how you can't help but sniff a little bleach every morning when you wake up, or complain that you are fat and your hair always looks as if it had just been rinsed with drool. And they'll say, I'll help you with that bleach habit that has debilitated you separately but equally from your physical illness, that dreadful habit that's keeping you from becoming more perfectly who you are. Or they may offer to teach you how the homeless are to be shunned and not fellated, or promise to wash your hair with the very shampoo of the gods. But they come and go, these interns and residents and attendings, nurses and Child Life specialists and social workers and itinerant tamale-ladies—only you and the hospital and the illness are constant. The interns change every month, and if you gave yourself to each of them they'd use you up as surely as an entire high-school football team would use up their dreamiest cheerleading slut, and you'd be left like her, compelled by your history to lie down under the next moron to come along.

Accidental confidences, or accidentally fabricated secrets, are no safer. Margaret misunderstands; she thinks I am fishing for validation. She is a professional validator, with skills honed by a thousand hours of role playing—she has been both the querulous young lesbian and the supportive adult. "But there's no reason to change," she tells me. "You don't have to be ashamed of who you are."

This is a lesson I learned long ago, from my mother, who really was a lesbian, after she was a nun but before she was a wife. "I did not give it up because it was inferior to anything," she told me seriously, the same morning she found me in the arms of Shelley Woo, my neighbor and one of the few girls I was ever able to lure into a sleepover. We had not, like my mother assumed, spent the night practicing tender, heated frottage. We were hugging as innocently as two stuffed animals. "But it's all *right*," she kept saying against my protests. So I know not to argue with Margaret's assumption, either.

It makes me pensive, having become a perceived lesbian. I wander the ward thinking, "Hello, nurse!" at every one of them I see. I sit at the station, watching them come and go, spinning the big lazy Susan of misfortune that holds all the charts. I can imagine sliding my hands under their stylish scrubs—not toothpaste-green like Dr. Chandra's scrubs, but hot pink or canary yellow or deep-sea blue, printed with daisies or sun faces or clouds or even embroidered with dancing hula girls—and pressing my fingers in the hollows of their ribs. I can imagine taking off Nancy's rhinestone granny-glasses with my teeth, or biting so gently on the ridge of her collar-bone. The charge nurse—a woman from the Philippines named Jory—sees me opening and closing my mouth silently, and asks if there is something wrong with my jaw. I shake my head. There's nothing wrong. It's only that I am trying to open wide enough for an imaginary mouthful of her soft brown boob.

If it's this easy for me to do, to imagine the new thing, then is he somewhere wondering what it would feel like to press a cheek against my scarred belly, or to gather my hair in his fists? When I was little my pediatrician, Dr. Sawyer, used to look in my pants every year and say, "Just checking to make sure everything is *normal*." I imagine an exam, and imagine him imagining it with me. He listens with his ear on my chest and back, and when it is time to look in my pants he stares for a long time and says, "It's not just *normal*, it's *extraordinary*!"

A glowing radiance has just burst from between my legs, and is bathing him in converting rays of glory, when he comes hurrying out of the doctor's room across from the station. He drops his clipboard and apologizes to no one in particular, and glances at me as he straightens up. I want him to smile and look away, to duck his head in an aw-shucks gesture, but he just nods stiffly, then walks away. I watch him pass around the corner, then give the lazy Susan a hard spin. If my own chart comes to rest before my eyes, it will mean that he loves me.

See the monkey? He has chronic kidney doom. His kidneys are always yearning toward things—other monkeys and trees and people and different varieties of fruit. He feels them stirring in him and pressing against his flank whenever he gets near to something that he likes. When he tells a girl monkey or a boy monkey that his kidneys want to hug them, they slap him or punch him or kick him in the eye. At night his kidneys ache wildly. He is always swollen and moist-looking. He smells like a toilet because he can only pee when he doesn't want to, and every night he asks himself, how many pairs of crisp white slacks can one monkey ruin?

Suffer, monkey, suffer!

*　　*　　*

Every fourth night he is on call. He stays in the hospital from six in the morning until six the following evening, awake all night on account of various intern-sized crises. I see him walking in and out of rooms, or peering at the two-foot-long flow sheets that lean on giant clipboards on the walls by every door, or looking solemnly at the nurses as they castigate him for slights against their patients or their honor—an unsigned order, an incorrectly dosed medication, the improper washing of his hands. I catch him in the corridor in what I think is a posture of despair, sunk down outside Wayne's door with his face in his knees, and I think that he has heard about me and Wayne, and it's broken his heart. But I have already dismissed Wayne days ago. We were like two IV poles passing in the night, I told him.

Dr. Chandra is sleeping, not despairing, not snoring but breathing loud through his mouth. I step a little closer to him, close enough to smell him— coffee and hair gel and something like pickles. A flow sheet lies discarded beside him, so from where I stand I can see how much Wayne has peed in the last twelve hours. I stoop next to him and consider sitting down and falling asleep myself, because I know it would constitute a sort of intimacy to mimic his posture and let my shoulder touch his shoulder, to close my eyes and maybe share a dream with him. But before I can sit Nancy comes creeping down the hall in her socks, a barf basin half full of warm water in her hands. A phalanx of nurses appears in the hall behind her, each of them holding a finger to her lips as Nancy kneels next to Dr. Chandra, puts the bucket on the floor, and takes his hand away from his leg so gently I think she is going to kiss it before she puts it in the water. I just stand there, afraid that he'll wake up as I'm walking away, and think I'm responsible for the joke. Nancy and the nurses all disappear around the corner to the station, so it's just me and him again in the hall. I drum my fingers against my head, trying to think of a way to get us both out of this, and realize it's just a step or two to the dietary cart. I take a straw and kneel down next to him. It's a lot of volume, and I imagine, as I drink, that it's flavored by his hand. When I throw it up later it seems like the best barf I've ever done, because it is for him, and as Nancy holds my hair back for me and asks me what possessed me to drink so much water at once I think at him, it was for you, baby, and feel both pathetic and exalted.

I follow him around for a couple call nights, not saving him again from any more mean-spirited jokes, but catching him scratching or picking when he thinks no one is looking, and wanting, like a fool, to be the hand that scratches or the finger that picks, because it would be so interesting and gratifying to touch him like that, or to touch him in any way, and I wonder and wonder what I'm doing as I creep around with increasingly practiced nonchalance, looking bored while I sit across from him, listening to him cajole the radiologist on the phone at one in the morning, when I could be sleeping, or riding my pole, when he is strange-looking, and cannot like me, and talks funny, and is rumored to be an intern of small brains. But I see him stand in the hall for five minutes staring at an abandoned tricycle, and he puts his palm against a window and bows his head at the blinking lights on the bridge in a way that makes me want very much to know what he is thinking, and I see him, from a hiding place behind a bin full of dirty sheets, hopping up and down in a hall he thinks is empty save for him, and I am sure he is trying to fly away.

Hiding on his fourth call night in the dirty utility room while he putters with a flow sheet at the door to the room across the hall, I realize that it could be easier than this, and so when he's moved on, I go back to my room and watch the meditation channel for a little while, then practice a few moans, sounding at first too distressed, then not distressed enough, then finally getting it just right before I push the button for the nurse. Nancy is off tonight. It's Jory who comes, and finds me moaning and clutching at my belly. I get Tylenol and a touch of morphine, but am careful to moan only a little less, so Jory calls Dr. Chandra to come evaluate me.

It's romantic, in its way. The lights are low, and he puts his warm, freshly washed hands on my belly to push in every quadrant, a round of light palpation, a round of deep. He speaks very softly, asking me if it hurts more here, or here, or here. "I'm going to press in on your stomach and hold my hand there for a second, and I want you to tell me if it makes it feel better or worse when I let go." He listens to my belly, then takes me by the ankle, extending and flexing my hip.

"I don't know," I say, when he asks me if that made the pain better or worse. "Do it again."

See the bunny? She has high colonic ruin, a very fancy disease. Only bunnies from the very best families get it, but when she cries bloody tears and the terrible spiders come crawling out of her bottom, she would rather be poor, and not even her fancy robot bed

can comfort her, or even distract her. When her electric pillow feeds her dreams of happy
bunnies playing in the snow, she only feels jealous and sad, and she bites her tongue
while she sleeps, and bleeds all night while the bed dabs at her lips with cotton balls
on long steel fingers. In the morning a servant drives her to the Potty Club, where she
sits with other wealthy bunny girls on a row of crystal toilets. They are supposed to
be her friends, but she doesn't like them at all.

Suffer, bunny, suffer!

When he visits I straighten up, carefully hiding the books that Margaret
brought me, biographies of Sappho and Billie Jean King and HD. She
entered quietly into my room, closed the door, and drew the blinds before
producing them from out of her pants and repeating that my secret was
safe with her, though there was no need for it to be secret, and nothing to
be ashamed of, and she would support me as fully in proclaiming my homo-
sexuality as she did in the hiding of it. She has already conceived of a banner
to put over my bed, a rainbow hung with stars, on the day that I put away
all shame and dark feelings. I hide the books because I know all would really
be lost if he saw them and assumed the assumption. I do not want to be just
his young lesbian friend. I lay out refreshments, spare cookies and juices
and puddings from the meal trays that come, though I get all the food I can
stand from the sauce.

I don't have many dates, on the outside. Rumors of my scarred belly or
my gastrostomy tube drive most boys away before anything can develop,
and the only boys that pay persistent attention to me are the creepy ones
looking for a freak. I have better luck in here, with boys like Wayne, but
those dates are still outside the usual progressions, the talking more and
more until you are convinced they actually know you, and the touching more
and more until you are pregnant and wondering if this guy ever even liked
you. There is nothing normal about my midnight trysts with Dr. Chandra,
but there's an order about them, and a progression. I summon him and he
puts his hands on me, and he orders an intervention, and he comes back to
see if it worked or didn't. For three nights he stands there, watching me for
a few moments, leaning on one foot and then the other, before he asks me
if I need anything else. All the things I need flash through my mind, but
I say no, and he leaves, promising to come back and check on me later, but

never doing it. Then, on the fourth night, he does his little dance and asks, "What do you want to do when you grow up? I mean, when you're bigger. When you're out of school, and all that."

"Medicine," I say. "Pediatrics. What else?"

"Aren't you sick of it?" he asks. He is backing toward the door, but I have this feeling like he's stepping closer to the bed.

"Maybe. But I have to do it."

"You could do anything you want," he says, not sounding like he means it.

"What else could Tarzan become, except lord of the jungle?"

"He could have been a dancer, if he wanted. Or an ice-cream man. Whatever he wanted."

"Did you ever want to do anything else, besides this?"

"Never. Not ever."

"How about now?"

"Oh," he says. "Oh, no. I don't think so. No, I don't think so." He startles when his pager vibrates. He looks down at it. "I've got to go. Just tell Jory if the pain comes back again."

"Come over here for a second," I say. "I've got to tell you something."

"Later," he says.

"No, now. It'll just take a second." I expect him to leave, but he walks over and stands near the bed.

"What?"

"Would you like some juice?" I ask him, though what I really meant to do was to accuse him, ever so sweetly, of being the same as me, of knowing the same indescribable thing about this place and about the world. "Or a cookie?"

"No thanks," he says. As he passes through the door I call out for him to wait, and to come back. "What?" he says again, and I think I am just about to know how to say it when the code bell begins to chime. It sounds like an ice-cream truck, but it means someone on the floor is trying to die. He jumps in the air like he's been goosed, then takes a step one way in the hall, stops, starts the other way, then goes back, so it looks like he's trying to decide whether to run toward the emergency or away from it.

I get up and follow him down the hall, just in time to see him run into Ella Thims's room. From the back of the crowd at the door I can see him standing at the head of the bed, looking depressed and indecisive, a bag mask held up in his hand. He asks someone to page the senior resident, then puts the mask over Ella's face. She's bleeding from her nose and mouth, and from her ostomy sites. The blood shoots around inside the mask when he squeezes the bag, and he can't seem to get a tight seal over Ella's chin. The mask keeps slipping while the nurses ask him what he wants to do.

"Well," he says. "Um. How about some oxygen?" Nancy finishes getting Ella hooked up to the monitor and points out that she's in a bad rhythm. "Let's get her some fluid," he says. Nancy asks if he wouldn't like to shock her, instead. "Well," he says. "Maybe!" Then I get pushed aside by the PICU team, called from the other side of the hospital by the chiming of the ice-cream bell. The attending asks Dr. Chandra what's going on, and he turns even redder, and says something I can't hear, because I am being pushed farther and farther from the door as more people squeeze past me to cluster around the bed, ring after ring of saviors and spectators. Pushed back to the nursing station, I am standing in front of Jory, who is sitting by the telephone reading a magazine.

"Hey, honey," she says, not looking at me. "Are you doing okay?"

See the cat? He has died. Feline leukemic indecisiveness is always terminal. Now he just lies there. You can pick him up. Go ahead. Bring him home and put him under your pillow and pray to your parents or your stuffed plush Jesus to bring him back, and say to him, "Come back, come back." He will be smellier in the morning, but no more alive. Maybe he is in a better place, maybe his illness could not follow him where he went, or maybe everything is the same, the same pain in a different place. Maybe there is nothing all, where he is. I don't know, and neither do you.

Goodbye, cat, goodbye!

Ella Thims died in the PICU, killed, it was discovered, by too much potassium in her sauce. It put her heart in that bad rhythm they couldn't get her out of, though they worked over her till dawn. She'd been in it for at least a while before she was discovered, so it was already too late when they put her on the bypass machine. It made her dead alive—her blood was moving in her, but by midmorning of the next day she was rotting inside.

Dr. Chandra, it was determined, was the chief architect of the fuck-up, assisted by a newly graduated nurse who meticulously verified the poisonous contents of the solution and delivered them without protest. Was there any deadlier combination, people asked each other all morning, than an idiot intern and a clueless nurse?

I spend the morning on my IV pole, riding the big circle around the ward. It's strange, to be out here in the daylight, and in the busy morning crowd—less busy today, and a little hushed because of the death. I go slower than usual, riding like my grandma would, stepping and pushing leisurely with my left foot, and stopping often to let a team go by. They pass like a family of ducks, the attending followed by the fellow, resident, and students, all in a row, with the lollygagging nutritionist bringing up the rear. Pulmonary, Renal, Neurosurgery, even the Hypoglycemia team are about in the halls, but I don't see the GI team anywhere.

The rest of the night I lie awake in bed, waiting for them to come round on me. I could see it already: everybody getting a turn to kick Dr. Chandra outside my door, or Dr. Fell standing casually with his foot on Dr. Chandra's neck as the team discussed my latest ins and outs. Or maybe he wouldn't even be there. Maybe they send you home early when you kill somebody. Or maybe he would just run and hide somewhere. Not sleeping, I still dreamed about him, huddled in a linen closet, sucking on the corner of a blanket, or sprawled on the bathroom floor, knocking his head softly against the toilet, or kneeling naked in the medication room, shooting up with Benadryl and morphine. I went to him in every place, and put my hands on him with great tenderness, never saying a thing, just nodding at him, like I knew how horrible everything was. A couple rumors float around in the late morning— he's jumped from the bridge; he's thrown himself under a trolley; Ella's parents, finally come to visit, have killed him; he's retired back home to Virginia in disgrace. I add and subtract details—he took off his clothes and folded them neatly on the sidewalk before he jumped; the trolley was full of German choir boys; Ella's father choked while her mother stabbed; his feet hang over the end of his childhood bed.

I don't stop even to get my meds—Nancy trots beside me and pushes them on the fly. Just after that, around one o'clock, I understand that I am following after something, and that I had better speed up if I am going to catch it. It seems to me, who should really know better, that all the late, new sadness of the past twenty-four hours ought to count for something, ought to do something, ought to change something, inside of me, or outside in the world. But I don't know what it is that might change, and I expect that nothing will change—children have died here before, and hapless idiots have come and gone, and always the next day the sick still come to languish and be poked, and they will lie in bed hoping, not for healing, a thing which the wise have all long given up on, but for something to make them feel better, just for a little while, and sometimes they get this thing, and often they don't. I think of my animals and hear them all, not just the cat but the whole bloated menagerie, crying and crying, *make it stop*.

Faster and faster and faster—not even a grieving short-gut girl can be forgiven for speed like this. People are thinking, *she loved that little girl* but I am thinking, *I will never see him again*. Still, I almost forget I am chasing something and not just flying along for the exhilaration it brings. Nurses and students and even the proudest attendings try to leap out of the way but only arrange themselves into a slalom course. It's my skill, not theirs, that keeps them from being struck. Nancy tries to stand in my way, to stop me, but she wimps away to the side long before I get anywhere near her. Doctors and visiting parents and a few other kids, and finally a couple security guards, one almost fat enough to block the entire hall, try to arrest me, but they all fail, and I can hardly even hear what they are shouting. I am concentrating on the window. It's off the course of the circle, at the end of a hundred-foot hall that runs past the playroom and the PICU. It's a portrait frame of the near tower of the bridge, which looks very orange today against the bright blue sky. It is part of the answer when I understand that I am running the circle to rev up for a run down to the window that right now seems like the only way out of this place. The fat guard and Nancy and a parent have made themselves into a roadblock just beyond the turn into the hall. They are stretched like a Red-Rover line from one wall to the other, and two of them close their eyes, but don't break, as I come near them. I make the fastest turn of my life and head away down the hall.

It's Miss Margaret who stops me. She steps out of the playroom with a crate of blocks in her arms, sees me, looks down the hall toward the window, and shrieks "Motherfucker!" I withstand the uncharacteristic obscenity, though it makes me stumble, but the blocks she casts in my path form an obstacle I cannot pass. There are twenty of them or more. As I try to avoid them I am reading the letters, thinking they'll spell out the name of the thing I am chasing, but I am too slow to read any of them except the farthest one, an R, and the red Q that catches under my wheel. I fall off the pole as it goes flying forward, skidding toward the window after I come to a stop on my belly outside the PICU, my central line coming out in a pull as swift and clean as a tooth pulled out with a string and a door. The end of the catheter sails in an arc through the air, scattering drops of blood against the ceiling, and I think how neat it would look if my heart had come out, still attached to the tip, and what a distinct, once-in-a-lifetime noise it would have made when it hit the floor.

THEY ALL STAND
UP AND SING

by JULIE HECHT

(nonfiction from Issue 39)

I WAS SOMEWHERE IN a big room in an old apartment in New York. The room was in a brownstone, or limestone, and had what appeared to be twenty-foot-high ceilings. There were baroque moldings around the ceilings, around the tops of the radiator covers and on the mantelpiece. The apartment was on the fifth floor and there was no elevator, but it was near Gramercy Park.

This was during the era when very young women could afford such places with a roommate or two. The roommates in this apartment were happy that they'd found this great deal. I was so young that I lived in a much-worse situation, which I didn't notice at the time but now look back upon with horror and disbelief. I accepted the fact that graduate students lived in better circumstances than high school or college students did. This was before the arrival of the yuppie generation who thought they could have

photo: The author wearing a Marimekko dress, sometime in the 1980s. Nantucket, Massachusetts.

everything they wanted immediately, and proceeded to get it.

We all wore Marimekko cotton dresses—not by plan, or necessarily at the same time. I myself had at least five or six, or seven or ten. What does it matter now? Who cares about our Marimekko dresses? Sleeveless for summer, long-sleeved for winter, short-sleeved for spring. They were the only clothes that were desperately wanted by artistic, intellectual, highbrow or hip girls and young women. We were called girls at the time. One of the highbrow girls in the apartment happened to have an actual low brow—a monkey's low brow, even though she was highly intelligent.

Each dress was a work of art. Some were Op Art. We knew the fabric had originally been painted by Finnish women artists—we knew some story like that. We were too crazed by the dresses to care much how they came to be. One design was striped, thin stripes, as if painted with a watercolor paintbrush so that the lines were all in uneven waves. One line was the blue the sky sometimes turns right before the sunset, the other was green, the color of lichen growing on a tree. This was one of the best. The style of the dresses was almost completely plain—as plain and simple as a dress a child would draw. Just two lines like a capital A. The neckline would be round and high, or maybe a small V-neck, or thin, silver-looking buttons going up to a little stand-up collar.

The Marimekko design came right after the completely opposite kinds of designs, designs of the neat and perfect fifties. No one's form was visible under the loose A of the dress—so unlike today's tramp-ware—all that was seen was a face, a head of hair, and the personality and brain behind the face. Then the dress, and the legs. The legs didn't have to be perfect legs. The person counted.

People met, went out, fell in love, or not; some got married and lived happily ever after, or not. All the girls looked like adorable girls from a child's book. Even those who were not that adorable. How much fun were the end of the sixties and part of the seventies, when girls and women were people. Most men were still what were later called sexist pigs, but they didn't need to know exactly what was under the dress at first glance. In present times we know this is a must—seeing everything on everyone all the time.

In a documentary about Bob Dylan, Joan Baez can be seen singing at the Newport Film Festival. She's wearing a plain white sleeveless dress with a high, round neck. The dress has no shape, but her shape is visible when she moves. Her long dark hair is hanging down and around her shoulders, just natural and plain—she could have been anyone. A college student, or a teacher, or even a librarian. Only her arms are bare and the hem of her dress is just below her knees, not much different from a dress Jacqueline Kennedy might have worn.

I recently read that Jacqueline Kennedy owned eight Marimekkos, which she wore during the summer of the 1960 presidential campaign. Since I read it on Wikipedia the information was suspect. She would have had many more than eight. Maybe eighteen or eighty.

The mania and fascination with Marimekkos began with student-girls at Radcliffe. In the beginning, Cambridge was the only place to get the dresses. Design Research on Brattle Street was a holy shrine. Next there was Design Research on East Fifty-seventh Street in New York, but that was less holy. We'd been told that some architect, Ben Thompson, was the store's founder, and that he was responsible for bringing all this stuff here—Finnish dresses, Scandinavian furniture, glasses, everything from these superior-design countries. We didn't wonder about him, we cared only about the dresses. We didn't understand that all the designs were part of a revolution. We were so young we didn't have the experience of buying things. We didn't know how ugly things had been before.

Every day, the song "Get Off of My Cloud" was played on speakers throughout the store in New York. It got us all high—all of us who were lucky enough to be working there instead of Max's Kansas City. We were too high to have been working in this shrine. The Rolling Stones–induced madness wasn't right for staring at fabric in the fabric-bolt area—a short, wide, light-wood stairway open to the space of the whole store, going up to a small second floor of a wall of shelves and floor-to-ceiling bolts of too many colors to take in. A special, beautiful, light-wood rolling ladder was used to reach the bolts on the top shelves.

The dresses were not short enough, so we shortened them. My bad-mannered, good-looking boyfriend directed mine to be shortened even more. We stood in front of a mirror in his apartment and he kept pulling the hem up two more inches. He didn't appreciate the subtlety of the dresses. When he'd first seen the Marimekkos, he had told me in his crude way, "It's what my old lady would have called a 'shmata.'

"No, like this," he'd say, turning the work of art into a minidress. "I want to see legs." I was surprised—this after my mother had always found fault with my legs, saying, "I won prizes for my legs in college." The boyfriend didn't know about perfect legs. I'd heard that his former girlfriend's legs were thick and clunky.

Later on, those of us in the fabric department were told that many male customers would ask for the bolts high on the wall so that when we climbed the ladder they could view our legs and underpants—modestly cut bikinis. At that time, that thing, the t _ _ _g, had not yet been invented. One must remember to be grateful for this.

I recall hearing an older woman, "older," in her forties, complain that the music was too loud. "And the same music every day," she said. She always came in at exactly 10 a.m., I assumed right after her psychoanalyst appointment, which apparently was not helping her. So angry at the Rolling Stones.

The music certainly wasn't loud like the loud music of today. People could hear each other speak. In present times many people can't go to stores because of all the so-called music and the loudness of it.

The frenzy about these Marimekko dresses was such that when describing a fellow student, one might say, "She has ten Marimekko dresses," or "She has seventeen Marimekkos." One student was reputed to have all of them.

The world was small. There was New York. There was Cambridge. There was Out West, but I didn't know about that.

It was a few years after the Marimekko era had begun, in the apartment near Gramercy Park, that the film student was discussing movies, or "films," as they were beginning to be called. She and an intellectual roommate were talking about *Casablanca*. They were friends and roommates of one of my older siblings. Without this crew I wouldn't have known anything. I was a young idiot still thinking about Elvis Presley and the Beatles. Sometimes Nietzsche and Pirandello. But ever since I'd heard Elvis Presley sing

"Heartbreak Hotel," I'd been hooked for life. I was a rock-and-roll fanatic but this was a secret, even to me.

The *Casablanca* talk continued.

"Is that the one where they all stand up and sing?" I asked.

The roommates knew that I was not a complete ignoramus, as evidenced by the fact that my favorite movie was *The Red Shoes*, which I had first seen at age five. The film student laughed. She repeated my question while shaking her head in disbelief. She had a large, thick puff-head of long brown hair that she set on giant pink plastic rollers every day or night to make it even straighter and bigger, as was the way of the time. Not "big" like the hair of the Ronettes or the Supremes—just thicker and more "bouffant," a word from the sixties, used over and over to describe Jacqueline Kennedy's hair, the describing starting with the inauguration. It's no fun to think about that day.

The film student would sit and read, or take a nap—needed from over-work—while her head was under the hood of the kind of portable home hair dryer almost every female person owned, except for me. I still had long, straight blond hair down to my waist the way I'd had during my whole life of being a girl.

I remember the film student's head of hair bobbing and floating all around as she shook her head and laughed when I asked the *Casablanca* question. Is naïveté funny or stupid? I couldn't be sure what she was thinking. The others laughed, too. Maybe they just kept me around for entertainment. They couldn't stop smiling. The film student later went on to win many awards and rose to the top of her profession, whatever that is.

It may be this: I was told at some point, maybe fifteen years later, that she had to go to the original Henri Bendel on West Fifty-seventh Street to buy a dress to wear to the Oscars.

"Why?" I asked. "Why does she have to go to that Hollywood thing?"

"She's nominated for one," was the answer.

After another few years, I heard that she'd won the award. I wouldn't have known since I never watched the dastardly proceedings.

By then, as a grown-up idiot, I was acquiring an understanding of misery, tragedy, and history. I became one of the many *Casablanca* fanatics and believed I had seen it more times than the writer-director whose first movie was *Take the Money and Run*. Unlike that person, I would never besmirch the film by using it for my own purposes.

I believed I understood every other part of *Casablanca*, too—the love story, the writing, the directing, the length and beauty of Ingrid Bergman's white gloves. And then there was her white sun hat. I always wondered how she kept her clothes so well pressed and clean and perfect looking, in her circumstances—in hot, hot Casablanca. This is never shown.

More time passed. A decade or two.

One night, when desperately flipping around the TV channels, I saw that *Casablanca* was on. It had started twenty minutes before. I said to my husband, "Oh, *Casablanca* is on. We missed the beginning." He ignored that and went into the kitchen to slice vegetables, his only job for dinner. I called him a couple of times and said, "What are you doing?" How long does it take to slice a few vegetables for two people? Even for a dinner of all vegetables. I didn't want to sit alone with the PAUSE button. One of the times I called, he said he was washing lettuce. He was not supposed to be washing lettuce. He doesn't know how.

But the third time he said, "What do you care what I'm doing?"

Then I became suspicious that he was doing something bad, like drinking cheap wine, alone, before dinner.

"Come in," I said. "You can't miss this part."

He walked a few steps and was standing in the doorway.

"Is it the part when they sing the Marseillaise?" he said.

"Yes, yes!" I said. I hit the PLAY button.

"I'm tired of that," he said in his coldhearted way. "Aren't you?"

"I'll never get tired of it," I said.

"Do you cry?" he asked without interest.

"Almost," I said as a lie. Because I was already crying. With him it was a case of: "Cry and you cry alone."

I thought about the fact that this movie and the history that inspired it—this all happened before we were born. It's then that I always realize that we're not very important. Especially when I hear Humphrey Bogart say, "What of it? I'm going to die in Casablanca. It's a good spot for it." The use of the word "spot"—the two words, "good spot"—I'm just no one compared with that sentence. Our parents were more clever before we existed. This leads to other dreadful thoughts.

*   *   *

I watched the rest of the movie while my husband went back into the kitchen to drink his wine.

After a while he brought out the vegetables and offered me some. I said, "No thanks."

"Just because I'm having a glass of wine you're mad at me?" he asked.

"It's just that you're drinking alone in the kitchen while they're singing the Marseillaise."

He ate his vegetables and brought his dishes back into the kitchen. Then he came out and sat down in the antique, upholstered man-chair. I looked over there a few times. His eyes were closed and he was falling asleep. He kept trying to wake himself and eventually succeeded. He got up and sat next to me on the couch where I was lying down and thinking about life on this planet. Especially the times of life shown in that movie.

The second part of the double feature was starting. It was *The African Queen*. He was pretending that he could stay awake and watch it.

I remembered something that happened before we were married. It had to do with the filmmaker from the apartment in Gramercy Park. It was a Sunday in November a few months after I met this pre-husband. He was watching football in my apartment I never watched TV after childhood until I found out that there were old movies on Channel Thirteen. My former roommate had temporarily left her TV in the living room when she moved out.

The apartment was in a brownstone on the third floor. It was the back half of one floor and had a view of other backs of other brownstones—trees and little backyards. I no longer worked at Design Research. In a productive mania, I had started my real work on my first book of photographs.

I wanted to go out for a walk in the park. He said, "When the game is over at four." But at four, that thing happened where more minutes get added to the game. He said, "Ten more minutes." When I went back he said, "That was game-minutes, not regular minutes."

"How much in human time?" I asked.

Later on in our life together he told some friends that I referred to these sports-minutes as not being human time. They all laughed. Ha, ha, for the waste of those minutes of life.

He said he didn't know how much time.

I fell into a wretched state. I saw that I was with a twenty-four-year-old man who wanted to watch sports on TV all the time—it wasn't even baseball.

The weather was the damp, gray kind—not hot, humid, and sunny like the new Novembers of this century. I called the number of the next apartment where the film students and my sibling were living. The apartment had a few gigantic rooms with a view of the Hudson River. The formerly laughing, serious filmmaker answered. I described my plight. She offered to go for a walk in Riverside Park. I said I'd see about the minutes and call her back.

I waited, but by the time the unreal-minutes were over, it was getting dark. I'd lost the desire to go walk with the football-watching man. In a hopeless state, I forgot about calling the filmmaker.

If I had called her, maybe we would have gone for the walk. Sometimes I'd meet her on the street, then, out on ugly upper Broadway. She was often with one filmmaker or another. Later, they'd ask if I wanted to be in this or that film they were putting together. I always declined, assuming the film would be serious and spooky, not funny or absurd. That was their preferred, intellectual inclination.

Maybe on that walk she would have said just one illuminating thing, like every psychiatrist-psychoanalyst I'd ever seen, but it would have made an impression, because she was a real person, and we knew each other as humans, not the way psychiatrists know you only when you're in their offices and are part of a game invented for their own interest and business. I'd have seen that the TV-watching was not just a phase of youth. I would have returned to the slew of arty, film-y, musician-men I used to know as boyfriend material.

Somewhere along the line I had unconsciously started a list in my head of the one true thing each psychiatrist had said.

One: This concerned some plants. In the early years of our marriage, every summer we left the hot and filthy city of Manhattan, which for some reason is still called the "greatest city in the world"—if it's so great, why are there gigantic black plastic bags of garbage piled high on every corner? Why doesn't David Letterman ask that question of the mayor when he appears on the show? We left the greatest city for Nantucket Island before Nantucket was ruined. My mother, at my parents' beach house, not that far from New York, had offered to take care of my plants.

When we arrived with the small collection of maidenhair ferns, my mother started her comments. I was on the screen porch when I heard her say about me: "She's putting her plants to bed." Then she laughed in a mean way. Although I later forgave my mother for everything she ever said, and felt only sadness and grief for her tragic life, I became enraged at the time. She meant that she wanted her three daughters to produce babies when they were only in their twenties and barely formed beings themselves. She wanted them to be putting these imagined babies to bed.

She'd often said "Children are overrated," and "Children ruin your life—you lose everything—your youth, your looks, your figure, your soul." We'd heard this all our lives, and she wanted us to join right in.

The next week when I told the psychiatrist about the plants, he said, "But then, why did you go there?"

I said, "To have the plants taken care of."

He said, "Some people care more about themselves than their plants."

I didn't think much of that at the time as he was as stupid and dangerous as are most in his profession. As Thomas Bernhard, the great Austrian writer and truth-teller, wrote: "Psychiatrists are the real demons of our age... constrained by neither law nor conscience."

In recent years, when I have had no mother and more and more plants and I have lived in a little house where the plants can stay outside in my absence and be watered by a plant-watering person, I have still been compelled to pack two gigantic pots of four-foot, pale peach-pink dahlias rather than be parted from them for the whole summer.

One summer, the local nursery-man helped me pack a five-foot, tree-form lavender heliotrope. It smelled like vanilla and the blossoms, made up of many tiny petals, were hanging from the little branches like bunches of grapes. As we filled the carton and stuffed it with paper and bubble wrap and plastic air-pillows, wasting an hour or two, the sentence of the psychiatrist popped into my mind, but I went on packing. All this, on the globally warmed-up, hot June days—and at night—ordering extra-large triple-walled cartons, spending hours looking at the bubble wrap from the Uline company's bubble-wrap choices on the Mac-whichever. This Mac-thing would be heating up and burning the tops of my thighs, leaving red burn marks, but I kept going.

There were large bubbles and small bubbles. There was stick-bubble with large bubbles, and stick-bubble with small bubbles. There was a patient customer-service person to discuss these bubble choices with. I heard myself saying, "Two rolls of small stick-bubbles, two rolls of regular large bubbles, one roll of large stick-bubbles." A lot of thinking had gone into the decision. This was before I'd read in a PETA magazine that glue is an animal by-product. And there is no eco–bubble wrap. The whole bubble-wrap thing is a vast eco-crime.

There was one other thing this psychiatrist had told me when I couldn't stop thinking about a number of minor incidents: "You remind me of the myth of '…'"—a name I couldn't ever remember.

It was about a boy who got stuck to anything he touched and couldn't get unstuck. Later, when I told other psychiatrists—and this is what psycho-therapy is, you tell the same things over and over until you go mad and would be institutionalized if there were any good institutions left—they didn't know what the myth was, either. They are an even more ignorant crew now. I guess I could google the myth, but life is short.

Next on my list there was the great German psychoanalyst who saw patients for consultation and then sent them on to someone way beneath him in every way. He asked me, "Are you happily married?" I said, "Yes, but it's not too exciting."

He said, "Well, you had enough excitement with your mother." I guessed he meant a bad kind of excitement. In the frenzy of youth, or manic depres-sion, I'd never thought of that myself. There was no time to explain about the football-watching. Basketball, too. Even hockey was watched.

The third of the one true things was the one concerning the shirt of the German woman-psychoanalyst-psychiatrist.

These were the days when my husband would ask me to buy wedding presents and such for people he worked with—people I'd never met and about whom I knew nothing. But trying to buy this one present seemed to be an easy task. There was a French store on Madison Avenue and

Sixty-something Street, when Madison Avenue was still normal and wasn't that expensive. The store was a branch of a store in France for the middle and upper-middle classes.

The towels they sold were white, or light pink, the color of a certain rose—there was even a middle-aged American saleswoman whose name was Rose—or they were dusty blue, or moss green. The loops of the towels were long and sewn wide apart so that the towels were soft and floppy like nothing I'd seen before or after. I see them now in the linen closet and they look the same.

I thought of going to this store to buy some special pillowcases for the wedding gift. The cases were white Euro-squares. I'd seen them in a catalog sent by the store. This was in the era when people received one or two catalogs per week. The cases were plain with cotton lace appliquéd onto the border. When I asked the very young French salesclerk for them, she said there was no such thing. I insisted that they were in a picture in the catalog. I asked to see the catalog. The pillowcases were right there, on the cover.

She became more and more infuriated. I could see her mental temperature rising. She was in her twenties. There was no reason for this behavior. She wasn't at the hysterical stage of life but her almost-pretty face was getting redder and redder and soon she was shrieking at me in her French accent, "We don't have these!" This was before the condition, now called PMS, had been named, but in retrospect it could have been that, or the rage part of manic-depressive psychosis.

At last she went to look in the basement stockroom—it might have been Rose, the older, sensible American saleswoman, who prompted her to do so—and after a lot of barely muffled screaming and the sound of boxes crashing around, she stomped up the stairs and threw the requested white European square pillowcases in my direction. Perhaps Rose took over the task of the white monogram, necessary for the newlyweds—I never remember that part—but by the time I left I had only a small fragment of my former self remaining.

Later I learned that the young couple for whom I'd purchased the pillowcases were divorced. The bride was a privileged, crazy bitch. The groom—a hapless nerd. When I heard about the matter of the divorce, I wondered about the fate of the white monogrammed cases because of the monogram. At which thrift shop might they be sitting on a shelf or thrown into a bin?

*   *   *

A year passed. When I dared to enter the store again, the French psycho-girl was still there. It was winter and people in the store were discussing the weather.

"So what of it?" the girl was screaming. "So it snowed a lot of feet in Buffalo!"—pronouncing the name of that city, "Boofalo"—"I am so sick of hearing this—nine feet of snow in Boofalo, fifteen feet in Boofalo—Boofalo! Who cares!"

These two incidents were what I described to the German doctor. "This has happened to me, too," she said. "I saw in a catalog from Saks Fifth Avenue a plain white shirt that was just what I needed." This was before the Internet. People had to go all over the place to hunt for things. The places we went—the things we did. At least people burned a lot of calories walking miles all over, up and down, from top to bottom and around New York, even down to Canal Street. We wore regular shoes, too, sometimes heels, or, the irony is, shoes called buffalo sandals. They had three-inch wedges. I found some with vegan, non-leather straps, but the cork wedges were hard as cement. Kork-Ease, they were dishonestly named. No ease involved.

That same uncouth, good-looking boyfriend who didn't understand the Marimekko dresses once told me as part of his screwed-up life story that he'd spent his first year in college going downtown every day to every department store, searching for a maroon corduroy suit. He did this instead of studying. Sometimes he'd cut classes. His "therapist" had cured him of the behavior and "helped him put things into perspective."

I thought this suit-searching was an interesting and good thing, not something to be cured of. It was one of his only admirable qualities. The other was his love for the Beatles.

About fifteen years later, sometime in the eighties, he came to New York from the other coast, where he had become, of course, a psychotherapist. His therapist from the corduroy-suit era had been his "role model," he'd once said.

We arranged to meet on some unpleasant corner in Greenwich Village. I immediately detected the odor of garlic. When he mentioned he'd had lunch at a Chinese restaurant and the dish he'd chosen was pork with garlic sauce, I figured: Well, he must not care about me anymore—I certainly almost gagged when he said the word "pork."

*　　*　　*

"So I went down there," the psychiatrist-analyst continued, "on Saturday morning—you know how little free time I have—and this stupid little salesclerk made no effort to find out where the shirt was located in the store. I had brought the catalog, and she refused to look for it, and argued that she couldn't find out if they had it at all."

I pictured the German doctor, in her mid- or late sixties, with her gray hair cut in long bangs in a modified, less-severe Buster Brown style—plain, but not at all ridiculous or undignified. She was an obviously educated woman from a European culture. I imagined her trudging down to Saks Fifth Avenue from her simple yet perfectly situated apartment building in the upper East Sixties between Central Park and Madison Avenue. She probably walked—in sensible shoes, not sneakers. This was still before sneakers for walking. Or maybe she took the Fifth Avenue bus—or even a taxi down to Forty-eighth Street, if she was in a hurry. And then to encounter this attitude, as she put it, this rudeness and stupidity. To say nothing of going into any department store on Saturday.

I felt badly for her because at the time I was so young that most salesclerks were relatively nice to me, but she was at that age where clerks like that one didn't bother with her. As she told the story I could see she was still angry. She was looking at me as if she were talking to a friend, not a patient.

"I knew she was just a rude, ignorant clerk and it was no reflection on me. I was annoyed, but why should you feel so badly if a neurotic clerk behaves this way to you about some pillowcases?"

The answer was a long story, the telling of which had never helped with the increasingly uncivilized behavior in our society.

The last on the list of psychiatrists was a colleague of the German woman's— possibly more eminent. Kind and even-tempered, and even a friend of Anne Freud's. She also did consultations and the visit was one of those. This consulting-thing later became just a racket for others—to help younger, incompetent trainees in the field—those who needed patients.

I was leaving her spartan but pleasant-enough office, the kind with an ordinary plant here and there. She was older than the other woman—maybe eighty, her hair was white, and she wore a plain skirt and blouse. The wood floors weren't well finished—I made a note, mental or psychological, to tell our friend, the artist floor-man, about them. "Probably old cheap oak with polyurethane," I figured he'd guess. That was another thing to figure out years later—your work is more important than your floors. Maybe floors didn't need to be tung-oiled by hand-rubbing, over and over, time after time with a cloth. Or maybe the floors really are important.

A UPS man with a heavy box was standing outside when the doctor opened the door to let me go out. This doctor was a tiny German analyst and she asked in her kind, polite way: "Could you please put it inside the door?" He did so, while shooting an angry, disrespectful glance in her direction—this was before crystal meth, before people were murdered for asking a serviceman to do something—but she didn't even notice his face.

I believed I'd once come close to being killed by a Verizon man in Nantucket. They had missed three appointments and he was a few hours late when he finally appeared. When I questioned him about this situation, he flew into a wild rage, even growled out the sound of the rage, and made two fists in the air—almost screaming the way I have done, not the fists-in-the-air part but the scream—until I felt a pressure in my chest and thought of the book *Anger Kills*, kills the person who feels it, and thought that this kind of anger might bring on a heart attack or stroke, even though I was young and my vegan-powered blood pressure was low and my lipid panel just perfect.

At one time, when we first went to Nantucket, I used to go to the all-night supermarket searching for Ball Jelly Jars. This was during the era when I still had the desire and psychic energy to pick beach plums and make jelly—hours of picking and separating and cleaning—hanging a cheesecloth bag of berries from the faucet to get every last drop of juice to drip out into a pot, and then boiling the juice for hours with apple juice and no sugar.

It was a late-night visit to the supermarket then called Finast, the spelling of which my cousin's precocious little boy misunderstood and laughed at with great fun every time he heard the name. "Fine Ass, how could that be the name? Like, 'She's sure got a fine ass!'" No matter how it was explained to the five-year-old boy he couldn't get it, or pretended he couldn't. My cousin later proudly told me that the child had not invented the commentary himself, but had learned it from the master, his father.

In any case, on this night a most cheerful and helpful customer-service woman told me where the jars were—high up above the shelves, where they couldn't be reached. She said she knew the shelf so well because her husband made beach-plum jelly. Then she said he made every kind of jelly—wild grape, rosehip, even low-bush blueberry, a notoriously difficult find. He knew the blueberry patches all over the island. It turned out that he knew where every kind of berry and all the beach plums were hidden. One thing he didn't do was cut open each rosehip and remove the seeds with a demitasse spoon, as I did after reading an old recipe: "Scoop out all the seeds."

"He just boils them whole," she said. "He's a man."

When I asked how he knew where all the secret berries were, she said, "He works for the cable company. He sees them on the way to his jobs." I asked when he had time to pick them. She said, "Then. Whenever he sees them on the way to a job."

So now you know why you wait all day for the Cablevision man.

One year, recently, I was driving in the blazing heat past Finast—now a Stop & Shop, on Nantucket—on the way to the health-food store. A pedestrian crosswalk had been painted onto the road after the population and development boom of the eighties and nineties. A stocky woman with short red hair—she was wearing blue jeans and a plaid shirt in this heat, and no sunglasses—this woman dashed out into the crosswalk. I used my vegan-mesh-clog-shoed foot to hit the brakes, and she stood there and raised her fists while yelling and pointing at the small, four-foot, faded-outline area. This area does not mean that people should rush out into it without first looking to see whether cars are right there. As we both tried to recover, I saw that she was the formerly calm and pleasant customer-service clerk and wife of the jelly-making Cablevision man.

The tiny psychiatrist-analyst was looking at the box and still smiling as the UPS man left. That is when I realized, it's not me, it's them—the angry people are angry before they even meet you. I learned this from watching the doctor—she didn't have to say a word. The UPS man had acted as if she was just some old lady. I bet he'd never heard of the members of the Freud family or the history of all that. Of course not, why would he?

There was another thing I'd learned from this doctor, although she wasn't a cognitive therapist—this therapy probably hadn't been named yet—she'd said to me, "I wouldn't think you were twenty-seven—you look younger." And I said, "Oh, no, I look older. Some days I think I look forty." As if that was really old. A cruel joke, when I review it.

"Well, on certain days we all look older or younger," she said.

Now, that had never occurred to me.

Last year we were in a restaurant with a couple. They were both artists and the woman-artist and I were discussing the tight Lycra clothing available and worn in present times. She said she'd seen a mourner wearing a tight Lycra miniskirt at a memorial service. I myself had seen on the news that one of Caroline Kennedy's daughters had worn a very short, pleated miniskirt to the funeral service of Jacqueline Kennedy at Arlington National Cemetery.

At the time I was too grief-stricken to dwell on the subject. But at least it shocked me out of the reality of the moment, and distracted me from the memory of all those films and photographs of the many tragedies, and from all the photographs of Jacqueline Kennedy burned into my mind forever. Especially the one on the plane, when they got her to stand there, still in her blood-drenched, Chanel-pink suit while the other guy was sworn in. The look on her face—if only I could get it out of my mind.

We quickly remembered our Marimekko dresses.

We asked each other whether we still had them. We both said, "Of course."

I thought I saw some form of despair as I was looking at her. She'd been brought up by *Mayflower*-descended parents and wasn't about to burst into tears. I'd been crying since 1963 and much more so in the last decades.

We discussed what to do with the Marimekkos. She said she was thinking of cutting them up and using the fabric for some of her work.

"Oh, don't cut them up," I said. "They're already art."

"They are," she said, as if she'd never thought of that before. Or as if she had, but didn't care.

After trying to figure out what we could do, I said, "I think we should frame them. They're small enough."

She looked into my eyes and I looked into hers. They were a beautiful blue color but I could see beyond them into what she was thinking: What will become of our Marimekkos?

A psychiatrist once asked me, "Are you a mind reader?" Because I could tell what people were thinking.

"No, I'm a face reader," I said. "And a voice reader."

Most people are, in varying degrees. Why didn't he know that?

Somehow we got onto the subject of the conspiracy theories. The husband was a ferocious, left-wing artist. His paintings had such extreme social content that he was not as well known as he deserved to be. He and his wife lived near Canal Street. As a young man, he'd had stationery printed with a picture of his face and the caption: *Robert Cenedella, Unknown Artist*. He was on my list of the three funniest men in the world.

But as for the Three Conspiracies, they were:

1. The attack on the World Trade Center—did Bush and his gang of four, or five, or however many evil ones he had around him—did they know and even collude with the terrorists?

2. The moon landing—was it fake or real?

3. Last—but really first, just further back in time—the assassination of President Kennedy.

We asked each other which conspiracy theories we believed were real conspiracies. The artist believed they were all conspiracies. His wife and I agreed on the first and third. My husband believed only Kennedy.

Then, as a form of comic relief, the artist-husband reminded us about the letter he'd received in the sixties from Nixon's secretary, Rose Mary Woods. The artist had created a wooden dartboard with Nixon's face on it and sent this to Nixon at his campaign office. In return he received a form thank-you letter with a signature from Rose Mary Woods.

He opened his art-messenger bag and took out a copy of the letter. The original had been framed and hung in his studio. Here's the copy:

NIXON FOR PRESIDENT COMMITTEE,
P. O. BOX 1968, TIMES SQUARE STATION,
NEW YORK, NEW YORK 10036
PHONE (212) 661-6400

May 2, 1968

Mr. Robert Cenedella
Oggi Products, Inc.
61 E. 11th Street
New York, N. Y. 10003

Dear Mr. Cenedella:

  Your letter of April 17 has arrived in Mr.
Nixon's absence from New York. I know he will
appreciate your courtesy in requesting a better
picture of him for use in your dart board project.

  I am enclosing a picture which I believe
compares more favorably with the picture of Mayor
Lindsay which you forwarded.

  Mr. Nixon, I know, would want me to extend
his best wishes to you.

        Sincerely,

        Rose Mary Woods
        Executive Secretary
         to Mr. Nixon

We passed the letter around and we laughed. We laughed hard. We laughed more. But it was a different kind of laughter—laughter with sadness behind it. It was a new kind of laughing and not that much fun.

We started talking about the clothes of former and present White House secretaries and presidents' wives. We don't want to say one bad thing about Michelle Obama, but why did she wear a diamond necklace in broad daylight on Inauguration Day? Why this, why that—many questions about her advisers. Hillary's, too, but her case was not as urgent anymore.

Then we moved on—to my favorite attire, the kind of clothes worn in *The Best Years of Our Lives* by Wilma, the fiancée of Homer Parrish, who was played by Harold Russell, a real soldier in World War II whose wounds really had caused the amputation of both his hands and forearms, leaving him with metal hooks for replacements. Not an actor, but as most everyone knows, he played himself in this part.

In the movie, Wilma wore pleated skirts, plain shirts, and little sweaters from the 1945 era, from before I was born, but the kind I still have. Because her part was acted with such heart-wrenching purity, goodness, and inner beauty radiating from every expression, I immediately looked, I'm ashamed to say, on IMDb, to find out who the actress was and what had become of her.

This is what: in spite of William Wyler's objections, she'd married his brother, Robert Wyler, disappeared from movies, and had a long happy marriage until the cruel and early end to her life at age forty-six. Her name was listed in the credits as Cathy O'Donnell, but her real, and better, name was Ann Steely. It probably sounded too film-noir for her pure inner light and beauty.

Other than this actress, only Teresa Wright had qualities of such purity and goodness. I read on IMDb that *The Best Years of Our Lives* was a big-cry movie, even though it had been unrealistically cheered up in scenes here and there.

Eventually we got around to talking about clothes in other old movies from the 1940s. We got to Ingrid Bergman's clothes. Then we got to *Casablanca*. We agreed about those, too. We didn't like a few wardrobe items from *Notorious*.

I started thinking about *Casablanca* again. Then I started thinking about the big room in that apartment near Gramercy Park and the laughing that went on there. And I was remembering the moment when I saw that *The African Queen* was better than I'd first realized. I was thinking about being very young and not knowing much about anything. And I thought that was a better time, when I had no understanding of *Casablanca*.

ORAL HISTORY WITH HICCUPS

by LYDIA DAVIS

(fiction from Issue 6)

MY SISTER DIED last year leaving two dau   ghters. My husband and I have decided to ad   opt the girls. The older one is thirty-three and a b   uyer for a department store, and the yo   unger one, who just turned thirty, works in the st ate budget office. We have one ch   ild still living at home, and the house is not b   ig, so it will be a tight fit, but we are willing to do this for their s   ake. We will move our son, who is eleven, out of his ro   om and into the small room I have been using as a s   ewing room. I will set up my machine d   ownstairs in the living room. We will put a bunk bed for the girls in my s   on's old room. It is a fair-sized room with one cl   oset and one window, and the bathroom is just down the h   all. We will have to ask them not to bring all their th   ings. I assume they will be willing to m   ake that sacrifice in order to be part of this family. They will also have to w   atch what they say at the d   inner table. With our younger son present we don't want open c   onflict. What I'm worried about is a c   ouple of pol   itical issues. My older niece is a f   eminist, while my husband and I feel the tables have been turned against m   ales nowadays. Also, my younger niece is probably more pro-g   overnment than either my older niece or my h   usband and me. But she will be away a good deal, traveling for her j   ob. And we have d   eveloped some negotiating skills with our own ch   ildren, so we should be able to w   ork things out with the two of them. We will try to be firm but f   air, as we always were with our older b oy before he left h   ome. If we can't w   ork things out right away, they can always go to their r   oom and c   ool off until they're ready to come back out and be c   ivil. Ex   cuse me.

A MOWN LAWN

by LYDIA DAVIS

(fiction from Issue 4)

S HE HATED A *mown lawn*. Maybe that was because *mow* was the reverse of *wom*, the beginning of the name of what she was—a *woman*. A *mown lawn* had a sad sound to it, like a *long moan*. From her, a *mown lawn* made a *long moan*. *Lawn* had some of the letters of *man*, though the reverse of *man* would be *Nam*, a bad war. A *raw war*. *Lawn* also contained the letters of *law*. In fact, *lawn* was a contraction of *lawman*. Certainly a *lawman* could and did *mow* a *lawn*. *Law and order* could be seen as starting from *lawn order*, valued by so many Americans. *More lawn* could be made using a *lawn mower*. A *lawn mower* did make *more lawn*. *More lawn* was a contraction of *more lawmen*. Did *more lawn* in America make *more lawmen* in America? Did *more lawn* make *more Nam*? *More mown lawn* made *more long moan*, from her. Or a *lawn mourn*. So often, she said, Americans wanted *more mown lawn*. All of America might be one *long mown lawn*. A *lawn* not *mown* grows *long*, she said: better a *long lawn*. Better a *long lawn* and a *mole*. Let the *lawman* have the *mown lawn*, she said. Or the *moron*, the *lawn moron*.

WHICH WAS DEDICATED TO A MAMMOTH TREASURY
OF THRILLING TALES

by MICHAEL CHABON

F OR THE LAST year or so I have been boring my friends, and not a few strangers, with a semi-coherent, ill-reasoned, and doubtless mistaken rant on the subject of the American short story as it is currently written. The rant goes something like this (actually this is the first time I have so formulated it): Imagine that, sometime about 1950, it had been decided, collectively, informally, a little at a time, but with finality, to proscribe every kind of novel from the canon of the future but the nurse romance. Not merely from the critical canon, but from the store racks and library shelves as well. Nobody could be paid, published, lionized, or cherished among the gods of literature for writing any kind of fiction other than nurse romances. Now, because of my faith and pride in the diverse and rigorous brilliance of American writers of the last half-century, I do believe that from this bizarre decision, in this theoretical America, a dozen or more authentic masterpieces would have emerged. Thomas Pynchon's *Blitz Nurse*, for example, and Cynthia Ozick's *Ruth Puttermesser, R.N.* One imagines, however, that this particular genre—that any genre, even one far less circumscribed in its elements and possibilities than the nurse romance—would have paled somewhat by the year 2002. Over the last year in that oddly diminished world, somebody, somewhere, would be laying down Michael Chabon's *Dr. Kavalier and Nurse Clay* with a weary sigh and crying out, "Surely, oh, surely there must be more to the novel than this!"

Instead of "the novel" and "the nurse romance," try this little *Gedankenexperiment* with "jazz" and "the bossanova," or with "cinema" and "fish-out-of-water comedies." Now, go ahead and try it with "short fiction" and "the contemporary, quotidian, plotless, moment-of-truth revelatory story."

Suddenly you find yourself sitting right back in your very own universe.

Okay, I confess. I am that bored reader, in that circumscribed world, laying aside his book with a sigh; only the book is my own, and it is filled with my own short stories, plotless and sparkling with epiphanic dew. It was in large part a result of a crisis—a word much beloved of tedious ranteurs—in my own attitude toward my work in the short story form that sent me back into the stream of alternate time, back to the world as it was before we all made that fateful and perverse decision.

As late as about 1950, if I referred to "short fiction," I might have been talking about any one of the following kinds of stories: the ghost story; the horror story; the detective story; the story of suspense, terror, fantasy, or the macabre; the sea, adventure, spy, war, or historical story; the romance story. Stories, in other words, with plots. A glance at any dusty paperback anthology of classic tales proves the truth of this assertion, but more startling are the names of the authors of these ripping yarns: Poe, Balzac, Wharton, James, Conrad, Graves, Maugham, Faulkner, Twain, Cheever, Coppard. Heavyweights all, some considered among the giants of modernism, source of the moment-of-truth story that, like homo sapiens, appeared relatively late on the scene but has worked very quickly to wipe out all its rivals. Short fiction, in all its rich variety, was published not only by the pulps, which gave us Hammett, Chandler, and Lovecraft among a very few other writers now enshrined more or less safely in the canon, but also in the great slick magazines of the time: the *Saturday Evening Post*, *Collier's*, *Liberty*, and even the *New Yorker*, that proud bastion of the moment-of-truth story that has only recently, and not without controversy, made room in its august confines for the likes of the Last Master of the Plotted Short Story, Stephen King. Very often these stories contained enough plot and color to support an entire feature-length Hollywood adaptation. Adapted for film and radio, some of them, like "The Monkey's Paw," "Rain," "The Most Dangerous Game," and "An Occurrence at Owl Creek Bridge," have been imitated and parodied and have had their atoms scattered in the general stream of the national imagination and the public domain.

About six months ago, I was going on in this vein to the editor of this magazine, saying things like, "Actually, horror stories are all psychology," and "All short stories, in other words, are ghost stories, accounts of visitations and reckonings with the traces of the past." Emboldened by the fact that he had not completely succumbed to unconsciousness, I went on to say that it was my greatest dream in life (other than hearing Kansas's "Dust in the Wind" performed by a mariachi orchestra) someday to publish a magazine of my own, one that would revive the lost genres of short fiction, a tradition I saw as one of great writers writing great short stories. I would publish works both by "non-genre" writers who, like me, found themselves chafing under the strictures of the Ban, and by recognized masters of the genre novel who, fifty years ago, would have regularly worked and published in the short story form but who now have no wide or ready market for shorter work. And I would toss in a serialized novel, too, carrying the tradition all the way back to the days of *The Strand* and *Argosy*. I would—

"If I let you guest-edit an issue of *McSweeney's*," he said, "can we please stop talking about this?"

The *McSweeney's Mammoth Treasury of Thrilling Tales* is the result of this noble gesture. Whether the experiment has been a success, I leave to the reader to judge. I will say, however, that while they were working on their stories, a number of the writers reported to me, via giddy e-mails, that they had forgotten how much fun writing a short story could be. I think that we have forgotten how much fun reading a short story can be, and I hope that if nothing else, this treasury goes some small distance toward reminding us of that lost but fundamental truth.

THE BEES

by DAN CHAON

(*fiction from the* Mammoth Treasury of Thrilling Tales)

G ENE'S SON FRANKIE wakes up screaming. It has become frequent, two or three times a week, at random times: midnight—three a.m.—five in the morning. Here is a high, empty wail that severs Gene from his unconsciousness like sharp teeth. It is the worst sound that Gene can imagine, the sound of a young child dying violently—falling from a building, or caught in some machinery that is tearing an arm off, or being mauled by a predatory animal. No matter how many times he hears it he jolts up with such images playing in his mind, and he always runs, thumping into the child's bedroom to find Frankie sitting up in bed, his eyes closed, his mouth open in an oval like a Christmas caroler. Frankie appears to be in a kind of peaceful trance, and if someone took a picture of him he would look like he was waiting to receive a spoonful of ice cream, rather than emitting that horrific sound.

"Frankie!" Gene will shout, and claps his hands hard in the child's face. The clapping works well. At this, the scream always stops abruptly, and Frankie opens his eyes, blinking at Gene with vague awareness before settling back down into his pillow, nuzzling a little before growing still. He is sound asleep, he is always sound asleep, though even after months Gene can't help leaning down and pressing his ear to the child's chest, to make sure he's still breathing, his heart is still going. It always is.

There is no explanation that they can find. In the morning, the child doesn't remember anything, and on the few occasions that they have managed to wake him in the midst of one of his screaming attacks, he is merely sleepy and irritable. Once, Gene's wife Karen shook him and shook him, until finally he opened his eyes, groggily. "Honey?" she said. "Honey? Did you have a bad dream?" But Frankie only moaned a little. "No," he said, puzzled and unhappy at being awakened, but nothing more.

They can find no pattern to it. It can happen any day of the week, any time of the night. It doesn't seem to be associated with diet, or with his activities during the day, and it doesn't stem, as far as they can tell, from any sort of psychological unease. During the day, he seems perfectly normal and happy.

They have taken him several times to the pediatrician, but the doctor seems to have little of use to say. There is nothing wrong with the child physically, Dr. Banerjee says. She advises that such things are not uncommon for children of Frankie's age group—he is five—and that more often than not, the disturbance simply passes away.

"He hasn't experienced any kind of emotional trauma, has he?" the doctor says. "Nothing out of the ordinary at home?"

"No, no," they both murmur, together. They shake their heads, and Dr. Banerjee shrugs.

"Parents," she says. "It's probably nothing to worry about." She gives them a brief smile. "As difficult as it is, I'd say that you may just have to weather this out."

But the doctor has never heard those screams. In the mornings after the "nightmares," as Karen calls them, Gene feels unnerved, edgy. He works as a driver for the United Parcel Service, and as he moves through the day after a screaming attack, there is a barely perceptible hum at the edge of his hearing, an intent, deliberate static sliding along behind him as he wanders through streets and streets in his van. He stops along the side of the road and listens. The shadows of summer leaves tremble murmurously against the windshield, and cars are accelerating on a nearby road. In the treetops, a cicada makes its trembly, pressure-cooker hiss.

Something bad has been looking for him for a long time, he thinks, and now, at last, it is growing near.

When he comes home at night everything is normal. They live in an old house in the suburbs of Cleveland, and sometimes after dinner they work together in the small patch of garden out in back of the house—tomatoes, zucchini, string beans, cucumbers—while Frankie plays with Legos in the dirt. Or they take walks around the neighborhood, Frankie riding his bike in front of them, his training wheels recently removed. They gather on the couch and watch cartoons together, or play board games, or draw pictures with crayons. After Frankie is asleep, Karen will sit at the kitchen table and study—she is in nursing school—and Gene will sit outside on the porch, flipping through a newsmagazine or a novel, smoking the cigarettes that he has promised Karen he will give up when he turns thirty-five. He is thirty-four now, and Karen is twenty-seven, and he is aware, more and more frequently, that this is not the life that he deserves. He has been incredibly lucky, he thinks. Blessed, as Gene's favorite cashier at the supermarket always says. "Have a blessed day," she says, when Gene pays the money and she hands him his receipt, and he feels as if she has sprinkled him with her ordinary, gentle beatitude. It reminds him of long ago, when an old nurse had held his hand in the hospital and said that she was praying for him.

Sitting out in his lawn chair, drawing smoke out of his cigarette, he thinks about that nurse, even though he doesn't want to. He thinks of the way she'd leaned over him and brushed his hair as he stared at her, imprisoned in a full body cast, sweating his way through withdrawal and D.T.'s.

He had been a different person, back then. A drunk, a monster. At nineteen, he'd married the girl he'd gotten pregnant, and then had set about to slowly, steadily, ruining all their lives. When he'd abandoned them, his wife and son, back in Nebraska, he had been twenty-four, a danger to himself and others. He'd done them a favor by leaving, he thought, though he still felt guilty when he remembered it. Years later, when he was sober, he'd even tried to contact them. He wanted to own up to his behavior, to pay the back child support, to apologize. But they were nowhere to be found. Mandy was no longer living in the small Nebraska town where they'd met and married, and there was no forwarding address. Her parents were dead. No one seemed to know where she'd gone.

Karen didn't know the full story. She had been, to his relief, uncurious about his previous life, though she knew he'd had some drinking days, some bad times. She knew that he'd been married before, too, though she didn't know the extent of it, didn't know that he had another son, for example, didn't know that he had left them one night, without even packing a bag, just driving off in the car, a flask tucked between his legs, driving east as far as he could go. She didn't know about the car crash, the wreck he should have died in. She didn't know what a bad person he'd been.

She was a nice lady, Karen. Maybe a little sheltered. And truth to tell, he was ashamed—and even scared—to imagine how she would react to the truth about his past. He didn't know if she would have ever really trusted him if she'd known the full story, and the longer they knew one another the less inclined he was to reveal it. He'd escaped his old self, he thought, and when Karen got pregnant, shortly before they were married, he told himself that now he had a chance to do things over, to do it better. They had purchased the house together, he and Karen, and now Frankie will be in kindergarten in the fall. He has come full circle, has come exactly to the point when his former life with Mandy and his son, DJ, had completely fallen apart. He looks up as Karen comes to the back door and speaks to him through the screen. "I think it's time for bed, sweetheart," she says softly, and he shudders off these thoughts, these memories. He smiles.

He's been in a strange frame of mind lately. The months of regular awakenings have been getting to him, and he has a hard time getting back to sleep after an episode with Frankie. When Karen wakes him in the morning, he often feels muffled, sluggish—as if he's hung over. He doesn't hear the alarm clock. When he stumbles out of bed, he finds he has a hard time keeping his moodiness in check. He can feel his temper coiling up inside him.

He isn't that type of person anymore, and hasn't been for a long while. Still, he can't help but worry. They say that there is a second stretch of craving, which sets in after several years of smooth sailing; five or seven years will pass, and then it will come back without warning. He has been thinking of going to A.A. meetings again, though he hasn't in some time—not since he met Karen.

It's not as if he gets trembly every time he passes a liquor store, or even as if he has a problem when he goes out with buddies and spends the evening drinking soda and non-alcoholic beer. No. The trouble comes at night, when he's asleep.

He has begun to dream of his first son. DJ. Perhaps it is related to his worries about Frankie, but for several nights in a row the image of DJ—aged about five—has appeared to him. In the dream, Gene is drunk, and playing hide and seek with DJ in the yard behind the Cleveland house where he is now living. There is the thick weeping willow out there, and Gene watches the child appear from behind it and run across the grass, happily, unafraid, the way Frankie would. DJ turns to look over his shoulder and laughs, and Gene stumbles after him, at least a six-pack's worth of good mood, a goofy, drunken dad. It's so real that when he wakes, he still feels intoxicated. It takes him a few minutes to shake it.

One morning after a particularly vivid version of this dream, Frankie wakes and complains of a funny feeling—"right here," he says—and points to his forehead. It isn't a headache, he says. "It's like bees!" he says. "Buzzing bees!" He rubs his hand against his brow. "Inside my head." He considers for a moment. "You know how the bees bump against the window when they get in the house and want to get out?" This description pleases him, and he taps his forehead lightly with his fingers, humming, "zzzzzzz," to demonstrate.

"Does it hurt?" Karen says.

"No," Frankie says. "It tickles."

Karen gives Gene a concerned look. She makes Frankie lie down on the couch, and tells him to close his eyes for a while. After a few minutes, he rises up, smiling, and says that the feeling has gone.

"Honey, are you sure?" Karen says. She pushes her hair back and slides her palm across his forehead. "He's not hot," she says, and Frankie sits up impatiently, suddenly more interested in finding a matchbox car he dropped under a chair.

Karen gets out one of her nursing books, and Gene watches her face tighten with concern as she flips slowly through the pages. She is looking at Chapter Three: Neurological System, and Gene observes as she pauses here and there, skimming down a list of symptoms. "We should probably take him back to Dr. Banerjee again," she says. Gene nods, recalling what the doctor said about "emotional trauma."

"Are you scared of bees?" he asks Frankie. "Is that something that's bothering you?"

"No," Frankie says. "Not really."

When Frankie was three, a bee stung him above his left eyebrow. They had been out hiking together, and they hadn't yet learned that Frankie was "moderately allergic" to bee stings. Within minutes of the sting, Frankie's face had begun to distort, to puff up, his eye welling shut. He looked deformed. Gene didn't know if he'd ever been more frightened in his entire life, running down the trail with Frankie's head pressed against his heart, trying to get to the car and drive him to the doctor, terrified that the child was dying. Frankie himself was calm.

Gene clears his throat. He knows the feeling that Frankie is talking about—he has felt it himself, that odd, feathery vibration inside his head. And in fact he feels it again, now. He presses the pads of his fingertips against his brow. Emotional trauma, his mind murmurs, but he is thinking of DJ, not Frankie.

"What are you scared of?" Gene asks Frankie, after a moment. "Anything?"

"You know what the scariest thing is?" Frankie says, and widens his eyes, miming a frightened look. "There's a lady with no head, and she went walking through the woods, looking for it. 'Give... me... back... my... head....'"

"Where on earth did you hear a story like that!" Karen says.

"Daddy told me," Frankie says. "When we were camping."

Gene blushes, even before Karen gives him a sharp look. "Oh, great," she says. "Wonderful."

He doesn't meet her eyes. "We were just telling ghost stories," he says, softly. "I thought he would think the story was funny."

"My God, Gene," she says. "With him having nightmares like this? What were you thinking?"

*   *   *

It's a bad flashback, the kind of thing he's usually able to avoid. He thinks abruptly of Mandy, his former wife. He sees in Karen's face that look Mandy would give him when he screwed up. "What are you, some kind of idiot?" Mandy used to say. "Are you crazy?" Back then, Gene couldn't do anything right, it seemed, and when Mandy yelled at him it made his stomach clench with shame and inarticulate rage. I was trying, he would think, I was trying, damn it, and it was as if no matter what he did, it wouldn't turn out right. That feeling would sit heavily in his chest, and eventually, when things got worse, he hit her once. "Why do you want me to feel like shit," he had said through clenched teeth. "I'm not an asshole," he said, and when she rolled her eyes at him he slapped her hard enough to knock her out of her chair.

That was the time he'd taken DJ to the carnival. It was a Saturday, and he'd been drinking a little so Mandy didn't like it, but after all—he thought—DJ was his son, too, he had a right to spend some time with his own son, Mandy wasn't his boss even if she might think she was. She liked to make him hate himself.

What she was mad about was that he'd taken DJ on the Velocerator. It was a mistake, he'd realized afterward. But DJ himself had begged to go on. He was just recently four years old, and Gene had just turned twenty-three, which made him feel inexplicably old. He wanted to have a little fun.

Besides, nobody told him he couldn't take DJ on the thing. When he led DJ through the gate, the ticket-taker even smiled, as if to say, "Here is a young guy showing his kid a good time." Gene winked at DJ and grinned, taking a nip from a flask of Peppermint Schnapps. He felt like a good Dad. He wished his own father had taken him on rides at the carnival!

The door to the Velocerator opened like a hatch in a big silver flying saucer. Disco music was blaring from the entrance and became louder as they went inside. It was a circular room with soft padded walls, and one of the workers had Gene and DJ stand with their backs to the wall, strapping them in side by side. Gene felt warm and expansive from the Schnapps. He took DJ's hand, and he almost felt as if he were glowing with love. "Get ready, Kiddo," Gene whispered. "This is going to be wild."

The hatch door of the Velocerator sealed closed with a pressurized sigh. And then, slowly, the walls they were strapped to began to turn. Gene tightened on DJ's hand as they began to rotate, gathering speed. After a moment the wall pads they were strapped to slid up, and the force of velocity pushed them back, held to the surface of the spinning wall like iron to a magnet. Gene's cheeks and lips seemed to pull back, and the sensation of helplessness made him laugh.

At that moment, DJ began to scream. "No! No! Stop! Make it stop!" They were terrible shrieks, and Gene grabbed the child's hand tightly. "It's all right," he yelled jovially over the thump of the music. "It's okay! I'm right here!" But the child's wailing only got louder in response. The scream seemed to whip past Gene in a circle, tumbling around and around the circumference of the ride like a spirit, trailing echos as it flew. When the machine finally stopped, DJ was heaving with sobs, and the man at the control panel glared. Gene could feel the other passengers staring grimly and judgmentally at him.

Gene felt horrible. He had been so happy—thinking that they were finally having themselves a memorable father and son moment—and he could feel his heart plunging into darkness. DJ kept on weeping, even as they left the ride and walked along the midway, even as Gene tried to distract him with promises of cotton candy and stuffed animals. "I want to go home," DJ cried, and "I want my mom! I want my mom!" And it had wounded Gene to hear that. He gritted his teeth.

"Fine!" he hissed. "Let's go home to your Mommy, you little crybaby. I swear to God, I'm never taking you with me anywhere again." And he gave DJ a little shake. "Jesus, what's wrong with you? Lookit, people are laughing at you. See? They're saying, 'Look at that big boy, bawling like a girl.'"

This memory comes to him out of the blue. He had forgotten all about it, but now it comes to him over and over. Those screams were not unlike the sounds Frankie makes in the middle of the night, and they pass repeatedly through the membrane of his thoughts, without warning. The next day, he finds himself recalling it again, the memory of the scream impressing his mind with such force that he actually has to pull his UPS truck off to the side of the road and put his face in his hands: Awful! Awful! He must have seemed like a monster to the child.

Sitting there in his van, he wishes he could find a way to contact them— Mandy and DJ. He wishes that he could tell them how sorry he is, and send them money. He puts his fingertips against his forehead, as cars drive past on the street, as an old man parts the curtains and peers out of the house Gene is parked in front of, hopeful that Gene might have a package for him.

Where are they? Gene wonders. He tries to picture a town, a house, but there is only a blank. Surely, Mandy being Mandy, she would have hunted him down by now to demand child support. She would have relished treating him like a deadbeat dad, she would have hired some company who would garnish his wages.

Now, sitting at the roadside, it occurs to him suddenly that they are dead. He recalls the car wreck that he was in, just outside Des Moines, and if he had been killed they would have never known. He recalls waking up in the hospital, and the elderly nurse who had said, "You're very lucky, young man. You should be dead."

Maybe they are dead, he thinks. Mandy and DJ. The idea strikes him a glancing blow, because of course it would make sense. The reason they'd never contacted him. Of course.

He doesn't know what to do with such premonitions. They are ridiculous, they are self-pitying, they are paranoid, but especially now, with their concerns about Frankie, he is at the mercy of his anxieties. He comes home from work and Karen stares at him heavily.

"What's the matter?" she says, and he shrugs. "You look terrible," she says.

"It's nothing," he says, but she continues to look at him skeptically. She shakes her head.

"I took Frankie to the doctor again today," she says, after a moment, and Gene sits down at the table with her, where she is spread out with her textbooks and notepaper.

"I suppose you'll think I'm being a neurotic mom," she says. "I think I'm too immersed in disease, that's the problem."

Gene shakes his head. "No, no," he says. His throat feels dry. "You're right. Better safe than sorry."

"Mmm," she says, thoughtfully. "I think Dr. Banerjee is starting to hate me."

"Naw," Gene says. "No one could hate you." With effort, he smiles gently. A good husband, he kisses her palm, her wrist. "Try not to worry," he says, though his own nerves are fluttering. He can hear Frankie in the backyard, shouting orders to someone.

"Who's he talking to?" Gene says, and Karen doesn't look up.

"Oh," she says. "It's probably just Bubba." Bubba is Frankie's imaginary playmate.

Gene nods. He goes to the window and looks out. Frankie is pretending to shoot at something, his thumb and forefinger cocked into a gun. "Get him! Get him!" Frankie shouts, and Gene stares out as Frankie dodges behind a tree. Frankie looks nothing like DJ, but when he pokes his head from behind the hanging foliage of the willow, Gene feels a little shudder—a flicker—something. He clenches his jaw.

"This class is really driving me crazy," Karen says. "Every time I read about a worst-case scenario, I start to worry. It's strange. The more you know, the less sure you are of anything."

"What did the doctor say this time?" Gene says. He shifts uncomfortably, still staring out at Frankie, and it seems as if dark specks circle and bob at the corner of the yard. "He seems okay?"

Karen shrugs. "As far as they can tell." She looks down at her textbook, shaking her head. "He seems healthy." He puts his hand gently on the back of her neck and she lolls her head back and forth against his fingers. "I've never believed that anything really terrible could happen to me," she had once told him, early in their marriage, and it had scared him. "Don't say that," he'd whispered, and she laughed.

"You're superstitious," she said. "That's cute."

He can't sleep. The strange presentiment that Mandy and DJ are dead has lodged heavily in his mind, and he rubs his feet together underneath the covers, trying to find a comfortable posture. He can hear the soft ticks of the old electric typewriter as Karen finishes her paper for school, words rattling out in bursts that remind him of some sort of insect language. He closes his eyes, pretending to be asleep when Karen finally comes to bed, but his mind is ticking with small, scuttling images: his former wife and son, flashes of the photographs he didn't own, hadn't kept. They're dead, a firm voice in his mind says, very distinctly. They were in a fire. And they burned up. It is not quite his own voice that speaks to him, and abruptly he can picture the burning house. It's a trailer, somewhere on the outskirts of a small town, and the black smoke is pouring out of the open door. The plastic window frames have warped and begun to melt, and the smoke billows from the trailer into the sky in a way that reminds him of an old locomotive. He can't see inside, except for crackling bursts of deep orange flames, but he's aware that they're inside. For a second he can see DJ's face, flickering, peering steadily from the window of the burning trailer, his mouth open in an unnatural circle, as if he's singing.

He opens his eyes. Karen's breathing has steadied, she's sound asleep, and he carefully gets out of bed, padding restlessly through the house in his pajamas. They're not dead, he tries to tell himself, and stands in front of the refrigerator, pouring milk from the carton into his mouth. It's an old comfort, from back in the days when he was drying out, when the thick taste of milk would slightly calm his craving for a drink. But it doesn't help him now. The dream, the vision, has frightened him badly, and he sits on the couch with an afghan over his shoulders, staring at some science program on television. On the program, a lady scientist is examining a mummy. A child. The thing is bald—almost a skull but not quite. A membrane of ancient skin is pulled taut over the eyesockets. The lips are stretched back, and there are small, chipped, rodentlike teeth. Looking at the thing, he can't help but think of DJ again, and he looks over his shoulder, quickly, the way he used to.

The last year that he was together with Mandy, there used to be times when DJ would actually give him the creeps—spook him. DJ had been an unusually skinny child, with a head like a baby bird and long, bony feet, with toes that seemed strangely extended, as if they were meant for gripping. He can remember the way the child would slip barefoot through rooms, slinking, sneaking, watching, Gene had thought, always watching him.

It is a memory that he has almost, for years, succeeded in forgetting, a memory he hates and mistrusts. He was drinking heavily at the time, and he knows now that alcohol had grotesquely distorted his perceptions. But now that it has been dislodged, that old feeling moves through him like a breath of smoke. Back then, it had seemed to him that Mandy had turned DJ against him, that DJ had in some strange way almost physically transformed into something that wasn't Gene's real son. Gene can remember how, sometimes, he would be sitting on the couch, watching TV, and he'd get a funny feeling. He'd turn his head and DJ would be at the edge of the room, with his bony spine hunched and his long neck craned, staring with those strangely oversized eyes. Other times, Gene and Mandy would be arguing and DJ would suddenly slide into the room, creeping up to Mandy and resting his head on her chest, right in the middle of some important talk. "I'm thirsty," he would say, in imitation baby-talk. Though he was five years old, he would play-act this little toddler voice. "Mama," he would say. "I is firsty." And DJ's eyes would rest on Gene for a moment, cold and full of calculating hatred.

Of course, Gene knows now that this was not the reality of it. He knows: He was a drunk, and DJ was just a sad, scared little kid, trying to deal with a rotten situation. Later, when he was in detox, these memories of his son made him actually shudder with shame, and it was not something he could bring himself to talk about even when he was deep into his twelve steps. How could he say how repulsed he'd been by the child, how actually frightened he was. Jesus Christ, DJ was a poor wretched five-year-old kid! But in Gene's memory there was something malevolent about him, resting his head pettishly on his mother's chest, talking in that sing-song, lisping voice, staring hard and unblinking at Gene with a little smile. Gene remembers catching DJ by the back of the neck. "If you're going to talk, talk normal," Gene had whispered through his teeth, and tightened his fingers on the child's neck. "You're not a baby. You're not fooling anybody." And DJ had actually bared his teeth, making a thin, hissing whine.

He wakes and he can't breathe. There is a swimming, suffocating sensation of being stared at, being watched by something that hates him, and he gasps, choking for air. A lady is bending over him, and for a moment he expects her to say, "You're very lucky, young man. You should be dead."

But it's Karen. "What are you doing?" she says. It's morning, and he struggles to orient himself—he's on the living room floor, and the television is still going.

"Jesus," he says, and coughs. "Oh, Jesus." He is sweating, his face feels hot, but he tries to calm himself in the face of Karen's horrified stare. "A bad dream," he says, trying to control his panting breaths. "Jesus," he says, and shakes his head, trying to smile reassuringly for her. "I got up last night and I couldn't sleep. I must have passed out while I was watching TV."

But Karen just gazes at him, her expression frightened and uncertain, as if something about him is transforming. "Gene," she says. "Are you all right?"

"Sure," he says, hoarsely, and a shudder passes over him involuntarily. "Of course." And then he realizes that he is naked. He sits up, covering his crotch self-consciously with his hands, and glances around. He doesn't see his underwear or his pajama bottoms anywhere nearby. He doesn't even see the afghan, which he had draped over himself on the couch while he was watching the mummies on TV. He starts to stand up, awkwardly, and he notices that Frankie is standing there in the archway between the kitchen and the living room, watching him, his arms at his sides like a cowboy who is ready to draw his holstered guns.

"Mom?" Frankie says. "I'm thirsty."

He drives through his deliveries in a daze. The bees, he thinks. He remembers what Frankie had said a few mornings before, about bees inside his head, buzzing and bumping against the inside of his forehead like a windowpane they were tapping against. That's the feeling he has now. All the things that he doesn't quite remember are circling and alighting, vibrating their cellophane wings insistently. He sees himself striking Mandy across the face with the flat of his hand, knocking her off her chair; he sees his grip tightening around the back of DJ's thin, five-year-old neck, shaking him as he grimaced and wept; and he is aware that there are other things, perhaps even worse, if he thought about them hard enough. All the things that he'd prayed that Karen would never know about him.

He was very drunk on the day that he left them, so drunk that he can barely remember. It was hard to believe that he'd made it all the way to Des Moines on the interstate before he went off the road, tumbling end over end, into darkness. He was laughing, he thought, as the car crumpled around him, and he has to pull his van over to the side of the road, out of fear, as the tickling in his head intensifies. There is an image of Mandy, sitting on the couch as he stormed out, with DJ cradled in her arms, one of DJ's eyes swollen shut and puffy. There is an image of him in the kitchen, throwing glasses and beer bottles onto the floor, listening to them shatter.

And whether they are dead or not, he knows that they don't wish him well. They would not want him to be happy—in love with his wife and child. His normal, undeserved life.

When he gets home that night, he feels exhausted. He doesn't want to think anymore, and for a moment, it seems that he will be allowed a small reprieve. Frankie is in the yard, playing contentedly. Karen is in the kitchen, making hamburgers and corn on the cob, and everything seems okay. But when he sits down to take off his boots, she gives him an angry look.

"Don't do that in the kitchen," she says, icily. "Please. I've asked you before."

He looks down at his feet: one shoe unlaced, half-off. "Oh," he says. "Sorry."

But when he retreats to the living room, to his recliner, she follows him. She leans against the door frame, her arms folded, watching as he releases his tired feet from the boots and rubs his hand over the bottom of his socks. She frowns heavily.

"What?" he says, and tries on an uncertain smile.

She sighs. "We need to talk about last night," she says. "I need to know what's going on."

"Nothing," he says, but the stern way she examines him activates his anxieties all over again. "I couldn't sleep, so I went out to the living room to watch TV. That's all."

She stares at him. "Gene," she says after a moment. "People don't usually wake up naked on their living room floor, and not know how they got there. That's just weird, don't you think?"

Oh, please, he thinks. He lifts his hands, shrugging—a posture of innocence and exasperation, though his insides are trembling. "I know," he says. "It was weird to me, too. I was having nightmares. I really don't know what happened."

She gazes at him for a long time, her eyes heavy. "I see," she says, and he can feel the emanation of her disappointment like waves of heat. "Gene," she says. "All I'm asking is for you to be honest with me. If you're having problems, if you're drinking again, or thinking about it. I want to help. We can work it out. But you have to be honest with me."

"I'm not drinking," Gene says, firmly. He holds her eyes, earnestly. "I'm not thinking about it. I told you when we met, I'm through with it. Really." But he is aware again of an observant, unfriendly presence, hidden, moving along the edge of the room. "I don't understand," he says. "What is it? Why would you think I'd lie to you?"

She shifts, still trying to read something in his face, still, he can tell, doubting him. "Listen," she says, at last, and he can tell she is trying not to cry. "Some guy called you today. A drunk guy. And he said to tell you that he had a good time hanging out with you last night, and that he was looking forward to seeing you again soon." She frowns hard, staring at him as if this last bit of damning information will show him for the liar he is. A tear slips out of the corner of her eye and along the bridge of her nose. Gene feels his chest tighten.

"That's crazy," he says. He tries to sound outraged, but he is in fact suddenly very frightened. "Who was it?"

She shakes her head, sorrowfully. "I don't know," she says. "Something with a 'B.' He was slurring so badly I could hardly understand him. B.B. or B.J. or..."

Gene can feel the small hairs on his back prickling. "Was it DJ?" he says, softly.

And Karen shrugs, lifting a now teary face to him. "I don't know!" she says, hoarsely. "I don't know. Maybe." And Gene puts his palms across his face. He is aware of that strange, buzzing, tickling feeling behind his forehead.

"Who is DJ?" Karen says. "Gene, you have to tell me what's going on."

But he can't. He can't tell her, even now. Especially now, he thinks, when to admit that he'd been lying to her ever since they met would confirm all the fears and suspicions she'd been nursing for—what?—days? weeks?

"He's someone I used to know a long time ago," Gene tells her. "Not a good person. He's the kind of guy who might... call up, and get a kick out of upsetting you."

They sit at the kitchen table, silently watching as Frankie eats his hamburger and corn on the cob. Gene can't quite get his mind around it. DJ, he thinks, as he presses his finger against his hamburger bun, but doesn't pick it up. DJ. He would be fifteen by now. Could he, perhaps, have found them? Maybe stalking them? Watching the house? Gene tries to fathom how DJ might have been causing Frankie's screaming episodes. How he might have caused what happened last night—snuck up on Gene while he was sitting there watching TV and drugged him or something. It seems farfetched.

"Maybe it was just some random drunk," he says at last, to Karen. "Accidentally calling the house. He didn't ask for me by name, did he?"

"I don't remember," Karen says, softly. "Gene..."

And he can't stand the doubtfulness, the lack of trust in her expression. He strikes his fist hard against the table, and his plate clatters in a circling echo. "I did not go out with anybody last night!" he says. "I did not get drunk! You can either believe me, or you can..."

They are both staring at him. Frankie's eyes are wide, and his puts down the corn cob he was about to bite into, as if he doesn't like it anymore. Karen's mouth is pinched.

"Or I can what?" she says.

"Nothing," Gene breathes.

There isn't a fight, but a chill spreads through the house, a silence. She knows that he isn't telling her truth. She knows that there's more to it. But what can he say? He stands at the sink, gently washing the dishes as Karen bathes Frankie and puts him to bed. He waits, listening to the small sounds of the house at night. Outside, in the yard, there is the swingset, and the willow tree—silver-gray and stark in the security light that hangs above the garage. He waits for a while longer, watching, half-expecting to see DJ emerge from behind the tree as he'd done in Gene's dream, creeping along, his bony hunched back, the skin pulled tight against the skull of his oversized head. There is that smothering, airless feeling of being watched, and Gene's hands are trembling as he rinses a plate under the tap.

When he goes upstairs at last, Karen is already in her nightgown, in bed, reading a book.

"Karen," he says, and she flips a page, deliberately.

"I don't want to talk to you until you're ready to tell me the truth," she says. She doesn't look at him. "You can sleep on the couch, if you don't mind."

"Just tell me," Gene says. "Did he leave a number? To call him back?"

"No," Karen says. She doesn't look at him. "He just said he'd see you soon."

He thinks that he will stay up all night. He doesn't even wash up, or brush his teeth, or get into his bedtime clothes. He just sits there on the couch, in his uniform and stocking feet, watching television with the sound turned low, listening. Midnight. 1 a.m.

He goes upstairs to check on Frankie, but everything is okay. Frankie is asleep with his mouth open, the covers thrown off. Gene stands in the doorway, alert for movement, but everything seems to be in place. Frankie's turtle sits motionless on its rock, the books are lined up in neat rows, the toys put away. Frankie's face tightens and untightens as he dreams.

2 a.m. Back on the couch, Gene startles, half-asleep as an ambulance passes in the distance, and then there is only the sound of crickets and cicadas. Awake for a moment, he blinks heavily at a rerun of *Bewitched*, and flips through channels. Here is some jewelry for sale. Here is someone performing an autopsy.

In the dream, DJ is older. He looks to be nineteen or twenty, and he walks into a bar where Gene is hunched on a stool, sipping a glass of beer. Gene recognizes him right away—his posture, those thin shoulders, those large eyes. But now, DJ's arms are long and muscular, tattooed. There is a hooded, unpleasant look on his face as he ambles up to the bar, pressing in next to Gene. DJ orders a shot of Jim Beam—Gene's old favorite.

"I've been thinking about you a lot, ever since I died," DJ murmurs. He doesn't look at Gene as he says this, but Gene knows who he is talking to, and his hands are shaky as he takes a sip of beer.

"I've been looking for you for a long time," DJ says, softly, and the air is hot and thick. Gene puts a trembly cigarette to his mouth and breathes on it, choking on the taste. He wants to say, I'm sorry. Forgive me. But he can't breathe. DJ shows his small, crooked teeth, staring at Gene as he gulps for air.

"I know how to hurt you," DJ whispers.

*　　*　　*

Gene opens his eyes, and the room is full of smoke. He sits up, disoriented: for a second he is still in the bar with DJ before he realizes that he's in his own house.

There is a fire somewhere: he can hear it. People say that fire "crackles," but in fact it seems like the amplified sound of tiny creatures eating, little wet mandibles, thousands and thousands of them, and then a heavy, whispered whoof, as the fire finds another pocket of oxygen.

He can hear this, even as he chokes blindly in the smoky air. The living room has a filmy haze over it, as if it is atomizing, fading away, and when he tries to stand up it disappears completely. There is a thick membrane of smoke above him, and he drops again to his hands and knees, gagging and coughing, a thin line of vomit trickling onto the rug in front of the still chattering television.

He has the presence of mind to keep low, crawling on his knees and elbows underneath the thick, billowing fumes. "Karen!" he calls. "Frankie!" but his voice is swallowed into the white noise of diligently licking flame. "Ach," he chokes, meaning to utter their names.

When he reaches the edge of the stairs he sees only flames and darkness above him. He puts his hands and knees on the bottom steps, but the heat pushes him back. He feels one of Frankie's action figures underneath his palm, the melting plastic adhering to his skin, and he shakes it away as another bright burst of flame reaches out of Frankie's bedroom for a moment. At the top of the stairs, through the curling fog he can see the figure of a child watching him grimly, hunched there, its face lit and flickering. Gene cries out, lunging into the heat, crawling his way up the stairs, to where the bedrooms are. He tries to call to them again, but instead, he vomits.

There is another burst that covers the image that he thinks is a child. He can feel his hair and eyebrows shrinking and sizzling against his skin as the upstairs breathes out a concussion of sparks. He is aware that there are hot, floating bits of substance in the air, glowing orange and then winking out, turning to ash. The air thick with angry buzzing, and that is all he can hear as he slips, turning end over end down the stairs, the humming and his own voice, a long vowel wheeling and echoing as the house spins into a blur.

* * *

And then he is lying on the grass. Red lights tick across his opened eyes in a steady, circling rhythm, and a woman, a paramedic, lifts her lips up from his. He draws in a long, desperate breath.

"Shhhhh," she says, softly, and passes her hand along his eyes. "Don't look," she says.

But he does. He sees, off to the side, the long black plastic sleeping bag, with a strand of Karen's blond hair hanging out from the top. He sees the blackened, shriveled body of a child, curled into a fetal position. They place the corpse into the spread, zippered plastic opening of the body bag, and he can see the mouth, frozen, calcified, into an oval. A scream.

A NOTE ON *RETREAT*

S HORT STORIES ALWAYS look really easy to write before you actually start writing them, and when an editor at *McSweeney's* wrote me asking if I had a piece of short fiction for an upcoming issue, I told him I'd have it for him in a week. Three weeks later, I told him it wouldn't be possible to write this story and that I was sorry and would he please leave me alone.

One thing that was screwing me up was all the long-form nonfiction work I'd been doing. Nonfiction—even "literary" nonfiction—calls for tools and processes that are pretty much useless when it comes to making short stories. In metalworking, they have this term, "cold connection," which is when you take two pieces of metal and a rivet. A few smart bashes, and you've got a bracelet with lots of nice bangles on it, and you've spared yourself the hot, tedious business of soldering and sweating joints. In a pinch, nonfiction can squeak by on cold connections. You go out and witness things, and if you've got at least a few compelling scenes, you can fuse them with the cold rivets of journalistic writing—the transition, the fraudulent hardware of arc and angle. Nine times out of ten the reader won't feel gypped, never mind that there's no real heart thumping in the thorax of your tin man.

Fiction can't be approached in such calculated fashion; at least I can't approach it that way and feel good about myself in the morning. But I'd been given a firm deadline for the story, so I started cold-connecting a bunch of spare parts I had lying around. I had an idea for two brothers who didn't get along, and an old man who would serve as a kind of ball joint between them, and also this story about a moose hunt for which I was trying to find a home.

(The moose story I'd heard from a guy named Clay Whitebear whom I met ten years ago during a job in a salmon cannery in Alaska. Clay was a long-term Alaska man, and one autumn he had a visit from his brother-in-law, a Californian, who was determined to go out and kill a moose. Clay knew what an ordeal killing a moose was. A good-size moose can weigh well above 1,000 pounds, and Alaska law requires you to take 80 percent of the meat, or they can lock you up for squandering the corpse. The day of the hunt was rainy and miserable, but the eager brother-in-law kept Clay out there all day. Finally, after eight fruitless hours, Clay convinced the other man that they should pack the project in. They'd just climbed into the boat when a moose walked out of the woods and the delighted brother-in-law shot it dead. So they dismantled it, an exhausting, gory affair, and just as they'd gotten the last haunch stacked, a second moose walked out of the woods. Before Clay could stop him, the brother-in-law shot that one, too.

In the first draft of "Retreat," I borrowed the whole two-moose anecdote, and then deleted it. It astounds me, by the way, how much of the fiction writer's job involves finding ways for fewer things to happen.)

At any rate, after a few more weeks, I'd finally lashed together something that resembled a story. I had some conflict and some decent descriptions. The sentences were tidy enough. The old-man character, called "Bob" in that first draft, said a few desperately wacky things in hopes of getting the reader to chuckle. Yet when I sat down to give it another look before signing off on my collection of short stories, *Everything Ravaged, Everything Burned*, I read the first few pages and was horrified. After all the work I'd done on it, the story looked cheap and inadequate and shameful. Reading it, I suffered the breathless revulsion that some of us feel when looking in the mirror, thinking, "Oh my God. I can't believe that's my actual face."

An emotional niggardliness seemed to pervade the story. A brief synopsis might have read, "A smug narrator perceives his brother to be obnoxious, and his perceptions are ratified when his brother ultimately ingests a ration of possibly lethal moose flesh." The story aspired to stingy ends, a kind of glib, just-deserts satisfaction at best. The stuff I'd liked most, the gag lines perpetrated by the Bob character, looked on second glance like a bunch of shucking and jiving: ha-cha-cha-cha! You could hear where the rimshots were supposed to go.

One question a smart teacher of mine liked to ask in fiction workshops is, "Was this written in good faith?" I took this to mean: did the writer make himself as vulnerable to the story's possibilities as he wishes his readers to be? Or, more simply put: does the writer believe in what he wrote? That first draft, with the bitter younger brother narrating, felt like it flunked the good-faith test.

So I took another stab at it, tasking myself with a mission of greater narrative generosity, a more complicated balance of sympathies, fewer cheap tricks. In order to liberate Matthew, the older brother, from his simple role as a bungling blowhard, it seemed necessary to let him tell the tale. It struck me as a sadder and more interesting story if we could get to know Matthew as a plenary human being, an aware, discerning narrator who nonetheless can't stop alienating people despite what he believes are his best intentions. I worked on that idea for about two months, hammering, hammering at the human-sympathy forge. When I proudly started passing the draft around, the editor of my collection, and a few others I showed it to, sort of shrugged and went Eh. The new draft wasn't as funny. Matthew had become too sympathetic, too verbally capable, too written, plus I'd crammed on a sentimental new ending that didn't work. I felt sick at heart. So much for magnanimity.

But then on a second read, my editor decided that there might be some promise in the new draft after all. She had the bright idea of borrowing a bit or two from the first draft, purging some of the verbal algae blooms I'd clotted the pages with, and trimming the mawkish closer. After another few weeks' worth of work, we had a story we both felt okay about.

It may be the case that the first draft, the younger-brother one, is the more successful story. Nevertheless, I prefer the second. It feels to me as though it grapples harder with our universal tendency to vex ourselves. Or, at the very least, the last time I read it, I didn't get that sinking, face-in-the-mirror feeling, which is enough for me for now.

My only real regret about the story is that I wasn't able to slip in another fine piece of moose lore I picked up in Alaska. One day, as I was getting ready to push off on a kayak trip across a big cold lake on the Kenai Peninsula, a park ranger came over and told me to beware of swimming moose. It was rut season, when the bulls go crazy. They'll put a hoof through your boat in a second, the ranger told me, just for the fun of it. But the really interesting thing he said was that when he's in rut, a bull moose standing on one side of the lake might suddenly get a very strong hunch that a cow moose is waiting for him on the far side of the lake, which might be as much as two or three miles away (these are big lakes). Off he'll swim. But when he's just about gotten to the distant shore, he'll take a contrary notion that, actually, all the ladies are probably on the shore he just swam from. So he does an about-face and paddles back the way he came. Just as the moose is finally reaching terra firma, he doubts himself again, and again with the U-turn. A lot of moose, the ranger said, kill themselves this way. As I was revising and revising this story and others, I thought often about those indecisive, waterlogged creatures. As much as I believe in the radical rewrite, I hope that someday I'll get better at picking a single course and sticking with it. The pond is always bigger than it looks. —WELLS TOWER

RETREAT

by WELLS TOWER

(fiction from Issue 23)

I HAD NOT SPOKEN to my brother Matthew in thirteen months when he telephoned me last autumn.

"Hey there, buddy. Ask you a question. What's your thinking on mountains?"

"I have no objection to them," I told him.

"Good, good," he said. "Did you hear I bought one? I'm on top of it right now."

"Which one? Is it Popocatepetl?"

"Hey, go piss up a rope." The mountain didn't have a name, as far as he knew. He said it was in the north of Maine, which is where he'd been living since July. Wind was blowing into the phone.

"You didn't move again."

"Oh, yes I did," said Matthew. You could hear he was talking through a grin. "I'm gone, little man. Must have been certifiable to stay in Myrtle Beach so long."

Maine sounded nice, I told him. Could he see the ocean from where he was?

"Hell no, I'm not on the *coast*," he roared. "I'm through with coasts. Didn't move twelve hundred miles just to come up here and bark my shins on a bunch of Winnebago people in lobster bibs."

Then his tone softened and he told me that the winter was coming, and that he'd like to see my face before the snows sealed him off from the world.

I said I probably couldn't spare the time, and Matthew began to emit an oral brochure of the property's virtues, its bubbling brooks, forests, and glassy ponds, and the "bold, above-canopy views" from his cabin on the summit, which he described to the last nailhead and bead of caulk. "And I got a guy out here with me who's your type of man. My buddy Bob, my neighbor. I've got him working on the crib. Outstanding guy. Mathematical opposite of those douchebags down in Myrtle. You guys could talk some good shit together. Let me put him on."

I tried to protest, but Matthew had taken his ear from the phone. The sound of a banging hammer rose in the receiver. Then the banging stopped, and a thin, chalky voice came on the line. "Yup, Bob Brown here. Who'm I talking to?"

"This is Alan—"

"Not Alan Dupree?"

"No. I'm Matthew's brother. I'm Alan Lattimore."

"Well, I can believe that over Alan Dupree. Good to know you."

The hammering started up again, and Matthew came back on the line.

"That's the wild man for you," Matthew said with a kind of chuckling pride. "Just him and me—pretty much a two-dude nation is what we've got out here. You'd go bananas for it. When can we put you on a plane?"

It was hard not to share Matthew's pleasure at his departure from Myrtle Beach. The world he'd inhabited there was every bit as worth fleeing as a Vietnamese punji trap—a shadowless realm of salt-scalded putting greens, of russet real-estate queens with sprawling cleavages pebbled up like brain-fruit hide, of real-estate men with white-fleeced calves, soft bellies, and hard, lightless eyes, men who called you "buddy-ro" as they talked up the investment value of condominiums already tilting into the Atlantic.

I would have applauded Matthew more heartily for abandoning his life down there had he not already insisted, over the years, that I applaud him for dropping out of law school at Emory, for quitting a brokerage in Memphis, for pulling out of a venture-capital firm he'd launched in Fort Lauderdale, for divorcing his first wife (a quiet, freckled woman I'd liked very much) on the grounds, as he put it to me, that she was "hard of hearing and her pussy stank," and for engaging himself to Kimberly Oosten, Esq., the daughter of an Oldsmobile dealer in Myrtle Beach.

You could trace Matthew's rotations to his early days at school. He'd been an awkward boy, eager to be liked, with eyes as large and guileless as a mule's. He spent his school years chasing acceptance to one social set or another— gerbil enthusiasts, comic-book collectors, the junior birders, the golf club, the hot-rod men, et cetera, without much success. He had a way of coming off as both fawning and belligerent. He was routinely ridiculed and occasionally beaten up by the boys whose friendship he most ardently pursued. His discarded careers notwithstanding, Matthew, at age forty, had accumulated a good amount of money, and I imagine could have bought himself permanent membership in whatever society he liked. But it seemed to me that years ago, this had stopped being the point. Somehow, he'd gotten to a place where he wasn't happy if he didn't pause every four or five years and abort the life he'd had before. After a few years of living comfortably in a place, he would grow restless and hostile, as though he suspected he was being deliberately swindled out of the better life owed to him someplace else.

I live in Arcata, California, where I earn a slim livelihood as a music therapist, an occupation of so little consequence in my brother's eyes that he can never seem to remember exactly what it is that I do for a living. Though I did not have spare time or money to squander on a trip to Maine, as Matthew's pitch wore on I found it heartening that he had once again called me, the sole emissary from his past, to preside over his latest metamorphosis, and in the end I booked a ticket.

I left the first Thursday in November, along a cheap and brutal route. I flew out of Arcata midday to the San Francisco airport, where I spent four listless hours in the company of a man with a wristwatch the size of a plaster ceiling medallion. He tugged ceaselessly at the thighs of his trousers, currying the spare fabric into a blousy pavilion at his crotch. "Edward is really riding roughshod when it comes to our intentionality" is a sentence I heard him utter in two different conversations on his cellular phone. I caught the overnight flight from San Francisco to Boston, hunkered in the lee of an enormous woman whose bodily upholstery entirely swallowed our mutual armrest. I had no place to rest my head. She saw me eyeing the cushioned cavern formed by her shoulder and wattle, and she said, "Go on, stick it right in there." I did so. The woman gave off a clean, comforting aroma of the sea, and I slept very well.

From Boston, I caught a dawn flight to Bangor. In Bangor, I was ushered onto a tiny six-seater that sat on the tarmac for two hours while a mechanic who did not look fifteen peered learnedly at the wing. At last, the engines cranked, and the plane lifted in quavering flight for northern Aroostook County.

Unimaginable vastnesses of spruce and pine forests passed beneath the plane, unbroken by town or village. We landed at an airport that was little more than a gravel landing strip with a Quonset hut off to one side. A solid chill was on the air. The four people I'd flown in with grabbed their luggage from where an attendant had strewn it on the blue gravel, and jogged for the parking lot. The small plane absorbed a fresh load of travelers and vanished over the spruce spires on shuddering wings.

I walked to the shoulder of the country boulevard that ran past the airfield and waited for my brother. Ten minutes went by, then fifteen, then twenty. As the time passed, I was gored repeatedly by a species of terrible, cold-weather mosquito I had never come across before. In the time it took to beat one of their number to death, a half dozen more would perch on my arm, their engorged, translucent bellies glowing like pomegranate seeds in the cool white sun.

I'd been smacking mosquitoes for three-quarters of an hour when a red Nissan pickup truck with darkly tinted windowglass rounded the curve. It pulled to a stop in the far lane, the calved asphalt on the shoulder crunching under its tires. Matthew stepped out and crossed the road. His appearance startled me. In the year since I had last seen him, he had put on a lot of spare flesh—a set of jowls that seemed to start at his temple and a belly that could have held late-term twins. His extra weight, and the milky pallor of it, conveyed an impression of regal corpsehood, like the sculpture on the lid of an emperor's sarcophagus. I felt a mild rush of worry.

"You're late," said Matthew.

"I've been standing here for forty-five minutes."

He snorted, as though forty-five were an insufficient number of minutes for me to have been kept waiting.

"We showed up here two hours ago. Now the whole day's shot to shit."

"Look, Matthew—"

He broke in.

"My point, Alan, is that I don't just sit around out here with my hand up my ass. I had plenty on my plate today, but instead we had to come in to town and wait around, and now Bob's drunk and I'm half in the bag, and now we won't get anything done at all."

"That's good," I said. "Because I asked them specifically to hold the plane just to piss you off. I'm glad it all worked out."

"You could have called me with the status, is what I'm saying." He took his cell phone from his pocket. "Telephone, you know? They're great. You use them to tell things to people who aren't where you're at."

I wanted very much to smash my brother's nose. I picked up my bag instead. "Screw it, you asshole," I said. "I'll leave. I'll take the next plane out."

I'd walked three steps when Matthew grabbed me by the back of the neck and spun me around. His anger had evaporated, and he was giggling at me now. Nothing delights my brother like the sight of me in a rage. He kissed my eye with a rasping pressure of stubbled lip. "Who's an angry little man?" he cooed at me. "Who's an angry little man with fire in his belly?"

"I am, and you're a big fat cock," I said. "I didn't ride a plane all night to take this crap from you."

"He's all upset," said Matthew. "He's a frustrated little man."

He grabbed my duffel from me and, still laughing, marched toward the idling truck.

Through the pickup's open door, I saw the form of a man in the passenger's seat. He was slight and so deeply tanned that he was hard to make out in the dim interior.

"Alan, Bob—Bob, Alan, my baby brother," he said, though I stand six foot three, beneath a head of thinning hair, with violet half-moons of adult fatigue under my eyes.

Bob nodded once. "Good to know you, baby brother," he said. His voice creaked like an over-rosined bow. "And as the French have it, *bienvenue*."

"Bob's a very slick ticket," said Matthew, tossing my bag into the bed with a thud. "He's a man of the world."

"Slick as a brick, and a genius in the bargain," said Bob. "I'm often told I should be president."

Matthew levered the driver's chair forward so that I could crawl into the cab's tiny rear compartment. Three large-bore rifles lay across the gun rack: the old Weatherby .300 magnum Matthew had claimed without asking from our father's estate, a sleek, black fiberglass rifle with a Nikon sight, and a cheap-looking 30.06. I had to crane my neck forward to keep my hair from touching the oiled barrels. The truck rolled onto the road.

Bob leaned around the seat to talk to me. He was older, in his sixties, I supposed. His rucked brown cheeks were roughened with whiskers the color of old ivory, and sparse white curls poked out from under his baseball cap. "I *should* be president," Bob continued. "Don't you think? Tell me, baby brother, would you or would you not give this face your vote?" He showed me a set of teeth that looked artificially improved.

"I'd have to know where you stand on the issues," I said.

Matthew cut me a look in the rearview mirror. "I'd appreciate it if you wouldn't get him started, really."

"Alan has every right to be apprised as to where I stand," said Bob. He tapped a philosophical finger against his pursed lips and pretended to ponder his platform. After a moment, he said, "Well, here's something: I believe that anybody who wants to ought to be able to drink a cocktail with the commander-in-chief and ask the man what's what. Once a week, we hold a lottery and an ordinary citizen gets to sit down for drinks with the president. The citizen brings the booze. The constitution doesn't provide for people going around getting soused on the taxpayers' dime."

"Fair enough."

"Number two: Every municipality in the United States has a cookout the last Sunday of the month. The grills are set up on the public square. You bring the fixings, the government brings the charcoal. Why not? It's good for the community."

"Sounds sensible," I said.

"And I'm proud of number three. The federal government imposes a single sensible standard for menus in Chinese restaurants. It's my position that if you walk into the goddamned Noodle Express in Toledo, Ohio and order a number forty-two, you know that's going to be the Kung Pao Chicken, rain or shine. Any chef who won't play ball gets a kick in the rump."

"It sounds like a hell of a country," I said.

"You're damn right it does," Bob said, his voice rising. "And I've got a cabinet all picked out. You know that girl from the tire commercials? Well—"

"I'm sorry, I'm sorry," said Matthew. "But is there any way you could please shut up with this? I apologize, Bob, but how many times have I heard this bit? Just change up the fucking jukebox, please."

Bob gazed back at Matthew in wordless malice. I gathered that in the three weeks since he'd called me, the "two-man nation" he and Bob had started building here was already showing signs of ugly schism.

Matthew steered the truck through a rural abridgement of a town—a filling station, a red gambrel-roofed barn with a faltering neon sign identifying it as a pizza restaurant, and a grocery store with newspaper coupon circulars taped to the window glass. At last, Matthew spoke, trying to dispel the sour silence that had congealed in the cab.

"Hey, Alan, you didn't say anything about my new truck."

I told him I liked it.

"Just bought it. Best vehicle I've ever owned. V-6. Sport package. Got a carriage-welded, class-four trailer hitch. I'd say you're looking at a three-ton towing capacity. Maybe three and a half."

"You're really not going back to Myrtle Beach?" I asked.

"Why would I? Stick a fork in me, as far as that town's concerned. I dissolved the partnership. Hugh Auchincloss—"

"The notorious Mister Auchincloss," said Bob wearily. Matthew narrowed his eyes at him, as though he was going to say something, but didn't.

"Yes, Hugh Auchincloss, the conniver. Because of him, I took a hard fucking on this EIFS deal."

"On what deal?" I said.

"EIFS," said Matthew. "Exterior Insulation Finish System. Nonbreathable synthetic cladding. Fake stucco, is what it is, and the deal is, it fosters mold." Matthew held forth at cruel length on the perils of EIFS and moisture intrusion and the tort liabilities involved in selling condominiums that were rotten with noxious spores. Hugh Auchincloss had evidently overseen the sale and construction of five infected buildings. He had homeowners coming at him, claiming respiratory ailments, and a couple talking about brain damage to their infant kids. The courts had handed down no penalties yet, but Matthew was sure there wouldn't be much left of him when the attorneys' knives stopped flashing.

"And Kimberly, the engagement?"

"Who, Kim Jong Il?" he said in a low growl. "She's done. Dead to me."

"Why?"

"She's a gold-plated bitch is why, with an ass like a beanbag."

"You left her?"

"Something like that."

In my opinion, this was not sad news. I'd met Kimberly once, over dinner at a high-class restaurant a year ago in January. I remember that she said that she wished Matthew "would quit being such a Jew" when he declined to order a $90 bottle of champagne. Then she told us about her brother, a Marine pulling his third tour in Iraq. She said she endorsed his idea for bringing the insurgency under control, which, if I was hearing her right, involved providing drinking water only to those districts that could behave themselves, and permitting the rest of the country to parch to death or die of dysentery. Kimberly was a churchgoer, and I asked her how the water tactic would square with "Thou Shalt Not Kill." She told me that "Thou Shalt Not Kill" was from the Old Testament, so it didn't really count.

"I'm sorry," I said. "I really saw that one working out."

Matthew took a tube of sunflower seeds from the ashtray and shook a long gray dose into his mouth. Then he spit the chewed hulls into a paper cup he kept in a holder on the dash.

"To be honest with you," he said after a time, "I just don't see the rationale for anyone purchasing a vehicle that doesn't come with a carriage-welded, class-four trailer hitch."

Bob lit a cigarette and rolled the window down. I heard the sharp lisp of beer cans being opened. Bob handed one to Matthew and one to me. Then he turned around in his seat and asked me, "Baby brother, would you like to see a magic trick?"

"Sure," I said.

He picked up an orange from the floor of the truck and held it out to me.

"Feast your eyes on it, touch it. Get the image firmly in your mind. Got it?"

It was a navel orange, flattened slightly on one side.

"Now watch closely," he said, and threw the orange out the window of the truck. "Presto," he said.

"You just tossed my fucking orange, Bob," said Matthew. "I was looking forward to eating that."

"And so you can," said Bob. "Whenever you want it, it'll be waiting for you right back there."

Matthew steered the truck through a narrowing vasculature of country roads that wound into high-altitude boondocks, past trailer homes and cedar-shake cottages with reliquaries of derelict appliances and discarded automotive organs in their yards. He turned at last down a rilled trail of blond gravel. High weeds grew on the spine between the tire tracks and brushed the truck's exhaust system with a sound of light sleet.

Bob watched the forest going by. "Once we get Alan's gear stowed, we should head to the lake and get some shots in."

"Not me," said Matthew. "We already shitcanned four days this week, and nothing. I've got a house to finish up. You want to go out, go."

"You know," said Bob, "if you weren't such a know-it-all son of a bitch, you might pay some heed to the fact that it's pretty much last-chance-thirty out here as far as getting something in the freezer this year. I don't think we've got seven good days left in the season. I like to eat meat in the winter-time. Stovewood is hard on my teeth."

Matthew shrugged, but Bob had warmed to his topic, and poured forth a suite of recollections of the bitter winters he'd endured out here and the miseries of waiting for the thaw without a freezer brimming with game. Ten miles of dirt track lay between Bob's house and the blacktop road. From Matthew's cabin, it was closer to eleven, and twenty more into town. When the snow was up to the eaves of your house, you couldn't ride into town for groceries any time you felt like it. It was all right by Bob if Matthew wanted to spend his winter making the frozen trek for supermarket pork chops that tasted like silly putty while Bob fattened up on homemade venison sausage and kidney pies.

"You've lived out here awhile?" I asked Bob before the two men's bickering could start up again.

"I spent my childhood running these woods," he said. "My family owned all of this."

"When was that?"

"Well, until your fatter half persuaded it away from me."

"You want it back? Make me an offer," Matthew said. "I'll let you have it cheap."

Matthew braked the truck at Bob's house, a khaki modular home at a fork in the track. Bob made no move to get out. "Go on," said Matthew. "Don't let us keep you from making your big kill."

Bob squinted at the sky, which was opaque and the color of spackle. "Rain coming."

"Come on now, Bob, don't let a little moisture hold you back," said Matthew.

Bob did not get out. Matthew winked at me in the rearview. "Bob can't actually shoot, is the problem. His eyes are bad. He couldn't shoot his way out from under a wet napkin."

"I'm going to have them tuned up soon," said Bob. "As soon I get used to the idea of somebody chopping up my eyeballs I'll have them good as new."

"Are you staying or going?"

"What's for dinner at your place?"

"You know what: beef stroganoff."

"Hm. Stroge again. I'd hate to miss that. We'll hunt tomorrow. Drive on, sir."

The truck bumped along the path and up Matthew's "mountain," which turned out to be a low-lying hill not much loftier than a medium-volume landfill. Matthew's cabin stood in a granite clearing at the summit. Beyond it, sunlight flamed the dark surface of a pond. The cabin, to my surprise, was a modest, handsome structure built of newly peeled logs and roof shingles the color of fresh pine needles. One curious thing was that the gable ends and eaves were trimmed out with a fussy surfeit of gingerbread curlicues, ornate scrollworks, and filigreed bargeboard, giving the place the look of a tissue-paper snowflake.

"This is amazing," I said. "You built this, Matthew?"

"It was mostly Bob," Matthew said, as though it were an accusation. "Bob called the shots."

"It's a hell of a good-looking place."

Bob's features lifted in an elfin smile. "The secret ingredient is wood," he said.

Matthew led me up the front stairs, along a gangplank nailed over the bare joists of the porch. In contrast to the cabin's outward fripperies, its interior was close to raw. The floors were bare, dusty plywood and half the walls were unfinished, just pink insulation trapped behind cloudy plastic sheeting.

"Just to spite me, Bob won't hang sheetrock," said Matthew. "All day long, I'm in here, mudding joints, and he's out there with his jigsaw turning my house into a giant doily. I get after him about it, but he threatens to quit and not come back."

Matthew let out a mirthless chuckle, and with the instep of his boot he herded a pile of sawdust against the wall. "It's pathetic, isn't it? I don't guess this is where you saw me winding up."

"I'm being honest, man," I said. "I think you've got a great spot. Once you get the finishing touches on it, you'll have a little palace out here."

His vast head tilted in a leery attitude, as though he couldn't be sure I wasn't making fun of him, so I went on. "I'd kill for something like this," I said. "Look at me. I live in a studio apartment above a candle shop."

Matthew's wariness relaxed into a kind of smirking disgust. "You're still renting?"

"Yes."

"Jesus Christ. You're how old, thirty-seven?"

"I turned thirty-eight in August."

"You got a girlfriend?"

"No."

"No shit? Still nobody since what'shername? Nothing on the side?"

"No."

Matthew raised his eyebrows, gazed at the floor, loosed a long sigh. "Well, fuck," he said. "I guess things could be worse."

I spent the afternoon with Bob, finishing up the porch, while Matthew worked indoors, where he kept up a steady racket, dropping tools and swearing importantly. The boards Matthew had bought for his porch were so drastically buckled that to make them lie straight you had to strain against them until you were purple in the face. While I was grunting over a plank that was warped to a grin, Bob raised his hammer and said, heraldically, "I proclaim this to be the sorriest excuse for a piece of one-by-six decking ever touched by human hands, and I proclaim Matthew Lattimore the cheapest, laziest son of a bitch to ever tread the grand soil of Maine."

I laughed, and then I brought up something that had been on my mind.

"Hey, Bob, what'd Matthew pay you for this place, if you don't mind the question."

"I do not. He paid me one hundred and eighty-nine thousand dollars in green cash."

"Ah," I said.

"How's that?"

"Nothing," I said. "I'm not surprised. You can always trust my brother to leave you holding the brown end of the stick."

"Oh, I've got no complaints," Bob said, and then drove another nail home. "The land's close to worthless, as a matter of fact. The county put its pecker to largeholders like myself. They require fifty-acre plots to build out here. You can't subdivide it. Can't develop it, can't anything with it, and it's already been timbered to hell. I got a fair price. In exchange, I've got retirement, sir! I've got new teeth in my head and a satellite dish. No, if Matthew hadn't come along when he did, I'd be at the bottom of the proverbial well of shit."

Matthew stepped onto the porch with a flask in his hand.

"So, Alan," Bob said. "You're from California. What part did you say?"

I told him that it was the northern part.

"Ah, the north! Now that's real fine. What do you do up there? I suppose you run around with men."

"I do what?"

"That you're a homosexual, sir—a queer, a punk, one of the modern Greeks."

I wasn't sure how to take this. I assured him I was not.

He nodded, and slapped another board into place. He took a nail from a pouch on his belt and sunk it in a single pistonlike stroke. "Oh no? I used to be one myself, or half of one, at least. In my twenties, I lived with my ex-wife in Annapolis, Maryland. We had a good friend in the naval academy, a corporal with a head of blond hair and a prick like a service baton. We used to take him home and wrestle him, if the mood struck us of a Saturday night."

Matthew leaned against the doorjamb and drank deeply from the flask. "He's not joking, by the way," said Matthew. "He really used to do that sort of thing."

"Oh, I did, by God, I did," said Bob. "Yes, I have fucked and sucked all across this noble land, from the burning Mojave sands to the clement shores of Lake Champlain. I took a turn with all who would have me—man, woman, and child; bird, leaf, and beast."

"God have mercy," said Matthew.

I was enjoying Bob, so I urged him on. "And what now, Bob? Have you a steady mate out here?"

He set the hammer down. "I do not, Alan. I don't have the need for one. That's why I returned to my ancestral land like a doomed old salmon-fish. I've learned in my old years that I don't really care for people. I don't like *Homo sapiens*, and I don't like to have coitus with them. Church is for noodleheads, but I'll agree with the Holy Rollers that intercourse is deplorable—somebody climbing all over you, trying to get themselves a gumdrop. Repulsive. The last time someone tricked me into it, I was angry for a week. No, sir, I'm off it for good. Of course, unless Matthew makes me a tempting offer some chill midwinter night."

"Oh, would you please shut up," Matthew said. His cheeks stood out in little quaking hillocks. For an instant I thought he would break into tears. "Oh god, my life is on fire."

We had our dinner on the porch, where a soft, warm wind was blowing in. We ate beef stroganoff that Matthew made from a kit, and drank cold gin from coffee cups because Bob felt that eating "stroge" without gin to go with it was like a kiss without a squeeze.

"Alan," Matthew said.

"Yes," I said. "What is it?"

"That money, your money from Gram Gram. Have you got it still, or did you blow it already?"

I told him that I hadn't done a thing with it at all. It was sitting in the bank.

This news invigorated him. "What is it, twenty thousand or so?"

"Yes." It was closer to forty, but I saw no need to mention that.

"Outstanding, because there's something I've been meaning to bring to your attention."

"What sort of something?"

A slow wind rattled the leaves still clinging to their limbs. On the crest of the hill, a flock of bats tumbled in the day's last light.

"This is the thing," he said. "Now listen to me. How many guys like us, like me, do you think there are out there? Ballpark figure."

"What does 'like us' mean?"

"I'm talking about jackasses who marriage isn't working out for them, they've got jobs that make them want to put a bullet in their face. Guys out in wherever, Charlotte or Brookline or Chattanooga, sitting there watching their lawns get tall. Just broke-down, broke-dick dudes with nothing to look forward to. How many guys like that you think there are?"

"It'd be tough to put a number on it, Matthew."

"Bet you there's twenty million of them, maybe more. What do these guys want? Bunch of half-dead Dagwoods. They don't want much. What they want is to do like me, come out somewhere like this, get away from all the bullshit, is all they're after."

He went on to spin a vision in which this very mountain would be gridded into a hatchwork of tiny lots, and on each lot would stand a tiny cabin, and in each cabin a lonely man would live. He was going to start a website, place ads in the back pages of men's magazines. As early as next spring, these desolated men would flock here by the hundreds to dwell in convalescent solitude, with Matthew as their uncrowned king. It would be a free and joyous land, a place where the thrill of living, unknown since childhood, would be restored to one and all. He would set up a shooting range and snowmobile trails. He might even open a mountaintop saloon where he'd show movies in the summer, and where touring bands would play.

"I'm serious," he said. "It's happening. I've already got some people on the line. I ran it past Ray Broughton, and he was wild about it. Broughton, and Tim Hayes, and Ed Little. All of them are crazy about it. They're all in for fifty."

"Fifty what?" I said.

He gave me a look. "They already sent the checks. But my point is I could let you in, even just with that twenty. If you could kick that twenty in, I'd set you up with an even share."

"I can't do it."

"Sure you can. You're not losing any money here, Alan. I'll cover it myself."

"Look, Matthew. I don't have investments, don't have a 401(k). If my practice tanks, that twenty thousand is the only thing between me and food stamps."

Matthew held up his hand, his fingers splayed and rigid. "Would you shut up a second and let me talk? Thank you. The thing you're not understanding here, Alan, is that I *make* money. I take land, and a little bit of money, and then I turn it into lots of money. That's what I do, and I am very, very good at what I do. I am not going to lose your money, Alan. What I am probably going to do is make you very rich. Now, if it wasn't for that fucking monkey Auchincloss, I wouldn't be coming to you like this, but here we are. All I'm asking is to basically just *hold* your twenty grand for a couple of months, and in return you'll be in on something that could literally change your life."

"I can't do it," I said.

He took a breath, his nostrils flaring. "Well, goddamit, Alan, what can you do? Could you go ten? Ten for a full share? Could you put in ten?"

"I'm sorry—"

"Five? Three? Two thousand? How about eight hundred, or two hundred? Would two hundred work for you, or would that break the bank?"

"Two hundred would be fine," I told him. "Put me down for that."

"Let's don't borrow trouble," said Bob. "No point in fighting over something that could never happen in a million years."

"Oh, it'll happen," said Matthew. "And I'd appreciate it if you kept out of something you don't know anything about."

"First off, there's a fifty-acre—"

Matthew swatted the idea out of the air. "Irrelevant. You file a variance, is all you do. Pay a few bucks, go to a hearing. You're done. The county's starved for development. Tax base is on the respirator. It'd sail through like corn through a goose. I'm quoting the guy at the county on that."

Bob mulled over this. "It still wouldn't work."

"Don't get down on it, Bob," said Matthew. "There'd be something in it for you, too. Who do you think would build the cabins? You'd have more money than you'd know what to do with."

Bob shook his head. "It still wouldn't work," he said.

"You've got no expertise here, Bob," Matthew said. "It's *already* working. The wheels are rolling. The ball is in play."

Bob was quiet for a moment.

"Well, for one thing," he said, "I think you'd be looking at a serious fire hazard, having all those people up here."

Matthew coughed in scorn. "What, lightning? Chimney fires? Bullshit."

"Yep, there's that," said Bob. "But what I've got in mind, if you tried to bring a couple hundred swinging dicks in here, I think what I'd probably have to do is go around with a gas can and light everybody's house on fire."

"Don't be an idiot," Matthew said.

The sound of Bob's laughing echoed in his coffee mug. "You don't know anything about me, Matthew. You don't know what I'd do."

"Here's what *I'd* do," said Matthew. "I'd crack your head open, and then I'd have you put in jail and by the time you get out you'll be wearing diapers, if that sounds like your idea of a good plan."

Bob drained his gin. Then he licked his plate a couple of times, set it down, and fixed Matthew with a smile. "Do you know who J. T. Dunlap is?"

"The guy at the service station? The guy with the bubble in his eye?"

Bob's perfect smile didn't fade. "That's right. Go ask J. T. Dunlap what went on between his brother and Bob Brown. He'll tell you some things you ought to know before you go around making threats."

For all the joy that Matthew finds in provoking other people, he has never been a violent man. My brother is comfortable only in contests he is sure to win, and the chaos of physical violence muddies his calculi of acceptable risk. In his school years, I had seen Matthew run from boys whose throats he could have danced on rather than take his chances in a fight.

Matthew chewed his bottom lip and stared at Bob with cautious, hooded eyes. Then he stood up and hurled his plate against the side of the cabin. It bloomed into smithereens just below the porch light. He stood there long enough to watch a pale clod of creamed noodles fall wetly to the floor. Then he walked inside, slamming the door hard enough to make the gutters chime.

Bob clicked his tongue and said it was time to turn her in. He stood and held his hand out to me. I took it with some reluctance. "So we'll see you dark and early, then," said Bob. "And if Mister Grouchy Bear isn't in a mood to hunt, then you and me will just have to go ourselves. *Bonsoir.*" Bob straightened his cap and winked at me and strolled into the night.

Matthew's only furniture was the sheetless mattress he was sprawled on in the center of the living-room floor. He did not stir when I came in. I folded myself into the warm embayment formed of my brother's knees and outflung arms and fell into a sturdy sleep.

*   *   *

The door creaked open before dawn. "Out of the fartsack, gentlemen," said Bob, clapping his hands. "Come on, get to it, boys."

Bob tramped to the stove. He lit a lantern and boiled water for coffee. I rose and dressed. The air in the cabin was dense with cold.

Matthew hadn't moved. I rocked his shoulder with my foot.

"Leave me alone," said Matthew.

"All righty," Bob said brightly. "The big man's sleeping in. Alan?"

I nudged him again. Matthew sighed a quick, harsh sigh and got up with a crashing of bedclothes and thudding of knees and feet. He pulled on a camouflage bib, a parka, and an elaborate hunter's vest, busy with zippered compartments, ruffled across the breast with cartridge loops. Matthew retrieved the guns from the pickup and carried them to Bob's old white Ford, which sat in the driveway, an aluminum skiff on the trailer it was towing. We climbed in and rode off down the hill. I sat wedged between Bob and my brother. Matthew rested his head against the dew-streaked window, drowsing, or pretending to. Bob was ebullient. Last night's hostilities seemed to have passed from his mind. He prattled at a manic clip on topics ranging from rumors of prehistoric, sixty-foot sharks living along the Mariana Trench to the claim of a Hare Krishna he had met that poor black Americans were white slave owners in their prior lives.

We rode for half an hour on a two-lane state highway, and then Bob turned the Ford down a narrow road, where the leprous trunks of silver birch flared in the headlights. The road carried us to the shore of a lake. Bob nimbly backed the trailer to the water's edge and winched the boat down a mossy slip into the water. Bob and I carried the gear into the boat. Matthew took a seat near the bow with the guns across his lap, facing east, where the sky was rusting up with the approaching dawn.

Bob pulled the cord on the motor, and the skiff skimmed out of the cove. We headed north, hugging the shore, past worlds of marsh grass, and humped expanses of pink granite that looked like corned beef hash. After a twenty-minute ride, Bob stopped the boat at a stretch of muddy beach where he said he'd had some luck before. We pulled the skiff ashore, and Matthew and I followed Bob into the tree line.

Bob browsed the woods on quiet, nimble feet, stopping now and again to check for sign. At the edge of a grassy clearing, Bob waved us over to have a look at a pine sapling whose limbs had been stripped by a rutting buck. He knelt, and scooped a handful of deer shits into his palm. He raised his hand to his face with such savor and relish that for a moment I thought that he was going to tip the turds into his mouth. "That's fresh all right," he said, and cast them away. "I think we'll make some money here."

We sat in ambush back in the trees, in view of the wrecked sapling, and waited. A loon moaned on the lake. Crows bitched and cackled overhead. Before the dawn had fully broken, a fine, cold rain started sifting down. We drew our collars in. The rainwater slid from our chins down the front of our shirts. Nothing moved in the clearing. After two hours, a sparrow walked out of a bush and then walked back in again.

Far be it from me to guess at what goes on in my brother's rash head, but it seemed to me that the black and hollow silence enclosing him that morning was something new for him. In Matthew's idle moments, I could usually see on his face the turnings of distant gears—negotiations being schemed over, old lovers being recalled, iced tumblers of strong alcohol being thirstily imagined. I had never seen his face this way before, slack and unblinking, a vacant, lunar emblem of irreparable regret.

"Doing okay?" I asked him.

"Yeah, of course," he said in a listless monotone. "No sweat."

It took Bob until ten o'clock to decide that nothing was happening for us there. We trudged back to the skiff, and Bob drove us to the far end of the lake, where he knew about a big deer stand which would at least get our asses off of the wet ground. Instead, we killed another couple of hours huddled together up there in the stand, spying down on some empty woods while the sky kept leaking on us. I didn't talk and neither did Matthew. At one point Bob said, "This is why they call it hunting," and an hour or so later he said it again.

Around noon, Bob broke out the lunch he'd brought along, which was bologna sandwiches with cold wads of margarine lumped under the soggy bread. Out of swooning hunger and politeness, I ate my sandwich. Matthew took one bite of his and pitched it off the stand. Bob saw him do it but didn't say anything.

We got back in the boat and thrummed out over the lake, which was stuccoed just faintly with light rain. We skimmed across the broads to a wide delta where a river paid out into a marshy plain, a spot where Bob claimed to have killed a buck four or six or eight years ago. The bank sloped up to a little rocky promontory. We hiked up there and got down behind some big white pines. We hadn't been there long when Matthew sat up, rapt. "There we go," he said.

On the far side of the delta, a large bull moose had stepped from the tree line and was drinking in the shallows, maybe three hundred yards away, an impossible distance. "Jesus, shit," Bob said in a whisper, and then he made an urgent motion for one of us to slip back down the bank and get the moose into clear range. But Matthew seemed not to hear. He got on his feet, raised his rifle, took a breath, and fired. The moose's forelegs crumpled beneath it, and an instant later I saw the animal's head jerk as the sound of the shot reached him. The moose tried to struggle upright but fell again. The effect was of a very old person trying to pitch a heavy tent. It tried to stand, and fell, and tried, and fell, and then gave up its strivings.

Matthew rubbed his eye with the heel of his hand. He gave us a quizzical look, as though he half suspected that the whole thing was a trick that Bob and I had somehow rigged up. It surprised me that he didn't promptly launch into the gloating fanfare and brash self-tribute that generally attend the tiniest of his successes. "Trippy," was all he said as he gazed toward his kill.

"One shot—are you shitting me?" said Bob. "That's the goddamnedest piece of marksmanship I've ever seen."

We made our way down to the carcass. The moose had collapsed in a foot of icy river water and had to be dragged onto firm ground before it could be dressed. What a specimen it was, shaggy brown velvet going on forever, twelve hundred pounds at least, Bob guessed. Matthew and I waded out to where the creature lay. We passed a rope under his chest. We looped the other end around a tree on the bank, using it as a makeshift pulley, and then tied the rope to the stern of the skiff. Bob gunned the outboard, and Matthew and I stood calf-deep in the shallows heaving on the line. By the time we'd gotten the moose to shore, our palms were puckered and torn raw, and our boots were full of water.

Matthew took Bob's hunting knife and bled the moose from the throat, and then made a slit from the bottom of the rib cage to the jaw, revealing the gullet and a pale, corrugated column of windpipe. The scent was powerful. It brought to mind the dark, briny smell that seemed always to hang around my mother when I was a child. Gorge rose faintly in my throat.

Matthew's face was intent, nearly mournful, as he worked, and he didn't say a word. Gingerly, he opened the moose's belly, careful not to puncture the intestines or the stomach. With Bob's help, he carefully dragged out the organs, and Bob set aside the liver, the kidneys, and the pancreas. The hide proved devilishly hard to remove. To get it loose, Bob and I had to brace against the creature's spine and pull with all our might while Matthew sawed at the connective tissues. Then Matthew sawed the hams and shoulders free. We had to lift the legs like pallbearers to get them to the boat. Blood ran from the meat and down my shirt with horrible warmth.

When we had the moose loaded in the boat, the hull rode low in the water. So the bow wouldn't swamp on the ride back to the truck, Matthew, the most substantial ballast of the three of us, sat in the stern and ran the kicker. Clearing the shallows, he opened up the throttle, and we sped off with a big white whale's fluke of churned water arcing out behind us. The wind blew his clotted hair from his forehead. The old unarmored smile I knew from Matthew's early childhood brightened his face. His lips parted in the familiar compact bow. He raised his eyebrows and wagged his tongue at me in pleasure. There is no point in my trying to describe the love I can still feel for my brother when he looks at me this way, when he is briefly free from worries over money, or his own significance, or how much liquor is left in the bottle in the freezer. Ours is not the kind of brotherhood I would wish on other men, but we are blessed with a single, simple gift. Though sometimes I think I know less about Matthew than I do about a stranger passing on the street, when I am with him in his rare moments of happiness, I can feel his pleasure, his sense of fulfillment, as though I were in his very heart. The killing had restored him, however briefly, to the dream of how he'd imagined life would be for him here. As the skiff glided over the dimming lake, I could feel how satisfying the gridded rubber handle of the Evinrude must have felt humming in his hand, and the air rushing through his whiskered cheeks, drying the moose's fluids and the brine of his own exertions. I could sense the joy of his achievement in having felled the animal, all the more pure because he had not made much of it, and his pride in knowing that its flesh would nourish two men until the spring.

With the truck loaded, and the skiff rinsed clean, we rode back to Matthew's hill. It was past dinnertime when we reached the cabin. Our stomachs yowled. Matthew asked if Bob and I wouldn't mind trimming and wrapping up his share of the meat while he put some steaks on the grill. Bob said sure, but that before he did any more work he was going to need to sit in a dry chair for a little while and drink two beers. While Bob was doing that, Matthew waded into the bed of the Ford, which was heaped nearly flush with the maroon dismantlings. With the knife in his hand, he browsed the mass. Then he bent over, sawed at the carcass for a while, and then held up a tapered log of flesh that looked like a peeled boa constrictor. "Tenderloin. You ever seen anything so pretty, Alan? If you had a thousand dollars, you couldn't buy yourself one of these, not fresh anyway."

He carried the loin to the porch and lit the grill. With a sheet of plywood and a pair of sawhorses, Bob and I rigged up a butcher station on the driveway in the headlights of Bob's truck.

I'd had enough of work by then. A swooning fatigue was settling on me. Not long into the job, I was not sure I'd feel it if I ran the knife into my hand. Bob, too, was unsteady on his feet. When he blinked, his eyes stayed closed a while. We had been at it for a time, when I began to take conscious notice of the dark aroma that had been gathering by degrees in the air around us, a sour diarrheal scent. The awful thought struck me that the old man, in his exhaustion, had let his bowels give way. I said nothing. A while later, Bob wrinkled his nose and looked at me. "Are you farting over there?" he said.

I told him no.

"What *is* that? My God, it smells like someone cracked open a sewer." He sniffed at his sleeve, then at his knife, then at the block of meat in front of him. "*Hruk*," he said, recoiling. "Oh, good Christ—it's off."

He went around to the truck bed and stood on the tailgate, taking up pieces at random at putting them to his face. "Son of a bitch. It's contaminated. It's something deep in the meat."

I sniffed my fingers, and caught a whiff of grave breath, the unmistakable stink of decay.

Out on the porch, Matthew had a radio turned up loud, and had set out a bottle of wine to breathe. On the patio table, three filets the size of wall clocks rested on paper plates, already pink and sodden. Matthew was ladling out servings of yellow rice when we walked up.

"Not possible," he said calmly, after Bob broke the news. "We broke it down perfectly. I'm sure of it. Nothing spilled at all. You saw."

"It was sick," said Bob. "That thing was dying on its feet when you brought it down."

"Oh, bull-*shit*. You figured that out, how?"

"Contaminated, I promise you," said Bob. "I should have known it when the skin hung on there like it did. He was bloating up with something, just barely holding on. The second he died, and turned that infection loose, it just started going wild."

Matthew rubbed his thumb across the slab of meat he'd intended for himself, and licked at the juice. "Tastes okay to me," he said. With a brusque swipe of his knife, he cut off a dripping pink ingot. He speared it with his fork and touched it to his tongue. "Totally fine. A little gamy, maybe, but they don't call it game for no reason. What?"

He licked it once more and then he squinted at the meat, the way a jeweler might look at a gem he could not quite identify.

"Poison," said Bob.

"No big thing, we go back out tomorrow," I said. "You'll get another one, no sweat."

But Matthew was not listening. He cocked his head and held it still, as though the sound of something in the woods beyond the cabin had suddenly caught his ear. Then he turned back to the table and slipped the fork into his mouth.

RETREAT #2

by WELLS TOWER

(*fiction from Issue 30*)

SOMETIMES, AFTER SIX or so large drinks, it seems like a sane idea to call my little brother on the phone. Approximately since Stephen's birth, I've held him among the principal motherfuckers of my life, and it takes a lot of solvent to bleach out all the dark recollections I've stashed up over the years. Pick a memory, any memory. My eleventh birthday party at Ernstead Park, how about? I'd just transferred schools, trying to turn over a new leaf, and I'd invited all the boys and girls of quality. I'd been making progress with them, too, until Stephen, age eight, ran up behind me at the fish pond and shoved me face-first into the murk. The water came up only to my knees, so I did a few hilarious staggers before flopping down, spluttering, amid some startled koi. The kids all laughed like wolves.

Or ninth grade, when I caught the acting bug and landed a part in our high school's production of *Grease* playing opposite a girl named Dodi Clark. We played an anonymous prancing couple, on stage only for the full-cast dance melees. She was no beauty, a mousy girl with a weak chin and a set of bonus, overlapping canine teeth, but I liked her somewhat. She had a pretty neat set of breasts for a girl her age. I thought maybe we could help each other out with our virginity problems. Yet the sight of Dodi and me dancing drove Stephen into a jealous fever. Before I could get my angle going, Stephen snaked me, courting her with a siege of posters, special pens, stickers, and crystal whim-whams. The onslaught worked and Dodi fell for him, but when she finally parted her troubled mouth to kiss him, he told me years later, he froze up. "I think I had some kind of primeval prey-versus-predator response when I saw those teeth. It was like trying to make out with a sand shark. No idea why I was after her to begin with."

But I know why: in Stephen's understanding, nothing pleasant should ever flow to me on which he hasn't exercised first dibs. He wouldn't let me eat a turd without first insisting on his cut.

He's got his beefs, too, I suppose. I used to tease him pretty rigorously. We had these little red toads that hopped around my mother's yard, and I used to pin him down and rub them into his clenched teeth. Once, when we were smoking dope in high school, I lit his hair on fire. Another time, I locked him outside in his underwear until the snot froze in scales on his face. Hard to explain why I did these things, except to say that I've got a little imp inside me whose ambrosia is my brother's wrath. Stephen's furies are marvelous, ecstatic, somehow pornographic, the equally transfixing inverse of watching people in the love act. That day I locked him out, I was still laughing when I let him in after a cold hour. I even had a mug of hot chocolate ready for him. He drained it and then grabbed a can opener from the counter and threw it at me, gouging a three-inch gash beneath my lower lip. It left a white parenthesis in the stubble of my chin, the abiding, sideways smile of the imp.

But give me a good deep rinse of alcohol and our knotty history unkinks itself. All of the old crap seems inconsequential, just part of the standard fraternal rough-and-tumble, and I get very soppy and bereft over the brotherhood Steve and I have lost.

Anyhow, I started feeling that way one night in October just after I'd crossed the halfway point on a fifth of Meyer's rum. I was standing at the summit of a small mountain I'd recently bought in Aroostook County,

Maine. The air was wonderful, heavy with the watery sweetness of lupine, moss, and fern. Overhead, bats hawked mosquitoes in the darkening sky, while the sun waned behind the molars of the Appalachian range. I browsed the contacts on my phone, wanting to call someone up, maybe just deliver an oral postcard of this place into someone's voicemail box, but I had a reason not to dial each of those names until I got to Stephen's.

I dialed, and he answered without saying hello.

"In a session," he said, the last syllable trilling up in a bitchy way, and hung up the phone. Stephen makes his living as a music therapist, but session or not, you'd think he could spare a second to at least say hello to me. We hadn't spoken in eight months. I dialed again.

"What the fuck, fool, it's Matthew."

"Matthew," he repeated, in the way you might say "cancer" after the doctor's diagnosis. "I'm with a client. This is not an optimum time."

"Yeah," I said. "Question for you: mountains."

There was a wary pause. From Stephen's end came the sound of someone doing violence to a tambourine.

"What about them?"

"Do you like them? Do you like mountains, Stephen?"

"I have no objection to them. Why?"

"Well, I bought one," I said. "I'm on it now."

"Congratulations," Stephen said. "Is it Popocatepetl? Are you putting 7-Elevens on the Matterhorn?"

Over the years, I've made a hell of a lot of money in real estate, and this seems to hurt Stephen's feelings. He's not a church man, but he's big on piety and sacrifice and letting you know what choice values he's got. So far as I can tell, his values include eating ramen noodles by the case, getting laid once every fifteen years or so, and arching his back at the sight of people like me—that is, people who have amounted to something and don't reek of thrift stores.

But I love Stephen. Or I think I do. We've had some intervals of mutual regard. Our father came down with lymphoma when Stephen was four, so we pretty much parented ourselves while our mother nursed our father through two exhausting cycles of remission and relapse.

At any rate, the cancer got our father when I was ten. Liquor killed our mother before I was out of college, and it was right around then that we went on different courses. Stephen, a pianist, retreated into a bitter fantasy of musical celebrity that was perpetually being thwarted—by his professors at the Eastman School, by the philistines in his ensembles, and by girl-friends who wanted too much of his time. He had a series of tedious artistic crackups, and whenever we'd get together, he'd hand me lots of shit about how drab and hollow my life was.

Actually, my life was extremely full. I married young, and married often. I bought my first piece of property at eighteen. Now, at forty-two, I've been through two amicable divorces. I've lived and made money in nine American cities. Late at night, when rest won't come and my breathing shortens with the worry that I've cheated myself of life's traditional rewards (long close-nesses, offspring, mature plantings), I take an astral cruise of the hundreds of properties that have passed through my hands over the years, and before I come close to visiting them all, I droop, contented, into sleep.

When no orchestras called Stephen with commissions, he exiled himself to Eugene, Oregon, to buff his oeuvre while eking out a living teaching the mentally substandard to achieve sanity by blowing on harmonicas. When I drove down to see him two years ago after a conference in Seattle, I found him living above a candle store in a dingy apartment which he shared with a dying collie. The animal was so old it couldn't take a leak on its own, so Stephen was always having to lug her downstairs to the grassy verge beside the sidewalk. Then he'd straddle the dog and manually void its bladder via a Heimlich technique horrible to witness. You hated to see your last blood relation engaged in something like that. I told Stephen that from a business standpoint, the smart thing would be to have the dog put down. This caused an ugly argument, but really, it seemed to me that someone regularly seen by the roadside hand-juicing a half-dead dog was not the man you'd flock to for lessons on how to be less out of your mind.

"The mountain doesn't have a name yet," I told him. "Hell, I'll name it after you. I'll call it Brown Cloud Hill"—my old nickname for the gloomy man.

"Do that," said Stephen. "Hanging up now."

"I send you any pictures of my cabin? Gets its power off a windmill. I'm telling you, it's the absolute goddamned shit. You need to come out here and see me."

"What about Charleston? Where's Amanda?"

I spat a lime rind into my hand and tossed it up at the bats to see if they'd take a nibble at it. They didn't.

"No idea."

"You split?"

"Right."

"Oh, jeez, big brother. Really? Wedding's off?"

"Yep."

"What happened? "

"Got sick of her, I guess."

"Why?"

"She was hard of hearing and her pussy stank."

"That's grand. Now look—"

Actually, like about fifty million other Americans, I'd been blindsided by sudden reverses in the real-estate market. I'd had to borrow some cash from my ex-fiancée, Amanda, an Oldsmobile dealership heiress who didn't care about money just so long as she didn't have to loan out any of hers. Strains developed and the engagement withered. I used the last of my liquidity to buy my hill. Four hundred acres, plus a cabin, nearly complete, thanks to my good neighbor George Tabbard, who'd also cut me a bargain on the land. The shit of it was I'd have to spend a year up in residence here, but I could deal with that. Next fall I could subdivide, sell the plots, dodge the extortionary tax assessment the state charges non-resident speculators, and float into life's next phase with the winds of increase plumping my sails and a vacation home in the deal.

"Anyway," I went on. "Here's a concept. Pry the flute out of your ass and come see me. We'll have real fun. Come now. I'll be under a glacier in six weeks."

"And get the airfare how? Knit it? Listen, I've got to go."

"Fuck the airfare," I told him. "I'll get it. Come see me." It wasn't an offer I really wanted to make. Stephen probably had more money in the bank than I did, but his poor mouthing worked an irksome magic on me. I couldn't take a second of it without wanting to smack him in the face with a roll of doubloons. Then he said he couldn't leave Beatrice (the collie was still alive!). Fine, I told him, if he could find the right sort of iron lung to stable her in, I'd foot the bill for that too. He said he'd think it over. A marimba flourish swelled on the line, and I let Stephen go.

The conversation left me feeling irritable, and I walked back to my cabin in a low mood. But I bucked up right away when I found George Tabbard on my porch, half of which was still bare joists. He was standing on a ladder, nailing a new piece of trim across the front gable. "Evening, sweetheart," George called out to me. "Whipped up another *objet* for you here."

George was seventy-six, with a head of scraggly white hair. His front teeth were attached to a partial plate that made his gums itch so he didn't wear it, and his breath was like a ripe morgue. At this point, George was basically my best friend, a turn I couldn't have imagined ten months ago when life was still high. His family went back in the area two centuries or so, but he'd moved around a good deal, gone through some wives and degrees and left some children here and there before moving back a decade ago. He'd pretty much built my cabin himself for ten dollars an hour. He was good company. He liked to laugh and drink and talk about road grading, women, and maintaining equipment. We'd murdered many evenings that way.

A couple of groans with his screw gun and he'd secured the item, a four-foot battery of little wooden pom-poms, like you'd see dangling from the ceiling of a Mexican drug dealer's sedan. I'd praised the first one he'd made, but now George had tacked his lacework fancies to every eave and soffit in sight, so that the house pretty well foamed with them. An otherwise sensible person, he seemed to fear a demon would take him if production slowed, and he slapped up a new piece of frippery about every third day. My house was starting to resemble something you'd buy your mistress to wear for a weekend in a cheap motel.

"There we are," he said, backing away to get the effect. "Pretty handsome booger, don't you think?"

"Phenomenal," I said.

"Now how about some backgammon?"

I went inside and fetched the set, the rum, and a jar of olives. George was a brutal prodigy, and the games were dull routs, yet we sat for many hours in the cool of the evening, drinking rum, moving the lacquered discs around the board, and spitting olive pits over the rail, where they landed quietly in the dark.

*   *   *

To my surprise, Stephen called me back. He said he'd like to come, so we fixed a date, two weeks later. It was an hour and twenty minutes to the village of Aiden, where the airfield was. When George and I arrived, Stephen's plane hadn't come in. I went into the Quonset hut they use for a terminal. A little woman with a brown bomber jacket and a bulb of gray hair sat by the radio, reading the local newspaper.

"My brother's flight was due in from Bangor at eleven," I told the woman.

"Plane's not here," she said.

"I see. Do you know where it is?"

"Bangor."

"And when's it going to arrive?"

"If I knew that, I'd be somewhere picking horses, wouldn't I?"

Then she turned back to her newspaper and brought our chat to an end. The front-page story of the Aroostook *Gazette* showed a photograph of a dead chow dog, under the headline, "Mystery Animal Found Dead in Pinemont."

"Quite a mystery," I said. "The Case of What Is Obviously a Dog."

"'Undetermined origin,' says here."

"It's a dog, a chow," I said.

"Undetermined," the woman said.

With time to kill, we went over the lumberyard in Aiden and I filled the bed of my truck with a load of decking to finish the porch. Then we went back to the airfield. Still no plane. George tried to hide his irritation, but I knew he wasn't happy to be stuck on this errand. He wanted to be out in the woods, gunning for deer. George was keen to get one before the weather made hunting a misery. Loading your freezer with meat slain by your hand was evidently an unshirkable autumn rite around here, and George and I had been going out about every fourth day since the opener three weeks ago. I'd shot the head off a bony goose at point-blank range, but other than that, we hadn't hit a thing. When I'd suggested that we go in on a side of beef from the butcher shop, George had acted as though I'd proposed a terrible breach of code. Fresh venison tasted better than store-bought beef, he argued. Also you were not out big money in the common event that your freezer was sacked by the meat burglars who worked the outer county.

To buck George up, I bought him lunch at a tavern in Aiden, where we ate hamburgers and drank three whiskey sours each. George sighed a lot and didn't talk. Already, I felt a coursing anger at Stephen for not calling to let me know that his plane was delayed. I was brooding heavily when the bartender asked if I wanted anything else. I told him, "Yeah, tequila and cream."

"You mean a Kahlúa and cream," he said, which was what I'd meant, but I wasn't in a mood to be corrected.

"How about you bring what I ordered?" I told him, and he got to work. The drink was bilious, vile, but I forced it down. The bartender told me, sneering, that I was welcome to another, on the house.

When we rolled back by the airport, the plane had come and gone. A light rain was sifting down. Stephen was out by the gate, on the lip of a drainage gully, perched atop his luggage with his chin on his fist. He was thinner than when I'd last seen him, and the orbits of his eyes were dark, kind of buttholish with exhaustion. The rain had wet him through, and what was left of his hair lay sad against his skull. His coat and pants were huge on him. The wind gusted and Stephen billowed like a poorly tarped load.

"Hi, friend!" I called out to him.

"What the shit, Matthew?" he said. "I just stayed up all night on a plane to spend two hours sitting in a ditch? That really happened?"

Of course, Stephen could have waited with the radio woman in the Quonset hut, but he'd probably arranged himself in the ditch to present a picture of maximum misery when I pulled up.

"You could have let me know you got hung up in Bangor. I shitcanned three hours waiting for you. We had stuff on our plate, but now George is drunk and I'm half in the bag and the whole day's shot. Frankly, I'm a little heated at you here."

Stephen bulged his eyes at me. His fists clenched and un-clenched very quickly. He looked about to thrombose. "Extraordinary! This is my fault now? Oh, you are a remarkable prick. This is your fucking... region, Matthew. It didn't occur to me that you'd need to be coached on how not to leave somebody in the rain. Plus call you how, shitball? You know I don't do cell phones."

"Come get in the truck."

I reached for him and he tore his arm away.

"No. Apologize to me." He was red-eyed and shivering. His cheeks and forehead were welted over from repeated gorings by the vicious cold-weather mosquitoes they had up here. Right now, one was gorging itself on the rim of his ear, its belly glowing like a pomegranate seed in the cool white sun. I didn't swat it away for him.

"Mother*fucker*, man. Just get in the truck."

"Forget it. I'm going home." He shouldered his bag and stormed off for the airfield. His tiny damp head, and squelching shoes—it was like watching the tantrum of a stray duckling.

Laughing, I jogged up behind Stephen and stripped the bag from his shoulder. When he turned I put him in a bear hug and kissed his brow.

"Get off me, you ape," he said.

"Who's a furious fellow?" I said. "Who's my little Brown Cloud?"

"Fucking asshole, I'll bite you, I swear," he said into my chest. "Let me go. Give me my bag."

"Ridiculous," I said.

I walked to the truck and levered the seat forward to usher Stephen into the club cab's rear compartment. When Stephen saw that we weren't alone, he stopped grasping for his bag and making departure threats. I introduced Stephen to George. Then my brother clambered in and we pulled onto the road.

"This is Granddad's gun, isn't it?" said Stephen. Hanging in the rack was the .300 Weatherby magnum I'd collected from my grandfather's house years ago. It was a beautiful instrument, with a blued barrel and a tiger-maple stock.

"Yes," I said, marshalling a defense for why I hadn't offered the gun to Stephen, who probably hadn't fired a rifle in fifteen years. Actually, Stephen probably had a stronger claim to it than I did. As kids, we'd gone out for ducks and rabbits with our grandfather, and Stephen, without making much of it, had always been the more patient stalker and a better shot. But he did not mention it.

"Hey, by the way," he said. "The tab comes to eight-eighty."

"What tab?" I said.

"Eight hundred and eighty dollars," Stephen said. "That's what the flight came to, plus a sitter for Beatrice."

"Your daughter?" George asked.

"Dog," said Stephen.

"George, this is a dog that knows where it was when JFK was shot,"

243

I said. "Stephen, are you still doing those bowel lavages on her? Actually, don't tell me. I don't need the picture in my head."

"I'd like my money," Stephen said. "You said you'd reimburse me."

"Don't get a rod-on about it, Steve-O. You'll get paid."

"Lovely. When?"

"At some future fucking juncture when I don't happen to be operating a moving motor vehicle. Is that okay with you?"

"Sure," said Stephen. "But just for the record, me being colossally shafted is how this is going to conclude."

"You little grasping fuck, what do you want, collateral? Want to hold my watch?" I joggled the wheel a little. "Or maybe I'll just drive this truck into a fucking tree. Maybe you'd like that."

George began to laugh in a musical wheeze. "How about you stop the car and you two have yourselves an old-fashioned rock fight."

"We're fine," I said, my face hot. "Sorry, George."

"Forget it," Stephen said.

"Oh, no, Steve, money man, let's get you squared away," I said. "George, my checkbook's in the glove box."

George made out the check, and I signed it, which hurt me deeply. I passed it to my brother, who folded it into his pocket. George patted my shoulder. "His name shall be called Wonderful Counselor, the Everlasting Father, the Prince of Peace," he said.

"Oh, suck a dong," I said.

"If there's no way around it," sighed George. "How's clearance under that steering wheel?"

"Fairly snug."

"A little later, how about, when I can really put my back into it?"

"That's a big ten-four," I said.

At all this, Stephen tittered. Then, after being such a childish shit about the check, he began a campaign of being very enthusiastic about everything going past the windows of the truck. The junky houses with appliances piled on their porches? "Refreshing" compared with the "twee fraudulence of most New England towns." Two hicks on a four-wheeler, blasting again and again through their own gales of dust, knew "how to do a weekend right." "Wagnerian" is how he described the storm clouds overhead. Then Stephen began plying George with a barrage of light and pleasant chatter.

Had he lived here long? Ten years? Amazing! He'd grown up here, too? How fantastic to have escaped a childhood in the exurban soul vacuum we'd been reared in. And George had gone to Syracuse? Had he heard of Nils Aughterard, the music biographer on the faculty there? Well, his book on Gershwin—

"Hey, Stephen," I broke in. "You haven't said anything about my new truck."

"What'd you pay for it?"

"Best vehicle I've ever owned," I said. "V-8, five liter. Three-and-a-half-ton towing capacity. Carriage-welded, class-four trailer hitch. Four-wheel drive, max payload package. It'll pay for itself when the snow hits."

"So you and Amanda, that's really off?"

"Yeah."

"I'm so sorry, Matty," Stephen said. "You were so hot on her."

Stephen had despised her. Amanda was a churchgoer, and a Republican. They'd argued about the war in Iraq. Over dinner, Stephen had baited her into declaring that she'd like to see the Middle East bombed to a parking lot. He'd asked her how this tactic would square with "Thou Shalt Not Kill." She'd told him "Thou Shalt Not Kill" was from the Old Testament, so it didn't really count.

"Anyway, I'm sorry," he went on. "I know it's got to hurt."

I took a tube of sunflower seeds from the dashboard and shook a long gray dose into my mouth.

"To be honest with you," I said, cracking a seed with my back teeth. "I just don't see the rationale for anybody owning a vehicle without a carriage-welded, class-four trailer hitch."

In silence, we rode through bleary, rural abridgements of towns, down a narrowing vasculature of country roads, to the rilled and cratered fire trail that served as a driveway to my and George's land. High weeds stood in the spine of earth between the tire grooves, brushing the truck's undercarriage with a sound of light sleet. We passed George's handsome cedar-shake cottage, I dropped the truck into four-wheel drive, and the Dodge leapt, growling, up the hill.

My home hove into view. I was ready for Stephen to bust my balls a little over George's fancy trim, but he took in the place without a word.

George ambled off to take a leak in the trees. I grabbed Stephen's bag and led him indoors. Though my cabin's exterior was well into its late Rococo phase, the interior was still raw. Stephen gazed around the living room. I felt newly conscious of the squalor of the place. The floors were still dusty plywood. The drywall stopped four feet from the floor, and pink insulation lay like an autopsy specimen behind the cloudy plastic sheeting. The sheet-less mattress I'd been sleeping on sat askew in the center of the room.

"Feel free to do a little embellishing when you send out the Christmas letter this year," I told him.

Stephen went to the window and gazed out at the wiry expanse of leafless trees sloping down the basin of the valley. "Hell of a view," he said. Then he turned away from the window and looked at the mattress. "You got a place for me to sleep?"

I nodded at a sleeping pad rolled up in the corner. "Top-of-the-line pad, right there. Ever get down on memory foam?"

"You didn't tell me we'd be camping."

"Yeah, well, if it's too much of a shithole for you, baby brother, I can run you back to the motor lodge in Aiden."

"Of course not," Stephen said. "The place is great. I think you're making real progress, Matthew. Honestly, I was expecting a modular chalet with tiered Jacuzzis and an eight-car garage."

"Next time you visit, I'll strip nude and wear a barrel, maybe get a case of hookworm going," I said. "You'll really be proud of me then."

"No, I'm serious. I'd kill for something like this," he said, reaching up to rub his hand along a smooth log rafter. "I mean, God, next month I'm forty. I rent a two-room apartment full of silverfish and no bathroom sink."

"That same place? You're kidding," I said. "What about that condo you were looking at?"

"Cold feet, I guess, with the economy and all. I figured I'd just get rooked."

"It's still on the market? You should've called me. I'd get you set up."
"No."

"But that money, your Gram-Gram cash? Still got it for a down payment?"
He nodded.

"Listen, you get back to Oregon, we'll find you something. Look around, send me some comps, I'll help you through it. We'll get you into a place."

Stephen gave me a guarded look, as though I'd offered him a soda and he wasn't sure I hadn't pissed in it first.

I wanted to get the porch wrapped up before dark, and I suggested that Stephen take a drink up to the summit, where I'd hung a hammock, while George and I nailed the decking down. Stephen said, "Why don't I help you guys? I'm acquainted with Manuel."

"Who?"

"Manuel Labòr," he said, and giggled.

So we unloaded the wood and he and George got to work while I stayed inside, slathering auburn Minwax on sheets of beadboard wainscot. Whenever I poked my head out the front door, I saw Stephen vandalizing my lumber. He'd bend every third nail, and then gouge the wood with the hammer's claw trying to correct his mistake. Water would pool in those gouges and rot the boards, but he seemed to be enjoying himself. Through the closed windows, I could hear George and Stephen chatting and laughing as they worked. I'd learned to tolerate long hours of silence in the months I'd been up here, to appreciate it, even. But it warmed me to hear voices coming from my porch, though in the back of my mind I suspected they were laughing about me.

George and Stephen took until nightfall to get all the decking in place. When they were finished, we made our way down to the tiny pond I'd built by damming a spring behind my house. We shed our clothes and pushed off into the pond, each on his own gasping course through the exhilarating blackness of the water. "Oh, oh, oh, *God* it feels good," cried Stephen in a voice of such carnal gratitude that I pitied him. But it was glorious, the sky and the water of a single world-ending darkness, and we levitated in it until we were as numb as the dead.

Back at the house, I cooked up a gallon or so of beef stroganoff, seasoned as George liked it, with enough salt to make you weep. A run of warm nights was upon us, thanks to a benevolent spasm of the Gulf Stream, and we dined in comfort on the newly finished porch. Over the course of the meal, we put away three bottles of wine and half a handle of gin. By the time we'd moved on to brandied coffee to go with the blueberry pie George fetched from his place, the porch was humid with bonhomie.

"Look at this," Stephen said, stomping heavily on one of the new boards. "Man, I put this bastard here. Some satisfying shit. God bless 'em, there's 'tards I've worked with ten years and we still haven't gotten past chants and toning. But look—" he clogged again on the board. "Couple hours with a hammer. Got something you can stand on. I ought to do like you, Matty. Come out here. Build me a spot."

"Hell yeah, you should," I said. "By the way, how big's that wad you've got? What's it, twenty grand or something?"

"I guess," he said.

"Because look, check it out," I said. "Got a proposition for you. Listen, how many guys like us do you think there are out there? Ballpark figure."

"What's that mean, 'like us'?" Stephen said.

Then I began to spell out for him an idea I'd had on my mind lately, one that seemed rosiest after a wine-soaked dinner, when my gladness for the land, the stars, and the bullfrogs in my pond was at its maximum. I'd get to thinking about the paunchy hordes, nightly pacing carpeted apartments from Spokane to Chattanooga, desperate for an escape hatch. The plan was simple. I'd advertise one-acre plots in the back pages of men's magazines, put up a few spec cabins, handle the contracting myself, build a rifle range, some snowmobile trails, maybe a little saloon on the summit. In they'd swarm, a hill of pals, a couple of million in it for me, no sweat!

"I don't know," said Stephen, helping himself to another fat dollop of brandy.

"What don't you know?" I asked him. "That twenty grand, you're in for an even share. You'd be getting what the other investors are getting for fifty."

"What other investors?" Stephen asked.

"Ray Lawton," I lied. "Lawton, Ed Hayes, and Dan Welsh. My point is I could let you in, even just with that twenty. If you could kick that twenty in, I'd set you up with an even share."

"No, yeah, I like it," Stephen said. "It's just I need to be careful with that money. That's my whole savings and everything."

"Now goddammit, Stephen, I'm sorry but let me explain something to you. I *make* money, that's what I do," I said. "I take land, and a little bit of money, and then I turn it into lots of money. You follow me? That's what I do. What I'm asking is to basically just *hold* your cash for five months, max, and in return you'll be in on something that, guaranteed, will change your life."

"Can't do it," he said.

"Okay, Stephen, what can you do? Could you go ten? Ten grand for a full share? Could you put in ten?"

"Look, Matthew—"

"Five? Three? Two thousand?"

"Look—"

"How about eight hundred, Stephen, or two hundred? Would that work for you, or would two hundred dollars break the bank?"

"Two hundred's good," he said. "Put me down for that."

"Go fuck yourself," I said.

"Matthew, come on," said George. "Cool it. "

"I'm totally cool," I said.

"No, you're being a shit," said George. "And anyway, your dude ranch thing isn't worth all this gas. Never work."

"Why not?"

"First of all, the county'd never let you do it in the watershed. The ten-acre buffer—"

"I already talked to them about a variance," I said. "Wouldn't be—"

"And for another thing, I didn't move back here to get among a bunch of swinging dicks."

"Due respect, George, I'm not talking about your land."

"I know that, Matthew," George said. "What I'm saying is, you carve this hill up and sell it out to a bunch of cock-knockers from Boston, I'd say the chance is pretty good that some night in the off-season, I'd get a few too many beers in me and I'd get it in my head to come around with a few gallons of kerosene."

George was staring at me with an irritating, stagy intensity. "Forget the kerosene, George—a hammer and nails'll do it," I said, turning and sweeping a hand at the wooden dainties on my gable. "Just sneak up some night and do a little raid with your scrollsaw. Turn everybody's camp into a huge doily. That'll run them off pretty quick."

I laughed and went on laughing until my stomach muscles ached and tears beaded on my jaw. When I looked back at George, he had his lips set in a taut little dash. He was evidently vain about his scrollsaw work. I was still holding my pie plate, and without giving it much thought, I flung it into the woods. A crash followed, but no rewarding tinkle of shattered crockery.

"Ah, fuck," I said.

"What?" said Stephen.

"Nothing," I said. "My life is on fire."

Then I went into my cabin and got down on my mattress, and before long I was sleeping very well.

I woke a little after three, hungover and thirsty as a poisoned rat, but I lay paralyzed in superstition that staggering to the sink would banish sleep for good. My heart raced. I thought of my performance on the porch, then of a good thick noose creaking as it swung. I thought of Amanda, and my two ex-wives. I thought of my first car whose engine seized because I didn't change the timing belt at 100,000 miles. I thought of how two nights ago I'd lost thirty dollars to George in a cribbage game. I thought of how in the aftermath of my father's death, for reasons I couldn't recall, I stopped wearing underwear, and of a day in junior high when the cold rivet in a chair alerted me to a hole in the seat of my pants. I thought of everyone I owed money to, and everyone who owed me money. I thought of Stephen and me and the children we'd so far failed to produce, and how in the diminishing likelihood that I did find someone to smuggle my genetic material into, by the time our little one could tie his shoes, his father would be a florid fifty-year-old who would suck the innocence and joy from his child as greedily as a desert wanderer savaging a found orange.

I wanted the sun to rise, to make coffee, to get out in the woods with George and find his trophy buck, to get back to spinning the blanket of mindless incident that was doing an ever-poorer job of masking the pit of regrets I found myself peering into most sleepless nights. But the sun was slow in coming. The montage wore on until dawn, behind it the soothing music of the noose, *crik-creak, crik-creak, crik-creak*.

At the first bruised light in the eastern windows, I got up. The air in the cabin was dense with chill. Stephen wasn't on the spare mattress. I put on my boots, jeans, and a canvas parka, filled a thermos with hot coffee, and drove the quarter mile to George's house.

The lights were on at George's. George was doing sit-ups and Stephen was at the counter, minting waffles. A very cozy pair. The percolator was gasping away, making me feel forlorn with my plaid thermos.

"Hey, hey," I said.

"There he is," Stephen said. He explained that he'd slept on George's couch. They'd been up late at the backgammon board. He handed me a waffle, all cheer and magnanimity, on his way toward another social heist in the Dodi Clark vein.

"What do you say, George," I said, when the old man had finished his crunches. "Feel like going shooting?"

"I suppose," he said. He turned to Stephen. "Coming with, little brother?"

"I don't have a gun for him," I said.

"Got that .30-.30 he can use," George said.

"Why not?" said Stephen.

Our spot was on Pigeon Lake, twenty miles away, and you had to boat out to the evergreen cover on the far shore. After breakfast, we hooked George's skiff and trailer to my truck, and went jouncing into the white fog that blanketed the road.

We dropped the boat into the water. With Stephen in the bow, I took the stern. We went north, past realms of marsh grass and humps of pink granite, which, in the hard red light of morning, resembled corned beef hash.

George stopped the boat at a stretch of muddy beach where he said he'd had some luck before. We beached the skiff, and trudged into the tree line.

My calamitous hangover was worsening. I felt damp, unclean, and suicidal, and couldn't concentrate on anything except the vision of a cool, smooth-sheeted bed and iced seltzer water and bitters. It was Stephen who found the first heap of deer sign, in the shadow of a pine sapling stripped orange by a rutting buck. He was thrilled with his discovery, and he scooped the droppings into his palm and carried them over to George, who sniffed the dark pebbles so avidly that for a second I thought he might eat them.

"Pretty fresh," said Stephen, who hadn't been out hunting since the eleventh grade.

George said, "Looks like he winded us. Good eyes, Steve."

"Yeah, I just looked down and there it was," said Stephen.

George went off to perch in a nearby stand he knew about and left the two of us alone. Stephen and I sat at adjacent trees with our guns across our laps. A loon moaned. Squirrels rasped.

"So Matty, you kind of put a weird bug in my ear last night."

"That a fact?"

"Not that ridiculous bachelor-campus thing. But this place is fantastic. George said he sold it to you for ninety bucks an acre. Is that true?"

"Market price," I said.

"Astounding."

"You'd hate it out here. What about your work?"

"I'd just come out here for the summers when my gig at the school slacks off. I need to get out of Eugene. It's destroying me. I don't go out. I don't meet people. I sit in my apartment, composing this crap. I'm done. I could have spent the last two decades shooting heroin and the result would be the same, except I'd have some actual life behind me."

I lifted a haunch to let a long, low fart escape.

"Charming," said Stephen. "How about you sell me two acres? Then I've got twelve thousand to put into a cabin."

"I thought you had twenty."

"I *had* twenty-three," he said. "Now I've got about twelve."

"You spent it? On what?"

"Investments," he said. "Some went to this other thing."

"What other thing?"

Distractedly, he pinched a few hairs from his brow. I watched him put the hairs into his mouth and nibble them rapidly with his front teeth. "I've got a thing with this girl."

"Hey, fantastic," I said. "You should have brought her. What's her name?"

"Luda," Stephen said. "She's Hungarian."

"Far fucking out," I said. "What's a Hungarian chick doing in Eugene?"

"She's still in Budapest, actually," Stephen said. "We're trying to get the distance piece of it ironed out."

"How'd you meet her?"

"That's sort of the weird part. I met her online."

"Nothing wrong with that."

Stephen coughed and ripped another sprig from his brow. "Yeah, but, I mean, it was one of these things. To be totally honest, I met her on this site. Really, pretty tame stuff. I mean, she wasn't, like, fucking people or anything. It was just, you know, you pay a few bucks and you can chat with her, and she's got this video feed."

I looked at him to see if he was kidding. His face was grim and earnest. "You and like fifty other guys, right?" I said after a while.

"No, no. Well, yeah," Stephen said. "I mean, there is a group room or whatever, but if you want to, you can, like, do a private thing where it shuts out all the other subscribers and it's just the two of you. And over time, we started really getting to know each other. Every once in a while, I'd log in under a different name, you know, to see how she'd act with other guys, and almost every time she guessed it was me! A few months ago, I set up a camera so she could see me, too. A lot of the time, we don't even do anything sexual. We just talk. We just share our lives with each other, just stuff that happens in our day."

"But you pay her, Stephen," I said.

"Not always," he said. "Not anymore. She's not a whore. She's really just a normal woman. She's getting her degree in computer science. She's got a little son, Miska. I've met him, too. But, yeah, I try to help them when I can. I ought to show you some of her e-mails. She's very smart. A good writer. She's probably read more books than I have. It's not as weird as it sounds, Matty. We're talking about me maybe heading over there in the new year, and, who knows, just seeing where it goes from there."

"How much money have you given her?"

He took a breath and wiped his nose. "I haven't added it all up. Seven grand? I don't know."

I didn't say anything. My heart was beating hard. I wasn't sure why. Minutes went by and neither of us spoke. "So, Stephen—" I finally said. But right then, he sat up and cocked an ear. "Hush," he whispered, fussing with the rifle. When he managed to lever a round into the chamber, he raised the gun to his shoulder and drew a bead on the far side of the clearing.

"There's nothing there," I said.

He fired, and then charged off into the brush. I let him go. The shot summoned George. He jogged into the clearing just as Stephen was emerging from the scrub.

"Hit something, little brother?" George asked him.

"Guess not," he said.

"At least you got a look," he said. "Next time."

At noon, we climbed back in the boat. There wasn't another craft in sight, and the loveliness of the day was enough to knock you down, but it was lost on me. The picture of gaunt Stephen, panting at his monitor as his sweetheart pumped and squatted for him, her meter ticking merrily, was a final holocaust on my already ravaged mood. I couldn't salvage any of the low glee I've wrung in the past from my brother's misfortunes. Instead, I had a close, clammy feeling that my brother and I were turning into a very ugly pair of men. We'd traced such different routes, each disdaining the other as an emblem of what we were not, only to fetch up, together, in the far weird wastes of life.

The boat plowed on. No planes disturbed the sky. Swallows rioted above the calm green lid of the lake. Birch trees gleamed like filaments among the evergreens. I was dead to it, though I did take a kind of comfort in the fact that all of this beauty was out here, persisting like mad, whether you hearkened to it or not.

George steered us to another stretch of lakefront woods, and I went and hunkered alone in a blueberry copse. My hands were cold, and my thighs and toes were cold, and my cabin would be cold when I got back, and to take a hot shower I would have to heat a kettle on the stove and pour the water into the rubber bladder hanging over my bathtub. The shower in my house in Charleston was a state-of-the-art five-nozzler that simultaneously blasted your face, breasts, and crotch. The fun was quickly going out of this, not just the day, but the whole bit up here, the backbreaking construction hassles, and this bullshit, too—crouching in a wet shrub, masquerading as a rugged hardscrabbler just to maintain the affection of an aged drunk.

Off to my right, I could hear George coughing a wet, complicated, old-man's cough, loud enough to send even the deafest herd galloping for the hills. I leaned out of my bush to scowl at him. He sat swabbing his pitted scarlet nose with a hard green hankie, and disgust and panic overwhelmed me. Where was I? Three months of night were coming on! Stuck in a six-hundred-square-foot crate! I'd probably look worse than the old man when the days got long again! Sell the truck! Sell the cabin! Get a Winnebago! Drive it where?

The sun was sinking when George called out, and the three of us slogged back to the soggy delta where we'd tied the boat.

Glancing down the beach, I spotted something that I thought at first might be a driftwood sculpture, but which sharpened under my stare into the brown serrations of a moose's rack. It was standing in the shallows, its head bent to drink. Well over three hundred yards, and the moose was downwind, probably getting ready to bolt in a second. I was tired. I raised my gun. George started bitching at me. "Goddammit, Matthew, no, it's too far." I didn't give a shit. I fired twice.

The moose's forelegs crumpled beneath it, and an instant later I saw the animal's head jerk as the sound of the shot reached him. The moose tried to struggle upright but fell again. The effect was of a very old person trying to pitch a heavy tent. It tried to stand, and fell, and tried, and fell, and then quit its strivings.

We gazed at the creature piled up down there. Finally, George turned to me, gawping and shaking his head. "That, my friend," he said, "has got to be the goddamnedest piece of marksmanship I've ever seen."

Stephen laughed. "Unreal," he said. He moved to hug me, but he was nervous about my rifle, and he just kind of groped my elbow in an awkward way.

The moose had collapsed in a foot of icy water and had to be dragged onto firm ground before it could be dressed. I waded out to where it lay and Stephen plunged along after me.

We had to crouch and soak ourselves to get the rope under its chest. The other end we looped around a hemlock on the bank, and then tied the rope to the stern of the skiff, using the tree as a makeshift pulley. George gunned the outboard, and Stephen and I stood calf-deep in the shallows heaving on the line. By the time we'd gotten the moose to shore, our palms were torn and puckered, and our boots were full of water.

With George's hunting knife, I bled the moose from the throat, and then made a slit from the bottom of the ribcage to the jaw, revealing the gullet and a pale, corrugated column of windpipe. The scent was powerful. It brought to mind the dark, briny smell that seemed always to hang around my mother in summertime when I was a child.

George was in a rapture, giddy at how I'd put us both in six months of meat with my preposterous shot. "We'll winter well on this," he kept saying. He took the knife from me and gingerly opened the moose's belly, careful not to puncture the intestines or the sack of his stomach. He dragged out the organs, setting aside the liver, the kidneys, and the pancreas. One strange hitch was the hide, which was hellish to remove. To get it loose, Stephen and I had to take turns, bracing our boots against the moose's spine, pulling at the hide while George slashed away at the fascia and connective tissues. I saw Stephen's throat buck nauseously every now and again, yet he wanted to have a part in dressing it, and I was proud of him for that. He took up the game saw and cut off a shoulder and a ham. We had to lift the legs like pallbearers to get them to the boat. Blood ran from the meat and down my shirt with hideous, vital warmth.

The skiff sat low under the weight of our haul. The most substantial ballast of our crew, I sat in the stern and ran the kicker so the bow wouldn't swamp. Stephen sat on the cross bench, our knees nearly touching. We puttered out, a potent blue vapor bubbling up from the propeller. Clearing the shallows, I opened the throttle, and the craft bullied its way through the low swells, a fat white fluke churning up behind us. We skimmed out while the sun sank behind the dark spruce spires in the west. The gridded rubber handle of the Evinrude thrummed in my palm. The wind dried the fluids on my cheeks, and tossed Stephen's hair in a sparse frenzy. With the carcass receding behind us, it seemed I'd also escaped the blackness that had plagued me since Stephen's arrival. The return of George's expansiveness, the grueling ordeal of the butchery, the exhaustion in my limbs, the satisfaction in having made an unreasonably good shot that would feed my friend and me until the snow melted—it was glorious. I could feel absolution spread across the junk-pit of my troubles as smoothly and securely as a motorized tarp slides across a swimming pool.

And Stephen felt it, too, or something anyway. The old unarmored smile I knew from childhood brightened his haunted face, a tidy, compact bow of lip and tooth, alongside which I always looked dour and shabby in the family photographs. There's no point in trying to describe the love I can still feel for my brother when he looks at me this way, when he's stopped tallying his resentments against me and he's briefly left off hating himself for failing to hit the big time as the next John Tesh. Ours isn't the kind of brotherhood I would wish on other men, but we are blessed with a single, simple gift: in these rare moments of happiness, we can share joy as passionately and single-mindedly as we do hatred. As we skimmed across the dimming lake, I could see how much it pleased him to see me at ease, to have his happiness magnified in my face and reflected back at him. No one said anything. This was love for us, or the best that love could do. I brought the boat in wide around the isthmus guarding the cove, letting the wake push us through the shallows to the launch where my sturdy blue truck was waiting for us.

With the truck loaded, and the skiff rinsed clean, we rode back to the mountain. It was past dinnertime when we reached my place. Our stomachs were yowling.

I asked George and Stephen if they wouldn't mind getting started butchering the meat while I put a few steaks on the grill. George said that before he did any more work he was going to need to sit in a dry chair for a little while and drink two beers. He and Stephen sat and drank and I waded into the bed of my pickup, which was heaped nearly flush with meat. It was disgusting work rummaging in there. George came over and pointed out the short ribs and told me how to hack out the tenderloin, a tapered log of flesh that looked like a peeled boa constrictor. I held it up. George raised his can in tribute. "Now there's a pretty, pretty thing," he said.

I carried the loin to the porch and cut it into steaks two inches thick, which I patted with kosher salt and coarse pepper. I got the briquettes going while George and Stephen blocked out the meat on a plywood-and-sawhorse table in the headlights of my truck.

When the coals had grayed over, I dropped the steaks onto the grill. After ten minutes, they were still good and pink in the center, and I plated them with yellow rice. Then I opened up a bottle of burgundy I'd been saving and poured three glasses. I was about to call the boys to the porch when I saw that something had caused George to halt his labors. A grimace soured his features. He sniffed at his sleeve, then his knife, then the mound of meat in front of him. He winced, took a second careful whiff and recoiled.

"Oh good Christ, it's turning," he said. With an urgent stride, he made for the truck and sprang onto the tailgate, taking up pieces of our kill and putting them to his face. "Son of a bitch," he said, "It's going off, all of it. Contaminated. It's something deep in the meat."

I walked over. I sniffed at the ham he'd been working on. It was true, there was a slight pungency to it, a diarrheal tang gathering in the air, but only faintly. If the intestines had leaked a little, it certainly wasn't any reason to toss thousands of dollars' worth of meat. And anyway, I had no idea how moose flesh was supposed to smell.

"It's just a little gamy," I said. "That's why they call it game."

Stephen smelled his hands. "George is right. It's spoiled. *Gah*."

"Not possible," I said. "This thing was breathing three hours ago. There's nothing wrong with it."

"It was sick," said George. "That thing was dying on its feet when you shot it."

"Bullshit," I said.

"Contaminated, I promise you," said George. "I should have known it when the skin hung on there like it did. He was bloating up with something, just barely holding on. The second he died, and turned that infection loose, it just started going wild."

Stephen looked at the meat strewn across the table, and at the three of us standing there. Then he began to laugh. I went to the porch and bent over a steaming steak. It smelled fine. I rubbed the salt crust and licked at the juice from my thumb.

"There's nothing wrong with it," I said.

I cut off a dripping pink cube and touched it to my tongue. Stephen was still laughing.

"You're a fucking star, Matty," he said, breathless. "All the beasts in the forest, and you mow down a leper moose. God, that smell. Don't touch that shit, man. Call in a hazmat team."

"There's not a goddamned thing wrong with this meat," I said.

"Poison," said George.

The wind gusted suddenly. A branch fell in the woods. A squad of leaves scurried past my boots and settled against the door. Then the night went still again. I turned back to my plate and slipped the fork into my mouth.

A NOTE ON *MR. SQUISHY*

"M R. SQUISHY" ORIGINALLY ran in *McSweeney's* 5, under the pseudonym Elizabeth Klemm. When David Foster Wallace sent it to me, he asked that this pen name be used, and for the life of me now I can't remember why. I didn't even question it, really, because we had already published a bunch of stuff in the journal under other authors' pseudonyms, and I knew there are plenty of good reasons to occasionally write under a different name. We wanted of course to publish it under his given name, because the story was brilliant and was the longest DFW story we ever got hold of. We were so proud to publish it, but we respected his wishes.

This was the first and only piece of his we ever published that I attempted to edit. And it was a pretty basic thing I tried to do. His work, as everyone knows, was very difficult to edit, because he made no mistakes, really, and could outthink and outlast anyone when it came to debating changes to his work. It wasn't that he was combative, but more that he had thought pretty much everything through, and had good reasons for every comma.

Which made it all the more surprising that I got him to break up a few paragraphs. I didn't think I had a right to ask, but, at the same time, I wanted people to read "Mr. Squishy," and I felt that some of the paragraphs were both very long and possessing some pretty comfortable places to start anew. So I wrote a note explaining all this, with a copy of the story indicating about 10 or 15 places we could start new paragraphs.

I didn't expect him to even entertain the notion, but he did. What became relatively clear in our exchange was that he hadn't really ever considered breaking up these or any long paragraphs. It was as if he were visiting the notion—sometimes exceedingly long paragraphs can impede one's enjoyment of a story—for the first time. He was that kind of genius, whose understanding of the workings of his own fiction was, I think, largely separate from ideas of audience.

But he went with the changes. There's room for debate whether or not they were best for the story.

We published "Mr. Squishy" with the fake name, but I don't think we fooled anyone for very long. Dave had at least four distinct styles, maybe more, but "Mr. Squishy" was written in his most recognizable. (Okay, acknowledging that this is ill-thought-out and incomplete, a stab at his four most clear-cut styles would be: (1) the plainspoken and fluid journalistic style demonstrated in his McCain piece [this is the style that goes down the easiest, and where his passion and opinions are most unguarded]; (2) the ramped-up journalistic style of the cruise-ship piece and similar pieces of epic observation [these pieces have the more elaborate footnotes and digressions]; (3) the humor-isolating and accessible style of *Brief Interviews* and the "Porousness of Certain Borders" stories; and (4) the dense, discursive, and insanely detailed style of his novels and certain stories.)

"Mr. Squishy" was probably closer to *Infinite Jest* in style than any other short story he wrote, so I wondered aloud to him whether anyone would really buy that it was written by someone named Elizabeth Klemm. And even if they did buy it, wouldn't they accuse Ms. Klemm of aping DFW's style? We both sort of laughed it off and agreed to let the whole thing play out.

About a day after shipping the issue, we started getting letters and e-mails, even phone calls to the office, demanding to know whether Wallace was the author of this incredibly Wallace-like story. And the jig was up shortly thereafter, because he went on a book tour, and everyone was asking him about it, and I think he felt bad about fibbing about the authorship issue. At the same time, a few of us *McSweeney's* people were doing events, too, and people kept asking. It was killing us, fibbing about it to very nice (though very intense) DFW fans. We'd perfected a non-answer answer, which was something like "Well, it came through the mail, and the byline on it was Elizabeth Klemm." Usually, the fans would walk away, feeling that, with this non-answer answer, their suspicions had been confirmed.

Not too long after, Dave owned up to the story, and we did, too. He was too honest to fib, too recognizable to hide, too singular to fool anyone. —DAVE EGGERS

MR. SQUISHY

by DAVID FOSTER WALLACE

(fiction from Issue 5)

THE FOCUS GROUP was reconvened in another of Reesemeyer Shannon Belt's 19th-floor conference rooms. Each member returned his Individual Response Profile packets to the facilitator, who thanked each in turn. The long conference table was equipped with leather executive swivel chairs; there was no assigned seating. Bottled spring water, soft drinks, and caffeinated beverages were made available to those who thought they might want them. The exterior wall of the conference room was a thick tinted window with a broad high altitude view of points NE, creating a spacious, attractive, and more or less natural-lit environment that was welcome after the bland fluorescent enclosure of the testing cubicles. One or two members of the Focus Group unconsciously loosened their neckties as they settled into the comfortable chairs.

There were more samples of the product arranged on a tray at the conference table's center.

This facilitator, just like the one who'd led the large Product Test and

Initial Response assembly earlier that morning before all the members of the different Focus Groups had been separated into individual soundproof cubicles to complete their Individual Response Profiles, held degrees in both Descriptive Statistics and Behavioral Psychology and was employed by Team Δy, a cutting-edge market research firm that Reesemeyer Shannon Belt Advertising had begun using almost exclusively in recent years. This Focus Group's facilitator was a stout, palely freckled man with an archaic haircut and a warm if somewhat nervous and irreverent manner. On the wall next to the door behind him was a presentation whiteboard with several Dry Erase markers in its recessed sill.

The facilitator played idly with the edges of the IRP forms in his folder until all the men had seated themselves and gotten comfortable. Then he said: 'Right, so thanks again for your part in this, which as I'm pretty sure Mr. Mounce told you this morning is always an important part of deciding what new products get made available to consumers versus those that don't.' The facilitator had a graceful, practiced way of panning his gaze back and forth to make sure he addressed the entire table, a skill that was slightly at odds with the bashful, fidgety presentation of his body as he spoke before the assembled men. The fourteen members of the Focus Group, all male and several with beverages before them, engaged in the slight gestures and expressions of men around a conference table who are less than 100% sure what is going to be expected of them. The conference room was very different in appearance and feel from the sterile, almost lab-like auditorium in which the PT/IR had been held an hour earlier. The facilitator, who did have the customary pocket-protector with three different colored pens in it, wore a crisp striped dress shirt and wool tie and cocoa-brown slacks, but no jacket or sportcoat. His shirtsleeves were not rolled up. His smile had a slight wincing quality, several members observed, as of some vague diffuse apology. Attached to the breast pocket on the same side of his shirt as his nametag was also a large pin or button emblazoned with the familiar Mister Squishy brand icon, which was a plump and childlike cartoon face of indeterminate ethnicity with its eyes squeezed partly shut in an expression that somehow connoted delight, satiation, and rapacious desire all at the same time. The icon communicated the sort of innocuous facial affect that was almost impossible not to smile back at or feel positive about in some way, and it had been commissioned and introduced by one of Reesemeyer Shannon Belt's senior creative people over a decade ago, when the regional Mister Squishy Company had come under national corporate ownership and had rapidly expanded and diversified from extra-soft sandwich breads and buns into sweet rolls and flavored doughnuts and snack cakes and soft confections of nearly every conceivable kind; and without any particular messages or associations anyone in Demographics could ever produce data to quantify or get a handle on, the crude line-drawn face had become one of the most popular, recognizable, and demonstrably successful brand icons in American advertising.

Traffic was brisk on the street far below, and also trade.

It was, however, not the Mister Squishy brand icon that concerned the carefully chosen and vetted Focus Groups on this bright cold November day in 1995. Under third-phase Focus Testing was a new and high-concept chocolate-intensive Mister Squishy–brand snack cake designed primarily for individual sale in convenience stores, with 12-pack boxes to be placed in upmarket food-retail outlets first in the Midwest and upper East Coast and then, if the test-market data bore out Mister Squishy's parent company's hopes, nationwide.

Twenty-seven of the snack cakes were piled in a pyramidic display on a large rotating silver tray in the center of the conference table. Each was wrapped in the airtight transpolymer material that looked like paper but tore like thin plastic, the same retail packaging that nearly all U.S. confections had deployed since M&M Mars pioneered the composite and used it to help launch the innovative MilkyWay Dark line in the mid-1980s. This new product's wrap had the same distinctive Mister Squishy navy-and-white design scheme, but here the Mister Squishy icon appeared with its eyes and mouth rounded in cartoon alarm behind a series of microtextured black lines that appeared to be the bars of a jail cell, around two of which lines or bars the icon's plump and dough-colored fingers were curled in the universal position of inmates everywhere. The dark and exceptionally dense and moist-looking snack cakes inside the packaging were *Felonies!*®, a risky and multivalent trade name meant both to connote and to parody the modern health-conscious consumer's sense of vice/indulgence/transgression/sin vis à vis the consumption of a high-calorie corporate snack. The name's association-matrix included as well the suggestion of adulthood and adult autonomy: in its real-world rejection of the highly cute, cartoonish, 'n'- and 'oo'-intensive names of so many other snack cakes, the product tag

'Felony!' was designed and tested primarily for its appeal to the 18–41 Male demographic, the single most prized and fictile demotarget in high-end marketing. Only two of the Focus Group's members were over 40, and their profiles had been vetted not once but twice by Scott R. Laleman's Technical Processing team during the demographic/behavioral voir dire for which Team Δy Focus Group data was so justly prized.

Inspired, according to agency rumor, by an RSB Creative Director's epiphanic encounter with something billed as Death By Chocolate in a Near-North cafe, *Felonies!* were all-chocolate, filling and icing and cake as well, and all-'real' chocolate instead of the hydrogenated cocoa and high-F corn syrup, the *Felony!* conceived thus less as a variant on rivals' Zingers, Ding Dongs, HoHos and Choc-o-Diles than as a radical upscaling and re-visioning of same. A domed cylinder of flourless maltilol-flavored sponge cake covered entirely in 2.4mm of a high-lecithin chocolate frosting manufactured with trace amounts of butter, cocoa butter, baker's choco-late, chocolate liquor, vanilla extract, dextrose, and sorbitol (a relatively high-cost frosting, and one whose butter-redundancies alone required heroic innovations in production systems and engineering—an entire production line had had to be remachined and the line-workers retrained and produc-tion and quality-assurance quotas recalculated more or less from scratch), which high-end frosting was then also injected by high-pressure confec-tionery needle into the 26 x 13mm hollow ellipse in each *Felony!*'s center (a center which in for example Hostess Inc.'s products was packed with what amounted to a sweetened whipped lard), resulting in double doses of an ultrarich and near-restaurant-grade frosting whose central pocket—given that the thin coat of outer frosting's exposure to the air caused it to assume traditional icing's hard-yet-deliquescent marzipan character—seemed even richer, denser, sweeter, and more felonious than the exterior icing, icing that in most rivals' field-tests' IRPs and GRDS was declared consumers' favorite parts (Hostess's lead agency Chiat/Day I.B.'s 1991–2 double-blind Behavior series' videotapes recorded over 45% of younger consumers actually peeling off HoHos' matte icing in great dry flakes and eating it solo, leaving the low-end cake itself to sit ossifying on their tables' Lazy Susans, film clips of which had reportedly been part of RSB's initial pitch to Mister Squishy's parent company's Subsidiary Product Development boys).

In an unconventional move, some of this quote-unquote 'Full-Access' information re ingredients, production innovations, and even demotargeting was being relayed to the Focus Group by the facilitator, who used a Dry Erase marker to sketch a diagram of Mister Squishy's snack-cake production sequence and the complex adjustments required by *Felonies!* at select points along the automated line. The relevant information was relayed in a skillfully orchestrated QA period, with many of the specified questions supplied by the two 'members' of the Targeted Focus Group who were in fact not civilian consumers but employees of Team Δy assigned to help orchestrate the unconventionally informative QA and to observe the deliberations of the other twelve men when the facilitator had left the room, taking care not to influence the Focus Group's arguments or verdicts but later adding personal observations and impressions that would help round and flesh out the data provided by the Group Response Data Summary and the digital videotape supplied by what appeared to be a large smoke detector in the conference room's northwest corner, whose lens and parabolic mike, while mobile and state-of-the-art, failed to catch certain subtle nuances in individual affect and low-volume interchanges between adjoining members. One of the UAFs,* a slim young man with waxy blond hair and a complexion whose redness appeared more abraded than ruddy or hale, had been allowed by Team Δy's UAF Coordinator to cultivate an eccentric and (to most Focus Group members) irritating set of personal mannerisms whose very conspicuousness served to disguise his professional identity: he had small squeeze bottles of both contact lens lubricant and intranasal saline before him on the table, and not only took notes on the facilitator's presentation but did so with a Magic Marker that squeaked loudly and had ink you could smell, and whenever he asked one of his assigned 'Full-Access' questions he did not tentatively raise his hand or clear his throat as other UAFs were wont but rather would just tersely bark out, 'Question:', as in: 'Question: is it possible to be more specific about what "Natural and Artificial Flavors" means, and is there any substantive difference between what it really means and what the average consumer is expected to understand it to mean,' without any sort of interrogative lilt or expression, his brow furrowed and rimless glasses very askew.

---

* Team Δy's term for their Focus Groups' moles was 'Unintroduced Assistant Facilitators,' whose identities were theoretically unknown to the facilitators in pure Double-Blinds, though in practice they were usually child's play to spot.

As any decent small-set univariable probability distribution would predict, not all members of the Focus Group were listening closely to the facilitator's explanation of what Mister Squishy and Team Δy hoped to achieve by leaving the Focus Group alone very shortly *in camera* to compare the results of their Individual Response Profiles and speak openly and without interference amongst themselves and attempt to come as close as possible to a unanimous univocal Group Response Data Summary of the product along sixteen different radial Preference and Satisfaction axes. A certain amount of this inattention was factored into the matrices of what the facilitator had been informed was the actual test underway on today's 19th floor. This secondary (or 'Nested') test sought quantifiable data on quote-unquote 'Full-Access' manufacturing and marketing information's effects on Targeted Focus Groups' perceptions of both the product and its corporate producer; it was a double-blind series, designed to be replicated along three different variable grids with random TFGs throughout the next two fiscal quarters, and sponsored by parties whose identities were being withheld from the facilitators as part (apparently) of the Nested test's conditions.

Three of the Focus Group's members were staring absently out the large tinted window that gave on a delicately muted sepia view of the street's north side's skyscrapers and beyond and between these different bits of the northeast Loop and harbor and several feet of severely foreshortened Lake. Two of these members were very young men at the extreme left of the demotarget's x axis who sat slumped in their tilted swivels in attitudes of either reverie or stylized indifference; the third was feeling absently at his upper lip's davit.

The Focus Group facilitator, trained by the requirements of what seemed to have turned out to be his profession to behave as though he were interacting in a lively and spontaneous way while actually remaining inwardly detached and almost clinically observant, possessed also a natural eye for behavioral details that often revealed tiny gems of statistical relevance amid the rough raw surfeit of random fact. Little things sometimes made a difference. The facilitator's name was Terry Schmidt and he was 34 years old, a Virgo. Eleven of the Focus Group's fourteen men wore wristwatches, of which roughly one-third were expensive and/or foreign. A twelfth, by far the TFG's oldest member, had the platinum fob of a quality pocketwatch running diagonally left–right across his vest and a big pink face and the permanent look in his eyes of someone older who had many grandchildren and spent so much time looking at them that the benevolent expression becomes almost ingrained. Schmidt's own grandfather had lived in a north Florida retirement community where he sat with a plaid blanket on his lap and coughed constantly both times Schmidt had ever been in his presence, addressing him only as 'boy.' Precisely 50% of the room's men wore coats and ties or had suitcoats or blazers hanging from the back of their chair, three of which coats were part of an actual three-piece business wardrobe; another three men wore combinations of knit shirts, slacks, and various crew- and turtleneck sweaters classifiable as Business Casual. Schmidt lived alone in a condominium he had recently refinanced. The remaining four men wore bluejeans and sweatshirts with the logo of either a university or the garment's manufacturer; one was the Nike *Swoosh* icon that to Schmidt always looked vaguely Arabic; three of the four men in conspicuously casual/ sloppy attire were the Focus Group's youngest members, two of whom were among the three making rather a show of not paying attention. Team Δy favored a loose demographic grid. Two of the three youngest men were slightly under 21. All three of the youngest men sat back on their tailbones with their legs uncrossed and their hands spread out over their thighs and their faces arranged in the mildly sullen expressions of consumers who have never once questioned their entitlement to satisfaction or meaning. Schmidt's initial undergraduate concentration had been in Statistical Chemistry; he still enjoyed the clinical precision of a lab. Less than 50% of the room's total footwear involved laces; one man in a knit shirt had small brass zippers up the sides of low-cut boots shined to a distracting gleam. Unlike Schmidt's and Mounce's, Darlene Lilley's marketing background was in computer-aided design; she'd come into Research because she said she'd discovered she was more a people person at heart. There were four pairs of eyeglasses in the room, although one of these pairs were sunglasses and possibly not prescription, another with heavy black frames that gave their wearer's face an earnest aspect above his dark turtleneck sweater. There were two mustaches and one probable goatee; a stocky man in his late twenties had a sort of sparse, mossy beard. It was indeterminable whether this man was just starting to grow a beard or whether he was the sort of person whose beard simply looked this way. Among the youngest men, it was obvious which were sincerely in need of a shave and which were just affecting an unshaved look. Two members had the distinctive blink-patterns of men wearing contact lenses in the conference room's astringent air. Five of the room's men were more than 10% overweight, Terry Schmidt himself excluded. His highschool P.E. teacher had once referred to Terry Schmidt in front of his peers as 'The Crisco Kid,' which he had then laughingly said meant 'fat in the can.' Schmidt's own father, a decorated combat veteran, had recently retired from a company that sold seed, phosphate fertilizer, and broad-spectrum herbicides in downstate Galesburg. The affectedly eccentric UAF was asking the men on either side of him, one of whom was Hispanic, whether they'd care for a chewable Vitamin C tablet. The Mister Squishy icon reappeared twice in the conference room as the stylized finials of two fine tan ceramic lamps on side tables at either end of the windowless interior wall. There were two African American males in the Targeted Focus Group, one over 30, the one under 30 with a shaved head. Three of the men had hair classifiable as brown, two gray or salt/pepper, another three black (excluding the African Americans and the Group's one oriental, whose nametag and overwhelming cheekbones suggested either Laos or the Socialist Republic of Vietnam—for complex but solid statistical reasons, Scott Laleman's team's Profile grids specified distributions for ethnicity but not national origins); three could be called blond or fair-haired. These distributions included the UAFs, and Schmidt had a reasonably good idea who this Group's other UAF was. Rarely did RSB Focus Groups include representatives of the very pale or freckled red-haired physical type, though Foote, Cone & Belding and D.D.B. Needham both made regular use of such types because of certain data suggesting meaningful connections between melanin quotients and continuous probability distributions of income and preference on the U.S. East Coast, where over 70% of upmarket products tested. Some of the trendy 'hypergeometric' techniques on which these data were based had been called into question by more traditional demographic statisticians, however.

By industry-wide convention, Focus Group members received a per diem equal to exactly 300% of what they would receive for jury duty in the state where they resided. The reasoning behind this equation was so old and tradition-bound that no one of Terry Schmidt's generation knew its origin. It was, for senior test-marketers, both an in-joke and a plausible extension of verified attitudes about civic duty and elective consumption, respectively. The Hispanic man to the off-blond UAF's left, who did not wear a wrist-watch, had evidence of large tattoos on his upper arms through the fabric of his dress shirt, which fabric the natural lighting's slightly tinted hue rendered partly translucent. He was also one of the men with mustaches, and his nametag identified him as NORBERTO, the first such Norberto to appear in any of the over 845 Focus Groups Schmidt had led so far in his career as a statistical market researcher for Team Δy. Schmidt kept his own private records of statistical correlations between product, client-agency, and certain variables in Focus Groups' constituents and procedures. These were run through various basic discriminant-analysis programs on his Apple-brand computer at home and the results collected in three-ring binders which he labeled and stored on gray steel shelves in the utility room of his condominium. The central problem of descriptive statistics was discrim-inating between what made a difference and what did not. The fact that Scott R. Laleman now both vetted Focus Groups and helped design them was just one more sign that his star was ascending at Team Δy. The other rising star was A. Ronald Mounce, whose background was also in Technical Processing. 'Question.' 'Question:' 'Comment:' One man with a kind of long chinless face wished to know what *Felonies!*' retail price was going to be and either didn't understand or disliked Terry Schmidt's explanation that retail pricing was outside the purview of the Group's focus today and was in fact the responsibility of a whole different RSB research vendor. The reasoning behind the separation of price from consumer-satisfaction grids was technical and parametric and was not included in the putative 'Full-Access' information Schmidt was authorized to share with the Focus Group under the terms of the study. There was one obvious hairweave in the room, as well as two victims of untreated Male Pattern Baldness, both of whom, either interestingly or by coincidence, were among the group's four blue-eyed members.

When Schmidt thought of Scott Laleman, with his all-season tan and sunglasses pushed musslessly up on his pale hair's crown, it was as something with the mindless malevolence of a carnivorous eel or skate, something that hunted on autopilot at terrible depths. The African American man whose head was unshaved sat with the rigidity of someone who has back problems and understands the dignity with which he bears them as an essential part of his character; the other wore sunglasses indoors in such a way as to make some sort of statement about himself. There was no way of knowing whether it was a general statement or one specific to this situation. Scott Laleman was only

27 and had come on board at Team Δy three years after Darlene Lilley and two-and-a-half years after Schmidt himself, who had helped Darlene train Laleman to run chi-square and t distributions on raw phone-survey data and had taken surprising satisfaction in watching the boy's eyes glaze and tan go sallow under the fluorescent banklights of Δy's data room, until one day Schmidt had needed to see Alan Britton personally about something and had knocked and come in and Laleman was sitting in the office's recliner across the room and he and Britton were both smoking very large cigars and laughing.

The figure who began his climb up the building's steadily increscent north facet just before 11:00 a.m. was outfitted in tight windproof Lycra® leggings and a snug hooded GoreTex® sweatshirt w/ fiber-lined hood up and tied tight and what appeared to be mountaineering or rock-climbing boots except that instead of crampons or spikes there were suction cups lining the instep of both boots. Attached to both palms and wrists' insides were suction cups the size of a plumber's helper; the cups' color was the same shrill orange as hunting jackets and road crews' hard hats. The Lycra pants' color scheme was one navy-blue leg and one white leg. The sweatshirt and hood were blue with white piping. The mountaineering boots were an emphatic black. The figure moved with numerous moist popping suction-noises up the display window of the Gap, a large retail clothier, then pulled himself up and over onto the narrow ledge at the base of the 2nd-floor window, rose complexly to his feet, affixed his cups, and commenced moving up the glass, which gave onto the Gap's second floor but had no promotional items displayed in it. The figure appeared lithe and expert. His manner of climbing appeared almost more reptilian than mammalian, you'd have to say. He was halfway up the window of a management consulting firm on the fifth floor when a small crowd of passersby began to gather on the sidewalk below. Winds at ground level were moderate.

In the conference room, the north window's tint made the half-cloudy sky appear raw and the froth of the waves on the distant windblown lake look dark; it brindled the sides of the other tall buildings in view as well, which were all partly in one another's shadow. Fully seven of the Focus Group's men had small remains of *Felonies!* either on their shirtfront or hanging from the hair on one side of their mustache or at the inner corner of their mouth or in the small crease between the fingernail of their dominant hand and that nail's surrounding skin. Two of the men wore no socks; both these men's shoes were unlaced leather; only one pair had a tassel. One of the youngest men's denim bellbottoms were so terrifically long that even with his legs out splayed and both knees joggling his sock-status was unclear. One of the older men wore black silk or rayon socks with small red lozenges on them. Another of the older men had a mean little slit of a mouth, another a face far too leathery and seamed for his demographic status. As was often the case, the youngest men's faces appeared not quite yet fully or humanly formed, with the clean generic quality of items still under construction. Terry Schmidt sometimes sketched his own face's outlines in caricature form as he spoke on the phone or waited for software programs to run. One man had a pear-shaped head, another a kite-shaped face; the room's second-oldest man had cropped gray hair and an overdeveloped upper lip that gave his face a simian aspect. The men's demoprofiles and initial Systat scores were in Schmidt's valise on the carpet next to the whiteboard; he also had an over-shoulder bag he kept in his cubicle. I was one of the men in this room, the only one wearing a wristwatch who never once glanced at it. What looked just like glasses were not. I was totally and complexly wired. A small LCD at the bottom of my right scope ran both Real Time and Mission Time. My brief script for the GRDS caucus had been memorized in toto but a redundant copy on a laminated card was just inside my sweater's sleeve, held in place with small tabs I could release by depressing one of the buttons on my watch, which was not a watch at all. There was also the emetic prosthesis. The cakes, of which I had already made a show of eating three, were so sweet they made your teeth hurt. Terry Schmidt himself was hypoglycemic and could eat only confections prepared with fructose, aspartame, or very small amounts of $C_6H_8(OH)_6$, and sometimes he found himself looking at trays of the product with the expression of a poor child at a toystore's window.

Down the hall past the MROP[*] Division's green room, in another RSB conference room whose window faced NE, Darlene Lilley was leading twelve consumers and two UAFs into the GRDS phase of Focused Response without any structured QA or 'Full-Access' background; neither Schmidt nor Darlene had been told which of today's TFGs represented the Nested test's Control, though it was pretty obvious. You had to work on the building's upper floors for some time before you noticed the very slight sway

---

[*] = Market Research Oversight and Planning

with which the building's structural design accommodated the winds off the Lake. 'Question: just what is polysorbate 80.' Schmidt was reasonably certain that none of the Focus Group felt the sway. It was not pronounced enough to cause any movement in the coffee in any of the iconized mugs on the table that Schmidt, standing and rotating the Dry Erase marker in his hand in an absent way that connoted both informality and a slight humanizing nervousness in front of groups, could see down into. The conference table was heavy pine with lemonwood inlays and a thick coat of polyurethane, and without the window's sepia tint there would be blinding pockets of reflected sun that changed angle as one's own angle with respect to the sun and table changed. Schmidt would also have had to watch dust and tiny clothing fibers swirl in columns of direct sunlight and fall very gently onto everyone's heads and upper bodies, which occurred in even the cleanest conference rooms and was one of Schmidt's least favorite things about the untinted interiors of certain other agencies' conference rooms around the metropolitan area. Sometimes when waiting or on Hold on the phone Schmidt would put his finger inside his mouth and hold it there for no good reason he could ever ascertain. Darlene N. Lilley, who was married and the mother of a large-headed toddler whose photograph adorned her desk and hutch at Team Δy, had, three fiscal quarters past, been subjected to sexual advances by one of the four Senior Research Directors who liaisoned between the Field and Technical Processing teams and the upper echelons of Team Δy under Alan Britton, advances and duress more than sufficient for legal action in Schmidt's and most of the rest of their Field Team's opinions, which advances she had been able to deflect and defuse in an enormously skillful manner without raising the sort of hue and cry that could divide a firm along gender or political lines, and things had been allowed to cool down and blow over to such an extent that Darlene Lilley, Schmidt, and the three other members of their Field Team all now still enjoyed a good working relationship with this dusky and pungent older Senior Research Director, who was now in fact overseeing Field research on the Mister Squishy–RSB project, and Terry Schmidt was personally in awe of the self-possession and interpersonal savvy Darlene had displayed throughout the whole tense period, an awe tinged with an unwilled element of romantic attraction, and it is true that Schmidt at night in his condominium sometimes without feeling as if he could help himself masturbated to thoughts of having moist slapping semiviolent intercourse with Darlene Lilley on one of the ponderous blinding conference tables of the firms they conducted statistical market research for, and this was a tertiary cause of what practicing social psychologists would call his 'Manual Adjusting Mechanism' with the Dry Erase marker as he used a modulated tone of off-the-record confidence to tell the Focus Group about some of the more dramatic travails Reesemeyer Shannon Belt had had with establishing the product's brand-identity and coming up with the test name *Felony!*, all the while imagining in a more autonomic part of his brain Darlene delivering nothing but the standard minimal pre-GRDS instructions for her own Focus Group as she stood in her dark Hanes hosiery and the burgundy high heels she kept at work in the bottom right cabinet of her hutch and changed out of her crosstrainers into every morning the moment she sat down and rolled her chair with small pretend whimpers of effort over to the hutch's cabinets, sometimes (unlike Schmidt) pacing slightly in front of the whiteboard, sometimes planting one heel and rotating her foot slightly or crossing her sturdy ankles to lend her standing posture a carelessly demure aspect, sometimes taking her delicate oval eyeglass frames off and not chewing on the arm but holding the glasses in such a way and in such proximity to her mouth that one got the idea she could, at any moment, put one of the fragile arm's plastic carguards just inside her mouth and nibble on it absently, an unconscious gesture of shyness and concentration at once.

The conference room's carpeting was magenta pile in which wheels left symmetrically distended impressions when one or more of the men adjusted their executive swivel chairs slightly to reposition their legs or their bodies' relation to the table itself. The ventilation system laid a pale hum over tiny distant street and city noises which the window's thickness itself cut to almost nothing. Each of the Targeted Focus Group's members wore a blue-and-white nametag with only his first name inscribed thereon by hand. 42.8% of these inscriptions were cursive or script; three of the remaining eight were block capitals, all of which block-cap first names, in a remarkable but statistically meaningless coincidence, began with H. Sometimes, too, Schmidt would as it were take a step back inside his head and view the Focus Group as a unit, a mass of busts in flesh and fiber; he'd observe all the faces at once, qua Group, so that nothing but the broadest commonalities passed through his filter. The faces were well-fed, mid- to upscale, neutral, provisionally attentive, the blood-fed minds behind them occupied with their own owners' lives, jobs, problems, plans, desires, & c. None had been hungry a day in their lives—this was the real commonality, and for Schmidt it did ramify. It was rare that the product really penetrated a Focus Group's consciousness. One of the first things a market researcher learns is that the product is never going to have as important a place in the TFG's minds as it did in the client's. Advertising is not voodoo. The client could hope only to create the impression of a connection or resonance between the brand and what was important to consumers. And what was important to consumers was always: themselves, what they conceived themselves to be. The Focus Groups made little difference in the long run; the only real test was actual sales, in Schmidt's personal opinion. Part of today's design was to go past lunch and keep the members eating only confections, and then assuming a normal breakfasttime one could expect their blood sugar to start going down hard by 11:30. The ones who ate the most *Felonies!* would be hit the hardest. Low blood sugar causes oscitance, irritability, lowered inhibitions; their game-faces would start to slip a little. Some of the TFGs' strategies could be extremely manipulative and even abusive in the name of data. A bleach-alternative detergent's agency had once hired Team Δy to convene primipara mothers aged 29 to 34 whose TATs had indicated insecurities at three key loci and then to administer questionnaires whose items were designed to provoke and/or heighten those insecurities—Do you ever have negative or hostile feelings toward your child? How often do you feel as if you must hide or disguise the fact that your parenting skills are inadequate? Have teachers or other parents ever made remarks about your child which embarrassed you? How often do you feel your child looks shabby or inadequately parented in comparison to other children? Have you ever neglected to launder, bleach, mend, or iron your child's clothes because of time constraints? Does your child ever seem sad or anxious for no reason you can understand? Can you think of a time when your child appeared to be frightened of you? Does your child's behavior or appearance ever provoke negative feelings in you? Have you ever shouted at or thought negative things about your child? & c.—which, over eleven grueling hours and six separate rounds of carefully designed questionnaires, brought the women to such an emotional state that truly invaluable data on how to pitch Cheer Xtra in terms of very deep maternal anxieties and conflicts emerged... data that as far as Schmidt had been able to see went wholly unexploited in the campaign the agency had finally sold P&G on. Darlene Lilley had said she later had felt like calling the Focus Group's women and apologizing and letting them know that they'd been totally set up, emotionally.

Some of the products and agencies whose branding campaigns Terry Schmidt and Darlene Lilley's Field Team had also worked on for Team Δy were: Downyflake Waffles for D'Arcy Masius Benton & Bowles, Diet Caffeine Free Coke for Ads Infinitum U.S., Eucalyptamint for Pringle Dixon, Citizens Business Insurance for Krauthammer-Jaynes/SMS, the G. Heileman Brewing Co.'s Special Export and Special Export Lite for Bayer Bess Vanderwarker, Winner International's *HelpMe* Personal Sound Alarm for Reesemeyer Shannon Belt, Isotoner Comfort-Fit Gloves for PR Cogent Partners, Northern Bathroom Tissue for RSB, and Rhône-Poulenc Rorer's new Nasacort and Nasacort AQ Prescription Nasal Spray, also for RSB.

The only way for an observer to detect anything unusual or out of the ordinary about the two UAFs' status would be to note that the facilitator never once looked directly at them, whereas Schmidt did look at each of the other twelve men at various intervals, making brief and candid eye-contact with first one man and then another at a different place around the conference table and so on, a subtle skill (there is no word for it) that often marks those who are practiced at speaking before small groups, neither holding any man's eye so long as to discomfit nor simply panning automatonically back and forth and brushing only lightly against each man's gaze in such a way that the men in the Focus Group might feel as though this representative of Mister Squishy and *Felonies!* were talking merely at them rather than to or with them; and it would have taken a practiced small-group observer indeed even to notice that there were two men in the conference room—one being the terse eccentric member surrounded by personal-care products, the other a silent earnest-eyed bespectacled man who sat in blazer and turtleneck at the table's far corner, which latter Schmidt had decided was the second UAF: something a tiny bit too composed about the man's mien and blink-rate gave him up—on whose eyes the facilitator's never quite alit. Schmidt's lapse was very subtle and an observer would have to be highly experienced and attentive to find any meaning in it.

The figure wore also a mountaineer's tool apron and a large nylon back-pack. Visually, he was both conspicuous and complex. On each slim ledge he appeared to use the suction cups on his right hand and wrist to pull himself lithely up from a supine position to a standing position, cruciform, facing inward, hugging the window with his arms' cups to keep from falling backward as he raised his left leg and turned the shoe outward to align the instep's cups with the glass's reflective surface. The suction cups appeared to be the kind whose vacuum action could be activated and deactivated by slight rotary adjustments that probably took a great deal of practice to learn how to perform as deftly as the figure performed them. The backpack and boots were the same color. Most of the passersby who looked up and stopped and accreted into the small watching crowd found their attention compelled by the mechanics of the figure's climb. He climbed each window by lifting his left leg and right arm and pulling himself lithely up, then attaching his dangling right leg and left arm and activating their cups' suction and leaving them to hold his weight while he deactivated the left leg and right arm's suction and moved them up and reactivated their cups. There were high degrees of both precision and economy in the way the figure orchestrated his limbs' complex tasks. His overall movement was lizardlike. The day was very crisp and winds aloft were high; whatever clouds there were moved very quickly across the slim square of sky visible above the tall buildings that flanked the street. The autumn sky itself the sort of blue that seems to burn. People with hats tipped them back on their heads and people without hats shaded their eyes with their gloves as they craned to watch the figure's progress. The clabbering skies over the Lake were not visible from the canyon's base. There was one large additional suction cup affixed to the back of the hood with a white Velcro strap. When the figure cleared another ledge and for a moment lay on his side facing out into the chasm below, the onlookers far enough back on the sidewalk to have some visual perspective could see another large orange suction cup, the hood's cup's twin, attached to his forehead by what was presumably Velcro although this Velcro band must have run beneath the hood. And either reflective goggles or very strange eyes indeed.

Schmidt was just giving the Focus Group some extra background, he said, on the product and on some of the marketing challenges it had presented, but he said in no way shape or form was he giving them anything like the whole story. One of the men sneezed violently. Schmidt explained that this was because Reesemeyer Shannon Belt Adv. wanted to make sure to give the Focus Group a generous interval to convene together *in camera* and discuss their experiences and assessments of *Felonies!* as a Group, to compare notes if you will, on their own, qua Group, without any marketing researchers yammering at them or standing there observing them as if they were psychological guinea pigs or something, which meant that Terry would soon be getting out of their hair (a small slip—even one case of Male Pattern Baldness in the room dictated the alternative casualism 'off your backs') and leaving them to perpend and converse in private amongst themselves and that he wouldn't be coming back until whatever Foreman they elected pushed the large red button next to the room's lights' rheostat that in turn activated—the red button—an amber light in the office down the hall where Terry Schmidt said he would be twiddling his metaphorical thumbs waiting to come collect the hopefully univocal Group Response Data Summary packet, which the elected Foreman here would be receiving *ex post hasto*. Eleven of the room's men had now consumed at least one of the products on the table's central tray; five of them had had more than one. Terry Schmidt, who was no longer playing idly with the Dry Erase marker because some of the men's eyes had begun to follow it in his hand and he sensed it was becoming a potential irritant, said he now also proposed to give them just a little of the standard spiel on why after all the solo time and effort they'd all already put in on their Individual Response Profiles he was going to ask them to start all over again and consider the GRDS packet's various questions and scales as a collective. He had a trick for disposing of the Dry Erase marker where he very casually placed it in the slotted tray at the bottom of the whiteboard and gave the pen's butt a hard fillip with his finger, sending it the length of the tray to stop just short of shooting out the other end altogether, with its cap's tip almost precisely aligned with the tray's end, which he performed with Focus Groups about 70% of the time and performed now. The trick was even more impressively casual-looking if he performed it while he was speaking, because it gave both what he was saying and the trick itself an air of distracted informality. Robert Awad (the Team Δy Senior Research Director who would later harass and be so artfully defused by Darlene Lilley) himself had casually performed this little trick in one of his orientation presentations for new Field Team researchers 27 fiscal quarters past. This, Schmidt said, was because one of Reesemeyer Shannon Belt Advertising's central tenets, one of the things that set them apart from other agencies in their bailiwick and so was of course something in which they took great pride and made much of in their pitches to clients like Mister Squishy and North American Soft Confections Inc., was that IRPs like the 20-page questionnaires the men so kindly had filled out in their separate airless cubicles were of definite but only partial research utility, since corporations whose products had national or even regional distribution depended on appealing not just to individual consumers but of course it almost went without saying very large groups of them, groups yes comprised of individuals but nevertheless groups, collectives. These groups as conceived and understood by market researchers were strange and protean entities, Schmidt told the TFG, whose tastes—referring to groups, or small-m 'markets' as they were known in the industry jargon—whose tastes and whims and predilections were not only as the men in the room were doubtless aware subtle and fickle and susceptible to influence from myriad tiny factors in each individual consumer's appetitive makeup but also, paradoxically, functions of the members of the group's influences upon each other, all in a set of interactions and recursively exponential responses-to-responses so complex and multifaceted that it drove statistical demographers half nuts and required a whole Sysplex series of enormously powerful low-temperature Cray-brand supercomputers even to try to model.

And if all that sounded like a lot of marketing doubletalk, Terry Schmidt told the Focus Group with an air of someone loosening his tie after something public's end, maybe the easiest example of what RSB was talking about in terms of intramarket influences was probably say for instance teenage kids and the fashions and fads that swept like wildfire through markets composed mostly of kids, meaning highschool and college kids and markets such as for instance popular music and clothing fashions. If the members saw a lot of teenage kids these days wearing pants that looked way too large for them and rode low and had cuffs that dragged on the ground, for one obvious example, Schmidt said as if plucking an example at random out of the air, or even if as was surely the case with some of the more senior men in the room (two, in fact) they themselves had kids who'd taken in the last couple years to suddenly wanting and wearing clothes that were far too big for them and made them look like urchins in Dickens stories even though as the men probably knew all too well with a grim chuckle the clothes cost a pretty penny indeed over at the Gap or Galleria, and if you wondered why your kid was wearing them of course the majority of the answer is that *other* kids were wearing them, for of course kids as a demographic market today were notoriously herdlike and their individual choices in consumption were overwhelmingly influenced by other kids' consumption-choices and so on in a fadlike pattern that spread like wildfire and usually then abruptly and mysteriously vanished or changed into something else. This was the most simple and obvious example of the sort of complex system of large groups' intragroup preferences influencing one another and building exponentially on one another, more like a nuclear chain reaction or an epidemiological transmission-pattern than a simple case of each individual consumer deciding privately for himself what he wanted and then going out and judiciously spending his disposable income on it, on what he wanted. The wonks in Demographics' buzzword for this phenomenon was MCP or 'Metastatic Consumption Pattern,' Schmidt told the Focus Group, rolling his eyes in a way that invited those who were attending closely to laugh with him at the statisticians' nomenclature. Granted, the facilitator went on, the model he was so rapidly sketching for them was overly simplistic—e.g. it left out advertising and the media, which in today's hypercomplex business environment sought always to anticipate and fuel these sudden proliferating movements in group choice, aiming for a tipping point at which a product or brand became so popular and widespread that it became like unto actual cultural news and-slash-or fodder for cultural critics and comedians, plus also a plausible placement-prop for mass entertainment that sought to look real and in-the-now, and so thereupon a product or style that got hot at a certain ideal apex of the MCP ceased to require much actual paid advertising or marketing at all, the hot brand becoming as it were cultural information rather than corporate promotion.

Of the 67% of the twelve real Focus Group members who were still concentrating on listening closely to Terry Schmidt, two wore the expressions of men who were trying to decide whether to be slightly offended; both of these were well over 30. Also, some of the individual adults across the conference table from one another began to exchange glances, and since these men had no prior acquaintance or connection (Schmidt believed) on which to base meaningful eye-contact, it seemed indisputable that the looks were in reaction to the facilitator's analogy to teen fashion fads. One of the men had classic peckerwood sideburns that came all the way down to his mandibular joints and ended in sharp points. Of the three youngest men, none were attending closely, and two were still established in postures and facial configurations designed to make this apparent. The third had removed his third *Felony!* from the table's display and was working the wrapper to make as little noise as possible, looking around him to determine whether anyone cared that he'd now taken more than his technical share. Schmidt, improvising slightly, was saying, 'I'm talking here about juvenile fads, of course, only because it's the simplest, most intuitive sort of example. The marketing people at Mister Squishy know full well that you gentlemen aren't kids,' with a small slight smile at the younger members, all three of whom could vote, purchase alcohol, and enlist in the armed forces after all; 'or nor that there's anything like a real herd mentality we're trying to spark here by leaving you alone to confer amongst yourselves qua Group. If nothing else keep in mind that soft-confection marketing doesn't work this way, it's much more complicated, and the group dynamics of the market are much harder to really talk about without computer modeling and all sorts of ugly math up on the board that we wouldn't even dream of trying to get you to sit still for.'

A single intrepid sporting boat was making its way right to left across the portion of the Lake the large window gave out on, and once or twice an automobile horn far below on E. Huron sounded at such insistent length that it intruded on the attention of Terry Schmidt and some of the well-vetted consumers in this conference room, a couple of whom Schmidt had to admit to himself that he felt he could frankly dislike—both somewhat older, one the man with the hairweave, something hooded about their eyes, and the way they looked at Schmidt and made little self-satisfied adjustments to parts of themselves and their wardrobes, sometimes in a very concentrated way, as if to communicate that they were men so important that their attention itself was highly prized, that they were old and experienced hands at sitting in rooms like this having earnest young men with easels and full-color charts make presentations and try to solicit favorable responses from them, and that they were well above whatever mass-consumer LCD Schmidt's clumsy mime of candid spontaneity was pitched at, that they'd taken cellular phone calls during or even walked out of far more nuanced, sophisticated, assuasive pitches than this. Schmidt had had several years of psychotherapy and was not without some perspective on himself; and he knew that some percentage of his reaction to the way these older men coolly inspected their cuticles or pinched at the crease in the trouser of the topmost leg as they sat back on their coccyx joggling the foot of their crossed leg was his own insecurity, that he felt vaguely sullied and implicated by the whole enterprise of contemporary marketing and that this sometimes manifested via projection as the conviction that people he was just trying to talk candidly to always believed he was making some sales pitch or other and trying to manipulate them in some way, that merely being employed, however ephemerally, in the great grinding U.S. marketing machine had somehow colored his whole being and that something essentially shifty or pleading in his expression now seemed inherently false or manipulative and turned people off, and not just in his career—which was not his whole existence, unlike so many at Δy, or even all that terribly important to him; he had a vivid and complex inner life, and introspected a great deal—but in his personal affairs as well, and that somewhere along the line his professional marketing skills had metastasized throughout his whole character so that he was now the sort of man who, if he were to screw up his courage and ask a female colleague out for drinks and over drinks open his heart up to her and reveal that he respected her enormously, was in certain ways in awe of her in a way that mixed both professional and personal respect, and that he spent a great deal more time thinking about her than she probably had any idea he did, and that if there were anything at all he could ever do to make her life happier or easier or more satisfying or fulfilling he hoped she'd just say the word, for that is all she would have to do, say the word or snap her short thick fingers or even just look at him in a meaningful way, and he'd be there, instantly and with no reservations at all, would in all probability be viewed as just wanting to sleep with her or fondle her or as having some creepy obsession with her, and maybe even a small creepy secretive kind of almost shrine to her in one corner of the unused second bedroom of his condominium, consisting of personal items fished out of her cubicle's wastebasket or the occasional short dry witty notes she passed him during especially deadly or absurd Team Δy staff meetings or orientations, or that his home Apple Powerbook®'s screensaver was an Adobe® 1440-dpi blowup of a digital snapshot of the two of them with his arm over her shoulder and just the arm and shoulder of the other Team Δy Fieldworker with his arm over her shoulder from the other side at a 4th of July picnic that A.C. Romney–Jaswat & Assoc. had thrown for its research subcontractors at Navy Pier two years past, Darlene holding her cup and smiling in such a way as to show almost as much upper gum as small white even teeth, the ale's cup's red digitally enhanced to match her lipstick and the small scarlet hairbow she wore just right of center as a sort of personal signature or statement.

The crowd on the sidewalk's growth was still inconstant. For every two or three passersby who joined the sidewalk's group, craning upward, someone else in the crowd looked anxiously at his watch and exited the crowd and hurried off either northward or across the street to make some sort of appointment. From a certain perspective the small crowd, then, looked like a living cell engaged in trade and exchange with the linear flows that fed it. There was no evidence that the climbing figure saw the fluctuantly growing crowd so far below. He at any rate never made any of the sort of motions or facial expressions people associate with someone at a great height looking down. No one in the sidewalk's group of spectators pointed or yelled; they simply watched. What children there were held their guardians' hand. There were some remarks and small conversations between adjoining onlookers, but these took place out of the sides of mouths as all parties looked up at what appeared to be a sheer and sky-high column of alternating glass and stone. The figure averaged roughly 230 seconds per story; a commuter timed him. Both the backpack and apron looked very full of some sort of equipment that caused them to bulge. There were loops along his GoreTex top's shoulders and also—unless it was a trick of the building's windows' reflected light—small strange almost nipplelike protuberances at the figure's shoulders, knees' backs, and directly in the center of the odd navy-and-white bullseye at the figure's seat. The crampons on mountaineering boots can be removed with a small square tool so they can be sharpened or replaced, a long-haired man supporting a ten-speed bicycle against his hip told the people around him. He knew what the protuberances were. New members of the crowd always asked the people around them what was going on, whether they knew. The costume was airtight, the guy was inflatable or designed to look that way, the long-haired man said. He appeared to be talking to his bicycle; no one acknowledged him. His pantcuffs were clipped for easy cycling. On every third or fourth ledge the figure paused for a time on his back on the narrow ledge with scrollwork at the cornices, resting. A man who had at one time driven an airport shuttlebus opined that the figure on the ledge looked to be idling, timing out his ascent to conform to some schedule; the child attached to the hand of the woman he said this to looked briefly over at him with her face still upturned. Anyone looking straight down would have seen a shifting collection of several dozen faces with bodies so foreshortened as to be suggestions only.

'Yes, so not at all,' Terry Schmidt said in response to a sort of confirmational question from a man with a heavy slablike face and a partly torn tag (two of the room's cursive nametags were ripped or sectional, the result of accidents during their removal from the adhesive backing) that read FORREST, a 35ish fellow with large and hirsute wrists and a frayed collar, whose air of rumpled integrity—along with two separate questions that actually helped advance the presentation's agendas—made this fellow Schmidt's personal choice for Foreman. 'What it is is just that RSB feels your Focus Group responses qua Group instead of just as the sum of your personal individual responses is an equally important market-research tool for a product like the *Felony!*. "GRDS" as well as "IRPs" as we say in the trade,' with a breeziness he did not feel. One of the younger members—age 22 according to the tiny Charleston Code worked into the scrollwork at his nametag's lower border, and handsome in a sort of blank, provisional way— wore a reversed baseball cap and a soft wool V-neck sweater with no shirt underneath, displaying a powerful upper chest and forearms (the sleeves of the sweater were carefully pushed up to reveal the forearms' musculature in a way designed to look casual, as if the sweater's arms had been thoughtlessly pushed up in the midst of his thinking hard about something other than himself), had crossed his leg ankle-on-knee and slid so far down on his tailbone that his cocked leg was the same height as his chin, thereupon holding the salient knee with his fingers laced in such a way as to apply pressure and make his forearms bulge even more. It had occurred to Terry Schmidt that, even though so many home products from Centrum Multivitamins to Visine AC Soothing Antiallergenic Eye Drops to Nasacort AQ Prescription Nasal Spray now came in conspicuous tamperproof packaging in the wake of the Tylenol poisonings of a decade past and Johnson & Johnson's legendarily swift and candid response to the crisis—pulling every bottle of every variety of Tylenol off every retail shelf in America and spending millions on setting up overnight a smooth and hassle-free system for every Tylenol consumer to return his or her bottle for an immediate NQA refund plus an added sum for the gas and mileage or postage involved in the return, writing off tens of millions in returns and operational costs and recouping untold exponents more in positive PR and consumer goodwill and actually enhancing the brand Tylenol's association with compassion and concern for consumer well-being, a strategy that had made J&J's CEO and their PR vendors legends in a marketing field Schmidt had just then begun idly considering getting into as a practical and potentially creative, rewarding way to use his double-major in Descriptive Statistics + Bv. Psych and imagining himself in plush conference rooms not unlike this one using the sheer force of his personality and command of the facts to persuade tablesful of well-dressed hard-eyed corporate officers that legitimate concern for consumer well-being was both emotionally and economically Good Business, that if RJ Reynolds opted to be forthcoming about its products' addictive qualities, and GM to be up-front in its national ads about the fact that vastly greater fuel-efficiency was totally feasible if consumers would be willing to spend a couple hundred dollars more and settle for slightly fewer aesthetic amenities, and shampoo manufacturers to concede that the 'Repeat' in their product instructions was hygienically unnecessary, and Tums' General Brands were to spend a couple million to announce candidly that Tums-brand antacid tablets should not be used regularly for more than a couple weeks at a time because after that the stomach lining automatically started secreting more HCl to compensate for all the neutralization and made the original stomach trouble worse—the gains in corporate PR and brand-associations with integrity and trust would more than outweigh the short-term costs and stock-price repercussions, that yes it was a risk but it was not a wild or dicelike risk, that it had on its side both precedent cases and demographic data as well as the solid reputation for both caginess and integrity of T.E. Schmidt & Subordinates, to concede that yes gentlemen he was in a way asking them to risk some of their narrow short-term margins and equity on the humble say-so of Terence Eric Schmidt Jr., whose own character's clear marriage of virtue, pragmatism, and oracular marketing savvy were his best and final argument; he was saying to these upper-management men in their vests and Cole Haans just what he proposed to have them say to a sorry and cynical U.S. market: Trust Me You Won't Be Sorry, which when he thinks of the starry-eyed puerility and near-Himalayan narcissism of these fantasies now, a rough decade later, Schmidt experiences a kind of full-frame internal wince, that kind of embarrassment-before-self that makes our most mortifying memories objects of fascination and repulsion at once, though in Terry Schmidt's case a certain amount of introspection and psychotherapy (the latter the origin of the self-caricature doodling during down-time in his beige cubicle) had enabled him to understand that his professional fantasies were not in the main all that unique, that a large percentage of bright young men and women locate the impetus behind their career-choice in the belief that they are, fundamentally, different from the common run of man, unique and in some ways kind of superior, more as it were fundamental, meaningful, important—what else could explain the fact that they themselves are at the *exact center* of everything they've experienced for the whole two dozen years of their conscious lives?—and that they can and will make a difference in their chosen field simply by the fact of their unique and central presence in it... and but so (Schmidt still declaiming professionally to his TFG all this while) so but even though so many upmarket consumer products now were tamperproof, Mister Squishy–brand snack cakes—and Hostess, Little Debbie, Pepperidge Farm, the whole soft-confection industry, with its flimsy neopolymerized wrappers and cheap thin cardboard Economy Size containers—were decidedly not, i.e. not tamperproof, that it would take nothing more than one thin-gauge hypodermic and 24 infinitesimal doses of KCN, As_2O_3, ricine, $C_{21}H_{22}O_2N_2$, acincetilcholine, botulinus, even merely Tl or some aqueous base-metal compound, to bring almost an entire industry down on one knee; for even if the soft-confection manufacturers survived the horror and recovered some measure of consumer trust, the relevant products' low cost was an essential part of its established Market Appeal Matrix, and the costs of reinforcing the Economy packaging and rendering the individual snack cakes visibly invulnerable to a thin-gauge hypodermic would push the products out so far right on the demand curve that mass-market snacks would become both economically and emotionally untenable, corporate soft confections going the way of unsupervised Trick-or-Treating, hitchhiking, door-to-door sales, & c.

While the limbic portions of Schmidt's brain pursued this line of thinking in fact while a whole other part of his mind surveyed these memories and fantasies and was both fascinated and repelled by the way all these thoughts and feelings could be entertained in total subjective private while Schmidt ran the Focus Group through a brief 'Full-Access' description of Mister Squishy's place in the soft-confection industry and some of the travails of developing and marketing what these men were experiencing as

Felonies! (referring offhandedly to nascent plans for bite-sized *misdemeanors!* [*sic*] if the original product established a foothold), at least half the room's men listening with what's called only ½ an ear while pursuing their own private lines of thought... and Schmidt had a quick vision of them all as like icebergs, only the sharp caps showing, unknown and -knowable to one another, and imagined that it was probably only in marriage—and a good marriage, not the decorous dance of loneliness he'd watched his mother and father do for seventeen years but true conjugal intimacy—where the partners allowed each other to see below the berg's cap's flat public mask and consented to be really *known*, maybe even to the extent of not only letting the partner see the repulsive nest of moles under their left arms or the way after any sort of cold or viral infection the nails on both feet turned a weird deep yellow for several weeks but even perhaps every once in a while sobbing in each other's arms late at night and pouring out the most ghastly private fears and thoughts of failure and impotence and *smallness* inside a grinding professional machine you can't believe you once had the temerity to think you could help change or make a difference or ever be more than a tiny cog in, the shame of being so hungry to have some sort of real impact on an industry that you'd fantasize over and over about deciding that making a dark difference with a hypo and eight c.c.'s of castor-bean distillate was better, somehow more true to your own inner centrality and importance, than being nothing but a faceless cog and doing a job that untold thousands of other bright young men and women could do at least as well as you, or rather now even better than you because they still believed deep inside they were made for something bigger and more central than shepherding preoccupied men through an abstracted sham-caucus and yet still believed they could (the bright young men could) begin to manifest their larger potential for impact and effectiveness by being the very best darn Targeted Focus Group facilitator that Team Δy and RSB had ever even dreamed of seeing, better than the data they'd seen so far had even shown might be possible, establishing via sheer candor and integrity and a smooth informal rhetoric that let their own very special qualities manifest themselves and shine forth such a level of connection and intimacy with a Focus Group that the TFG's men or women felt, within the special high-voltage field of the relationship the facilitator created, an interest in and enthusiasm for the product and for RSB's desire to bring the product out into the U.S. market in the very most effective way that matched or even exceeded the agency's own. Or that even just the possibility of expressing any of this trite, wide-eyed heartbreak to someone seemed impossible except in the context of the mystery of true marriage, meaning not just a ceremony and financial union but a true communion of souls, and Schmidt now lately felt he was coming to understand why the Church all through his childhood catechism and pre-con referred to it as the Holy Sacrament of Marriage, for it seemed every bit as miraculous and transrational and remote from the real possibilities of actual lived life as the crucifixion and resurrection and transubstantiation did, that is to say appeared not as a goal to expect ever to really reach or achieve but as a kind of navigational star, as in in the sky, something high and untouchable and miraculously beautiful in the sort of distant way that reminded you always how ordinary and unbeautiful and incapable of miracles you yourself were, which was another reason why Schmidt had stopped looking at the sky or going out at night or even usually ever opening the lightproof curtains of his condominium's picture window when he got home at night and instead sat with his satellite TV's channel-changer switching quickly from channel to channel to channel out of fear that something better was going to come on unexpectedly on another of the cable provider's 220 regular and premium channels and he was about to miss it, spending three hours this way before it was time to stare with drumming heart at the telephone that wholly unbeknownst to her had Darlene Lilley's home number on Speed Dial so that it would take only one moment of the courage to risk looking prurient or creepy to use just one finger to push one beige button to invite her for one cocktail or even a soft drink over which he could take off his mask and open his heart to her before quailing and deferring the call one more night and waddling into the bathroom and/or then the cream-and-beige bedroom to lay out the next day's crisp shirt and tie and say his dekate and then masturbate himself to sleep again. Schmidt was sensitive about the way his weight and body-fat percentage increased with each passing year and imagined that there was something about the way he walked that suggested a plump, flabby, prissy fat man's waddle, when in fact his stride was 100% average and unremarkable and nobody except Terry Schmidt had any opinions about his manner of walking one way or another. Sometimes this last quarter when shaving in the morning with WLS News and Talk Radio on over the intercom he stopped, Schmidt did, and looked at his face and the lines and slack pouches that seemed to grow a little more pronounced each day and would call himself, right to his mirrored face, *Mister Squishy*; the name would come unbidden into his mind, and despite his attempts to ignore or resist it the large subsidiary's name and logo had become the dark part of his latest taunt, so that when he thought of himself now it was as something he called *Mister Squishy*, and his face and the plump and wholly innocuous icon's face tended to bleed in his mind into one face, crude and line-drawn and clever in a small way, a design that someone might find some small selfish use for but could never love or hate or possibly even know.

Some of the shoppers inside the first-floor display window of the Gap observed the small crowd on the sidewalk craning upward and wondered what was up. At the base of the 8th floor the figure shifted himself carefully around so that he was seated on the ledge with his legs dangling. He was 238 feet up in the air. The square of sky right overhead a shrill blue. The growing crowd watching him could not discern that there was in turn a growing collection of shoppers inside looking out at them because the building's glass, which appeared tinted on the inside, was reflective on the outside; it was One-Way® glass. The figure now crossed his legs lotus-style on the ledge beneath him, paused, and then in one lithe movement drove himself upright, losing his balance slightly and windmilling his arms to keep from pitching forward off the ledge altogether. There was a brief group-exhalation from the sidewalk's crowd as the figure now snapped its hooded head back and with a tiny distant wet noise affixed the suction cup at his head's rear to the window. A couple young men in the crowd cried up at the 8th floor for the figure to jump, but their tone was ironic and it was clear that they were simply parodying the typical cry of jaded onlookers to a figure balanced on a slim ledge 240 feet up in a high wind and looking down at a crowd on the sidewalk so far below. Still, one or two much older people shot optical daggers at the youths who'd shouted; it was unclear whether they knew what parody even was. Inside the window of the building's north facet's 8th floor—which space happened to comprise the Circulation and Subscription departments of *Playboy* Magazine—the employees' response to the sight of the back of a lithe blue-and-white figure attached to the window by a suction cup on its head can only be imagined. It was the Gap's floor manager in Accessories who called the police, and merely because the press of customers at the window's display bespoke some kind of disturbance on the street outside; and because the nature of the disturbance was unknown, none of the roving television vans who monitored the city's police frequencies were alerted, and the scene remained media-free for a good 500 feet in every direction.

What Terry Schmidt sketched for the all-male Focus Group was a small eddy or crosscurrent in the tide that demomarketers called MCPs—these were known as Antitrends or sometimes Shadow Markets. In the area of corporate snacks, Schmidt pretended to explain, there were two basic ways a new product could position itself in a U.S. market for which health, fitness, nutrition, and attendant indulgence-vs.-discipline conflicts had achieved a metastatic status. A Shadow snack simply worked to define itself against the overall trend (one, yes, often age- and class-based) against HDL fats, sugars, refined flours, trans-fatty acids, i.e. the consumption of what some subgroups variously termed 'empty calories,' 'sweets,' 'junk food,' or in other words the whole brilliantly orchestrated obsession with nutrition and exercise and stress-management that went under the demographic heading Healthy Lifestyles. Schmidt said he could tell from the Focus Group's faces—whose expressions ranged from sullen distraction in the youngest to a kind of studious anxiety in the older men, faces tinged with the slight guilt-about-guilt that Schemm, Halter-Deight's legendary Peter E. Fish, the mind behind both shark-cartilage and odor-free garlic supplements, had called at a high-priced seminar that both Scott Laleman and Darlene Lilley had attended '...the knife-edge that Healthy Lifestyles Marketing had to walk along,' which unfortunate phrase was reproduced by a Hewlett-Packard digital projector that cast Fish's key points in bold-fonted outline form against one wall to facilitate effective note-taking (the whole industry seminar business was such bullshit, Terry Schmidt believed, with its leather binders and Mission Statements and war-game nomenclature, marketing truisms to marketers, who when all was said and done were probably the most plasticly gullible market around, although there was no disputing P.E. Fish's importance or his statements' weight)—Schmidt said he could tell from their faces that they knew quite well what Antitrend was about, the Shadow Markets like Punk contra Disco and Cadillacs contra high-mileage compacts and Sun and Apple contra the MS juggernaut. He said they could if the men wished talk at some length about the stresses on individual consumers between their natural God-given herd instincts and their deep fear of sacrificing their natural God-given identities as individuals, and

about the way these stresses were tweaked and/or soothed by skillfully engineered trends and then but by sort of the 3rd Law of Motion of Marketing
spawned also their Antitrend Shadows, the spin inside and against the larger
spin of in this instance Reduced-Calorie and Fat-Free foods, nutritional
supplements, Lowcaf and Decaf, NutraSweet® and Olestra®, jazzercise and
liposuction and kava-kava, good and bad cholesterol, free-radicals and antioxidants, time-management and Quality Time and the brilliantly managed
stress that everyone was made to feel about staying fit and looking good and
living long and squeezing the absolute maximum productivity and health
and self-actuation out of every last vanishing second, but that of course the
men's time was valuable and he'd—here one or two of the older Focus Group
members who had wristwatches glanced at them by reflex, and the over-
stylized UAF's pager went off by prearrangement, which allowed Schmidt
to gesture broadly and pretend to chuckle and to concede that yes see their
time *was* valuable, that they all felt it, they all knew what he was talking
about because after all they all lived in it didn't they, and that so in this case
it would perhaps suffice just to simply for example utter the words Jolt®
Cola, Starbucks, Häagen-Dazs, Ericson's All Butter Fudge, premium cigars,
conspicuous low-mileage 4WDs, Hammacher Schlemmer's all-silk boxers,
whole Near-North Side eateries given over to exotic desserts—enterprises
in other words that rode the transverse Shadow, that said or sought to say
to the consumer bludgeoned by herd-pressures to achieve, forebear, trim
the fat, cut down, discipline, prioritize, be sensible, self-parent that Hey,
you deserve it, you work hard, reward yourself, brands that in essence
said what's the use of living longer and healthier if there aren't those few
precious moments in every day when you stopped, sat down, and took a
few moments of hard-earned pleasure just for you? and various myriad other
pitches that aimed to remind the consumer that he was an individual, with
individual tastes and preferences and freedom of individual choice, that he
was not a herd-animal who had no choice but to go go go on U.S. life's
digital-calorie-readout treadmill, that there were still some rich and refined
and harmless-if-judiciously-indulged-in pleasures out there to indulge in if
he snapped out of his high-fiber hypnosis and realized that life was also to
be enjoyed, that the unenjoyed life was not worth living & c & c. That just
as Hostess Inc. was coming out with Low-Fat Twinkies and Cholesterol-Free
Ding Dongs, Jolt Cola's own branders had hung its West Coast launch on

the inverted Twice the Sugar Twice the Caffeine®, and that meanwhile the stock of Ericson's A.-B. Fudge and individual bite-sized Fudgies®' parent company U.S. Brands had split three times via D.D.B. Needham's series of ads that featured people in workout clothes running into each other in closets where they'd gone to eat Ericson's ABF in secret, with all the ingenious and piquant tag lines that played against the moment their mutual embarrassment turned to laughter and a kind of convoled esprit de corps. (Schmidt knew full well that RSB had lost the U.S. Brands/Ericson account to D.D.B. Needham's spectacular pitch for a full-out Shadow strategy, and thus that the videotape of his remarks would raise at least three eyebrows among RSB's MROP team and force Robert Awad to behave as though he believed Schmidt hadn't known anything about the Ericson–D.D.B. Needham thing and to come [Awad] lean pungently over the wall of Schmidt's cubicle and try to 'fill in Terry' on certain facts of life of interagency politics without unduly damaging Schmidt's morale over the 'boner' & c.)

Nor was the high-altitude figure in fact gazing down at them, the street's keener onlookers discerned; he was looking down at himself and gingerly removing a shiny packet of what appeared to be Mylar® from his mountaineer's tool apron and giving it a delicate little towel-like snap to open it out and then reaching up with both hands and rolling it down over his head and hood and fixing it in place with small Velcro tabs at his shoulders and throat's base. It was some sort of mask, the long-haired cyclist who always carried a small novelty-type spy telescope in his fannypack opined, though except for two holes for eyes and a large one for his forehead's cup the whole thing appeared too wrinkled and detumesced-looking to make out who or what the shapeless arrangement of lines on the Mylar was supposed to represent, but even at this distance the mask looked frightening, baggy and hydrocephalic and cartoonishly inhuman, and there were now some louder cries, and several members of the watching crowd involuntarily stepped back into the street, fouling traffic and causing a brief discordance of horns, as the figure placed both hands on his head's white bag and with something like a wet kissing noise from his skull's rear cup performed a lithe *contra face* that left him now facing the window with the sagged mask's nose and lips and forehead's very orange cup pressed tight against it—again provoking God only knows what reaction from the *Playboy* Magazine corporate staff on the glass's inside—whereupon he now reached around and removed from the backpack what appeared to be a small generator or perhaps SCUBA-style tank with a hoselike attachment that was either black or dark blue and ended in a strange sort of triangular or arrowhead- or Δ-shaped nozzle or attachment or mortise, which tank he connected with straps and a harness to the back of his GoreTex top and allowed the dark hose and nozzle to hang unfettered down over his concentricized rear and the leggings' tops, so that when he resumed his practiced-looking opposite-leg and -arm climb up the 8th-floor window he now also wore what appeared to be a deflated cranial balloon, dorsal airtank, and demonic or impish-looking tail, and presented a sight so complex and unlike anything iconic from any member of the (now larger and more diffuse, some still in the street and beginning to roil) crowd's visual experience that there were several moments of dead silence as everyone on the sidewalk's individual neocortices worked to process the visual information and scan their memories for any thing or combination of live or animated things the figure might resemble or suggest. A small child in the crowd began to cry because someone had stepped on its foot.

Now that he appeared less conventionally human, the way the figure climbed by moving his left arm / right leg and then right arm / left leg looked even more arachnoid or saurian; in any event he was just lithe as hell. Some of the shoppers inside the display windows of the Gap now had come out and joined the sidewalk's growing crowd. The figure scaled the 8th, 9th, 10th, 11th, and 12th floors with ease, then paused attached to the 13th- (or 14th-) floor window to apply some sort of cleaner or moisturizer to his suction cups. The winds at 425 (or 459) feet must have been very strong, because his tail-like hose swung wildly this way and that.

It was also impossible for some people in the street and sidewalk's crowd to resist looking at their own and the whole crowd's reflection in the Gap's display window. There were no more screams or cries of 'Jump!', but among some of the crowd's younger and somewhat more media-savvy members there began to be speculation about whether this was a Publicity Stunt for some product or service or whether the climbing figure was one of those post-modern renegade daredevils who climbed skyscrapers and then parachuted to the ground below and allowed himself to be arrested while blowing kisses to network news cameras. The well-known Sears Tower or even Hancock Center would have been a way better high-visibility site for a stunt like this if such it was, some of them felt. The first two squad cars arrived as the figure—by this time very small, even through a novelty telescope, and obscured almost entirely from view when he negotiated ledges—was hanging attached by his forehead's central cup to the 15th-floor window (or 16th, depending whether the building had a 13th floor) and appeared to be pulling more items from his nylon pack, fitting them together and using both hands to telescope something out to arm's length and attaching various other things to it. It was probably the squad cars and their garish lights at the curb that caused so many other cars on Huron Ave. to slow way down and pull over to see if there'd been a death or arrest, forcing one of the officers to spend all his time trying to control traffic and keep cars moving so that the avenue stayed passable. The older woman talking to a policeman asked whether the strangely costumed figure's climb could be a licensed stunt for a feature film or television or cable program, and this was when it occurred to some of the other spectators that the lithe figure's climb was possibly being filmed from the upper stories of one of the other commercial skyscrapers on the street and that there might in particular be cameras, film crews, and/or celebrities in the tall gray vertiginously flèched older building directly opposite 1101 E. Huron's north facet, and a certain percentage of the crowd's rear turned around and began craning and scanning windows on that building's south side, none of which windows were open, although this signified nothing because by City Ordinance 920-1247(d) no commercially zoned structure could possess, or authorize by terms of lease or contract its lessees to possess, operable windows above the 3rd floor. It was not clear whether this older opposite building's glass was One-Way or not because the angle of the late-a.m. sun, now almost directly overhead in the street's slot of sky, caused blinding reflections in that older spired building's windows, some of which brilliant reflections the windows focused and cast almost like mirrors or polished steel against the surface of the original building the masked figure with the rank and tail and real or imitation semiautomatic weapon—for verily that is what the new item was, slung over the subject's back at a slight transverse angle so that its unfolded stock rested atop the small blue-and-white tank for what might even conceivably be a miniaturized combat-grade gas mask or even maybe Jaysus help us all if it was a flamethrower or Clancy-grade biochemical aerosol nebulizer gizmo thing the officer with the CPD-issue high-X binoculars reported, using a radio that was somehow attached like an epaulette to his uniform's shoulder so that he had only to cock his head and touch his left shoulder to be able to confer with other officers, whose blue-and-white bored-out Montegos' sirens could be heard approaching from what sounded like Loyola U.—scaled, viz. 1101 E. Huron, so that squares and small rectangles and parallelo-grams of high-intensity light swam around him and lit up the 17th- (or 16th-) floor window he was even then scaling with nerveless ease, the fully automatic-looking M-16's barrel and folded stock inserted through several presewn loops along the left shoulder of his GoreTex top so that he retained full use of his left arm and hand's cup as he scaled the window and then sat again on the next story's ledge, the long nozzle arranged beneath him and only a couple feet of it protruding from between his legs and wobbling stiffly in the high wind. Reflected light swam all around him. A group of pigeons or doves on the ledge of the adjoining window was disturbed and took flight across the street and reassembled on a ledge of the exact same height at the opposite building. The figure now appeared to have removed some sort of radio, cellular phone, or recording device from his mountaineer's apron and to be speaking into it. At no time did he appear to look down or in any way to acknowledge the sidewalk and street's crowds, their shouts and cheers as each window was negotiated, or the police cruisers which by this time were parked at several different angles on the street, with two more squad cars blocking off E. Huron at the major intersections on either side.

A CFD truck arrived and firefighters in heavy slickers exited and began to mill about for no discernible reason. There were no evident media vans or rigs or mobile cameras at any time, which struck the savvier members of the crowds as further evidence that the whole thing was some sort of licensed prearranged corporate promotion or stunt or ploy. A few arguments ensued, mostly good-natured and inhibited by the number of auditors nearby. The stiff new ground-level breeze carried the smell of fried foods. A foreign couple arrived and began to hawk T-shirts whose silkscreen designs had nothing to do with what was going on. A detachment of police and fire-fighters entered 1101's north facet in order to establish a position on the building's roof, the firemen's axes and hats causing a small panic in the Gap and causing a jam-up at the building's revolving door that left a man in Oakley sunglasses bent over and holding his shoulder. Several people in the crowd cried out and pointed at what they claimed had been movement and/or the flash of lenses on the roof of the older building opposite. There was counter-speculation in the crowd that the whole thing was maybe designed to only *look* like a media stunt and that the weapon the figure was now sitting back against was genuine and that the idea was for him to look as eccentric as possible and climb high enough to draw a large crowd and then to spray automatic fire indiscriminately down into the crowd. The driverless autos along the curb at both sides of the street now had tickets under their windshield wipers. A helicopter could be heard but not seen from the canyon or crevasse the commercial structures made of the street below. One or two fingers of cirrus were now in the sky overhead. Some people were eating vendors' pretzels and brats, the winds whipping the paper napkins tucked into their collars. One policeman had a bullhorn but seemed unable to activate it. Someone had stepped backward onto the steep curb and injured his ankle or foot; a paramedic attended him as he lay on his topcoat and stared straight up at the tiny figure, who by this time had gained his feet and was splayed beneath the 18th or 17th floor, appearing to just stay there, attached to the window and waiting.

Terry Schmidt's father had served in the U.S. armed forces and been awarded a field commission at the age of just 21 and received both the Purple Heart and the Bronze Star, and the decorated veteran's favorite civilian activity in the whole world — you could tell by his face as he did it—was polishing his shoes and the buttons on his five suitcoats, which he did every Sunday afternoon, and the placid concentration on his face as he knelt on newspaper with his tins and shoes and chamois had formed a large unanalyzable part of the young Terry Schmidt's determination to make a difference in the affairs of men someday in the future. Which was now. Time had slipped by.

In the last two years Team Δy had come to function as what the advertising industry called a 'Captured Shop'; the firm occupied a contractual space somewhere between a subsidiary of Reesemeyer Shannon Belt and a contract vendor. Under Alan Britton's stewardship, Team Δy had joined the industry's trend toward 'Captured Consolidation' and reinvented itself as more or less the research arm of Reesemeyer Shannon Belt Adv. Team Δy's new status was designed both to limit RSB's paper overhead and to maximize the tax advantages of Focus Group research, which now could be both billed to Client and written off as an R&D subcontracting expense. There were substantial salary and benefit advantages to Team Δy (which was

itself structured as an employee-owned S Corporation under USTC §1361-
1379) as well. The major disadvantage, from Terry Schmidt's perspective,
was that there were no mechanisms in place by which a Captured Shop
employee could make the horizontal jump to Reesemeyer Shannon Belt
itself, within whose MROP division actual marketing-research strategies
were developed, enabling someone like T. E. Schmidt to have an at least
marginal impact on actual research design and analysis. Within Team Δy,
Schmidt's only possible advancement was to the Senior Research Director
position now occupied by the same swarthy, slick, glad-handing émigré
(with college-age children and a wife who always looked about to ululate)
who had made Darlene Lilley's professional life so difficult over the past
year; and of course even if the Team did indeed vote in such a way as to
pressure Alan Britton to ease Robert Awad out and then even if (as would
be unlikely to say the least) the thunderingly unexceptional Terry Schmidt
were picked and successfully pitched to the rest of Team Δy's upper echelon
as Awad's replacement, the SRD position really involved nothing more
meaningful than the supervision of 16 cog-like Field Researchers just like
Schmidt himself, plus conducting desultory orientations for new hires,
plus of course overseeing the compression of the TFGs' data into various
statistically differentiated totals, all of which was done on commercially
available software and entailed nothing more significant than adding a
certain number of four-color graphs and a great deal of acronym-heavy
jargon designed to make a survey any competent 10th-grader could conduct
look more sophisticated and meaningful than it really was. Although plus
of course the preliminary lunches and golf and glad-handing with RSB's
MROPs and the actual three-hour presentation of Field Research results
in the larger and more expensively appointed conference room upstairs
where Awad, his audio-visual team, and one chosen member of the relevant Field Team presented the numbers and graphs and facilitated RSB's
MROPs and Creative and Marketing heads' brainstorming on the research's
implications for the actual campaign RSB was already at this stage far too
heavily invested in to do anything more than modify some of the more
ephemeral elements of. (Neither Schmidt nor Darlene Lilley had ever been
selected to assist Bob Awad in these PCAs,[*] for reasons that in Schmidt's

---

[*] = Presentations to Client Agency

case seemed all too clear.) Meaning, in other words, that without anyone once ever saying it outright, Team Δy's real function was to present test-data to Reesemeyer Shannon Belt that RSB could then turn around and present to Client as confirming the soundness of the OCC* that RSB had already billed Client in the millions for and couldn't turn back from even if the actual test-data was resoundingly unpromising, which it was Team Δy's real job to make sure never happened, which real job Team Δy accomplished simply by targeting so many different Focus Groups and foci and varying the format and context of the tests so baroquely and facilitating the different TFGs in so many different ways that in the end it was child's play to selectively weight and rearrange the data in pretty much whatever way RSB's MROP boys wanted, and so Team Δy's ultimate function was not to provide information or even a statistical approximation of information but rather textbook entropy, a cascade of random noise meant to so befuddle the firm and its Client that no one would feel anything but relief at the decision to proceed with an OCC which by this time the Mister Squishy Company itself was so heavily invested in that it couldn't possibly turn away from and would in fact have fired RSB if its testing had indicated any sort of substantive problems, because Mister Squishy's parent company had very strict ratios for R&D marketing costs (RDM) to production volume (PV), ratios based on the Cobb-Douglas Function whereby $\frac{RDM(x)}{PV(x)}$ must, after all the hemming and hawing, be $0 < \frac{RDM(x)}{PV(x)} < 1$, a textbook formula that any first-term MBA student had to memorize in Management Stats, which was in fact where North American Soft Confections Inc.'s CEO had doubtless learned it, and nothing inside the man or at the four large U.S. corporations he had helmed since taking his degree from Wharton in 1968 had changed; no no all that changed were just the jargon and mechanisms and gilt rococo with which everyone in the whole huge blind grinding mechanism conspired to convince each other that they could figure out how to give the paying customer what they could prove he could be persuaded to believe he wanted without anybody once ever saying Stop a second! or pointing out the absurdity of calling what they were doing collecting 'information' or ever even saying aloud—even Team Δy's Field Researchers together over drinks at Beyers' Market Pub on E. Ohio together on Fridays

---

* = Overall Campaign Concept

before going home alone to stare at the phone—what was going on or what it obviously meant or what the simple truth was. That it made no difference. None of it. One RSB Senior Creative Director in his gray ponytail had been at one upscale cafe someplace and had ordered one trendy Death By Chocolate dessert on the same day he was making notes for a Creative Directors brainstorming session on what to pitch to the Subsidiary P.D. boys over at North American Soft Confections, and had had one idea, and one or two dozen gears already machined and set in place in various craggy heads at RSB and North American's Mister Squishy had needed only this one single spark of $C_{12}H_{22}O_{11}$-inspired passion from an SCD whose whole reputation had been made equating toilet paper with clouds and helium-voiced teddybears and all manner of things innocent of shit in some abstract Ur-consumer's mind to set in movement a machine of which no one single person now—least of all the Squishy Mr. T.E Schmidt, forgetting himself enough almost to pace a little before the conference table's men and toying dangerously with the idea of dropping the involved farce and simply telling them the truth—could be master.

Not surprisingly, the marketing of a conspicuously high-sugar, high-cholesterol, Shadow-class snack cake had presented substantially more costs and challenges than the actual kitchenwork of development and production. As with most Antitrend products, the *Felony!* had to walk a fine line between a consumer's resentment of the Healthy Lifestyles trend's ascetic pressures and the guilt and unease any animal instinctively felt when it left the herd—or perceived itself as leaving the herd—and the successful Shadow product was one that managed to position and present itself in such a way as to resonate with both these drives at once, the facilitator told the Focus Group, using slight changes in intonation and facial expression to put tone-quotes around 'herd.' The perfectly proportioned mixture of shame, delight, and secret alliance in the Ericson-D.D.B.N. spots were a seminal example of this sort of multivalent pitch, Terry Schmidt said, tweaking Awad again and letting the small secret thrill of it almost make him throw a puckish wink at the smoke detector, as too was Jolt Cola's brand-name's double-entendre of a 'jolt' to both the individual nervous system and the tyranny of dilute and innocuous soft drinks in an era of trendy asceticism, as well of course as Jolt's well-packaged can's iconic face with its bulging novelty-shop eyes and electrolized hair and ghastly fluorescent computer-room pallor—for Jolt had worked to position itself as a recreational beverage for digital-era Phreaks and managed at once to acknowledge, parody, and evect the Phreak as an avatar of individual rebellion.

Schmidt had also adopted one of Darlene Lilley's signature physical mannerisms when addressing TFGs, which was sometimes to put one foot forward with his or her weight on its heel and to lift the remainder of that foot slightly and to waggle it idly back and forth along the x axis with the planted heel serving as pivot, which in Lilley's case was slightly more effective and appealing because a burgundy high heel formed a better pivot than a cocoa-brown cordovan loafer. Sometimes Schmidt had dreams in which he was one of a Focus Group's consumers being led by Darlene Lilley as she crossed her sturdy ankles or waggled her 9DD high heel back and forth along the floor's x axis and had her eyeglasses off, which were small and oval with tortoiseshell-design frames, and had one of the glasses' delicate arms in closer and closer proximity to her mouth, and the whole dream was Schmidt and the rest of the Focus Group for the nameless product hovering right on the edge of watching Darlene actually put the glasses' arm inside her mouth, which she came incrementally closer and closer to doing without ever quite seeming to be aware of what she was doing or the effect it was having, and the feeling of the dream was that if she ever did actually put it in her mouth something very important and/or dangerous would happen, and the ambient unspoken tension of the dream's constant waiting often left Schmidt exhausted by the time he awoke and remembered again who and what he was, opening the lightproof curtains.

In the morning at the sink's mirror shaving sometimes Schmidt would examine the faint lines beginning to appear and connect the dots of pale freckle in meaningless ways on Mister Squishy's face and could envision in his mind's eye the deeper lines and sags and bruised eye-circles of his face's predictable future and imagine the slight changes required to shave his 44-year-old cheeks and chin as he stood in this exact spot ten years hence and checked his moles and nails and brushed his teeth and examined his face and did precisely the same series of things in preparation for the exact same job he had been doing now for eight years, sometimes carrying the vision further all the way and seeing the ravaged lineaments and bloblike body propped upright on wheels with a blanket on its lap against some sundrenched pastel backdrop, coughing. So even if the almost vanishingly unlikely were to happen and Schmidt did get tagged to replace Robert Awad or one of the other SRDs the only substantive difference would be that he would receive a larger share of Team Δy's after-tax profits and so would be able to afford a nicer and better-appointed condominium to masturbate himself to sleep in and more of the props and surface pretenses of someone truly important but he wouldn't be important, he would make no more substantive difference in the larger scheme of things than he did now. The almost 35-year-old Terry Schmidt had nothing left anymore of the delusions that he differed from the great herd of the common run of men, not even in his despair at not making a difference or the great hunger to have an impact that in his early 30s he'd clung to as evidence that even though he was emerging as sort of a failure the grand ambitions against which he judged himself a failure were somehow exceptional and superior to the common run's, not anymore, since now even the phrase 'Make a Difference' had become a platitude so familiar that it was used as the tag-mnemonic in low-budget Ad Council PSAs for Big Brothers/Big Sisters and the United Way, which used 'Make a Difference in a Child's Life' and 'Making a Difference in Your Community' respectively, with B.B./B.S. even acquiring the telephonic equivalent of *DIF-FER-ENCE* to serve as their Volunteer Hotline number in the metro area. Schmidt, then at the cusp of 30, at first had rallied himself into what he knew was a classic consumer delusion, viz. that the B.B./B.S. tag-line and telephone number were a meaningful coincidence and directed somehow particularly at him, and had called and volunteered to act as Big Brother for a boy age 11–15 who lacked significant male mentors and/or positive role models, and had sat through the two three-hour trainings and testimonials with what was the psychological equivalent of a rigid grin, and the first boy he was assigned to as a Big Brother had worn a tiny black leather jacket with fringe hanging from the shoulders' rear and a red handkerchief tied over his head and was on the tilted porch of his low-income home with two other boys also in expensive jackets, and all three boys had without a word jumped into the back seat of Schmidt's car, and the one whose photo and heartbreaking file identified him as Schmidt's mentorless Little Brother had leaned forward and tersely spoken the name of a large shopping mall in Aurora some distance west of the city, and after Schmidt had driven them on the nightmarish I-88 Tollway all the way to this mall and been directed to pull over at the curb outside the main entrance the three boys had all jumped out without a word and run inside, and after waiting at the curb for over three hours without their returning—and after two $40.00 tickets and a tow-warning from the Apex MegaMall Security officer, who was totally indifferent to Schmidt's explanation that he was here in his capacity as a Big Brother and was afraid to move the car for fear that his Little Brother would come out expecting to see Schmidt's car right where he and his friends had left it and would be traumatized if it appeared to have vanished just like so many of the other adult male figures in his case file's history—Schmidt had driven home; and subsequent telephone calls to the Little Brother's home were not returned. The second 11–15-year-old boy he was assigned to was not at home either of the times Schmidt had come for his appointment to mentor the boy, and the woman who answered the apartment door—who claimed to be the boy's mother although she was of a completely different race than the boy in the file's photo, and who the second time appeared to be intoxicated—claimed to have no knowledge of the appointment or the boy's whereabouts or even the last time she'd seen him, after which Schmidt had finally acknowledged the delusory impression that the Ad Council's PSAs had succeeded in making on him and had—now 30, older, wiser, more indurate—given up and just gone about his business.

In his spare time Schmidt read, watched satellite television, collected rare and uncirculated U.S. coins, ran discriminant analyses of TFG statistics on his Apple Powerbook, worked in the small home laboratory he'd established in his condominium's utility room, and power-walked on a treadmill in a line of eighteen identical treadmills on the mezzanine-level CardioDeck of a Bally's Total Fitness franchise just east of the Prudential Center on Mies van der Rohe Way, where he also sometimes used the sauna. Favoring beige, rust, and cocoa-brown in his professional wardrobe, short and soft and round-faced and vestigially freckled, with a helmetish haircut and a smile that always looked forced no matter how real the cheer, Terry Schmidt had been described by one of Scott R. Laleman's toadies in Technical Processing as looking almost exactly like a '70s yearbook photo come to life. Agency MROPs he'd worked with for years had trouble recalling his name and always greeted him with an exaggerated bonhomie designed to obscure this fact. Ricin and botulinus were about equally easy to cultivate. They were actually both quite easy indeed, if you were comfortable in a laboratory environment and exercised due care in your procedures. Schmidt himself had personally overheard some of the other young men in Technical Processing refer to Darlene Lilley as 'Lurch' or 'Herman' and make fun of her height and physical solidity.

41.6% of what Schmidt mistakenly believed were the TFG's twelve actual consumers were now presenting with the classic dilated eyes and shiny pallor of low-grade insulin shock as Schmidt announced to the men that he'd decided to 'privately confide' to them that the product's original proposed trade-name had been *Devils*, a name meant both to connote the chocolate-intensive composition and to simultaneously invoke and parody associations of 'sin,' 'sinful indulgence,' 'yielding to temptation,' (with the proposed tag-line being 'Sinfully Delicious' or something equally unsubtle), and that considerable resources had been devoted to developing, refining, and target-testing the product inside various combinations of red-and-black individual wrappers with various cartoonishly demonic incarnations of the familiar Mister Squishy icon, presented here as rubicund and heavy-browed and grinning maniacally instead of endearingly, before negative test-data scrapped the whole strategy—both Darlene Lilley and Trudi Keener had worked some of these early Focus Groups, which apparently some inträ-agency political enemy of the Creative Packaging Director at Reesemeyer Shannon Belt who'd pitched the trade-name *Devils* had used his (meaning the CPD's enemy's) influence with RSB's MROP coordinator to stock heavily with consumers from downstate IL, a region that as Terry Schmidt knew all too well tended to be rural and Republican and Bible-Beltish, and without going into any of the Medicean intrigues and retaliations that had ended up costing three mid-level RSB executives their jobs and resulted in at least one six-figure settlement to forestall WT* litigation (which was the only truly interesting part of the story, Schmidt himself believed, jingling a pocket's contents and watching his cordovan rotate slowly from 10:00 to 2:00 and back again as straticulate clouds in the Lake's upper atmosphere began to lend the sunlight a pearly cast that the conference room's windows embrowned), the stacked Groups' responses to tag-lines that included 'Sinfully Delicious,' 'Demonically Indulgent,' and 'Why Do You Think It's Called [in red] **Temptation**?' as well as to video storyboards in which shadowed and voice-distorted figures in hoods 'confessed' to being regular

* = Wrongful Termination

upstanding citizens and consumers who unbeknownst to anyone 'Worshipped the Devil' in 'Secret Orgies of Indulgence,' had been so uniformly extreme as to produce markedly different 'Taste' and 'Overall Satisfaction' aggregates for the snack cakes on IRPs and GRDSs completed before and after exposure to the lines and boards themselves—which after much mid-level headrolling and high-level caucuses had resulted in the present *Felonies!*®, with its milder penal and thus renegade associations designed to be much lighter and to offend absolutely no one except maybe anticrime wackos and prison-reform fringes. With facilitator Schmidt's stated point being let none of those assembled here today doubt that their judgments and responses and the hard evaluative work they had already put in and would shortly plunge into again qua Group in the vital GRDS phase were important or were taken very seriously indeed by the folks over at Mister Squishy.

A man in his early 30s with a vaguely kite-shaped face showing no signs of polypeptide surfeit was staring, from his place at the corner of the conference table nearest Schmidt and the whiteboard, either absently or not at Schmidt's valise, which was made of a pebbled black synthetic-leather material and was quite a bit wider and squatter than your average-type briefcase or valise, resembling almost more a doctor's bag or a computer technician's upscale toolcase. Among the periodicals to which Schmidt subscribed were *U.S. News & World Report*, *Numismatic News*, *Advertising Age*, and the quarterly *Journal of Applied Statistics*, the last of which was divided into four stacks of two years each which supported a sanded-pine plank and sodium work lamp that functioned as a laboratory table with various decanters, retorts, flasks, vacuum jars, filters, and Reese-Handey-brand alcohol burners in the small utility room that was separated from Schmidt's condominium's kitchen by a foldable door of flimsy louvered enamel composite. Ricin and its close relative abrin, both powerful phytotoxins, are derived from castor and jequirity beans respectively, whose attractive flowering plants can be purchased at most commercial nurseries and require three months of cultivation to yield mature beans, which are lima-shaped and either scarlet or lustrous brown and historically were, Schmidt had gotten that eerie Big Brothers/Big Sisters—like sensation again when he discovered during his careful researches, apparently employed as rosary beads, possibly by medieval flagellants. Castor beans' seed hulls must be removed by soaking 1–4 oz of the beans in 12–36 oz of distilled water with 4–6 tablespoons of NaOH or 6–8 ts of commercial lye (their natural buoyancy requires that the beans be weighed down with marbles, sterilized gravel, or low-value coins combined and tied in an ordinary Trojan® condom). After one hour of soaking, the beans can be taken out of solution and dried and the hulls carefully removed by anyone wearing quality surgical gloves. (Ordinary rubber household gloves are too thick and unwieldy for removing castor hulls.) Schmidt had step-by-step instructions stored on both the hard-drive and backup disks of his Apple home computer, which possessed a three-hour battery capacity and could itself be set up on the pine work table in order to keep a very precise and time-indexed experimental log, which is one of the absolutely basic principles of proper lab procedure. A blender (on Purée) is used to grind the hulled beans plus commercial acetone in a 1:4 ratio. Discard blender after use. Pour castor-acetone mixture into a sterile covered jar and let stand for 72–96 hours. Attach a sturdy commercial coffee filter to an identical jar and pour the mixture slowly and carefully through the filter. You are not decanting; what you're after is what's being filtered out. Wearing two pairs of surgical gloves and at least two standard commercial filtration-masks, use manual pressure to force as much acetone as possible out of the sediment in the filter. Bear down as hard as due caution permits. Weigh the remainder of the filter's contents and place them in a third sterile jar along with x4 their weight in fresh CH_3COCH_3. Repeat standing, filtering, and squishing process 3–5 times. The residue at the procedures' terminus will be nearly pure ricin, of which 0.04mg is lethal if injected directly; note that 9.5–12 times this dose is required for lethality through ingestion. Saline or distilled water can be used to load a 0.4mg ricin solution in a standard fine-gauge hypodermic injector, available at better pharmacies everywhere under Diabetes Supplies. Ricin requires 24–36 hours to produce initial symptoms of severe nausea, diarrhea, vomiting, disorientation, and cyanosis. Terminal VF and circulatory collapse follow within twelve hours. Note that *in situ* concentrations under 1.5 mg are undetectable by standard forensic reagents.

More than just a few among the crowds and police initially used the words *sick*, *gross*, and/or *nasty* when the tank's deltate nozzle was affixed to the protuberance at the center of the figure's rear end's bullseye. These comments were silenced by the figure's inflation. First the bottom and belly and thighs ballooned, forcing the figure out from the window and contorting him slightly to keep his forehead's cup affixed. The airtight Lycra rounded and became shiny. The long-haired man on Dexedrine patted his bicycle's rear tire and told the young lady he'd lent the field glasses to that he knew all along what they (presumably meaning the little protuberances) were. One shoulder's valve inflated the left arm, the other the right arm, & c., until the figure's whole costume had become large and bulbous and doughily cartoonish. There was no coherent response from the crowd, however, until a nearly suicidal-looking series of nozzle-to-temple motions from the figure began to fill the head's baggy mask, the crumpled white Mylar at first collapsing slightly to the left and then coming back up erect as it filled with gas, the face's black and patternless lines rounding to resolve into something that produced from 400+ ground-level adults loud cries of recognition and an almost childlike delight.

...That the time, Schmidt told the Focus Group, had—probably not at all to their disappointment, he said with a tiny pained smile—that the time had now arrived for them to elect a Foreman and for Schmidt himself to withdraw and allow the Focus Group's constituents to take counsel together here in the darkening conference room, to compare their individual responses and opinions of the taste, texture, and overall satisfaction of *Felonies!* and to try now together to come up with agreed-upon GRDS-ratings for same. In some of the fantasies in which he and Darlene Lilley were having high-impact intercourse on the firms' conference tables Schmidt kept finding himself saying "Thank you. Oh, thank you' in rhythm to the undulatory thrusting motions of the coitus, and was unable to stop himself, and couldn't help seeing the confused and then distasteful expression the rhythmic 'Oh God, thank you's produced on Darlene Lilley's face even as her eyeglasses fogged and her crosstrainers' heels drummed thunderously on the table's surface, and sometimes it almost spoiled the fantasy. If, after time and a reasonable amount of discussion, the Focus Group for whatever reason found that they could not get together on certain specific numbers to express the Group qua Group's feelings, Schmidt told them (by this time three of the men actually had their heads down on the table, including the overeccentric UAF, who was also emitting tiny low moans, and Schmidt had decided he was going to give this fellow a very low TFG Performance Rating on the evaluations all Team Δy facilitators had to fill out on UAFs at the end of a research cycle), what he'd ask is that the Focus Group then go ahead and submit two separate Group Response Data Sheets, one GRDS comprising each of the numbers on which the Focus Group's two opposed camps had fixed—there was no such thing as a Hung Jury in TFG-testing, he said with a grin he hoped wasn't rigid—and that if splitting into even two such subgroups proved unfeasible because one or more of the men at the table felt that neither subgroup's number adequately captured their own individual feelings and preferences, why then if necessary three separate GRDS should be completed, or four, and so on—but with the overall idea being kept in mind that Team Δy, Reesemeyer Shannon Belt, and the Mister Squishy Co. were asking for the very lowest possible number of GRDS responses an intelligent group of discerning consumers could come up with today. Schmidt in fact had as many as thirteen separate GRDS packets in the manila folder he now held rather dramatically up as he mentioned the GRDS forms, though he removed only one packet from the folder, since there was no point in doing anything actually to encourage the Focus Group to atomize and not unite. The fantasy would of course have been exponentially better if it were Darlene Lilley who gasped 'Thank you, thank you' in rhythm to the damp lisping pelvic slaps; Schmidt was well aware of this, and of his apparent inability to enforce his preferences even in fantasy. It made him wonder if he even had what common convention called a 'will' at all. Only two of the room's fifteen total males noticed that there had been no hint of distant window-muffled exterior noise in the conference room for quite some time; neither of these two were actual test-subjects. Schmidt knew also that by this time—the exordial presentation had so far taken 23 minutes, but it felt, as always, much longer; and even the upright and insulin-tolerant members' restive expressions indicated that they too were feeling hungry and tired and felt that the preliminary presentation was taking an excessively long time, when in fact Robert Awad had confirmed that Alan Britton himself had allotted up to 35 minutes for the putatively experimental 'Full-Access' TFG presentation, and had said that Schmidt's reputation for relative conciseness and the smooth preemption of digressive questions and ephemera was one of the reasons he (meaning R. Awad) had selected Schmidt to facilitate the experimental TFG's GRDS phase—Schmidt knew that by this time Darlene Lilley's own Focus Group was *in camera* and deeply into its own GRDS caucus, and that Darlene was back in the RSB Research Green Room making a brisk cup of Lipton Flo-Thru® Tea in the microwave, what she liked to call her 'grownup' shoes off and resting—one perhaps on its burgundy side—with her briefcase and purse beside one of the comfortable chairs opposite the Green Room's four-part viewing screen, Darlene now facing the microwave and with her great massive back to the door so that

Schmidt would have to sigh loudly or cough or jingle his keys as he came down the hall to the Green Room in order to avoid making her jump and lay her palm against the flounces of her blouse's front by 'coming up behind [her] like that' as she'd once accused him of doing during the six-month period when SRD Awad had indeed been 'coming up behind' her and her own and everyone else's nerves were understandably strung out and on edge. Schmidt would pour a cup of RSB's strong sour coffee and join Darlene Lilley and today's experimental project's other two Field Researchers and perhaps one or two silent and very intense young RSB Market Research interns in the row of cushioned chairs in front of the screens, Schmidt next to Lilley and somewhat in the shadow of her very tall hair, and Ron Mounce would as always produce a pack of cigarettes and Trudi Keener laugh at the way Mounce always made a show of clawing a cigarette desperately out of the pack and lighting it with a trembling hand, and the fact that neither Schmidt nor Darlene Lilley smoked—Darlene had grown up in a household with heavy smokers and was now allergic—would cause a slight alliance of posture as both leaned slightly away from the smoke—Schmidt had once swallowed hard and mentioned the smoking issue with Mounce, cavalierly claiming the allergy as his own, but since RSB equipped its Green Room with both ashtrays and exhaust fans and it was 18 floors down and a hundred yards out the Gap's rear service doors into a small cobbled area where people without private offices gathered on breaks to smoke, it wasn't the sort of issue that could be pressed without appearing like either a militant crank or someone putting on a show of patronizing chivalry for Darlene, who often crossed her legs ankle-on-knee and massaged her instep with both hands as she watched her Focus Group's private deliberations and Schmidt tried to concentrate on his own. There was never much conversation; the four facilitators were still technically 'on,' ready at any time to return to their TFG's conference room if the screen showed their Foreman moving to press the button that the Groups were told activated an amber signal-light.

Team Δy chief Alan Britton, M.S. & J.D., of whom one sensed that no one had ever even once made fun, was an immense and physically imposing man, roughly 6'1" in every direction, with a large smooth shiny oval head in the precise center of which were extremely tiny close-set features arranged in the calm, concentrated smile of a man who'd made a difference in all he'd ever tried.

There was, of course, the problem of taste/texture. Ricin, like most phyto-toxins, is extraordinarily bitter, which meant that the requisite 0.4mg must present for ingestion in a highly dilute form. But the dilution seemed even more unpalatable than the ricin itself: injected through the thin wrapper into the 26x13mm ellipse of frosting at the *Felony!*'s hollow center, the distilled water formed a soggy caustic pocket whose contrast with the deliquescent high-lipid filling itself fairly shouted adulteration. Injection into the moist flourless surrounding cake itself turned an area the size of a 1916 Flowing Liberty Quarter into maltilol-flavored sludge. A promising early alterna-tive was to administer 6–8 very small injections to different areas of the *Felony!* and hope that the subject got all or most of the snack cake down (like Twinkies and Choc-o-Diles, the *Felony!* was designed to be a 'Three-Biter,' but also to be sufficiently light and saliva-soluble that an especially ambitious consumer could get the whole thing into his mouth at once, with predictably favorable consequences for TPMC* and concomitant sales-volume) before anything presented as amiss. The problem here was that each injection, even with a fine-gauge hypodermic, produced a puncture of .012mm diameter (median) in the flimsy transpolymer wrapper, and in individually packaged cakes at average Midwest–New England humidity levels these punctures produced topical staleness/desiccation within 48–72 hours of shelving (as with all Mister Squishy products, *Felonies!* were engineered to be palpably moist and to react with salivary ptyalin in such a way as to literally 'melt in the mouth,' qualities established in very early Field Research to be associated with both freshness and a luxe (almost sensual) indulgence.† The botulinus exotoxin, being tasteless as well as 97% lethal at .00003g., was far more practical, though because its source is an anaerobic it must be injected into the direct center of the product's creamy filling, and even the microscopic

---

* = Total Periods of Multiple Consumption
† The emetic prosthesis consisted of a small polyurethane bag taped under one arm and a tube of ordinary clear plastic running up the rear of my left shoulder blade to emerge from the turtleneck through a small hole just under my chin. The contents of the bag was six of the snack cakes mixed with mineral water and real bile harvested via emetic first thing this a.m. The bag's power cell and vacuum were engineered for one high-volume emission and two or three smaller spurts and dribbles afterward; they were to be activated by a button on my 'watch.' The material wouldn't actually be coming out of my mouth per se, but it was a safe bet that nobody would be looking very closely at the stuff's exit; people's automatic reaction is to avert their eyes. The CPD's transmitter's clear earpiece was attached to my glasses. The scope's Mission Time said 24.30 and change, but the presentation seemed endless; everyone was anxious to get down to business already.

air-pocket produced by evacuation of the hypodermic will begin to attack the compound, requiring ingestion within a week for predictable result. The anaerobic saprophyte *Clostridium botulinum* is simple to culture, requiring only an airtight home-canning jar in which are placed 2–3 oz. of puréed Aunt Nellie-brand beets, 1–2 oz. of common cube steak, two tablespoons of fresh topsoil from beneath the noisome pine chips under the lollipop hedges flanking the pretentiously gated front entrance to Briarhaven Condominiums, with enough ordinary tap water (chlorinated OK) added to the other ingredients to fill the jar to the absolute top. This was the only exacting part: the absolute top. If the water's meniscus comes right to the absolute top of the jar's threaded mouth and the jar's lid is properly applied and screwed on very tightly w/vise and wide-mouth Sears Craftsman pliers so as to allow 0.0% trapped O_2 in the jar, ten days on the top shelf of a dark warm utility closet will produce a moderate bulge in the jar's lid, and extremely careful double-gloved and masked removal of the lid will reveal a small tan-to-brown colony of *Clostridium* awash in a green-to-tan penumbra of botulinus exotoxin, which is, to put it delicately, a byproduct of the mold's digestive process, and can be removed in very tiny amounts with the same hypodermic used for administration. Botulinus had also the advantage of directing attention to defects in manufacturing and/or packaging rather than product tampering, which would of course heighten the overall industry impact.

The real principle behind running Field Research in which some of the TFGs completed only IRPS and some were additionally convened in juridical Groups to hammer out a GRDS was to allow Team Δy to provide Reesemeyer Shannon Belt with two distinct and statistically complete sets of market research data, allowing RSB to use and evince whichever data best reinforced the research results they believed Mister Squishy and N.A.S.C. most wanted to see. Schmidt, Darlene Lilley, and Trudi Keener had been given tacitly to understand that this same principle informed the experimental subdivision of today's TFG juries into 'No-Access' and 'Full-Access' Focus Groups, which latter were to be given preliminary 'behind-the-scenes' information on the genesis, production, and marketing goals of the product; i.e. that whether retroscenic access to marketing agendas created substantive differences in the Focus Groups' mean GRDSs or not, Team Δy and RSB wanted access to different data-fields from which they could pick and choose and use slippery hypergeometric statistical techniques to manipulate as they believed Client saw fit. In the Green Room, only Ronald R. Mounce, M.S. (who is Robert Awad's personal mentee and probable heir-apparent and his mole among the Field Researchers whose water-cooler chitchat Mounce distills and reports via special #0302 Field Concerns and Morale forms that Awad's earnest young Administrative Asst. provides Mounce with in the same manila envelopes all the day's IRPS and GRDS packets are distributed to Field Teams in) Mounce alone knows that the unconventional 'Full-' and 'No-Access' Mister Squishy TFG design is in fact part of a larger Field-experiment that Alan Britton and Team Δy's upper management's secret inner executive circle—said circle incorporated by Britton as a §543 Personal Holding Company under the dummy name 'Δy^2'—is conducting for its own sub rosa research into TFGs' role in the ever more self-conscious and media-savvy marketing strategies of the future. The idea, as Robert Awad saw fit to explain to Mounce on Awad's new catamaran one June day when they were becalmed and drifting four nautical miles off Montrose Wilson Beach's private jetties, was that as the ever-evolving U.S. consumer became ever more savvy and discerning about media and marketing and tactics of product-positioning—an insight into the individual consumer mind that Awad said he had achieved in his health club's sauna after handball one day when the intellectual-property attorney he had just decisively beaten at handball was complimenting an A.C. Romney– Jaswat campaign for the new carbonated beverage Surge® whose tightly demotargeted advertisements everyone had been seeing all over the metro area that quarter, and remarked (the intellectual-property attorney* did) that he probably found these modern youth-targeted ads utilizing guitar-riffs and epithets like 'Dude' and the whole ideology of rebellion-via-consumption so interesting and got such a hoot out of them because he himself was 'so far out of the demographic' (using the actual word *demographic*) for a campaign like *Surge*'s that he found himself disinterestedly analyzing the ads' strategies and pitches and appreciating them more like pieces of art or fine pastry, then had (the J.D. had, right there in the sauna, wearing only rubber thongs and a towel wrapped Sikh-style around his head, according to Awad) proceeded casually to deconstruct the strategies and probable objectives of the *Surge* campaign with such acuity that it was almost as if the attorney had been right

---

* (who in fact, unbeknownst to Awad, was an old friend and Limited-Partnership crony of Alan Britton from the previous decade's Passive Income Tax Shelter heyday)

there in the room at A.C. Romney–Jaswat MROP team's brainstorming and strategy confabs with Team Δy, who as Mounce was of course aware had done some first-stage Focus work for ACR-J/Coke on *Surge* six quarters past before the firm's gradual emigration to RSB as a Captured Shop. Awad, whose knowledge of small-craft operation came entirely from a manual he was now using as a paddle, told Mounce the idea's gist's thrust here was that it seemed more and more feasible to make a new product's marketers' strategy and travails themselves a part of that product's essential 'story'—as in for historic examples the 'story' that outer Chicago's own Keebler Inc.'s hard confections were manufactured by elves in a hollow tree, or that Pillsbury's Green Giant–brand canned and frozen vegetables were cultivated by an actual virid giant in his eponymous Valley—but with the added narrative twist now of, say, for instance, advertising Mister Squishy's new *Felony!* line as gourmet snack cakes conceived and marketed by beleaguered legions of nerdy admen under say a tyrannical mullah-like A.S.C. CEO who was such a personal fiend for high-cost luxury-class chocolate that he was determined to push *Felonies!* onto the U.S. market no matter what the cost- or sales-projections, such that (in the proposed campaign's 'story') A.S.C. subsidiary Mister Squishy had to force Team Δy to manipulate and cajole Focus Groups into producing just the sort of 'objective' statistical data needed to green-light the project and get *Felonies!* on the shelves, all this in other words an arch tongue-in-cheek pseudo-behind-the-scenes 'story' that appealed to young consumers' imagined savvy about marketing tactics and 'objective' data and flattered their sense that in this age of metastatic spin and trend and the complete commercialization of every last thing in their world they were extremely jaded and discerning and canny and well-nigh impossible to manipulate by any sort of clever multimillion-dollar marketing campaign. This was, as of the second quarter of 1995, a fairly bold and unconventional marketing concept, Awad conceded modestly over Ron Mounce's cries of admiration and excitement, tossing (Mounce did) another cigarette over the catamaran's side to hiss and bob forever instead of sinking; and Awad further conceded that an enormous amount of very careful and carefully controlled research would have to be done and analyzed in all sorts of hypergeometric ways before he could even conceive of jumping ship and starting his own R. Awad & Associates agency and pitching the idea to various farsighted companies—certain of the U.S. Internet's new start-ups, with their young and self-perceivedly renegade top management, looked like a promising market—to forward-looking companies that craved a fresh, edgy, cynicism-friendly corporate image, rather like FedEx and Subaru in the previous decade, and also Wendy's when Settlemeyer had briefly ruled the industry landscape. In point of fact none of what Robert Awad had brought his mentee four miles out onto the Lake to drop in his ear was conventionally 'true' except as the agreed-upon cover-narrative to be fed select Team Δy SRDs and Field Researchers as part of the control-conditions for the really true Field-experiment, which Alan Britton and Scott R. Laleman (there was no §543-structured 'Δy^2'; that little fiction was part of the cover-narrative Britton had fed Bob Awad, who unbeknownst to him [=Awad] was already being gradually eased out in favor of Mrs. Lilley, whom Laleman said was a whiz on both Systat and HTML and on whom Britton had had his particular eye ever since he'd sent Awad around with covert instructions to behave in such a way as to test for fault-lines in Field Team morale and the girl'd shown such an extraordinary blend of personal stones and political aplomb in defusing Awad's stressors) so but yes which Field-experiment Britton and his mentee Scott Laleman had been told by no less a personage than T. Cordell ('Ted') Belt himself was designed to produce data on the way(s) certain preconceived ideas of market research's purposes affected the way Field Researchers facilitated their Targeted Focus Groups' GRDS phase and thus influenced the material outcome of the TFGs' *in camera* deliberations and GRDSs. The experiment was the second stage of a campaign, Britton had later told Laleman over almost zeppelin-sized cigars in his inner office, to finally after all this time start bringing U.S. marketing research into line with the realities of modern Hard Science, which had proved long ago (Science had) that the presence of an observer affects any process and thus by clear implication that even the tiniest, most ephemeral details of a Field Test's set-up can have a profound impact on the data it produces. The ultimate idea was to eliminate all unnecessary random variables in those Field Tests, and of course by your most basic managerial Ockham's Razorblade this meant doing away as much as possible with the Human Element, the most obvious of which Element was the TFG facilitators, viz. Team Δy's nerdy beleaguered Field Researchers, who now, with the coming digital era of abundant data on whole markets' preferences and patterns available via computer links, were soon to be dinosaurs (the Field Researchers were) anyway, Alan Britton said. A passionate and imposing rhetor, Britton liked to draw invisible little illustrations in the air with his cigar's red tip as he spoke. The mental image Scott Laleman associated with Alan Britton was of an enormous macadamia nut with a tiny little face painted on it. Laleman did unkind impersonations of Britton's voice and facial expressions for some of the boys in Technical Processing when he was sure Mr. B. was nowhere around. The whole thing from soup to nuts could be done via computer network, as Britton said he was sure he didn't have to sell Laleman on. Scott Laleman didn't even like cigars. Meaning the coming WWW cybercommerce thing, which there'd already been countless professional seminars on and all of U.S. marketing and advertising and related support industries were very excited about. But where most agencies still saw the coming WWW primarily as just a new, fifth venue for high-impact ads,* part of your more forward-looking Reesemeyer Shannon Belt–type vision for the coming era involved finding ways to exploit cybercommerce's staggering research potential as well. Undisplayed little tracking codes could be designed to tag and follow each consumer's W3 interests and spending patterns—here Laleman once again told Alan Britton what these algorithms were commonly called and averred that he personally knew how to design them; he did not of course tell Britton that he had already secretly helped design some very special little tracking algorithms for A.C. Romney–Jaswat's & Assoc.'s sirenic Chloe Jaswat and that two of these 'cookies' were even at that moment nested in Team Δy's SMTP/POP protocols. Britton said that Focus Groups and even n-sized test markets could be assembled abstractly via ANOVAs† on consumers' known patterns, that the TFG vetting was built right in—as in e.g. who showed an interest? who bought the product or related products and from which site via which link thing?—that not only would their be no voir dire and no archaic per diem expenses but even the unnecessary variable of consumers even knowing they were part of any sort of market-test was excised, since a consumer's subjective consciousness of his identity as a test-subject instead of a pure desire-driven consumer had always been one of the distortions that market research swept under the rug and ignored because they had no way of calculating subjective identity-consciousness on any known ANOVA. TFGs would go the way of

---

* (venues 1–4 historically comprising TV, Radio, Print, and 'Outdoor' [= mainly billboards])

$\dagger$ = 'ANalysis Of VAriance model,' a sort of hypergeometric multiple-regression technique used by Team Δy to study the statistical relations between dependent and independent variables in market tests.

the dodo and bison and art deco. Britton had already had versions of this conversation with Scott R. Laleman several times; it was part of Britton's way of pumping himself up. Laleman had a vision of himself sitting at a very large oak desk, Chloe Jaswat behind him kneading his trapezius muscles, while an enormous macadamia nut sat in a low chair before the desk and pleaded for a livable severance package. Sometimes, on the very rare occasions when he masturbated, Laleman's fantasy involved a view of himself, shirtless and adorned with war-paint, standing with his boot on the chest of various supine men and howling upward at what was out of the fantasy's frame but might be the moon. That in other words the exact same wonkish technology Laleman's boys in TP now used to run analyses on the TFG paperwork could *replace* the paperwork. No more small-sample testing; no more β-risks or variance-error probabilities or 1-α confidence intervals or regression-inferences or entropic noise. In his junior year at Cornell U. Scott Laleman had once been in an ACS Dept. lab accident and had breathed halon gas and for several subsequent days went around campus with a rose clamped in his teeth and tried to tango with everyone he saw and insisted they all call him 'The Magnificent Enriqué' until several of his fraternity brothers finally ganged up and knocked some sense back into him, but most people thought he was still never quite the same after the halon thing. For now, in Belt and Britton's binocular vision, the market becomes its own test. Territory = Map. Everything encoded. And no more facilitators to muddy the waters by impacting the tests in all the tiny ephemeral unnoticeable infinite ways human beings always kept impacting each other and muddying the water. Team Δy would be 100% TP, a totally Captured Shop. All they needed was some actual study-data showing unequivocally that human facilitators made a difference, that their attitudes and appearance and manner and syntax and/or even small personal tics of individual personality affected the Focus Groups' findings. Something on paper, with all the Systat *t*'s crossed and *i*'s dotted and even maybe yes a high-impact full-color graph—these were professional statisticians, after all, the Field Researchers. They knew the numbers wouldn't lie. If they saw that the data entailed their own subtraction they'd go quietly, most probably even offering to resign, for the good of the Team. Plus then Laleman pointed out that the study-data'd also come in handy if some of them tried to fight it or squeeze the Team for a better severance by threatening some kind of bullshit WT suit. He could almost feel the texture of Mr.

B.'s sternum under his heel. Not to mention (said Britton, who sometimes then held the cigar like a dart and jabbed it at the air when stipulating or refining a point) that not all would have to go. The Field Researchers. That some could be kept. Transferred. Retrained to work the machines, to follow the cookies and run the Systat codes and sit there amusing themselves while it all compiled. The others would have to go. It was a tough business; Darwin's tag-line still fit. Britton usually addressed Scott Laleman as 'Laddie' or 'Boyo,' but of course never even once as 'The Magnificent Enriqué.' Mr. B. had absolutely 0% knowledge of what and who Scott R. Laleman really was inside, as an individual, with a very special and above-average destiny, Laleman felt. He had practiced his smile a great deal, both with and sans rose. Britton said the *sub rosa* experiments' stressors would, as always in Nature and Science, determine survival. Fitness. Who fit the new pattern. Versus who made too much difference, see, and where, *in camera*. This was 100% bullshit. Britton poked holes in the air above the desk. See how the facilitators reacted to different stimuli, how they responded to their Focus Groups' own reactions. All they needed were stressors. High-stress stimuli. Rattle the cage. Up the voltage, see what fell out, he said. This was known in the game as Giving Someone Enough Rope. The big man leaned back, his smile both warm and expectant. Inviting the Boyo he'd chosen to mentor to brainstorm with him on some possible stressors right here and now. As in with Britton himself, to flesh out the tests. No time like now. Scott Laleman felt a kind of vague latent dread as the big man made a show of putting out his Fuente. A chance to step up to the plate with the big dogs, get a taste of real front-lines creative action. Right here and now. A chance for Δy's golden boy to strut his stuff. Impress the boss. Run something up the pole. Anything at all. Spontaneous flow. To brainstorm. The trick was not to think or edit, just let it all fly.[*] The big man counted down from five and put one hand to his ear and came down with the other hand to point at Scott Laleman as if to say You're On The Air, his eyes now two nailheads and tiny mouth turned down like a Greek mask. The finger had something dark's remains in the rim around its nail. Laleman sat there smiling at it, his mind a great flat blank white screen.

---

[*] Britton knew all about Laleman trying to jew him out to Romney–Jaswat; who did the smug puppy think he was dealing with; Alan S. Britton had been infighting and surviving when this kid was playing with his little pink toes.

DAYS

a twenty-minute story by ALEKSANDAR HEMON

ON MAY 24, 1968, I was brought back to consciousness by cold water my Uncle Bogdan poured on my face. I had fallen into a ditch full of cow shit, mud, and yucky sludge. The cup was beaten tin, and I drank from it later.

On September 1, 1971, my father brought me a blazing-white sweater from his trip to Monaco. On the chest, there was a resplendent emblem for the Casino Royale.

September 7, 1971: my mother made me wear it to school. I was embarrassed because I stuck out, and some kids thought that my family was rich. So after school, I rolled in the dirt behind the school. I told my mother I had been tripped by a bully named Ziojutro.

January 15, 1974: I had a dream in which hordes of armored knights were sledding. There were three knights per sled, and I could hear the din of clattering visors and squealing knights and swords and armors clashing when the sleds turned over. I couldn't see the knights' faces. Another part of the same dream—though what the relation was I could not tell—was the feeling that my big toes were enlarged to the size of a horsehead.

April 19, 1974: I wrote a poem entitled "Is This Death or Rebirth?" It was based on an untested assumption of mine that when you die, you go to a place thickly populated with dinosaurs and other gigantic reptiles.

May 9, 1974: I gave that poem to a girl I was in love with so much that I couldn't imagine her not being in love with me, and she wasn't. She thought "Is This Death or Rebirth?" to be weird, and it was.

July 29, 1982: I scored a goal with a bicycle kick. It was a school soccer tournament, played on a concrete surface. I dislocated my shoulder, and we lost.

October 3, 1984: I slept under my bed in the platoon dorm, successfully hidden from the platoon commander, who stupidly expected me to dwell over the freedom of our people and be on guard against the enemy, inner and outer. Neither the inner nor the outer enemy ever slept, but I did, every day, under the bed.

February 11, 1987: I got drunk on a bitter herbal digestive, normally consumed by the worst of drunks, who liked to believe that being wasted on a digestive was good for their ulcers. I wore a navy blue trench coat and my father's pseudo-Irish hat, which was thereafter marked by a barely visible vomit stain on its rim.

August 25, 1990 (a Tuesday): My girlfriend came to our date with a postcoital glaze over her eyes. There were so many fornication candidates (including numerous women) that I couldn't be jealous. I was just sad, because when I embraced her, it was like embracing an empty coat.

November 11, 1991: I saw my dog—a beautiful, flaming-red Irish Setter—running uphill (the same hill, come to think of it, down which the knights were sledding in my dream) with a unit of military police shooting with blanks, getting ready for the use of live ammo. I had let my dog out of the mountain cabin I was spending my time and wasting my mind in, because he started licking my face at 6 a.m. So at 10 a.m. my dog was running alongside military policemen with gas masks. I couldn't see their faces, but I could hear their panting and the chatter of their helmets, as I stood outside in my pajamas and whistled, calling my dog. My dog ignored me, thinking it was all a game, the military police charging at the imaginary enemy. I whistled.

March 30, 1993: I told the story of my life to a restaurant manager in Chicago. I was trying to get a busboy job. He had a sword tattoed on his arm.

December 10, 1998: In a graduate Shakespeare class I pronounce the word *akin* as "achin'."

January 2, 2000: I washed my face with cold water and noticed that the toothpaste sprinkles on the mirror formed a pattern.

On Ocotber 23, 2002, in Chicago, I wrote this down—it took me some thirty minutes. After I finished, I felt a quick emptiness looking out the window at the garage roofs and fences and back alleys, where kids in helmets rode their skateboards. The only thing moving in my room was a pot with a plant that calls itself snowstorm, swinging like a pendulum.

—October 23, 2002, 10:30–11:02 a.m., Chicago, IL

A NOTE ON *GENTLEMEN, START YOUR ENGINES*

IT WAS A sunny day on my back porch when I got a call. "Hey Andy," the voice said cheerfully. "We're making a broadsheet newspaper. We were wondering if you'd do a sports column." I have many fine qualities, including a mean paella and a magic eye in a consignment store, but writing amazing sports pieces is not among them. I do, however, have a sporty husband, who can meet a stranger and guess what car they drive in three tries.

"We were thinking you and David should go to a NASCAR rally. It'll be classic." The absurdity of the idea rocked the back porch on its shaky pilings. "And we were thinking a really long piece. Like thirty pages." This seemed absolutely impossible. But David brightly said it sounded great, I should totally do it. I called up my mother and told her, proudly, that I was going to be a sports writer and she laughed and laughed. I could hear her sighing and wiping tears from her face. "Well, bless your heart" was the best she could do.

I was off to an artist colony, and David was traveling for work, so, looking at the NASCAR schedule, we discovered the only date we could meet up was in August. In Michigan. My heart sank; I had a fantasy of visiting South Carolina, where my family is from. Michigan didn't seem… foreign enough. But we booked flights into Detroit and I talked with the Michigan Speedway lady about what tickets to get ("Everything, honey!") and waited a month and a half before meeting up at a hotel in Detroit and readying for our journey.

The results are here. There is a tiny tent, Mardi Gras beads, and Bud Light Lime. I had done an enormous amount of research into NASCAR, and Michigan, and certainly had enough material from the event to write something very funny. But after the trip, when I sat down to write, I found myself stumped. Things had not turned out as I'd expected; I did not feel, anymore, that I wanted to make fun of anyone we met, or anything we saw. I realized the only comical character was me. And the only hero was my husband.

I picked two inspirations (Wallace and Whitman) and two points of view (first and second) and stared at the screen. It was not a new realization that I am a ridiculous creature. To sit before a manuscript and understand that I had to toss out the pages I'd written and start all over, this time with myself as the object of ridicule, was similar to the thought going through the head of the bowl of petunias called into being by the Improbability drive in *The Hitchhiker's Guide to the Galaxy* before it is dashed out of existence: "Oh no, not again!" But I did it. And here it is. Again. —ANDREW SEAN GREER

GENTLEMEN, START
YOUR ENGINES

by ANDREW SEAN GREER

(nonfiction from Issue 33; The San Francisco Panorama)

SING TO ME, America, of stock-car racing! Of four hundred miles driven in four hours. Sing to me of Goodyear tires and Sunoco gasoline, of Gatorade Victory Lane and of ServiceMaster Clean, of the Sprint Cup and of Nationwide and Craftsman Truck, of Bud and Bud Light and Bud Light Lime. Sing to me of Jeff Gordon and Jimmie Johnson, of Joey Logano and Juan Pablo Montoya, of Dale Earnhardt and Dale Earnhardt Jr., of Jack Daniel's and Jameson. Sing to me, America, of beer bongs and beads for boobies. Sing to me of Sin City.

Say you find yourself, America, with all your fellow NASCAR fans, gathered around the campfire and throwing menthol cigarettes into its embers, tossing back beers, entranced by the story Lucky tells about Cupcake, the midget stripper he once hired for a bachelor party. You and your husband sit in camping chairs as Lucky's wife Jennifer delivers shots of something they invented called a Cherry Bomb. Say you are a gay man; say tonight is your first wedding anniversary, at least in California where you married while it was legal, and you have chosen to celebrate it here, with strangers, at the Michigan International Speedway. Say Lucky and his friends do not know this. For all you know, they take your two-man tent as simply another strange California way of doing things, your Joey Logano beer coozies (he is the youngest and cutest driver) as one of the whims of NASCAR fandom, and your wedding rings as proof of wives you left behind, as they have left their children. The group toasts with their Cherry Bombs and downs them all together; you and your husband do as well. It tastes like cotton candy. It tastes delicious. Then Lucky tells you about how Cupcake arrived at the party, a much younger girl than he expected, and had the time of her life, giving the groom-to-be a lap dance that took place entirely on his lap. Later he came to understand that this was her first time.

"The variety of human experience," you say, perhaps too loudly, too grandly after all the beers and shots, as the faces turn toward you all at once, "it's vast and wonderful, isn't it?"

There is a pause, and you can hear the beer cans warping slightly in the fire and cracking from the heat. The smell of cotton candy seems omnipresent. Faces glow in firelight, and from somewhere far away, a car alarm goes off.

"Ain't that the truth?" says Lucky, and everyone laughs, and Jennifer pours you another Cherry Bomb. And say this middle-aged man, tanned and big-bodied and happy, just say he murmurs, "Now fellas," nodding at you and your husband very seriously before you down your shots, "since it's your first NASCAR, maybe we should take y'all to Sin City—"

"Oh, Lucky," Jennifer says, shaking her head.

"It's their first time! They gotta see Sin City!"

"What's Sin City?" your dear husband asks, and of course that question can only be answered one way. Lucky looks up at you with a wide grin and shrugs.

"Oh," you interrupt, "oh, we have to get up early for the race tomorrow. We've got pit passes—" In truth, you do not really know what pit passes are.

"Well you gotta see Sin City. You gotta see it to believe it," he says. And within a few minutes he has persuaded the entire group to take you to the secret wild part of NASCAR nightlife, a place found only by chance or by listening for the faint beat of dance music. They call it Sin City, but that's just something they have made up over the years to describe it. There is no real name for what you are trying to find, and now, for you, there is no turning back.

Give me, O America, the strength to tell the tale!

We had come to Michigan in search of NASCAR racing, a weekly event that crisscrosses America and brings with it all the great stars of stock-car racing and their fans, which at the Michigan event numbered above a hundred and twenty thousand on the day of the CARFAX 400. Now, I would not call myself a NASCAR fan. In fact, in my first conversation with my husband about the idea, he asked me to tell him what NASCAR stood for, and I answered, "National Stock Car Racing." Then I paused. "Wait, I think I left out some A's there, didn't I? National... wait... North American Stock Car... Association... Racing?" Then he asked me what I thought a stock car was. "Oh, well a stock car is like... an ordinary car that they've tricked out for racing, with a bigger engine and things, like a turbo Honda Accord." I grinned with pleasure at my answer. Then he asked: "And what direction do the drivers turn?" I figured I had even odds at that one. I guessed they turned right. David nodded his head in amazement.

What NASCAR stands for is National Association for Stock Car Auto Racing. What it is—well, perhaps it's better to say what it's not. It's not what it started as, which was moonshiners evading revenuers in the Appalachian Mountains, modifying their cars with faster engines and learning tricks to take on the rough roads and turns of hill country. In 1948, a man named Bill France came up with the idea of setting a "shiner" race in Daytona Beach, known as the hub of high-speed land records since the early twentieth century. France established a governing body and rules and regulations, and stipulated that the cars be "strictly stock." NASCAR is still run by the France family today. The CEO is Bill's grandson, Brian France, a fact that seems unfair to many fans. Until the fifties, cars ran with virtually no modifications at all, but by the sixties cars were being specifically manufactured for racing. Though they still bear the badges of their putative "stock" models, NASCAR cars are designed from the ground up purely for winning, just as sharks are designed purely for killing.

It is not the Indy 500. It is also not Formula One. As I was informed by my husband, the thrill of NASCAR is that, while the cars are no longer "strictly stock," there is at least a nod toward the originals. NASCAR fans enjoy the idea that these are modified American cars, and while there is no rule to this effect, any deviation brings an uproar; note the fury following the recent inclusion, along with the Chevy Monte Carlo and the Ford Fusion, of the Toyota Camry as an eligible model. Toyota, though not an American company, manufactures the Camry in the States, but I beg you not to visit the numerous forums where the topic of whether Toyota has "ruined" NASCAR usually devolves into whether "Jap" or "redneck" is the more racist term.

Another thrill of NASCAR, apparently, is that the cars have fenders. Unlike Indy and Formula One racing (with their long-necked, big-tired vehicles), this allows cars to scrape up next to each other for seat-hugging suspense without fear of tangled tires. NASCAR also isn't merely a matter of who wins the race: the NASCAR Sprint Cup (as opposed to the Nationwide Series and the Craftsman Truck Series) awards points over its ten-month-long series of thirty-six races, and after twenty-six races the top twelve drivers are awarded a base point level and are now "in the chase" for the Cup. The Michigan Carfax 400 we were attending was race number twenty-three.

And that is all I know. I am sure I have it completely wrong. I always get this kind of thing wrong, much to my husband's dismay. I am the sort of man who, before attending a baseball game, must yet again have a full explanation of the rules. Nine innings, right? So why are we standing at the seventh? Why does that hitter not have to play in the field? Somehow, I cannot keep this stuff in my head.

Oh, and also: the drivers turn left. When it comes to cars, I cannot get anything right.

This is not for lack of trying. At our house, we subscribe to five car magazines, and one of them is called *AutoWeek*. That magazine arrives, as you've no doubt guessed, *weekly*. I cannot get through a weekly *New Yorker*, but David gets through *AutoWeek* in no time. In addition, David often purchases copies of his favorite car magazine, a British publication called *CAR*, which is also my favorite car magazine, because it is very glossy and has high-quality photographs of glamorous cars that I can look at in the bathroom. We also travel to auto shows, sometimes three a year, and usually David goes to each show three or four times in order to see all the cars completely, and to get to sit in each one. I try to find interest in all this, I really do. When we go to an auto show, I give David fifteen slips of paper, representing fifteen cars he can make me sit inside, and he has to pay me a slip of paper every time. I do this to prevent him from making me sit in hundreds of cars; I do this to prevent my own untimely death. But I try. I read the car magazines. I listen to his ideas about what cars he thinks everyone we know should get. I look at pictures online of cars he would really like to get himself. I tell him what cars I myself would like to get if I lived in the suburbs, or Germany, or Alaska, or in the 1950s, or on a farm. I listen, I look, I tell. But really, I couldn't care less. Cars, to me, are appliances, just like my microwave. They do their job, sometimes they're pretty, but I don't think about them when they're not around.

David does.

The Michigan International Speedway lies about seventy miles southwest of Detroit, and if you're gay or Jewish or an Obama liberal, you will probably pass through Ann Arbor and pick up four Reuben sandwiches from Zingerman's deli, visit the Farmer's Market for local greengage plums and apples, discover an astounding invention called Pie Bites (which David plans to market), and visit the local Target for a cooler and cans of Starbucks Espresso & Cream for the morning. Later down the road, you will pick up ice at the liquor store and stand in a walk-in beer cooler and puzzle over the many varieties, all of them light beer, none of which your India-pale-ale-only husband is willing to drink. Finally you will have an argument in the walk-in beer cooler about whether Bud Light Lime is a gay beer or merely a girl's beer, and surely the clerks watch your lovers' spat through the glass of the sealed sound-proof door, faces blocked by stickers of NASCAR drivers. You will also argue over how many beers are needed, and end up buying twenty. Bud Light Lime wins, and you will gaily purchase it from the clerk, confident that you will now have plenty of Bud Light Lime to give away. Turns out you get a free NASCAR poster with every case of Bud.

Husband loads the beer into the cooler. Off you go, confident that everything is taken care of. The notes, the camera, the tickets and camping site. The twenty Bud Light Limes floating in their dream of ice. Of course, twenty will not be nearly enough. Not for NASCAR camping.

The Irish Hills of Michigan host a number of tourist attractions, including the expected Hill of Mystery, shamrock-laded bars and clubs, and numerous BBQ places (one with a gigantic cow bearing the message SAVE A COW, EAT PORK), but none are as attractive as the Prehistoric Forest Amusement Park, which lies with its animatronic dinosaurs frozen over the pathways, forced to endure yet another extinction, this one revealed by the FOR SALE sign out front, and you have a brief fantasy of telling your friends that you've decided to leave San Francisco and open a theme park in rural Michigan, and that the out-of-scale T. Rex will once more attack the meek Diplodocus, and rivers of blood will run again in the Irish Hills. But the fantasy fades as soon as the signs for NASCAR appear.

Tens of thousands of fans camp outside the Michigan International Speedway for each race, but of all the myriad campsites surrounding the track, only one of them offers tent camping. The rest are exclusively for RVs. The cost of a campsite is surprisingly high—one hundred and thirty dollars—but it is a flat fee for the week, and considering that many race fans arrive on Wednesday and don't leave until the following Monday, it's not outrageous. Of course, tickets to the Sunday Sprint Cup race are one hundred and ten dollars each, pit passes fifty, tickets to the Saturday Nationwide race fifty as well, and that doesn't count travel costs, RV rental, and food and beverages, so that leaves a family of four spending up to a thousand dollars for a NASCAR weekend, something completely out of the question for most of the people camping there, and a number that makes one wonder how "anti-elitist" the NASCAR circuit can really be. (For the 2010 season, the Michigan International Speedway is lowering weekend prices for all Grandstand seats, with teenagers half off and young kids free.)

To economize, many race fans pay their campsite fee but don't purchase tickets in advance except for the Sunday race. Some are able to borrow tickets, for instance on Saturday when there are two races, or pit passes, which last through long hot hours, from those who have gone earlier in the day and don't plan to use them again. It is crucial to get pit passes, however, in whatever way one can, because for many fans pit passing allows them their sole moment to meet their favorite driver in the pit and, perhaps, to collect his autograph. It is common to see fans wearing their pit passes around their necks on lanyards, the passes covered with signatures, as a way of showing their status as an autograph-seeker. You and your husband have pre-ordered pit passes. You will, however, fail completely to get anybody's autograph.

And so you arrive at the Northwoods campsite, stopping at the ranger's station to get an entry sticker, and it is there, talking to the rather dykey red-haired Ranger Dawn, that you receive the first of many NASCAR shocks: she is absolutely friendly and welcoming. In fact, *everyone* who works here is welcoming: the security guards who search your bags, the teenagers who take your tickets, even Brian at Will Call who sits in a hot booth and listens to a race he never gets to see. Dawn takes the time to make it clear where your site is, how to find the markers, where the shower-trailer is (with hot water!), the Porta-Johns, and the entrance to the track itself. You then enter NASCAR camping proper, past RVs and pop-up trailers, into the tent campsites all aflutter with flags. Canadian flags, NASCAR driver flags (many for 24, Jeff Gordon, and 48, Jimmie Johnson), and yes of course Confederate flags. "But we're in Michigan!" your husband exclaims. "What could a Confederate flag mean to a Michigander? That you wish the South had seceded from the Union? Wasn't this still a territory? I don't get it!" And you tell your husband to be quiet, because you have arrived. Spot P-14. And there, where in every other site campers have erected their tents, you see that yours, in a sweet ironic gesture from the gods, is completely taken up by a tree.

You emerge from your Camry, taking stock of the situation and opening a Bud Light Lime, and a burly suntanned man walks over from another camp, thrusting out his hand and saying, "I like your style! Hi, I'm Lucky!"

I want to make it clear that I have been camping before, and I'm not just talking about Burning Man. I'm trying to say that I've lived in Montana and backpacked for hours into the wilderness, just me and a friend, where we set up our camp beside a little-known hot spring, and while my friend napped I got in *au naturel* and was promptly joined by an enormous female moose. There we sat, me and the moose, enjoying the steaming water, looking out blissfully at the sunset together like a honeymooning couple, while I summoned the courage to call in a wee voice: "Help me!" If I had been wearing pants I would have peed them. But I survived my wildlife encounter, and made a fire, and bear-proofed our foodstuffs, and did all the things one does when one is camping. This is not a story of gay San Franciscans setting up a Moroccan hideaway among all the army-surplus tents, complete with mirrored pillows and a Porta-John covered in veils. I am proud to say it is quite the opposite.

My husband is, in fact, from Montana. That's where we met, thirteen years ago, in the food court of the mall, in front of Orange Julius. Because of this, he does all sorts of guy things, not the least of which is his car obsession, but which include the very straight-male habit of buying the most expensive and elaborate sports equipment available, even for the briefest contact with that sport. David was entrusted with bringing a new tent and sleeping bags; what emerges from his check-in bag is a small miracle in outdoor sciences. He explains to me that the tent weighs only four pounds, the sleeping bags only two, and that they are good down to thirty degrees. The total cost is more than the Comme des Garçons jacket I purchased in Paris, which kept me awake for two weeks with pangs of regret (though it, too, is good down to thirty degrees). David is so pleased to see his tent in action. It springs from his hand, Cat in the Hat–style, and unfurls before us with a titanium spine.

"Quite a setup!" Lucky exclaims. "Where are you two from?"

"California," David says, to Lucky's absolute astonishment. We will come to learn that this is the most astonishing place to be from. "We needed a light tent for a bike trip through Sonoma." This is the first I have heard of a bike trip through Sonoma. But the tent is impressive, and assembled in a flash. By comparison, we will later watch, with our campmates, as ten young Canadian men try to put together an old metal-pole tent. It will take them three hours, though we will consider they are probably stoned out of their minds, and it probably won't help when Lucky sneaks over and steals one of their poles. Just for giggles. Put against these poor suckers, we are practically Grizzly Adams.

"Well what the heck brought you all this way?" Lucky's wife Jennifer asks us. She is a small, attractive woman with a tightly pulled-back ponytail and wire glasses that exaggerate her blue eyeliner. She wears the number 48 prominently on every item of her clothing.

We tried to prepare for this question the night before, while visiting a Detroit gay bar. I suggested saying we were on a road trip across the country, but David said the rental car would give things away. So my husband gives the simplest possible explanation: "We just always wanted to see NASCAR."

Amazingly, this answer requires no further elaboration. Of course it doesn't. We are among NASCAR fans, all of whom have sacrificed and worked hard to come to this event. No enthusiasm is too outrageous. Lucky pats us on the back and introduces us to his mother and father-in-law, who sit eating beans under a flag-draped canopy.

"Now, this is Andy and David, they came all the way from California!"

The mother asks where in California. "San Francisco," David answers. We wait while this answer makes its presence known. San Francisco means only one thing.

"Well, we're thinking of going out there for a race," the mother offers. There is a NASCAR track in Southern California, outside Rancho Cucamonga.

We will later learn, while sitting by the campfire, that the mother has a son, Jennifer's brother, who just went off to Iraq. He had tried to forestall things, but in order to stay in the Marines he has to see action, and so he put in to go overseas. She is half-sick over it, something she admits only while sipping her Jack and Coke. It will turn out that her husband, sitting there eating potato salad, went off to Vietnam one month after their wedding. It is clear this was the worst portion of life she ever had to swallow, and she is terrified of facing another. Both events are on her mind, always.

"Hey David," Lucky calls out, "you going to the Kenny Wayne Shepherd concert tonight?"

"Yep, but first we're gonna see the Nationwide race. Sounds like it already started."

"Yeah, we're ditching," Lucky says. "We got beat by a hot day in the pits."

I offer everyone a Pie Bite, but David cuts in to say we'll come by later and walk with them to the concert.

Lucky responds happily: "It's a deal! Have fun!"

And off we go for our first day at the races.

The first time I really understood David's obsession was on our first road trip, which happened about a month or so after we started dating. He had told me something vague about an interest in cars, and mainly showed interest in *my* car, an eighties Subaru GL Wagon, which I took, flatteringly, as a sign of the fetishization that comes with early love. Of course he would show an interest in anything of mine! We both lived in Montana at the time, and it didn't seem too strange to talk about how to get places and what you drove; everything was far away and took some thought and planning. I never noticed that the car topic came up more than any other. I lived, you could

say, in a cloud of innocence. But it was on a trip we took to Seattle, for a plan
to move there I'd made long before David showed up, that I truly saw down
to the depths of his soul and glimpsed what swam in the darkness there. It
was a few hours outside Missoula, on the long valley highway, in those few
years when the speed limit sign read only REASONABLE AND PRUDENT.
That was when it happened, when I saw. He presented it very casually, with a
smile, perhaps the way a cardsharp might suggest a friendly round of poker.
"Hey, I have an idea," he said, letting his left arm drift out the open window.
"Why don't you identify the cars as they go by?"

Later I would meet his mother and father, his two sisters, one of whom
lived in Canada with two daughters, his brother, who lived out on the streets
of Seattle, and various other close and distant friends and relations. But none
of those meetings were anywhere near as important as the one that happened
that day, with that casual little suggestion. Only now do I understand how
beautiful and poignant the moment was, introducing me, in his way, to the
real love of his life. To cars.

"I can't," I said.

"'Course you can! Look, what's that one?"

I am of course very good at this game now; we hardly need to play it. I've
learned all the insignias, but this is cheating; the point is to identify cars by
their shape, their color, the obvious details that set them apart from all other
makes and models, the way Nabokov could identify some butterflies by their
shadows. David, after all, could by the age of five identify the cars passing
his house simply from the sound of their motors. This is not expected of
me; I am meant only to be able to follow a conversation about parked cars
we pass on our way to the coffee shop. But back then I couldn't tell a Dodge
from a Jaguar. And not only that—I was supposed to be identifying cars in
the oncoming lane *as they drove by*. The speed limit, remember, was REASON-
ABLE AND PRUDENT. That meant at least ninety miles an hour.

"I can't do it," I said. "It's like, it's like you're a geologist and you want
me to identify rocks—"

"Well, I guess so—"

"Only you want me to identify the rocks while *throwing them at me!*"
I shouted, somewhat desperately. "What's this?" I said, miming tossing
something at him. "And this! And *this!*"

"Come on, here's an easy one. See the grille?"

"Porsche."

"What? Porsche? What? It's a Cadillac! Porsche?"

And on it went. For nine hours. I learned the telltale vertical taillight of the Cadillac, the Continental Kit of the Lincoln Continental, the "portholes" distinctive of the Buick brand, the kidney-shaped grille found on every BMW, and so on. And I saw, every time I misidentified a car, his mouth twitch with frustration, because of course to him it was close to heresy to think a Mitsubishi was a BMW. But I also saw, when I correctly guessed a make (and I was mostly guessing), a glow of happiness take over his body for a moment. It wasn't me, the fact that I was learning his world, the things he cared about. The names themselves caused that pleasure. Ford. Toyota. Audi. It was the happiness of a gourmet as you described the foods he loved. Honda. Dodge. Renault. Or an astronomer as you named his beloved constellations. Volkswagen. Fiat. Saab. Or perhaps a zealot, as you called forth his gods.

I learned early on in our relationship that if you found my husband staring into space, and wondered if he was perhaps recalling the past or dreaming of the future or even thinking of you, his life's great love, you could ask him, "What are you thinking about, honey?" and he would always turn and give the same answer:

"Cars."

What is the most boring thing you've ever seen? I know, I know, it's hard to remember, precisely because it was so boring. Boring events, Thomas Mann once noted, seem interminable to live through, yet these events contract in our memory into no time at all. It is only the intense, sublime experiences of life that, though over in a flash, expand to take up most of our remembered past. In just this way I am tempted to skip over the Nationwide Series racing and move straight into Sin City, but I know for a fact we spent three hours watching the race and only about an hour and a half wandering around in search of stripper poles. Isn't it funny how the mind works?

As we arrive at the track that first afternoon, I expect some resistance from my brain. But there is so much else to entertain me—the blow-up dinosaur slide, the T-shirt hawkers, the trailers with driver paraphernalia (where we buy our Logano beer coozies), along with the XXL clientele, each with the one soft-sided six-pack cooler and one transparent bag allowed at the track—that I have not yet confronted the idea that I am about to watch cars. I have already contacted the Michigan International Speedway, intending to have the announcer mention the first wedding anniversary of the somewhat androgynous "Andy and David" (and hoping the camera wouldn't turn to our row), but was told they didn't do announcements of that type. I am a little disappointed, and try not to mention it to David. Our seats are high in the stands (which the lady on the phone recommended), so we have to climb a series of ramps, all the time hearing the *vroom, vroom, vroom* of the cars rushing by. It is exciting, I have to admit. The whole metal structure trembles and there is the very Roman sense of a coliseum crowd come to watch a huge exotic creature, possibly a dinosaur, pacing and roaring its way around the track. And when we finally emerge from beneath the grandstands—spectacular! A red-and-yellow curve of seats pitched at a stomach-churning angle, an oval D track laid out for all to see, little Matchbox cars making their way past each other and a blue sky blazing everywhere overhead. On the infield, rows of RVs and VIP tents are encamped, and Pit Row sits right before us, painted orange, with pit crews at the ready for a crew chief calling in a driver for gas or tires or an adjustment. And the roar! We see that everyone wears thick headsets in gray or yellow, and almost immediately we find ourselves putting our earplugs into our ears. It is absolutely deafening, like a god crying out in agony, the sound of those engines! Earplugs in, all is quiet. Peacefully quiet. Painfully quiet. And around they go. And around. And around.

And around and around and around and around and around.

Here it is, and I had not known it would come so soon: the most boring moment of my life.

Yet thousands of people are loving it. Wearing their bright headsets, or watching on TV, or listening on radios and loving it. The variety of human experience—it's vast and wonderful, isn't it?

I turn to my husband. He gives me a sheepish smile and offers me another Bud Light Lime. I feel Devil Time hunched over us like a farmer with his chickens, plucking the minutes from our hides. My husband mouths something and mimes frantically. I remove an earplug and he shouts each word over the din: "GET... US... SCANNERS!"

We saw these for rent at little booths among the stuffed animals (there is a NASCAR groundhog named Digger, with some very gay badger friends, and I now have a T-shirt featuring them in police hats that says BADGERS ON A MISSION), and I ignored them the way I ignore most things I don't understand. But now down the ramp I go, past the tequila stands and Dove Ice Cream Bar carts, throwing myself at the mercy of the woman behind the counter, Stacey, with lemonade hair and caramel tan. "Well, this is the way to go," she tells me, showing me a handheld monitor attached to two bright yellow headsets. "It's the Sprint FanView." This is, in fact, what we had witnessed most of the other fans using: scanners and monitors, most of them Sprint products. (Sprint sponsors the major NASCAR race.) One can rent or buy a scanner at any NASCAR event, which allows one to hear the sportscasters that one cannot hear trackside due to road noise, but also allows one access to the intimate conversations between driver and pit-crew chief about how the tires are doing, fuel levels, the condition of the road, and—most mysteriously and importantly of all—whether the car is "tight" or "loose." The Sprint FanView takes it a step further: it allows you, in addition to rankings and car placement, access to cameras *inside the drivers' cars!* I know David will thank me dearly for being able to sit beside Joey Logano later this weekend. I rent the FanView plus two headsets. It is sixty dollars for the entire weekend. When I arrive with the clear bag of yellow plastic and see David's face, I know it is the best present I have ever given him. It is love. It is the way to go.

It turns out that for me, the key to enjoying any sporting event—for that matter, any dull event where one watches people who are astoundingly skilled at their work, like modern dance—is to have a knowledgeable, enthusiastic companion who, like a guide through a Masonic ritual, will narrate the mysteries. My husband is knowledgeable (he claims not to follow NASCAR, by which he means he only reads the stats in magazines and does not watch it on TV), and damned if he's not enthusiastic, but he is no guide. Here, though, on my Sprint FanView, at last I have found one! Suddenly I can tell who is in the lead (how to guess with them spread out in a circle?) and who is running out of gas, and who has blown a tire and is trying to catch up by sprinting along the straightaways, and who is the outside young kid from Michigan slowly making his way up car after car, unseen by the two leaders (that would be Brad Keselowski, who will go on to win). We get to watch close-ups of pit crews jacking up cars, throwing tires on, tipping gas into the capless tanks, and jumping back as the cars take off. David shows me drivers' views of the track, including Keselowski's (Logano does not race in the Nationwide Series), and animated versions of the very scene we see before us. Most importantly of all, however, my magic headphones explain the rules of the road.

I suppose there are many other sports based on a cumulative point system—all kinds of glorious things exist in this fine world—but I am too ignorant to know much about them. I'm sure, also, that the knowledge I've gained about NASCAR is soon to drain from my mind through the sports-leak I developed as a child when I stepped on a rusty nail, so I should put this down as quickly as I can. It seems that NASCAR drivers can get points in two ways: by their final placement in the race, and by leading a lap. Placement seems obvious: the higher your placement, the greater your points. First place, for instance, gets one hundred and eighty-five points. But (in a lovely little palindrome) forty-third place still gets thirty-four points, which apparently explains why even wrecked cars will try to hump their way through to the finish line. It does give one hope, doesn't it?

A driver can also earn five points for leading any single lap (meaning crossing the finish line first) and five points for leading the most laps in the race. Drivers can lead a lap during both the green and yellow flags, which is why, when other cars are heading into the pits, a driver might forgo a pit stop in order to take the lead that lap and gain his extra points. O, but heavens! I haven't explained about the flags!

Don't you really come to NASCAR to see a car crash? I did. So did Brian at Will Call, who when we picked up our tickets told us "You just missed a great crash!" Can you blame him? After all, the cars drive so close to one another, literally scraping metal, and sometimes follow the outside edge of the track to within an inch of the concrete barrier. I think I explained about the fenders. Because of this, crashes and other problems are bound to occur. This is what actually makes the race interesting to some and manipulative to others. At the least puff of smoke or shred of tire a yellow caution flag goes up, a Chevy Camaro Pace Car arrives, and all drivers are forced to slow to a crawl, keeping their lap positions, while the Servicemaster Clean trucks take to the track and vacuum up any debris (or, as we would learn Saturday, dry it of rain). The green flag comes out when the hazard has been cleared from the track.

There is also a "lucky dog" rule that allows the closest driver who has been lapped by the leader to make up the lap and join the main group. Since 2007, at least seven drivers have taken advantage of the "lucky dog" rule to win a race. To some, these cautions break or even manipulate the action (a few drops of rain seems an unlikely hazard). To others, they are similar to the "leveling" features in most board games, giving bad-luck players a chance and preventing the same dull order of cars from going around and around until the finish.

Because they do go around and around. The first race we witness, the CARFAX 250 Nationwide Series, is two hundred and fifty miles long, which, on a two-mile track like Michigan's, means a hundred and twenty laps. We come in halfway through, so we only have to sit through sixty. That takes about two hours, and we only have six Bud Light Limes with us.

The next day, hung over from our quest for Sin City, we will be watching the race we came for: the CARFAX 400.

That is four hundred miles.

Two hundred laps.

Vroom.

Say, America, that you drink ten Bud Light Limes in a row, on top of two Cherry Bombs and a sip of something pink and curdled involving Malibu Coconut Rum, and decide to go in search of NASCAR debauchery. Perhaps, to get into the spirit of things, you bum a menthol Newport and smoke it until green sparkles appear in the corners of your eyes. Say half a dozen of you, similar substances coursing through your veins, head out from Northwoods through a gap in the chain-link fence while the security guard isn't looking. What would you see?

RVs and pop-ups decorate the dark, rolling landscape, packed together like Chiclets, each strung with Christmas or rope lights or, more elaborately, light-up Budweiser signs and disco balls. Couples, families, or groups of guys are huddled around fires, each encircled (for safety's sake) by rings of dead beer cans piled up in careful structures some three or four cans high. No solo women campers, or groups of women. There are cardboard cut-outs of women, naturally, holding beer signs, loaded with Mardi Gras beads, beside large hand-lettered signs reading BEADS FOR BOOBIES! Some camps are set up as tiki huts, some with simple plywood bars, but most are fold-up chairs around a fire, a cooler for the beer. There are over nine thousand camp-sites, around fifty thousand campers, and during racing events the city of Brooklyn, which contains this state park, becomes the third-largest city in Michigan. South of us the racetrack is afire with floodlights, and the glow of it rises above the trees like the Northern Lights. From time to time, above us float flame-powered red lanterns that drift higher with the air currents, then head west and disappear into the stars. Who knows who is lighting them?

One canopy is decorated with brassieres, and you casually ask where they got them all. "Last night, donations, every one!" says one of the men inside. He then takes you on a tour of each bra, and says a judge came by an hour before, smelling each, and awarded the prizes. First is a red and black lace brassiere, second a pink one, and third something in black. None of the bras are for small women. "Nice work, gentlemen!" your husband says, and Lucky pats him on the back, saying, "I like your style!" You shoot your husband a glance: *Oh, so we're going to bond over the degradation of women now?*

Suddenly a pretty thirtyish woman appears from between the RVs. "Have you seen two small blond girls?" she asks. She wears her hair in a long braid and is dressed in cut-off jeans decorated with caution tape. She is very drunk.

"Well, no," Lucky says, pondering the idea. "What are they up to?"

"They goddamn ditched us, that's what! Sixteen and seventeen. You see them, Britney and Caitlin, you tell them get the hell home!"

"What's your cell number?" Lucky asks.

"Ain't got a cell. They live here in town. You tell them I called the cops!"

"Will do."

And off she staggers, her long braid swinging. You comment that looking for a Britney or a Caitlin at a NASCAR rally would be like looking for hay in a haystack.

"Ain't that the truth," Lucky says happily.

You have basically spent the night with Lucky and Jennifer, from the Kenny Wayne Shepherd concert until now, far past midnight, in a camp-ground called Juniper Hills where you have no right to be. The concert took place after the Nationwide race, at the water tower where anyone with a race pass could enter the grasslands; thousands of people were gathered around, drinking cans of beer, and every other man seemed to know Lucky. Ahead, on a stage and magnified by monitors, Kenny Wayne Shepherd played his country guitar and rocked his head gently, so his longish blond hair fell over his face. "Who is Kenny Wayne Shepherd?" you had asked on the way over, and Jennifer answered, "Oh you'll recognize him, 'Blue on Black'? 'Deja Voodoo'?" You shook your head. You wondered aloud what would happen to all the crushed beer cans underfoot, and only later saw Onsted Boy Scout Troop 637 moving through the crowd like hyenas, tan and spotted with merit badges, picking up the cans and tossing them into recycling bags, secretly jiggling them to see if they were empty. Men with beer bongs wandered around the audience, offering their services by pointing a finger at your chest. You shook your head. The man beside you took one, and his buddies emptied their beers into the funnel as the man struggled to swallow the foam that overwhelmed him.

Beer bongs are everywhere tonight. You pass a double one strung on a pulley from a tree and watch as it is lowered, filled with beer, then raised again so two strapping young men can stand up to the tubes and, as the umpire shouts and releases the catch, race to the finish. You pass another, deeper in the Brooklyn Trails campground (Lucky is following an instinct northwest, saying he needs to be drunker to find it), and this one is twenty feet high, decorated with rope lights, with a cut-out lady standing beside it and a cartoon bubble reading: LADIES, YOU KNOW WHAT WE WANT TO SEE! Lucky points out that this is the fucker they tried to get him to do the night before, but he doesn't do beer bongs anymore, not since last year in a race when he found out, after finishing his bong, that they'd put whiskey in at the end. He was drunk for days. "No more," he says, "no more, but you should give it a try." David says no thanks, he's had plenty in his time. Then your husband turns to you.

"How about you, Andy? Ever done a beer bong?"

You recognize the little smile on his face. You will never forgive him.

For years I lived under the impression that the first word people said when they thought of me was "fun!" But I discovered, on one drunken night a year ago, that the first word was actually "forbidding." These are very different words. I also recall a townie college boyfriend who said he liked my "British accent," a comment that, after pondering it for twenty years, I can only conclude meant I sounded like Charles Winchester from *M*A*S*H*, the one from Penobscot, Maine. That I sounded like an Ivy League prig. I don't think of myself this way, but I suppose I'm at an age where I no longer get to have illusions about myself. I *am* an Ivy League prig. I grew up the son of chemistry professors in suburban Maryland, went to a left-wing private school, a left-wing Ivy, and moved promptly to the West Village in New York. I will admit it: Montana baffles me. The South, where my family came from, baffles me. And NASCAR baffles me. "Forbidding," apparently that's me in a word. And let's get down to it, shall we? By "forbidding" they really mean *snob*.

But not David. And this is the main thrust of my defense. David grew up very poor, in a Mormon family in rural Idaho. He was the first to go to college, which he paid for entirely by himself. David has been supporting himself consistently since he was fifteen years old. He has worked every possible job under the sun, and he is always willing to fall back on waiting tables if it becomes necessary. Once in a while he likes to point out that I have no job skills to fall back on when the novel breathes its last breath. I have not had a normal, regular job in at least ten years, and have only once held a salaried position, as an executive secretary for a non-profit foundation whose name I could not pronounce. My last job? As a contract worker, naming toys for a toy company. Yes, I'm the one who named their floating radio toy "The Sound Turtle."

So say what you like about me. It's all true or possibly true, and I've heard it all. A famous writer, for instance, once provided my recommendation for grad school. It was only after multiple rejections that, puzzled, I broke into the office files and discovered, to my horror, one solitary sentence on his page. *Andrew Sean Greer*, he had written, *is a self-conscious Dudley Do-Right.*

But please, leave my husband out of it. No one would call David "forbidding." Or "self-conscious." Or Dudley anything. The one time David visited my grandparents in rural South Carolina—that's right: *my gay lover visited my Southern grandparents alone*—my grouchy bigoted grandfather's comment was: "That David's a good ol' boy." As even this night at NASCAR is proving, my husband always finds himself loved and embraced. He fits in everywhere. In this way, he will always betray me.

So why is he with me? I ask myself that all the time. Thirteen years. Why does he possibly put up with it? I must be incredibly cute.

*　　*　　*

It is not so bad, a beer bong. Just a crouching stance, an upward gaze, and people around you yelling "Don't panic! Just relax! Just let it go down!" Some hooting and hollering. And then it comes: the rush of Bud Light Lime—official sponsor, I suppose, of tomorrow morning's hangover. From the height of twenty feet, it is a hard thing to deny. Down it goes—well, about half of it. The rest just dribbles out of your mouth. You look up in fear that you've failed, again, but everyone seems elated. There is no bad beer bong, you're told. Just good and better and best.

"Nice job, Andy!" Lucky says, patting you on the back. Your husband just laughs. And so you are no longer a virgin.

David comes up and whispers: "You are incredibly cute."

Say you wandered drunk for an hour or so among the lit-up RVs and fold-out bars decorated with glowing chili peppers and shots of tequila and found yourself called to, time after time, by people sitting around a fire. "What's your hurry?" they ask, and "Come on in here!" And while you are aware they especially want the girls, there is a certain generosity to their tone. Bring your own beer, of course, but sit in one of our chairs. They don't know you spent last night at a bar called Club Gold Coast, which turned out (to your surprise) to be a hustler bar, where nobody would talk to you and David but the prostitutes, one of whom, Justin, wore a pair of green underwear with BELIEVE IN THIS! spelled in sparkles across the butt and offered to give you a private dance. They don't know any of it, and don't care to know. All they know is that you are here for the racing, and are therefore part of their tribe. Waving at you from a fire, taking you on a tour of the campground, handing you a spare beer. At first it seems like a terrible fraud. But then, of course, you *are* here for the racing. For tonight, you *are* part of their tribe. You and David both. It is certainly a friendlier crowd than Club Gold Coast.

"Hey guys!" a young man implores you, "Come in here and draw on my drunk friend."

"There's always one," Jennifer says.

In you go, all of you, and are given magic markers. The poor guy is in his early twenties, black hair and pale skin, sitting in a chair with his head lolling back, aware of nothing. People have drawn all over his white shirt—mostly obscene imagery—and you merely find a blank spot and write: WASH ME. Lucky writes, directly on the fellow's neck, LUCKY WAS HERE! "Hey!" the friend objects. "Hey, you wrote right on him!" A shrug and a laugh. But there's no real problem here; it's all the price you pay for passing out at NASCAR.

And then there is the glowing sign of a racing car. And there are the women who, indeed, will bare their boobies for beads. And there is the giant Jenga set, each piece half the size of a man, where people are crowded around to watch the action. But nothing more licentious than that; nothing more than anything you might find at Golden Gate Park.

At last you find the secret entrance to Sin City. Here it is, everyone insists, right here where a path leads through the dark junipers. The entrance to Hell.

But there, where we should find lines of drunken fans staggering through the trees, an RV is parked. A dozen folks are gathered around a fire circle, as if the entrance were merely another camping spot, and Lucky asks and discovers that Sin City is closed this year. Not because the rangers found it too outrageous for NASCAR, but because the usual campers didn't come back. They couldn't afford the tickets.

"Recession always hits the partiers first," Lucky notes. "They've got shitty jobs, and they're no good at their jobs 'cause they're always partying. So they're the first fired. Dammit, always the first to go."

Ain't it the truth?

"Sin City's gone!" Jennifer repeats in disbelief. "It's just gone!"

"Sorry, boys!" Lucky says, shaking his head. "Guess you'll have to settle for San Francisco fun." A wide smile. Do they know we're a couple? Of course they do. They knew the instant we stepped out of the car.

Down the street we find a little party going in a brightly lit E-Z UP, where some young girls are playing a strip version of Red and Black, and tell people the news. They nod their heads. "We called that place Purgatory," one comments. He is wearing a rubber mullet. Another says her friends called it Sodom and Gomorrah. Whatever they called it, the economy ate it alive. A reverent hush passes over the crowd.

Drunk from your beer bong, you ask the crowd if Bud Light Lime is a girl's beer.

"No!" the answers arrive in a rush. "No, no, of course not!" The answers all come from girls.

Then you notice the youngsters playing cards. The two teenage boys with them have already lost their shirts, but the girls have everything on, clearly in control of this game. Both are blond, one is very short, but the ringleader is pretty and confident as she yells to her friend: "Hey Britney, tell him to take off his shoes!"

You nudge Lucky and whisper: "Listen to these girls." A moment later, he turns to the ringleader and asks, "Hey, Caitlin, you want another beer?"

"No thanks!"

It's them. It's Britney and Caitlin. You may not have found Sin City, but you have found the wayward girls.

Within minutes the RV owner is shouting, "Party's over, girls!" and shutting off the lights. Lucky has let them know this is a sixteen- and seventeen-year-old who have taken control of their party and are drinking their beers, and Jennifer has pulled the girls aside and told them their mother wants them home immediately and is calling the cops.

Caitlin's face is shaking with fury. Her bleached blond hair is frizzed from the humidity, her lipstick smeared from kissing, and she turns to Britney, her shorter sister or cousin or friend—it has never been clear—and hisses: "That crazy fucking bitch!"

And then, brave and drunk little girl that she is, she turns to the entire crowd and shouts: "This is *my* town! Get the hell out of here!"

Lucky suggests that perhaps the evening is over. You all need to rest up well for the Sprint Cup tomorrow, after all. And what shocks you most, as you and your husband will speak about later, in whispers, in your four-pound tent, is how kind they all have been to you. Lucky and Jennifer and the others. There was not a moment of wariness or suspicion; that was all on your side. These people walked over the instant you arrived and led you around every moment of the day, from concerts to dinner to drinks, wanting nothing other than to show you hospitality, the NASCAR way, with the wish that you would return to the same campground beside them, Lucky and Jennifer, telling now about the strippers he once hired who poured red wax over each other until it hardened into molds like armor breastplates. Somehow the image sticks with me. Laughing, walking away from Britney and Caitlin, who can still be heard screaming at us all: "Get the hell out of my town!"

And tomorrow, at last, is the Sprint Cup.

*   *   *

America, how beautiful you are in multitudes! One hundred twenty thousand of you, fanned across the metal bleachers, wearing T-shirts boldly numbered with your favorite drivers, or, in most cases, wearing no shirts at all, pale and tanned and sunburned in fascinating shadows of yesterday's clothing, tattooed with feathered cow skulls across your backs and barbed wire around your biceps and Celtic spirals on your shoulders—who knows what it all means to you?—lathering each other with sunblock or sun oil, watching the camouflaged roofless Humvees make their way around the track, each carrying one of the drivers you adore, waving at you with a smile.

"And today!" the announcer says, "The Canadian National Anthem will be performed by Amy Rivard! You know her from the TV show *What's Up Canuck?*! A big welcome to... Amy Rivard!"

How beautiful in families, gathered together with your headsets daisy-chained along the row, connected at last to dad's bought-not-rented scanner, each with your legal six-pack cooler and transparent bag, with Buds and Bud Lights kept cold in coozies with those same glorious numbers—48! and 24! and 88! Your big pale girls in tank tops and little wire glasses, their white hair tied up high in the heat, and tall tan lanky boys with boxers showing and a heart-shape of sweat already forming on their shirtfronts, and dads hunkered down over their FanViews, and moms standing and rooting for their drivers, then turning and asking if anybody *wants* anything, waiting for headsets to be removed and repeating loudly *"Anybody WANT anything?"* before heading out for a cigarette.

"And today!" the announcer says, "the national anthem will be performed by Chris Young! You know him as Nashville's rising star... and *Country Weekly*'s Hottest Bachelor! A big welcome to... Chris Young!"

How beautiful in Pit Row, earlier that morning, under the sweltering sun, as you gathered by the cars you loved, and wrote messages on the white concrete barriers, and paid a dollar for a yellow Joey Logano lugnut, watching as a crewman painted putty on the wheels and placed new lugnuts, lovingly, on the soft adhesive so they could be thrown onto the car and bolted quickly. How lovely standing on the track itself, shimmering in the heat, taking pictures of yourself against the vertiginous slope of the asphalt, the announcer's tower, the climb of the stadium behind you in yellow and red.

How glorious standing by the fence, waiting for each driver to arrive, as they always do, and sign your pit pass for you—for of all the sports, these stars are the most accessible to fans, the most touchable, the most *real*.

"And today!" the announcer says, "We are being assisted by the A-10 Warthogs from Selfridge Air Force Base! Here they come!"

We sit in giddy expectation, hats in hands, hands still over our hearts from the National Anthem. Our drivers are there; Joey Logano has just gotten into his car after the last words. Embraced by our campmates, enlarged by the event itself, barely touching fingers in an encoded sign of love—and a sign floats overhead: BILLY WILL YOU MARRY ME? AMANDA, and why didn't I think of that? An airplane banner, brilliant. Amanda is more of a romantic than I, who can only think of irony when planning an anniversary. NASCAR indeed. And what is that roar behind us? A squadron of fighters, flying up from the horizon in strict V formation. The heart drops.

Look up! Look up, here they come!

"And today!" the announcer says, "Our Grand Marshals are Jordan and Jacob Vanderstel of Hudsonville, Michigan!"

The screen cuts to two boys in baseball caps, one wearing Gordon's number and the other Jimmie Johnson's. They are in wheelchairs. Apparently both have muscular dystrophy. They wave to the crowd.

How wonderful what we are about to watch, over four hours of race cars zooming through the miles, the crowd braving three rainstorms, waiting out the long stretches as the ServiceMaster trucks dry up the track, the caution when Robby Gordon blows a tire, watching Dale Earnhardt Jr. work his way car by car up the stretch, making up time on the straightaways and hugging the outer groove, calculating the fuel consumption, as Jimmie Johnson, after leading nearly every lap of the race, is forced to pit two laps shy of the finish and allows Brian Vickers to pull into the lead just a second and a half ahead of Jeff Gordon. How wonderful to see my husband bent over his FanView, watching the image of each car along the track, each driver, each pit stop, his childhood fantasies come true—of seeing cars not as vehicles but as creatures of grace and power. How nice it will be to have a good shower in a hotel, and a good dinner and a beer back in Detroit, but for now the Bud Light Lime is cold and right. The hot dogs are right. The crowd is right, and somewhere out there Lucky and Jennifer are in their seats, the western ones with the sun at their backs, the same seats they get year after year, with friends beside them, standing to watch the cars get in their row from qualifying. A man leans in with the green flag. I see David laughing soundlessly and he grabs my hand, turning to me and mouthing "HAPPY ANNIVERSARY!" and I mouth back "HAPPY ANNIVERSARY!" We listen as, in the high bland tone of sick children called on to do their best, the Vanderstel brothers shout:

"Gentlemen, start your engines!"

How lovely to be married in America.

CAN A PAPER MILL
SAVE A FOREST?

THE STRANGE POSSIBILITY THAT THE
TRANSFERRING OF INFORMATION
DIGITALLY IS MORE ENVIRONMENTALLY
DESTRUCTIVE THAN PRINTING IT

by NICHOLSON BAKER

(nonfiction from Issue 33: The San Francisco Panorama*)*

T HERE ARE TWO paper mills in the town of Jay, in Maine, on the Androscoggin River. One mill, now owned by Verso Paper Corp., makes the paper for *Martha Stewart Living*, *National Geographic*, *Cosmopolitan*, and other magazines. It's a big plant, built by International Paper in the sixties.

The other mill is older and made of brick and stone. It's called the Otis Mill, and it was built by Hugh Chisholm, the founder of International Paper, in 1896. Back then it was a prodigy—"The Largest Paper Mill Plant in the World," according to a headline in the *Lewiston Weekly Journal*, which was exaggerating, but only a little.

The Otis Mill has produced all sorts of paper over the years—paper for postcards, ornate playing cards, wallpaper, copier paper, inkjet paper, and the shiny, peel-off paper backing for sticky labels. Now, though, the Otis Mill doesn't make anything. The paper industry is in a slump. The new owner, Wausau Paper Company, shut down one of Otis's two paper machines in August 2008. The number of employees dropped from about two hundred and fifty to ninety-six. Then, this spring, Wausau's CEO, Thomas J. Howatt, closed the plant altogether. The closure was a difficult decision, he said in a press release, but it was necessary in order to "preserve liquidity and match capacity with demand during a period of severe economic difficulty." The final reel of paper came off the mill at 6:50 a.m. on June 1, 2009. It was parchment paper, the kind bakers use to bake cookies.

I drove up to Jay on a fine day in mid-October, thinking as I drove about forests with logging trails, and about 400,000-square-foot Internet data centers going up around the country with cooling towers and 28,000-gallon backup tanks of diesel fuel, and about mountaintop coal removal, and about relative carbon footprints. I'd been talking on the phone to Don Carli, a research fellow at the Institute for Sustainable Communication. Carli said that the risk to Maine's forests—and to forests in Washington and Wisconsin and elsewhere—was not from logging, but from what happens if the logging stops. A thinned or even completely felled woodland grows back, but when a landowner loses his income from cutting down trees, he has to find another way to make money. Low-density development, with all of its irrevocabilities—paved roads, parking lots, power lines, propane depots, sewage plants, and mini-malls—is one way of getting a return. "Hamburgers and condos kill more trees than printed objects ever will," Carli told me. "If the marketplace for timber, harvested sustainably from Maine's forests, collapses because of the propagation of a myth—which some might say is a fraud—that says that using the newspaper is killing trees, then what happens is the landholder can no longer generate the revenue to pay a master logger for sustainable timber harvesting, and can't pay the taxes. Then a developer offers to buy the land at a steep premium over what it was worth as a forest, and the developer clear-cuts the land and turns it into a low-density development. Then it really is deforested."

I drove through Auburn and Turner, north on Route 4, past many FOR LEASE signs, past the Softie Delight (closed), past the White Fawn Trading Post, which once sold deerskin gloves (closed), past the Antique Snowmobile Museum (open), the apple-processing factory (closed), and Moose Creek log-cabin homes (open). The road curves as you come into Jay and you drive along the railroad track toward the Otis Mill. The tower is made of brick and, oddly, looks a little like the Campanile in Venice. It still says, at the top: INTERNATIONAL PAPER CO. / 1906.

At a little variety and pizza shop I bought a Coke and three newspapers. The headline on one of the papers, the *Franklin Journal*, was WAUSAU MILL SOLD, CLOSING. The *Lewiston Sun Journal* had a big front-page article: OTIS MILL SOLD. A couple from Jay, owners of Howie's Welding & Fabrication, had bought the mill from Wausau with financing from a consortium of local towns. They were just figuring out what to do with it, according to the *Sun Journal*. They wanted to save the building and get some people back to work. As for the machinery, "We'll be doing a lot of liquidating."

I drove through Otis's plant gate and into one of the parking spaces near the railroad tracks. When I got out, a man was standing near a shiny red pickup truck. I told him I was writing about the paper industry for a newspaper in San Francisco and he said I should talk to Larry, because Larry had been there over thirty years. He himself had only been there for ten, he said. He asked me inside.

We walked into a low white room with blue trim. Fabric banners announcing yearly corporate safety awards hung from the ceiling. So did the American flag. There were several corkboards for union announcements, but the announcements had all been taken down and the colored pushpins neatly clustered in the cork. There was a bench strewn with flyers for employment retraining and adult education—also brochures from church groups, job-loss support groups, and workshops on starting a new business. Something from the United Way said: "YOU CAN SURVIVE UNEMPLOYMENT!"

Larry, a man in his sixties, gestured me upstairs to the darkened, unkempt office suite. Larry's own office was still well organized, though. It was officially his last day as an employee of Wausau—October 15, 2009. He'd worked at the plant for thirty-three years, first in maintenance and then in engineering. Schematics and electrical diagrams of the mill that he knew better than almost anyone else were neatly ranked in a file caddy, and pictures of his grandchildren were angled on the bookcase behind him. "When I first started here," he said, "they were making copier-type paper. Then those markets grew so big that we couldn't compete with bigger mills. We started getting into specialty grades, like release-base paper—the paper that you throw away behind a self-sticking stamp or a bumper sticker. We did a lot of that. We did some inkjet early in the inkjet era. Again, we got competed out of that. Our niche was specialty grades, small orders."

Larry didn't smile much, except when he talked about taking care of his grandchildren. Everyone knew everyone in the plant, he said, and the closing of the second paper machine came as a shock to the town. "It's not good news, for sure," Larry said. "The expectation was that we had a few years left to run the one machine."

Could the plant be brought back online by another owner, I asked, if paper markets picked up? No, said Larry: Wausau had sold the plant under the condition that its machines never again be used to make paper in North or South America. "It was sold with a non-compete clause," he explained. Wausau had not only closed the plant down, it had effectively ended any possibility of its resurrection as a paper mill.

As he was shaking my hand, Larry told me I should get in touch with Sherry Judd, who was in charge of Maine's Paper and Heritage Museum.

I got in the car, sighed, and drove on down the road, trying to figure out where to go next. Passing the Otis Federal Credit Union, I saw an electric sign, which said: BENEFIT SPAGHETTI SUPPER FOR PAPER & HERITAGE MUSEUM SATURDAY OCTOBER 17 4:30 TO 7 P.M. ST. ROSE PARISH HALL JAY. I stopped and took a picture of the sign. Then I drove a few miles upriver to the big Verso Paper mill—"Andro," as the locals call it—where they make the paper for *Cosmo* and *Martha Stewart Living*. More than nine hundred employees work there. I parked near a vintage green Jaguar in the parking lot.

I stood for a while, looking at the sun as it sank behind the two digester towers with their mane-like plumes of steam. Not smoke—steam. The plant was enormous and boxy and clean and, I thought, elegant in its own way. It was heavy industry, but it carried its weight well. There was no sulphurous paper-mill stench. I felt a surge of pride that the paper for many magazines—filled with photographs of food and jungles and expensive New York City interiors and classy brassieres—was being made right here, in Jay, Maine. The biggest building said VERSO in big letters on the side.

We may not make steel anymore, in our hollowed-out husk of a country, I thought, and we may not make shoes or socks or shirts or china or TVs or telephones or much of anything else except pills and pilotless drones—but we do make very heavy, twenty-four-foot rolls of clean-smelling, smooth-surfaced paper.

I took some pictures of trucks filled with cut logs queued up in one of the feeder roads. Then I went to the security desk and announced myself and drove home. A few days later I got a call from Sondra Dowdell, one of Verso's corporate spokespersons. She explained how efficient the Verso plant was—that it used river power, tree bark, and "black liquor," the lignin-rich waste product of papermaking—as sources of energy. She forwarded me Verso's sustainability report, "A Climate of Change." A chart diagrammed the sources of Verso's energy: more than 50 percent came from recycled biomass—i.e., bark and black liquor—and another 1.2 percent came from hydroelectric power. Dowdell had visited one of Verso's customers, Quad Graphics, in Wisconsin, which prints many magazine titles. "It is amazing," she said, "the talent of the graphic artists and the technical savvy of the people who can lay lovely ink on paper. It is just beautiful to watch."

That Saturday, my wife and I drove back to Jay to go to the spaghetti fundraiser. We got there early, so that we could have a tour of Maine's Paper and Heritage Museum, which is in a mansion on Church Street in Livermore Falls, where mill managers and their families once lived. The front walk is dug up now, because they're installing a new community walkway and wheelchair ramp.

Walter Ellingwood and Norman Paradis, whose father and grandfather worked at the Otis Mill and whose son now works at Andro, gave us the museum tour. Walter showed us the burst tester, and the opacity and absorption tester, and a piece of wood that helped you compute the speed of the paper machine—and the two of them pointed out the old steam whistle from the Otis Mill. Walter said that one night long ago he got lost in the swamp in Chesterville and they blew the steam whistle for him so that he could find his way home. Norm showed us a diagram of Andro, with light-up buttons, and he pointed out the medal that his father had gotten for working for International Paper for forty years. It had four diamonds, one for each decade. "He thought that was really really something from International Paper company. It didn't take much to make these people say, 'Jeez, look how nice that is.'" Norm himself also worked for International Paper for forty years, first as a kid in school and eventually as a supervisor at Andro, with four hundred people under him. "These are some of my buckles that I won," he said, showing us some metal pieces in a glass case. His grandfather, who came from Quebec, had worked in the Otis Mill barefoot, he said, because the chemicals ruined any shoes you wore.

We paused in front of an aerial photograph of the Otis Mill in winter. Norm pointed out the town's skiing hill, just on the other side of the river. The old mill's hydro plant had always powered the ski lifts; now, Norm said, he didn't know what would happen. Then he and Walter had to hurry on over to work at the spaghetti event. We went there, too, to the Saint Rose Church Parish Hall.

There were two other public fundraisers happening in town that night, but even so, a good crowd came out to have the seven-dollar dinner. Mostly they were retired millworkers, but there were some who had just lost their jobs. Norm greeted everyone—he knew everyone. We sat next to two women who had, long ago, cleaned the offices at the mill. "You can't be delicate eating spaghetti," said one of the women—she was about seventy—when I wiped my mouth. There were two sculptures of saints on the walls, each nearly life-size.

Sherry Judd, the founder of the museum, a smiley woman with short curly hair who wore a western-style blue shirt, was serving the spaghetti. Sherry had worked at both Otis and Andro, and also at a paper mill in California, and her father had been a mason at Otis Mill. She started raising money for the museum several years ago, she said. "I had a vision that someday there was not going to be papermaking in these towns," she told me. "Somebody needs to tell the children about what their ancestors did, how hard they worked to develop this community and the communities around it." For two years she raised money for the museum by towing around a caboose replica filled with papermaking artifacts and giving talks on the need to preserve the past. She had a video made, "Along the Androscoggin," about the history of papermaking in the area, with good clips from millworkers, including Norm Paradis and his son. She wants people to walk into the museum and hear the sound of the papermaking machinery, and see how it worked. "I have a lot of ideas up here," she said, tapping her head, "but we need a curator. And a grant writer."

We bought some tickets for the quilt raffle and a brick to go into the museum's new front walkway, and then we drove home talking about Sherry, Norm, Walter, and the skiing hill next to the river.

Don Carli, of the Institute for Sustainable Communication, told me that this year eighteen paper mills have closed in the United States, and more than thirty-four papermaking machines have been permanently put out of commission. Meanwhile, the power demand from the Internet is growing hugely. "If you do a simple extrapolation of the consumption of energy by data centers, we have a crisis," Carli said. In 2006, the Energy Information Administration estimated that data centers consumed about 60 billion kilowatt hours of electricity—just the centers themselves, not the wireless or fiber-optic networks that connect them or the end-user computers that they serve—while paper mills consumed 75 billion kilowatt hours of electricity, of which more than half was green power from renewable sources. "And that was in 2006," Carli said, "when print wasn't kicked to the curb and declared all but dead and buried. It was still fighting the good fight." Not only is there now a roughly comparable carbon footprint between server farms and paper mills, but the rate of growth in server and data-center energy consumption is "metastasizing," he said. "It doubled between 2000 and 2005, and it's due to double again at current rates by 2010." That's one reason why gigantic data centers are now going up far away from cities, Carli added. "You can't go to ConEd and get another ten megawatts of power. You can buy the computers, you can buy the servers. You just can't get juice for them, because the grid is tapped out."

"That's kind of amazing," I said.

"So when we start thinking about transforming more and more of our communication to digital media," Carli said, "we really do have to be asking, 'Where will the electrons come from?'"

I nodded and looked out at the trees.

A NOTE ON *THE GIRL WITH BANGS*

MY FIRST NOVEL was published in the spring of 2000. Somehow—I can't remember how—I was convinced to come on some kind of mini-tour for this new journal, *McSweeney's*. I can't remember where we went. I remember Arthur Bradford singing and smashing guitars, and maybe someone dressed as Spiderman, and John Hodgman being a crazed literary agent, and me reading, I guess, but I don't remember what I read. Perhaps this all culminated at the Philadelphia Free Library? Perhaps not.

Anyway: it was during that period that *McSweeney's* said they were going to do a music issue and that They Might Be Giants had written a song and would I write a story about it. It is also totally possible that I wrote the story and then TMBG wrote a song based on it. [The former is true.—Ed.]

Again, I don't remember. I *do* remember being thrilled that it was TMBG. The last time I'd seen them was on television (them, not me), aged fourteen (me, not them), as they bounced around the *Top of the Pops* studio to "Birdhouse in My Soul." Even back then I can remember looking at those two profoundly white American nerdy people and looking at my own state of British black nerdery and thinking: These might be my people.

Ten years later so it proved to be: I loved their song, and still love it. I felt incredibly excited to be any part of this magazine that had once had a David Foster Wallace short story printed along its spine. I was young, I was in America. I was surrounded by nerds. It was heaven. I haven't read my story since I wrote it. I hope it's still okay. —ZADIE SMITH

THE GIRL WITH BANGS

by ZADIE SMITH

(fiction from Issue 6)

I FELL IN LOVE with a girl once. Some time ago, now. She had bangs. I was twenty years old at the time and prey to the usual rag-bag of foolish ideas. I believed, for example, that one might meet some sweet kid and like them a lot—maybe even marry them—while all the time allowing that kid to sleep with other kids, and that this could be done with no fuss at all, just a chuck under the chin, and no tears. I believed the majority of people to be bores, however you cut them; that the mark of their dullness was easy to spot (clothes, hair) and impossible to avoid, running right through them like a watermark. I had made mental notes, too, on other empty notions—the death of certain things (socialism, certain types of music, old people), the future of others (film, footwear, poetry)—but no one need be bored with those now. The only significant bit of nonsense I carried around in those days, the only one that came from the gut, if you like, was this feeling that a girl with soft black bangs falling into eyes the color of a Perrier bottle must be good news. Look at her palming the bangs away from her face, pressing them back along her hairline, only to have them fall forward again! I found this combination to be good, *intrinsically* good in both form and content, the same way you think of cherries (life is a bowl of; she was a real sweet) until the very center of one becomes lodged in your windpipe. I believed Charlotte Greaves and her bangs to be good news. But Charlotte was emphatically bad news, requiring only eight months to take me entirely apart; the kind of clinically efficient dismembering you see when a bright child gets his hand on some toy he assembled in the first place. I'd never dated a girl before, and she was bad news the way boys can never be, because with boys it's always possible to draw up a list of pros and cons, and see the matter rationally, from either side. But you could make a list of cons on Charlotte stretching to Azerbaijan, and "her bangs" sitting solitary in the pros column would outweigh all objections. Boys are just boys after all, but sometimes girls *really seem to be* the turn of a pale wrist, or the sudden jut of a hip, or a clutch of very dark hair falling across a freckled forehead. I'm not saying that's what they really are. I'm just saying sometimes it seems that way, and that those details (a thigh mole, a full face flush, a scar the precise shape and size of a cashew nut) are so many hooks waiting to land you. In this case, it was those bangs, plush and dramatic; curtains opening on to a face one would queue up to see. All women have a backstage, of course, of course. Labyrinthine, many-roomed, no doubt, no doubt. But you come to see the show, that's all I'm saying.

I first set eyes on Charlotte when she was seeing a Belgian who lived across the hall from me in college. I'd see her first thing, shuffling around the communal bathroom looking a mess—undone, always, in every sense—with her T-shirt tucked in her knickers, a fag hanging out of her mouth, some kind of toothpaste or maybe mouthwash residue by her lips and those bangs in her eyes. It was hard to understand why this Belgian, Maurice, had chosen to date her. He had this great accent, Maurice, *elaborately* French, like you couldn't *be* more French, and a jaw line that seemed in fashion at the time, and you could tick all the boxes vis-à-vis personal charms; Maurice was an impressive kind of a guy. Charlotte was the kind of woman who has only two bras, both of them grey. But after a while, if you paid attention, you came to realise that she had a look about her like she just got out of a bed, no matter what time of day you collided with her (she had a stalk of a walk, never looked where she was going, so you had no choice) and this tendency, if put under the heading "QUALITIES THAT GIRLS SOMETIMES HAVE," was a kind of poor relation of "BEDROOM EYES" or "LOOKS LIKE SHE'S THINKING ABOUT SEX ALL THE TIME"—and it worked. She seemed always to be stumbling away from someone else, toward you. A limping figure smiling widely, arms outstretched, dressed in rags, a smoldering city as backdrop. I had watched too many films, possibly. But still: a bundle of precious things thrown at you from a third floor European window, wrapped loosely in a blanket, chosen frantically and at random by the well-meaning owner, slung haphazardly from a burning building; launched at you; it could hurt, this bundle; but look! You have caught it! A little chipped, but otherwise fine. Look what you have saved! (You understand me, I know. This is how it feels. What is the purpose of metaphor, anyway, if not to describe women?)

Now, it came to pass that this Maurice was offered a well-paid TV job in Thailand as a newscaster, and he agonized, and weighed Charlotte in one hand and the money in the other and found he could not leave without the promise that she would wait for him. This promise she gave him, but he was still gone, and gone is gone, and that's where I came in. Not immediately—I am no thief—but by degrees, studying near her in the library, watching her hair make reading difficult. Sitting next to her at lunch watching the bangs go hither, and, I suppose, thither, as people swished by with their food trays. Befriending her friends and then her; making as many nice noises about Maurice as I could. I became a boy for the duration. I stood under the window with my open arms. I did all the old boy tricks. These tricks are not as difficult as some boys will have you believe, but they are indeed slow, and work only by a very gradual process of accumulation. You have sad moments when you wonder if there will ever be an end to it. But then, usually without warning, the hard work pays off. With Charlotte it went like this: she came by for a herbal tea one day, and I rolled a joint and then another and soon enough she was lying across my lap, spineless as a mollusk, and I had my fingers in those bangs—teasing them, as the hair-dressers say—and we had begun.

*   *   *

Most of the time we spent together was in her room. At the beginning of an affair you've no need to be outside. And it was like a filthy cocoon her room, ankle deep in rubbish; it was the kind of room that took you in and held you close. With no clocks and my watch lost and buried, we passed time by the degeneration of things; the rotting of fruit, the accumulation of bacteria, the rising-tideline of cigarettes in the vase we used to put them out. It was a quarter past this apple. The third Saturday in the month of that stain. These things were unpleasant and tiresome. And she was no intellectual; any book I gave her she treated like a kid treats a Christmas present—fascination for a day and then the quick pall of boredom; by the end of the week it was flung across the room and submerged; weeks later when we made love I'd find the spine of the novel sticking into the small of my back, paper cuts on my toes. There was no bed to speak of. There was just a bit of the floor that was marginally clearer than the rest of it. (But wait! Here she comes, falling in an impossible arc, and here I am by careful design in just the right spot, under the window, and here she is, landing and nothing is broken, and I cannot believe my luck. You understand me. Every time I looked at the bangs, the bad stuff went away.)

Again: I know it doesn't sound great, but let's not forget the bangs. Let us not forget that after a stand-up row, a real screaming match, she could look at me from underneath the distinct hairs, separated by sweat, and I had no more resistance. *Yes, you can leave the overturned plant pot where it is. Yes, Rousseau is an idiot if you say so.* So this is what it's like being a boy. The cobbled street, the hopeful arms hugging air. There is nothing you won't do.

Charlotte's exams were coming up. I begged her to look through her reading list once more, and plan some strategic line of attack, but she wanted to do it her way. Her way meant reading the same two books—Rousseau's *Social Contract* and Plato's *Republic* (her paper was to be on people, and the way they organize their lives, or the way they did, or the way they should, I don't remember; it had a technical title, I don't remember that either)—again and again, in the study room that sat in a quiet corner of the college. The study room was meant to be for everyone but since Charlotte had moved in, all others had gradually moved out. I recall one German graduate who stood his ground for a month or so, who cleared his throat regularly and pointedly picked up things that she had dropped—but she got to him, finally. Charlotte's papers all over the floor, Charlotte's old lunches on every table, Charlotte's clothes and my clothes (now indistinguishable) thrown over every chair. People would come up to me in the bar and say, "Look, Charlotte did X. Could you please, for the love of God, stop Charlotte doing X, *please?*" and I would try, but Charlotte's bangs kept Charlotte in the world of Charlotte and she barely heard me. And now, please, before we go any further: tell me. Tell me if you've ever stood under a window and caught an unworthy bundle of chintz. Gold plating that came off with one rub; faked signatures, worthless trinkets. Have you? Maybe the bait was different—not bangs, but deep pockets either side of the smile or unusually vivid eye pigmentation. Or some other bodily attribute (hair, skin, curves) that recalled in you some natural phenomenon (wheat, sea, cream). Same difference. So: have you? Have you ever been out with a girl like this?

Some time after Charlotte's exams, after the 2.2 that had been stalking her for so long finally pounced, there was a knock on the door. *My* door—I recall now that we were in my room that morning. I hauled on a dressing-gown and went to answer it. It was Maurice, tanned and dressed like one of the Beatles when they went to see the Maharishi; a white suit with a Nehru collar, his own bangs and tousled hair, slightly long at the back. He looked terrific. He said, "Someone in ze bar says you might have an idea where Charlotte is. I need to see 'er—it is very urgent. Have you seen 'er?" I had seen her. She was in my bed, about five feet from where Maurice stood, but obscured by a partition wall. "No..." I said. "No, not this morning. She'll probably be in the hall for breakfast though, she usually is. So, Maurice! When did you get back?" He said, "All zat must come later. I 'ave to find Charlotte. I sink I am going to marry 'er." And I thought, *Christ, which bad movie am I in?*

*   *   *

I got Charlotte up, shook her, poured her into some clothes, and told her to run around the back of the college and get to the dining hall before Maurice. I saw her in my head, the moment the door closed—no great feat of imagination, I had seen her run before; like a naturally uncoordinated animal (a panda?) that somebody has just shot—I saw her dashing incompetently past the ancient walls, catching herself on ivy, tripping up steps, and finally falling through the swing doors, looking wildly round the dining hall like those movie time-travelers who know not in which period they have just landed. But still she managed it, apparently she got there in time, though as the whole world now knows, Maurice took one look at her strands matted against her forehead, running in line with the ridge-ways of sleep left by the pillows, and said, "You're sleeping with her?" (Or maybe, "You're sleeping with *her?*"—I don't know; this is all reported speech) and Charlotte, who, like a lot of low-maintenance women, cannot tell a lie, said "Er... yes. Yes" and then made that signal of feminine relief; bottom lip out, air blown upward; bangs all of a flutter.

Later that afternoon, Maurice came back round to my room, looking all the more noble, and seemingly determined to have a calm man-to-man "you see, I have returned to marry her / I will not stand in your way"-type of a chat, which was very reasonable and English of him. I let him have it alone. I nodded when it seemed appropriate; sometimes I lifted my hands in protest but soon let them fall again. You can't fight it when you've been replaced; a simple side-step and here is some old/new Belgian guy standing in the cobbled street with his face upturned, and his arms wide open, judging the angles. I thought of this girl he wanted back, who had taken me apart piece by piece, causing me nothing but trouble, with her bangs and her antisocial behavior. I was all (un)done, I realized. I sort of marveled at the devotion he felt for her. From a thousand miles away, with a smoldering city as a backdrop, I watched him beg me to leave them both alone; tears in his eyes, the works. I agreed it was the best thing, all round. I had the impression that here was a girl who would be thrown from person to person over years, and each would think they had saved her by some miracle when in actual fact she was in no danger at all. Never. Not even for a second.

*   *   *

He said, "Let us go, zen, and tell 'er the decision we 'ave come to," and I said yes, let's, but when we got to Charlotte's room, someone else was putting his fingers through her curls. Charlotte was always one of those people for whom sex is available at all times—it just happens to her, quickly, and with a minimum of conversation. This guy was some other guy that she'd been sleeping with on the days when she wasn't with me. It had been going on for four months. This all came out later, naturally.

Would you believe he married her anyway? And not only that, he married her after she'd shaved her head that afternoon just to spite us. All of us— even the other guy no one had seen before. Maurice took a bald English woman with a strange lopsided walk and a temper like a gorgon, back to Thailand and married her despite friends' complaints and the voluble protest of Aneepa Kapoor, who was the woman he read the news with. The anchor-woman, who had that Hitchcock style: hair tied back tight in a bun, a spiky nose and a vicious red mouth. The kind of woman who doesn't need catching. "Maurice," she said, "you *owe* me. You can't just throw four months away like it wasn't worth a bloody thing!" He e-mailed me about it. He admitted that he'd been stringing Aneepa along for a while, and she'd been expecting something at the end of it. For in the real world, or so it seems to me, it is almost always women and not men who are waiting under windows, and they are almost always disappointed. In this matter, Charlotte was unusual.

COOP*

a twenty-minute story by GLEN DAVID GOLD

IN 1943, GROUCHO Marx lived alone in Maine on a chicken farm he'd purchased with the proceeds from what the brothers swore was their last film, *The Big Store*. It had been a terrible film that no one had wanted to make, something rewritten from a Ritz Brothers program. Humiliated, Groucho had left California on a train, and since he was just another fifty-three-year-old man with thick glasses, he was ignored from station to station. He read books. He looked out the window. He called in for messages, and when there were none, he seethed. The worst place for anger is, of course, when it is worn on the surface of the skin. Groucho imagined it made out of that powder found on the wings of moths; touch it and the animal can no longer fly. But it had served him well, it was the fountain of his fame, and because he was Groucho, no one could touch it. It rendered him completely opaque.

When he arrived at his chicken farm, he found a caretaker's cabin at the edge of a nest of olive trees. It was deserted, and he collapsed onto a single cot in the center of the room, and closed his eyes and listened for the sounds of chickens. It was the heat of the day, they slept, so he listened for sleeping chickens. A middle-aged Jew who had received no phone calls asking where he'd gone to, and he was on a cot listening for sleeping chickens.

He loved this. He hated this. He was asleep until he heard, definitively, the flapping of wings, which satisfied him for just a moment. Then he explored the cabin. There was a standing wardrobe, half-splintered at the joints, filled with uniforms—nurses' uniforms, valets' uniforms, perhaps something worn by the local fire department. And next to it was a stove. And along two pieces of plywood propped up by cinderblocks, armed forces editions of novels: *Forever Amber*, Faith Baldwin trash, movie star magazines (none with him featured), photographs of a man in uniform.

There was no telephone, no refrigerator, no shower, no plumbing. Groucho was for the first time in his life actually alone rather than just feeling that way. His plan was to stay for months, or until someone missed him enough to come looking, but he, it turned out, was hardly that patient. To wish to be a lonely farmer is much different than actually to be one, and three days into his exile, when he walked to town and at the soda fountain made his daily call and heard from his manager only that Chico needed money again, and had started looking for him, he snapped.

When he returned, he entered the cabin, and for a few moments there was no sound, except for the clucking of the chickens. Then the stove, uniforms on hangers, shelves of books, magazines, and photographs, all flew into the olive grove.

—June 1, 2002, 11:54 p.m.–12:15 a.m., Los Angeles, CA

**This story contains a single sentence—a disputed sentence—found both in a Stephen Ambrose book (*Wild Blue*) and in his source material (George McGovern Grassroots: The Autobiography of George McGovern).*

A NOTE ON *BORED TO DEATH*

IN JANUARY OF 2007, I was commissioned by *Esquire Magazine* to write a short story. They told me that they wanted to make fiction relevant and of the moment, so each commissioned story—they were doing one piece of fiction every month—was to have as its title the date of the magazine's publication. That date was also supposed to figure, plot-wise, into the story—the idea being that the reader would feel like this piece of fiction was happening *now*.

The date and title I was given was April 20, 2007—the actual day that the magazine would hit the newsstands, despite being the May issue. This was all a bit nuts to me, but I needed the money, and I was pleased and flattered that a famous magazine wanted me in its pages.

I wrote most of the story in my mind one night as I lay in bed. It just sort of came to me, and I worked in April 20 by having it written on the back of a card another character hands to the narrator.

My word count was supposed to be five thousand words. When I sat down to write the thing, it took me a little over a week, and I produced about eleven thousand words. I made myself a character, because for the longest time when I wrote essays people would tell me that I was obviously making things up, but then when I wrote fiction they would ask me why I didn't have the guts to call it memoir. So with this story I decided to write a piece of fiction in the voice of my essays and see what happened.

Well, I sent it to *Esquire* and they rejected it. It wasn't what they were looking for—I hadn't made April 20 a big enough part of the plot, and it was too long. I asked feebly if they might consider serializing it if I made April 20 more important; that notion was squashed. I wrote another story for them—the erotic diary of a writer on a book tour, with April 20 very prominent—and they rejected that one as well. They paid me a nice kill fee, which sounds like something out of Mickey Spillane, and that was that.

So I had two stories titled "April 20, 2007" on my hands. I thought the first one, especially, was pretty good. I retitled it "Bored to Death" and sent it to a bunch of people in Hollywood and to *McSweeney's*. *McSweeney's* got back to me very quickly, said they liked it, wanted it, and asked me if it was true. My essay-fiction style had worked!

As for Hollywood, no one in Los Angeles wrote back to me. I thought the story could be like *After Hours* but darker, but I had unsuccessfully tried to make some money out there in the past and had more or less given up on it, so I wasn't surprised by the lack of response.

This all would have been around February of 2007. *McSweeney's* said they would publish the story in the fall or winter of that year. In late June, a producer who had a deal with HBO moved from Los Angeles to New York. She was meeting dozens of New York writers to see if anyone had something that could possibly work as an HBO show. I was on this list of writers, and a meeting was scheduled. The day of the meeting, I slept till around 11:30. My meeting was at 11:30. Subconsciously, because of my Hollywood track record, I must have self-sabotaged, thinking on some level that it was a waste of time.

I thought of not going, but, ultimately, I'm a momma's boy who tries to get good grades, so I called someone, begged forgiveness, and got there very sweaty—it was a disgusting, moist New York day—around 12:15.

I was asked what I had been working on lately and couldn't think of anything. Then I remembered my story.

I said, "I wrote this thing, I think it could be a movie, like *After Hours*. But it also could be, I imagine, a TV show."

I knew that the meeting was about TV, so I threw that bit in at the end. The producer asked me some questions about the story and said she'd like to read it. I e-mailed it to her the next day. She read it, liked it, and said that if I developed friends for the protagonist—Jonathan Ames—then maybe we could turn it into a show.

I obediently came up with two friends and a few other ideas, and two months later I went out to Los Angeles, met up with the producer, and pitched it to HBO. They said yes—they would commission me to write a pilot. Then there was a writer's strike, which slowed things down for about nine months, until, finally, in April 2008, I wrote a pilot script. Miraculously, HBO liked the script, and that September we shot the pilot. Then they liked that and ordered seven more episodes. The following September, the show's first season aired; it went on—another miracle—to last for three seasons. I wrote over seven hundred filmed screenplay pages, got out of debt for the first time in my adult life, and made some beautiful friends.

So I'm very pleased that *Esquire* asked me to write something, and very grateful that *McSweeney's* wanted it. If they hadn't, I might have just thrown the thing away. — JONATHAN AMES

BORED TO DEATH

by JONATHAN AMES

(fiction from Issue 24)

THE TROUBLE HAPPENED because I was bored. At the time, I was twenty-eight days sober. I was spending my nights playing Internet backgammon. I should have been going to AA meetings, but I wasn't.

I had been going to AA meetings for twenty years, ever since college. I like AA meetings. My problem is that I'm a periodic alcoholic, even with going to AA. Every few years, I try drinking again. Or, rather, drinking tries me. It tries me on for size and finds out I don't fit and throws me to the ground. And so I go crawling back to AA. Or at least I should. This last go-round, I was skipping meetings and just staying home and, like I said, playing Internet backgammon.

When I wasn't burning out my eyes on the computer, I was lying in bed, reading. I was going through the third Raymond Chandler phase of my adulthood. Read all his books in 1988, then 1999, and now 2007. Some people re-read Proust or Thomas Mann and improve themselves. Not me. Mixed in with the Chandler was some Hammet and Goodis. I needed murder and mayhem while I breathed my way to my own placid, dull, and boring death.

So that's all I was doing—reading and playing backgammon. I can afford such a lifestyle because I'm a writer. I'm not a hugely successful writer, but I'm my own boss. I've written six books—three novels and three essay collections—and at the time of the trouble I had roughly six thousand dollars in the bank, which is a lot for me. I also had a few checks for movie work coming in down the road.

By my economic standards it was a flush time. I had even paid my taxes early, at the end of March—it was now mid-April—and I was just trying to stay sober and keep a low profile in my own little life. I wasn't doing any writing, because, well, I didn't have anything to say.

Overall, I was being pretty reclusive. I only talked to a few people, primarily my parents, who are retired and live in Florida and who call me every day. They're a bit needy, my senior-citizen parents, but I don't mind, life is short, so if I can give them a little solace with a daily call, what the hell. My father is eighty-two and my mother is seventy-five. I have to love them now as best I can. The only other two people I really spoke to were the two close friends I have, one who lives here in New York and the other who's in Los Angeles. I have a lot of acquaintances, but I've never had a lot of friends.

One night a week, I did leave the apartment to go see this girl. It was nice. I guess you could say that she was a friend too, but I've never really thought of the women in my life as friends, which must be a flaw. Her name was Marie and we would have dinner, maybe go to a movie, and then we'd get into bed at her place, never my place, and the sex with her was good. But it wasn't anything serious. She was twenty-six and I'm forty-two, and I retired from being serious with women a few years ago. Somebody always got hurt, usually the girl, and I couldn't take it anymore.

Well, I'll shut up now about all this. It's not my drinking problem and my finances and my dead love life that I want to talk about. I only mention all this as some kind of way to explain why I had too much free time on my hands, because that's what got me into trouble. As I said, I was bored. Bored with backgammon and bored with reading and bored with being sober and bored with myself and bored with being alive.

I should make it clear that I wasn't at all bored by the books I was tearing through and loving, but bored by the fact that I wasn't actually doing anything, just reading. But the reading did something to me, made me delusional, I think. Sometimes when I read too much, I start living the books. For example, if I read a WWII spy thriller, I start walking around, looking over my shoulder, noticing things that aren't there, and I half-believe that the Nazis are still in power. Or if I read a prison novel, then I start feeling like I'm locked up, that I could be stabbed at any moment.

So because of all the Chandler and the Hammet, I got into my head this fantasy, this crazy notion that I wanted to play at being a private detective. I wanted to help somebody. I wanted to be brave. I wanted to have an adventure. And it's pathetic, but what did I do? I put an ad on Craigslist in the "services" section under "legal." It read as follows:

Private Detective For Hire
Reply to: serv-261446940@craigslist.org
Date: 2007-04-13, 8:31AM EST

Specializing: Missing Persons, Domestic Issues.
I'm not licensed, but maybe I'm someone who can help you.
My fee is reasonable.
Call 347-555-1042

There were two other private-detective ads on Craigslist and they offered all sorts of help—surveillance, undercover work, background checks, video and still photography, business investigations, missing persons, domestic issues, and two things I didn't quite grasp—"skip tracing" and "witness locates."

I figured the only thing I could help with was trying to find someone or maybe follow someone, which would most likely be a *domestic issue*—an unfaithful spouse or boyfriend or girlfriend. I didn't have any qualms about that, following an unfaithful lover, though in all the private-detective fiction I've read the heroes never do "marriage work," as if it's beneath them. But I didn't think it was beneath me. I thought it would be fun to follow somebody and to do so for the purposes of a real mission. Sometimes, probably because I want everything to be like it is in a book or a movie, I have followed people on the streets of New York, pretending I was a detective or a spy.

I did try to cover myself legally by writing in my ad that I wasn't licensed. I don't know who does license private detectives, but I figured it was a difficult process and, anyway, I just wanted to put the ad up, mostly as a lark, a playing out of a dream. But I didn't really think anybody would actually call me—I was offering far fewer services than the other private detectives and I was acknowledging in the ad that I wasn't exactly a professional.

If somebody did call, I figured after talking to me they would try somebody more reputable. Whatever came of it, even if nobody called, I thought it might be something I could write about, a comedic essay—"My Failed Attempt at Being a Private Detective." Often during my writing career, mostly for my essays, I've put myself in weird positions and then milked it for humor. This situation would be like the time I tried to go to an orgy but wasn't allowed in. Even when nothing happens, you can sometimes make a good story out of it.

Anyway, I got a thrill from posting the ad, but it was a short-lived thrill. For the first day, I would look at my ad, admiring my own handiwork, laughing to myself, wondering if something might happen, almost as if I checked out my ad enough times, other people would too. But then, after about a day, the thrill wore off. It was one more ridiculous thing in a ridiculous life, and, of course, no one called.

So I went back to the usual routine—I started a David Goodis novel, *Black Friday*, and once again I was spending hours playing backgammon. Then (around four o'clock in the afternoon) on Thursday, April 19, when I was in the midst of a good game, my cell phone rang. The number had an area code I couldn't immediately place—215. I answered the phone and kept on playing.

"Hello?" I said.

"I saw your ad," said a girl's voice.

"What? What ad?" I said. I had forgotten completely about my Craigslist posting. It had been six days.

"Craigslist? Missing persons?"

"Yes, of course, I'm sorry," I said, quickly rallying, remembering my little experiment. "I was distracted. I'm sorry. And most of my clients are word-of-mouth, so I forgot about my ad on Craigslist. How can I help you?"

Right away, I was trying to sound professional and the lie about the other clients just came to me naturally. I've always been a good liar.

"It's about my sister…" she started to say, then hesitated, and I glanced at my laptop, at the game. If I resigned, which is the same thing as losing and at the moment I was ahead, my ranking would go down, and I hate for my ranking to go down. I've worked very hard to get it to the second-highest level. I was momentarily conflicted, but I clicked a button and resigned from the game so that I could give my full attention to this other game, this one with the young-sounding girl on the phone.

"Your sister?" I said, prompting her.

"Well, I came in from Philadelphia this morning," she started slow and then her speech came fast, real fast, the way young girls talk, "and we're supposed to go to a show tonight. I know it's weird but we got tickets to *Beauty and the Beast*, we saw it when we were really young and loved it and now it's closing, so that's why we want to see it, but she didn't answer her phone all day yesterday or this morning, but I came in anyway, it was our plan, I figured she's just not picking up or it's not charged, she always forgets to charge her phone, but she's still not answering and now her voice mail is full, and no one at her dorm has seen her for a while and the guard let me in, but she's not in her room, the door is locked, she has a single, and I don't want to call my parents and freak them out, but I have a weird feeling, she's got this sleazy boyfriend, and I don't know what to do, and I'm at this Internet café and I always use Craigslist for everything, so I typed in 'missing persons' and found you."

This was a lot to digest. I tried to break it down.

"Your sister lives in a dorm? Where?"

"Twelfth Street and Third Avenue. It's an NYU dorm."

"And where are you?" I asked.

"This café. On Second Avenue. I don't know the side street, let me look out the window… Third Street."

"What's your name?"

"Rachel."

"Last name?"

"Weiss."

"Your sister's name?"

"Lisa…Weiss."

"And I'm Jonathan… Spencer, by the way… You can call me Jonathan. And you live in Philadelphia?" The lies were coming fast and easy. Spencer was my strange middle name. I'm Jewish but my parents loaded me up with a WASP assembly of names, Jonathan Spencer Ames.

"Yeah, I go to Temple," she said. "I'm a freshman."

"What year is your sister?"

"Junior."

"And where are your parents?"

"Maryland... Can you help me? I don't have anywhere to stay tonight, if I can't find her, and she has the tickets to *Beauty and the Beast*, and so I think I should just go back to Philly but I'm not sure what to do."

"I think I can help you. I can come meet you in about thirty minutes. I'm in Brooklyn, but it's a very quick subway ride. I know the café you're in... I charge one hundred dollars a day, but I bet I can find her by tonight or at least tomorrow. Can you afford a down payment of at least one hundred dollars to cover the first day?"

"Yes," she said. "I have money. I can go to an ATM."

"Just wait at the café. I'll be there in thirty minutes. Maybe twenty... What do you look like?"

"Why?"

"So I can recognize you."

"Oh... I have dark hair, almost black. Kind of long. I'm wearing a yellow dress and a kind of thick white sweater."

"Okay... I'll have a tan cap on. Not to frighten you but my most distinctive feature is my white eyebrows. I'm not an albino. The sun has bleached them over the years. I'll be there by four-thirty."

"I guess so," she said, a bit nonsensically. Her voice was practically a whisper. She wasn't sure she was doing the right thing. I cursed myself for possibly blowing it with the mention of the white eyebrows and sounding like a nut.

"Everything will be okay. I'll find your sister," I said.

"All right," she said, meekly.

"See you in a little bit," I said and hung up, before she changed her mind.

I put on a tie, loosened it at the collar, and undid the top button to give myself a rumpled, world-weary private detective look, and I threw on my gray tweed Brooks Brothers sport coat, since there was a slight chill in the air. Also, on all the covers of my Chandler novels, Philip Marlowe is always wearing a sport coat. Then, so the girl would recognize me, I put on my cap. I usually wear a hat of some kind, anyway, since I'm bald and buzz my hair down, and without hair it's a very drafty world. I was already wearing my favorite olive-green corduroy pants. Looking at myself in the mirror, I felt, overall, quite capable of finding this missing NYU coed, at least wardrobe-wise.

I grabbed *Black Friday* to read in the subway and was out of the apartment within five minutes of hanging up the phone.

The café had uncomfortable aluminum chairs and we sat with our legs practically touching. She was a cute little thing—very white skin and very dark hair. Her mind was soft, though, and that cut down the attraction and made it easier to keep my attention focused on the business at hand. I got the following information out of her, expanding on what she had told me on the phone: the sister, Lisa, about a year ago, had disappeared for a week with an older boyfriend (early thirties) and the family had gone into a panic; now she had a different boyfriend, but the same genus—thirtysomething, guitarist in a rock band, a bartender, and possibly a junkie; Rachel didn't want to get the parents or the police or NYU security involved, because it was probably nothing and her sister would kill her if she blew the whistle; at the same time, she had a bad feeling—she was worried that her sister had maybe started using heroin.

I figured the boyfriend was the key to this whole thing and she told me his name was Vincent, but she didn't have a last name. He worked at a bar called Lakes on Avenue B. Rachel, on an earlier trip to the city, had gone there with her sister. The NYU students liked it because the place was lax when it came to asking for proof of age.

"Do you have a picture of Lisa?" I asked.

"No," she said. Then she remembered that her sister had sent a picture of herself with Vincent to her cell phone. From Vincent's cell phone. This was a coup—I had a picture and a number to work with. She showed me the picture—Lisa was more severe than her sister, high cheekbones, a sensual mouth, but the same dark hair and marble-white skin. Vincent had a long, yellow-gray face, a tattoo of some kind on his neck, and a false look of rock-band confidence in his eyes.

I called Vincent's number; his voice mail, like Lisa's, was full. But at least

I had a number. I suggested to Rachel that we go over to Kinko's on Astor Place and that she e-mail me the picture and we print it up.

But first we called the sister, on the off-chance that this could be solved right here and now and the two girls could go see *Beauty and the Beast* as planned and live happily ever after. Not unexpectedly, the call went right to the filled-up voice mail. So then we swung by the dorm, with the same hope of an easy resolution, but the sister still wasn't in her room. I instructed Rachel to ask the guard in an offhand way if he had seen her sister—she showed him the cell-phone picture—and he said he hadn't.

It was now almost five thirty. As we walked over to Kinko's, I said, giving her an out and giving me an out, "Are you really sure you don't want to go to the cops or let your parents know?"

"I'm sure," she said. "Lisa'll go ballistic. She's probably forgotten about the play and is just having sex for hours. Somebody told me that if you do heroin you just keep having sex and don't want to stop."

"I think that's crystal meth," I said, "but I could be wrong." My problems have always been with alcohol and cocaine, so I wasn't too sure about these other drugs.

"Whatever," she said. "I don't even like beer. She always goes with the worst guys possible. He's either shooting her up with heroin or giving her crystal meth. It's like it turns her on to find a serial killer or something."

We stopped at the Chase Bank on Astor Place and she gave me one hundred dollars. At Kinko's, I printed up a blurry but recognizable portrait of the two lovebirds.

At Fourth Avenue, we waited for a cab to take her to Penn Station. From there she'd catch the next train to Philly.

"Are you really a professional?" she asked.

"I'm not licensed," I said, "but I've been at this awhile." I had been reading pulp fiction for nearly twenty years. It was an apprenticeship of sorts and was the little bit of truth that made the lie sound sincere. I may have been having a bipolar episode. "The first thing I'm going to do is find Vincent, and when I find Vincent I'll find your sister."

She got in a cab and as I closed the door, I said, "I'll call you later tonight."

"Okay," she said, and she looked scared and dumb. But she was a sweet kid. The cab drove off and the six o'clock light was beautiful, day darkening into night.

*   *   *

I stood on the corner and called information and got the number for Lakes Bar.

"Lakes." It was a woman's voice, mid-twenties. I could hear a jukebox in the background.

"Is Vincent there?" I asked. "The bartender."

"He comes in after me, at eight," she said. "Works eight to four."

"Okay, thanks… Listen, I owe him some money and I'm going to bring him by a check and I'm a terrible speller. Can you spell out his last name for me?"

"What? Yeah. I know. It's a weird name. I'm pretty sure there are two *t*'s. *E-t-t-i-n.*"

"Thanks so much," I said and hung up.

People will give you anything if you just ask directly. I called information and there was only one Vincent Ettin listed in Manhattan and this Ettin still had a landline and lived at 425 West Forty-seventh Street. I had two hours to kill before he was to be at work at eight. Maybe I could find him beforehand, so I called the number and got an answering machine. It was a no-nonsense message: "This is Vincent. You know what to do." It could have been the guy in the picture or some other Vincent Ettin. I didn't leave a message.

I walked over to West Eighth Street and took the A train up to Forty-second Street. When I got out of the subway the last of the light was gone and it was evening. Number 425 was an old five-story walk-up. Apartment 4F had the name *Ettin* next to the buzzer. I buzzed 4F. Nothing. I buzzed 2F. A voice, that of an old lady, came through the intercom: "Who is it?"

"Building inspector, let me in."

"Who?"

"City building inspector, fire codes, let me in."

The door buzzed open. I went up to the fourth floor. I knocked at 4F. No answer. I knocked again. Silence. Out of instinct I didn't know I had I tried the doorknob and the place was unlocked. Heart pounding with the feeling of transgression, I stepped in. The lights were on, and I called out, "Hello," like a fool, and then I got hit by a bad smell. There were two large mounds of shit on the floor, right near the door, and I nearly stepped on them. There was also a pool of piss, which I *had* stepped in. What the hell is this? I thought. I closed the door and again called out, "Hello?"

I stepped over the shit and the piss, and separate from those two grosser elements it was definitely a ragged dump of a place and reminded me of my own apartment. There was a futon couch with white hairs all over it, an old TV, a good-looking stereo, a cluttered coffee table, and at the far end a miniature nasty New York kitchen. There were no pictures anywhere, so I had no idea if this was the apartment of the Vincent Ettin that I was looking for.

A little black-and-white mutt came from some back room off the kitchen, probably the bedroom. Its tail was between its legs and it looked defeated and humiliated. Not much of a watchdog, it came over to me and I petted its head. I went through the kitchen and looked in the bedroom—nobody was there, just an unmade futon bed, and a lot of musical equipment, several amps, and three guitars, all of it new and expensive looking. The bathroom, which was off the bedroom, was a squalid closet and also empty of human life.

The dog was following me around and I got the idea that if he hadn't been walked for a while, at least two days for the two dumps, he also probably hadn't been fed. I found a bowl and dry dog food in the kitchen and set him up. Then I headed for the front door and noticed two things—the window behind the futon couch was wide open with no screen and it led to a fire escape, which would make the place pretty vulnerable to a break-in (though the unlocked door made things even easier), and I also saw that there was a cell phone on the coffee table.

The musical equipment had pretty much convinced me that this was the V. Ettin I was looking for, but then to confirm it I called the cell number I had for him. The phone on the coffee table vibrated but didn't ring. The dog looked up but then kept on eating, and the phone moving on the coffee table, like a living thing, gave me a spooked feeling. So I hung up my phone, but Ettin's phone, because of some delay in the system, still shuddered, like something twitching before dying, until it finally did stop. Then I got the hell out of there.

I took the train back downtown and then made the long walk east over to Avenue B. By the time I got to Lakes, which was at the corner of Eleventh, it was eight thirty. It was a dark, stripped-down place. It had a scarred wood bar, plenty of booze, three taps for beer, stools, some booths, and a jukebox. It wasn't too crowded, and there was a man behind the bar but it wasn't Ettin. This fellow was short and very skinny and had a shiny shaved head. My head is shaved but I always leave it stubbly, using old-fashioned barber's clippers. This guy went at his head with a razor.

I took a stool and for a moment I thought of ordering a beer. I wavered, then regained the old sober thinking, and when the bartender came over to me, I ordered a club soda. I gave him three bucks, sipped my drink, and he took care of some other customers. I wondered if Ettin was running late or wasn't going to show up. I waited a few minutes, then I waved the bartender over, deciding to show him my full hand. I took out the picture of Lisa Weiss and Vincent Ettin, which I had folded up and put in the Goodis novel.

"Do you know these two?"

"Yeah," he said, wary. "What's this about?"

"What are their names?"

"That's Vincent and Lisa. What the fuck is going on?"

"I've been hired by Lisa's family to find her. She's been missing for a few days and she doesn't answer her phone and neither does Vincent. Do you know where they might be?"

The bartender looked at me and then looked down the bar and out the window by the front door, not for any real reason except to avoid my eye. I took forty dollars out of my wallet and put it on the bar. I don't know who I thought I was, but I had all the moves. Shiny-head saw the money.

"Tell me what you know," I said.

"Lisa is missing?"

"Yes, and her family is very concerned."

"Well... okay, I don't know where she is. But Vince was supposed to work tonight but he called me a few hours ago and asked me to cover for him. He said he was upstate, that his band had a gig in Buffalo."

"Buffalo?"

"That's what he said. But my phone has caller ID and it said that he was calling from the Senton Hotel and it was a 212 number, Manhattan."

"What do you think he's doing at the Senton?"

"He might be on a run."

"Drugs?"

"Yeah. He was on methadone but he went off about a month ago. First he was just snorting lines and then he started shooting it again."

Shiny realized that maybe he was saying too much—he was a natural gossip and hadn't been able to help himself. I pushed the forty over to him.

"I appreciate the information," I said.

"I'm only telling you all this because of Lisa. She's a young kid." He looked down at the forty bucks, which he still hadn't touched.

"I hear you," I said.

"What are you going to do?" he asked.

"Go to the Senton. That's probably where Lisa is."

I sat up from the stool. Shiny pocketed the forty, and said, "Listen, before you came in another guy was looking for Vincent and gave me his card to give to Vincent. You'll probably see him before I do, so here's the card."

He pulled the card out of his pocket and handed it to me. On the card was the letter *G* in the middle and a 917 number. Below the number, hand-written, was *4/20/2007*, which would be the next day.

"So you didn't know this guy?"

"No."

"What was he like?"

"Spanish. A tough guy. About your height, six foot, but he looked like he lifted weights."

"How old?"

"My age. Thirties. To be honest, he kind of scared me."

I went outside, got the Senton's number, and called. They had no Vincent Ettin registered, but that didn't mean anything. I knew the Senton. It was on Twenty-eighth Street and Broadway and it was a flop hotel. Unless they were stupid, people didn't give their real names when they registered. You only went to the Senton to do drugs and hide out with prostitutes. It was run, like most flop hotels, by Indians. I knew the place because in the mid-'90s I had a booze-and-coke relapse and holed up there myself for two days with a prostitute. For some reason, you never want to do such things in your own home. Better to go on a run in an anonymous hotel room, and then when it's over you walk away and don't have to clean up the mess. I figured if the Senton was still in business it probably hadn't changed much.

I got a taxi. On the ride over to the hotel, I tried Lisa Weiss's number for the hell of it and was directed to her filled-up voice mail. I called both of Vincent Ettin's numbers, just in case he had returned to Forty-seventh Street, but no luck on that end. I thought of that sweet dog alone in the apartment. It had nice eyes.

The Senton hadn't changed and neither had that stretch of Twenty-eighth Street. All of Manhattan is being turned into one big, glossy high-end mall, but Twenty-eighth Street was still a dark and empty corridor, at least at night, and had an illicit feeling to it that was kind of comforting, like you couldn't drain all the life out of New York, even if that life was the kind that was trying to kill itself.

The hotel was just as I remembered it. It didn't have much in the way of a lobby, more of a narrow hallway, with a small alcove off to the right with one old stuffed chair, and at the end of the hallway there was an Indian in an office, behind a thick bulletproof piece of glass, with an opening at the bottom of the glass for the passing back and forth of money and keys. Past the office was the beat-up door to the elevator.

I approached the office and the Indian, a pockmarked, exhausted fellow, said he hadn't seen the two people in the picture, which I held up to the glass, but even if he had I don't think he would have told me. I asked him if I could wait in the alcove in case they were in the hotel and I could talk to them if and when they headed out. I explained to him that I very much needed to find them, the young girl in particular.

"You could wait there, if you rent a room," he said. "It's sixty dollars for three hours, ninety for the night."

I thought of just staking out the place from the sidewalk, but I didn't know how long I would be out there and it was a bit cold, even for an April night. I decided to rent the room for three hours, see if I got lucky. Between my tip for Shiny back at the bar, not to mention the subway rides and the cab, I was losing money on this deal, not that I was in it for the money, but still. I kicked myself for not telling Rachel that there would be expenses. What had I been thinking? Marlowe always quoted a day rate *plus expenses*.

I registered as Philip Marlowe and got the key to my room but I didn't go up to it. I went and sat in the alcove. If Vincent and Lisa headed out to get something to eat or go for cigarettes, I would be right there. I took out my Goodis novel and started reading, looking up from the page every few minutes when somebody walked past me, which meant I was eyeballing a variety of prostitutes—females, trannies, gay hustlers—and the usual ragged assortment of middle-aged married johns, plus other sundry types who were using the Senton just to party.

I read for about an hour, and then I put the book down and kind of meditated, mulling things over, trying to make sense of it—Lisa, the pretty girl in the picture with the dark hair and beautiful mouth; Vincent's empty apartment with the dog shit and the left-behind cell phone and the open window and unlocked door; and this card from "G" with tomorrow's date written on it. In the midst of all this cogitating, my parents called. My mother had taken a t'ai chi class for seniors at the Y and my father's ring finger had bent in and he couldn't straighten it out.

We eventually rang off, and I thought some more about my "case." I didn't know what to make of anything, but in my own sick way I was having a good time. Then around eleven p.m., after sitting there for nearly two hours, I really had to go to the bathroom. I wasn't sure what to do about this. I couldn't recall Marlowe or the Continental Op, Hammett's detective, having to give up a stakeout position because of the toilet. What if during the time I was in the bathroom, I missed the two I was looking for? That would be bad luck, and from playing backgammon, I know that you get a lot of bad luck when you play a game. Mostly I had been rolling good—Ettin being listed and the door not being locked at his apartment, the bartender having caller ID and being willing to feed me plenty of information. So it was all the more reason why something should go against me.

I went back to the Indian behind the glass. I asked him if there was a toilet on the ground floor that I could use.

"No," he said. "You have a toilet in your room."

"All right, listen," I said and I took the picture back out and again pressed it to the glass, "if these two come out while I'm in the bathroom, tell them there's someone here that needs to see them. Stall them for me."

"Fuck you," he said, but it wasn't a "fuck you" with malice. It was primarily a simple statement of refusal. It was vulgar, but there was room for negotiation.

I took twenty dollars out of my wallet and slid it through the movie-ticket opening at the bottom of the glass. He took the money and didn't say anything, but I thought he would do what I had asked.

I walked quickly over to the elevator and waited a good long time for it. I really needed to piss. Then I rode the thing at a glacial speed up to my room on the fifth floor. The room was clean enough, cigarette burns on most every surface, but the bed was made and there was one towel in the bathroom. I took a piss and felt profound relief. Sometimes a good piss is incredible.

I took the elevator back down, again waiting at least three minutes for it, and returned to the lobby. I had been gone about ten minutes, mostly because of the elevator. I went up to the glass. "You didn't see them, did you?"

"I saw the man," he said. "He came in right after you left and went up to his room."

"Shit. Came in? You mean, he didn't go out? And the girl wasn't with him?"

"Yeah, he came in. And no girl."

"So he went up to his room. That's excellent. What's his room number?"

"Fuck you."

"I need to talk to this guy," I said. "I'm a good person. I'm looking for this young girl for her family. I'm not going to make any trouble."

"Fuck you."

I took out another twenty and slid it through.

"Sixty-three," he said.

I waited nearly five minutes for the elevator and thought of walking up the stairs, but then kept on waiting. Finally, it came. I went up to the sixth floor, another long ride. I knocked at 63 and got no response. I could hear the TV playing inside, and playing in the other rooms on the hall. I knocked again, but with more force. I said, through the door, "I have a note for you from G." I waited. I put my ear against the door and didn't hear any movement. I tried the knob. Vincent Ettin was not big on locking doors. I let myself in. He was lying on the big queen-size bed, his arms splayed out. There was a band of rubber wrapped around Vincent's right arm and there was a needle still in his left hand.

I had never seen a dead body in my forty-two years and Vincent Ettin was my first.

Near a deli on Seventh Avenue and Twenty-eighth was a pay phone. It didn't work. I walked a few blocks south and found one that did work. It had been years since I'd used a pay phone. I called 911 and reported a dead body in the Senton Hotel on Twenty-eighth Street, room 63. The operator wanted my name and I hung up. I called 911 again, spoke to a different operator, and told that person the same thing and hung up. I wanted to make sure they got it right.

Fifteen minutes before those phone calls, I had been in his room, just staring at the body, terrified and disbelieving, but then I'd had the presence of mind to close the door and I got on the bed right next to him. I cursed myself for not knowing CPR. Do I pinch his nostrils and blow into his mouth? Do I pound on his chest? His eyes were open, but they were like the eyes of a doll. I felt his neck for a pulse, feeling the skin beneath the tattoo, which was some obscure Asian markings, and there wasn't anything there, no pulse, no life. Then I put my head against his chest and I couldn't hear anything. But I opened his lips, anyway, and held his nose shut—it's what I had seen on TV—and I suppressed a scream of terror and blew air into him. I thought I might be sick. I did it for maybe twenty seconds and it had no effect. I pulled away. My first animal instinct had been correct—he was dead.

I staggered out of the room, trembly and dizzy, but I walked down the six flights of stairs to get my head straight, and then went right out of the hotel, not handing in my key, not saying anything to my Indian pal. Just got out of there. Let him try to find Philip Marlowe.

After making the 911 calls and walking about twenty blocks in some kind of frenzied panic, I stopped at a bodega on Broadway, near Union Square, and bought an eight-ounce bottle of Listerine and gargled and spit out the piss-yellow liquid on the street, again and again. I had to get the taste of the dead man out of my mouth. I used up the whole thing, people passing by must have thought I was insane, and then I threw away the empty bottle and hailed a cab to take me back to Brooklyn. In the car, I tried calling Lisa Weiss, hoping to end this nightmare and find the damn girl, but got the same fucking filled-up voice mail. I then tried calling Rachel Weiss, but she didn't pick up. I left a message saying she should call me right away, though I tried to keep my voice calm. When I spoke to her, I was going to tell her to have her parents call the police right away. But I have to say, this scared me. What kind of trouble could I get into for taking on this whole thing and then anonymously reporting a dead body? But it didn't matter, I just had to get out of this mess.

I got home around twelve thirty and lay on top of my bed for hours, didn't even take off my sport coat or shoes, just lay there, numb, waiting for Rachel to call, but she never did. At some point, I passed out. I woke up around eight a.m. and called Rachel again and left another voice mail. At nine I tried her again and I got a recording telling me that the service at the number had been suspended. Fucking college student hadn't paid her bill and I needed to talk to her!

I thought of calling her parents but I didn't know where in Maryland they lived. I started pacing in my dirty apartment. I went on Craigslist and called one of the private detectives listed. I told him most of my story, kept it real tight, except I didn't say anything about my bogus ad, just that I was a friend trying to help out.

"Why did you make an anonymous call to the cops?" the PI asked; he had a gruff voice.

"I don't know. I was scared."

"That doesn't look good. Makes it seem like you did something wrong. You and your friend better go to the police. It sounds like you stepped in a big pile of shit."

"Could you help us?" I asked. I hadn't told him about Vincent's dog, so he didn't know how accurate his metaphor was.

He was silent a moment, then he said, "I'm busy," and he hung up. He must not have liked the sound of the whole thing. I didn't blame him.

I tried Rachel's number again and got the same recording. I called Temple University information and the number they had for her was her cell phone.

Stay cool, I told myself. Stay cool. I undressed and took a shower. I dried off, got dressed in the same clothes I had been wearing, except for the tie. Putting on fresh clothes seemed like too much to ask of myself. I tried Rachel and her sister just to torture myself, got the usual results, and I even thought for a moment of calling Vincent's number and then I remembered that he was dead. I was already unraveled and it was getting worse.

I sat at my desk, staring at the computer, and I thought of calling the cops or going to the cops, my local precinct, but what would I say? I had posted a bogus ad, then given a false name to some undergrad from Temple University, run around the city, found a dead body, and made an anonymous call to 911.

I filled my kettle to boil some water to make coffee in my French press.

Marlowe was always making himself coffee. The thing to do was to stay calm and not overreact, that's how Marlowe always handled himself. While the water did its thing, I started dialing 911 again, to get this over with, but then I couldn't go through with it. I was too scared. I hung up the phone.

I poured myself a cup of coffee and sat back down at my desk, like it was any other day, and because I'm a sick person I logged on to the backgammon site, thinking that a game might clear my head. On the site the time and the day were listed: April 20, 2007. I didn't start playing. I remembered the card from G. I took it out of my wallet. I held it, and sipped my coffee.

There were two competing thoughts in my head: (1) Go to the cops right now, and (2) call G. Calling G had the appeal of a first drink on a relapse. You know you're going horribly against the grain, doing the wrong thing, what they call in the AA *Big Book* "a sickening rebellion," but there's some kind of mad force of nature that makes you do it, that demands that you do it. So before I could stop myself—in the grips of it, the impulse to self-destruct, to get deeper into this mess—I dialed *70 to block my number and then dialed the number on the card.

"Yeah." It was a deep voice. I was going off the deep end, but for once at least I didn't get somebody's fucking voice mail and that was a relief.

"Is this G?" I asked.

"Who's this?" There was some trace of a Spanish accent, but not much. "How'd you get my number?"

"I... I went to Lakes Bar, the bartender gave me your card. I've been looking for the girlfriend of Vincent Ettin. Lisa Weiss. Do you, by any chance, know where she is?"

"Where's Vincent at? Who is this?"

"Do you think you can help me?"

"What the fuck are you talking about? Help you with what?" The voice was angry, hostile, fierce.

"Finding this girl."

"Where's Vincent. I need to speak to him."

"This is going to sound strange. I don't know if you're good friends. But he's dead."

"What the fuck you saying?"

"I was looking for this girl, Lisa Weiss, and I found Vincent. He was in a hotel and he OD'd."

"This is fucked up. You're a friend of Vincent's? Where are you?"

"I'm not a friend. I'm looking for the girl."

"How do you know he's dead if you're not a friend?"

"I found him dead."

"You're fucking lying to me. Who are you? Tell me your fucking name."

"Jonathan Spencer. Do you know where the girl is?"

"Okay," he said, less heated. He was suddenly all calm and gentle. "I know Lisa. She's a friend. She's a good girl. You and I should meet up and talk this out. Figure out what is going on. Where do you live?"

"I'm in Brooklyn, but I'll meet you somewhere. Where are you?"

"I'm in Brooklyn. Red Hook. Come to where I work. You know Coffey Street, off of Van Brunt? You know Red Hook?"

"Yeah, it's not far from me. Where do you work?"

"C and L."

"What's C and L?"

"Beverage distributor."

"Okay... How about we meet at this restaurant in Red Hook—Hope and Anchor, you know that place? It's open for breakfast."

"Yeah, sure, I know it. We deliver to them."

"Want to meet there in half an hour?"

"Okay."

"And you'll tell me where Lisa is?"

"Yeah. Yeah."

"Can you just tell me on the phone then?"

"Listen you f..." He reined himself in. "I want to talk to you about Vincent, this shit about OD'ing. It's not something to talk about on the phone, hearing that someone you know is dead, if he is dead. So let's meet up and talk this shit out."

"All right, see you at the restaurant in half an hour. I'll be wearing a tan cap and a gray sport coat."

"I'll find you," he said and hung up.

Like somebody sleepwalking out a ten-story window, not knowing what they were doing, I called Promenade Car Service, the one I always use. They came in fifteen minutes and ten minutes after that I was at Hope and Anchor, which I had been to a few times. It was almost ten thirty in the morning. It was a faux-rustic little place—a cutesy, gentrified outpost in the old waterfront neighborhood of Red Hook, which in the last five years has started attracting artists, the kinds of people who fifteen years before had been colonizing the Williamsburg neighborhood of Brooklyn. They colonized it so well that they can't afford to live there anymore. So now it's Red Hook.

The place was empty at ten thirty in the morning on a Friday, except for a scruffy twentysomething fellow drinking coffee and reading the *New York Times*, and the waitress, a cute hippie-looking blond, also in her twenties. I ordered a coffee. I wasn't thinking about much. I was sort of high or something. High on the folly of all that I had been doing. But not high in a good way, more like I was out of it, dazed. It didn't help that I had slept only about three hours.

Then G came in. He was my height, about six feet, and had a muscular V-shaped torso discernible underneath a gray sweatshirt with a hood. He had shiny black hair, which was greased back, and he was good-looking, nice features—a straight, elegant nose, big eyes, masculine chin. He had light brown skin and, like Shiny the bartender said, was probably in his early thirties. There was a scar on his right cheek, not too pronounced but visible. We made eye contact and I didn't like the way he looked at me. My heart stopped and he came over to me, sat right next to me, instead of across from me, and put a switchblade right against my belly and said, "Let's talk outside. I'll rip you up. I don't give a shit. Just walk out with me."

"I haven't paid for my coffee," I said. Why this occurred to me, I don't know.

"Put the money on the table and fucking walk out," he said. The waitress was sitting at the bar, with her back to me, and the boy with his paper didn't even look up. Music was playing loudly on the stereo system. They were in their own worlds.

I put a five on the table, it was the smallest bill I had, and G walked behind me and led me outside to a big car, a sky-blue Chevy Caprice with fancy rims. I knew it was a Caprice. I'd had one years ago. He had a friend in the front seat at the wheel and we sat in the back.

We drove a few blocks and then turned right on Coffey, which is a long block of warehouses that leads to the waterfront and the moribund Red Hook piers. Manhattan was across the river and to the right, gleaming and rich. Straight ahead, about half a mile away, was the Statue of Liberty. It was a beautiful day out—clear and bright.

Spanish music played on the radio and they didn't say anything. I hadn't gotten a good look at the driver, but he seemed younger than G, probably in his early twenties, and from the backseat I looked at his shiny black hair, which was cut close to his scalp so that you could see the skin between each individual hair. His neck and shoulders were fat. He was a fat boy.

"Is G your full name or just an initial?" I asked.

"Shut up," he said, and then said something in Spanish to the driver.

"Where's Lisa?" I said, pretending to be brave and tough, and I sort of fooled myself, in that I actually felt somewhat courageous.

"I told you to shut up."

We pulled into a garagelike warehouse, not too big, but room enough for the car and a van that had C & L BEVERAGES stenciled on its side. Toward the back of the garage there were dozens of piled-up cases of soda and water and beer.

We got out of the car. G pushed me toward the far left corner, where there was a battered steel door. He stayed behind me, and I didn't feel the knife, but I knew it wasn't far away. His fat friend followed after us. We went through the door and into a crowded office that had more cases of water and soda stacked along its walls. On a little couch was Lisa Weiss, with thick gray tape over her mouth. Her wrists and ankles were bound by the same kind of tape. She was wearing a short black skirt and a white blouse, which was dirty and ripped by the right shoulder, like she had been yanked. Because of the tape around her ankles, her knees were close together and prim looking. The hollows of her eyes were darkened from exhaustion and smeared mascara, and she stared at me.

There was a battered desk next to the couch, and behind it was a squat older man with gray in his short, close-cropped hair. He had a black mustache, also with traces of gray, and, like G and the fat boy, he was Spanish, with yellow-brown skin. He appeared to be in his mid-fifties and was wearing a blue short-sleeved sport shirt, with only two buttons near his opened collar. He was smoking a cigarette and had a thin-lipped, ugly mouth underneath his mustache. G pushed me forward so that I was standing right by the edge of the desk. The older man spoke to me.

"Where's Vincent?"

"I told G here that I found him dead last night of an overdose. At the Senton Hotel." The girl kicked out her legs, but nobody paid attention to her.

"Don't fucking lie to me," said the old man.

"I'm not, I swear... He had just shot up. He OD'd. I'm just looking for this girl." I pointed to Lisa. She kicked her legs again. "Her sister asked me to find her and I tracked down Vincent and found him dead."

"Are you fucking with me?" the old man asked, and G stuck me in the back with the knife, just enough so that I could feel the point coming through my sport coat.

"I'm not. I promise. I just want to take this girl and leave. I don't know what's going on."

"Your friend Vincent owes me seventy-five thousand dollars. One key. I told him he had to have it to me by *today*."

"He's not my friend."

"I gave him all the bars on Avenue B for dealing and he fucked me over. You can never trust a junkie. I have to say that it's my own damn fault." He seemed to be speaking more to G and the fat boy than to me.

"I don't know what's going on," I said. "But he's dead. I'm telling you the truth. You could call the Senton Hotel and ask them if someone died there last night. He was in room sixty-three."

The old man was quiet. "If he died, it wasn't our shit," he then said, not really to anyone.

He opened a drawer in his desk and then came around to my side. He was shorter and more squat than I realized, maybe five foot five, but there was a large, black gun in his hand and so it didn't really matter. He said something to G in Spanish and G shoved me down to my knees. I don't think the old man liked me towering over him.

Then he pushed the gun against my mouth. "Open up," he said. I didn't. I glanced for a second at the girl; her eyes were terrified and she was kicking out her legs. G took a step toward her and she stopped the kicking. The old man said it again, "Open up," but I didn't. Then he smacked me across the jaw with the handle of the gun, making sure to hit the bone. I opened my mouth then and he put the gun inside. I tasted the grease and the metal.

"That bastard has nine lives. All junkies do. I don't think he's dead. He got away from these two *maricons*, jumping out a window, should have broken his neck then, and they bring me this Jewish bitch. I don't need her and I don't need you. G, you fucked up bringing this girl... I need Vincent. I want my money." He swirled the gun around in my mouth, knocking it gently against my teeth. I stared at his yellow hand holding the gun, his thick blunt fingers. Lisa must have been with Vincent at the apartment when G and the fat boy showed up; Vincent went out the window, left his cell phone, and they took the girl. I thought of that dog. "But he doesn't have my money," the old man went on, "and tells you to call G and act like he's dead to get out of it. So you fucking tell me where Vincent is hiding!"

"He's dead. OD'd," I said and with the gun in my mouth I sounded horrific, like a deaf-mute, my words all strangled.

He violently raked the gun sideways out of my mouth, breaking my front teeth on purpose. I screamed and my mouth filled with blood.

Then he hit me across the face with the gun, doing it very hard this time, using the barrel like a knife and opening up my cheek.

"Is he really dead? Don't lie to me!"

"Yes. Please. Please. I'm sorry." I was begging and my mouth was bleeding, and my teeth were sharp, broken things. I put my hand to my face, to try to keep my cheek in one piece, I could feel it flapping open; I might have been going into shock. It was like I wasn't really there. I was detached and drifting away, passive and submissive. I had always wondered how so many Jews could be killed in Germany, but now I knew why they would get on their knees and be shot into their own open graves.

Then there was a spark of life in my mind, what I thought was a solution, and I said, "I went to his apartment. There was a lot of musical equipment in his bedroom. You could sell it and probably make some of the money back. I'll help you, I promise."

My words were all mangled and came out sibilant because of my teeth, and the old man looked at me like I was crazy. Then he handed the gun to G and muttered something in Spanish, and I couldn't have possibly seen it, but I felt like I did, some kind of Darwin thing where an animal, a human animal like me, can see things it shouldn't. So I saw G swinging the gun down at the back of my head and then my head and eyes were filled with a red-orange color and there was a burning pain at the base of my neck, my spine itself was in an agony it had never felt before, and then there was blackness, like a sudden, violent suffocation.

*   *   *

When I came to I thought I was in a dark metal box. I couldn't really see anything, and there was something soft next to my face. I reached across myself and ran my hand over the soft thing and my eyes adjusted to the minimal light and I saw that I was touching Lisa Weiss's leg. She was still taped up and she had passed out. We were moving, and I realized I was lying in the back of what must have been the van I had seen in the garage. There were a few cases of Poland Spring water and there were two frosted-over windows on the back doors and they let in just enough milky light for me to make things out. It was a closed-off compartment, and whoever was driving the van was on the other side of the aluminum-sheet wall behind me. I touched my face. It was dried and swollen, but there was a long hole, a groove I could put my finger in. I was horrified. My face wasn't my own. I was disfigured. I ran my tongue over my jagged teeth and just lay there stunned.

Then I looked at my watch. It was almost nine p.m.; I had been out for hours. I reached behind my head and felt a swelling back there that was the size of a tennis ball. I shook Lisa but she didn't wake up.

I felt for my cell phone and wallet, but they were both gone. I slid down to the doors, but there were no inside handles. I tried to look out the windows, but I couldn't see anything. I was incredibly thirsty and it seemed like odd luck that there were cases of water. I pulled a bottle out of one of the boxes and I took a sip but I could barely swallow.

We were driving somewhere very bumpy and I spilled most of the water on myself, but what little I was able to get down tasted good. I looked again at my watch. I couldn't believe how long I had been out. I figured they had waited until it was dark so that they would have the cover of night for killing us and getting rid of our bodies.

They must have followed up on what I told them about Vincent, and without him the girl was just a liability, no longer a bargaining chip, just somebody they had kidnapped, so better to get rid of her. And me, well, I was a fool that they had absolutely no use for, and if I was dead then I couldn't make trouble for them. They had a good setup: they distributed beverages and heroin, and that's probably how they met Vincent. The beverages got them in the door at bars and then they hooked up bartenders to deal for them. They dealt in two substances that people needed, and the liquids probably cleaned the cash from the drugs.

I looked around me. I didn't want to die. I had to do something to help myself and this girl. In the murky shadows I made out a spare tire attached to the wall of the van. I thought maybe I could use the tire to bang open the door. It was a futile thought, but I tried to take the tire off the wall and I saw that inside it was a jack and a tire iron. I yanked out the iron. One end was shaped like an egg-holder for unscrewing lug nuts and the other end was a sharpish wedge for prying off hubcaps. The van came to a stop. I got to my feet. I could just about stand near the two doors, bending over a little. My head was pounding. I held the tire iron like a club, the lug nut end in my fist.

The doors opened up and it was the fat boy and I came down on his face with the tire iron as hard as I could and the thing went right through his nose and deep into his face and got stuck there. I fell forward and he fell back onto the ground and I landed on top of him and it was a freakish thing but that tire iron, with my weight behind it, pierced deeper into his flesh and must have gone right into his brain.

A car door slammed toward the front of the van and I scrambled around and saw that the fat boy had a gun tucked into his pants. I yanked that out, sprawling across him, my stomach on his thick legs, and G came around, talking on his cell phone, probably to a girl, he was saying, "Okay, baby," and he was five feet from me and he said, "Oh, fuck," and I had the gun pointed right at him. I pulled the trigger and nothing happened. It was on safety.

G dropped his phone and reached for what must have been a gun in the side pocket of his baggy pants, and I flipped the safety—my dad had guns when I was a kid and I knew where the safety was—and I shot at G and somehow I missed and he was bent over, struggling with the Velcro on his pocket, and I fired again and it went right through the top of his sleek black head and he went down.

I looked around me. We were near the water, the edge of the Atlantic Ocean. I could see the Verrazano Bridge to the north. We were on some bumpy, broken-up service road off the Belt Parkway. High weeds and concrete barriers hid us from view, but high-powered streetlights from the highway, about two hundred yards away, cast everything in silvery shadows. Light came off the water like a mirror.

G and the fat boy were probably going to shoot us and then dump us in the current. I dropped the gun and went into the van. I shook Lisa and poured a bottle of water on her face and she still wouldn't wake up. I worried about hurting her, but I yanked off her mouth tape and vomit spilled out. I realized she was dead. She must have vomited behind that tape and choked to death.

Somehow, shifting their bodies a little at a time, I got G and his friend into the back of the van and closed them in there with Lisa. I looked for my phone on G and the fat boy, but they didn't have it, and they also didn't have my wallet. I thought of using G's phone to call the police, but I felt like I had to keep moving; I didn't want to wait for the cops to come to me. I started the van up, found my way out to the highway, and decided to go to my own neighborhood, to go to *my* precinct. It was some kind of muted desire to just go home, but I knew I couldn't go home just yet, so the best I could do was go to the police *near my home*.

And I knew I had to go to them. I had killed two men and I had more or less killed this girl I had never really met. If I hadn't interfered, they might have let her go. Without me bringing the news, it could have been a while before they found out Vincent was dead, if they ever did find out, and so they probably would have just threatened her, said they'd be watching her until Vincent showed up. She'd still have value to them as a link to their money and so she'd be alive, and maybe she would have been smart and gotten far away from New York. She could have been safe. But I had complicated everything and so because of me she was dead.

I drove north on the Belt, and the light of the oncoming traffic was killing my eyes. I knew I must have had a bad concussion and I couldn't stop morbidly running my tongue over my fractured teeth, which made me think of the old man in the garage. I didn't like the fact that he probably had my phone and my wallet. Maybe I wouldn't be able to pin anything on him and he'd come after me. He could find me.

So I changed my mind and I didn't go to the police. I drove over to Coffey Street and pulled into the garage. The blue Caprice was there and there was a light under the door in the corner. I don't think he was expecting me and I had the fat boy's gun in my hand.

THERE IS NO TIME
IN WATERLOO

by SHEILA HETI

conceived with MARGAUX WILLIAMSON

(from Issue 32, which was dedicated to stories set in the year 2024)

EVERYONE IN WATERLOO was an amateur physicist, and they endlessly bugged the real physicists as the physicists sat in cafés talking to each other. The amateurs would approach and put questions to them; simple questions, obvious ones. Or else they asked questions that even a physicist couldn't answer, or questions that weren't in the realm of physics at all, but had more to do with biology or straight computation. People who know almost nothing about what they're talking about are often more enthusiastic than the ones who know a lot, so they do all the talking, while the ones who know their stuff stay silent and get red in the face.

Whenever a real physicist would start to correct or explain a point, the amateur would smile and nod, and loudly proclaim that they'd read something about that in a magazine or a book recently. Then they would start to explain and the physicist would listen, tight-lipped, or else abruptly put an end to the conversation in frustration.

Then the physicist would return to the Perimeter Institute, which was built on the top of a gently sloping hill, and sigh in relief to be home again, standing at the chalkboard, working out equations.

One afternoon in March, a rumor went around town that some boy's Mothers had predicted that a kid was going to blow up the mall on the left side of town, so all the teenagers got on their scooters and sped off toward the parking lot there.

As Sunni was leaving her apartment, her mother called out from her usual place on the couch and asked where she was going. Sunni returned and explained about the rumor, and admitted that she was really eager to see the mall be blown up; that she and her friends had so much pent-up energy— they were wild with energy, and simply couldn't wait.

Sunni's mother felt a bit of regret that Sunni was going to watch the mall explode, but she didn't object; after all, if that was Sunni's destiny, who was she to interfere?

At the mall the teenagers spoke excitedly with each other, drawing together and apart, eager for the show to begin. They asked around to discover whose Mothers had predicted the explosion, but no one seemed to know. When, after an hour and a half, the mall remained standing, undisturbed, they started checking their Mothers to see if they were the one destined to blow it up. It appeared that none of them were.

Now they began to grow tense and upset. It was not the first time something like this had happened. The week before, some boy's Mothers had predicted a fight, but no one had thrown the first punch. A month ago, there was supposed to have been an orgy in the back of the other mall, the nice one, but after standing around awhile they had checked their Mothers and learned that the probability of their participating in an orgy was really low.

It started to rain, as a weatherman had predicted. Dispirited, the teenagers began to drift off. Only Sunni and a few of her friends remained, to finish the conversation they'd been having about film. They each had their own distinct opinions about art, but came together in agreement that drama was an inaccurate reflection of life; the best stories followed the path of greatest likelihood. Indeed, when you thought about the best stories down through time, their greatness and terror came from the fact that the most predictable and most probable thing always occurred.

"Like in Oedipus," Sunni said. And in that moment, one of Sunni's friends tossed a match into the air, having just used it to light his cigarette. It landed smack on Sunni's Mothers, igniting a little flame.

"Oh, *fuck!*" Sunni cried, batting her Mothers into the air. It arced, smoking, and dropped onto the pavement.

"Oh my God, Sunni—is your Mothers dead?" Danny gasped.

"Nope! Nope! Luckily no!" Sunni replied, picking it up. It was burning hot, and she tossed it from hand to hand. Looking down at it as it cooled, she saw that the screen had been melted into a squinty little eye. The keys were matted down to their wires, and the casing was tarry and charred.

"Still works!" Sunni announced. Then she got onto her scooter, feeling like she was about to faint, and rode to the parking lot around the other side of the mall, her Mothers propped up against the windshield. She kept glancing down at it, but no glance transformed it from the twisted, charry mess it had been in the glance before.

In the back parking lot, she stopped her scooter and got off and doubled over, hyperventilating a bit, then ran a distance to throw up. When she returned to her scooter and saw her Mothers there, she was overtaken by another spell of dizziness. It wasn't clear yet whether this was the worst, most tragic thing that had ever happened to her, or if this was the most exciting moment of her life. She only knew that she had never felt such vertigo before, and upon asking herself what to do now, then glancing down reflexively at her Mothers for the answer, she was overwhelmed by vertigo once more.

Twenty years earlier, the citizens of Waterloo had become enthralled by a book written by a physicist who had been invited to spend some time working at Perimeter. The book was called *The End of Time*, and its author, Julian Barbour, had argued in a persuasive and beautiful way that time did not exist; that the universe was static. There were a slightly less than infinite number of possible futures hanging about, like paintings in an attic, all real but out of reach, and each person's destiny was nothing more and nothing less than the most probable of those possible futures.

The people most taken with this idea led fervent discussions on how best to realize the theory in one's own life. Like humans anywhere, they didn't want to waste time. They hoped to reach their destinies as quickly and efficiently as possible—not their ultimate destinies, just their penultimate ones. And so it made sense to try and act as much in accordance with probability as they could.

The executives at the BlackBerry headquarters in Waterloo decided they would capitalize on this desire, and they began producing a machine they tagged *The Mother of All BlackBerrys*. It remained a phone you could e-mail from, but it had an added, special feature: given ongoing inputs, it was calibrated to determine for each user what they were destined to do next.

"It will be a device that determines a person's most likely next action based on previous behaviors. If the input is one's life, then the outcome is one's life," an executive explained to the rest as they sat around a table.

"Brilliant!" said another executive, reaching for a Danish. And they all reached for Danishes, and toasted each other, smiling.

The Mothers—as people began calling them—were at once a huge success. They eclipsed everything in the culture at that moment, like any great fad down through time. People in Waterloo consulted their Mothers at every turn, and it quickly became as impossible to live without a Mothers as it had once been to not check e-mail. People wondered how they had managed their lives before their Mothers. They bought Mothers for their babies.

If life became somewhat more predictable as a result, it was also more comforting, and soon the citizens of Waterloo didn't even notice that they were going in circles; that it was always the same thing over and over again.

The physicists, though nominally to blame for the proliferation of the Mothers, were largely skeptical and had a hundred doubts. It was not unusual to be standing in a supermarket line and hear one of them testily provoke and challenge an amateur physicist who was checking his Mothers, if the physicist was having a particularly bad day. "So do these Mothers calculate quantum or classical probabilities?" the physicist might ask; a question over which the amateur might stumble, only to regain his footing upon consulting his Mothers about whether continuing the conversation would be to his benefit, to which the Mothers would reply that the probability was low.

*   *   *

What will Sunni do without her Mothers? I sometimes ask myself a similar question. What would I do if I didn't know what was to come? If the inputs of my past were to disappear, I'd have no idea how I'd behaved in relationships past, and would not know how to behave in them now. I would play it all differently, not knowing how I was most likely to play it. I might forget how much I once hated to be on a soccer pitch, and how I had avoided soccer ever since. I might, while lounging in a park, say to the soccer players, while rising, *Do you need an extra player?*

If you draw a line across a piece of paper, that is King Street. Now draw a small, perpendicular line crossing King Street near the center. That is Princess Street. That is the part of town where the losers, misfits, and orphans hang out. It's where someone crosses the street drunk, and someone else crosses the street with ripped jeans and a lazy eye.

On either end of King Street, draw a square. These are the two malls. The mall at the right end of town is in the richer neighborhood, near the Perimeter Institute, the University, and the Institute for Quantum Computing—all the institutions representing the heights of Waterloo's excellence. The other mall, the one that the teenagers gathered at, is situated near the Old Town Hospital, City Hall, and the more run-down establishments that deal with the humanities and the human body.

Now watch Sunni speed along the long line of King Street, arriving within minutes at Princess.

"No," said one of the physicists, standing in the park under the gazebo, to the twenty-odd citizens picnicking around her. "We *don't* all believe that time is static."

The picnickers smiled up at the physicist. They continued to eat their bread and sandwiches and throw their strawberries into the grass.

*   *   *

Sunni was like all her friends. And all her friends were like Sunni. Their machines resembled the part of the brain that sees patterns and nothing but patterns. To that part of the brain, everything fits. There is no randomness to life, no chance. If ever their Mothers missed something, or something not predicted occurred, they would correct for the future, learning from what happened and fitting this new thing into a better, more complete image of the whole. In this way, if not everything was already accounted for, Sunni and her friends had faith that in time all would be. Life would proceed as anticipated. One had only to walk the determined path.

Sunni had always avoided Princess Street, since only losers hung out there. But since nearly every teenager whose Mothers broke somehow wound up on Princess, it was where she decided to go. She still had the instincts of someone with a Mothers, and wanted to waste no time before moving on to the likeliest next stage of her destiny. She parked her scooter and walked straight into one of the bars, pushing its red door open.

Two teenagers she had never seen before were sitting on tall stools, smoking and drinking, and upon entering Sunni could hear them whisper: *Doesn't she look like Shelly? No, but she reminds me a lot of my grade-four gym teacher. Actually, today in its entirety reminds me a lot of grade four.*

She went to perch on the stool beside them, and then she said hi. They regarded her blankly. Without waiting for a sign of their interest, she explained that she had lost her Mothers that day.

The boy nodded solemnly. He knew that once your Mothers is dead, it's gone for good. The factory had shut down seven years before due to lack of any demand for the Mothers beyond Waterloo, and not a single repair shop in town knew how to fix the machines.

The boy explained that the very same thing had happened to him four years ago, but told Sunni not to worry; life would not be as different as she feared. Having said this he turned to face his friend, finishing up the anecdote he had been telling about his childhood, concluding, "And I still feel its reverberations today." Then they put down their money and began packing their bags to leave.

"Wait! Wait! Where are you going?" Sunni cried anxiously, and the boy sighed deeply and said, "Relax. Personality is as static as time; it's a fixed law. People don't change. As long as you remember that, you'll be all right. Now we have to go and write in our diaries." Then they left.

Sunni, still sitting there, glanced down at her Elders pin as it began to blink and beep.

Time is a measurement of change. The change in the position of quantum particles cannot always be known, because they don't seem to exist in any fixed spots. At the level of human bodies, we can see that time has passed because one moment I'm here at this table, the next I'm there at the stove. But at the quantum level, everything is cloudy. This is the mechanism for the disappearance of time. The people of Waterloo liked this theory because, deep down, they felt it. Their lives, in many ways, reflected it. *The End of Time* simply stamped their intuition with the air of authority and truth.

Though Sunni sped down to City Hall as soon as she received the call, she arrived a little later than everyone else, as was typical for her. The other Elders were already there, waiting for the emergency meeting to begin.

The teenagers of Waterloo, whose Mothers had been receiving inputs since the day they were born, were believed by everyone to have a more accurate grasp of what the future would bring. Compared to their Mothers, their parents' Mothers were deeply lacking: twenty, thirty years unaccounted for. So a special place in Waterloo was reserved for the teenagers. They were given much respect. They bore the official title Double Special Elders, since having a particular destiny is the essence of being Special. They were paraded about on ceremonial occasions and called in to advise the city on all the important matters.

Sunni crept quietly through the side door and up to her seat in the fourth row of the dais, which seated thirty across. Already the city's two hundred and fifty-eight native-born teens were in their seats, and they glanced at Sunni and watched her take her place, though she had tried to make her entrance subtle. The mayor, standing at the podium before them, was in the midst of explaining the current crisis, but after two minutes Sunni was still totally lost, so she whispered to the boy beside her, asking him what she had missed.

He replied quickly, "This morning Perimeter received word from Africa that all the problems in physics have been solved."

"*What?*" she whispered back. "Are you *sure?* The measurement problem and—"

"Yes, yes, *everything*," he insisted hotly. Then he rolled his eyes. "Don't ask me."

Sunni sat back in her chair, stunned. The mayor was now on to the mundane, municipal details, explaining how much it cost the city to fund the institute, claiming that it would be humiliating for Waterloo to carry on the project of physics when the field was now kaput. He gestured toward the two physicists who had come to explain the proof, should anyone want to hear it. He said that they represented the physicists who believed the institute should be kept alive—not because the African proof was wrong; it wasn't—but for reasons that he, the mayor, did not completely understand, though if one of the Elders wanted to hear their reasoning, the physicists could give it. As for the rest of the physicists, they were too preoccupied with going over the proof to attend the meeting that day.

"Would any of the Elders like to see the African proof?" the mayor asked.

Sunni looked around tentatively. No one else seemed to want to hear it, but she was interested, so she raised her hand. The mayor nodded at the physicists, and the younger of them stood and went to the whiteboard and began drawing an equation and a little diagram. He turned to the Elders and began to speak. He was only a few sentences into his elucidation when the mayor interrupted him to exclaim:

"Aha—look! It's like an earthworm praying!"

At which point the physicist violently threw his marker onto the ground and left the whiteboard and sat down beside his friend. He was too upset by the events of the day to push forward. It wasn't even so awful that a proof had been found; the pain in his heart was because of how unsatisfying a proof it was. It just wasn't the beautiful, elegant thing that everyone had been hoping for.

Sunni wanted to ask the physicists what the African proof said about the absence of time, but just as she was about to raise her hand again, the boy next to her leaned over and pointed at Sunni's Mothers, which she still reflexively clasped tightly.

"Is your Mothers *dead?*" he gasped.

Sunni, hiding it quickly under her coat, replied with feigned ease, "Nah, it's just a new sleeve. My architect friend made it. He's cool."

"I wouldn't want a sleeve that looked like that."

"Never mind."

"You should take that sleeve off."

"One day I will."

Then the mayor turned to the teenagers and asked, "Should Perimeter be closed?" In this way the voting began.

The first Elder spoke: "Yes."

The second Elder looked up from her Mothers, which knew that once you began talking about ending something, usually that thing ends. "Yes!" she said.

The third Elder spoke. "Yes."

And on and on it went: yes yes yes yes yes yes yes.

Now it was Sunni's turn. She hesitated, glancing down at the blank screen of her Mothers, which she had pulled from under her coat. It was still a twisted, black, charry mess. She took a deep breath and said very quietly, though loud enough for everyone to hear: "I am no longer Special."

Then she stood up from her place on the dais and climbed carefully down the steps. It was a humiliating walk, one others had performed before her while she had watched in pity and fear. Behind her there rose a wall of whispers; it was the world Sunni had been part of, sealing itself closed behind her.

She walked past the mayor and the physicists, toward the doors at the end of the hall. Just before she slipped out, she heard the mayor announce the tally of the vote: it was unanimous. Perimeter was to be shut down within the hour.

"Fucking teenagers," the older physicist muttered.

Sunni stepped out into the warm air of the afternoon, blinking and adjusting to the brightness of the day. She stood on the steps of City Hall, thinking nothing, a blank, faintly bewildered. Her eyes rested on a tree that stood a short distance away in the grass, and she watched it gently sway, moved by the breeze. What would move Sunni, now that her Mothers was dead? With each day, she felt, her destiny would be less and less clear, and less and less would what was probable be the law that ran her life. She tried to imagine what other law might come to replace it, but no other laws came to mind.

Perhaps, she mused, she could learn about living from this tree—let the laws that moved it move her as well. At base, she knew, she was made up of the very same particles as the tree; she must, in some sense, be treelike. She stepped down onto the lawn.

But at that moment her attention was distracted by vague sounds in the distance. She squinted her eyes; there seemed to be a lethargic parade approaching from the far end of King Street. After a moment, she realized what it was: a small tide of dejected physicists was flowing out from the doors of Perimeter. They came closer, heaving down King Street with stooped posture, dazed, carrying boxes of computers, papers and chalk, streaming toward their cars, which would take them back to the university towns from which they had come.

"How pathetic," came a small voice.

Sunni turned and noticed that sitting cross-legged beneath the tree was a scrawny boy around her own age. From the first glance she could tell that he was a loser, but such a loser he wasn't even a Princess Street loser.

"They don't have to leave," he said.

"But it's their destiny," Sunni replied. "I was in the meeting. I saw it happen."

The boy looked at her skeptically, pushing his bangs away. "Destiny? There's no destiny. These physicists don't believe in the future. Most of them don't, anyway. I know. I'm good friends with some of them."

"But—" Sunni shook her head. "If there's no destiny, how can you tell what's going to happen next?"

The boy, whose name was Raffi, frowned. He paused a moment, and then he went on to quietly explain, barely raising his voice above a whisper, so that Sunni had to move closer to hear.

He told her that last year's Bora Bora proof, which contributed to the African proof, revealed that not everything that comes to pass can be known in advance, that everything is in a continuous state of cocreation and coevolution with everything else. The universe is utterly non-computable and non-predictable—possibly not mathematical, at essence, at all. No future can exist until it exists, since we create reality together in a radically flexible present. "Things can go in different ways," he said. "The possibility of creating genuine novelty, while rare and precious, is real."

Sunni sat back hard against the tree. The Bora Bora proof was impossible! She turned her head as the Double Special Elders emerged from the tall doors of City Hall and began spreading across the lawn, moving off, heads bent low over their Mothers as they decided what to do next. She was about to say something when, in the distance, a blue spiral exploded into the sky.

Sunni gasped and turned to Raffi, scared.

"It's the action," Raffi said quietly. "It's coming closer, I see."

"What action?" Sunni asked.

He said slowly, "You're a Double Special Elder through and through. You didn't even know."

Now another spiral burst wildly in the distance, near the mall. A high-pitched radial whistle could be heard emanating from it. Raffi got up like a smooth animal. He bent over and started rummaging in the large duffel bag that had been lying beside him in the grass.

Sunni pushed herself closer to the tree, astonished. In the distance, a physicist in a red overcoat had turned around and begun to walk back toward them. Raffi looked up to answer the question on Sunni's face and explained, "It's a Turquoise bomb. We might know how to handle this." The physicist came near and Raffi walked off with her, in the direction of the institute and through its front doors.

Now Sunni was alone. She stood up from the ground and watched the Elders, most of whom were gazing up into the distance, where the spiral still hung. She watched as they looked down at their Mothers to make sense of it; to know how to respond. But their Mothers had no valuable insight; could not fit the spiral into the pattern; had never encountered such a thing before.

Get on your scooter and go home, was the instruction on their screens; an instruction applicable to many situations, and the most common one.

The teenagers made their way to their scooters, sure in their movements, for deep in their hearts they felt a cool reassurance: it was not that their Mothers lacked insight, but that the question they had posed about the explosions was not a pertinent one. What happened in the distance had nothing to do with the patterns in their lives. It had nothing to do with all the ways they were special. They got on their wheels and, like the physicists, sped off from the heart of town.

Sunni looked up as an acorn fell from the tree and landed on her head. She thought about what she knew.

*Thanks to physicists Sean Gryb, Aaron Berndsen,
Julian Barbour, and Lee Smolin for conversations and advice.*

A NOTE ON *THE DOUBLE ZERO*

I WAS THERE AT the beginning with *McSweeney's*, or, at least, just after the beginning. I was asked to contribute to the first issue, and I did, not really having any idea what I was getting into. The "new journal" in question had the most inadvisable name for a journal I had ever heard. It was, I should say now, extremely gratifying to be involved in those early issues, and to see how the revolution took place. I can't remember exactly when they approached me for an issue they had in mind to be composed of "cover" stories, the word "cover" in this case being used exactly as it was used in rock and roll circles—that is, we were for this issue of *McSweeney's* to make stories that were adaptations of prior stories.

The details are slightly fuzzy at this remove, but I recall that I was worried that I would be asked to do a "cover" of a John Cheever story, because in those days I was known as a sort of John Cheever acolyte. Anyhow, I can't remember exactly how Sherwood Anderson came up. I had read *Winesburg, Ohio* at an impressionable age and loved it as I loved all gothic and macabre things—Poe and that band called the Cramps, and people with missing limbs.

Upon rereading "The Egg," I grasped immediately how much fun it would be to rewrite it. It was grim, funny, and memorable. The ostrich part of the resulting Rick Moody story was grafted onto the work from life: I had recently been to an ostrich ranch in Picacho, AZ, which had traumatized and fascinated me. As I recall "The Double Zero," without looking back closely, it has an unmistakably anti-capitalist last page, despite the comic flavor of the whole, and I believe this resulted in at least one subscriber canceling his subscription to *McSweeney's*. The reader in question may re-subscribe, if he wishes, based on my promise that my economic critique has grown subtler over the years (if not programmatically different). —RICK MOODY

THE DOUBLE ZERO

by RICK MOODY

(fiction from Issue 4, with apologies to Sherwood Anderson)

M Y DAD WAS for Midwestern values; he was for families; he was for a firm handshake; he was for a little awkward sweet-talking with the waitress at the HoJo's. Until he grew to the age of thirty-four he worked at one of those farms owned by a big international corporation that's created from family farms gone defunct. Looked like a chessboard, if you saw it from the air. This was near Bidwell, Ohio. Don't know if it was Archer Daniels Midland, Monsanto, some company like that. The particular spread I'm talking about got sold to developers later. Guess it was more lucrative to sell the plot and buy some other place. The housing development that grew up on that land, it was called Golden Meadow Estates even though it didn't have any meadows. That's where we lived after Dad got laid off. He'd been at the bar down by the railroad when the news came through.

So he took the job at Sears, in the power tools dept. About the same time he met my mom. She'd once won a beauty contest, Miss Scandinavian Bidwell. They got married after dating a long while. My mom, probably on account of her beauty crown, was eager for my dad (and me, too, because I showed up pretty soon) to get some of that American fortune all around her. She was hopeful. She was going to get her some. The single-story tract house over in Golden Meadow Estates, well, it was a pretty tight fit, not to mention falling down, and they were stuck next door to a used-car salesman nobody liked. I heard a rumor that this guy Stubb, this neighbor, had dead teenagers in the basement. The Buckeye State had a national lead in serial killers, though, so maybe that wasn't any big surprise. My mother convinced my dad that he had to get into some other line of work, where there was a better possibility of advancing. *Was he going to spend his whole life selling power tools?* Her idea was raising Angora rabbits. He went along with it. They really multiplied, these rabbits, like I bet you've heard. They were my chore, as a matter of fact. You'd get dozens of these cages with rabbits that urinated and shat all over everything if you even whispered at them, and then you had to *spin* their fur, you know, on an *actual loom.* If you wanted to make any kind of money at all. I didn't have to spin anything back then. I was too little. But you get the idea. Turned out my mother didn't have the patience for all that.

Next was yew trees. Some chemical in the yew tree was supposed to be an ingredient in the toxins for fighting cancers. Maybe my mother was thinking about that cluster in town. I mean, just about everybody in Golden Meadow Estates sported a wig, and so it wasn't newsworthy later when they found that the development had been laid out on an old chromium dump. Meantime, we actually had a half acre of yew trees already planted on some land rented from the nylon manufacturer downtown, and there were heavy metals there too, must have been fatal to the yew trees. The main thing is they made this chemical, the yew chemical, in the laboratory by the end of the year.

Mom made a play for llamas. She went down to the Bidwell public library. To the business section. Read up about llamas. But what can you do with them anyway? Make a sweater? *Well, that's how we settled on ostriches.* The ostrich is a poetic thing, let me tell you. Its life is full of dramas. The largest of birds on planet earth. The ostrich is almost eight feet tall and weighs three hundred pounds and it has a brain not too much bigger than a pigeon's brain. It has two toes. It can reach speeds of fifty miles an hour, and believe me, I've seen them do it. Like if you were standing at the far end of the ostrich farm we had, the Rancho Double Zero, and you were holding a Cleveland Indians beer cup full of corn, that ostrich would come at you about the speed an eighteen-wheeler comes at you on the interstate. Just like having a pigeon swoop at you, except that this pigeon is the size of a minivan. The incredible stupidity on the ostrich's face is worth commenting on, too, in case you haven't seen one lately. They're mouth-breathers, or anyhow their beaks always hang open a little bit. That pretty much tells you all you need to know. Lights on, property vacant. They reminded me of a retarded kid I knew in grammar school, Zechariah Dunbar. He's dead now. Anyway, the point is that ostriches are always trying to hold down other ostriches, by sitting on them, in order to fuck these other ostriches, without any regard to whether it's a boy or girl animal they're trying to get next to. And speaking of sex and ostriches, I'm almost sure that the men who worked on my father's farm tried to have their way with the Rancho Double Zero product. With a brain so small, it was obvious that the ostrich would never feel loving congress with some heartbroken Midwestern hombre as any kind of bodily insult. Actually, it's amazing that the pea-sized brain in those ostrich skulls could operate the other end of them. Amazing that electrical transmissions could make it that far, what with that huge bulky midsection that was *all red meat*, hundreds of pounds of it, as every brochure will tell you, *but with a startlingly low fat content. In fact, it tastes like chicken*, my grandma said before the choking incident. Okay, it was almost like the ostrich was some kind of bird. But it didn't look like a bird, and when there were three or four hundred of them, running around in a herd at fifty miles an hour, flattening rodents, trying to have sex with each other, three or four hundred of them purchased with a precarious loan from Buckeye Savings and Trust, well, they looked more like conventioneers from some Holiday Inn assembly of extinct species. You expected a mating pair of wooly mammoths or a bunch of saber-toothed tigers to show up any moment.

I'm getting away from the story, though. I really meant to talk about ostrich eggs. After ten years of trying to get the Rancho Double Zero to perform fiscally, my parents had to sell the whole thing and declare bankruptcy. That's the sad truth. And it was no shame. Everybody they knew was bankrupt. Everybody in Bidwell, practically, had a lien on their bank account. When we were done with the Double Zero, we had nothing left but a bunch of ostrich eggs, the kind that my parents used to sell out in front of the farm, under a canopy, for people who came out driving. There were three signs, a quarter-mile apart, SEE THE OSTRICHES! TWO MILES! And then another half-mile. OSTRICH EGGS!

FIVE DOLLARS EACH! Then another. FEED THE OSTRICHES! IF YOU DARE!

I remember giving the feeding lecture myself to a couple from back East. They were the only people who'd volunteered to feed the ostriches in weeks. I handed them the Cleveland Indians cups. They were dressed up fine. *You can either put some of this corn in your hand and hold it out for the ostriches, but I sure wouldn't do that myself, because I've seen them pick up a little kid and whirl him around like he was a handkerchief and throw him over a fence, bust his neck clean through. Or you can hold out the cup and the ostriches will try to trample each other to death to get right in front of you, and then one of those pinheads will descend with incredible force on you, steal the entire cup away. Or else you can just scatter some corn at the base of the electrified fence there and get the heck out of the way, which is certainly what I'd do if I were you.* Who would go from Bidwell to anywhere, I was asking myself, unless they were trying to avoid a massive interstate manhunt? Probably this couple, right here, laughing at the poor dumb birds, probably they were the kind of people who would sodomize an entire preschool of kids, rob a rich lady on Park Avenue, hide her body, grind up some teenagers, and then disappear to manage their investments.

Anyhow, that ranch came and went and soon we were in a used El Dorado with 120,000 miles on it. I was in the backseat, with five dozen ostrich eggs. Dad was forty-eight, or thereabouts, and he was bald, and he was paunchy, and, because of the failure of all the gold-rush schemes, he was discouraged and mean. If he spoke at all it was just to gripe at politicians. He was an independent, in terms of gripes. Just so you know. Nonpartisan. And the only hair left on his ugly head, after all the worrying, was around those two patches just above his ears, just like if he were an ostrich chick himself. Because you know when they came out of the shell, these chicks looked like human fetuses. In fact, I've heard it said that a human being and an ostrich actually share 38 percent of their DNA, which is pretty much when you think about it. So Dad looked like an ostrich. Or maybe he looked like one of those cancer survivors from Golden Meadow Estates who were always saying they felt like a million bucks even though it was obvious that they felt like about a buck fifty. Mom, on the other hand, despite her bad business decisions, only seemed to get prettier and prettier. She still spent a couple of hours each morning making up her face with pencils and brushes in a color called *deadly nightshade*.

In terms of volume, one ostrich egg is the equivalent of two dozen of your regular eggs. It's got two liters of liquefied muck in it. That means, if you're a short-order cook, that one of these ostrich eggs can last you a long time. A whole day, maybe. The ostrich shell is about the size of a regulation football, but it's shaped just like the traditional chicken eggshell. Which is something I was told to say to tourists, *Note your traditional eggshell styling.* The ostrich egg is so perfect that it looks fake. The ostrich egg looks like it's made out of plastic. In fact, maybe the guys who came up with plastics got the idea from looking at the perfection of the ostrich egg. Myself, I could barely eat one of those ostrich eggs without worrying about seeing a little ostrich fledgling in it, because it looked so much like a human fetus, or what I imagined a human fetus looked like based on some pictures I'd seen in the *Golden Books Encyclopedia.* What if you accidentally ate one of the fledglings! Look out! They made pretty good French toast, though.

Over the years, my dad had assembled an ostrich freak exhibition. There were lots of genetic things that could go wrong with an ostrich flock, like say an ostrich had four legs, or an ostrich had two heads, or the ostrich didn't have any head at all, just a gigantic midsection. Maybe the number of genetic abnormalities in our stock had to do with how close the farm was to a dioxin-exuding paper plant, or maybe it was the chromium or the PCBs, whatever else. It was always something. The important part here is that the abnormalities made Dad sort of happy and enabled him to have a *collection* to take away from the Rancho Double Zero, and what's the harm in that. Not a lot of room for me in the back seat, though, what with the eggs and the freaks.

The restaurant we started wasn't in Bidwell, because we had bad memories of Bidwell, after the foreclosure and all. There wasn't much choice but to move farther out where things were cheaper. We landed in Pickleville, where it was real cheap, all right, and where there wasn't anything to do. People used to kill feral cats in Pickleville. There was a bounty on them. Kids learned to obliterate any and all wildlife. Pickleville also had a train station where the out-of-state train stopped once a day. Mom figured what with the train station right nearby there was a good chance that people would want to stop at a family-style restaurant. So it was a diner, Dizzy's, which was the nickname we had given our ostrich chick with two heads. The design of our restaurant was like the traditional style of older diners, you know, shaped like a suppository, aluminum and chrome, jukeboxes at every booth. We

lived out back. I was lucky. I got to go to a better school district and frat-
ernize with a better class of kids who called me *hayseed* and accused me of
intimate relations with brutes.

My parents bought a neon sign, and they made a shelf where Dad put
his ostrich experiments, and then they got busy cooking up *open-faced turkey
sandwiches* and *breaded fish cutlets* and *turkey hash* and lots of things with
chipped beef in them. Just about everything in the restaurant had chipped beef
in it. Mom decided that the restaurant should stay open nights (she never
had to see my dad that way, since he worked a different shift), for the freight
trains that emptied out their passengers in Pickleville occasionally. Freight
hoboes would come in wearing that hunted expression you get from never
having owned a thing and having no fixed address. Sometimes these guys
would order an egg over easy, and Dad would attempt to convince them that
they should have an ostrich egg. He would haul one of the eggs down, and
the hoboes would get a load of the ostrich egg and there would be flourishing
of *change money*, and then these hoboes would be gone.

My guess is that Dad had concluded that most Midwestern people were
friendly, outgoing folks, and that, in spite of his failure in any enterprise
that ever had his name on it, in spite of his galloping melancholy, he should
make a real attempt to put on a warm, entertaining manner with the people
who came into the diner. It was a *jolly innkeeper* strategy. It was a last-chance
thing. He tried smiling at customers, and even at me, and he tried smiling
at my mother, and it caught on. I tried smiling at the alley cat who lived in
the trailer with us. I even tried smiling at the kids at school who called me
hayseed. But then an ostrich egg ruined everything.

One rainy night I was up late avoiding homework when I heard a really
scary shriek come from the restaurant. An emergency wail that couldn't be
mistaken for anything but a real emergency. Made goosebumps break out on
me. My dad burst into the trailer, weeping horribly, smashing plates. What
I remember best was the fact that my mother, who never touched the old
man, caressed the bald part of the top of his head, as if she could smooth out
the canals of his worry lines.

It was like this. Joe Kane, a strip-club merchant in Bidwell, was waiting
for his own dad, Republican district attorney of Bidwell, to come through
on the train that night. There'd been a big case up at the state capital. The
train was late and Joe was loafing in the restaurant, drinking coffees, playing

through all the Merle Haggard songs on the jukebox. After a couple of hours of ignoring my dad, Joe felt like he ought to try to say something. He went ahead and blurted out a pleasantry,

—Waiting for the old man. On the train. Train's running late.

Probably, Dad had thought so much about this body that was right there in front of him, this body who happened to be the son of the district attorney, that he started getting really nervous. A white foam began to accumulate at the corners of his mouth. And like in your chess games that kind of pile outward from the opening, maybe dad was attempting to figure out *every possible future conversation* with Joe Kane, ahead of time, so he would have something witty to say, becoming, in the process, a complete retard.

He said the immortal words, —How-de-do.

—How-de-do? said Joe Kane. Did anyone still say stuff like this? Did kiddy television greetings still exist in the modern world of schoolyard massacres and religious cults? Next thing you know my father'd be saying *poopy diapers, weenie roast, tra la la, making nookie.* Just so he could conduct his business. He'd locate in his playbook the conversational gambit entitled *withering contempt dawns in the face of your auditor*, and, according to this playbook, wasn't anything else for him to do but go on being friendly, and he would.

—Uh, well, have you heard the one about how Christopher Columbus, discoverer of this land of ours, was a cheat? Sure was. Said he could make an egg stand on its end, which obviously you can only do when the calendar's on the equinoxes. And when he couldn't make the egg stand, why he had to crush the end of the egg. Maybe it was a hard-boiled egg, I don't know. Obviously, he can't have been that great a man if he had to crush the end of the egg in order to make it stand. I wonder, you know, whether we ought to be having all these annual celebrations in honor of him, since he was a liar about the egg incident. Probably about other things too. He claimed he hadn't crushed the end of the egg when he had. That's not dealing fair.

To make his point, my father took an ostrich egg from the shelf where a half-dozen were all piled up for use at the diner. The counter was grimy with a shellac of old bacon and corn syrup and butterfat and honey and molasses and salmonella. He set the egg down here.

—Helluva egg, Joe Kane remarked. —What is that, some kind of nuclear egg? You make that in a reactor?

—I know more about eggs than any man living, my father mumbled.

—Don't doubt that for a second, Joe Kane said.

—This egg will bend to my will. It will succumb to my powers of magic.

—If you say so.

My dad attempted to balance the ostrich egg on its end without success. He tried a number of times. Personally, I don't get where people thought up this idea about balancing eggs. You don't see people trying to balance gourds or footballs. But people seem like they have been trying to balance eggs since there were eggs to balance. Maybe it's because we all come from some kind of *ovum*, even if it doesn't look exactly like the kind that my father kept tipping up onto its end in front of Joe Kane, but since we come from some kind of *ovum* and since that is the closest we can get to any kind of real point of origin, maybe we're all kind of dumb on the subject of *ova*, although on the other hand, I guess these *ova* probably had to come from some chicken, and vice versa. Don't get me confused. Joe had to relocate his cup of coffee out of the wobbly trajectory of the shell. A couple of times. My father couldn't get anything going in terms of balancing the ostrich egg and so why did he keep trying?

Next, Dad got down the formaldehyde jars from up on the shelf, and started displaying for Joe Kane some deformed ostriches. In his recitation about the abnormalities he had names for a lot of the birds. He showed Joe the fetus with two heads, Dizzy; *she was the sweetest little chick*, and then showed Joe one with four legs. He showed Joe two or three sets of Siamese twin ostriches, including the set called Jack 'n Jill. *This pair could run like a bat out of hell.* My dad's voice swelled. He was a proud parent. He gazed deeply into yellowed formaldehyde.

Joe Kane tried to figure an escape. He looked like an ostrich himself, right then, a mouth-breather, a shill waiting for the sideshow, where the real freaks, the circus owners themselves, would go to any lengths, glue a piece of bone on the forehead of a Shetland pony and call it a unicorn, for the thrill of separating crowds from wallets. Wasn't there any other place for Joe to take shelter from the buckets of rain falling from the sky? Must have been a lean-to or something. On the good side of the tracks.

—This bird here has two *male appendages*, and I know a number of fellows would really like it if they had two of those. Imagine all the trouble you could get into with the ladies.

Ever notice how in the Midwest no one ever kisses anyone? That little peck on the cheek people are always giving one another back East? *Nice to see you!* Much less in evidence here in the Midwest. It accounts for the ostrich farmhands and their romantic pursuits, turned down by wives, just looking for some glancing contact somewhere, with a mouth-breather, if necessary. They came home, these working men, to wives reciting lists of incomplete chores, because of which they'd just get right back into their pickups and head for the drive-thru. They'd sing their lamenting songs into drive-thru microphones. My father had seen a man once slap another man good-naturedly on the shoulder after a friendly exchange about a baseball. This was at a fast-food joint. He was sick with envy right then. And that's why, since he'd just shown Joe Kane an ostrich fetus with two penises, he decided *to chuck Joe under the chin*, as a sign of neighborly good wishes. My father came out from around the counter—he was a big man, I think I already said, 250 pounds, and over six feet—and as Joe Kane attempted to get up from his stool, my father *chucked him under the chin*.

—Take a weight off for a second, friend; I'm going to show you how to get an ostrich egg into a Coke bottle. And when the magic's done you can carry this Coke bottle around with you as a souvenir. I'll give it to you as a special gift. Here's how I do it. I heat this egg in regular old vinegar, kind you get anyplace, and that loosens up the surface of the egg, and then I just slip it into this liter bottle of Coke, which I also bought at the mini-mart up the road, and then when it's inside the Coke bottle, it goes back to its normal hardness. When people ask you how you did it, you just don't let on. Okay? It's our secret. Is that a deal?

What could Joe say? Dad already had the vinegar going on one of the burners. When the egg had been heated in this solution, my dad began attempting to cram the thing into the Coke bottle, to disappointing results. Of course, the Coke bottle kept toppling end over end. Falling behind the counter. Dad would have to go pick it up again. Meantime, the train was about to come in. Hours had passed. The train was wailing through the crossing. My father jammed the ostrich egg, which didn't look like it had loosened up at all, against the tiny Coke bottle opening, without success. Maybe if he had a *wide-mouth bottle* instead.

—Last time it worked fine.

—Look, I gotta go. Train's pulling in. My dad's—

—*Sit down on that stool.* Damned if you're going to sit in here for two hours on a bunch of coffees, eighty-five-cent cups of coffee, and that's going to be all the business I'm gonna have all week, you *son of a bitch*. I know one place I can get this egg to fit. Goddamn you.

And this is where the ostrich egg broke, of course, like a geyser, like an explosion at the refinery of my old man's self-respect. Its unfertilized gunk, pints of it, splattered all over the place, on the counter, the stools, the toaster, the display case of stale donuts. Then Joe Kane, who was already at the door, having managed to get himself safely out of the way, *laughed bitterly*. My father, his face pendulous with tusks of egg white, reached himself down an additional ostrich egg and attempted to hurl it at Joe Kane. But, come on, that was like trying to be a shot-put champion. He managed to get it about as far as the first booth, where it shattered on the top of a jukebox, obscuring in yolk an entire run of titles by the Judds.

Next thing that happened, of course, was the blood-curdling shriek I already told you about. I'm sorry for it turning up in the story twice, but that's just how it is this time. My father, alone in the restaurant, like the proverbial bear in the trap, screamed his emergency scream, frightened residents of Pickleville for miles around, especially little kids. People who are happy when they're speculating about other people's business, they might want to make a few guesses about that scream, like that my dad was ashamed of himself because the trick with the ostrich egg didn't work, or my dad was experiencing a crisis of remorse because he couldn't ever *catch a break*. And these people would be right up to a point, but they'd be missing a crucial piece of information that I have and which I'm going to pass along. My father screamed, actually, because he was experiencing a shameful gastrointestinal problem. That's right. It's not really, you know, a major part of the story, but there was this certain large food company that was marketing some cheese snacks with a simulated fatty acid in them, and that large company was test marketing the cheese snacks guess where? Buckeye State. Where these companies test marketed lots of products for people they thought were uninformed. These cheese snacks were cheap, all right, a real bargain when compared to leading brands, and they had a cheddar flavor. Only problem was, since your large and small intestines couldn't absorb the fatty acid, it was deposited right out of you, usually in amounts close to two or three tablespoons. Right in your briefs, an oily residue that didn't come out in the wash. Depended on how fond you were of the cheese snacks. If you ate a whole bag, it could be worse. So the truth is, on top of having *egg on his face*, my dad messed his pants. It was a rough day.

You'll be wanting to know how I know all this stuff, all these things, that happened to my father in the restaurant, especially since I wasn't there and since Dad would never talk about any of it. Especially not *anal leakage*. Wouldn't talk about much at all, after that, unless he was complaining about Ohio State during football season. You'll want to know how I know so much about the soul of Ohio, since I was a teenager when all this happened and was supposed to be sullen and hard to reach. Hey, what's left in this breadbasket nation, but the mystery of imagination? My mother lay in bed, hatched a plan, how to get herself out of this place, how to give me a library of books. One night she dreamed of escaping from the Rust Belt, from a sequence of shotgun shacks and railroad apartments. A dream of a boy in the shape of a bird in the shape of a story, a boy who has a boy who has a boy: each generation's dream cheaper than the last, like for example all these dreams now feature Chuck E. Cheese (*A special birthday show performed by Chuck E. Cheese and his musical friends!*) or Cracker Barrel or Wendy's or Arby's or Red Lobster or the Outback Steakhouse or Boston Chicken or Taco Bell or Burger King or TCBY or Pizza Hut or Baskin Robbins or Friendly's or Hard Rock Cafe or KFC or IHOP or Frisch's Big Boy. Take a right down by Sam's Discount Warehouse, Midas Muffler, Target, Barnes & Noble, Home Depot, Wal-Mart, Super Kmart, Ninety-Nine Cent Store. My stand's at the end of the line. Eggs in this county they're the biggest darned eggs you ever seen in your whole life.

A NOTE ON *K IS FOR FAKE*

C ARTER SCHOLZ AND I had conceived this collaborative book, *Kafka Americana*, pegged on the notion of a series of conflations of Kafka's life and material with American cultural subjects, American milieus, American pop iconography, and so forth. He and I each had to write one further "major" story to flesh out the project, so he went off to do his—the brilliant "The Amount to Carry," where Kafka the insurance adjuster meets up with Wallace Stevens and Charles Ives, who labor in the same trade—leaving me to my somewhat broader pastiche, where I leveraged Kafka's "The Trial" back through Orson Welles's uncelebrated (but great) film version, and gathered up the "crying clown" painters Walter and Margaret Keane, and also the legendary suppressed Jerry Lewis holocaust film *The Day the Clown Cried*—what a constellator of ephemera I was, back then! This "blizzard of reference" style is a mode I've worked in, sporadically, in stories like "The Insipid Profession of Jonathan Hornebom" and "Their Back Pages," and I suppose it also relates to my collage-essay "The Ecstasy of Influence." Here, it enters into a productive tension with a sincere attempt to work my way into something like Kafka's prose style, which might be a kind of opposite to that other methodology, being as it is helplessly self-enclosed, hermetically intense, burrowing into fictional situations like a creature into its burrow, and utterly oblivious to the sort of effects generated by straying cultural signifiers.

This is also a sideways story about World War Two, which is possibly a subject that can't be approached sideways. (More lately I've been feeling that it is a subject I'll be writing about directly, soon, as intimidating as that prospect may be; in this way, the story now strikes me as an early unconscious flare of a slow-developing interest in the war as a subject for my work.) Is it good? I don't know! I like how particular and unrepeatable it seems to me. A reader's experience might depend on being either deeply familiar with the Welles film, and the facts in the cases of Keane and Lewis, or blissfully—mercifully?—oblivious to any of it; being stuck somewhere in between, I fear a reader might find it pretty irritating to read. My friend Will Amato did an illustration for the piece, based on a notion of a Kafka postage stamp, and *McSweeney's* bound it in a sickly pea-green pamphlet. From time to time collectors still bring it out for me to autograph, and I'm always staggered to be reminded it exists, or once did. —JONATHAN LETHEM

K IS FOR FAKE

by JONATHAN LETHEM

(fiction from Issue 4)

"The birth of the sad-eyed waifs was in Berlin in 1947 when I met these kids," Mister Keane said. "Margaret asked for my help to learn to paint, and I suggested that she project a picture she liked on a canvas and fill it in like children do a numbered painting. Then the woman started copying my paintings."

While he has sought redress in the courts twice, Margaret Keane has thus far emerged the winner. A lawsuit against her for copyright infringement was dismissed; she then sued Mister Keane for libel for statements he made in an interview with *USA Today*, and to back her suit, she executed a waif painting in front of the jury in less than one hour. She won a $4 million judgment. Walter Keane declined to participate in the paint-off, citing a sore shoulder.

—*The New York Times*, Feb. 26, 1995

K.'S PHONE RANG while he was watching cable television, an old movie starring the Famous Clown. In the movie the Famous Clown lived in a war-torn European city. The Famous Clown walked down a dirt road trailed, like the Pied Piper, by a line of ragged children. The

Famous Clown juggled three lumps of bread, the hardened heels of French loaves. K.'s phone rang twice and then he lifted the receiver. It was after eleven. He wasn't expecting a call. "Yes?" he said. "Is this painter called K.?" "Yes, but I'm not interested in changing my long distance—" The voice interrupted him: "The charges against you have at last been prepared." The voice was ponderous with authority. K. waited, but the voice was silent. K. heard breath resound in some vast cavity. "Charges?" said K., taken aback. K. paid the minimums on his credit cards promptly each month. "You'll wish to answer them," intoned the voice. "We've prepared a preliminary hearing. Meanwhile a jury is being assembled. But you'll undoubtedly wish to familiarize yourself with the charges."

On the screen the Famous Clown was being clapped in irons by a pair of jackbooted soldiers. The ragamuffin children scattered, weeping, as the Famous Clown was dragged away. Through the window beyond K.'s television the cityscape was visible, the distant offices, lights now mostly extinguished, and the nearby apartments, from whose open windows gently arguing voices drifted like mist through the summer air. On the phone the sonorous breathing continued. "Is it possible to send me a printed statement?" said K. He wondered if he should have spoken, whether he had in fact now admitted to the possibility of charges. "No," sighed the voice on the phone. "No, the accused must appear in person; hearing first, then trial. All in due course. In the meantime a defense should be readied." "A defense?" K. said. He had hoped that whatever charges he faced could be cleared by rote and at a remove, by checking a box or signing a check. K. had once pleaded no contest to a vehicular infraction by voicemail. "Press One for No Contest," the recorded voice had instructed him. "Press Two for Not Guilty. Press Three for Guilty With An Explanation." "A defense, most certainly," said the voice on K.'s telephone now. "Be assured, you are not without recourse to a defense." The voice grew suddenly familiar, avuncular, conspiratory. "Don't lose heart, K. That is always your weakness. I'll be in touch." With that K.'s caller broke the connection. More in curiosity than fear K. dialed *69, but his caller's number had a private listing. K. replaced the receiver. On his television the Famous Clown was in shackles in a slant-roofed barracks, his head being shaved by a sadistic commandant. Wide-eyed children with muddy cheeks and ragged hair peered in through a window. In the distance past them a sprawling barbed wire fence was visible, and at the corner of the fence a high wooden tower topped with a gunnery. K. thumbed the remote. The Sci-Fi channel was in the course of a *Twilight Zone* marathon. A man awoke alone in terror, in sweats, in a shabby black-and-white room. The camera boxed at him, the score pulsed ominously. K. fell asleep, comforted.

* * *

"The central European Jewish world which Kafka celebrated and ironized went to hideous extinction. The spiritual possibility exists that Franz Kafka experienced his prophetic powers as some visitation of guilt…"

—George Steiner

* * *

"I consider him guilty… he is not guilty of what he's accused of, but he's guilty all the same."

—Orson Welles, on *The Trial*

* * *

K. was on his way to visit his art dealer, Titorelli, when the Waif appeared in the street before him. It was a cold day, and heaps of blackened snow lay everywhere in the street. The Waif wasn't dressed for the cold. The Waif stood shivering, huddled. Titorelli's gallery was in Dumbo (Down Under the Manhattan Bridge Overpass) and though it was midday the cobblestone streets were empty of passersby. Above them loomed the corroded pre-war warehouses, once Mafia-owned, now filled with artists' studios and desirable loft apartments. The sky was chalky and gray, the chill wind off the East River faintly rank. The Waif's huge eyes beckoned to K. They gleamed with tears, but no tears fell. The Waif took K.'s hand. The Waif's grip was cool, fingers squirming in K.'s palm. Together they walked under the shadow of the vast iron bridge, to Titorelli's building. K. wanted to lead the Waif to shelter, to warmth. Through the plate glass window on which was etched Titorelli's name and the gallery's hours K. saw Titorelli and his art handler, Lilia, animatedly discussing a painting which sat on the floor behind the front desk. K. glanced at the Waif, and the Waif nodded at K. K. wondered how the Waif would be received by Titorelli and Lilia. Perhaps in the refrigerator in the back of the gallery a bit of cheese and cracker remained from the gallery's most recent opening reception, a small snack which could be offered to the Waif. K. pictured the Waif eating from a saucer on the floor, like a pet. In his imaginings the Waif would always be with him now, would follow him home and take up residence there. Now K. pushed the glass door and they stepped inside. Immediately the Waif pulled away from K. and ran silently along the gallery wall, moving like a cat in a cathedral, avoiding the open space at the center of the room. The Waif vanished through the door into the back offices of the gallery without being noticed, and K. found himself alone as he approached Titorelli and Lilia. The art dealer and his assistant contemplated a canvas on which two trees stood on a desolate grassy heath, framing a drab portion of gray sky. As K. moved closer he saw that the floor behind the desk was lined with a series of similar paintings. In fact they were each identical to the first: trees, grass, sky. "The subject is too somber," said Titorelli, waving his hand, dismissing the canvas. Lilia only nodded, then moved another of the paintings into the place of the first. "Too somber," said Titorelli again, and again, "Too somber," as Lilia presented a third example of the indifferently depicted heathscape. Lilia removed it and reached for another. "Why don't you hang them upside down?" remarked K., unable to bear the thought of hearing Titorelli render his verdict again, wishing to spare Lilia as well. "Upside down?" repeated Titorelli, his gaze still keenly focused on the painting as though he hadn't yet reached a complete judgement. "That may be brilliant. Let's have a look." Then, looking up: "Oh, hello, K." K. greeted Titorelli, and Lilia as well. The assistant lowered her gaze shyly. She had always been daunted and silent in K.'s presence. "Quickly, girl, upside down!" commanded Titorelli. K. craned his neck, trying to see into the back office, to learn what had become of the Waif. "Have you got anything to drink, Titorelli?" K. asked. "There might be a Coke in the fridge," said Titorelli, waving distractedly. K. slipped through the doorway into the back room, where a cluttered tumult of canvases and shipping crates nearly concealed the small refrigerator. K. didn't see the Waif. He went to the refrigerator and opened the door. The Waif was inside the refrigerator. The Waif was huddled, arms wrapped around its shoulders, trembling with cold, its eyes wide and near to spilling with tears. The Waif reached out and took K.'s hand again. The Waif stepped out of the refrigerator and, tugging persistently at K.'s hand, led him to the vertical racks of large canvases which lined the rear wall of the office. Moving aside a large shipping tube which blocked its entrance the Waif stepped into the last of the vertical racks, which was otherwise empty. K. followed. Unexpectedly, the rack extended beyond the limit of the rear wall, into darkness, alleviated only by glints of light which penetrated the slats on either side. The Waif led K. around a bend in this narrow corridor to where the space opened again into a tall foyer, its walls made of the same rough lath which lined the racks, with stripes of light leaking through faintly. In this dark room K. discerned a large shape, a huge lumpen figure in the center of the floor. The glowing end-tip of a cigar flared, and dry paper crackled. As the crackle faded K. could hear the sigh of a long inhalation. The Waif again released K.'s hand and slipped away into the shadows. K.'s eyes began to adjust to the gloom. He was able to make out the figure before him. Seated in a chair was a tremendously fat man with a large, stern forehead and a shock of white eyebrows and beard. He was dressed in layers of overlapping coats and vests and scarves and smoked a tremendous cigar. K. recognized the man from television. He was the Advertising Pitchman.

The Advertising Pitchman was advocate for certain commercial products: wine, canned peas and pears, a certain make of automobile, et cetera. He loaned to the cause of their endorsement his immense gravity and bulk, his overstuffed authority. "It is good you've come, K.," said the Advertising Pitchman. K. recognized the Advertising Pitchman's voice now as well. It was the sonorous voice on the phone, the voice which had warned him of the accusation against him. "We're overdue to begin preparations for your defense," continued the Pitchman. "The preliminary hearing has been called." The Advertising Pitchman sucked again on his cigar; the tip flared; the Pitchman made a contented sound. The cigar smelled stale. "By any chance did you see a small child—a Waif?" asked K. "Yes, but never mind that now. It is too late to help the child," said the Pitchman. "We must concern ourselves with answering the charges." The Pitchman rustled in his vest and produced a sheaf of documents. He placed his cigar in his lips to free both hands, and thumbed through the papers. "Not now," said K., feeling a terrible urgency, a sudden force of guilt regarding the Waif. He wondered if he could trouble the Pitchman for a loan of one of his voluminous scarves; one would surely be enough to cloak the Waif, shelter it from the cold. "I want to help—" K. began, but the Pitchman interrupted. "If you'd thought of that sooner you wouldn't be in this predicament." The

Pitchman consulted the papers in his lap. "Self-absorption is among the charges." K. circled the Pitchman, feeling his way through the room by clinging to the wall, as though he were a small bearing circling a wheel, the Pitchman the hub. "Self-absorption, Self-amusement, Self-satisfaction," continued the Pitchman. K. found himself unable to bear the sound of the Pitchman's voice, precisely for its quality of self-satisfaction; he said nothing, instead continued his groping search, moving slowly enough that he wouldn't injure the Waif should he stumble across it. "Ah, here's another indictment—Impersonation." "Shouldn't that be Self-impersonation?" replied K. quickly. He believed his reply quite witty, but the Pitchman seemed not to notice, instead went on shuffling papers and calling out charges. "Insolence, Infertility, Incompleteness—" By now K. had determined that the Waif had fled the cul-de-sac he and the Pitchman currently inhabited, had vanished back through the corridor behind them, through the gallery racks, perhaps even slipping silently between K.'s legs to accomplish this feat. "See under Incompleteness: Failure, Reticence, Inability to Achieve Consummation or Closure; for reference see also Great Chinese Wall, Tower of Babel, *Magnificent Ambersons*, et cetera," continued the Pitchman. K. ignored him, stepped back into the narrow corridor. "See under Impersonation: Forgery, Fakery, Ventriloquism, Impersonation of the Father, Impersonation of the Gentile, Impersonation of the Genius, Usurpation of the Screenwriter—" K. moved through the corridor back toward the gallery office and the Pitchman's voice soon faded. K. made his way through the glinted darkness of the gallery racks to Titorelli's office. The Waif was nowhere to be seen, but Lilia waited there, and when K. emerged she came near to him and whispered close to his ear. "I told Titorelli I had to go to the bathroom in order to come find you," she said teasingly. "I didn't really have to go." The shyness Lilia exhibited in front of Titorelli was gone now. Her sleek black hair had fallen from the place where it had been pinned behind her ears, and her glasses were folded into her blouse pocket. "Perhaps you've seen a child," said K. "A little—Waif. In tatters. With big eyes. And silent, like a mouse. It would have just run through here a moment ago." Lilia shook her head. K. felt that there only must be some confusion of terms, for Lilia had been standing at the entrance to the racks, apparently waiting for K. "A small thing—" K. lowered his hand to indicate the dwarfish proportions. "No," said Lilia. "We're alone here." "The Waif has been with me in the gallery all this time," said K. "We entered together. You and Titorelli were distracted and didn't notice." Lilia shook her head helplessly. "The Waif is like a ghost," said K. "Only I can see it, it follows me. It must have some meaning." Lilia stroked K.'s hand and said, "What a strange experience. It's practically Serlingesque." "Serlingesque?" asked K., unfamiliar with the term. "Yes," said Lilia. "You know, like something out of *The Twilight Zone*." "Oh," said K., surprised and pleased by the reference. But it wasn't exact, wasn't quite right. "No, I think it's more—" K. couldn't recall the adjective he was seeking. "Titorelli was very happy with your suggestion," whispered Lilia. She put her lips even closer to his ear, and he felt the warmth of her body transmitted along his arm. "He's hung them all upside down—you'll see when you go back into the gallery. But don't go outside yet." K. was faintly disturbed; he'd intended the remark to Titorelli as a joke. "What about the artist's intentions?" he asked Lilia. "The artist's intentions don't matter," said Lilia. "Anyway, the artist is dead, and his intentions are unknown. He left instructions to destroy these canvases. You've saved them; the credit belongs to you." "There's little credit to be gained turning a thing upside down," said K., but Lilia seemed oblivious to his reflections. She pulled at his collar, then traced a line under his jaw with her finger, closing her eyes and smiling dreamily while she did it. "Do you have any tattoos?" she whispered. "What?" said K. "Tattoos, on your body," said Lilia, tugging his collar farther from his collarbone, and peering into his shirt. "No," said K. "Do you?" "Yes," said Lilia, smiling shyly. "Just one. Do you want to see it?" K. nodded. "Turn around," commanded Lilia. K. turned to face the rear wall of the gallery office. He wondered if Titorelli was occupied, or if the gallery owner had noticed K.'s and Lilia's absence. "Now, look," said Lilia. K. turned. Lilia had unbuttoned her shirt and spread it open. Her brassiere was made of black lace. K. was nearly moved to fall upon Lilia and rain her throat with kisses, but hesitated: something was evident in the crease between her breasts, a mark or sign. Lilia undid the clasp at the center of the brassiere and parted her hands, so that she concealed and also gently parted her breasts. The tattoo in her cleavage was revealed. It was an image of the Waif, or a child very much like the Waif, with large, shimmering eyes, a tiny, downturned mouth, and strawlike hair. Looking more closely, K. saw that the Waif in the tattoo on Lilia's chest also bore a tattoo: a line of tiny numerals on the interior of the forearm. "I should go," said K. "Titorelli must be wondering about us." "You can visit me here anytime," whispered Lilia, quickly buttoning her shirt. "Titorelli doesn't care." "I'll call," said K., "or e-mail—do you e-mail?" K. felt in a mild panic to return to the front of the gallery, and to pursue the Waif. "Just e-mail me here at the gallery," said Lilia. "I answer all the e-mails you send, anyway. Titorelli never reads them." "But you answer them in Titorelli's voice!" said K. He was distracted from his urgency by this surprise. "Yes," said Lilia, suddenly dropping her voice in impersonation to a false basso, considerably deeper than Titorelli's in fact, but making the point nonetheless. "I pretend to be a man on the Internet," she said in the deep voice, dropping her chin to her neck and narrowing her nostrils as well, to convey a ludicrous satire of masculinity. "Don't tell anyone." K. kissed her cheek quickly and rushed out to the front of the gallery, where he found Titorelli adjusting the last of the small landscapes in its place on the wall. The paintings were hung upside down, and they lined the gallery now. "There you are," said Titorelli. He thrust a permanent marker into K.'s hand. "I need your signature." "Did you see a—a child, a Waif?" said K., moving to Titorelli's desk, wanting to sign any papers quickly and be done with it. "A wraith?" said Titorelli. "No, a Waif, a child with large, sad eyes," said K. "Where are the papers?" K. looked through the front window of the gallery and thought he saw the Waif standing some distance away, down the snowy cobblestone street, huddled again in its own bare arms and staring in his direction. "Not papers," said Titorelli. "Sign the paintings." Titorelli indicated the nearest of the upside-down oils. He tapped his finger at the lower right-hand corner. "Just your initial." In irritation K. scrawled his mark on the painting. "I have to go—" he said. The Waif waited out in the banks of snow, beckoning to him with its sorrowful, opalescent eyes. "Here," said Titorelli, guiding K. by the arm to a place beside the next of the inverted heathscapes. K. signed. Outside, the Waif had turned away. "And the next," said Titorelli. "All of them?" asked K. in annoyance. Outside, the Waif had begun to wander off, was now only a speck barely visible in the snowy street. "Please," said Titorelli. K. autographed the remaining canvases, then headed for the door. "Perhaps now we can market these atrocities," said Titorelli. "If they move I'll have her paint a few more; she can do them in her sleep." "I'm sorry," said K., doubly confused. Market atrocities? Paint in her sleep? Outside, the Waif had vanished. "Isn't the painter of these canvases dead?" K. asked. "Not dead," said Titorelli. "If you really think she can be called an artist. Lilia is responsible for these paintings." Outside, the Waif had vanished.

*　　*　　*

CITIZEN KAFKA

—name of punk band on flyer, San Francisco, circa 1990

*　　*　　*

As the babyfaced wunderkind awoke one morning from uneasy dreams he found himself transformed in his bed into a three-hundred-pound advertising pitchman.

As Superman awoke one morning from a Red K Dream he found himself transformed in his bed into two Jewish cartoonists.

As the laughing-on-the-outside clown awoke one morning from uneasy dreams he found himself transformed in his bed into a gigantic crying-on-the-inside clown.

As the painter of weeping children awoke one morning from uneasy dreams he found himself transformed in his bed into his own defense attorney, a man who in his previous career in Hollywood had himself been accused of charlatanism, plagiarism, and dyeing Rita Hayworth's hair black. Great, he thought, this is just what I need. He found that he was so heavy he had to roll himself out of bed.

As Modernism awoke one morning from uneasy dreams it found itself transformed in its bed into a gigantic Postmodernism.

The Waif didn't have a bed.

Gregor Samsa ducked into a nearby phone booth. "This looks," he said, "like a job for a gigantic insect."

*　　*　　*

"In my masterwork I wanted to portray the unsolved problems of mankind; all rooted in war, as that vividly remembered sight of the human rats amid the rubble of Berlin so poignantly signified… endless drawings, the charcoal sketches lay scattered along the years. Each in its groping way had helped lead me to this moment…"

—Walter Keane, in *Walter Keane: Tomorrow's Master Series*

*   *   *

"I've come up against the last boundary, before which I shall in all likelihood again sit down for years, and then in all likelihood begin another story all over again that will again remain unfinished. This fate pursues me."

—Kafka, *Diaries*

*   *   *

On a gray spring morning before K.'s thirty-first birthday K. was summoned to court for his trial. He hadn't thought a trial so long delayed would ever actually begin, but it had. Go figure. K. was escorted from his apartment to the court by a couple of bailiffs, men in black suits and dark glasses and with grim, set expressions on their faces that struck K. as ludicrous. "You look like extras from the *X-Files*!" he exclaimed, but the bailiffs were silent. They held K.'s arms and pressed him close from both sides, and in this manner K. was guided downstairs and into the street. In silence the bailiffs steered K. through indifferent crowds of rush-hour commuters and midmorning traffic jams of delivery trucks and taxicabs, to the new Marriott in downtown Brooklyn. A sign in the lobby of the Marriott said: WELCOME TRIAL OF K., LIBERTY BALLROOM A/B, and in smaller letters underneath: A SMOKE-FREE BUILDING. K. and the bailiffs moved through the lobby to the entrance of the ballroom which now served as a makeshift court. The ballroom was already packed with spectators, who broke into a chorus of murmurs at K.'s appearance at the back of the room. The bailiffs released K.'s arms and indicated that he should precede them to the front of the court, where judge and jury, as well as prosecuting and defending attorneys, waited. K. moved to the front, holding himself erect to indicate his indifference to the craning necks and goggling eyeballs of the spectators, his deafness to their murmurs. As he approached the bench K. saw that his defending attorney was none other than the Advertising

Pitchman. The Pitchman levered his bulk out of his chair and rose to greet K., offering a hand to shake. K. took his hand, which was surprisingly soft and which retreated almost instantly from K.'s grip. Now K. saw that the prosecuting attorney was the Famous Clown. The Famous Clown was dressed in an impeccable three-piece suit and tremendously wide, pancake-like black shoes which were polished to a high gloss. The Famous Clown remained in his seat, scowling behind bifocal lenses at a sheaf of papers on his desk, pretending not to have noticed K.'s arrival. Seated at the high bench in the place of a judge was the Waif. The Waif sat on a tall stool behind the bench. The Waif wore a heavy black robe, and on its head sat a thickly curled wig which partly concealed its strawlike thatch of hair but did nothing to conceal the infinitely suffering black pools of its eyes. The Waif toyed with its gavel, seemingly preoccupied and indifferent to K.'s arrival in the courtroom. K. was guided by the Pitchman to a seat at the defense table, where he faced the Waif squarely, the Prosecuting Clown at his right. The jurors sat at a dais to K.'s left, and he found himself resistant to turning in their direction. K. wanted no pity, no special dispensation. "Don't fear," stage-whispered the Pitchman. He winked and clapped K.'s shoulder, conspiratorial and garrulous at once. "We've practically ended this trial before it's begun," the Pitchman said. "I've exonerated you of nearly all of the charges. Incompleteness, for one. It turns out their only witnesses were the Unfinished Chapters and the Passages Deleted by the Author. They were prepared to put them on the stand one after another, but I disqualified them all on grounds of character." "Their character was deficient?" asked K. "I should say so," boasted the Pitchman, arching an eyebrow dramatically. "Why, just have a look at them. You've left them woefully underwritten!"

K. hadn't understood himself to be the *author* of the Unfinished Chapters and the Passages Deleted by the Author, but rather a fictional character, one subject to the deprivations of being underwritten himself. However, one glance at the Unfinished Chapters and the Passages Deleted by the Author, all of whom sat crowded together in the spectators' gallery, muttering resentfully and glaring in K.'s direction, told K. that they did not themselves understand this to be the case. The Unfinished Chapters held themselves with a degree of decorum, their ties perhaps a little out-of-fashion and certainly improperly knotted, but they at least wore ties; the Passages Deleted by the Author were hardly better than unwashed rabble.

Still, K.'s instinct was for forgiveness. He reflected that for Chapters and Passages alike it must have been bitter indeed to be denied their say in court after so long. "Additionally," continued the Pitchman, "you've been cleared of the various charges of Impersonation, Ventriloquism, Usurpation, and the like." "How was this achieved?" asked K., a little resentfully. "Which other witnesses had to be smeared in order that I not need defend myself in this matter in which, incidentally, I am entirely innocent?" The Pitchman was undeterred, and said with a guttural chuckle, "No, not witnesses. This was a side bargain with my counterpart on the opposite aisle." K. glanced at the Famous Clown, who just at that moment was staring across at the Advertising Pitchman with poisonous intensity, even as he readjusted his false buck teeth. K. heard a sharp and rhythmic clapping sound and saw that the Famous Clown was slapping his broad, flat shoes against the floor beneath his desk. The Pitchman seemed not to notice or care. He said, "Let's just say you're not the only one in this room with skeletons in his closet—or perhaps I should say with a dressing room full of masks and putty noses." The Pitchman groped his own bulbous proboscis, and grew for one moment reflective, even tragic in his aspect. "I speak even for myself…" He seemed about to digress into some reminiscence, then apparently thought better of it, and waved his hand. "Still, congratulations would be premature. One charge against you remains—a trifle, I'm sure. This charge you can eradicate with a few swift brushstrokes." "How with brushstrokes?" asked K. "You stand charged with Forgery," said the Pitchman. "Patently absurd, I know, yet it is the only jeopardy that still remains. A woman has stepped forward and claimed your work as her own. I negotiated with the prosecution a small demonstration before the jury, knowing how this opportunity to clear yourself directly would please you." "A demonstration?" asked K. "Yes," chuckled the Pitchman. "One hardly worthy of your talents. A hot-dog eating contest would be more exalted. Regardless, it should provide the flourish these modern show trials require." K. saw now that the bailiffs had dragged two painting easels to the front of the courtroom and erected them before the Waif's bench. Blank canvases were mounted on each of the easels, and two sets of brushes and two palettes of oils were made available on a table to one side. The Waif was now rolling the handle of its gavel back and forth across the desktop, in an uncharacteristic display of agita-tion. "A masterpiece isn't required," said the Pitchman. "Merely a display of competence, of facility." "But who is this woman?" asked K. "Here she is now," whispered the Pitchman, nudging K.'s shoulder. K. turned. The woman who had entered the courtroom was Lilia, Titorelli's art handler. There was a buzz from the jury box, like a small hive of insects. Lilia wore a prim white smock and a white painter's hat. Her gaze was fiercely determined, her eyes never lighting on K.'s. "Go now," whispered the Pitchman. "A sentimental subject would be best, I think. Something to stir the hearts of the jurors." K. stood. He saw now that the jury box was full of ragged children, much like the Waif who stood now in its robes and clapped its gavel to urge the painters to commence the demonstration. Lilia seized a brush and began immediately to paint, first outlining two huge orbs in the center of the canvas. K. wondered if they were breasts, then saw that in fact they were two enormous, bathetic eyes: Lilia was initiating a portrait of the Waif. K. moved for the table. As he reached to take hold of a brush he felt a sudden clarifying pain in the shoulder where the Pitchman had nudged him a moment before, a pain so vivid that he wondered if he would be at all able to paint, or even to lift his arm; it now felt heavy and inert, like a dead limb. Lilia, meanwhile, continued to work intently at her easel.

(Note: It is here the fragment ends. Nevertheless, I believe this sequence, taken in conjunction with the completed chapters which precede it, reveals its meaning with undeniable clarity. —Box Dram, Editor)

*   *   *

"I don't like that ending. To me it's a "ballet" written by a Jewish intellectual before the advent of Hitler. Kafka wouldn't have put that after the death of six million Jews. It all seems very much pre-Auschwitz to me. I don't mean that my ending was a particularly good one, but it was the only possible solution."

—Orson Welles, on *The Trial*

*   *   *

See K. awaken one morning from righteous dreams to find himself transformed in his bed into a caped superhero: Holocaust Man!

See Holocaust Man stride forth in the form of the golem, with a marvelously powerful rocklike body and the Star of David chiseled into its chest!

See Holocaust Man and his goofy sidekick, Clown Man, defeat Mister Prejudice, Mister Guilt, Mister Tuberculosis, Mister Irony, Mister Paralysis, and Mister Concentration Camp!

See Holocaust Man and Clown man lead a streaming river of tattered, orphaned children to safety across the battlefields of Europe!

Laugh on the outside! Cry on the inside!

FURTHER INTERPRETATIONS OF REAL-LIFE EVENTS

by KEVIN MOFFETT

(fiction from Issue 30)

A FTER MY FATHER retired, he began writing trueish stories about fathers and sons. He had tried scuba diving, had tried being a dreams enthusiast, and now he'd come around to this. I was skeptical. I'd been writing my own trueish stories about fathers and sons for years, stories that weren't perfect, of course, but they were mine. Some were published in literary journals, and I'd even received a fan letter from Helen in Vermont, who liked the part in one of my stories where the father made the boy scratch his stepmom's back. Helen in Vermont said she found the story "enjoyable" but kind of "depressing."

The scene with the stepmom was an interpretation of an actual event. When I was ten years old my mother died. My father and I lived alone for five years, until he married Lara, a kind woman with a big laugh. He met her at a dreams conference. I liked her well enough in real life but not in the story. In the story, "End of Summer," I begrudged Lara (changed to "Laura") for marrying my father so soon after my mother died (changed to five months).

"You used to scratch your ma's back all the time," my father says in the final scene. "Why don't you ever scratch Laura's?"

Laura sits next to me, shucking peas into a bucket. The pressure builds. "If you don't scratch Laura's back," my father says, "you can forget Christmas!"

So I scratch her back. It sounds silly now, but by the end of the story, Christmas stands in for other things. It isn't just Christmas anymore.

The scene was inspired by the time my father and Lara went to Mexico City (while I was marauded by bullies and blackflies at oboe camp) and brought me home a souvenir. A tin handicraft? you guess. A selection of cactus-fruit candy? No. A wooden back-scratcher with extended handle for maximum self-gratification. What's worse, TE QUIERO was embossed on the handle. Which I translated at the time to mean: *I love me.* (I was off by one word.)

"Try it," my father said. His tan had a yolky tint and he wore a shirt with PROPERTY OF MEXICO on the back. It was the sort of shirt you could find anywhere.

I hiked my arm over my head and raked the back-scratcher north and south along my vertebrae. "Works," I said.

"He spent all week searching for something for you," Lara said. "He even tried to haggle at the *mercado*. It was cute."

"There isn't much for a boy like you in Mexico," my father said. "The man who sold me the back-scratcher, though, told me a story. All the men who left to fight during the revolution took their wives with them. They wanted to remember more…"

I couldn't listen. I tried to, I pretended to, nodding and going *hmm* when he said *Pancho Villa* and *wow* when he said *gunfire* and then *some story* when it was over. I excused myself, sprinted upstairs to my bedroom, slammed my door, and snapped that sorry back-scratcher over my knee like kindling.

A boy like me!

You'll never earn a living writing stories, not if you're any good at it. My mentor Harry Hodgett told me that. I must've been doing something right, because I had yet to receive a dime for my work. I day-labored at the community college teaching Prep Writing, a class for students without the necessary skills for Beginning Writing. I also taught Prep Prep Writing, for those without the skills for Prep Writing. Imagine the most abject students on earth, kids who, when you ask them to name a verb, stare like you just asked them to cluck out a polka with armpit farts.

Literary journals paid with contributors' copies and subscriptions, which was nice, because when your story was published you at least knew that everyone else in the issue would read your work. (Though, truth be told, I never did.) This was how I came to receive the Autumn issue of *Vesper*—I'd been published in the Spring issue. It sat on my coffee table until a few days after its arrival, when I returned home to find Carrie on my living-room sofa, reading it. "Shh," she said.

I'd just come back from teaching, dispirited as usual after Shandra Jones in Prep Prep Writing told a classmate to "eat my drippins." A bomb I defused with clumsy silence, comma time!, early dismissal.

"I didn't say anything," I said.

"Shh," she said again.

An aside: I'd like to have kept Carrie out of this because I haven't figured out how to write about her. She's tall with short brown hair and brown eyes and she wears clothes and—see? I could be describing anybody. Carrie's lovely, her face is a nest for my dreams. You need distance from your subject matter. You need to approach it with the icy, lucid eye of a surgeon. I also can't write about my mother. Whenever I try, I feel like I'm attempting kidney transplants with a can opener and a handful of rubber bands.

"Amazing," she said, closing the journal. "Sad and honest and free of easy meanness. It's like the story was unfolding as I read it. That bit in the motel: wow. How come you never showed me this? It's a breakthrough."

She stood and hugged me. She smelled like bath beads. I was jealous of the person, whoever it was, who had effected this reaction in her: Carrie, whom I met in Hodgett's class, usually read my stories with barely concealed impatience.

"Breakthrough, huh?" I said casually (desperately). "Who wrote it?"

She leaned in and kissed me. "You did."

I picked up the journal to make sure it wasn't the Spring issue, which featured "The Longest Day of the Year," part two of my summer trilogy. It's about a boy and his father (I know, I know) driving home, arguing about the record player the father refuses to buy the boy, even though the boy totally needs it since his current one ruined two of his Yes albums, including the impossible-to-find *Time and a Word*, and—*boom*—they hit a deer. The stakes suddenly shift.

I turned to the contributors' notes. *FREDERICK MOXLEY is a retired statistics professor living in Vero Beach, Florida. In his spare time he is a dreams enthusiast. This is his first published story.*

"My dad!" I screamed. "He stole my name and turned me into a dreams enthusiast!"

"Your *dad* wrote this?"

"And turned me into a goddamn dreams enthusiast! Everyone'll think I've gone soft and stupid!"

"I don't think anyone really reads this journal," Carrie said. "No offense. And isn't he Frederick Moxley, too?"

"Fred! He goes by *Fred*. I go by Frederick. Ever since third grade, when there were two Freds in my class." I flipped the pages, found the story, "Mile Zero," and read the first sentence: *As a boy I always dreamed of flight.* That makes two of us, I thought. To the circus, to Tibet, to live with a nice family of Moonies. I felt tendrils of bile beanstalking up my throat. "What's he trying to do?"

"Read it," Carrie said. "I think he makes it clear what he's trying to do."

If the story was awful I could have easily endured it, I realize now. I could've called him and said if he insists on writing elderly squibs, please just use a pseudonym. Let the Moxley interested in truth and beauty, etc., publish under his real name.

But the story wasn't awful. Not by a long shot. Yes, it broke two of Hodgett's six laws of story-writing (Never dramatize a dream, Never use more than one exclamation point per story), but he'd managed some genuine insight. Also he fictionalized real-life events in surprising ways. I recognized one particular detail from after Mom died. We moved the following year, because my father never liked our house's floor plan. That's what I'd thought, at least. Too cramped, he always said; wherever you turned, a wall or closet blocked your path. In the story, though, the characters move because the father can't disassociate the house from his wife. Her presence is everywhere: in the bedroom, the bathroom, in the silverware pattern, the flowering jacaranda in the backyard.

She used to trim purple blooms from the tree and scatter them around the house, on bookshelves, on the dining-room table, he wrote. *It seemed a perfectly attuned response to the natural world, a way of inviting the outside, inside.*

I remembered those blooms. I remembered how the house smelled with her in it, though I couldn't name the smell. I recalled her *presence*, vast ineffable thing.

I finished reading in the bath. I was no longer angry. I was a little jealous. Mostly I was sad. The story, which showed father and son failing to connect again and again, ends in a motel room in Big Pine Key (we used to go there in December), the father watching a cop show on TV while the boy sleeps. He's having a bad dream, the father can tell by the way his face winces and frowns. The father lies down next to him, hesitant to wake him up, and tries to imagine what he's dreaming about.

Don't wake up, the father tells him. *Nothing in your sleep can hurt you.*

The boy was probably dreaming of a helicopter losing altitude. It was a recurring nightmare of mine after Mom died. I'd be cutting through the sky, past my house, past the hospital, when suddenly the control panel starts beeping and the helicopter spins down, down. My body fills with air as I yank the joystick. The noise is the worst. Like a monster oncoming bee. My head buzzes long after I wake up, shower, and sit down to breakfast. My father, who's just begun enthusing about dreams, a hobby that even then I found ridiculous, asks what I dreamed about.

"Well," I say between bites of cereal. "I'm in a blue—no, no, a golden suit. And all of a sudden I'm swimming in an enormous fishbowl in a pet store filled with eager customers. And the thing is, they all look like you. The other thing is, I *love* it. I want to stay in the fishbowl forever. Any idea what that means?"

"Finish your breakfast," he says, eyes downcast.

I'd like to add a part where I say *just kidding*, then tell him my dream. He could decide it's about anxiety, or fear. Even better: he could just backhand me. I could walk around with a handprint on my face. It could go from red to purple to brownish blue, poetic-like. Instead, we sulked. It happened again and again, until mornings grew as joyless and choreographed as the interactions of people who worked among deafening machines.

In the bathroom I dried myself off and wrapped a towel around my waist. I found Carrie in the kitchen eating oyster crackers. "So?" she said.

Her expression was so beseeching, such a lidless empty jug.

I tossed the journal onto the table. "Awful," I said. "Sentimental, boring.

I don't know. Maybe I'm just biased against bad writing."

"And maybe," she said, "you're just jealous of good writing." She dusted crumbs from her shirt. "I know it's good, you know it's good. You aren't going anywhere till you admit that."

"And where am I trying to go?"

She regarded me with a look I recalled from Hodgett's class. Bemused amusement. The first day, while Hodgett asked each of us to name our favorite book, then explained why we were wrong, I was daydreaming about this girl in a white V-neck reading my work and timidly approaching me afterward to ask, What did the father's broken watch represent? and me saying *futility*, or *despair*, and then maybe kissing her. She turned out to be the toughest reader in class, far tougher than Hodgett, who was usually content to make vague pronouncements about *patterning* and *the octane of the epiphany*. Carrie was cold and smart and meticulous. She crawled inside your story with a flashlight and blew out all your candles. She said of one of my early pieces, "On what planet do people actually talk to each other like this?" And: "Does this character do anything but shuck peas?"

I knew she was right about my father's story. But I didn't want to talk about it anymore. So I unfastened my towel and let it drop to the floor. "Uh-oh," I said. "What do you think of this plot device?"

She looked at me, down, up, down. "We're not doing anything until you admit your father wrote a good story."

"*Good?* What's that even mean? Like, can it fetch and speak and sit?"

"Good," Carrie repeated. "It's executed as vigorously as it's conceived. It isn't false or pretentious. It doesn't jerk the reader around to no effect. It lives by its own logic. It's poignant without trying too hard."

I looked down at my naked torso. At some point during her litany, I seemed to have developed an erection. My penis looked all eager, as if it wanted to join the discussion, and unnecessary. "In that case," I said, "I guess he wrote one good story. Do I have to be happy about it?"

"Now I want you to call him and tell him how much you like it."

I picked up the towel, refastened it, and started toward the living room.

"I'm just joking," she said. "You can call him later."

Dejected, I followed Carrie to my room. She won, she always won. I didn't even feel like having sex anymore. My room smelled like the bottom of a pond, like a turtle's moistly rotting cavity. She lay on my bed, still talking about my father's story. "I love that little boy in the motel room," she said, kissing me, taking off her shirt. "I love how he's still frowning in his sleep."

I never called my father, though I told Carrie I did. I said I called and congratulated him. "What's his next project?" she asked. Project! As if he was a famous architect or something. I said he's considering a number of projects, each project more poignant-without-trying-too-hard than the project before it.

He phoned a week later. I was reading my students' paragraph essays, feeling my soul wither with each word. The paragraphs were in response to a prompt: "Where do you go to be alone?" All the students, except one, went to their room to be alone. The exception was Daryl Ellington, who went to his rom.

"You sound busy," my father said.

"Just getting some work done," I said.

We exchanged postcard versions of our last few weeks. I'm fine, Carrie's fine. He's fine, Lara's fine. I'd decided I would let him bring up the journal.

"Been writing," he said.

"Here and there. Some days it comes, some days it doesn't."

"I meant me," he said, then slowly he paddled through a summary of how he'd been writing stories since I sent him one of mine (I'd forgotten this), and of reading dozens of story collections, and then of some dream he had, then, *finally*, of having his story accepted for publication (and two others, forthcoming). He sounded chagrined by the whole thing. "I told them to publish it as Seth Moxley but lines must've gotten crossed," he said. "Anyway, I'll put a copy in the mail today. If you get a chance to read it, I'd love to hear what you think."

"What happened to scuba diving?" I asked.

"I still dive. Lara and I are going down to the Pennecamp next week."

"Right, but—writing's not some hobby you just dabble in, Dad. It's not like scuba diving."

"I didn't say it was. You're the one who brought up diving." He inhaled deeply. "Why do you always do this?"

"Do what?"

"Make everything so damn difficult. I had to drink two glasses of wine before I called, just to relax. You were such an easygoing kid, you know that? Your mom used to call you Placido. I'd wake up panicked in the middle of the night and run to check on you, because you didn't make any noise."

"Maybe she was talking about the opera singer," I said.

Pause, a silent up-grinding of gears. "You don't remember much about your mother, do you?"

"A few things," I said.

"Her voice?"

"Not really."

"She had a terrific voice."

I didn't listen to much after that. Not because I'd already heard it, though I had—I wanted to collect a few things I remembered about her, instead of listening to his version again. Not facts or adjectives or secondhand details, but… qualities. Spliced-together images I could summon without words: her reaching without looking to take my hand in the street, the pockmarks on her wrist from the pins inserted when she broke her arm, her laughing, her crying, her warmth muted, her gone, dissolving room-by-room from our house. I'd never been able to write about her, not expressly. Whenever I tried she emerged all white-robed and beatific, floating around, dispensing wisdom, laying doomed hands on me and everyone. Writing about her was imperfect remembering; it felt like a second death. I was far happier writing about fathers making sons help drag a deer to the roadside, saying, "Look into them fogged-up eyes. Now that's death, boy."

"She always had big plans for you," my father was saying. It was something he often said. I never asked him to be more specific.

It occurs to me that I'm breaking two of Hodgett's laws here. Never write about writing, and Never dramatize phone conversations. Put characters in the same room, he always said. See what they do when they can't hang up. "We'd love to see Carrie again," my father said after a while. "Any chance you'll be home for Christmas?"

Christmas was two months away. "We'll try," I told him.

After hanging up, I returned to my students' paragraphs, happy to marinate for a while in their simple insight. *My room is the special place*, Monica Mendez wrote. *Everywhere around me are shelfs of my memory things*.

* * *

Imagine a time for your characters, Hodgett used to say, when things might have turned out differently. Find the moment a choice was made that made other choices impossible. Readers like to see characters making choices.

She died in May. A week after the funeral my father drives me and three friends to a theme park called Boardwalk and Baseball. He probably hopes it'll distract us for a few hours. All day long my friends and I ride roller coasters, take swings in the batting cage, eat hot dogs. I toss a ping-pong ball into a milk bottle and win a T-shirt. I can't even remember what kind of T-shirt it was, but I remember my glee after winning it.

My father follows us around and sits on a bench while we wait in line. He must be feeling pretty ruined but his son is doing just fine. His son is running from ride to ride, laughing it up with his friends. In fact, he hasn't thought about his mom once since they passed through the turnstiles.

My father is wearing sunglasses, to help with his allergies, he says. His sleeves are damp. I think he's been crying. "Having fun?" he keeps asking me.

I am, clearly I am. Sure, my mom died a week ago, but I just won a new T-shirt and my father gave each of us twenty dollars and the line to the Viper is really short and the sun is shining and I think we saw the girl from *Who's the Boss*, or someone who looks a lot like her, in line at the popcorn cart.

I cringe when I remember this day. I want to revise everything. I want to come down with food poisoning, or lose a couple of fingers on the Raptor, something to mar the flawless good time I was having. Now I have to mar it in memory, I have to remember it with a black line through it.

"I'm glad you had fun," my father says on the drive home.

Our house is waiting for us when we get back. The failing spider plants on the front porch, the powder-blue envelopes in the mailbox.

November was a smear. Morning after morning I tried writing but instead played Etch-a-Sketch for two hours. I wrote a sentence. I waited. I stood up and walked around, thinking about the sentence. I leaned over the kitchen sink and ate an entire sleeve of graham crackers. I sat at my desk and stared at the sentence. I deleted it and wrote a different sentence. I returned to the kitchen and ate a handful of baby carrots. I began wondering about the carrots, so I dialed the toll-free number on the bag and spoke to a woman in Bakersfield, California.

"I would like to know where baby carrots come from," I said.

"Would you like the long version or the short version?" the woman asked.

For the first time in days I felt adequately tended to. "Both," I said.

The short version: baby carrots are adult carrots cut into smaller pieces.

I returned to my desk, deleted my last sentence, and typed, "Babies are adults cut into smaller pieces." I liked this. I knew it would make an outstanding story, one that would win trophies and change the way people thought about fathers and sons if only I could find another three hundred or so sentences to follow it. But where were they?

A few weeks after my father sent me his first story, I received the Winter issue of the *Longboat Quarterly* with a note: *Your father really wants to hear back from you about his story. He thinks you hated it. You didn't hate it, did you? XO, Lara*. No, Lara, I didn't. And I probably wouldn't hate this one, though I couldn't read past the title, "Blue Angels," without succumbing to the urge to sidearm the journal under my sofa (it took me four tries). I already knew what it was about.

Later, I sat next to Carrie on the sofa while she read it. Have you ever watched someone read a story? Their expression is dim and tentative at the beginning, alternately surprised and bewildered during the middle, and serene at the end. At least Carrie's was then.

"Well," she said when she was done. "How should we proceed?"

"Don't tell me. Just punch me in the abdomen. Hard."

I pulled up my shirt, closed my eyes, and waited. I heard Carrie close the journal, then felt it lightly smack against my stomach.

I read the story in the tub. Suffice it to say, it wasn't what I expected.

As a kid I was obsessed with fighter planes. Tomcats, Super Hornets, anything with wings and missiles. I thought the story was going to be about my father taking me to see the Blue Angels, the U.S. Navy's flight team. It wouldn't have been much of a story: miserable heat, planes doing stunts, me in the autograph line for an hour, getting sunburned, and falling asleep staring at five jets on a poster as we drove home.

The story is about a widowed father drinking too much and deciding he needs to clean the house. He goes from room to room dusting, scrubbing floors, throwing things away. The blue angels are a trio of antique porcelain dolls my mother held on to from childhood. The man throws them away, then regrets it as soon as he hears the garbage truck driving off. The story ends with father and son at the dump, staring across vast hillocks of trash, paralyzed.

I remembered the dump, hot syrup stench, blizzard of birds overhead. He told me it was important to see where our trash ended up.

When I finished, I was sad again, nostalgic, and wanting to call my father. Which I did after drying off. Carrie sat next to me on the sofa with her legs over mine. "What are you doing?" she asked. I dialed the number, waited, listened to his answering-machine greeting—*Fred and Lara can't believe we missed your call*—and then hung up.

"Have I ever told you about when I saw the Blue Angels?" I asked Carrie.

"I don't think so."

"Well, get ready," I said.

I quit writing for a few weeks and went out into the world. I visited the airport, the beach, a fish camp, a cemetery, a sinkhole. I collected evidence, listened, tried to see past my impatience to the blood-radiant heart of things. I saw a man towing a woman on the handlebars of a beach cruiser. They were wearing sunglasses. They were poor. They were in love. I heard one woman say to another: *Everyone has a distinct scent, except me. Smell me, I don't have any scent.*

At the cemetery where my mother was buried, I came upon an old man lying very still on the ground in front of a headstone. When I walked by, I read the twin inscription. RUTH GOODINE 1920–1999, CHARLES GOODINE 1923–. "Don't mind me," the man said as I passed.

At my desk, I struggled to make something of this. I imagined what happened before and after. What moment made other moments impossible. He had come to the cemetery to practice for eternity. I could still picture him lying there in his gray suit, but the before and after were murky. Before, he'd been on a bus, or in a car, or a taxi. Afterward he would definitely go to... the supermarket to buy... lunch meat?

"Anything worth saying," Hodgett used to declare, "is unsayable. That's why we tell stories."

I returned to the cemetery. I walked from one end to the other, from the granite cenotaphs to the unmarked wooden headstones. Then I walked into the mausoleum and found my mother's placard, second from the bottom. I had to kneel down to see it. Another of Hodgett's six laws: Never dramatize a funeral or a trip to the cemetery. Too melodramatic, too obvious. I sat against something called the Serenity Wall and watched visitors mill in and out. They looked more inconvenienced than sad. My father and I used to come here, but at some point we quit. Afterward we'd go to a diner and he would say, "Order anything you want, anything," and I would order what I always ordered.

A woman with a camera asked if I could take her picture in front of her grandmother's placard. I said, "One, two, three, smile," and snapped her picture.

When the woman left, I said some things to my mom, all melodramatic, all obvious. In the months before she died, she talked about death like it was a long trip she was taking. She would watch over me, she said, if they let her. "I'm going to miss you," she said, which hadn't seemed strange until now. Sometimes I hoped she was watching me, but usually it was too terrible to imagine. "Here I am," I told the placard. I don't know why. It felt good so I said it again.

"Why don't you talk about your mom?" Carrie asked me after I told her about going to the cemetery.

"You mean in general, or right now?"

Carrie didn't say anything. She had remarkable tolerance for waiting.

"What do you want to know?" I asked.

"Anything you tell me."

I forced a laugh. "I thought you were about to say, 'Anything you tell me is strictly confidential.' Like in therapy. Isn't that what they tell you in therapy?"

For some reason I recalled my mother at the beach standing in the knee-deep water with her back to me. Her pants are wet to the waist and any deeper and her shirt will be soaked, too. I wondered why I needed to hoard this memory. Why did this simple static image seem like such a rare coin?

"Still waiting," Carrie said.

My father published two more stories in November, both about a man whose wife is dying of cancer. He had a weakness for depicting dreams, long, overtly symbolic dreams, and I found that the stories themselves read like dreams, I suffered them like dreams, and after a while I forgot I was reading. Like my high-school band teacher used to tell us, "Your goal is to stop seeing the notes." This never happened to me, every note was a seed I had to swallow, but now I saw what he meant.

Toward the end of the month, I was sick for a week. I canceled class and lay in bed, frantic with half-dreams. Carrie appeared, disappeared, reappeared. I picked up my father's stories at random and re-read paragraphs out of order. I looked for repeated words, recurring details. One particular sentence called to me, from "Under the Light."

That fall the trees stingily held on to their leaves.

In my delirium, this sentence seemed to solve everything. I memorized it. I chanted it. *I* was the tree holding on to its leaves, but I couldn't let them go, because if I did I wouldn't have any more leaves. My father was waiting with a rake because that was his *job* but I was being too stingy and weren't trees a lot like people?

I got better.

The morning I returned to class, Jacob Harvin from Prep Writing set a bag of Cheetos on my desk. "The machine gave me two by accident," he said.

I thanked him and began talking about subject-verb agreement. Out of the corner of my eye, I kept peeking at the orange Cheetos bag and feeling dreadful gratitude. "Someone tell me the subject in this sentence," I said, writing on the board. *"The trees of Florida hold on to their leaves."*

Terrie Inal raised her hand. "You crying, Mr. Moxley?" she asked.

"No, Terrie," I said. "I'm allergic to things."

"Looks like you're crying," she said. "You need a moment?"

The word *moment* did it. I let go. I wept in front of the class while they looked on horrified, bored, amused, sympathetic. "It's just, that was so *nice*," I explained.

Late in the week, my father called and I told him I was almost done with one of his stories. "Good so far," I said. Carrie suggested I quit writing for a while, unaware that I already had. I got drunk and broke my glasses. Someone wrote *Roach* with indelible marker on the hood of my car.

*　　*　　*

One day, I visited Harry Hodgett in his office. I walked to campus with a bagged bottle of Chivas Regal, his favorite, practicing what I'd say. Hodgett was an intimidating figure. He enjoyed playing games with you.

His door was open, but the only sign of him was an empty mug next to a student story. I leaned over to see *S.B.N.I.* written in the margin in Hodgett's telltale blue pen—it stood for *Sad But Not Interesting*—then I sat down. The office had the warm, stale smell of old books. Framed pictures of Hodgett and various well-known degenerates hung on the wall.

"This ain't the petting zoo," Hodgett said on his way in. He was wearing sweatpants and an Everlast T-shirt with frayed cut-off sleeves. "Who are you?"

Hodgett was playing one of his games. He knew exactly who I was. "It's me," I said, playing along. "Moxley."

He sat down with a grunt. He looked beat-up, baffled, winded, which meant he was in the early days of one of his sober sprees. "Oh yeah, Moxley, sure. Didn't recognize you without the… you know."

"Hat," I tried.

He coughed for a while, then lifted his trash can and expectorated into it. "So what are you pretending to be today?" he asked, which was Hodgett code for "So how are you doing?"

I hesitated, then answered, "Bamboo," a nice inscrutable thing to pretend to be. He closed his eyes, leaned his head back to reveal the livid scar under his chin, which was Hodgett code for "Please proceed." I told him all about my father. Knowing Hodgett's predilections, I exaggerated some things, made my father sound more abusive. Hodgett's eyes were shut, but I could tell he was listening by the way his face ticced and scowled. "He sends the stories out under my name," I said. "I haven't written a word in over a month."

To my surprise, Hodgett opened his eyes, looked at me as if he'd just awoken, and said, "My old man once tried to staple-gun a dead songbird to my scrotum." He folded his arms across his chest. "Just facts, not looking for pity."

I remembered reading this exact sentence—*staple-gun*, *songbird*, *scrotum*—then I realized where. "That happened to Moser," I said, "at the end of your novel *The Hard Road*. His dad wants to teach him a lesson about deprivation."

"That wasn't a novel, Chief. That was first-person *life*." He huffed hoarsely. "All this business about literary journals and phone calls and hurt feelings, it's just not compelling. A story needs to sing like a wound. I mean, put your father and son in the same room together. Leave some weapons lying around."

"It isn't a story," I said. "I'm living it."

"I'm paid to teach students like you how to spoil paper. Look at me, man—I can barely put my head together." His face went through a series of contortions, like a ghoul in a mirror. "You want my advice," he said. "Go talk to the old man. Life ain't an opera. It's more like a series of commercials for things we have no intention of buying."

He narrowed his eyes, studying me. His eyes drooped; his mouth had white film at the corners. His nose was netted with burst capillaries.

"What happened to the young woman, anyway?" Hodgett asked. "The one with the nasty allure."

"You mean Carrie? My girlfriend?"

"Carrie, yeah. I used to have girlfriends like Carrie. They're fun." He closed his eyes and with his right hand began casually kneading his crotch. "She did that story about the burn ward."

"Carrie doesn't write anymore," I said, trying to break the spell.

"Shame," Hodgett said. "Well, I guess that's how it goes. Talent realizes its limitations and gives up while incompetence keeps plugging away until it has a book. I'd take incompetence over talent in a street fight any day of the week."

I picked up the Chivas Regal bottle and stood to leave. I studied the old man's big noisy battered redneck face. He was still fondling himself. I wanted to say something ruthless to him. I wanted my words to clatter around in his head all day, like his words did in mine. "Thanks," I said.

He nodded, pointed to the bottle. "You can leave that anywhere," he said.

Another memory: my mother, father, and me in our living room. I am eight years old. In the corner is the Christmas tree, on the wall are three stockings, on the kitchen table is a styrofoam-ball snowman. We're about to open presents. My father likes to systematically inspect his to figure out what's inside. He picks up a flat parcel wrapped in silver paper, shakes it, turns it over, holds it to his ear, and says, "A book." He sets it on his lap and closes his eyes. "A... autobiography."

He's right every time.

My mother wears a yellow bathrobe and sits under a blanket. She's cold again. She's sick but I don't know this yet. She opens her presents distractedly, saying *wow* and *how nice* and neatly folding the wrapping paper in half, then in quarters, while I tear into my gifts one after another. I say thanks without looking up.

That year, she and I picked out a new diver's watch for my father, which we wait until all the presents have been opened to give him. We've wrapped it in a small box and then wrapped that box inside a much larger one.

I set it in front of him. He looks at me, then her. He lifts the box. "Awfully light." He shakes it, knocks on each of the box's six sides. "Things are not what they seem."

My mother begins coughing, softly at first—my father pauses, sets his hands flat atop the box—then uncontrollably, in big hacking gusts. I bring her water, which she drinks, still coughing. My father helps her to the bathroom and I can hear her in there, gagging and hacking. For some reason I'm holding the remote control to the television.

The box sits unopened in the living room for the rest of the day. At night, with Mom in bed and me brushing my teeth, he picks it up, says "Diver's watch, waterproof up to a hundred meters," then opens it.

Carrie and I drove to Vero Beach the day before Christmas Eve. There seemed to be a surplus of abandoned cars and dead animals on the side of the road and, between this and the gray sky and the homemade signs marking off the fallow farms—PREPARE FOR THE RAPTURE; PRAISE HIM—I began to daydream about the apocalypse. I was hoping it would arrive just like this, quietly, without much warning or fanfare.

"I know it's fiction," Carrie was saying, referring to my father's most recent story, "but it's hard not to read it as fact. Did you actually tape pictures of your mom to the front door when Lara came over the first time?"

"Maybe," I said. "Probably. I don't really remember."

I taped the pictures in a circle, like the face of a clock. I waited at the top of the stairs for the doorbell to ring.

Carrie pointed to a billboard featuring the likeness of a recently killed NASCAR driver's car, flanked by white angel wings. "I hope they haven't started letting race cars into heaven," she said.

*   *   *

I finally talked to my father about his writing while we were in the garage looking for the styrofoam-ball snowman. We were searching through boxes, coming across yearbooks, macramé owls, clothes, and my oboe, snug in purple velvet. I always forgot how fit and reasonable-looking my father was until I saw him in person. His hair was now fully gray and his silver-rimmed reading glasses sat low on his nose.

"I didn't know we went to the dump to hunt for those dolls," I said. It sounded more reproachful than I meant it to.

He looked up from the box, still squinting, as if he'd been searching dark, cramped quarters. "You mean the story?"

"'Blue Angels,'" I said. "I read it. I read all of them, actually."

"That's surprising," he said, folding the flaps of the box in front of him. "Best not to make too much out of what happens in stories, right?"

"But you were looking for those dolls."

"I didn't expect to find them. I wanted to see where they ended up." He shook his head. "It's hard to explain. After your mom died—I'd be making breakfast and my mind would wander to Annie and I'd start to lose it. The only time I relaxed was when I slept. That's why I started studying dreams. I found that if I did a few exercises before falling asleep, I could dictate what I dreamed about. I could remember. I could pause and fast-forward and rewind. You're giving me a 'how pitiful' look."

"It's just strange," I said. "The dreams, the stories, it feels like I haven't been paying attention. I had no idea you were being all quietly desperate while I was waiting for my toast."

"It wasn't all the time." He pushed his glasses up on his nose and looked at me. "You should try writing about her, if you haven't already. You find yourself unearthing all sorts of things. Stories are just like dreams."

Something about his advice irritated me. It brought to mind his casually boastful author's note, *This is his first published story.* "Stories aren't dreams," I said.

"They're not? What are they, then?"

I didn't know. All I knew was that if he thought they were dreams, then they had to be something else. "They're jars," I said. "Full of bees. You unscrew the lid and out come the bees."

"All right," he said, moving the box out of his way. "But I still think you should try writing about her. Even if it means the bees coming out."

We searched until I found the snowman resting face-down in a box of embroidered tablecloths. A rat or weasel had eaten half of his head, but he still smiled his black-beaded smile.

"I remember when you made that," my father said.

I did, too. That is, I remembered *when* I made it, without remembering the actual making of it. I made it with my mom when I was three. Every year it appeared in the center of the kitchen table and every year she would say, "You and I made that. It was raining outside and you kept saying, 'Let's go stand in the soup.'" Maybe she thought that if she reminded me enough, I'd never forget the day we made it, and maybe I didn't, for a while.

I brought the snowman into the house and showed it to Carrie, who was sitting in the living room with Lara. "Monstrous," Carrie said.

Lara was looking at me significantly. An unfinished popcorn string dangled from her lap. "Carrie was sharing her thoughts on your dad's stories," she said. "Do you want to add anything?"

My father walked into the living room holding two mismatched candlesticks.

"They," I said slowly, looking at Carrie, waiting for her to mouth the words, "were," she really was lovely, not just lovely looking, but lovely, "good." I breathed and said, "They were good."

Carrie applauded. "He means it, too," she said. "That slightly nauseous look on his face, that's sincerity." Then to me: "Now that wasn't so hard. Don't you feel light now, the weight lifted?"

I felt as if I'd swallowed a stone. I felt it settling and the moss starting to cover it.

"Frederick here's the real writer," my father said. "I'm just dabbling."

How humble, right? How wise and fatherly and kind. But I know what he meant: Frederick here's the fraud. He's the hack ventriloquist. I'm just dabbing at his wounds.

What more should be said about our visit? I want to come to my father's Mexico story without too much flourish. I hear Hodgett's voice: Never end your story with a character realizing something. Characters shouldn't realize things: readers should. But what if the character is also a reader?

We decorated the tree. We strung lights around the sago palms in the front yard. We ate breakfast in an old sugar mill and, from the pier, saw a pod of dolphins rising and rolling at dawn. I watched my father, tried to resist the urge to catalog him. His default expression was benign curiosity. He and Lara still held hands. They finished each other's sentences. They seemed happy. Watching my father watch the dolphins, I felt like we were at an auction, bidding on the same item. It was an ugly, miserly feeling.

I couldn't sleep on Christmas Eve. Carrie and I shared my old bedroom, which now held a pair of single beds separated by my old tricolor nightstand. All the old anxieties were coming back, the deadness of a dark room, the stone-on-stone sound of a crypt top sliding closed as soon as I began drifting to sleep.

I heard Carrie stir during the night. "I can't sleep," I said.

"Keep practicing," she said groggily. "Practice makes practice."

"I was wondering why you quit writing. You had more talent than all of us. You always made it look so easy."

She exhaled through her nose and moved to face me. I could just barely see her eyes in the dark. "Let's pretend," she said

I waited for her to finish. When she didn't I said, "Let's pretend what?"

"Let's pretend two people are lying next to each other in a room. Let's pretend they're talking about one thing and then another. It got too hard to put words in their mouths. They stopped cooperating." She rolled over, knocked her knee against the wall. "They started saying things like, I'm hungry, I'm thirsty, I need air. I'm tired of being depicted. I want to live."

I thought about her burn-ward story, the way boys were on one side of the room and girls were on the other. Before lights-out the nurse came in and made everyone sing and then closed a curtain to separate the boys from the girls. After a while I said, "You sleeping?" She didn't answer so I went downstairs.

I poured a glass of water, and looked around my father's office for something to read. On his desk were a dictionary, a thesaurus, and something called *The Yellow Emperor's Classic of Internal Medicine*, which I flipped through. *When a man grows old his bones become dry and brittle like straw and his eyes bulge and sag.* I opened the top drawer of his filing cabinet and searched through a stack of photocopied stories until I found a stapled manuscript titled "Mexico Story." I sat down on his loveseat and read it.

In Mexico, it began, *some men still remember Pancho Villa*. I prepared for a thinly veiled account of my father's and Lara's vacation, but the story, it turned out, followed a man, his wife, and their son on vacation in Mexico City. They've traveled there because the mother is sick and their last hope is a healer rumored to help even the most hopeless cases. The family waits in the healer's sitting room for their appointment. The son, hiding under the headphones of his new walkman, just wants to go home. The mother tries to talk to him but he just keeps saying *Huh? Huh?*

The three of us go into a dim room, where the healer asks my mother what's wrong, what her doctors said, why has she come. Then he shakes his head and apologizes. "Very bad," he says. He tells a rambling story about Pancho Villa, which none of us listens to, then reaches into a drawer and pulls out a wooden back-scratcher. He runs it up and down along my mother's spine.

"How's that feel?" he asks.

"Okay," the mother says. "Is it doing anything?"

"Not a thing. But it feels good, yes? It's yours to keep, no charge."

I must have fallen asleep while reading, because at some point the threads came loose in the story and mother, father, and son leave Mexico for a beach that looks a lot like the one near our house. Hotels looming over the sea oats. The inlet lighthouse just visible in the distance. I sit on a blanket next to my father while my mother stands in knee-deep water with her back to us.

"She's sick," my father says. "She doesn't want me to say anything, but you're old enough to know. She's really... sick."

If she's sick she shouldn't be in the water, I think. Her pants are wet to the waist and if she wades in any deeper her shirt will be soaked, too. I pick up a handful of sand and let it fall through my fingers.

"So it's like a battle," he's saying. "Good versus bad. As long as we stick together, we'll get through it okay."

My mother walks out of the water. She is bathed in light and already I can barely see her. She sits next to us, puts her hand on my head, and, in the dream, I realize this is one of those moments I need to prolong. I put my hand over hers and hold it there. I push down on her hand until it hurts and I keep pushing.

"You can let go," she says. "I'm not going anywhere."

*   *   *

The next morning I found my father in checked pajamas near the Christmas tree. He carefully stepped over a stack of presents onto the tree skirt and picked up a gift from Carrie and me. He shook it and listened. He tapped on it with his finger.

"It's not a watch," I said.

He turned to me and smiled. "I've narrowed it down to two possibilities," he said. "Here." He waved me over. "Sit down, I've got something for you."

I sat on the couch and he handed me a long, flat package wrapped in red-and-white paper. "Wait, wait," he said when I started to unwrap it. "Guess what it is first."

I looked at it. All that came to mind was a pair of chopsticks.

"Listen," he said, taking it from me. He held it up to my ear and shook it. "Don't think, just listen. What's that sound like to you?"

I didn't hear anything. "I don't hear anything," I said.

He continued shaking the gift. "It's trying to tell you what it is. Hear it?"

I waited for it, I listened. "No."

He tapped the package against my head. "Listen harder," he said.

PANTEENTOUM

a pantoum by BILL TARLIN

I'll kick your ass at State and Madison
Zero to the zero crosshair corner
Prepare to taste my downtown medicine
Feed a meter for the county coroner

Zero to the zero crosshair corner
I draw a bead on your unkempt head
Feed a meter for the county coroner
Or call street sweepers in instead

I draw a bead on your unkempt head
You called me out to stake a claim
Well call street sweepers in instead
You're dust, you're ash, before my flame

You called me out to stake a claim?
Don't think I didn't see her first
You're dust, you're ash, before my flame
She'll wear your nuts hung on her purse

Don't think I didn't see her first
She touched my gun, I met her mom
She'll wear your nuts hung on her purse
and go with me to the senior prom

She touched my gun, I met her mom
Prepare to taste my downtown medicine
Don't talk to me 'bout the senior prom
I'll kick your ass at State and Madison

FIRE:
THE NEXT SHARP STICK?

A CONVERSATION AMONG CAVEMEN

by JOHN HODGMAN

(fiction from Issue 2)

The offices of Ten Men Who Help Each Other But Are Not Brothers, a firm located Near the River That's Not as Wide as the Really Wide River.

(ONE WHO HELPS THE HAIRY ONE *is seated going over some notes. Enter* MAKER OF FIRE.)

ONE: (*standing*) Hey, it's good to see you. Thanks for coming by.

MAKER: Thank you, One Who Helps The Hairy One. I'm sorry I'm late. Somehow I ended up by the Really Wide River.

ONE: Really? When we met by the Sticky Tree, I thought I said Near the River That's Not as Wide as the Really Wide River.

MAKER: That is what you said. I must have gotten turned around at the

Sharp Shells.

ONE : Oh, yeah. That happens a lot.

MAKER: I must have just spaced.

ONE: No harm done. Do you want a Stick that Tastes Good to gnaw on?

MAKER: No thanks. I just had one. I'm a bear if I don't have one before Hot Part of the Day.

ONE: (*doesn't understand, a little afraid*) Excuse me?

MAKER: (*laughs*) Sorry. Sorry. I'm not *actually* a bear. I just mean that I'm *like* a bear if I don't have a Stick that Tastes Good.

ONE: You pretend to be a bear?

MAKER: No. I feel like a bear feels when he wakes up. You know, grumpy, impatient.

ONE: Do you become a bear when you say it?

MAKER: No. I just say it.

ONE: (*still doesn't understand*) Oh. Okay. I see. Well, in a way, that's exactly why I asked you to come down here. As you know, Ten Men Who Help Each Other But Are Not Brothers is a very old and established firm.

MAKER: I do know.

ONE: I mean, for me, it's a real honor to be associated with The Hairy One and to be his Helper. The Hairy One's a visionary, you know. But he's, how do I say it? He's older than The Old One, and as a result, I think that Ten Men needs to think about its future and think about how it can stay competitive in changing times.

MAKER: Naturally, I agree.

ONE: When we met by the Sticky Tree, I immediately thought, here's a guy who's ahead of the curve. Here's a guy who maybe can help Ten Men make the transition into That Day That Isn't This Day, But Also Isn't The Day Before or The Day Before That.

MAKER: At The Shallow Pond With a Terrible Odor, we call it "Tomorrow."

ONE: Really? "Tomorrow"? Very clever. But the point is, we were talking about fire. And it seemed to me after we spoke that this could be just the thing to carry Ten Men into "Tomorrow."

MAKER: Well, there's no question that fire has a lot to offer any firm, Ten Men included, and I'm happy to show you why. But I think you need to think seriously about what your fire needs are. The truth is, this technology is so revolutionary that I think the real question won't be whether fire is right for Ten Men, but whether Ten Men is ready for fire.

ONE: (*nodding seriously*) True. True. Well, what I have planned is pretty informal, just a meeting of the minds, so to speak. I've asked the Hairy One to sit in on this meeting, since he'll have to approve anything that might happen Not Now, But Another Time. You may have to take it a little slow with him—he's a bit of a neanderthal when it comes to this sort of thing, if you know what I mean.

MAKER: HA HA HA HA HA HA!

ONE: HA HA HA HA HA HA!

(*Enter* THE HAIRY ONE, *carrying a sharp stick.* ONE *immediately stops laughing and falls to the floor completely prostrate, arms and legs spread, face down.* MAKER *smirks and does not move.*)

ONE: (*speaking into the floor*) Oh, hey, Hairy One, how are you? Thanks for coming by.

HAIRY ONE: (*grunts. To* MAKER) Where are the Sticks That Taste Good?

MAKER: I think they're over there.

(HAIRY ONE *crosses to side table to get a stick and begins gnawing it.*)

ONE: (*starting to raise himself*) I just gathered them, Hairy One, so they're fresh. (*Pauses. Looks to* MAKER) You know me: I'm a bear if I don't have one before The Time You Tell Us When We Can Eat.

HAIRY ONE: (*stick drops from mouth in fear*) BEAR! BEAR! (*Raises sharp stick and crosses to begin hitting* ONE *with it*).

ONE: No! Not bear! Not bear!

MAKER: It's just a saying.

ONE: It's just a saying!

(HAIRY ONE *stops his attack and stares at both of them suspiciously*)

ONE: (*rising, then sitting down*) I'm not a bear.

MAKER: It's just something that he said.

HAIRY ONE: (*completely disinterested*) Whatever. (*Retrieves stick and sits down at head of table.*)

ONE: Hairy One, Maker of Fire. Maker of Fire, The Hairy One.

MAKER: My pleasure, Hairy One. I've followed your work with Ten Men for a long time. It's a remarkable firm.

HAIRY ONE: So you're the one with the fire?

MAKER: Yes.

HAIRY ONE: Is it here?

MAKER: Well, no.

HAIRY ONE: Where is it?

MAKER: Well, in a sense, Hairy One, fire is everywhere. Rather than being an object, say, like your sharp stick, it's really a process, and so it can't really be said to exist anywhere. In a sense, fire exists in its own imaginary, virtual space, where we can only talk about what is not fire, and what might become fire.

HAIRY ONE : Whoa whoa whoa! English, please!

ONE: I think that what the Maker of Fire is trying to say is that—and let me know if I have it right—while I may have one fire, and you may have another fire in another place, and The One Who Helps the Hairy One may be planning to make a fire, the truth is that it's all fire. It's all the same thing. It's all fire.

MAKER. That's true, in a rudimentary sense, but for our purposes it'll do fine.

ONE: What's great about fire, Hairy One, is that it combines many things in one. Light, heat, pain—all in one. It's all those things. It's multi-thing.

HAIRY ONE: I thought you said it was all the same thing.

ONE: It is!

HAIRY ONE: But now you say it's multi-thing?

(ONE *is confused; looks to* MAKER OF FIRE)

MAKER: It is and it isn't. It depends on how you define *thing*.

HAIRY ONE: And where does the bear come in?

MAKER: It doesn't.

ONE: That was just something I said.

HAIRY ONE: I get that, okay? I just wanted to know if a bear was involved in fire or not.

MAKER: It isn't.

HAIRY ONE: Good.

MAKER: See, the thing about fire is that it's totally interactive. Fire isn't a bear, but if you put fire on a bear, then the bear becomes fire. It's completely responsive to your needs at a given time, reacting specifically to your fuel input and usage paradigm...

HAIRY ONE: Okay, stop right there. Here's the thing. I've heard a lot about this fire already. Everyone is saying how shiny it is and how flickery it is. But you have to agree that that's very specialized. I know you folks at the Shallow Pond With a Terrible Odor are making a whole big deal about this, but we here by the River That's Not as Wide as the Really Wide River, well, we're simple folk. We want to know: what can it do for us? And the thing is, until people really figure out how fire can be used, I just can't see it becoming a staple of everyday life.

ONE: If I can just jump in here for a moment, Hairy One, think of it like the sharp stick. You know, Many Many Many Nights ago, everyone was using a blunt stick for clubbing and for poking at things we had no name for. We didn't even call it "blunt stick" back then. We just called it "stick."

MAKER: Exactly.

ONE: And then someone came along and said, hey, let's take this rock and push it on the stick and remove parts of the stick at one end until it's different than it was before. Everyone called this one Crazy One, until Crazy One took the sharp stick and put it in the Loud One's eye.

HAIRY ONE: *Someone* didn't do that. *I* did.

ONE: That's what I'm saying. Once we had the sharp stick, The Loud One became One Eye, and the Crazy One became The Big Hairy One.

HAIRY ONE: *I'm* The Big Hairy One.

ONE: That's what I'm saying. You don't want to be the One Who Didn't Like Fire. Fire is the Sharp Stick of... of... Tomorrow.

HAIRY ONE: What's tomorrow?

MAKER: Well, that's not entirely a correct analogy, since fire can't really be compared to anything that isn't fire, but...

HAIRY ONE: (*to* ONE) Okay, but I think you're both overlooking an important thing: fire is very very scary. Even when sharp stick got big, there were a lot of people still using blunt stick because they knew what blunt stick could do. People still love their blunt sticks, and it is many many days and nights later. So I can't see how this fire thing is going to work until people have a reason not to be scared.

MAKER: Well, before we go on, we have to all accept that not everything is going to appeal to Johnny Blunt Stick.

HAIRY ONE: Okay, but let me tell you that it's Johnny Blunt Sticks that made Ten Men one of the top firms by the River That's Not the Really Wide River. Johnny Blunt Sticks like me.

MAKER: Look, I didn't mean to offend anyone. Listen, I have to use the dungheap. Why don't I step out for a moment, and you two can decide how you want this meeting to go. Okay?

HAIRY ONE: No offense, no offense. We'll be here.

(MAKER *exits.*)

ONE: I'm sure he didn't mean to suggest that…

HAIRY ONE: I don't care about that. I know how they are by the Shallow Pond. You know I've met him before?

ONE: You have?

HAIRY ONE: Sure. Many many many many nights ago on a business trip. I was over by the Shallow Pond, and all the Shallow Ponders were laughing at him. You know what they used to call him? I mean, before all this "Maker of Fire" bullshit?

ONE: What?

HAIRY ONE: They used to call him The One Who Knocks Two Rocks Together Over Dry, Dead Plants.

ONE: Oh, man, really?

HAIRY ONE: He's a complete lunatic. Not just Not Like Us—not like anybody.

ONE: But what about fire?

HAIRY ONE: Oh, he may have fire, but "Maker of Fire"? He's an idiot. Where did you meet him?

ONE: Over by the Sticky Tree. He wanted to know if Ten Men would want to give him some food and then he would give us some fire.

HAIRY ONE: He what?!

ONE: He called it "barter."

HAIRY ONE: Well, I call it bullshit. He's obviously deranged. I thought he was here to invite us to go to the Shallow Pond and kill everyone and *take* fire.

ONE: No, he wants to "trade."

HAIRY ONE: Now I just feel sorry for him.

(Re-enter MAKER OF FIRE*)*

MAKER: Well, have you thought it over?

HAIRY ONE: Maker of Fire, you do us great honor by traveling so far to visit we Two Men of the Ten Men Who Help Each Other But Are Not Brothers. But until I get a sense of how fire could ever be useful, I'm afraid we're just going to have to muddle along without it.

MAKER: I understand. Not all are fire-ready.

HAIRY ONE: And I'm sorry about the Johnny Blunt Stick business. Please, come over here and join hands.

MAKER: *(goes to join hands.* THE HAIRY ONE *stabs him with the stick, and then beats him until he is dead.)*

ONE: What are you doing?

HAIRY ONE: There, he's out of his misery, poor fellow. Now go through his skins and his magic bag.

ONE: What? Why?

HAIRY ONE: We're looking for fire, my Helper! We're looking for fire!

ONE: Oh, you truly are the Wise and Big Hairy One!

FINIS.

MISS GREENBURGER

a twenty-minute story by PETER ORNER

JENNY HAFNER'S FATHER showed up at school in his pajamas drunk and roaring. The pajamas looked comfortable and lived-in, softened, the way pajamas should look. He wasn't wearing any socks or even slippers and even more amazing than his sputtering rumpus were his awful feet, not so much big as grotesque. His toes were black, as if for years he'd been stubbing them on the sidewalk. Nobody had ever seen Mr. Hafner's feet before, much less him in his pajamas, although of course it wasn't a secret that he was a raving public drunk (he was on the school board) so his sudden appearance in our classroom didn't come as much of a shock to anybody, except the new teacher, Miss Greenburger. Imagining her now, she was so young, so greenly bendable.

It was her first year teaching. It was fourth grade. She tried to love us all equally. She was like a new mother with twins, kissing one and then the other to not play favorites. She was almost pretty even though her nose didn't point directly at you. I loved her more for this. We all did. She taught us cursive though she said in most schools you had to wait another two years. She didn't waste a hell of a lot of time on math. Her breasts were like anthills that my hand craved smoothing. Her hair was short but still somehow got in her eyes. We all hated her name and once passed around a scrawled petition begging her to change it to something more appropriate to her delicacy and petite wrists. We refused to leave for recess without her. She was pigeon-toed. She wore swishy skirts that sometimes brushed our knees. Once she put two pencils behind her ears by accident. She said she hated chalk. She didn't grow her fingernails longer than *ours*. Sometimes she stopped in midsentence to look out the window. Some days her breasts were more like small balloons than anthills. We would have died for her, all of us, which is why I remain ashamed.

It wasn't his feet that got her. When Mr. Hafner ranted into Room A-14 that morning in late October, barefoot and foozled in his comfortable pajamas, his open fly allowing Miss Greenburger to see more of Mr. Hafner than she ever needed to see—she cried. She hunched over her desk and wept. She shrank more than we ever imagined she could. And we did zero. Maybe for a fleeting moment we were more interested in him than her. Prevaricators! You're not children, you evil midgets! Or maybe in those two perfect months our love had waned inexcusably. I wish I could say. To our credit, we never talked about it after. We focused solely on our dereliction of duty. Yet that didn't absolve us then and never has. What would it have taken for one of us to stand up from his or her desk and go to her and block her view? After Mr. Hafner staggered away, Miss Greenburger thrust her head back and sneezed, viciously, her face awash in tears and snot. Marlin Lavanhar shouted Gesundheit! from the back of the room, but nothing, not even being polite in German could have brought her back to us then. She'd aged. We all had.

—April 7, 2002, 1:15–1:45 a.m., San Francisco, CA

BENJAMIN BUCKS

by JENNIE ERIN SMITH

(nonfiction from Issue 39)

BENJAMIN BUCKS'S FATHER was a lapsed Mormon from Lehi, Utah, who moved to Zurich in the 1970s along with a small collection of milk snakes and king snakes that he tucked into rolled-up socks in his luggage. The senior Bucks was a biochemist, and it seemed natural that Benjamin, a pretty, precocious, fluffy-haired youth who loved reptiles as much as his father did, would endeavor to become a man of science himself.* But just a few months after penning his first and only scientific article—"Further contributions to the knowledge of *Bradypodion uthmoelleri* (Müller, 1938) from Tanzania," for the German herpetology journal *Salamandra*—Benjamin bought a plane ticket and took off for Uganda, his parents unable or unwilling to stop him. It was 1994, and Bucks was sixteen.

This was not Bucks's first African trip; he'd gone on safari almost annually with one parent or another since the age of seven, and had once smuggled

---

* Bucks's name, and the names of some of his associates, have been changed.

a chameleon—the same *Bradypodion uthmoelleri* he'd written about—back to Zurich using the sock-stuffing technique his father had taught him. He arrived at Entebbe airport in the fall of '94 with a vague idea that he would make a living exporting reptiles. At his hostel outside Kampala, though, he wound up in conversation with a former Tutsi rebel in the Rwandan Patriotic Front, and he decided on the spot to visit Rwanda.

Bucks took a bus across the border, not thinking anything could go wrong until he saw the shot-up walls and burnt, abandoned houses of Kigali. He hid in a hotel until the next day, when he managed to make it to the American embassy. "I'd like to go see some gorillas," he told the staff, and they told him to leave immediately. After that he ran into an Austrian relief worker who told him, with more patience, that he couldn't go see the gorillas because the forests were mined and he would be blown up.

Two years later American reptile dealers started receiving mysterious, crude price lists hand-scribbled on stationery from Kenyan hotels. They didn't know Bucks was a teenager; they didn't know anything about him except that he was selling such rare and seldom-offered snakes as *Atheris ceratophora*, a little horned viper from a small range in Tanzania. Bucks's snakes made it out thanks to an arrangement he'd struck with the Kenyan agricultural ministry. That ministry didn't have the authority to approve snake exports—only the wildlife service did—but American and European customs inspectors didn't necessarily know that.

Bucks, by then a tall, blond young man with a nicely chiseled jaw, slept in an apartment behind a Mombasa nightclub where in the wee hours the bouncers tied petty thieves to chairs and beat them for stealing empty beer bottles. After losing his virginity to a Kenyan woman ten years his senior who refereed boxing matches, he began keeping a computer spreadsheet of the names, ages, and "habitats" of his partners, making sure to list what he paid in exchange for sex—two eggs and a tomato in one case, a can of coke in another. He built and lost three businesses, including a doomed venture to smuggle hippopotamus teeth to Hong Kong. Just as his sex diary was getting epic, Kenyan officials confiscated Bucks's computer and put him on a plane to Switzerland.

Bucks returned to Kenya in short order. He met a barmaid who became pregnant and left with him for Uganda, where they were soon estranged. For a while afterward he moved between that country and Kenya, once again attracting scrutiny for exporting protected snakes: his new specialties were *Bitis worthingtoni* and *Bitis parviocula*, highland adders from Kenya and Ethiopia. On New Year's Eve 2005, Bucks was arrested and thrown into a Kenyan jail. The official charge was something about illegal frogs in one of his terrariums, but Kenya now had a long list of grievances against him, as did Uganda and Ethiopia.

Bucks slept on the concrete floor of his cell for four nights before they let him out. This wouldn't have been so terrible except for the fact that two weeks earlier, Bucks's night bus from Kampala had crashed, breaking several of his vertebrae. But nine of his fellow passengers had died, so Bucks felt relatively lucky.

He was thinking about giving up Africa for good when, that March, he visited his brother in Zurich. When he tried to return, Kenya blocked his reentry.

Bucks managed to return to East Africa a few months later. I met him on the tarmac at Entebbe airport in the fall of 2006, while working on a book about reptile smugglers; it was the second time I'd seen him in three years. His hair was cropped and he wore camouflage pants, and he looked very handsome except for one long, chipped canine that extended from his mouth like a lateral fang. It was the type of thing, he said, that would have caused him enough embarrassment in Switzerland that he wouldn't have ventured out; in Uganda he barely gave it any thought.

It was Bucks's dual citizenship that had helped him slide back in. In previous years, Bucks had used his passports interchangeably—it seemed that it was his E.U. passport that had set off the most recent alarm. Thus, during his sojourn in Switzerland, Bucks had claimed to have lost his American passport, and received a clean one no stamps from the American embassy. Now it bore a fresh Ugandan visa.

At Bucks's side, at the airport, stood a good friend of his whom he called Captain. Captain was three decades older and a foot shorter than Bucks; he looked like the late King Hussein of Jordan, smelled very boozy, and held a plastic flask of Ugandan *waragi*, a local rotgut made from bananas. Captain smiled steadily, like a friendly demon. His teeth were black and decayed, with some shards of incisor bound together with gold.

The two were very close. It was Captain who'd pulled an unconscious Bucks out of the wrecked bus the previous winter, and Captain who, Bucks said, had gotten him started in a new business after the reptile-smuggling flamed out. Kenyan and Ethiopian wildlife officials were still on the lookout for him; if he was to stay in Africa, he needed a new line of work.

Bucks had written me months before about Captain, so that I would know what to expect.

> There is this Captain as we all call him. He is a Pakistani who was trained under Ghadaffi in Libya in the early 1980s. He came to Uganda as a pilot supplying the NRM (National Resistance Movement) which is Pres. Museveni's party with weaponry to oust Milton Obote. Anyhow he has been on death row for conspiracy in the later 80s and managed to escape only by unfortunately needing to kill his warden who was a very friendly young guy who even brought him food from home. He was in for murder 2 years ago again. He was cheated by an Italian in Uganda for like $10,000 and a couple days later the Italian was found on the side of the road with his dick cut off and in his mouth and his eyes pierced out. The police checked his phone and checked the last received calls. Second last was Captain. So prime suspect. The facts are that 3 months later he was out and the Italian officially committed suicide ;-) In Uganda THE SHIT happens. Anyways he is a really good guy...

It was a Monday night, and when we left the airport we headed for a club. "The kind of place with loud music and a lot of whores," Bucks explained on the way.

The club comprised a giant courtyard with a dance floor and a tiki island in the middle. It was the kind of place that attracted foreign men, mostly white and up to no good: A white man in Africa was up to a lot of good or absolutely no good, Bucks said. You were Médecins Sans Frontières or you were a Russian cocaine smuggler with tattoos all over your forearms and your own plane.

"Captain!" a woman yelled when we walked in, beckoning with one long, manicured finger. Her dress was sheer black gauze, her bare breasts visible beneath. Captain grabbed one, then grumbled.

"He's been fucking her for a few weeks," Bucks said, and ordered himself a warm beer, a habit he'd developed over the years.

Behind Bucks stood a girl of about twenty in a tracksuit, eyeing Captain and looking very mad. When the woman in the gauze dress noticed this she squatted, for some reason, and turned up two middle fingers at her challenger. The girl in the tracksuit lunged. Bucks tried, unsuccessfully, to direct the fight away from us. Captain leaned back and laughed, arms wide, half ecstatic from all the attention. Then he hunched over to cough up a lung.

By the time Bucks settled on a girl for himself, a third seething woman had come to the bar to stare Captain down. "I have a baby with him," she said. "And he won't even buy me a beer!"

"Does she really?" Bucks asked Captain.

Captain shrugged. "Maybe," he conceded.

Bucks shook his head. Nobody bought her a beer.

Outside the bar, the earthen pockmarked streets of Kampala were dark— scheduled blackouts limited power to alternate days, since the whole country faced electricity shortages. Only gas stations were consistently lit at night, and grasshoppers swarmed the lamps. Women swung large nets over their heads, catching all that they could. They would tear off the insects' legs, fry them, and sell them in little grease-stained paper bags the next morning. Bucks sometimes ate the bugs for breakfast.

For the last few months he'd been living with the sister of the Ugandan woman he'd had a child with a few years earlier. She was fourteen years old and hadn't been in school for some time. They had a half-furnished apartment on a street clogged with ducks, chickens, and burning garbage. The girl cared for Bucks's daughter there; her other duties included scratching Bucks's head on demand and washing his shirts. In exchange for these services, he fed her.

Bucks's building alone sustained a small village of laundry boys and housemaids, young women who hacked their hair short and wore ill-fitting dresses and had the inscrutable faces of the impossibly poor. In a tiny shack by the door lived a middle-aged security guard and his teenage companion, whom I'd find nursing their baby in the building's dark stairwell. The lock on Bucks's apartment would have befitted a bank.

Inside, the place was devoid of animals save for a scorpion in a tank and two frogs in a jar by the window. Bucks was trying to ease reptiles and amphibians out of his life, but he could not completely do it. His new business, he said, helped keep his mind off them.

The morning after my arrival, Bucks and I collected Captain from an apartment down the hall, where we found him sitting at his dining-room table having his morning waragi. This time it came in a little plastic packet, which he cut with scissors and emptied into a glass. Bucks had under his arm a copy of *National Geographic*. He didn't want to wait for Captain to finish his drink. They were late for a meeting.

Bucks and Captain did not travel far for meetings; this one was at a grocery-cum-outdoor-café a hundred feet from their apartment building. From its aluminum roof came the sound of scurrying animals, and seated in plastic chairs were three men—two in suits, and one in a tracksuit.

Bucks began. "All right," he said. "I'm going to show you the samples." He pulled from his *National Geographic* a sheet of uncut fifty-dollar bills and another sheet of fives. Bucks passed them around. Flies gathered in my glass of juice while the men rubbed and regarded the money. Then Bucks demanded it back.

The currency came from Switzerland and was available in blocks of $1 million, he said, for 40 percent of face value. A long discussion on bank transfers ensued. One of the suits, who spoke with a refined English accent, turned out to be a banker. The other was a lawyer.

I sat next to Captain, who wasn't paying attention. He stared alternately at the waitress and at me. "This is all bullshit," he would slur in my ear, before making a gurgling, semi-obscene outburst to the table. Captain had been deteriorating, mentally and physically, Bucks had told me, and was becoming something of a hindrance.

When the suits departed twenty minutes later—looking happy—Bucks and Captain remained, as did the tracksuit man, a very big and very fit Nigerian. The Nigerian had quietly deferred to Bucks during the meeting, but now took over, speaking in a theatrically deliberate baritone. From mid-morning he drank waragi from those same little plastic packets Captain used. Unlike Captain, he never seemed drunk. People called him the Lion, since he liked to remind them that he ate like a lion, hunting ruthlessly but sharing the kill. His body gave off an aroma detectable for yards. It was his natural smell, but it was sort of like incense, and it suited so lordly a man to have a trailing scent.

Bucks and the Lion conferred briefly about laser-cutting machinery. The machines would have to come from South Africa, the Lion explained, and would cost three hundred thousand dollars. Bucks listened attentively, then countered by insisting that the machines would come from Germany.

It took me a while to figure out that the machines were a fiction, part of the narrative with which they would further their con. It was all a con. Bucks's currency sheets were merely uncut legal tender, readily available as souvenirs from the U.S. Bureau of Engraving and Printing; he was passing them off as splendid counterfeits. The bankers who had been with us a moment ago were the *mugus*, the name that Nigerians called their marks. The Lion specialized in currency scams like this one—baroque, multinational, executed by a team of Europeans and Africans in concert. Some of the scams the Lion ran were already getting worn out, like the black-dollars trick; the UN, according to this story, dyed currency black for security in transit, and the mugu would be persuaded to invest in a chemical that removed the pigment. The Lion still ran the black dollars once in a while, if a mugu seemed ripe for it, but he was eager for newer things.

The Lion was a very good scammer, famous for stringing mugus along. Once a man was invested by even just a few hundred dollars, he said, that man would be overcome by a kind of tunnel vision, and after that he could be picked clean in stages. "It is better for the hungry man never to have tasted food, than to have a little taste," was a Lion maxim. The Lion was full of maxims and pronouncements. He was also, Bucks said, a born-again Christian who did not do business or even answer his phone on Sundays.

Bucks had only recently joined the company, via introduction by Captain— Captain and the Lion had known each other for years. But I could see that the Lion favored Bucks: Bucks had ideas. This real-fake-currency scam was Bucks's. The Lion now talked about taking it to Dubai.

Bucks believed that his luck as a scammer would be as disproportionately good as his luck as a reptile smuggler had been bad. "The reptiles I did out of passion," he said, and passion had its pitfalls. He was firmly on the Kenyan government's radar now, blacklisted among the ivory and rhino-horn and hippo-tooth poachers, which irked him, since he didn't feel he deserved to be classed with such scum. At this point his days mostly consisted of meetings with Captain and fellow members of the Lion's organization.

One afternoon Bucks and Captain met with a middle-aged German who smoked menthol cigarettes constantly without inhaling. "I do it for the pleasure," the German said. He was gently spoken, with eyes that scanned about like a nervous rodent's, and his teeth were almost as bad as Captain's. The German, named Burkhard, was an old friend of Bucks's, a trained electrician who had moved to Kenya for reasons that had more to do with his sexual tastes than anything else. Burkhard liked his girlfriends young, no older than fourteen or fifteen. When he couldn't find work as an electrician, he smuggled drugs from Brazil to Africa and then sometimes on to Europe. For years Burkhard had lived in Mombasa without incident, but Kenya, as Bucks had recently learned, was purging itself of white opportunists. Burkhard had found himself suddenly among the purged.

He'd crossed the Kenya-Uganda border by bicycle, finding employment with Bucks and Captain and the Lion, supplying them with the foreign SIM cards they needed to appear to be calling from Switzerland or Germany, as their scams sometimes required. Burkhard also acted as company bookkeeper, tracking everyone's activities—the clean phone numbers, the dirty phone numbers, who'd been seen with whom—in a logbook. For this he employed German words written with Cyrillic letters. The Cyrillic-German was a code that a junior FBI clerk would have cracked over half a cup of coffee, but Burkhard was quite confident that the Ugandan authorities would be too daunted to bother.

Burkhard's first African girlfriend had died of AIDS. His neighbors accused him of sorcery when he kept her coffin aboveground, right next to his house, for days—he was waiting for her mother to arrive from the countryside before burying her, he told them, but they refused to believe it. Eventually he buried the girlfriend and took up with a series of ever-younger girls, until he was imprisoned in Kenya, Bucks said, for "defilement." Now he was broke and stuck in Uganda, where he slept in a seven-dollar-a-night hotel with no hot water. Impressively, he had already managed to get himself a Ugandan girlfriend, a fifteen-year-old who ate only chicken and chips, the national fast food. She looked, with her matted hair and glum expression, like she'd arrived on a slow bus from a very remote village. She'd had sex with Captain once, but everyone kept that a secret from Burkhard. For now, while Burkhard scratched up some money, it was Bucks who kept her in chicken and chips.

During one of their interminable daily meetings, Burkhard and Bucks sent the girl, along with Bucks's child and her fourteen-year-old aunt, to an amusement park. Once they were gone, Burkhard sifted through his SIM cards and smoked while Bucks wandered over to an Internet café across the street. Captain disappeared into a seamstress's shop. The seamstress, it turned out, was a part-time prostitute. Half an hour later, when Captain sat back down, I noticed that his right shoulder protruded strangely.

Captain explained. Once upon a time, he had flown for a major American carrier, but he'd been dismissed. "We need caring pilots, not daring pilots," his bosses told him. So Captain bought two planes in the Gambia and started a business flying charters. On an early-morning flight from Dakar to a Club Med resort on the coast, Captain crashed. Thirty-one of Captain's passengers, all of them French tourists, were killed. He severed a shoulder muscle in that accident, and had to have a steel plate put in his chest. Sometimes the plate still bothered him, he said.

The story, as Captain told it, was much longer, sadder, and rigorous in a way that suggested he'd perfected it over the years. He emphasized certain mitigating details, such as weather information that had failed to arrive, and a mistake made by the tower. When he was done talking he stared soberly out at the street.

After the crash Captain returned to flying around weapons and killing people, a better job for daring pilots.

I came down with malaria. Captain, the daring pilot and murderer, was the only one who noticed my symptoms—he pitied me enough to take me to the hospital, where I paid five dollars for tests and another five dollars for medicine. Bucks was by then deeply involved in the planning of a con involving the Lion, Burkhard, and a mugu from Dubai, scouted for the Lion by his contacts in London. "You thought you would have to go to Dubai," the Lion told Bucks, "but I have brought Dubai to you."

Since Bucks was preoccupied, and his hospitality had been a little lacking all along anyway, I checked into a lakeside resort to recover.

Lake Victoria had sunk by more than six feet in the previous eight years, turning the lakefront half of the resort—with its boat slips and careful landscaping—into an amorphous swamp. It gave off an overwhelming stench in the sun and burst into a deafening concert of frog calls at night. Bucks showed up there the second morning of my stay, dressed as a "legitimate

Swiss businessman," as he described himself, in an Oxford shirt, khakis, and a wedding ring. His plan was to sell the mugu from Dubai some black dollars. Coincidentally, the mugu had just checked in to my hotel, so the control center of the operation would, it seemed, be my sick room.

The setup was decided: Burkhard would play a courier from Germany, newly arrived with the black dollars. He would check in to the hotel himself as part of the setup, and meet with the mugu first, over drinks at the bar. After Burkhard collected the money, the scam would be turned over to Bucks, the legitimate Swiss businessman and vendor of the magic pigment-removing chemicals. The Lion would supervise things from a distance.

It was 6 p.m. now. The scam would commence in an hour.

The Lion went home for dinner, promising to check in later. I was feeling a little better, so Bucks and I went for a walk. Bucks wanted to hunt some of the reed frogs that were making such a racket in the hotel swamp, and for a while we did so, with a flashlight Bucks had brought along, but by 8 p.m. a terrible nervousness had overcome him. He suddenly felt he could not trust Burkhard. Burkhard was desperate and broke—he would take the mugu's down payment and escape with it, Bucks just knew it. He might be tempted to do the same thing himself, he realized.

"First the German, then the frogs," Bucks said.

Bucks called Burkhard's cell phone, but it was turned off. He cursed himself. Why hadn't he thought to spy on Burkhard at the restaurant? We stopped by the restaurant—no Burkhard, no mugu. Bucks was too scared to call the Lion with his suspicions. The Lion, he was sure, would blame him.

At 10 p.m., Burkhard called back. The mugu had been tired when he arrived, so Burkhard had met with him in his room. The mugu could only manage two thousand dollars for a down payment, it turned out, and that wouldn't be until the next morning.

By then the mugu had disappeared.

The Lion wasn't all that mad about the lost mugu; it happened. Within a week he had produced at least four new marks for his team, including a high-ranking bureaucrat in Uganda's water ministry.

The company converged at an Ethiopian restaurant in Kampala to discuss their progress with the water minister. It was the Lion; Burkhard;

two Somalians; a good-looking Englishman named Andy; Bucks and his little daughter, whose caretaker had briefly run off after Bucks whacked her across the face; and me. I had gotten over my malaria. Captain was home feeling wheezy and sick, which was happening a lot lately.

The Lion was not feeling well, either. He had on the table a little box of medicine called Vermex.

"Worms," he explained.

The scam currently under way was referred to as the "ball-bearings scam." It required three con artists—two white men, to pose as foreign businessmen, and one African. The first white guy poses as the buyer of a special type of ball bearing needed, supposedly, for an oil-exploration project in the Sudan. His local accomplice approaches the mugu and says, "I know a guy who wants these special bearings—he'll pay seventeen hundred dollars apiece for them. I think I know where to get some for three hundred." He introduces the mugu to the buyer. The buyer agrees to buy as many ball bearings as the mugu can get, at seventeen hundred dollars apiece.

The local then puts the mugu in touch with the seller of the bearings, who is played by the other white guy. The bearings, the white seller confirms, are three hundred dollars apiece. He produces them. The mugu-middleman buys as many of the three-hundred-dollar bearings as he can afford, thinking he's about to make a fourteen-hundred-dollar profit on each one. Then the buyer and seller disappear.

This time the buyer was being played by the Englishman, Andy. Burkhard was playing the seller. The "local" was one of the two Somalians at the table, Isaac, who had just come from a meeting with Andy and the mugu. Isaac was protesting that he would have to move now, because the mugu had seen where he lived. The Lion, he was hinting, should give him extra money because of this.

Andy, on the other hand, was exuberant. He'd picked a fight with Isaac at the meeting, he told us, just to make things look less conspiratorial. When he recounted how he'd called the Somalian a "fucking Dinka," the whole table erupted with laughter, the Lion the hardest.

Andy told me he'd never been a criminal until now. In the late 1970s he'd married a Ugandan fashion model, and they'd moved to Kampala from London. Now their kids were about to enter college, and money had become a little tight. He loved this work. "I was an actor in college—a poor one," he said. The con artistry brought back the thrill of the stage.

The Lion returned to his agenda—the state of the mugu. "Can he buy eight but only pay for four today?" he started in. "No, okay. Can he buy six and pay for four?"

While the Lion talked, Burkhard hoisted Bucks's young daughter onto his knee. Bucks gave him a hard look.

Just then a stream of young men in white shirts and black pants entered the restaurant. All but a few were white; a disproportionate number were blond. More followed, dozens of them, all milling around seeking seats.

Mormons! The rest of the table looked mildly annoyed at this invasion, but Bucks was excited. He stood.

"Any of you guys from Lehi?" he called out.

The Lion and his teammates looked up, incredulous. They did not know, and could not bring themselves to believe, that Benjamin Bucks was a Mormon.

Captain died two weeks after I left. The morning it happened, Bucks ran into Captain and Burkhard eating breakfast at the café near their apartment building; all three planned to go elsewhere that afternoon, for another meeting, but Captain said he needed to lie down first, so Bucks ran an errand. When he returned, Captain's roommates told him that Captain had begun to have trouble breathing, and that they had taken him to the hospital. Captain was dead by the time Bucks found him there, his body still warm.

Bucks e-mailed to say how sad he was. *Captain was like a father and a brother to me*, he wrote. He wanted to know if I could look up Captain's crash in Senegal, back in 1992. He had always been curious about it.

I did find a brief report. There was no mention of weather, or any message from the tower. The pilot had simply mistaken the lights of a hotel for the airstrip. Survivors remembered him announcing that they would be landing in five minutes; seconds later, they crashed.

This scenario made more sense to Bucks than Captain's own tortured account. *I pretty much can imagine him aiming for the hotel thinking it's the runway. He used to get really confused on waragi even in Kampala*, Bucks wrote. Club Med's owners were charged with criminal negligence in the affair, but

Captain, somehow, was not.

On the fourth day after his death, Captain's autopsy results came back. Bucks, Burkhard, and the Lion went to look at them, and to collect his body for burial. They thought they knew Captain's real name—it was Sajjad Heider Soorie, he'd told them, or perhaps Sorie—but none of them had been able to find his family. His body was a painful sight, having decomposed rapidly in the unrefrigerated morgue.

The autopsy stated that Captain had died of a massive brain aneurysm. It made no mention of any steel plate in Captain's chest. Bucks asked about it. It didn't exist, he was told.

Captain's neighbors in the building, meanwhile, decided that Bucks had poisoned Captain, and reported as much to the police. Bucks managed to persuade them that he had done no such thing, but the neighbors persisted in their talk.

The police wouldn't leave Bucks alone. Even the Lion, whom the police relied on for bribes, couldn't keep them at bay. Officers kept coming by, often when Bucks wasn't home, alleging that they were continuing to investigate the poisoning rumors. *I can only think that they are some fucking asshole Cops who think they can lock me up claiming that I am a suspect of having murdered Captain in order to extort money from me*, Bucks wrote to me. He wasn't hanging around Kampala to find out.

The Lion sent Bucks to Hong Kong, to embark on a black-dollars scam there; then on to Dubai, and the Philippines. Within months he was back in Switzerland, living at his brother's. His daughter and her aunt were still in Kampala, subsisting on whatever money Bucks could send—an arrangement that would persist indefinitely.

Bucks's older brother, an upright Zurich entrepreneur, was both proud of and embarrassed by Benjamin. He wanted to arrange some sort of job for him in Zurich, but Bucks wasn't having it. Instead he began receiving government subsidies, claiming mental illness. His father and brother had paid into the Swiss social system all their lives, he said—it was only right that a family member should benefit.

Swiss welfare merely covered the basics, though. If he wanted luxuries, he would have to smuggle reptiles.

*   *   *

A year after my visit to Uganda, I flew from Florida to Germany to see Bucks again. He made me fill half my suitcase with boxes of Jell-O, which, like many Mormons, he was addicted to.

It had been a few months since he'd left Africa, and his whole life had changed. He was back in the reptile business, making trips to Mexico and Mauritius. He had a new girlfriend, a seventeen-year-old Mauritian who now lived with Bucks in the government-subsidized apartment his mental illness had earned him. His snaggletooth had been fixed.

I asked him what had happened to his old associates. The Lion was still running scams in Kampala, he said; the irrepressible Burkhard, meanwhile, had recently accompanied Bucks to Mauritius, where Bucks had outfitted him with what looked like an exoskeleton of small, lizard-stuffed PVC pipes. Once Burkhard had thrown some clothes over that, he'd flown to Europe.

A few weeks later, after returning to Africa, Burkhard had received an offer from a group of Nigerians to fly to Europe again with a rather sizable amount of cocaine. Burkhard had elected to divert the shipment and sell it himself.

Unfortunately, aside from the cocaine's intended recipient, the German had no real drug connections in Europe. He had been living near Bucks while he attempted to figure out what to do, and he was wearing out his welcome. Knowing nobody with the wherewithal to buy the shipment, Burkhard had been trying to sell it bit by tiny bit. He was broke again, as usual.

Bucks, meanwhile, had been cultivating his Mexican operation. He was interested in a few species of lizards that sold as cheap pets there—because Mexico banned wildlife exports, the lizards were worth substantial sums overseas. A new friend of Bucks's named Guillermo, a Mexican living in Spain, had arranged for his mother to accrue them on Bucks's behalf. When Bucks flew in, every month or so, he mailed the lizards from Mexico to Switzerland himself, choosing to save his suitcase space for Jell-O.

During Bucks's last Mexican foray, Burkhard had shown up at Bucks's apartment. Bucks had flown his girlfriend's even-younger teenage cousin up from Mauritius to keep her company during his absence; now Burkhard was demanding that Bucks's girlfriend "arrange" for him a sexual encounter with the cousin, and getting increasingly angry when she wouldn't. Bucks's horrified girlfriend had called him in a panic.

Bucks was furious. "He thinks he's still in Africa!" he told me later. It made Bucks wish that Captain were still alive—Captain would have taken care of Burkhard, and with flair.

Instead, when Bucks returned from Mexico, he bought Burkhard a round-trip ticket to Africa for an errand that would have him back in Switzerland within days. Burkhard would not be there long enough for the Nigerians to notice, Bucks assured him. But then, after the German had left, Bucks canceled Burkhard's return flight.

This was still going on at the time of my visit, with Burkhard calling frantically from somewhere in Africa and Bucks looking at his cell phone and laughing. We were en route to Hamm, Germany, to the Terraristika reptile show, where Bucks hadn't shown his face in four years. He had become, in the interim, something of a legend.

Some fifty thousand people had come in for Terraristika—smugglers, pet-store owners, private collectors, industrial-quantity snake breeders, Asian and African exporters. Bucks drove to the fairgrounds in the early-morning darkness, the highway exits clogged with reptile people, his girlfriend beside him. I sat in the back with a duffel bag full of Mexican alligator lizards and Bucks's friend Guillermo, a very boyish twenty-five-year old with a funny, loping gait who smiled a lot and wore a backpack everywhere.

When we arrived in Hamm, the fairground complex was cold and smelled faintly of farm animals; by 10 a.m. it was overheated and stinking of human sweat. Guests stood five or six deep at each tiny vendor table, elbowing for a glimpse of the merchandise. Many species that were highly controlled in the United States, thanks to the Endangered Species Act, could be sold openly in Europe. At lunch, in the fairground's cafeteria, Bucks entertained a pitch from a middle-aged Swiss gentleman in a safari vest, a collector who knew Bucks by reputation and had a smuggling assignment for him. "This dead-butterfly type wants me to go to Australia!" said Bucks, who was having none of it. He had better ideas. He was at the stage now, he said, where he didn't want to smuggle anymore—he wanted someone to do his smuggling for him.

Bucks was grooming Guillermo for that. The young Mexican certainly seemed ripe for such assignments. While Bucks was selling lizards surreptitiously out of a soft-sided cooler, Guillermo paced the tables in the venomous-snake rooms, bug-eyed with excitement. He spoke very little English, but mustered together enough of it to tell me that this day, the day of the Terraristika Hamm reptile show, had been the best day of his entire life.

At the end of it, Bucks paid him two thousand euros. It was Guillermo's share of the proceeds from the Mexican lizards, and Guillermo immediately blew the whole sum. He bought deli cups full of baby cobras, which he stacked in his backpack. He bought big, heavy coffee-table books on rattlesnakes and Asian vipers, some of them in German.

As we headed back toward Zurich on the autobahn, Guillermo ate beef jerky and ogled his snake books in joyful silence.

Guillermo turned out to be smarter than Bucks had thought. Not only did he not become Bucks's mule, but within a year he had cut Bucks out of his lucrative Mexican connection entirely—he was making tens if not hundreds of thousands of dollars mailing his lizards from Mexico to Spain, sometimes with the help of his mother, and Bucks was seeing none of it. Lately Guillermo was wearing a Breitling watch, a thing that looked like a dinner plate on his skinny wrist. He emerged from the next Hamm show thirty thousand dollars richer, though he tended to blow at least half of what he made on snakes for himself.

Bucks had no choice but to let Mexico go. He focused instead on an extraordinary reptile from Oman, *Uromastyx thomasi*, a stout, flat desert lizard with an alert dinosaur face and a fantastic dappling of orange down its back. It was rumored that the sultan of Oman was so personally fond of the colorful *Uromastyx thomasi* that he had imposed the death penalty on anyone caught stealing them. That rumor had apparently been a very clever marketing strategy by the one German who had so far managed to get the species out of Oman, but Bucks, who soon found his own way in, saw fit to perpetuate it.

Soon afterward Bucks reconciled with Burkhard, which surprised me, as did the fact that Burkhard was still alive, after what Bucks had done to him. But that was how people like Bucks and Burkhard were. Burkhard, a veteran smuggler always in need of work, was too useful for Bucks to stay mad at forever, though he would lose his patience when the German made slurping noises at young girls in the grocery store.

Reunited, Burkhard and Bucks made a quick, very successful run to South Africa. Bucks collected armadillo lizards, which curl into tight balls when they are scared, and taped them to Burkhard's legs for the ride home. This worked beautifully, but when they did it again with the fleshier, squirmier *Uromastyx thomasi*, Burkhard was stopped in the Dubai airport. "Had it been Oman, we really would have been fucked," Bucks told me. Instead, when he saw Burkhard being led away by airport police—"so relaxed, smiling and talking to them," Bucks said admiringly—he changed plans and got on another plane.

Burkhard was detained for a week in Dubai, insisting to officials that the lizards had been so plentiful on the roads in Oman that he'd collected them for fear of running them over, and then decided to bring some home for his daughter. As for taping them to his legs, he did that because the air conditioning in the airport was so cold. "All this he thought up on the spot," Bucks told me later. He had wired all the money he could to a sheikh friendly with the Lion once he'd made it back to Switzerland, and after two more days Burkhard was released. The lizards stayed behind.

A few weeks later Bucks returned to Oman alone, rented a car, and drove into the desert to collect *Uromastyx thomasi* himself. He showed up with four of the lizards in time for the next Hamm show, where he unloaded them for ten thousand euros.

Bucks had always been cocky, but he was getting cockier. He had recently discovered Facebook, and was now keeping his religious relatives in Lehi up to date on his Emirates Airlines upgrades, his hot chicks, his rare lizards. His American passport, so fresh and blank in Uganda, had extra pages in it now. The slender, fawn-like young man I'd met years before had become muscular and imposing, and had covered himself with tattoos. On the way to the Hamm shows from Zurich he'd drive 120 miles an hour in a cheap rental Skoda. While there he'd sleep two or three hours a night, and chide anyone who couldn't keep up. He was acting invincible again, which never befits a smuggler.

Two months before another Terraristika show, in 2010, a German man was arrested at the airport in Christchurch, New Zealand, with jeweled geckos sewn into an undergarment. The little green-and-white geckos were released back into the park from which they'd come, with much fanfare; not long afterward the German was sentenced and jailed. A month later, another German—Burkhard—was arrested walking around Christchurch with sixteen of the same creatures in his backpack, arranged in protective plastic pipes. A day after that, the police found Bucks and Guillermo and arrested them, too.

Guillermo and Bucks—who had reconciled in the interim—had arrived first in New Zealand and quickly plucked the geckos off trees. In Christchurch they'd waited for Burkhard, who had lingered in Fiji in an aborted attempt, orchestrated by Bucks and some Austrians, to steal some of that island's famous blue-and-green iguanas. Bucks and Guillermo had sent Burkhard a wire transfer that would allow him to fly to New Zealand and meet them; once he was in country, they communicated by cell phone, but only in Swahili. None of their precautions did any good, because Burkhard, exhausted and overwhelmed by what the police already seemed to know about him, told his interrogators the rest. The New Zealand newspapers identified Bucks as a "Swiss stockbroker" and Guillermo as a "Mexican chef" until it became clear that neither was employed in either capacity, or at all.

Bucks, Burkhard, and Guillermo spent the spring of 2010 in the well-appointed Manawatu prison, where Burkhard played cards with the other lizard-smuggling German, who was finishing out his term. Sometimes the incarcerated Maoris danced at night while everyone else circled around and watched. One tattooed Maori chastised Bucks and Guillermo for stealing lizards that his culture considered sacred; Bucks explained that they weren't the same lizards the Maori was thinking of, and that seemed to satisfy the man. Guillermo stole cigarettes and cookies from the other prisoners, and fell back on his near-total lack of English when confronted. Bucks let him get beat up. The younger man was first to be released, and soon turned up online under a new identity, "Joaquim," with more Mexican lizards for sale.

Burkhard, after his own release, decided that he needed to be back in Uganda. Africa pulled at him, always.

When I talked to Bucks again, just after his return to Europe, he seemed uncharacteristically maudlin and self-pitying, announcing that he would "probably end up working at McDonald's." Feeling mistrustful, he deleted most of his Facebook friends and braced himself for the numbing boredom of the normal-citizen world. This plan, however, did not last long. A month later he was bringing reptiles back from Egypt; within a year he would extend his reach to the Galapagos, Somalia, and Zanzibar, with Interpol having him stopped now and then to check for animals in his bags. They never found any.

At the first Hamm show after his release from prison, Bucks made the rounds in a New Zealand Department of Conservation T-shirt, earning himself laughs and a few high-fives. There, he told me what had happened with the jeweled geckos after he, Guillermo, and Burkhard had been arrested. His Austrian friends had flown to New Zealand and stolen themselves yet another batch, he said, this time with more success. The jeweled geckos that had put him in jail—perhaps even the same individual animals—were here in this fairgrounds, somewhere.

from the introduction to the

UNWRITTEN STORIES OF F. SCOTT FITZGERALD

A PROJECT INCLUDED IN McSWEENEY'S 22

by MICHELLE ORANGE

DURING F. SCOTT Fitzgerald's time at Princeton he became a fan of the so-called Note-Books of Samuel Butler, the Victorian novelist. Such a fan, in fact, that he was inspired to begin a notebook of his own, filling it with musings, sketches, snippets of conversation, and story ideas for future use, all meticulously cataloged and ordered. After his death in 1940, his friend and fellow Princeton alum Edmund Wilson collected these notebooks, along with some of Fitzgerald's letters and non-fiction essays, and in 1945 published them as *The Crack-Up*.

I have gone through numerous phases of Fitzgerald preoccupation in my life, and was in the middle of an intense bout last year when I finally tracked down *The Crack-Up*. I was impressed with his letters, as usual, and his essays about the breakdown that writers of that era seemed especially prone to, but what interested me most were those notebooks. They make up more than a third of the book, and run in alphabetical order. With "Descriptions of Girls" a close second, the section I returned to most was "Ideas": there were thirty-two of them in all, some just three words and others three sentences or more. Fitzgerald's short stories explored far broader terrain than his novels, and the potential of the notebook ideas encompassed almost every genre.

Time ran out before he was able to realize these ideas, and I wondered what the stories would have been like. Then I wondered what they could be like, say, if writers working today abandoned their own notebooks to take on the "to-do" list of F. Scott Fitzgerald.

And so the challenge was put to a group of writers: choose an idea and see what Fitzgerald's seed of inspiration inspires. We can't know whether "Girl and giraffe" was a code to spark a larger vision or something more concrete, but we do know that, of the thirty-two ideas, it was the first choice of nearly a third of the writers who took on the task.

F. SCOTT FITZGERALD'S IDEAS

Play in which revolutionist in big scene—"Kill me," etc.—displays all bourgeois talents hitherto emphasized, paralyzes them with his superiority, and then shoots them.

Lois and the bear hiding in the Yellowstone.

For Play.
Personal charm.
Elsa Maxwell.
Bert.
Hotels.
Pasts—great maturity of characters.
Children—their sex and incomprehension of others.
Serious work and worker involved.
    No more patience with idlers unless *about* them.

Helpmate: Man running for Congress gets hurt in line of other duty and while he's unconscious his wife, on bad advice, plans to run in his stead. She makes a fool of herself. He saves her face.

Family breaks up. It leaves a mark on three children, two of whom ruin themselves keeping a family together and a third who doesn't.

A young woman bill collector undertakes to collect a ruined man's debts. They prove to be moral as well as financial.

✳✳✳✳✳ ✳✳✳✳✳ running away from it all and finding that the new ménage is just the same.

Widely separated family inherit a house and have to live there together.

Fairy who fell for a wax dummy.

Three people caught in a triangle by desperation. Don't resolve it geographically, so it is crystallized and they have to go on indefinitely living that way.

Andrew Fulton, a facile character who can do anything, is married to a girl who can't express herself. She has a growing jealousy of his talents. The night of her musical show for the Junior League comes and is a great failure. He takes hold and saves the piece and can't understand why she hates him for it. She has interested a dealer secretly in her pictures (or designs or sculptures) and plans to make an independent living. But the dealer has only been sold on one specimen. When he sees the rest he shakes his head. Andrew in a few minutes turns out something in putty and the dealer perks up and says, "That's what we want." She is furious.

A Funeral: His own ashes kept blowing in his eyes. Everything was over by six and nothing remained but a small man to mark the spot. There were no flowers requested or proffered. The corpse stirred faintly during the evening but otherwise the scene was one of utter quietude.

Story of a man trying to live down his crazy past and encountering it everywhere.

A tree, finding water, pierces roof and solves a mystery.

Father teaches son to gamble on fixed machine; later the son unconsciously loses his girl on it.

A criminal confesses his crime methods to a reformer, who uses them that same night.

Girl and giraffe.

Marionettes during dinner party meeting and kissing.

Play opens with a man run over.

Play about a whole lot of old people—terrible things happen to them and they don't really care.

The man who killed the idea of tanks in England—his after life.

Play: *The Office*—an orgy after hours during the boom.

A bat chase. Some desperate young people apply for jobs at Camp, knowing nothing about wood lore but pretending, each one.

The Tyrant Who Had To Let His Family Have Their Way For One Day.

The Dancer Who Found She Could Fly.

There was once a moving picture magnate who was shipwrecked on a desert island with nothing but two dozen cans of film.

Angered by a hundred rejection slips, he wrote an extraordinarily good story and sold it privately to twenty different magazines. Within a single fortnight it was thrust twenty times upon the public. The headstone was contributed by the Authors' League.

Driving over the rooftops on a bet.

Girl whose ear is so sensitive she can hear radio. Man gets her out of insane asylum to use her.

Boredom is not an end-product, is comparatively rather an early stage in life and art. You've got to go by or past or through boredom, as through a filter, before the clear product emerges.

A man hates to be a prince, goes to Hollywood and has to play nothing but princes. Or a general—the same.

Girl marries a dissipated man and keeps him in healthy seclusion. She meanwhile grows restless and raises hell on the side.

PEASLEY

by SAM LIPSYTE

(from "The Unwritten Stories of F. Scott Fitzgerald," in Issue 22)

THE MAN WHO Killed the Idea of Tanks in England sipped tea in his parlor somewhere in England. Pale light trickled through the parlor's leaded windows in that trickling manner of English light as pictured by a person who would not know. The Man Who Killed the Idea of Tanks in England was an old man now. He passed his days sipping tea in his parlor and staining his mustache with smoke from his briar pipe. His legs, once strong enough to spur his horse at a Boer sniper's nest or leap a boulder to avoid the whirling blades of a Mahdi charge, lay withered beneath the double layer of his tweed trousers and his dear dead wife's favorite shawl.

It was difficult to believe it was 1983. How old was he? One hundred and twenty-five? He had lived to see so much, from the fall of the Czar to the Austrian paperhanger to the American moon shot, not to mention those urchins with pins through their eyeballs and their so-called music.

The Sex Pistols were the best of the lot.

Still and all, it would be better to die now. It seemed to him during these days of pale, pictured light that the only thing keeping him out of his coffin was an unanswered question: Why had he killed the idea of tanks in England? There had been reasons and he recalled them quite well, thank you. Tanks were clunky. Tanks were slow. Tanks looked silly compared to, for instance, a mounted regiment of the Scots Guard cresting a hill on a crisp autumn day. Yes, he had been present when Mr. Simms demonstrated his "Motor war-car," that boiler on wheels with the revolving Maxim guns. Impressive to a simpleton, perhaps, all those moving parts in the Daimler engine, but at the end of the day…

At the end of the day, what a terrifying phrase that was! The light trickling through the leaded windows was certainly pale. The air, which of course one could not see, was cold. This PiL business was a terrible mistake. Rotten had got it right the first time out. The Man Who Killed the Idea of Tanks in England had got it wrong, stood there that day on the muddy field, snorted in Mr. Simms's expectant face.

"Won't do. Won't do at all."

Was he supposed to be some seer, then? Nostradamus, a Delphic oracle? How could he predict such intractability, the endless trenches, all that wire, the Boche guns shredding so many tender poets? Surely he should be forgiven for killing the idea of tanks in England. Others, after all, had revived the idea, fetched it from conceptual purgatory. A little late to save the poets, perhaps, but there were too many about anyway. Besides, who is to say they would not have roasted inside those infernal kettles?

Then again, with a jump on the job England might have had a whole fleet of armored poet-preserving machines. (Maybe one would have rolled over Corporal Hitler in No Man's Land, saved everyone a considerable inconvenience.) Still, would it have been worth the price of watching Rupert Brooke die of prostate cancer?

It was the American Century, after all, or so the Americans kept proclaiming, and perhaps they had a point. Though not much of a book-fancier, The Man Who Killed the Idea of Tanks in England had always been keen on Yank writers. His favorite was that golden lush from Minnesota. *Gatsby* was tops. A secret part of him had always wished he could write such a bloody good novel. Or better yet, be the subject of some short magazine fiction penned by such a blazing talent. But the story of The Man Who Killed the Idea of Tanks in England would probably never have occurred to Mr.

Fitzgerald. The Man Who Killed the Idea of Tanks in England had spent most of the so-called Jazz Age pretending he had not killed the idea of tanks in England. It was not much of a story, was it? Then punk rock took off.

It could have been that The Man Who Killed the Idea of Tanks in England was actually one hundred and twenty-seven years old. There were no papers pertaining to his birth. A bastard, he was, born in a hedgerow to a chambermaid. His father the fake earl had been kind enough to pay for his schooling. The army seemed a natural choice. Charge some Boers, leap a Sudanese boulder, you might dodge certain questions of lineage. You might rise through the ranks until you have won enough medals to be asked your opinion of the idea of tanks in England.

Be ready, by God.

Now The Man Who Killed the Idea of Tanks in England heard the sound of an engine revving out past the garden, peered out the parlor window. It was that damned Peasley, the groundskeeper, on his new contraption, the mechanized lawnmower. Peasley had eaten up a good deal of the grounds budget with that pretty mechanical toy, which is what Kitchner dubbed the Simms car, come to think of it.

So it was not only The Man Who Killed the Idea of Tanks in England who killed the idea of tanks in England! Kitchner was a greater order of dolt than Peasley, and that was saying something! The Man Who Killed the Idea of Tanks in England could remember when men cut grass with whirling blades on the ends of sticks. What did they call those again? What did they call those sticks with blades on the ends at the end of the day again? Now here came Peasley riding high up on his little mower like a modish tank general, some kind of arrogant Total War twit.

Confound him.

The Man Who Killed the Idea of Tanks in England let his dear dead wife's shawl slip from his lap. He hobbled out to the garden gate. Peasley chugged by on his mower, waved.

"Won't do!" called The Man Who Killed the Idea of Tanks in England. "Won't do at all!"

He noticed Peasley wore some odd plastic muffs on his ears, probably had not heard him.

"Hello there!" he called, moved past the gate and onto the lawn. Peasley rounded a tree, headed straight away at The Man Who Killed the Idea of

Tanks in England. Could Peasley be driving with his eyes shut? The idiot looked lost in reverie. The Man Who Killed the Idea of Tanks in England stood motionless. His old bones, his rotted legs, felt staked to the earth. What he would not now give for Hal, his old Boer War war mount. Not a kingdom, though. Too late for that.

"Peasley! Peasley!"

One could not say his life flashed before his eyes. His life had been too long. The lawnmower was too slow, and clunky. He saw things, though, toys from his boyhood, tin lancers and hussars and cuirassiers, the gilt-edged pages of his beloved adventure books. He saw the nibs of examination pens, and the body of the girl who would become the woman who would become his wife, in moonlight. He saw himself and others in uniform, on parade, on maneuvers, and, finally, gut shot on pallets, gurneys. He saw Veldt grass and Sudanese sand and trench mud drying on his boots. He saw his mother in her maid's kit and he saw his father, far off in a sun-buzzed meadow, a quail gun in the crook of his arm. He saw the garish pink and green sleeve of *Never Mind the Bollocks*, his own palsied hand pawing at the precious vinyl inside.

It had been too bloody long, this life, everything hinging on one decision made when he was just a youngish fool with too many ribbons, too much fringe.

"Won't do," said The Man Who Killed the Idea of Tanks in England, and fell to his ruined knees. Peasley, eyes shut, recollecting a childhood fishing trip he had taken with his maternal uncle, a German who had helped develop mustard gas for the Kaiser, drove down upon The Man Who Killed the Idea of Tanks in England, the blades beneath the mower's carriage whirling like—that's it—scythes.

GIRL AND GIRAFFE

by LYDIA MILLET

(from "The Unwritten Stories of F. Scott Fitzgerald," in Issue 22)

G IRL SPENT THE first nine months of her life as a ward of one
Ronald Ryves, a sergeant in the Scots Guards. This was the early
1960s in Kenya, where the Second Battalion of the Scots Guards
was stationed to fight a mutiny in Dar-es-Salaam. It was the tail end of the
British empire in East Africa.

A man who had adopted Kenya as his home, name of George Adamson,
wrote about Girl in his autobiography. Girl was one of his success stories,
whereas her brother, Boy, was an extravagant failure; yet Boy was the one
that Adamson deeply loved.

Adamson lived a long life, long and rough and mostly in a large tent in
the bush, a tent with a thatch roof and dirt floor, full of liquor and books.
He smoked a pipe with a long stem; he sported a white goatee and went
around bare-chested in khaki shorts, a small, fit man, deeply tanned. He was
murdered in his eighty-third year by Somali lion poachers.

Joy Adamson, his wife and the famous author of *Born Free*, had been stabbed to death a few years before. She bled out alone, on the road where she fell.

They were somewhat estranged by the time of Joy's death. They had cats instead of children—George had raised scores of lions while Joy had moved on from lions to cheetahs to leopards—and lions and leopards could not cohabit, so George and Joy also lived apart. They maintained contact, but they were hundreds of miles distant.

When Girl and Boy were nine months old the Scots Guards brought them to the plains beneath Mount Kenya, to a farm where a British company was filming *Born Free*. Along with twenty-two other lions, Girl and Boy had roles in the movie. Afterward most of the lions were sent to zoos, where they would live out their lives in narrow spaces. But Girl and Boy were given to Adamson, and he took them to a place named Meru, where he made a camp. This was red-earth country, with reticulated giraffes browsing among the acacia and thornbush. Zebras roamed in families and the odd solitary rhino passed through the brush; there were ostriches and an aged elephant named Rudkin, who plundered tomatoes.

Girl had been fed all her life, but she took readily to the hunt. Her first kill was a jeering baboon, her second an eland with a broken leg, her third a baby zebra. From there she took down a full-grown cow eland and was soon accomplished. Meanwhile Boy did not feel moved to kill for himself; he merely feasted off the animals she brought down.

So Girl became a wild lion, but Boy did not. Boy remained close to Adamson all his life, often in camp, between two worlds. Though he made forays to the wild he did not vanish into it: and on one occasion, hanging around camp while people were visiting, he stuck his head into a jeep and bit the arm of a seven-year-old boy. This boy was the son of the local park warden; soon an order came down for Boy's execution.

But before Adamson could carry out the shooting—he was busy protesting to bureaucrats, who declined to listen—Boy was found under a bush with a porcupine quill through one eye and a broken leg. If not euthanized on the spot he would have to be moved; so Adamson sat on the ground beside him until the veterinarian could fly in, by turns sleeping, drinking whiskey, and brandishing his rifle.

After a surgery in camp, Adamson prepared for an airlift. The two of them would live on a private property of Joy's while Adamson nursed Boy back to health. And curiously, though Girl had barely seen her brother for a year, she emerged suddenly from the bush as they were loading him into Adamson's pickup to go to the airstrip. She jumped onto the back of the truck, where Boy lay sedated and wrapped in a blanket. No one was able to entice her away, so they began the drive to the airstrip with Girl along too.

But on the way she spotted a young giraffe by the road and was distracted. She jumped off the pickup. She had become a wild lion; wild lions are hungry.

This was the last time Adamson saw Girl and the last time she saw any of them. Afterward, when Adamson returned to Meru, he would search for her fruitlessly.

Boy grew irritable in temperament after the surgery, due to the steel rod in his leg; and who among us might not become cantankerous? Two years after he and Girl were parted he suddenly attacked a man named Stanley who had tended him with gentle care through illness and injury. Adamson heard a scream and went running with his rifle to find that Boy had bitten deep into Stanley's shoulder; he turned and shot his beloved lion through the heart and then tended to his friend, who bled to death from a severed jugular inside ten minutes.

In Adamson's autobiography the end of Boy is well-described while the end of Girl, who lived out her days in the wild, is invisible. Happy endings often are.

But there is one more report of Girl outside Adamson's published writings. It was made by a man who claimed to have visited Adamson in his camp the year before his murder, one Stefan Juncker, based in Tübingen, Germany. Juncker said he had made a pilgrimage to see Adamson at Kora, where he was living with his final lions. Because Adamson constantly welcomed guests to his camp such a visit would not have been uncommon.

The two men sat beside a fire one night and Adamson—in his cups, which the German implied was not rare—became melancholy. He remembered a time when he had not been alone, before his wife and his brother had died. He remembered his old companions, sitting there at the base of the hills among the boulders and the thornbush; he remembered all his lions, his women and men.

His brother Terence, who had lived with him at Kora, had in his dotage discovered that he had what Adamson called "a talent for divining." By wielding a swinging pendulum over a map he could determine the location of lost or wanted things. This included water, missing persons, and lions, which he correctly located about sixty percent of the time. Adamson was skeptical in theory, not being much given to magical thinking, but had to admit that his brother's method led him to his lions faster than spoor- or radio-based tracking. It was inexplicable, he said, but there it was.

Since Terence had died of an embolism two years before, he no longer had a diviner.

At this point Adamson gestured toward a flower bush a few feet away. That was where Terence lay now, he said. And there, he said, turning, over there by a tree was Boy's grave; he had buried his dear lion himself, though others had dug up the corpse later to have proof he was dead. He had been forced to rebury him several times.

The German was disturbed. He did not like the fact that Adamson had laid his brother to rest a stone's throw from a killer.

There was much that science had not yet understood, went on Adamson, about the minds of lions and men and how they might meet. Divining was one example—had the lions somehow told Terence where they could be found?—but he had also known others. In fact, he said, he would tell of an odd event he had once witnessed. Over the years he had thought of it now and then, he said; and at this point a warm, low wind sprang up from the Tana River and blew out the embers of their campfire, sinking them into darkness.

He had thought of it over the years, he repeated, but he had mentioned it to no one. He would tell it, if the German could keep a secret.

Of course, said the German.

It was when he was first taking Girl out to hunt. This was in Meru, he said, in the mid-1960s. Of course now, more than twenty years later, Girl would have to be long dead.

All your stories end with someone dead, said the German.

All *my* stories? asked Adamson.

He and Girl had been walking through the forest together and had emerged into a clearing, where they surprised a herd of giraffes browsing. The herd quickly took off, galloping away before Adamson even had a chance to count them, but they left behind a gangly foal without the sense to run. Perfect prey. It should fall easily. It stood stupidly, blinking, backed up against a large tree.

Girl charged, with Adamson standing by proudly. She had made several kills in the preceding days and he considered her a prodigy.

But abruptly she stopped, pulling up short. Her ears were flat; then they pricked. She and the foal seemed to be studying each other. Adamson was shocked, bordering on indignant, but he remained in the copse. Possibly she sensed something wrong with the giraffe, he thought; or possibly there were other predators behind it, competition in the form of a clan of hyenas he could not see.

As he waited Girl stood unmoving, crouched a few feet from her quarry. Then the giraffe reached up slowly and mouthed a branch with its mobile, rubbery lips. It chewed.

Adamson was flabbergasted. Possibly the animal recognized his lion as a neophyte hunter: but how could it? Giraffes were not insightful; they had the dullness of most placid grazers. Either way, the animal should be bolting. Girl would be on him in a second, fast as light.

He could only see Girl from the rear; her tail twitched, her shoulders hunched. He could not see her face, which frustrated him, he told the German, for a lion's face is extraordinary in its capacity for expression. What was she waiting for?

Then again, he thought as he watched the stillness between them and held his own breath, the foal was going nowhere. Maybe Girl was hypnotized by the future: maybe she saw the arc of her own leap, was already feeling the exhilaration of flight and the impact, the smell and weight of the foal as it crumpled beneath her, as she dragged and wrestled and tore it down, worried the tough hide and sweet flesh. Possibly she was waiting, pent up and ready.

But no. Girl straightened; she relaxed. She sniffed around the foal's long legs. She jumped onto a dry log. She yawned.

And the giraffe kept eating, munching and grunting softly. It shifted on its feet; it stooped down, head dipping toward Girl and up again to the branches, where it tore and chewed, tore and chewed with a complacent singularity of purpose.

There was sun on the log, glancing across the nape of the lion's neck so that her face was illuminated, the rest of her in shadow. She licked a paw and lay down.

Adamson, squatting in the bushes, stayed put. His body was still but his mind worked hard, puzzling. He considered giraffes. Terence had a weakness for elephants; himself, he was strictly a lion man. But giraffes, though morphological freaks, had never interested either of them. Artiodactyla, for one thing: the order of camel, swine and bovids. Not suited for long-term relationships. Strictly for riding, eating, or milking, really. He pitied them, but not much. There were no refrigerators in nature; meat and milk had to keep themselves fresh.

After years in the bush he saw all animals as predators or prey. The tourists that came through his camp wanting to pet the lions? Now those were strictly prey, he mused.

Then, recalled to the present after a pause: No offense.

None taken, said the German heartily.

In fact, the German felt a prickle of annoyance. The flight in, on a single-engine Cessna in jolting turbulence, had made him squeeze his eyes shut and pray silently to a God in whom he did not believe. For this?

An old alcoholic, he thought angrily, with poor hygiene: that was all. He had been eight years of age when he saw *Born Free*, living in a claustrophobic bourgeois household in Stuttgart. His father was fat as blood sausage and his mother used a bottle of hairspray a week. He thought Adamson and his beautiful wife were like Tarzan and Jane.

But Kirsten had disapproved of this trip and she was probably right: nothing more than a midlife crisis.

The smoke from Adamson's pipe was spicy. The German was disgusted by smoking—frankly, any man fool enough to do it deserved what he got—but he had to admit the pipe smelled far better than cigarettes.

You were saying, the German reminded him. Girl and giraffe?

Yes, said Adamson softly.

The old man was frail, thought the German, with the ranginess of a hungry dog; his muscles had no flesh between them. He had nothing to spare.

So Girl had lain there on the log in the sun, dozing while the giraffe moved from tree to tree. The sun crossed the sky and clouds massed, casting a leaden grayness over the low hills. Adamson stayed seated in the scrub, drank from a flask, and puffed on his pipe. There was a silver elegance to the day, which was unusually mild and breezy; he listened to the wind rattle the branches and whisper the dry grass. Birds alit in the trees and moved off—he noticed mostly black-headed weavers and mourning doves—and Girl and the giraffe ignored them. The shadows grew longer; the sun was sinking. Adamson began to feel impatient, pulled back to camp. He had things he should do before dark.

It was almost dusk when the giraffe moved. It ambled over and bent its head to Girl again, who stirred.

While it is not true, said Adamson solemnly to the German, that giraffes never lie down, as legend has it, it *is* true that they do so rarely and for a very short time. And never, he said, in his experience, did they lie down at the feet of their predators.

And yet this was what the foal did.

It had been a good day, said Adamson, and raised his glass.

As he talked, the German had built up the fire again and now he saw the flames reflecting off amber. He was regretting his choice. It had been this or Mallorca, where his wife was now tanning.

The foal lay down deliberately, said Adamson, right beside the dry log. It was deliberate.

And Girl stretched her legs, as a cat will do, luxurious and long, all four straight out at their fullest reach like table legs. She stretched and rose, jumped languidly off the log, and paused. Then she leaned down over the foal and sank in her teeth.

The movement, said Adamson, was gentle. The foal barely struggled; its legs jerked reflexively but soon it was still.

Later, he said, he almost believed he had dreamed the episode. But came to believe, over the years, that a call and answer had passed between Girl and the giraffe: the foal had asked for and been granted reprieve. She had given him a whole afternoon in which to feel the thorny branches and leaves in his mouth, the sun and shade cross his neck, his heavy lashes blink in the air.

It was a free afternoon, because all afternoon the foal had been free of the past and free of the future. Completely free.

It was almost, said Adamson, as though the possibilities of the world had streamed through Girl and the giraffe: and he, a hunched-over primate in the bushes, had been the dumb one, with his insistent frustration at that which he could not easily fathom, his restless, churning efforts to achieve knowledge. Being a primate he watched; being a primate he was separate forever. The two of them opened up beyond all he knew of their natures, suspended: they were fluid in time and space, and between them flowed the utter acceptance of both of their deaths.

They had been together, said Adamson, closer than he had ever been to anyone. They had given; they had given; they had shimmered with spirit.

Spirits, thought the German, glancing at the luminous dial of his watch: yes indeed. Bushmill's, J&B, Ballantine, Cutty Sark, and Glenlivet on special occasions.

This was in Kenya in the late 1980s, decades after the Mau Mau rebellion brought the deaths of two hundred whites and twenty thousand blacks. A new homespun corruption had replaced the old foreign repression; fewer and fewer lions roamed the grasslands of East Africa, and the British were long gone.

STAY WHERE YOU ARE

by DEB OLIN UNFERTH

(fiction from Issue 41)

A MAN IN FATIGUES stepped out of the brush and onto the gravel. He must have come off a small path of some sort because no branches snapped when he came out. He turned and pointed a machine gun at them—maybe more like *toward* them. He called out something neither of them understood.

"Now what," said Jane. "What's this soldier want?"

Max lifted a hand in greeting. "Hullo, we're waiting for the bus," he called.

The man in fatigues walked over and said some sentences in Spanish. He kept the gun casually pointed their way. He was young. One of his boots flapped on the ground.

"Maybe it's about the chairs," Jane suggested. Max had borrowed the chairs from the coffee farm off the road. She had told him not to, because there might not be time to run them back when the bus came, but Max had done it anyway.

"You can take the chairs back," Jane said to the gunman now. She stood and pointed at her chair.

The gunman didn't seem interested in the chairs. He moved the gun from side to side, explaining. He wore an army cap pulled low over his eyes.

"We're waiting for the bus," Max said. "The Tuesday bus?" He sighed. "They give these kids these weapons to go out and wave around like hands." He slapped his thighs and got to his feet. He was at least a full head taller than the gunman.

The gunman waited, listening. He spoke again, louder this time, and gestured with the gun toward the place in the trees he'd exited from.

"You want us to go with you? Take us to the station, is that it?" Max turned to Jane. "Could be there's a hurricane coming through. An evacuation?"

"Hummm," said Jane. She studied the sky for a storm. "Too bad he doesn't speak English."

Max frowned.

They'd argued the night before because she wanted to stop in the next country and take a language. Six weeks. Spanish school. Learn something. Hordes of people were doing it and it looked like fun. But Max detested school—being rooted to the ground, potted. He'd been to fifty-eight countries and never learned a language other than his own. He was no good at language. He never had a problem making himself understood. He could pantomime. "Besides, everybody speaks English these days," he'd said.

So they would accompany the gunman. But now what were they supposed to do with their packs? Max and Jane stood over the packs, deciding. The gunman waited. If they weren't going to be long, they could just leave the packs here. No one came down this road. Max and Jane had been walking up and down it for days and had seen hardly a soul. Even if someone did come along, Max didn't think they'd make off with the packs. On the other hand, Jane said, the two of them might be kept awhile at the station.

What damn luck.

The gunman interrupted them irritably.

Max and Jane looked up. "We'll probably miss the bus, you understand,"

Max said. "The Tuesday bus?"

They got their packs on.

The three of them entered the rainforest in the same spot the gunman had come out. Indeed it was a very small footpath, so small it could overgrow itself in days. It must have been well used despite its thinness. Max, then Jane, stepped through the trees, the gunman behind. Max and Jane walked easily, without the usual timidity of the tourist. Wet leaves hit their faces and arms. The rainforest hung in loops around them.

In fact they'd been stopped by the authorities before, many times— mostly in order to be herded back onto the tourist tracks or pumped clean of any cash they were carrying, and once in Morocco to make Jane put on more clothes (she'd been wearing a [really rather modest] bathing suit). Never been delayed more than a few hours but it would be unfortunate to miss the bus, Max thought. On the other hand these military men might arrange a ride back to town for them, might even bring them themselves in a jeep. You never knew. Might as well make the best of it. Was Jane listening to all these species of bird?

"How close are we to the river?" Max called back to the gunman, who didn't respond. "We saw a waterfall yesterday that couldn't be beat. I say, my dear, was that a waterfall?"

"All right," she said. "Okay."

"Would you believe," Max called back to the gunman, "I have a wife who complains about being on a tropical vacation? Other women say, 'You never take me anywhere.'"

"Vacation?" said Jane. "Who takes a vacation for eighteen years?"

She'd been sixteen when they met, an English schoolgirl. He liked to say he stole her from her father and it wasn't a big stretch. He'd been working on an oil rig twenty miles out on the ocean. Three-month shifts. All men. The boss, her father, had brought her on board. What sort of a dull-headed move was that, to bring your sixteen-year-old daughter out to a place like that?

Oil rig: square island, salt and steel, concrete, fish, everything the color of water.

Max had been thirty-four at the time, married with a daughter in Sussex. He was thirty-six and divorced when he took Jane away. The first place they'd gone was Africa, where they'd stayed for years, far from anything she'd ever known, Max the only familiar object for thousands of miles, anyone else days away. It was like being the last two people on Earth. It was like you yourself had sent everyone off, except for the man with you—the only man left on Earth. It was like being in one of those movies about that, about you being the only ones who had ever done this, your great idea, and his. At first.

But then the movie keeps going, five years, eight years, twelve. Eventually you want a movie like that to be over, you want to see a different movie, change the channel, but it keeps going. Then one day fifteen, sixteen years in, you're suddenly sick of it—not horrified, not scared—just annoyed and sick to death of it, sick of yourself, sick of him. It was like waking up in someone else's bed and knowing just how you'd gotten there.

They'd been going like this for eighteen years, half her life, never stopping.

The gunman prodded Jane with the gun when she stopped behind Max. "Ow," she said. "Max, he just stabbed me with that monstrous weapon!"

The gunman said something angrily in Spanish.

"Hey, watch where you direct that thing, kiddo," Max said, and moved Jane, rubbing her elbow, around him. "You go ahead of me."

They all continued walking.

Of course they stop, Max would counter. They ran out of money every few years. Remember she'd been a postal lady in New Zealand? Carried sacks of mail. And she'd swabbed decks on a ship like a man, all the way across the Indian Ocean. Spirited girl, always had been. One of the first things he'd liked about her.

And how about the time they became citizens of New Zealand? he'd say. You have to hold still for an honor like that. Nobody just throws citizenship papers into the airplane after you. Remember they got to meet the president on New Year's Day? They got to shake hands with the president.

His favorite defense. How about the time in New Zealand?

Yes, but they left the next day! The *very day* after they received their citizenship, they left, Jane would say. And now they didn't even own anything other than the belongings in their packs and it might be nice to.

Didn't own! Max said. They still had some carpets in New Zealand, remember? They'd gotten them in India and brought them along, left them with the neighbors in Wellington. They could go back and get those carpets anytime they liked. Is that what she wanted? Carpets?

She didn't want carpets.

Citizens of New Zealand, he'd say. Hands in pants. Looking around. As a matter of fact, this is a nice spot. Maybe they could be citizens here too.

They were deep in the rainforest now, dense damp foliage, vines like arms crossing in front of them, sun blocked by a canopy of leaf-knotted trees meters overhead. Bugs whipped past them, loud as motors, biting their hands and getting caught in their sweaty hair, sticking to an eye. Jane brushed them aside.

God she hated this now. She could almost imagine another story for herself but she had no faith in it. No faith in herself. She couldn't really imagine what that other story might be. It had been seven years since she'd seen her father. Nine since she'd seen her sister. Imagine going nine years without seeing your sister.

Max thought she didn't even like her family. He certainly didn't. But why not invite them out if she missed them so much? Meet up in Peru for some hiking. Like his daughter had done that one time. That had been good fun.

Was he referring to the time his daughter met them in Africa and got so sick she nearly died, and so afraid she flew home halfway through the trip? The time his own daughter had to fly six thousand miles and risk death to see her dad?

She used to not like her family.

Yes, well, she used to be a teenager.

*　　*　　*

The three of them rounded a corner, stepped into a clearing, a gathering of huts. "Ah, here we are," said Max. He stopped and surveyed the patch of border trees, the tents strung between the clotheslines, the overturned crates. "Not much of a station. What is this, an outpost camp?"

The three walkers rounded the corner, stepped into the clearing. The gunman looked around and stopped.

He was thinking (in Spanish): Where the fuck did they go? Fuck.

He kept his gun trained on the Americans.

The bus comes on Tuesday, Max thought. All the people at the coffee farm had told them that. Mimed it. Mimed Tuesday.

Jane was thinking: Shit.

The gunman was thinking: Shit. They'd gone off without him, the bastards. What, they'd woken up, seen he was gone, and left? Or, worse, had they not even noticed he was gone and just marched off without him? And here he'd been so crafty, bringing back two Americans, surprise, surprise! Now who's the champion? But no one was here.

He took out his cell phone.

He told the Americans to shut up.

And another thing was America. The argument always went like this: Max despised first-world countries, but Jane wanted to go. Might be fun to ride a tandem bike across America. Picnic basket on the back.

Oh no, Max always said. They'd been to America once already and they weren't going back. America had been exactly as they'd expected, exactly as they'd always heard. First thing that happens, they buy a cup of tea and the lady says, "Have a nice day!" Just like an American on the television. He and Jane got on a bus and a fight broke out between a young man and the driver. The two of them screaming at each other until the man got off the bus, cursing. Violent country. He's surprised they didn't get killed.

Jane: They spent one day in America on their way to Mexico. Nineteen hours.

Max: And it was just as they thought it'd be. No reason to go back.

Jane thought, Shit. That is, she was thinking about shit. She couldn't see a camp like this one—strung canvas, fire pit, encroaching foliage—without the image coming into her mind of a camp they'd stayed in at the edge of the Sahara. The latrine had filled to the top and then run over. People had to stand on the seat to shit into the pile. Soon the latrine was so full of shit, you just shat nearby it. It became a sort of "latrine area," and you tried to get your shit in the vicinity of it on the ground there without getting too close yourself and stepping in it and tracking it back into the camp. Then, of course, the rains came and drained all that shit right into the camp. It all came floating in, getting into everything. The tents, the mosquito nets, the clotheslines. It got onto hands and smeared onto hair.

The gunman now very decidedly had the gun pointed at them, which was unfriendly, for one, and dangerous, but Max and Jane were both determined not to make a thing of it. It wasn't as though they'd never had a gun pointed at them before, and to complain like an American usually made things worse.

"He's asking to see our passports," Max said. "Here you go, then."

The gunman took the passports. He noted they were not blue and didn't want to think about that. He put them in his pocket and paced. His boot flapped. Too big. He almost tripped. He'd been given a fucking mismatched set of shoes. He told the Americans to stop looking at him and go sit by the pit. He had to make some calls.

The gunman said something in Spanish. Max and Jane didn't understand, but they understood the waving gun and went where the gunman said.

*　　*　　*

Yes, they'd been captured before. In the late nineties, by a tribe. In order to pass through certain territories you had to ask permission of the head of the tribe. Usually it was no trouble. But one time a tribe took the opportunity to lock them up. Jane had been certain it was the end. But Max had charmed them all, chattered away in English—which none of them understood. The tribe leader had offered Max a dark mixture, the kind of thing that could kill a man not used to it, but Max had drunk it down and asked for more, and by the end of the night they were all singing songs.

They squatted in the dirt with their packs on. A line of ants was re-forming itself around them. The gunman poked at the tents with the gun, making agitated sounds into his cell phone.

Jane slapped the bugs. The ground was burnt moss and forest and soot. The sun coming on full by now, breaking into the clearing. Sweat was coming down their faces and arms. They took off their packs.

The gunman came back over to them with something else in his hand.

The gunman was thinking they had to be at the main camp by now. Were they not answering on purpose? He didn't have a second piece of rope, but in his experience, Americans were an obedient bunch, as long as you had a gun. They'd just stare, or weep—though they always talked, you couldn't shut them up. He couldn't herd these two fourteen kilometers, he knew. When were those assholes coming back?

Yes, Max could talk all day to people who didn't understand him, but with tourists who spoke English, he did just shut up. He let her take over, had never been much for small talk. He'd nod out on the stair or watch the light play on the plaza tile though the trees—who knew what he was thinking—while she talked to the tourists about wristwatches that stopped in the tropical air, places to use the bathroom. All travelers love to talk about shit and bugs. He didn't need anyone but her.

Last month in Nicaragua, they'd met two sisters who had been too scared of getting robbed to do anything but hide in their room, mosquito nets lowered around them. Max and Jane had brought the sisters along with them for a few days, showed them the ropes. They'd been in awe of Max—in the old way. (People used to be so impressed with Max.) Last fun he and Jane had had.

What she herself had been in awe of at one time, she couldn't quite reach anymore when she looked at him. She'd been thinking for two years now about leaving him.

But what was left for him without her? Middle age giving way to old age and the difficulties of that, disenfranchised family, cemented-in views that were now outdated, no friends, no money, no hobbies that one could do while sitting still, no abilities of any kind other than not speaking fifty-eight languages, a keen knack for spotting animals no one else could see in the trees, a knack for drinking the locals' water anywhere in the world (this last was no cheap trick, you had to be determined, unafraid of illness or death, although in most places consuming water wasn't considered a special skill, you don't get a paycheck for being thirsty).

All either of them had was this thing they'd created, this two-ness between them. If she left (or made *him* leave, rather—there could be no question of her walking off and leaving him somewhere, unimaginable, he, the walking man), what was left for him?

Did he think about that? What did he think about? All these years with him and she still didn't know.

For her, sure, there was enough. She was still young enough to create more for herself, to make it someplace, find someone. An adequate life, a job in retail, maybe, or being a company rep or an exec or something. Maybe she'd find that life exotic after the one she'd led. Or nicely quaint. So far she hadn't done it, because of what it could become in the long run—what they'd always feared, what they'd always been running from, the drab, the dull, the stupid, and then death. She'd always said she could never go in for a regular job, house, kids, vacation a few weeks a year. Avoidance of this had been their mainstay, their mythology. But now this option seemed inviting compared to what Max would become by himself, alone, aging. Might as well be dead.

So that's how Jane thought of him, and Max, in a place deep inside himself, knew it. And knew, too, that she might be right. But he also knew it didn't matter, for he had already done the one great thing he would do (not travel all over the world, anyone could do that—didn't even need the resources, just the desire): he'd loved this one woman for eighteen years.

The gunman held the piece of rope in his hands. He put down his gun and began to forcibly tie Max's hands together behind him.

"Now is this really necessary, mate?"

Jane looked on, uncertain. All right, no, they'd never had their hands tied before, but that didn't mean they should get excited, right? She couldn't stop him somehow, could she? How? Grab the gun? "I wonder if this is a stitch-up," Jane said.

Max was nodding. "They've mistaken us for foreign intruders. These fellows are trained to think that anyone near the mountains is trying to take over their government."

They were sitting facing each other by the fire pit. The gunman was sulking by the clotheslines with his phone. Jane was parched.

"You know," Max said, "I don't think this is a military man. I believe what we have here is an insurgent. A rebel of some kind."

They both looked at the gunman.

"I'm sure I'm right about this," he said. "Look at the uniform. It's not a proper military uniform. The top and bottom don't match."

"That doesn't mean anything. Who can tell who wears what?" Jane said.

Max considered. "What war do they have going on here? Do they have one?"

"I thought it was over ages ago."

"Insurrections, maybe? Mountain revolts?"

"Well, if we read the paper," said Jane, smartly. "If we spoke Spanish."

She couldn't resist.

"Hey," Max called to the gunman, "are you a revolutionary or a soldier? We can't tell."

The gunman didn't know he was being spoken to.

"Some new revolution," Max said, looking back from the gunman.

"No doubt," Jane said. One they hadn't heard of, since they didn't read the papers, since they didn't speak the language, since they didn't care what was going on around them other than what they could see before them. Only way to know a country is just to be in it, he'd always said. Walk the land. Be among the people. The political stuff was so boring. It changed every month.

"This is the stupidest thing that's ever happened to us," she said.

"Get off," Max said. They'd been through worse, Max thought. This wasn't going to be something they always talked about. Besides, what was this—a situation? Were they being kidnapped? If so, Max wondered whom this guy thought they were going to call for money. No one in *Max's* family was going to donate to the cause. And these revolutionaries or whoever they were better have someone who spoke a little English, because if you thought *Max* was bad at languages, he doubted his family believed other languages *existed*.

Things had been better in Africa, Max was thinking. Things had been better in New Zealand. Only the Americas. The Americas got them all right. Every time.

"Cállate," the gunman called to the American, who blinked at him and stopped talking for a moment but then went on talking. The gunman went over and punched the American in the face and came back.

As for the gunman, we may wonder who he was and where he came from. He was much like a regular gunman for the insurgents: he'd been born not ten kilometers from this spot and loved it here, despite the rain, the poverty, the fighting. He'd grown up doing gunman activities and wanting to do them. He'd learned how to shoot at age nine (he was now nineteen), he knew people who'd died by bullet, he'd shot people he hadn't known, he loved the cool nights of the dry season, he'd had his share of fistfights and knife fights and preferred fists because knives were too psychological and fistfights ended fast. He believed in no land tariffs. He believed in school for kids (he himself had gone three years). He'd buried his mother and two brothers.

He was different from a regular gunman in that he'd been to the States once, had hated it, and had not wanted to stay. He preferred to stay here, where he had the hope of one day being a leader, though he knew those who knew him would say there was little chance of that: he lacked charisma, they would say. And maybe he was different in that he didn't hate all Americans, though he wished those two over there weren't there.

One other fact about the gunman: he'd never loved. He wasn't a psychopath or anything so ugly as that. He'd had women (and once a man) but he couldn't say he'd ever felt love, and he understood this was strange, since the men he knew were always loving their heads off all over the place. He just felt dry. He had desire and lust but never longing, and this bothered him.

But it was only a fact about him, not a defining characteristic, one short fact among others—another being that he could fall from anywhere and not hurt himself, had been like that since he was a kid, could fall out of trees, off roofs. He was known for it, had earned nicknames.

What was that sound? That faint roar in the distance? Was that the bus?

Jane looked over at Max. He'd heard it too. But what were they going to do about it?

The gunman listened for his men but heard only the Wednesday bus, a day early this week apparently.

As for Max, he'd already done the great thing he would do.

They were quiet, all of them, contemplating the glassy future. "Look," said Max at last. "There's going to be a moment when you can get away. I want you to take that moment and do something with it."

"What am I supposed to do with it?"

"Get away."

"How? Where? What about you?"

"Don't sit there asking questions like that when the moment comes, okay?"

Jane was thinking: See? He had a plan. If this fellow with his gun thought a piece of string would hold Max back, well, he had another think coming. There wasn't a knot Max couldn't untie. It was as if he'd been a sailor. And Max had vision. He knew how to see monkeys in the trees. When no one else could see anything but green, Max would spot dozens.

Max was brave, had always been brave. She knew that. He had talents. A punch in the face was nothing to him. She'd seen him stand still when the gorillas came after you. *That* was brave. They had gone to the gorilla preserve in Tanzania some years back, the one people make films about. The gorilla experts, they say to you, "Okay, listen up, folks. This is what's going to happen. The gorillas are going to come after you. They'll make a big noise and run right at you. It's something they do, the gorillas. It's a test. You have to just wait it out. When they charge, don't move—stay where you are." They tell you that and you repeat it in your mind, *Don't move, don't move*, but then when this five-hundred-pound gorilla charges at you, you just throw up your hands and run screaming. Supposedly it took months to learn how not to. Only way to make friends with the fellows, the guides said.

Max was the one who hadn't run. Even the experts—the newer ones, anyway—ran. The scientists ran, but Max didn't. Jane had been amazed. Everyone had been.

Maybe she'd go back to England, see her sister. Maybe she'd go back to New Zealand, where she had friends. She wouldn't go back to Africa, though things had been better there.

*   *   *

Jane looked up and realized Max had scooted to his feet, hands still behind him, so fast she hadn't heard him. The gunman strode over shouting and Max shouted back. The gunman raised the gun to his face. Jane was screaming. But she got up and ran screaming into the forest (didn't sit there asking questions) because what else was she supposed to do? He'd told her to do that and if he had told her to, it meant that this was his plan for her and so he had a plan for himself, too—which was what? That he get punched in the face again? That he get shot? That he get himself killed? That he not care about himself as long as she got away? What kind of a plan was that? She realized she was still screaming so she stopped. Then she heard a shot and started screaming again.

He would one day love. By the time he got around to it, this day with the two Americans would have been long ago (two years) and so much would have taken place in the meantime (he'd leave the insurgents, move to the city with his uncle) that he wouldn't even think of them anymore, except when he had to use his right arm (constantly), because that's where the American (Brit, actually, and New Zealander, but the gunman would never know that) had shot him, and the place still ached after all this time. The American had brought out his hands, untied, and grabbed the gun with a grip the gunman never would have expected—not so hard that he couldn't have wrenched it away, he was trained for this sort of thing, after all, had killed a man in four minutes with his hands. But the problem was the shoe. It was too big, his foot slid in it and at the very moment he needed to have it he couldn't get a good grip on the ground and the American toppled him over and shot him in the arm and then stood over him, staring like a fucking American, gun hanging at his side. The last thing the gunman saw, before the blood made him lower his head, was the two of them running, turning away, the woman pulling the man's arm.

Later that image, the two of them in that instant, would come into his mind again and again, but it would no longer be there when he finally did love, because his own image, his own love, came back at him instead. But the Americans (New Zealanders, rather) stayed in his mind for longer than most things.

*   *   *

You would have thought that going through something like that would keep them together and it did for a while, but humans go through all sorts of things, and it doesn't always settle their hearts.

At the end of it all, after she'd left—well, after he left (because she made him) and, not knowing what she was doing, she left too—and after they both found themselves in countries far away from each other, in places that didn't have the energy or beauty the two of them had once found in such places together (although there is nothing unique in that, the world dims over time—though maybe it wouldn't have had the evil tint that it eventually seemed to Max to have, or the lifeless, meaningless tint that it seemed to Jane to have, if they hadn't parted ways)—after all that, each of them installed on separate continents, she wrote a letter to no one of significance: one of the sisters they'd met in Nicaragua with whom they'd traveled for a few days. Jane wrote to explain, felt she had to explain to this stranger why she'd left him (or made him leave, the walking man) and what it had felt like.

It was like leaving him in the clearing with the gunman. That's how it felt. Like she'd been given a chance to get away, and he hadn't. He'd given her a chance and she'd taken it, knowing where she was leaving him and in what condition, knowing the fear and loneliness he must have felt, but she'd done it, run on a bed of leaves and needles, under a canopy of trees (didn't ask questions)—or that had been the plan, though it hadn't turned out that way.

At first she was running. She realized she was still screaming and she closed her mouth. She heard the shot and started screaming again. She was moving away, running over beds of leaves, the sun coming through the branches.

Then she slowed, and stopped. She didn't move, thinking.

She turned and went back.

She could see a break in the trees and was moving toward it. Should she go in there? She didn't know who had been shot—Max or the gunman. She was pushing away the branches, she was pushing herself through, and then she stepped out to greet him (*I came back for you*) or to be shot.

MILLTOWN AUSPICE

a pantoum by BEN JAHN

How to explain his death—with humor
The best jokes start serious:
He fell asleep on the beach with his pockets full of bread
Seagulls carried him away—

The best jokes start serious:
The Governor went north (the mills full of men) God knows
Seagulls carried him away—
It was a thick-fog day, and still

The Governor went north (the mills full of men) God knows
How to explain his death—with humor
It was a thick-fog day, and still
He fell asleep on the beach with his pockets full of bread

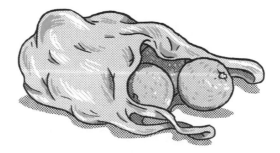

HOT PINK

by ADAM LEVIN

(*fiction from Issue 18*)

MY FRIEND JOE Cojotejk and myself were on our way to Nancy and Tina Christamesta's, to see if they could drive to Sensei Mike's housewarming barbecue in Glen Ellyn. Cojo's cousin Niles was supposed to take us, but last-minute he got in his head it was better to drink and use fireworks with his girlfriend. He called to back out while we were in the basement with the heavy bag. We'd just finished drawing targets on the canvas with marker. I wanted small red bull's-eyes, but Joe thought it would be better to represent the targets like the things they stood for. He'd covered a shift for me at the lot that week, so I let him have his way; a triangle for a nose, a circle for an Adam's apple, a space for the solar plexus, and for the sack a saggy-looking shape. The bag didn't hang low enough to have realistic knees.

When my mom yelled down the stairs that Niles was on the phone, I was deep into roundhouse kicks—I wanted to land one on each target, consecutively, without pausing to look at them, or breathing, and I was getting there; I was up to three out of four (I kept missing the circle)—so I told Cojo to take the call, and it was a mistake. Cojo won't argue with his family. Everyone else, but not them. He gets guilty with them. When he came back down the basement and told me Niles was ditching out, I bolted upstairs to call him myself, but all I got was his machine with the dumbass message: "You've reached Niles Cojotejk, NC-17. Do you love me? Are you a very sexy lady? Speak post-beep, baby."

I hung up.

My mom coughed.

I said, "Eat a vitamin." I took two zincs from the jar on the tray and lobbed one to her. She caught it in her lap by pushing her legs together. It was the opposite of what a woman does, according to the old lady in *Huckleberry Finn* who throws the apple in Huck's lap to blow his fake-out. Maybe it was Tom Sawyer and a pear, or a matchbox. Either way, he was cross-dressed.

The other zinc I swallowed myself. For immunity. The pill trailed grit down my throat and I put my tongue under the faucet.

"What happened to cups?" my mom said. That's how she accuses people. With questions.

I shut the tap. I said, "Did something happen to cups?"

"Baloney," she said.

Then I got an inspiration. I asked her, "Can you make your voice low and slutty?"

"Like this?" she said, in a low, slutty voice.

"Will you leave a message on Niles's machine?"

"No," she said.

"Then I'm going away forever," I said. "Picture all you got left is bingo and that fat-ass Doberman chewing dead things in the gangway. Plus I'll give you a dollar if you do it." I said, "You can smoke two cigarettes on that dollar. Or else I'll murder you, violently." I picked up the nearest thing. It was a mortar or a pestle. It was the empty part. I waved it in the air at her. "I'll murder you with *this*."

"Gimme a kiss!" she sang. That's how she is. A pushover. All she wants is to share a performance. To riff with you. It's one kind of person. Makes noise when there's noise, and the more noise the better. The other kind's a soloist, who only starts up when it's quiet, then holds his turn like it'll never come again. Cojo's that kind. I don't know who's better to have around. Some noise gets wrecked by quiet and some quiet gets wrecked by noise. So sometimes you want a riffer and other times a soloist and I can't decide which kind I am.

I dialed the number. For the message, I had my mother say, "You're rated G for Gypsy, baby." Niles is very sensitive about getting called a Gypsy. I don't know what inspired me with the idea to have my mom say it to him in a low, slutty voice, but then I got a clearer idea.

I dialed the number again and got her to say the same thing in her regular voice. Then I called four more times, myself, and I said it in four different voices: I did a G, a homo, a Paki, and a Dago. I'm good at those. I thought I was done, but I wasn't. I did it once more in my own voice, so Niles would know it was me telling people he's a Gypsy.

My mom said, "You're a real goof-off, Jack."

Cojo came upstairs, panting. "Tina and Nancy," he said.

I thought: Nancy, if only.

Cojo said, "They might have a car."

It was a good idea. I called. They didn't know for sure about a car, but said come over and drink. I kissed my mom's head and she gave me money to buy her a carton of Ultralights. I dropped the money in her lap and pulled a jersey over my T. Cojo said it was too hot out for both. It was too hot out for naked, though, so it wouldn't matter anyway. Except then I noticed Joe was also wearing a jersey and a T, and I didn't want to look like a couple who planned it, which Joe didn't want either, which is what he meant by too hot out, so I dumped the jersey for a Mexican wedding shirt and we split.

Five minutes later, Cojo and myself were feared, and soon after that, I learned something new about talking and how to use it to intimidate people.

How I knew we were feared was a full-grown man walking the other way on the other side of the street looked at us and nodded. It's a small thing to do but it meant a lot. My lungs tickled at the sight of it. I got this tightness down the center of my body, like during a core-strength workout. Or trying to first-kiss someone and you can't remember where to put your hands. Even thinking about it, I get this feeling. This stranger, nodding at you from all the way across the street.

It was late in the afternoon by then, and tropical hot, but overcast with small black clouds. And the wind—it was flapping the branches. Wing-shaped seed-pods rattled over the pavement and the clouds blew across the sun so fast the sky was blinking. It opened my nose up. The street got narrow compared to me. The cars looked like Hot Wheels. And in my head, my first thing was that I felt sorry for this guy who nods. It's like a salute, this kind of nod.

But then my second thing is: You better salute me, Clyde. And I get this picture of holding his ears while I slowly push his face into his brains with my forehead. I got massive neck muscles. I got this grill like a chimney and an ugly thing inside me to match it. I feel sorry for a person, it makes me want to hurt him. Cojo's the same way as me, but crueler-looking. It's mostly because of the way we're built. We're each around a buck-seventy, but I barrel in the trunk. Joe's lean and even, like a long Bruce Lee. He comes to all kinds of points. And plus his eyes. They're a pair of slits in shadow. I got comic-strip eyes, a couple black dimes. My eyes should be looking in opposite directions.

I ran my hands back over my skull. It's a ritual from grade school, when we used to do battle-royales at the pool with our friends. We got it from a cartoon I can't remember, or a video game. You do a special gesture to flip your switch; for me it's I run my hands back over my skull and, when I get to the bottom, I tap my thumb-knuckles, once, on the highest-up button of my spine. You flip your switch and you've got a code-name. We were supposed to keep our code-names secret, so no one could deplete their power by speaking them, but me and Cojo told each other. Cojo's special gesture was wiping his mouth cross-wise, from his elbow to the backs of his fingertips. Almost all the other special gestures had saliva in them. This one kid Winthrop would spit in his palms and fling it with karate chops. Voitek Moitek chewed grape gum, and he'd hock a sticky puddle in his elbow crooks, then flex and relax til the spit strung out between his forearms and biceps. Nick Rataczeck licked the middle of his shirt and moaned like a deaf person. I can't remember the gestures of the rest of the battle-royale guys. By high school, we stopped socializing with those guys and after we dropped out we hardly ever saw them. I don't know if they told each other their code-names. They didn't tell me.

Cojo's was War, though. Mine was Smith. It's embarrassing.

I coughed the tickle from my lungs and Joe stopped walking, performed his gesture and was War.

He said to the guy, "What," and the guy shuddered a little. The guy was swinging a net-sack filled with grapefruits and I hated how it bounced against his knee. I hated he had them. It made everything complicated. My thoughts were too far in the background to figure out why. Something about peeling them or slicing them in halves or eighths and what someone else might prefer to do. I always liked mine in halves. A little sugar. And that jagged spoon. It's so specific.

The guy kept moving forward, like he didn't know Joe was talking to him, but he was walking slower than before. It was just like the nod. The slowness meant the exact opposite of what it looked like it meant. I'm scared of something? I don't look at it. I think: If I don't see it, it won't see me. Like how a little kid thinks. You smack its head while it's hiding in a peek-a-boo and now it believes in God, not your hand. But everyone thinks like that sometimes. I'm scared my mom's gonna die from smoking, the way her lungs whistle when she breathes fast, but if I don't think about it, I think, cancer won't think about her. It's stupid. I know this. Still: me, everyone. Joe says, "What," to a guy who's scared of him, the guy pretends Joe's not talking to him. The guy pretends so hard he slows down when what he wants is to get as far the hell away from us and as fast as he can.

Joe says, "I said, 'What.'"

"I'm sorry," the guy says.

"Sorry for what?" Joe says, and now he's crossing the street and I'm following him.

I say, "Easy, Cojo," and this is when I learn something new about how to intimidate people. Because even though I say "Easy, Cojo," I'm not telling Cojo to take it easy. I'm not even talking to Cojo. I'm talking to the guy. When I say "Easy, Cojo," I'm telling the guy he's right to be scared of my friend. And I'm also telling him that I got influence with my friend, and that means the guy should be scared of me, too. What's peculiar is when I open my mouth to say "Easy, Cojo," I *think* I'm about to talk to Cojo, and then it turns out I'm not. And so I have to wonder how many times I've done things like that without noticing. Like when I told my mom I'd kill her and waved the empty thing at her, I wasn't really threatening her, it was more like I was saying, "Look, I'll say a stupid thing that makes me look stupid if you'll help me out." But that was different, too, from this, because my mom knew what I meant when I said I'd kill her, but this guy here doesn't know what I mean when I say "Easy, Cojo." He gets even more scared of Joe and me, but he gets that way because he thinks I really *am* talking to Joe.

I say it again. I say, "Easy, Cojo."

And Cojo says, "Easy what?"

And now the guy's stopped walking. He's standing there. "I'm sorry," he says.

"'Cause why?" Cojo says. "Why're you sorry? Are you sorry you nodded at me like I was your son? Like I was your boy to nod at like that? I don't know you."

"I'm sorry," the guy says. The guy's smiling like the situation is very lighthearted, but it's like yawning after tapping gloves on your way back to the corner. A lie you tell yourself. And I'm thinking there's nothing that's itself. I'm thinking everything is like something else that's like other something elses and it's all because I said "Easy, Cojo" and didn't mean it, or because this guy nodded.

I think like this too long, I get a headache and pissed off.

I put my arm around Cojo. I say, "Easy, Cojo."

"Fuck easy," Cojo says to me. And when Cojo says that, it's like the same thing as when I said "Easy, Cojo." I know Cojo isn't really saying "Fuck easy" to me. He wouldn't say that to me. He's saying "Fear us" to the guy. But I don't know if Cojo knows that that's what he's doing with "Fuck easy." That's the problem with everything.

"Give us your fruit," I tell the guy.

"My—"

"What did you say?" Joe says.

"Easy, Cojo," I tell him.

Then the guy hands his grapefruits to me.

I say to him, "Yawn."

He can't. Cojo yawns, though. And then I do.

Then I tell the guy to get out of my sight and he does it because he's been intimidated.

Nancy Christamesta is no whore at all. And I'm no Jesus, but still I want to wash her feet. Nancy's so beautiful, my mind doesn't think about fucking her unless I'm drunk, and even then it's just an idea: I don't run the movie through my head. Usually, I imagine her saying, "Yes," in my ear. That's all it takes. Maybe we're on a rooftop, or the 69th floor of the Hancock with the restaurant that spins, but the "Yes" part is what counts. It's a little hammy. I've known her since grade school, but I've only had it for her since she was fourteen. It happened suddenly, and that's hammy too. I was eighteen, and it started at the beach—sunny day and ice cream and everything. Our families went to swim at Oak Street on a church outing and I saw her sneak away to smoke a cigarette in the tunnel under the Drive. There's hypes and winos who live in there, so I followed her, but didn't let her know. I waited at the mouth, where I could hear if anything happened, and when she came back through, she was hugging herself around the middle for warmth. A few steps out of the tunnel, her left shoulder-strap fell down and, when she moved to put it back, a bone-chill shot her posture straight and a sound came from her throat that sounded like "Hi." I didn't know if it was "Hi" or just a pretty noise her throat made after a bone-chill. I didn't think it was "Hi," because I was behind her and I didn't think she'd seen me. I wanted it to be "Hi," though. I stood there a minute after she walked away, thinking it wasn't "Hi" and wishing it was. That was that. That's how I knew what I felt.

Now she's seventeen, and it's old enough, I think. But she's got this innocence, still. It's not she's stupid—she's on the honor roll, she wants to be a writer—but Joe and I were over there a couple months earlier, at the beginning of summer, right when him and Tina were starting up. They went off to buy some beer and Nancy and I waited in her room. Nancy was sitting in this shiny beanbag. She had cutoff short-shorts on, and every time she moved, her thighs made the sticking sound that you know it's leg-on-vinyl but you imagine leg-on-leg. I had it in my head it was time to finally do something. I laid down on the carpet, next to her, listening, and after a little while, I said, "What kind of name is Nancy for you, anyway?"

Nancy said, "Actually, I think Nancy's a pretty peculiar name for me. But I always thought that was because it's mine."

See, I was flirting. I was teasing her. It was my voice she was supposed to hear, not the words it said. But it was the words she heard, and not my voice. It was an innocent way to respond. And I didn't know what to do, so I told her she was nuts.

She said, "No. Listen: Jack... Jack... Jack... Does it sound like your name, still?"

It completely sounded like my name, but I didn't say that because hearing it was as good as "Yes" in my ear and I wanted her to keep going. I wanted to tell her I loved her. Instead, I said "it." I said, "I love it." She said, "Jack... Jack... Jack. I'm glad, Jack Jack."

If she didn't have innocence, she'd have heard what my voice meant and either shut me down or flirted back at me.

When we got to their house on the day of the nodding guy, she was sitting on the stoop with a notebook, wearing flip-flops, which made it easy to admire the shape of her toes. Most people's toes look like extra things to me, like earrings or beards. Nancy's look necessary. They work for her.

Joe went inside to find Tina.

Nancy said, "What's with the grapefruits?"

I said, "We intimidated a man. It's all words."

"I don't like that spoon," she said. "I clink my teeth. It chills me up." She was still talking about grapefruits.

"They're not for you," I said. "They're for your parents."

"What's all words?" she said.

I said, "You don't say what you mean. You pretend like you're talking about something else. It works."

"A dowry goes to the groom, not the other way around," she said.

I said, "What does that have to do with anything?"

She said, "Implications. Indirectness. And suggestion."

Was she fucking with me? I don't even know if she was fucking with me. She's a wiseass, sometimes, but she's much smarter than me, too. And plus she was high. I would've taken a half-step forward and kissed her mouth right then, except I wasn't also high, and that's not kosher. Plus I probably wouldn't have stepped forward and it's just something I tell myself.

"Come inside with me," she said.

She kicked off her sandals and I followed her to the kitchen. It's a walk through a long hallway and Nancy stopped every couple steps for a second so that I kept almost bumping her. She said, "You should take your shoes off, Jack. And your socks. The floor's nice and cold."

That was a pretty thought, but getting barefoot to feel the coldness of a floor is not something I do, so I told her, "You're a strange one." Nancy likes people to think she's strange, but she doesn't like people thinking that she likes them to think that, so it was better for me to say than it sounds, even though she spun around and smacked me on the arm when I said it, which also worked out fine because I was flexed. I was expecting a smack. I know that girl.

In the kitchen, Cojo was drinking beer with Tina and Mr. Christamesta. Mr. Christamesta was standing. He's no sitter. He's 6'5" and two guys wide. I can't imagine a chair that would hold him. He could wring your throat one-handed. If there was a black-market scientist who sold clones derived from hairs, he'd go straight for the clog in Mr. Christamesta's drain whenever the customer wanted a bouncer. That's what he looks like: the father of a thousand bouncers. Or a bookie with a sandwich-shop front, which is what he is. But it's a conundrum after you talk to him, because you don't think of him like that. You talk to him, you think: he's a sandwich-shop owner who takes a few bets on the side. Still, he's the last guy in Chicago whose daughter you'd want to date. Him or Daley. But a father-in-law is a different story.

He said to me, "Jack Krakow! What's with the grapefruits?"

I didn't want to think about the grapefruits. The grapefruits made me sad.

I said, "They're for you, Sir, and Mrs. Christamesta."

"You're so formal, Jack. You trying to impress me or something? Why you trying to impress me, now? You want to marry my daughter? Is that it? My Nancy? You want to take my Nancy away from her papa? You want to run away with her to someplace better? Like that song from my youth? If. it's. the. last. thing. you ever do? You want to be an absconder, Jack? With my daughter? So you bring me grapefruits? Citrus for a daughter? What kind of substitute is that? It's pearls for swine, grapefruits for Nancy. Irrespectively. It's swine for steak and beef for venison. You like venison? I love venison. But I also love deer, Jack. I love to watch deer frolic in the woods. Do you see what I mean? The world's complicated. It's okay, though. I am impressed with your grapefruits. You have a good heart. You're golden. I like you. Just calm down. We're standing in a kitchen. It's air-conditioned. Slouch a little. Have a beer."

He handed me a bottle. I handed him the grapefruits. He's got thumbs like ping-pong paddles, that guy. He could slap your face from across the country.

What sucked was, grapefruits or no, I *was* trying to impress him, and I *did* come for his daughter, and he wouldn't be so jolly about it if he knew that, so I knew there was no way he knew it. And since he didn't know it, I knew Nancy didn't know it, because those two are close. So I was like one of these smart guys like Clark Kent that the girl thinks of like an older brother. Except I'm not smart. And my alter ego isn't Superman, who she loves. At best I'm Smith, who no one knows his name but Cojo.

The one good thing about Mr. Christamesta going off on those tangents was it got Nancy laughing so hard she was shaking. She pushed her head against my shoulder and hugged around me to hold my other shoulder with her hands. For balance. And I could smell her hair, and her hair smelled like apples and girl, which is exactly what I would've imagined it smelled like in my daydreams of "Yes," if I was smart enough to imagine smell in the first place. I don't think I have the ability to imagine smell. I never tried, but I bet I can only do sound and sight.

An unfortunate thing about Nancy's laughing was how it drew her mom in from the living room. She's real serious, Mrs. Christamesta. So serious it messes with her physically. She's an attractive woman, like Nancy twenty years later and shorter-haired—see her through a window or drive by her in the car, it's easy to tell. If you're eating dinner with her, though, or at church, and she knows she's being looked at, the seriousness covers up the beauty. It's like she doesn't have a face; just her eyebrows like a V and all the decisions she made about her hairstyle. My whole life, I've seen Mrs. Christamesta laugh at three or two jokes, and I've never heard her crack a one.

"You, young lady," she said, "and you, too," to Tina, "have to quit smoking those drugs."

That got Nancy so hysterical that I had to force myself to think about the grapefruits again, about that guy coming home with no grapefruits and acting like he just forgot or, even worse, him going back to the store and getting more grapefruits and then, when he got home, making this big cere-mony around cutting them or peeling them, whatever his family did with them. I had to think about that so I wouldn't start laughing with Nancy. If I laughed, it would look like I was laughing at Mrs. Christamesta. And maybe I would be.

"It's because you give them beer," she said to her husband.

"Is it you want a beer, honey?" he said to her.

She bit her lip, but took a seat.

He got up real close to her and said it again. "Is all you want is a beer?" He crouched down in front of her chair so his shirt rode up and I saw his lower back. His lower back was white as tits, and not hairy at all, which surprised me. He held her neck, and touched those paddles to her ears. "Is it you want a grapefruit?" he said. "I'll cut you a grapefruit. I'll peel you a grapefruit. I'll pulp it in the juicer. I'll juice it in the pulper. Grapefruit in segments, in slices, or liquefied. And beer. All or any. Any combination. All for you. Am I not your husband? Am I not a good husband? Am I not a husband to prepare you citrus on a sunny weekend in the windy city? Have I ever denied you love in any form? Have I ever let your gorgeous face go too long unkissed? How could I? What a brute," he said. "What a drunken misanthrope. What a cruel, cruel man," he said. "I'll zest the peel with the zester and cook salmon on the grill for you. I'll sprinkle pinches of zest for you. On top of the salmon." Then he kissed her face. Thirty, twenty times.

That was the fourth time I ever saw Mrs. Christamesta laugh. Or the third. And thank God because I was done feeling sorry for that nodding guy. I lost it so hard that when the laughter was finished with me I was holding Nancy's hand and she was tugging on the front of my shirt and I didn't remember how we got that way.

I made a violent face at her, all teeth and nostrils. For comedy. Then she pinched me on my side and I jumped back fast, squealing like a little girl.

"Fucken girl," Cojo whispered. But he didn't mean it how it sounded. It was nice of him to say to me. Brotherly.

Mr. Christamesta threw a key at me. "You okay to drive?" he said. "You're okay," he said. He kissed his wife's neck and we went out the back door. To the garage.

The Christamestas have two cars. Both of them are Lincolns and both Lincolns are blue. I tried the key on the one on the left. It was the right choice.

Cojo called shotgun, but he was kidding. I held the shotgun door open for Nancy and Cojo tackled Tina into the back seat.

We stopped at the Jewel for some patties and nacho chips, and then we were on our way.

*   *   *

I forgot to mention it was furniture day. Two Sundays a year, Chicago's got furniture day. You put your old furniture in the alley, in the morning, and scavengers in vans take it to their houses and junk shops. If no one wants it, the garbage trucks come in the afternoon and they bring it to the dump. That's what makes it furniture day—how the garbage trucks come. That's why there were garbage trucks on a Sunday.

One of them had balloons tied to its grill with ribbon. We got stopped at a light facing it. Grand and Oakley. We were going south on Oakley. That light takes forever. Grand's a main artery. It's dominant. Grand vs. Oakley? Oakley gets stomped.

There were white balloons and blue ones and some yellows. I don't know what color the ribbon was, but I knew it wasn't string because it shined.

Nancy said, "Do you think it's a desperate form of graffiti, Jack?"

Jack. I checked the rearview. Tina had her feet in Joe's lap. Joe was pretending to look out his window, but what he was doing was looking *at* the window. It was tinted, and he was looking at Tina's legs, reflected. Tina has good legs. You notice them. You feel elderly.

I said to Nancy, "It's probably the driver had a baby."

She said, "I think maybe some tagger got his markers and his spray-cans taken, and he was sitting on the curb out front of his house, watching all the trucks making pickups and feeling worthless because he couldn't do anything about it. He didn't want to write 'wash me' with his finger in the dirt along the body since there's nothing original about that, and he didn't want to brick the windshield because he wasn't someone who wanted to harm things, but still he found himself reaching down into the weeds of the alley to grasp something heavy. He needed to let the world know he existed, and without paint or markers, bricking a windshield was the only way he could think to do it. Except then, right then, right when he gets hold of the brick—and it's the perfect brick, a cement quarter-cinderblock with gripping holes for his fingers, it fits right in his hand—he hears his little sister, inside the house. She's singing through the open window of her bedroom, above him. She's happy because yesterday was her birthday and she got all the toys she wanted, and it reminds the boy of the party they had for her, how he decorated the house all morning and his sister didn't even care because all she really wanted

518

was to unwrap her presents—the party meant nothing to her, not even the cake, much less the decorations—and so this boy races inside, to the hallway in his mom's house, and tears a balloon-cluster from the banister he tied it to, then races back out front, decorates the grill of the garbage truck."

Finally, the light turned green. If you're Oakley, you get about seven seconds before Grand starts kicking your ass again.

I said, "It could be the driver got married."

Nancy said, "And maybe it wasn't even today. Maybe it was sometime last week. Maybe those balloons have been there for nine, ten days because the driver thinks it's pretty. Because he understands what it means, you know? Or maybe because he doesn't understand what it means, because it's a conundrum, but it's a nice conundrum, something he wants to figure out."

"It could be his son," I said. "It could be it was his son got married or had a baby," I said.

Nancy said, "Oh." And I knew I shouldn't have said what I said. She was trying to start something with me and I kept ending it. She wanted me to tell her a fantasy story. I'm a meathead. A misinterpreter. Like hot pink? For years I thought it was regular pink that looked sexy on whoever was wearing it. And that Bob Marley song? I thought he was saying that as long as you stayed away from women, you wouldn't cry. Even after I figured it out, it's still the first thing I think when it comes on the radio. It's like when I'm wrong for long enough, I can't get right. I had a fantasy story in my head, but I didn't say it. And why not?

We were merging onto the Eisenhower when this guy in a Miata blew by us on the ramp and I had to hit the brakes a little. Everyone cussed except Nancy, who was spaced out, or pretending to be. Then we got quiet and Joe said, "What kind of fag drives a Miata?"

And Tina said, "Don't." Tina goes to college at UIC. She was a junior, like I would have been. "Don't say fag," she said.

"Fag faggot fag," Cojo said. "It's just words. It's got nothing to do with who anyone wants to fuck." He took out a cigarette. He said, "This is a fag in England." He lit the cigarette. He said, "I know fags who've screwed hundreds of women. I know fags who screw no one. Have a fag," he said. He gave the cigarette to Tina and lit a second one for himself. He said, "That rapist Mike Tyson's a fag. And my cousin Niles. He's screwing his girlfriend even as we speak to each other here in this very car. There's fags who like windmills and fags on skinny bicycles. I know fags who fix cars and fags who pour concrete. Regis Philbin's a fag. Kurt Loder and that fag John Norris. Lots of TV and movie guys. Rock stars. Pretty much all of them. So what? It's a word. It means asshole, but it's quicker to say and more offensive cause it's only fags who say asshole like it's any kind of insult. Even jerk's better than asshole. Asshole's a fagged-out word, and fag's offensive. And it should be offensive. I want it to be offensive. Someone calls me a Polack? I'm offended. But I'm a fucken Ukrainian, you know? I don't give a shit about the Polish people. No offense, Krakow, but I don't give a fuck for your people. Someone calls me Polack, though, I'll tear his jaws off at the hinge. And cause why? Cause he's saying I'm Polish? No. Cause he's saying Polish people are lowlifes? No. He's trying to offend me is why. When he's calling me Polack, he's calling me fag. He's calling me asshole. So fine. You're pretty. Okay. You smell good. You say smart things to me when you're not telling me the right way to talk. Good news. I like you. I want to spend all my money on you. I want to take you on vacation to an island where there's coconuts and diving. Miatas are for assholes if it makes you more comfortable. But the asshole in that Miata's got fagged-out taste is what I'm telling you."

Tina said, "You've thought about this a lot, Cojo."

"I got a gay cousin," he said. "A homosexual. Lenny. He fucks men, and that's not right and it makes me sick, but that's not why he's a fag. He's a fag because whenever someone calls him fag, it's me who ends up in a fight, not him. He's a fag because he won't stand up for himself. Imagine: your own cousin a fag like that. That's how it is to be me. Not just one but two fags in the family—Lenny the homofag and don't forget about Niles the regular fag who all he does is chase girls— but I'm the only one can say it, right? About how my family's got some fags in it, I mean. Don't you ever bring it up to me. It's like a big secret, and tell the truth it makes me uncomfortable to talk about, so let's just stop talking about it, okay?"

Joe was always talking to girls about Lenny. Sometimes Lenny had cancer and sometimes he was a retard. In 1999, he was usually Albanian. But there wasn't any Lenny. I know all Joe's cousins. So do the Christamestas. Lenny was fiction. But I didn't say. If he did have a cousin Lenny, and this Lenny was a gay, Cojo would defend his cousin Lenny against people who called Lenny fag. So Cojo was telling a certain kind of truth. And it never really mattered to Tina, anyway. She'd just wanted to know Joe cared what she thought of him, and the effort it took him to come up with that bullshit about fags and assholes—that made it obvious he cared. And Joe is definitely crazy for Tina. He discusses it with me. All the things he wants to buy her. Vacations on islands with sailboats and mangos, fucking her on a hammock. They'd still never fucked, but they mashed pretty often. So often it was comfortable. So comfortable they started in the back seat of the car, which was not comfortable for me, sitting next to Nancy, who's staring at the carton of patties in her lap while the sister gets mauled. I hit as many potholes as I could. The Ike's got thousands.

Finally we arrived at the wrong barbecue. We were supposed to go to 514 Greenway and we went to 415. It was my fault. I wrote it down wrong when Sensei Mike told us at the dojo on Friday.

But 415 was raging. Fifty, forty people. Mostly middle-aged guys, wearing Oxfords and sandals. Some of them had wives, but there weren't any babies, which always spooks me a little, a barbecue without babies. It's like if you ever had a father who shaved off his mustache.

It took us a few minutes of looking around for Sensei Mike before we noticed this banner hanging off the fence. It said, HAPPY TENURE, PROFESSOR SCHINKL! By then, we all had bottles of beer in our hands. The beers tasted yeasty. They were from Belgium. That's what set the whole thing off.

The four of us were half-sitting along the edge of the patio table, trying to decide if it was more polite to finish the beers there or take them with us to look for Sensei Mike's house when this guy came up and made a show of adjusting his sunglasses. First he just lowered them down the bridge of his nose so we could see one of his eyebrows raise up. But then he was squinting at us over the frames and he had a hand on his hip. He stayed that way for a couple of wheezy breaths, then tore the sunglasses off his face with the other hand and held them up in the air behind his ear like he was gonna swat us. Instead, he let the shades dangle and he said, "Hmmmmmmm." The sound of that got the attention of some other people. They weren't crowding up or anything, but they were looking at us.

The guy said, "Hmmmmmm," again, but with more irritation than the first time. Like a whining, almost.

"How ya doin'?" Cojo said to him. Nancy leaned into me, but it was instinct, nothing to make a big deal of. Tina held her beer close. Cojo was smiling, which is not a good thing for him to do around people who don't know him. His smile looks like he's asking you to stop making him smile. It's got no joy. It's because of his smile that I retrieve the cars when we work the lot together. If customers tip, it's usually on the way out.

Real slow and loud, the guy said, "How's. Your Belgian. Beer?"

So the beer was his and he was attached to it in some sick way. Like fathers and the end-piece of the roast beef. He wasn't anyone's father, though, this guy. He was being a real prick about the beer is what he was, but it was the wrong barbecue and he was harmless so far. He was tofu in khakis. About as rough as a high-school drama teacher. Still, he could've been Schinkl for all we knew, so he didn't get hit.

"You want one?" Cojo said. He said, "I think there's one left in the cooler by the grill."

The guy stared at Joe, just to let him know that he'd heard what Joe said, but was ignoring him. Then he spun on Nancy. He said, "Is that *ground chuck* in your lap, young lady? Do you mean to wash down those patties of *ground chuck* with my imported. Belgian. beer?" He poked the meat.

I said, "Hey."

"Hay's for horses," he said, the fucken creep.

A woman in the crowd—they were crowding up, now—said, "Calm down, Byron."

He poked the meat again, hard. Busted a hole in the plastic wrap. Nancy flinched and I had that fucker in an armlock before the meat hit the ground. Joe dumped his beer in the lawn and broke the bottle on the table edge. We moved in front of the Christamestas, like shields. I had Byron bent in front of me, huffing and puffing.

I didn't want the girls to see us get beat down, but I thought about afterward, about Nancy holding my hands at my chest and wiping the blood from my face with disinfected cottonballs, how I could accidentally confess my love and not be held responsible since I'd have a serious concussion.

Byron said, "Let go."

"You got a thin voice," I told him.

I pulled his wrist back a couple degrees. His fingers danced around.

Every guy in that yard was creeping toward us, saying "Hey" and "Hey, now." There were too many of them, broken bottle or no. All we had left was wiseass tough-guy shit. "Hey," they said. And Joe said, "Hay's for horses," and I forced a laugh through my teeth like I was supposed to. They kept creeping. Little baby steps. Tina whispered to Nancy, "Can we go? Let's just go."

"Just let go of me!" Byron said. "Let go of me!"

I said, "What!"

He shut his mouth and the crowd stopped moving. They stopped right behind where the patio met the grass. That's when it occurred to me the reason they weren't pummeling us was Byron. They didn't want me to damage him. And that meant that I controlled them. I thought: We got a hostage. I thought: All we have to do is take him out the gate on the side of the house, get him to the car, then drop him in the street and drive off. I was gonna tell Joe, but then Nancy started talking.

"Do you guys know Sensei Mike?" she said.

This chubby drunk guy was wobbling at the front of the crowd. He said, "What?" But it sounded like "Whud?" That's how I knew he was a lisper, even before he started lisping. Because he had adenoid problems. The first lisper I ever knew in grade school had adenoid problems. Brett Novak. He said his own name "Bred Novag." Mine he said "Jag Gragow." When people called him a lisper, I didn't know what a lisper was, so I decided he was a lisper not just because of what he did to s sounds, but because of what he did to t sounds and k sounds, too. So I thought this chubby drunk guy was a lisper, because I used to be wrong about what a lisper was and so "lisper" is the first thing I think when I hear adenoid problems. But since the chubby guy turned out to be a lisper after all, my old wrongness made it so I was right. It was like if Nancy wore hot pink. The color would look sexy on her, and because it would look sexy on her, I'd say it was "hot pink," and I'd be right, even though I didn't know what I was saying. I'd be right because of an old misunderstanding.

"Sensei Mike?" said Nancy. "We came for Sensei Mike." Her voice was trembling. I could've killed everybody.

The guy said, "Thenthaimigue? Ith that thome thort of thibboleth?"

This got laughs. The crowd thought it was very clever for the lisper to say a word like *shibboleth* to us.

But fuck them for thinking I don't know shibboleth. Some people don't, but I do. It's from the Old Testament. In CCD they told us we shouldn't read the Old Testament till we were older because it was violent and confusing and totally Christless, so I read some of it (I skipped Leviticus and quit at Kings). The part with shibboleth is in Judges: There were the Ephrathites who were these people who couldn't make the sound *sh*. They were at war with the Gileadites. The Gileadites controlled all the crossings on the Jordan River, and the main thing they didn't want was for the Ephrathites to get across the river. The problem was the Ephrathites looked exactly like the Gileadites and spoke the same language, too; so if an Ephrathite came to one of the crossings, the Gileadites had almost no way of telling that he was an Ephrathite. Not until Jephthah, who was the leader of the Gileadites, remembered how Ephrathites couldn't make the *sh* sound—that's when he came up with the idea to make everyone who wanted to cross the river say the word *shibboleth*. If they could say shibboleth, they could pass, but if they couldn't say it, it meant they were an enemy and they got slain. So shibboleth was this code word, but it didn't work like a normal code word. A normal code word is a secret—you have to prove you know what it is. Shibboleth, though—it wasn't any secret. Jephthah would tell you what it was. What mattered was how you said it. How you said it is what saved your life, or ended it.

I said to the lisper, "I know what's a shibboleth, and Sensei Mike's no shibboleth. And you're no Jephthah, either." It came out wormy and know-it-all sounding. I sounded like I cared what they thought of me. Maybe I did. I don't think so, though.

"Are you jogueing?" he said. "Whud gind of brude are you? Do you *offden* find yourthelf engaging in meda-converthathions?" He pronounced the *t* in *often*, the prick, and on top of it, he turned it into a fucken *d*.

All those guys laughed anyway. It was funnier to them than the shibboleth joke. It was the funniest thing they'd ever heard. And I was sick of getting laughed at. And I was sick of people asking me questions that weren't questions.

I pulled on Byron's arm and he moaned. Cojo slapped him on the chops and the lisper stepped back into the crowd, to hide.

The crowd started shifting. But not forward. Not in any direction really, not for too long. It swelled in one place and thinned in another, like a water balloon in a fist. It was in my fist.

I saw the lisper's head craned up over the shoulder of a guy who'd snuck to the front, and that's when I knew.

They didn't stop creeping up at the patio because they were scared of what I'd do to their friend and his arm. They stopped at the patio to give us space. They stopped at the patio so I could do whatever I'd do to Byron and they could watch.

I said to Nancy, "You and Tina go get the car, okay?" Nancy reached in my pocket for the keys and whispered, "Be careful." Then Tina kissed Joe. The girls ran off. It could've been a war movie. It could've been Joe and I going to the front in some high-drama war movie. It was a little hammy, but that didn't bother me.

As soon as I was sure the girls were clear, I asked Joe, with my eyes and eyebrows, if he thought we should run for it.

He told me with his shoulders and his chin that he thought it was a good idea.

Then I got an inspiration. I started yelling at the top of my lungs: "AHHHHHH!"

The whole crowd went pop-eyed and stepped back and stepped back and stepped back. I got a huge lung capacity. I think I yelled for about a minute. I yelled till my throat bled and I couldn't yell anymore. Then I dropped Byron, and we took off.

Nancy was just pulling out of the parking spot when we got to the car. Some of the sickos from the barbecue ran out onto the street, and one of them was shouting, "We'll call the police!"

We still didn't know Sensei Mike's right address and the girls decided it was probably better to get out of Glen Ellyn, so we headed back to Chicago. When we got to the Christamesta house, Tina and Joe went inside and I followed Nancy around the neighborhood on foot, not saying anything. I don't know how long that lasted. It was dark, though. We ended up at the park at Iowa and Rockwell, under the tornado slide, sitting in pebbles, our backs against the ladder. Nancy opened her purse and pulled out a Belgian beer. I popped it with my lighter and gave it to her. She sipped and gave it back. I sipped and gave it back.

I've told a lot of girls I was in love with them. There's some crack-ass wisdom about it being easier to say when you don't mean it, but that's not why I didn't say it to Nancy. I didn't say it because every time I've said it, I meant it. If I said it again, it would be like all those other times, and all those other times—it went away. And silence wasn't any holier than saying it. Just more drama for its own sake. All of it's been done before. It's been in TV shows and comic books and it's how your parents met. And there's nothing wrong with drama, I don't think. And there's nothing wrong with drama for it's own sake, either. What's wrong is drama that doesn't know it's drama. And what's wrong is doing the same thing everyone else does and thinking you're original, thinking you're unpredictable.

I said, "Maybe it's cause he wanted racing stri—" and the sound cut off. My throat was killing me from the yelling and it closed up.

Nancy said, "Your voice is broken."

And that was an unexpected way to put it, drama or no.

I swigged the beer again and told her, all raspy, "Maybe it's racing stripes. The guy wanted racing stripes."

"What?" she said.

"Don't what me," I said. I gulped more beer. I said, "He wanted to paint racing stripes and the city wouldn't let him. There's a code against painting stripes on city vehicles. So every day he ties the balloons on the grill. And maybe that's a half-ass way to have racing stripes, but then maybe he figures stripes on a garbage truck aren't really racing stripes to begin with, so he doesn't mind using balloons. Or maybe he does mind, but he keeps it to himself because he's not a complainer. Maybe he just keeps tying balloons on the grill, telling himself they're as good as racing stripes, and maybe one day they will be."

"That's a sad story," Nancy said. She carved SAD! in the pebbles with the bottle of beer.

"How's it *sad*?" I said.

Under SAD! she carved a circle with an upside-down smile. "It's not sad," I said.

She said, "I don't believe that."

"But I'm telling you," I said.

She said, "Then I don't believe you, Jack."

And did I kiss her then? Did Nancy Christamesta close her eyes and tilt her head back, away from the moon? Did she open her mouth? Did she open it just a little, just enough so I could feel her breath on my chin before she would kiss me and then did I finally kiss her?

Fuck you.

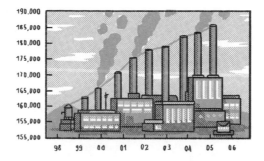

FOUR INSTITUTIONAL
MONOLOGUES

by GEORGE SAUNDERS

(fiction from Issue 4)

I.

(EXHORTATION)

MEMORANDUM
DATE: Apr 6
TO: Staff
FROM: Todd Bernie
RE: March Performance Stats

I WOULD NOT LIKE to characterize this as a plea, but it may start to sound like one (!). The fact is, we have a job to do, we have tacitly agreed to do it (did you cash your last paycheck, I know I did, ha ha ha). We have also—to go a step further here—agreed to do the job well. Now we all know that one way to do a job poorly is to be negative about it. Say we need to clean a shelf. Let's use that example. If we spend the hour before the shelf-cleaning talking down the process of cleaning the shelf, complaining about it, dreading it, investigating the moral niceties of cleaning the shelf, whatever, then what happens is, we make the process of cleaning the shelf *more difficult than it really is*. We all know very well that that "shelf" is going to be cleaned, given the current climate, either by you or by the guy who replaces you and gets your paycheck, so the question boils down to: Do I want to clean it happy or do I want to clean it sad? Which would be more effective? For me? Which would accomplish my purpose more efficiently? What is my purpose? To get paid. How do I accomplish that purpose most efficiently? I clean that shelf well and I clean it quickly. And what mental state helps me clean that shelf well and quickly? Is the answer: Negative? A negative mental state? You know very well that it is not. So the point of this memo is: Positive. The positive mental state will help you clean that shelf well and quickly, and thus accomplish your purpose of getting paid.

What am I saying? Am I saying whistle while you work? Maybe I am. Let us consider lifting a heavy dead carcass such as a whale. (Forgive the shelf/whale thing, we have just come back from our place on Reston Island, where there were 1) a lot of dirty shelves and 2) yes, believe it or not, an actual dead rotting whale, which Timmy and Vance and I got involved with in terms of the clean-up.) So say you are charged with, you and some of your colleagues, lifting a heavy dead whale carcass on to a flatbed. Now we all know that is hard. And what would be harder is, doing that with a negative attitude. What we found, Timmy and Vance and I, is that even with only a neutral attitude, you are talking a very hard task. We tried to lift that whale, while we were just feeling neutral, Timmy and Vance and I, with a dozen or so other folks, and it was a no-go, that whale wouldn't budge, until suddenly one fellow, a former Marine, said what we needed was some mind over matter and gathered us in a little circle, and we had a sort of a chant. We got "psyched up." We knew, to extend my above analogy, that we had a job to do, and we got sort of excited about that, and decided to do it with a positive attitude, and I have to tell you, there was something to that, it was fun, fun when that whale rose into the air, helped by us and some big straps that Marine had in his van, and I have to say that lifting that dead rotting whale on to that flatbed with that group of total strangers was the *high point of our trip*.

So what am I saying? I am saying (and saying it fervently, because it is important): let's try, if we can, to minimize the grumbling and self-doubt regarding the tasks we must sometimes do around here that maybe aren't on the surface all that pleasant. I'm saying let's try not to dissect every single thing we do in terms of ultimate good/bad/indifferent in terms of morals. The time for that is long past. I hope that each of us had that conversation with ourselves nearly a year ago, when this whole thing started. We have embarked on a path, and having embarked on that path, for the best of reasons (as we decided a year ago) wouldn't it be kind of suicidal to let our progress down that path be impeded by neurotic second-guessing? Have any of you ever swung a sledgehammer? I know that some of you have. I know some of you did when we took out Rick's patio. Isn't it fun when you don't hold back, but just pound down and down, letting gravity help you? Fellows, what I'm saying is, let gravity help you here, in our workplace situation: pound down, give in to the natural feelings that I have seen from time to time produce so much great energy in so many of you, in terms of executing your given tasks with vigor and without second-guessing and neurotic thoughts. Remember that record-breaking week Andy had back in October, when he doubled his usual number of units? Regardless of all else, forgetting for the moment all the namby-pamby thoughts of right/wrong etc etc, wasn't that something to see? In and of itself? I think that, if we each look deep down inside of ourselves, weren't we each a little envious? God he was really pounding down and you could see the energetic joy on his face each time he rushed by us to get additional clean-up towels. And we were all just standing there like, wow, Andy, what's gotten into you? And no one can argue with his numbers. They are there in the Break Room for all to see, towering above the rest of our numbers, and though Andy has failed to duplicate those numbers in the months since October, 1) no one blames him for that, those were miraculous numbers and 2) I believe that even if Andy never again duplicates those numbers, he must still, somewhere in his heart, secretly treasure the memory of that magnificent energy flowing out of him in that memorable October. I do not honestly think Andy could've had such an October if he had been coddling himself or entertaining any doubtful neurotic thoughts or second-guessing tendencies, do you? I don't. Andy looked totally focused, totally outside himself, you could see it on his face, maybe because of the new baby? (If so, Janice should have a new baby every week, ha ha.)

Anyway, October is how Andy entered a sort of, at least in my mind, de facto Hall of Fame, and is pretty much henceforth excluded from any real close monitoring of his numbers, at least by me. No matter how disconsolate and sort of withdrawn he gets (and I think we've all noticed that he's gotten pretty disconsolate and withdrawn since October), you will not find me closely monitoring his numbers, although as for others I cannot speak, others may be monitoring that troubling fall-off in Andy's numbers, although really I hope they're not, that would not be so fair, and believe me, if I get wind of it, I will definitely let Andy know, and if Andy's too depressed to hear me, I'll call Janice at home.

And in terms of why is Andy so disconsolate? My guess is that he's being neurotic, and second-guessing his actions of October—and wow, isn't that a shame, isn't that a no-win, for Andy to have completed that record-breaking October and now to sit around boo-hooing about it? Is anything being changed by that boo-hooing? Are the actions Andy did, in terms of the tasks I gave him to do in Room 6, being undone by his boo-hooing, are his numbers on the Break Room Wall miraculously scrolling downwards, are people suddenly walking out of Room 6 feeling perfectly okay again? Well we all know they are not. No one is walking out of Room 6 feeling perfectly okay. Even you guys, you who do what must be done in Room 6, don't walk out feeling so super-great, I know that, I've certainly done some things in Room 6 that didn't leave me feeling so wonderful, believe me, no one is trying to deny that Room 6 can be a bummer, it is very hard work that we do. But the people above us, who give us our assignments, seem to think that the work we do in Room 6, in addition to being *hard*, is also *important*, which I suspect is why they have begun watching our numbers so closely. And trust me, if you want Room 6 to be an even worse bummer than it already is, then mope about it before, after, and during, then it will really stink, plus, with all that moping, your numbers will go down even further, which guess what: They cannot do. I have been told in no uncertain terms, at the Sectional Meeting, that our numbers are not to go down any further. I said (and this took guts, believe me, given the atmosphere at Sectional): Look, my guys are tired, this is hard work we do, both physically and psychologically. And at that point, at Sectional, believe me, the silence was deafening. And I mean deafening. And the looks I got were not good. And I was reminded, in no uncertain terms, by Hugh Blanchert himself, that our numbers are not to go down. And I was asked to remind you—to remind us, all of us, myself included—that if we are unable to clean our assigned "shelf," not only will someone else be brought in to clean that "shelf," but we ourselves may find ourselves on that "shelf," *being* that "shelf," with someone else exerting themselves with good positive energy all over us. And at that time I think you can imagine how regretful you would feel, the regret would show in your faces, as we sometimes witness, in Room 6, that regret on the faces of the "shelves" as they are "cleaned," so I am asking you, from the hip, to try your best and not end up a "shelf," which we, your former colleagues, will have no choice but to clean clean clean using all our positive energy, without looking back, in Room 6.

This all was made clear to me at Sectional and now I am trying to make it clear to you.

Well I have gone on and on, but please come by my office, anybody who's having doubts, doubts about what we do, and I will show you pictures of that incredible whale my sons and I lifted with our good positive energy. And of course this information, that is, the information that you are having doubts, and have come to see me in my office, will go no further than my office, although I am sure I do not even have to say that, to any of you, who have known me these many years.

All will be well and all will be well, etc etc,

Todd Birnie
Divisional Director

II.
(DESIGN PROPOSAL)

It is preferable, our preliminary research has indicated, for some institutional space to be provided, such as corridor, hallway, etc, through which the group may habitually move. Our literature search indicated that a tiled area is preferable, in terms of preventing possible eventual damage to the walls and floors by the group moving through the space. The review of published literature also indicated that it is preferable that this area to move through (henceforth referred to, per Ellis et al., as the "Fenlen Space") be non-linear in areal layout, that is, should include frequent turning options (i.e., side hallways or corners), to give the illusion of what Ellis terms "optional pathway choices." Per Gasgrave, Heller et al., this non-linear areal layout, and the resulting apparent optional pathway choices, create a "Forward-Anticipating" mindset. Per Ellis et al., the Forward-Anticipating mindset (characterized by an Andrew-Brison Attribute Suite which includes "hope," "resolve," "determination," and "sense of mission") results in less damage to the Fenlen Space, as well as better general health for the Temporary Community, which in turn results in significantly lower clinic/medicinal costs.

Also in Ellis et al., the phrase "Forward-Anticipating Temporary Community" (FATC) is defined to designate a Temporary Community which, while moving through a given Fenlen Space, maintains NTEI (Negative Thought External Indicator) values below 3 per person/per hour. A "Non-Forward-Anticipating Temporary Community" (NFATC) is defined as one for which NTEI values are consistently above 3 per person/per hour. NTEIs are calculated using the Reilly Method, from raw data compiled by trained staff observing from inside what are termed "Amstel Booths," one-way mirror locales situated at regular intervals along the Fenlen Space.

For the purposes of this cost proposal, four Amstel Booths have been costed, along with the necessary ventilation/electrical additions.

As part of our assessment, we performed a statistical analysis of the NTEIs for four distinct Fenlen Spaces, using a standard Student's T-test, supplemented with the recently developed Anders-Kiley outlier correction model. Interestingly, the most important component of the Fenlen Space appeared to be what is referred to in the current literature as the Daley Realignment Device (DRD). The DRD allows for quick changes in the areal layout of the Fenlen Space during time periods during which the Temporary Community is moving through another, remote portion of the Fenlen Space. The purpose of the DRD is to prolong what Elgin et al. term the "Belief Period" in the Fenlen Space; that is, the period during which the Temporary Community, moving through the recently realigned DRD, fails to recognize that the portion of the Fenlen Space being traversed by them has already in fact been traversed by them. Rather, the altered areal layout leads to the conclusion that the portion of the Fenlen Space being traversed is an entirely unfamiliar and previously untraversed place, thus increasing the Temporary Community's expectation that, in time, they will arrive at what Allison and

Dewitt have termed the "Preferable Destination." At some facilities, a brief oral presentation is made to the Temporary Community shortly before the Community enters the Fenlen Space, during which it is strongly implied or even directly stated that the Community will be traversing the Fenlen Space in order to reach the Preferable Destination, which is described in some detail, especially vis-à-vis improvements in terms of cold/heat considerations, food considerations, crowding/overcrowding considerations, and/or perceived menace considerations. An "apology" may be made for any regrettable past incidents. It may also be implied that the individuals responsible for these incidents have been dismissed etc etc. Such presentations have been found to be extremely beneficial, significantly minimizing NTEIGs and prolonging the Belief Period, and several researchers have mentioned the enthusiasm with which the Temporary Community typically enters the Fenlen Space following such a presentation.

Should Building Ed Terry wish to supplement its DRD with such a pre-traversing oral presentation, Judson & Associates would be pleased to provide the necessary technical writing expertise, a service we have already provided successfully for nine facilities in the Northeast.

In any event, some sort of DRD is strongly recommended. In a study of a Fenlen Space located in Canton, New Jersey, a device which was not equipped with a DRD, it was reported that, toward the end of Day 1, the Temporary Community went, within a few hours, from a strong FATC (with very low NTEIs, ranging from 0–2 per person/per hour) to a very strong NFATC (with NTEIs as high as 9 per person/per hour). Perhaps the most striking finding of the Canton study was that, once the Temporary Community had devolved from an FATC to a NFATC (i.e., once the Belief Period had expired), NTEI values increased dramatically and catastrophically, until, according to one Amstel Booth observer, the NTEIs were occurring at a frequency that were "essentially impossible to tabulate," resulting in the event being classified as "Chaotic" (on the Elliot Scale), after which the Fenlen Space had to be forcibly cleared of the Temporary Community. In other words, once the Temporary Community perceived the Fenlen Space as a repetitious traversing of the same physical space, morale eroded quickly and, per clinical data, could not be restored. Needless to say, the forcible clearing of a Fenlen Space involves substantial risk and expense, as does the related interruption to the smooth flow of facility operations.

In contrast, since a DRD was added to the Canton facility, no further Chaos Situations have occurred, with one exception, which was later seen to be related to a small fire that occurred within one of the Amstel Booths.

Currently available DRDs range from manually rearranged units (typically featuring wallboard panels with quick-release bolts, which are placed into a floor-embedded grid) to electronic, track-based units which offer a large, practically unlimited range of configurations and are typically integrated using the ChangeSpace™ computer software package. The design we have submitted for Building Ed Terry includes cost estimates for the economical Homeway DRD6 (wallboard-grid model) as well as the higher-end Casio 3288 DRD (track-based, computer-operated unit). For the Homeway unit, we have included approximate costs for the physical labor involved in the manual rearrangement of the DRD. For the purposes of this proposal, we have assumed seven rearrangements a day, with four persons required for each rearrangement. This corresponds with a circumnavigation period of approximately three hours—that is, seven rearrangements a day, precluding the possibility that the Temporary Community would inadvertently encounter areal rearrangements in progress, which has been shown (in Percy et al.) to markedly decrease the belief period, for obvious reasons.

Judson Associates firmly believes that the enclosed proposal more than meets the needs described in your Request for Proposal of January 9. Should you desire further clarification, please do not hesitate to contact either Jim Warner or myself. We look forward to hearing from you, and to working with you on this exciting and challenging project, and on other projects yet to come.

Sincerely,

Mark Judson
President and CEO
Judson Associates

III.

(A FRIENDLY REMINDER)

We in Knuckles herebuy request that those of you in Sorting refran from calling the Fat Scrap Box the Pizza Hut Box and refran from calling the Bone Scrap Box the Marshmallow Box and refran from calling the Misc. Scrap Box the Dog Food Box because we think that is insulting to our work and workplace in terms of why do you have to make fun of what we all of us do for a living as if it is shameful. Even though it is true that some of our offal might get used for pizza topping and mashmallows and dog food we do not like it when you are saying those names in a sarcasmic voice. Because new hires can be infected by these attitudes which are so negative and soon they will not be working their best but only laughing at your smartass dumb jokes, so in the future use the correct names (Fat Scrap and Bone Scrap and Misc. Scrap) for these boxes if you feel like you have to talk at all while working although also we in Knuckles suggest you just shut up and just work. For example when one of us in Knuckles throws a Knuckle but it misses the belt you do not have to call it a "skidder" or act like you are a announcer on a basketball show by saying whoa he missed the hole. And also you dont have to say Ouch whenever one of our throwed Knuckles goes too far and hits the wall, it is not like the Knuckle could feel that and say Ow, because it is dead dumbass, it cannot feel its leg part hitting the wall, so we know you are being sarcasmic. And we dont think this is funny because when we miss the belt or hit the wall what do we have to do is we have to put down our knives and go get it which takes time. And already we are tired without that extra walking. Because what we do takes real muscle and you can easily see us if you look huffing and breething hard all day in the cold inside air, whereas you, although its true you are all hunched over, we never see you breething hard and you dont even work with knives and so never accidentally cut your friend. Which is why we think you have so much energy for yelling your "funny" taunts that you say at us and have so much energy for making up dumb names of your Belts. So to summarize we do not appreciate all the sarcasmic things that are daily said by you in Sorting in your snotty voices, as it is not something to be ashamed about, people need meat and people like meat, it is good honest work you should be glad you got it, so straighten up and fly right, in other words fucken shut up while working and just do your work silencely and try to appreciate the blessing god give you, like your job of work, it could be worse and is worse for many peeple who have no work

IV.

(93990)

A ten-day acute toxicity study was conducted using twenty male cynomolgous monkeys ranging in weight from 25 to 40 kg. These animals were divided into four groups of five monkeys each. Each of the four groups received a daily intravenous dose of Borazidine, delivered at a concentration of either 100, 250, 500, or 10,000 mg/kg/day.

Within the high-dose group (10,000 mg/kg/day) effects were immediate and catastrophic, resulting in death within 20 mins of dosing for all but one of the five animals. Animals 93445 and 93557, pre-death, exhibited vomiting and disorientation. These two animals almost immediately entered a catatonic state and were sacrificed moribund. Animals 93001 and 93458 exhibited vomiting, anxiety, disorientation, and digging at their abdomens. These animals also quickly entered a catatonic state and were sacrificed moribund.

Only one animal within this high-dose group, animal 93990, a diminutive 26 kg male, appeared unaffected.

All of the animals that had succumbed were removed from the enclosure and necropsied. Cause of death was seen, in all cases, to be renal failure.

No effects were seen on Day 1 in any of the three lower-dose groups (i.e., 100, 250, or 500 mg/kg/day).

On Day 2, after the second round of dosing, animals in the 500 mg/kg/day group began to exhibit vomiting and, in some cases, aggressive behavior. This aggressive behavior most often consisted of a directed shrieking, with or without feigned biting. Some animals in the two lowest-dose groups (100 and 250 mg/kg/day) were observed to vomit, and one in the 250 mg/kg/day group (animal 93002) appeared to exhibit self-scratching behaviors similar to those seen earlier in the high-dose group (i.e., probing and scratching at abdomen, with limited writhing).

By the end of Day 3, three of five animals in the 500 mg/kg/day group had entered a catatonic state and the other two animals in this dose group were exhibiting extreme writhing punctuated with attempted biting and pinching of their fellows, often with shrieking. Some hair loss, ranging from slight to extreme, was observed, as was some "playing" with the resulting hair bundles. This "playing" behavior ranged from mild to quite energetic. This "playing" behavior was adjudged to be typical of the type of "play" such an animal might initiate with a smaller animal such as a rodent, i.e., out of a curiosity impulse, i.e., may have been indicative of hallucinogenic effects. Several animals were observed to repeatedly grimace at the hair bundles, as if trying to elicit a fear behavior from the hair bundles. Animal 93110 of the 500 mg/kg/day group was observed to sit in one corner of the cage gazing at its own vomit while an unaffected animal (93222) appeared to attempt to rouse the interest of 93110 via backpatting, followed by vigorous backpatting. Interestingly, the sole remaining high-dose animal (93990, the diminutive male), even after the second day's dosage, still showed no symptoms. Even though this animal was the smallest in weight within the highest-dose group, it showed no symptoms. It showed no vomiting, disinterest, self-scratching, anxiety, or aggression. Also no hair loss was observed. Although no hair bundles were present (because no hair loss occurred), this animal was not seen to "play" with inanimate objects present in the enclosure, such as its food bowl or stool or bits of rope, etc. This animal, rather, was seen only to stare fixedly at the handlers through the bars of the cage and/or to retreat rapidly when the handlers entered the enclosure with the long poking sticks to check under certain items (chairs, recreational tire) for hair bundles and/or deposits of runny stool

By the middle of Day 3, all of the animals in the 500 mg/kg/day group had succumbed. Pre-death, these showed, in addition to the effects noted above, symptoms ranging from whimpering to performing a rolling dementia-type motion on the cage floor, sometimes accompanied by shrieking or frothing. After succumbing, all five animals were removed from the enclosure and necropsied. Renal failure was seen to be the cause of death in all cases. Interestingly, these animals did not enter a catatonic state pre-death, but instead appeared to be quite alert, manifesting labored breathing and, in some cases, bursts of energetic rope-climbing. Coordination was adjudged to be adversely affected, based on the higher-than-normal frequency of falls from the rope. Post-fall reactions ranged from no reaction to frustration reactions, with or without self-punishment behaviors (i.e., self-hitting, self-hair-pulling, rapid shakes of head).

Toward the end of Day 3, all animals in the two lowest-dose groups (250 and 100 mg/kg/day) were observed to be in some form of distress. Some of these had lapsed into a catatonic state; some refused to take food; many had runny brightly colored stools; some sat eating their stool while intermittently shrieking.

Animals 93852, 93881, and 93777, of the 250 mg/kg/day group, in the last hours before death, appeared to experience a brief period of invigoration and renewed activity, exhibiting symptoms of anxiety, as well as lurching, confusion, and scratching at the eyes with the fingers. These animals were seen to repeatedly walk or run into the cage bars, after which they would become agitated. Blindness or partial blindness was indicated. When brightly colored flags were waved in front of these animals, some failed to respond, while others responded by flinging stool at the handlers.

By noon on Day 4, all of the animals in the 250 mg/kg/day group had succumbed, been removed from the enclosure, and necropsied. In every case the cause of death was seen to be renal failure.

By the end of Day 4, only the five 100 mg/kg/day animals remained, along with the aforementioned very resilient diminutive male in the highest dose group (93990), who continued to manifest no symptoms whatsoever. This animal continued to show no vomiting, retching, nausea, disorientation, loss of motor skills, or any of the other symptoms described above. This animal continued to move about the enclosure normally and ingest normal amounts of food and water and in fact was seen to have experienced a slight weight gain and climbed the rope repeatedly with good authority.

On Day 5, animal 93444 of the 100 mg/kg/day group was observed to have entered the moribund state. Because of its greatly weakened condition, this animal was not redosed in the morning. Instead, it was removed from the enclosure, sacrificed moribund, and necropsied. Renal failure was seen to be the cause of death. Animal 93887 (100 mg/kg/day group) was seen to repeatedly keel over on one side while wincing. This animal succumbed at 1300 hrs on Day 5, was removed from the enclosure, and necropsied. Renal failure was seen to be the cause of death. Between 1500 hrs on Day 5 and 2000 hrs on Day 5, animals 93254 and 93006 of the 100 mg/kg/day dose group succumbed in rapid succession while huddled in the NW corner of the large enclosure. Both animals exhibited wheezing and rapid clutching and release of the genitals. These two animals were removed from the enclosure and necropsied. In both cases the cause of death was seen to be renal failure.

This left only animal 93555 of the 100 mg/kg/day dose group and animal 93990, the diminutive male of the highest dose group. 93555 exhibited nearly all of the aforementioned symptoms, along with, toward the end of Day 5, several episodes during which it inflicted scratches and contusions on its own neck and face by attempting to spasmodically reach for something beyond the enclosure. This animal also manifested several episodes of quick spinning. Several of these quick-spinning episodes culminated in sudden hard falling. In two cases, the sudden hard fall was seen to result in tooth loss. In one of the cases of tooth loss, the animal was seen to exhibit the suite of aggressive behaviors earlier exhibited toward the hair bundles. In addition, in this case, the animal, after a prolonged period of snarling at its tooth, was observed to attack and ingest its own tooth. It was judged that, if these behaviors continued into Day 6, for humanitarian reasons, the animal would be sacrificed, but just after 2300 hrs, the animal discontinued these behaviors and only sat listlessly in its own stool with occasional writhing and therefore was not sacrificed due to this improvement in its condition.

By 1200 hrs of Day 5, the diminutive male 93990 still exhibited no symptoms. He was observed to be sitting in the SE corner of the enclosure, staring fixedly at the cage door. This condition was at first mistaken to be indicative of early catatonia but when a metal pole was inserted and a poke attempted, the animal responded by lurching away with shrieking, which was judged normal. It was also noted that 93990 occasionally seemed to be staring at and/or gesturing to the low-dose enclosure, i.e., the enclosure in which 93555 was still sitting listlessly in its own stool occasionally writhing. By the end of Day 5, 93990 still manifested no symptoms and in fact was observed to heartily eat the preferred food and weighing at midday Day 6 confirmed further weight gain. Also it climbed the rope. Also at times it seemed to implore. This imploring was judged to be, possibly, a mild hallucinogenic effect. This imploring resulted in involuntary laughter on the part of the handlers, which resulted in the animal discontinuing the imploring behavior and retreating to the NW corner where it sat for quite some time with its back to the handlers. It was decided that, in the future, handlers would refrain from laughing at the imploring, so as to be able to obtain a more objective idea of the duration of the (unimpeded) imploring.

Following dosing on the morning of Day 6, the last remaining low-dose animal (93555), the animal that earlier had attacked and ingested its own tooth, then sat for quite some time writhing in its own stool listlessly, succumbed, after an episode that included, in addition to many of the afore-mentioned symptoms, tearing at its own eyes and flesh and, finally, quiet heaving breathing while squatting. This animal, following a limited episode of eyes rolling back in its head, entered the moribund state, succumbed, and was necropsied. Cause of death was seen to be renal failure. As 93555 was removed from the enclosure, 93990 was seen to sit quietly, then retreat to the rear of the enclosure, that is, the portion of the enclosure farthest from the door, where it squatted on its haunches. Soon it was observed to rise and move toward its food bowl and eat heartily while continuing to look at the door.

Following dosing on Day 7, animal 93990, now the sole remaining animal, continued to show no symptoms and ate and drank vigorously.

Following dosing on Day 8, likewise, this animal continued to show no symptoms and ate and drank vigorously.

On Day 9, it was decided to test the effects of extremely high doses of Borazadine by doubling the dosage, to 20,000 mg/kg/day. This increased dosage was administered intravenously on the morning of Day 9. No acute effects were seen. The animal continued to move around its cage and eat and drink normally. It was observed to continue to stare at the door of the cage and occasionally at the other, now-empty, enclosures. Also the rope-climbing did not decrease. A brief episode of imploring was observed. No laughter on the part of the handlers occurred, and the unimpeded imploring was seen to continue for approximately 130 seconds. When, post-imploring, the stick was inserted to attempt a poke, the stick was yanked away by 93990. When a handler attempted to enter the cage to retrieve the poking stick, the handler was poked. Following this incident, the conclusion was reached to attempt no further retrievals of the poking stick, but rather to obtain a back-up poking stick available from Supply. As Supply did not at this time have a back-up poking stick, it was decided to attempt no further poking until the first poking stick could be retrieved. When it was determined that retrieving the first poking stick would be problematic, it was judged beneficial that the first poking stick was now in the possession of 93990, as observations could be made as to how 93990 was using and/or manipulating the poking stick, i.e., effect of Borazadine on motor skills.

On Day 10, on what was to have been the last day of the study, upon the observation that animal 93990 still exhibited no effects whatsoever, the decision was reached to increase the dosage to 100,000 mg/kg/day, a dosage 10 times greater than that which had proved almost immediately lethal to every other animal in the highest-dose group. This was adjudged to be scientifically defensible. This dosage was delivered at 0300 hrs on Day 10. Remarkably, no acute effects were seen other than those associated with injection (i.e., small, bright purple blisters at the injection site, coupled with elevated heart rate and extreme perspiration and limited panic gesturing) but these soon subsided and were judged to be related to the high rate of injection rather than to the Borazadine itself.

Throughout Day 10, animal 93990 continued to show no symptoms. It ate and drank normally. It moved energetically about the cage. It climbed the rope. By the end of the study period, i.e., midnight of Day 10, no symptoms whatsoever had been observed. Remarkably, the animal leapt about the cage. The animal wielded the poking stick with good dexterity, occasionally implored, shrieked energetically at the handlers. In summary, even at a dosage 10 times that which had proved almost immediately fatal to larger, heavier animals, 93990 showed no symptoms whatsoever. In all ways, even at this exceptionally high dosage, this animal appeared to be normal, healthy, unaffected, and thriving.

At approximately 0100 hrs of Day 11, 93990 was tranquilized via dart, removed from the enclosure, sacrificed, and necropsied.

No evidence of renal damage was observed. No negative effects of any kind were observed. A net weight gain of 3 kg since the beginning of the study was observed.

All carcasses were transported off-site by a certified medical waste hauler and disposed of via incineration.

TO DO

a twenty-minute story by JENNIFER EGAN

1. Mow lawn
2. Get rid of that fucking hose
3. Wash windows
4. Spay cat
5. Dye hair
6. Do tarot cards
7. Pick up kids
8. Drop off kids at Mom's
9. Buy wig
10. See if small removable portions of fence can be cut QUIETLY
    a. Kinds of clippers
    b. Metal solvents
    c. Electrical devices
       1. How noisy?
       2. Flying metal chips?
       3. Danger of electrocution?
          a. Rubber gloves/goggles?
          b. Lethal?
             1. Sign will
          c. Does it make the body look really shitty at death?
             1. Get tooth capped
11. Send warning letter
    a. Newspaper cutouts?
    b. Get kids to write it?
    c. Write with left hand?
    d. Be vague. "Certain unpleasant things."
12. Mail letter
    a. Or drop it off while wearing wig
13. Renew meds
14. Investigate poisons
    a. Flammable
    b. Powders
    c. Gasses

d. Pills
e. Herbal
f. Chemical
g. Musical
   1. Ask kids
   2. Hamlet—ear
h. Ingestible
   1. Cookies?
i. Must look INNOCENT
15. Research cameras
    a. Affixed to fence
    b. Propped in hole cut in fence
    c. Small, undetectable
    d. Implanted in flowers
    e. How to use?
    f. Must be REASONABLY priced
    g. Take no shit from photo man
       1. Remind him of ruined prints
16. Pick up kids
17. Make dinner
18. Get ready for party
    a. Polka dots
    b. Black gloves
    c. Hair ribbon
    d. Veil
    e. Bring seltzer
    f. Remind Lou of pantry
    g. Plan two funny stories
    h. Breathing exercises to prepare for seeing THEM
       1. Kiss Kiss
       2. Hug Hug
       3. Remember: NO ONE CAN SEE YOUR THOUGHTS

—July 1, 2002, 12:35–1:00 p.m., in Central Park, NY

HOW TO SELL

by CLANCY MARTIN

(fiction from Issue 23)

BEFORE SHE KILLED my brother the Polack called me out of courtesy and told me what she was going to do. I explained to her that Baron was my big brother and I loved him and asked if there was anything I could do to stop her. First she laughed—"Ha!"—then she said "Fifty grand." But I didn't have fifty grand, or even twenty grand, and my word was useless with the Polack.

I first met the Polack when she worked at Fort Worth Gold. This was before I learned the jewelry business myself and joined Baron. I was only a customer when I met her, buying a stainless-steel Cartier for an institutional client of mine. It was almost Christmas, and the sales floor stood ten deep with buyers. It was the fat time. Those were the helpful, lazy days when I made good money. It came lightly to me and I didn't resist it.

After a while I grew bored and shouldered my way to the watchcase. There was the Polack. People said the Polack took the job as a jewelry salesperson because she was the most beautiful woman in Fort Worth, Texas.

She had won contests. But that was not it. She was there because there she found people all around her who didn't know any better, and she did. She was showing a big gold Rolex to an elderly black man in a black suit. I saw that she did not know how to sell. I stood next to the old man.

"I have one of those," I said to him. "See?" I pulled back my cuff to show him. I had won it two years before. Ten thousand Kirbys in one year. That's nearly thirty vacuum cleaners a day. Five million, seven hundred thousand dollars gross. It said Kirby right on the dial. Not every company can do that with a factory dial. We had a special deal with Rolex USA. "That looks good," he said to me. "You think so?" I asked her. This was the Polack I was asking about my Rolex, but neither of us knew that then. I shook the watch at her. My wrist was always too thin for a watch as big as a President. I wore Submariners too; it didn't matter to me. "Let me take the links out for you," she said. "To wear it like that is bad for the watch." "It's comfortable that way," I said. "You think it looks good?"

"It is handsome," she said. "Old," she said.

"Not old," I said. "Distinguished."

"That is what I said," she said. "Sophisticated. You listen," she said.

She wiped the Rolex she was selling with a diamond cloth. I saw the salesman next to her wince, but he didn't correct her. Dust from the diamonds would scratch the metal. Even I knew better than that.

"Try it on," I said to the man. "It helps to see it on your wrist."

She put the watch on the man. She handled the man's hand like she was fixing a broken machine.

"Do you have a mirror?" I asked her.

"Of course," she said. She went to find one. I nudged the man with my elbow as she walked away.

"Look at that. That's something."

"Not bad, huh?"

We grinned at each other. He had three gold teeth. He admired the watch on his wrist. He had thick, muscular wrists and it looked better on him than on me. The gold belonged on his dark skin. He could see himself feeding his enemies to the crocodiles in the moat behind his mansion. She returned with the mirror and angled it on its brass stand to show him the watch on his arm. There we were, together in his country. The date palms. The lions on hilltops. The hot wind in the sawgrass.

"Yes," he said. He was smiling happily. "Yes, that is the one."

You wait for that smile. You come to doubt you ever saw it. Then some customer smiles it at you and you recollect that you are not duping but helping them.

After he left the Polack found me on the showroom floor. "You sell for Rolex?" she said.

"I'm a vacuum salesman," I said. "But I'm here to buy. You want to sell another watch? Make it a big day."

"You don't look like a vacuum-cleaner man," she said. "My mother is someone who loves vacuum cleaners."

"Sensible woman," I said. "Everyone loves a good vacuum cleaner," I said. "Love is the word. But there are so many bad ones. A good vacuum cleaner you own for life. Pass it down to your grandkids. Change the belt every ten years and it will never age a day. Hardwoods, concrete, carpet. You think a Dyson will last twenty years? Cheap plastic, too many parts. You can buy one at Target. Can you buy a Rolex at Target? Manolo Blahniks? Kirby vacuum cleaners have been the world's leading professional vacuum cleaner for the home for more than half a century."

She laughed—"Ha!" That was the first time I heard that laugh, like a dog's bark. At first it disoriented you but then it made sense. And she knew when to do it. Maybe it was natural.

"I don't really sell them anymore," I said. "But I'm proud I know how. Never be ashamed of being a salesperson. It's a gift. Most people can never learn to sell. But you learn it, you can do anything. King of the practical professions, one of the few honest trades. Jesus Christ was a salesman. Mohammed. Allah. World's greatest. Paul. Those Jews. Think about Christ without Paul, huh? Ron Hubbard. Tom Cruise. So where are you from? Would you like to join me for lunch?"

"What about the watch you are buying?" she said. "You are buying today, yes?"

"That's right," I said. "Today I am a customer."

"I don't think I am a salesman," she said. "That is not a good business to be in."

I remember another time, much later. It was summer, after Baron and I had started up together and expanded the store, and the Polack was waiting outside my office. She was out on her own, hip-pocketing. For most of us hip-pocketing is like unemployment insurance, something to turn to between jobs or after bankruptcies. You pick all the cherries from the pawnshops—Swiss watches and good diamonds, antique pieces, pearl ropes, the things they pay nothing for because they don't understand real jewelry—and memo it out to the retail jewelers who need to fill up their cases. For the Polack this was regular business.

At this time, anyway, she dealt only in the big-name watches, Cartier, Rolex, Patek, that bunch, large turn-of-the-century finished pieces, some counterfeit cut color, and loose diamonds with fake certs she was printing herself. I remember she was wearing a white dress. I had a skinny redneck in a blue baseball cap at my desk selling me a cheap four-carat diamond. It was stolen, brown, and full of carbon, and I planned to offer him a hundred a carat. Five bills tops. It would flip to IDC or Pioneer for twenty-five hundred, maybe three grand. But first I wanted to show him several diamonds of mine so that he would understand how bad his diamond was. I had prepared several stones with fake cheap prices printed boldly on the diamond papers so that he would believe you could buy pretty four-carats for a thousand or less. I had bought from this kid before and I knew he was stupid and in a hurry so I was unconcerned. But then he jumped up, yelled some word I didn't catch, and pulled a gun on me. He was bouncing on his legs and I could see that he would shoot me accidentally. So I gave him the whole diamond box. I was already thinking of the numbers I had to call: first Ken our insurance agent, then Baron at his girlfriend's, then the police, next Jude Brown our angel (they were mostly his diamonds), then Idan at IDC about his memo stones in the box, also Paul over at the bank, then my wife. But as the kid ran out of my office the Polack was there and she took him by the shoulder calmly and shot him briskly four times in the stomach. From my office it looked like she was holding him up to shoot him. But she fired so quickly you couldn't tell. Then she stepped back and the kid fell. I looked for red blood on her white dress, but she was sparkling clean. Ignoring the fallen kid she picked up the diamond box from the floor and returned it to me. "Ha!" she said. "The young!" She could not have been twenty-five years old herself at the time. She sat down at my desk and opened her briefcase. "What you got for me today?" she said, smiling. Her teeth were like silver. "Now you owe me, Martin! Ha ha! You better call the cops! The ambulances!"

The Polack had a thick Eastern European brow and greasy lips. There were hail dents on the roof and the hood of her big green Mercedes. Later she had a wine-colored convertible Cadillac. My sales manager Dennis sold her his Blancpain for fifteen hundred bucks. That was a thousand shy of what it should have been. The Polack paid less than everyone else but she always paid cash. Dennis needed the money to square up with his divorce attorney. It was a dirty divorce with a child and the worthless remnants of Dennis's old repair business in the mall. He asked me, "How can I turn this watch into cash in a hurry?" It was a beautiful automatic chronograph with a stainless head and a hobnail bezel.

"Dennis, I'd buy it if I could," I told him. "You might ask Dave. But if you're in a hurry call the Polack."

"I don't like that woman," he said.

One time the Polack and I were playing backgammon at the coffee shop behind the store and I asked her why she would never let me take her out to lunch.

"You want to fuck me, Martin?" she said. "Why don't you just say it? Say 'Hey, Polack, let's go fuck. We will have some fun!' Maybe then you could get a woman."

I thought about saying it but I couldn't.

"You don't know anything about women, Martin," she said. "They should call you Mister Dumbshit Martin. How did you get a wife?"

"I'm getting divorced," I said.

"I am not surprised," she said. "She was stupid to marry you, but she's not that dumb! Ha!"

"She doesn't want the divorce," I said.

"Marriage is not love, Martin. It is not to be a coward. Are you going to be a coward all your life? Of course you are. Mister Dumbshit Martin. Liar, thief, coward. Nice names you got! Mister Dumbshit Martin the cowardly jeweler."

For three years the Polack was my connection. Mostly I dumped to her when we were in trouble at the bank. Or if one of my salespeople screwed up and bought a drilled-and-filled diamond or a piece of antique counterfeit, I called her. And she checked our cases during the slow season like all the Texas and Louisiana hip-pocketers. We had a name in the Southwest for several years there. But I couldn't hang on to the Polack. My brother Baron was the personality behind the store and sooner or later everyone doing real business with us took his business to Baron. I tried not to let this bother me. You shouldn't care who put the numbers on the board so long as the numbers were up there. He was my big brother, he brought me into the business, naturally he should be better at it than me. I was a better salesman. But he found a way to put together deals that eluded me.

Those two started up together and at first it was just South American Rolexes. I ran full-page color ads in the *Star-Telegram*, ten grand a pop, and we sold a hell of a lot of watches. That was another good time. But their success together gave them exaggerated hopes. Next thing you know Baron and the Polack were bringing in counterfeit stamps, paintings, fake antiquities, you name it. You tripped over Egyptian vases on the way to the bathroom. On Black Friday, the day after Thanksgiving, movers hauled in a seventeenth-century walnut partners' desk and angled it into Baron's office. They had to tear the frame off the door. This was not a knockoff, either. It was the real thing, gigantic, bigger than a vault, two thousand pounds. You had to squeeze around the corners of the room. I don't know how Baron managed to tuck his belly under it. And there was the Polack, her back to the showroom, working deals on the phone and counting cash with my big brother. I don't think they were sleeping together. She chained a gun to her chair and kept it on the desk while she made her calls. Most of the time she was out of the store and she left the gun, so if you wanted to sit in her chair and pretend you were the Polack you had to move the gun.

I was sitting in her chair when Ronnie Popper walked in the door. He had been in prison for wire fraud and was looking for work. Ronnie Popper was the marketing genius who once owned Fort Worth Gold and Silver Exchange, where the Polack got her start. It was Ronnie who created the Rolex aftermarket. There didn't used to be one. Ronnie invented guerilla jewelry markets, which had their heyday in the eighties and now are mostly dead. After Fort Worth Gold went bust Ronnie and Baron had been partners and started our place, and it was Ronnie who talked Baron into hiring me. He taught me the business while Baron was still keeping his distance, and when the FBI came in it was Baron and me who rolled over on him and sent him to prison. I wished I could give him a job. It was a Tuesday afternoon and there I was in the Polack's chair on Baron's phone. I stood up. That was lucky because the Polack came in right behind Ronnie. The Polack pretended she didn't see him. Ronnie was nervous, I could tell.

"She works for the Feds, you know," he told me when we were back in my office. I had proudly given him a tour of the showroom. That gave the Polack some time to sidle into Baron's office and get behind that desk of theirs. "Baron should know better. Your big brother should know better."

"It was his idea," I said. "They've been putting some deals together. And I think Baron may owe her some money." I doubted that last was true but I said it nevertheless.

"They must be fucking," Ronnie said. "She's a ride and a half, I'll give her that. I remember back in the day. That office of mine. I remember one time up against the office door. That was making butter. That's what she called it, making butter. Not very romantic but she knows what she's doing. I miss that office. But I hope you're wrong, I hope it's not money. He doesn't want to owe her money," Ronnie said. "That's expensive money." He shook his head with his face down, like a tortoise. He always did that when we were in trouble. I remembered that gesture and it made me miss him.

"I wish we could put you to work, Ronnie, but I just don't have it." I felt bad. I wanted Ronnie in the store. But with the Feds following him around and Baron and the Polack pulling their shenanigans it was not practical.

"No, that's fine," he said, eyeing the Polack. "I heard she's bringing in those twelve-karat Venezuelan bracelets? Maybe I'll talk to her."

"I think she's out of the Rolex business," I lied. "Anyway do you really want to get back into Rolexes?" It was selling hundreds of fictional Rolexes over the phone and running the credit cards that they got him on. Ronnie fingered the side of his nose and grinned that old grin of his. One thing about a great salesman is those familiar, lover-like idiosyncrasies. It's difficult to fake that.

"The Anteater's bad luck but she knows money," he said.

In Houston they called her the Anteater. When inspecting packages she'd lick out the diamond melee—the tiny round-cut diamonds smaller than a tenth of a carat—while your eye was turned and store it in her cheeks like a goddamn hamster. She did the same thing with packages of diamond baguettes. She had other industry names, too. When Simons heard we were working with her he called me and told me not to do business with the Gypsy. Almost no one else dared to use that name for her.

"I've known her since she was a kid, Granddad," I reassured him. "I helped her sell her first Rolex."

There were only half a dozen jewelers in the metroplex who could call Simons Granddad, and I was one of them. I was proud of that. He called each of us Grandson.

"She's Russian mob, Grandson," Simons said. "You don't want those guys in your store."

She wore a diamond ring on every finger. You might have thought that was why a few people who hated her called her the Gypsy. But Simons called her the Gypsy because of a different story that no one liked to talk about. It wasn't because she was a gypsy, but because of something she was supposed to have done to some gypsies.

That Christmas Ronnie opened an upstairs office place in Dallas, on the second floor of an old bank on McKinney, and started shipping Rolexes all over the country. He bought the watches from Baron and the Polack, who were using the money to put together a buy of twenty jewelers working in Russia at the jewelry house that used to be Fabergé. They were actually going to purchase the jewelers from the fellow who owned them in St. Petersburg, house them in a warehouse in Arlington, Texas, and have them make counterfeit Fabergé eggs, which they were then going to sell to museums and rich Arabs and African warlords. In the meantime they weren't paying their Rolex vendors in Venezuela. Eventually the South Americans got impatient and came to town and that's when Baron came into my office.

He poured scotch from my bureau into his coffee cup. "You want some?" he asked. I started to say No, it's my scotch, but he was my brother so I said "Why not" and pushed my cup toward him. He tipped in a heavy shot.

"I have to use our line at the bank," he said. "They've got Emily."

It was the first time I had heard anyone use the Polack's real name. "Who?"

"Come on, you know who. These fucking Venezuelans."

Personally I hate South Americans, except Argentinians and Chileans. There are no gemstones or gold that far south so they haven't been soiled by jewelry and the easy money that goes along with it. But the first time we were ever held up, at the JCK show in Vegas, it was by some Brazilians. Really it was some hookers in our hotel room who spun the safe after we passed out, but we blamed the Brazilians to everyone except the cops and our insurance agent, who had to know the truth. South Americans hit the JCK every year. They held us up with machine guns in the elevator, we said.

It was straight out of *Scarface*.

"How much?" I asked him.

He took a sip of coffee. He rubbed his temple with his fist in that way he had and twisted an odd smile out at me. "Three hundred grand," he said.

"We don't have three hundred grand on that line. We'd be lucky to get a hundred."

"I know. We need to call Jude, I guess. Can you call him? I don't want to call him."

"He can't bite you through the phone."

"Can't you call him? I always call him. I don't want to call him this time. Can't you be the one to call him for once?"

He was my big brother and I trusted him. Baron was the one who had first brought our angel Jude Brown in but I called Jude this time and this time it was me who met him at the bank and signed the new papers.

We met the Venezuelans at Legends over off of Harry Hines. That was not one of our regular titty bars because it was a favorite of the Cowboys and the Rangers, so we would always run into customers. Like all celebrities professional athletes expect to pay for nothing. So we would buy their table dances and their drinks and by the end it was a thousand-dollar night instead of just two hundred each.

We weren't buying these South Americans any dances. They were three short men whose features looked like they had been cut open on their faces. Even their ears were ugly. Two of them were nervous around the topless women; they laughed and pointed rudely, and I wondered if it was their Catholic upbringing. The third sat next to the Polack with his hand on her wrist. All three wore counterfeit Men's Presidents with lousy aftermarket diamond bezels. I had the three-hundred-thousand-dollar cashier's check folded in my pocket. It occurred to me that I might stand, fake a trip to the bathroom, and depart. I could live in Portugal, Thailand, or Indonesia for ten years on that money. But I gave them the check. I showed it to the girl on my lap before handing it over so that she would be impressed and would hesitate to leave me for the rest of our evening. The Polack winked at the one holding on to her and said loudly, over the music, "You see! You see how it works! Like I tell you!" He grinned, and I realized she was taking a piece of the check. They used her to collect and she got a cut. Maybe she was using them to collect. The whole thing was complicated.

I turned to Baron. He was in the middle of a dance and he knew this woman so she let him have his hands on her ass. He had that childish, menacing grin on his face he always displayed when he was receiving a lap dance.

"We make this money back," I said. "I signed the papers. I promised Jude. We can't screw this up with the bank."

"Of course," he said. "For chrissake it's a titty bar, Clancy. Have fun."

I wasn't lying to myself. I hate that ticklish taste of self-deception. But I sincerely did not expect it when, thirty days later, Baron and the Polack did not have the green.

The bad news always happened in my office. Baron held a jeweled Thai dagger in his hands and played with it as we talked. He spun it on its tip on my desk. I frowned about the leather. He was making a hole. "What are our options?" I asked him. I moved over to his side of my desk and sat beside him like I always did when we were in trouble. I put my arm around his shoulders. This time the screwup was his fault for a change. "Cheer up. We've been in worse places," I said, generously. The Polack came in then and sat down in my chair. She picked up my phone. I thought, That is not your phone, please put it down. She had a blue vein in her wrist that stood out when she handled something. You noticed it when she louped diamonds. She was getting older but she was getting sexier, too.

"You tell him?" she asked Baron. "Ha!" she said. "What a joke!" She held the phone with her chin. She was very slender but she had a round, gentle chin. It was unexpected. It looked like a chin your mother might have. "Do not worry, little brother," she said to me, "I will get your money! Tell him, Baron! That money is for me nothing." She laughed and dialed a number on my phone.

"Do you have anybody, Clancy?" Baron asked. "What about Ralston?"

"What about Ronnie?" I said.

"Ronnie owes us almost eighty. He might surprise us. But three hundred grand is rough."

"Well, Ralston's still dangling on that consignment necklace." I had sold Tom Ralston, my best customer, a platinum Art Deco ruby-and-diamond necklace on the premise that it would wholesale for twice what he paid for it—what won't a customer believe?—and he had immediately consigned it back to me. It had sat in the case ever since with a seven-hundred-and-fifty-thousand-dollar tag hanging off it. It was worth a hundred grand, maybe. The Polack teased me about it twice a week.

"How about Fadeen?" That was Baron's crow. He was an enormously wealthy Pakistani cancer specialist in Chicago who had bought his twin daughters matching tiaras for their coming-out party. He was always good for a big diamond from Pioneer, and we reserved him for situations like this.

"Sally says they're being investigated. They've been diagnosing people who aren't sick with cancer and treating them for the insurance money. She's worried."

"Ha!" the Polack said. "Wait," she said into the phone, and tucked the receiver under her arm. "That was smart! But they catch him!"

We often solved problems by driving, so Baron and I got into his Suburban and drove out to the old Plano store. "We could ask Emily to come," he said. "She might have an idea." "This is our problem," I said.

We had closed the Plano store a year before. They still hadn't rented the space. About half the cloth wallpaper had been ripped from the sheetrock; the rest of it hung there desperately. We shot thirty bucks a yard on that fabric. There's nothing as lonely or as sweet as a dead, vacant jewelry store in a little Texas strip mall. You want to carry it in your arms to a safer place.

"Are you sleeping with the Polack?" I asked him.

"I don't think she has sex, Clancy," he said. "We're partners."

"Partners."

"You know what I mean. Of course you're my partner. She's not my partner. She's a vendor for chrissake. Anyway it's not her fault. If you want to blame someone blame me. Not to mention that you talked Jude into it. If you hadn't signed the note we wouldn't be in this mess. Now we lost the bank. It's your fault as much as mine. We need the money. Without the bank we're dead."

"Why don't we use the Ronnie solution?" I asked him. "Blame it on her, since you're not sleeping with her. It could be a theft. The way she's in and out of the store all the time. She's got a key and the codes now, right? We make some invoices for imaginary diamonds, finger the Polack for stealing them, collect the insurance, pay off the bank. Nice and clean. It's the same stunt the Calabis pulled on their in-laws. They use Ken for their insurance same as we do. And Ken went for it. He'd go for it again. Hell, maybe we could cut Ken in."

"Nice, Clancy. Good idea," he said. "Anyway you know her better than that—think what she would do to us. She's not going to roll over and go to jail. She'd take the whole thing down with her."

I wanted to tell him, This is all your fault. But keeping quiet was more satisfying. That way it was his fault and I didn't lose the advantage by rubbing it in. We barely talked on the ride home. I wanted to call my wife on Baron's cell phone but I was too shy to ask. That's how it is with big brothers. We watched the yellow grass on the side of the highway. I knew it was that familiar time again, the time when you remembered how happy you were before.

When you declare bankruptcy it is not dramatic. It's a bit like cheating on your wife. You regard the mess from a distance. First you admit to yourself that there is no money to pay the note, then you call your banker who refuses to extend you, next there is a lunch with your angel who loses his temper, and last the call to your lawyer who summarizes your choices. He explains: "If you want to hang on to the store, it's an easy Chapter Eleven." Except from your lawyer's perspective, there's no such thing as an easy bankruptcy. You want to hang on to your store, so you hide what cash you can, trim down the inventory and make a sock, warn your favorite employees, and pull the trigger.

The Polack didn't like failure so she hustled out. "It smells bad here!" she said. I helped her wrap the delicate items in gauzy paper we bought at the Container Store. She put everything in red plastic milk crates. "You see they stack, Martin!" she said. "What are you complaining about? Spilt milk! Ha!" she said. She took the partners' desk too.

I caught them one night about a month after the Polack had moved out. It was after midnight and I had left my coke up at the store so that I wouldn't go through it all but I changed my mind. There they were, the Polack shouting in Russian or Polish on top of a jeweler's bench with her hands on the back of Baron's head. You never saw how red her skin was with her clothes on. I watched them for a few minutes. She looked better naked. Naked she didn't look like she thought about money as much as I knew she did. Naked she looked trustworthy. I thought, If you sold naked, no one could outsell you. In my desk I saw they'd found my cocaine and it was all gone. Naturally Baron's was gone too. So I rifled the cash box to let him know I'd been there before they got the same idea. But probably the Polack had plenty of cash. I skipped work the next day and when Baron called at a quarter after ten I didn't answer the phone. Let him open up the store and deal with the employees if he's going to stay up all night making butter with the Polack.

I wanted to kill her then. When I came in again I sat behind my desk with my diamond tweezers pinched around my pinkie finger or on the lobe of one ear and imagined her with that tiny red laser-targeting dot following the back of her slender skull. I contemplated that for nearly a year while I explained away the bankruptcy to my panicky, childish customers. "No, new layaways are fine, it's a Chapter Eleven." "No, your diamond won't disappear while it's being set, it's a Chapter Eleven." "No, I can't cut the price any lower. No, we're not going out of business. No, it's not all cash to me now. It's a Chapter Eleven."

After the Chapter Eleven I took over. I figured all we needed was one big season. But then Rolex USA flexed its lawyers and closed down our Rolex trade. We had to can the Christmas catalog. The last hundred grand we had I sunk into that thing. Even the trustee approved it. But those bastards knew what they were doing. They waited until days before the season started. The book was all South American counterfeit and used, reconditioned Swiss. I was debuting my new gimmick, knocking off Lexus: "Certified Pre-Owned Rolex." Rolex killed Christmas.

This was a nervous time for us. You can hide a lot while your business is running that you cannot hide once it is closed. People will wait and are careless about explanations if they think they're going to see some money out of you. When they hear that there will be no more money they become scientists and detectives, they want to see your books. At that point the best you can do is create confusion. Also you can act stupid.

By February we were converting the Chapter Eleven to a Seven, and Baron borrowed fifty grand from the Polack to pull us through the closing payroll. "We've put them through enough," he said. "I can't bounce their last paychecks." Bad idea, I said. I told him I didn't want my name near that money. "Clancy, it's a personal loan," Baron told me, but he was angry. He hinted that there was something morally wrong with me.

I took home the two bronze dogs that sat outside my office because my six-year-old admired them, and Baron took the electric MARTIN'S PRECIOUS JEWELS sign and hung it above his swimming pool. We barbecued out there a couple of times and sat in the hot tub under the green neon light. Baron planned to hip-pocket until a deal came together. Hit the pawnshops on the coast and flip diamonds and Swiss watches in the city to Dave and IDC. Suddenly we could talk the way we used to.

Between these times she called me. I remember thinking about it right after the initial meeting with creditors, while I watched everyone leave the courthouse. I was across the street, hiding in the park beneath a tree. I was hiding from the creditors, especially the customers with their consignments of their grandmothers' jewelry and their layaways for their wives' birthdays. It's a pleasant park, the only one downtown, and it has a series of forty or so short fountains arranged in a simple geometrical pattern, like a chessboard. The fountains bend when the wind blows, so it resembles a forest of very short trees made of water. The Polack had said she missed our backgammon games. I still wanted to sleep with her. Probably she wanted our customer list. I often masturbated with her in mind. There were only a hundred or so she would be interested in, but we had some good crows. Everybody in the business knew that. They knew I was the best jewelry salesman in DFW, they knew my older brother could be trusted, and they knew that somehow over the years we had accumulated the best crows.

After all the creditors were gone the Polack and I met at a Starbucks on Houston Street, not far from the courthouse and our old bank.

"I have not seen Baron," she said. She looked happy and thoughtful. "He is down here? He had the meeting with you? I see him."

"How's business?" I asked her. I didn't like her asking about Baron. "How's Ronnie?" I suspected they were fucking again. Her eyes were lidded, and I wanted to ask her if she'd been drinking. Baron said she drank before lunch. I doubt it was true. She was too cunning.

"He is old! Tell me, Martin, what am I doing with that old man? But he is smart. Smart man. You and your brother were not so smart. You were not good for me. Now no one wants to do business with the Martins. They are cheats, they say. Bad rent! That is what everyone says about you now."

"Smart enough not to go to prison."

"Ha! So you send Ronnie Popper! Again! Him first! Not me! But that time is over now. Good! No one goes to jail. I came to help you. What do you want? I am here to help you. You want money? You need something on the arm? No problem, Martin! What do you want? Just tell me! What's your plan now? You got a plan? You need help now. You know I am your friend. Old friends!"

"You said you wanted to talk to me," I said.

"I want to tell you a story. Something for you! Ha! Customers! When I was a girl, a young girl, a kid, my father took me fishing. He was a fisherman."

"I didn't know that."

"Yes, it is true. People think I am nobility but we are fishermen. He was looking for a fish. And he found it! He caught it. On a hook."

"That's how they catch them," I said.

"No, they use nets. You cannot make a living with hooks, Martin. You always talk like a Canadian. That's why you and Baron never make money. But when he pulled it up it was swollen. Like the baby in its belly. So he cuts it open with his knife. And what do you think was inside?"

"I don't know."

"Ha! Of course not. Guess!"

"I said I don't know."

"I know! A snake. A snake with an egg in its mouth! A duck egg!"

"I don't believe you."

"It does not matter. Why do I care if it's true? Then he cracks open the egg and what is inside the egg?"

"Another snake."

"No. Ha! That would be good. Good idea. No, something better. A diamond!"

"A diamond in the egg inside the fish."

"A duck egg! Don't forget the snake. In the snake's mouth! And then he said to me, 'You will be a jeweler.' My father called me like that. But he was right. But how did he know? Was it the diamond? No! Of course. It was because he told me. That is it. Power! Believing people, Martin. That is what I am telling you. Now you have to believe. Ha! That is not what I mean. I mean, a person you believe. Your brother. You believe him."

"You made that story up." For the first time since I originally met her, back at Fort Worth Gold, just down Houston Street from where we were sitting now, she seemed like a woman. She was lying to me to help me.

"No, it is a true story. But it is a good one. So, you help your brother."

Then I thought everything would be all right. It sounded like they were square. Maybe he had paid her back the fifty grand without telling me. But when Baron suddenly moved back to Canada I knew he was running from the Polack. I had left the jewelry business altogether and gone back to vacuums.

One morning a few minutes before a presentation I got a call in my car from Emily.

"How did you get this number?" I asked her.

"Ha!" she said. "I'm in Calgary, Martin," she said. I thought of her as Emily now that I was out of the business.

I asked her why she was calling me. She said, "You know. Ha ha!"

I explained that I didn't have any money but that I knew where to get some. This was a lie to create some room.

"You bet!" she said. "Fifty grand." I decided that Baron was already dead. That was the sort of thing the Polack could do. To prove she was cleverer than me. Or just as a joke.

I wondered what Ronnie Popper would say, or Granddad, if he were still alive. What if I called Bob and Jeremy at Pioneer, could they front me fifty grand? Or Dave? His money was always tied up in inventory but he could get liquid in a hurry if he would take the hit.

I remembered the buying trips Baron and I took together. Colombia, Thailand, Hong Kong, Israel. We had ridden elephants into the Vietnamese mountainside to buy untreated rubies and sapphires from the miners. We had slept in the same bed with the same hooker. We always planned to go with Nikhil to his cutters in Bombay but never made it.

I thought about the afternoon the Polack shot that kid outside my office. That was a happier time, I thought. You used to like my brother, I wanted to tell her. Think of all the money we made together. I almost told her about the time I saw the two of them together. I told myself I ought to hang up the phone. It was his fault. I should have fucked her.

"Let me talk to Baron," I said. "You want to buy something?" I asked her. Then I laughed. "Put Baron on the phone, Polack," I said. "That kind of money is nothing for us."

Tina Barney, *Marina and Peter*, 1997. © Tina Barney, courtesy Janet Borden, Inc., NY

FATHERS AND DAUGHTERS

TINA BARNEY PORTRAITS

by LAWRENCE WESCHLER

(nonfiction from Issue 8)

BOUT THREE YEARS ago, on an art walk through Soho, in a gallery off Broadway, I happened upon a large-scale color-saturated photograph that stopped me cold: Tina Barney's double portrait of what were clearly a father and his late-teenaged daughter, staring head-on into the camera. It stopped me cold, and immediately I started to warm to it. As it happened, this was the photo that was featured on the show's announcement postcard, so I was able to take that version of it home with me: I push-pinned it to the wall facing my desk and have, in the months and years since, had frequent occasion to lose myself in it.

Back in college, years ago, I'd had a girlfriend who looked remarkably like the girl in Barney's picture—and who'd look at me in a remarkably similar manner: self-assured, ironical, a drowsy-lidded gaze freighted with entendres and double-entendres. Occasionally we'd go up to visit her parents in San Francisco. I could be wrong, but something about the light and the furnishings makes me sure the bedroom in Barney's photo is also in

San Francisco. Anyway, my girlfriend's parents were of a certain class—comfortable haute-bourgeoisie, which is to say a situation slightly higher than my own family's—and every once in a while, she and her father would get themselves lined up, facing me, just like the pair in the photo: she'd be giving me that ironically freighted look, and her father, in turn, who looked remarkably like the guy in the photo, would also be giving me a look just like his: wary, somewhere between begrudged and resigned. Between the two of them, they had me nailed.

And years later, as, daydreamingly, I continued gazing back into the father and daughter in Barney's double portrait over my desk, they still had me nailed: I was back in college, it was as if I hadn't grown a day, I was still that slightly gawky and yet increasingly assured kid, right on the cusp, eternally on the cusp.

Do any of us ever grow up?

Anyway, as I say, that photo has been staring at me from across my desk for years now, slowly becoming festooned over with other cards and photos and announcements, but still pertinent, still sweetly charged, still capable of drawing me in in the midst of my otherwise busy days.

Days full of this and that, my writing work, my own family responsibilities, and this past year, increasingly, caring for Herb, the dear old man across the street, a ninety-eight-year-old geezer who until just recently had been wry and spry and sharp and funny and astonishingly nimble, an ongoing inspiration to everyone in the neighborhood, including me and my wife and our little daughter. Late some nights—say, three in the morning—our entire block would be dark save for two lights: me in my office, writing away at my desk; and Herb across the street in his front parlor, hunched over, his glasses pushed up onto his bald pate, gazing down, intently reading by the light of a single bulb. I knew that some months hence, when whatever piece I happened to be working on got published, Herb would read it and have me over to kibbitz about it: he'd be my best reader, and I was writing for him.

Though, it had to be said, over the last several months, Herb had suddenly started declining precipitously, and actually—it was tough to face but clearly true: he no longer sat there at night in the front parlor in that puddle of light, reading away. He was largely confined to his bed, which had been moved down into his living room because he could no longer make it up the stairs. A dear, spirited Trinidadian woman named Marjorie had moved into the house to care for him full-time. Herb was on his last legs. He no longer wanted to live: in considerable chronic pain and discomfort, all he anymore wanted was to be let to die.

Very early one morning a few months back, around four—it happened to be my birthday—I was startled awake by the phone. It was Marjorie, calling to tell me that Herb had just "breathed his last" and asking if I could come over to sit with her, she really didn't want to be alone with the body. My wife happened to be away, traveling, so after I got dressed, I went into my now-thirteen-year-old daughter's room to wake her and tell her what had happened. Sara took it pretty hard: she'd adored Herb, too. I told her where I'd be, how she should go back to sleep but if she wanted she could just look out her window and she'd be able to see me there across the street. I'd keep checking, I said, in any case.

And the morning proceeded like that: sitting by Herb's side, making the necessary calls, commiserating with Marjorie, occasionally peering through the window across the street to check on Sara (she was standing there, framed in her bedroom window, somber, intent, unmoving the entire time). Eventually the sun rose, the police arrived, then the coroners, and I headed back across the street to get Sara ready for school.

Sara came downstairs to greet me: she'd obviously been thinking. "Daddy," she said thoughtfully, "do you realize that Herb died on the very day that you became half his age? And that, for that matter, even though today is the thirteenth and I myself happen to be thirteen, in two days it will be seven days until I become exactly two-sevenths your age. Which is weird because at that point I will be two-times-seven and you are seven-squared and Herb was two-times-seven-squared, which of course also means that I will have become one seventh of Herb's age. And what's really weird, if you think about it"—clearly she'd been dwelling on all this, up there in the window her mind had been racing—"half of seven is 3.5 and you are going to be 3.5 times as old as me, or phrased differently, 35 years older than me."

I looked at her for a few long seconds and finally said, "Sara, get a life."

*   *   *

That evening I was back at my desk, working, when I happened to gaze up at the Barney photo. It had undergone a sudden transformation. Wait a second, I found myself thinking, I'm not the one the father and the girl are looking at—*I'm the father!* That's me, or almost: that's what I'm fast becoming. It was a startling, almost vertiginous shift in vantage.

A few weeks later, during a trip to Chicago, I happened into another gallery that happened to be staging a Tina Barney retrospective. I got to talking with the gallery owner, described the picture over my desk, and she averred as to how, yes, of course, she knew it, and in fact she happened to have a couple earlier pictures from the same series.

"The same series?" I asked.

Oh yes, she said, leading me into her storage vault and rifling among the framed images. Barney photographed the same father and daughter at least three times. Once when the girl was maybe ten or so—this one here (and indeed, there they were, draped on the same bed: the girl roughly the age my own daughter had been the day I happened on the later image at that Soho gallery)—and then another time, about three years after that, when the girl was thirteen or fourteen: this one… here. And indeed, there they were again, the same bedroom, the girl exactly my daughter's age: with exactly her haughty put-upon self-assurance ("Daaa-aaadie"). The gallery owner then pulled out a Barney book and turned to the last image in the series, the one over my desk. And yes, there they were again, same father, same girl.

Ten years: God, he had aged.

(NOTES FROM THE MIDDLE WORLD)

by BREYTEN BREYTENBACH

(essay from Issue 6)

"Who are you? Even when you know the answer, it is not an easy question."
— Leon Wieseltier, *Against Identity*

I'D LIKE TO taste the breeze and take a stroll through the Middle World which is, and is not, the same as the Global Village. Let's say that those of the Middle World—I think of them as *uncitizens*, the way you have un-American activities as opposed to those considered non- or anti-American—are global Village vagrants, knights of the naked star. They are defined by what they are not, or no longer, and not so much by what they oppose or even reject. They ventured into zones where truths no longer fit snugly and where certainties did not overlap, and most likely they got lost there.

In the course of doing so, proceeding by interrogation and comparison, discovering/uncovering the way and the ways of my hand, I hope to outline the territory and identify some of its inhabitants.

What I'm reaching for may be a fancy, a construct of the imagination, a conceit. I'm not even certain about the terminology. Let us rather think of it as a temporary name for what could be a passing phenomenon.

"Middle World" is probably confusing; unwittingly it resonates with "Middle Kingdom." (I'd feel more comfortable were it to evoke "the floating world" of old Japan, of actors and prostitutes and poets—though, aptly, to live in the Middle World is not unlike a long-nosed ghost living in Chinese.) In other languages, friends tell me, they find the term unsatisfactory: the French *monde du milieu* quite literally relates to the world of gangsters and politicians—not entirely inappropriate since narco-traffic, for example, like transnational business, has more of an international reach than the communion of intellectuals and artists. Carlos Fuentes, with whom I discussed the conceit, liked the notion but found the term in Spanish too wishy-washy. It may also put us in mind of Tolkien's "Middle Earth," where the hobbits live. In this instance I'd be quite delighted to accept the confusion. As for the "Middle Way," I leave that to your appreciation.

I call it Middle World because of its position somewhere equidistant from East and West, North and South, belonging and not belonging. Not of the Center though, since it is by definition and vocation peripheral, other, to be living in the margins and on the live edges. (The Center, both internationally and in any given country, is always elsewhere, to the North.) Also, to be there is to be "in the middle of the world." Maybe I should push my luck and suggest we call this emerging archipelago of self-enforced freedom and unintentional estrangement, partaking in equal parts of love and death, MOR. I like the sound: the land of MOR. To be the first of the Moricans.

(What if there were not one shared language in this world but as many tongues as you have uncitizens? And if no one could understand one another? And if the Middle World were the tower of Babel—not built upward as the Bible imagines (for the Bible is more the projection of collective imagination than the transcription of shared memory), but down into the earth, as Kafka intimated? What if it were no more that the area of being lost, the vacant lot of nothingness? Nothingness-making is not the upshot of Middle Worlders not having a common language; on the contrary, it is an expression of the one-language of imposed consensus and the convention of correct brainwashing.)

My immediate purpose is not now to suggest how this space and tribe of uncitizens came into being. We are all aware of paradigm-shattering changes in the world at moments accelerating into new patterns of power. We know—have been buffeted, alienated, awed—by the cave-in of empires; we are all consumer subjects to the monopoly of a capitalist free market masquerading as "globalization of the world economy"; most of us are already caught in the tele-technological web of virtual reality and virtual knowledge and virtual communication and thus virtual imagination and virtual truth; we observe shifts in population caused by war and famine and ethnic cleansing and sometimes national liberation; despite our best commitments we probably share the *Realmoral* that makes it plausible—or is it inevitable?—to live with the now irrevocable division between rich and poor, which makes it furthermore "normal" that certain states known to be "weak" or "failed" should implode, that is, "held to consequence" (I'm thinking of Somalia, Liberia, Sierra Leone, Congo, soon Angola and Ivory Coast and perhaps Nigeria and Indonesia and Zimbabwe...), normal too, that we should shrug our shoulders and ultimately forget these black holes.

This is not new. In one of his writings, Jacques Derrida speaks of "the first evil," the night from which so many anonymous people are struggling to emerge. He goes back to Hannah Arendt's description of *Heimatlosen*—the stateless ones, the nations of minorities and the peoples without a state (one could say the Kurds and the Palestinians of our times), and her analyses of how the principles of human rights had deteriorated. Derrida decries the erosion of "universal hospitality," that axiom Kant had considered a "cosmopolitical law."

But perhaps the situation is worse now. One may borrow Walter Benjamin's words to illustrate how, in civilized societies, police violence and intelligence control became faceless and all-pervasive (*gestaltlos* and *nirgends fassbar*), as if phantoms now directed life from the shadows. Even in France, *pays des droits de l'homme*, we came close a few years ago to a proposed legal dispensation in terms of which hospitality offered to "illegal foreigners" (*étrangers en situation irrégulière*) or simply to those "without papers" (*les sans-papiers*) would have been decreed a "terrorist action."

The purpose of Derrida's text, *Cosmopolites de tous les pays, encore un effort!*

(Cosmopolitans of the world, one more try!), was to explain and extol the proposal of "shelter cities" (*villes-refuges*), as in Biblical times or during the Middle Ages, and to argue for its implementation.

Refuge and asylum, persecution and hospitality, indifference and difference, solidarity, home and exile—all these concepts figure in the Middle World. Tolerance and diversity, as well. In fact, to live in MOR is to promote diversity, sometimes by default. Somehow I don't think "democracy" comes into the equation, and "peace" is unlikely to be on the agenda. Talking about these two notions is rather like asking Buddha whether he believes in God, when the answer was that we have here an unknowable question and why bother about what is far when we can't take care of what is near? Or should we say with Marcel Duchamp: "If no solution, maybe no problem"?

A West African poet, Ka'afir, someone I've known on and off over the years—an outsider in Africa, a heathen among those who grovel—recently wrote to me in a letter:

> The word "peace." Ah, how voluptuous. Like "democracy." It just fills the mouth with its familiar, well-sucked, inoffensive, satisfying taste. As if one were experiencing one's own *goodness*. No indigestion, no burnt lips. It won't cause constipation and you won't grow fat on it either. In fact, it carries no nutritional connotation whatsoever. And guaranteed to have no secondary effects: it won't provoke a rash of freedom, let alone the aches of justice. Ah, "peace," "democracy," soft drugs of self-absorption—how we love to talk sweet nothings with them tucked in the cheek hard by the tongue, chew them, take them out at international conferences to lick the contours before plopping them back into the mouth…

However much we may whistle in the dark, the Center is holding, redefining and regrouping and re-outlining itself. Be it by Internet—power flows there to form a stem, a spine of control. This is true for any given combination of tensions—nationally (as with cultural or religious orthodoxy), regionally, and internationally. You may wish to identify it as the One Superpower making the world safe for democracy, otherwise known as Pax Americana, or as the IMF, political correctness, the World Economic System built on the "moral" Law of History called Freedom… You may wish to name it True Faith or Jihad, which is just an unholy war, or Eretz Israel, or Hollywood, or CNN… Any number of power groupings may easily be recognized because their lowest common denominator will often be an acronym.

And yet, as if in a contradictory movement, there is a surge toward cultural diversity and ethnical affirmation, perhaps in a scramble for the supposed security of self recognition. The margins are heaving, throwing up new ideas and old contestations, positing chaos, respecting madness. Counterforces continually emerge. In the mountains, dreamers with hoods over their heads grope for the forgotten treasure of "revolution." Black thoughts are vomited on paper.

And indeed, the ways you are positioned to and in language may be one of the defining traits of the Middle World uncitizen. More often than not he/she will no longer be living untrammeled in the subtle regions of the birth-tongue, and memories of that "paradise" will now be travel jottings; just as often the contours of the other language(s) used will be potentially hostile shallows to be negotiated with great care and the precise circumspection of the trained orphan. But often too, these "new" spaces of self-othering will be invested with exuberance. (*And there you go again!* Ka'afir would warn me.)

Does the Middle World not also have a "ghost center"? Can there be continuing awareness outside the group, therefore beyond shared references? Aristotle postulated that the political animal (*zōon politikon*) was not just *any old bee* but distinguished itself by a collective ethical existence. Political animals don't live in groups by instinct or only for the sake of survival and not even for the happy hell of it. No, human nature strives for more than the satisfaction of needs and desires, for lightening the skin color or finding the right lotion to darken it. Man wants to live with justice. Or he used to.

For what do we still remember about the *common weal* now that our public spaces have been blighted by the barrenness of television soaps and the smirks of politicians looking for the soundbite? Do we still know and accept that the one thing we cannot be deprived of is our humanity? That, as Roger Antelme wrote after the death camps, *the SS may kill a man, but cannot change him into something else?* Isn't it this striving for transgression, transcendence, becoming other, that distinguishes us from the animals? Even when we cannot express it in words?

We seem forever incapable of grasping and expressing all the variations of our changes. The first effect of that Center which we combat or which repulses us, is to stultify language, to make it "official," to substitute it for memory, to make of it the privileged means of "communication and record," thus order and authority, to repress the contestation and creativeness of uncertainty.

Perhaps the ideal of shared and compound and irreducible marginality I'm talking about here was best expressed in Zarathustra's favorite "center" or never-never capital called "the multihued cow," Die bunte Kuh. Nietzsche must have had in mind a line from an ancient Greek's verse, where the wise man is described as being one who is painted in many colors...

Is the uncitizen not just a garden-variety internationalist, perhaps a multi-cultured person with a hyphenated social identity? No, because you can be all of that without leaving your premises of prejudice. A universalist, then? No, because "universal values" (as embodied in l'homme universel) are well understood to be Western; universalism is represented, I'd say, by a French-bound point of departure. Surely a cosmopolitan, of the déclassè intelligentsia, and how does he or she differ from what used to be termed "displaced persons"? Indeed, the Middle World has affinities with all these categories, but the above terms are fairly precisely circumscribed in specific historical periods and situations.

To be of the Middle World is to have broken away from the parochial, to have left "home" for good (or for worse) while carrying all of it with you, and to have arrived on foreign shores (at the onset you thought of it as "destination," but not for long) feeling at ease there without ever being "at home." Exile? Maybe. But exile is a memory disease expressing itself in spastic social behavior: people find it a mysterious ailment and pity you greatly. (J. M. G. Le Clézio has this evocative definition of exile as "he or she who has left the island"; the ex-ile, one assumes, leaves the I-land of self to become water lapping at the continent of we-ness, of belonging.)

Exile could be a passage and you may well speak of "passage people." Yet, the Middle World is a finality beyond exile. For a while at least the reference pole will remain the land from which you had wrenched yourself free or from where you were expelled. Then, exile itself will become the habitat. And in due time, when there's nothing to go back to or you've lost interest, MOR will take shape and you may start inhabiting the in-between. The terrain is rugged, the stage bathed in a dusty grey light. It is not an easy perch. Wieseltier, in another of his barbed aphorisms, says: "In the modern world, the cruelest thing you can do to people is to make them ashamed of their complexity."

One location of the Middle World is where the turfs of the outcast, the outsider, and the outlaw overlap. It could be a dominion of outers. Is it all shame, therefore? Not on your life! Listen to this poem, written around the year 1080 by a Chinese world-traveler, Su Tung-p'o, a functionary who had carnal knowledge of prison and banishment:

> A hundred years, free to go, and it's almost spring;
> for the years left, pleasure will be my chief concern.
> Out the gate, I do a dance, wind blows my face;
> Our galloping horses race along as magpies cheer.
> I face the wine cup and it's all a dream,
> pick up a poem brush, already inspired.
> Why try to fix the blame for troubles past?
> Years now I've stolen posts I never should have had.

(The translator, Burton Wallace, adds that the third line, "I do a dance," may as well be interpreted as, "I stop to piss.")

Now let me draw the line a little more clearly by proposing a very partial and partisan list of people I consider to be (or have been) of the Middle World; these well-known names make the night of the nameless ones even darker, of course.

I won't touch upon religion or science—the Dalai Lama is there by definition, and Einstein was surely an uncitizen of MOR; nor music (Mozart was one) or business (I suspect that Maxwell, the news-mogul who became a whale, was also an uncitizen), nor politics (Mandela, forever driven into self-preservation by prison, burnt clean of attachments, may just be of the Middle World, and so ultimately was Ghandi)...

You will take me to task for my choices which depend more on feeling than on verifiable assessment, but my sketchy picture includes: Kundera—for a while before he became French; Nureyev; Naipaul—adrift while denying it; Rushdie—neither East nor West but enjoying the party immensely; Homi Bhabha—*we now locate the question of culture in the realm of the beyond*; Pei, the international architect, and so was Gaudi; Juan Goytisolo; Eric von Stroheim, but somehow neither Dietrich nor Chaplin; Edward Said— very intermittently so; Bai Dao, the Chinese exile poet, is in the process of getting his uncitizen papers; Brecht from the time after he returned to East Germany; Adorno, who relished it, particularly in his late style; Borges— very nearly, tapping his white cane against the gates; Freud—unwittingly, which is not strange because he fancied himself a scientist when he was in fact but an interesting writer—and probably also Jung; Samuel Beckett,

who visualized the workrooms of Middle Worldness on stage; Pessoa, popu-
lating his head with alienated explorers of the self, that slippery slope to
damnation; Jean-Marie Le Clézio; Henri Michaux—*hell is the rhythm of the
other*; Rimbaud—both as poet and trader; Victor Segalen; Han Shan the Cold
Mountain poet, and Gary Snyder his disciple; the Andalusian explorers and
historians; Mahmoud Darwish—*Where should we go after the last frontiers?
Where should the birds fly after the last sky?*; Franz Fanon and Franz Kafka; Bessy
Head and Amos Tutuola in their worlds of spirits; Cervantes of the Missing
Hand and Goya with the Screaming Mind; Morandi and Giacometti; Carlos
Fuentes but not Octavio Paz and certainly not Vargas Llosa; Frida Kahlo
but not Diego Rivera; the Zapatistas of Chiapas but not the Shining Path
guerrillas; Passolini but not Fellini; Ryszard Kapuscinski; Robert Walser—
*how fortunate I am not to be able to see in myself anything worth respecting and
watching*; Albert Camus; Alexandra David-Neel; William Burroughs, maybe
Jack Kerouac—but, I imagine, somehow not Allen Ginsberg; the Chinese
wandering monks/artists/poets/exiles; Gauguin, maybe Degas; probably
Bacon with the raw meat of his thinking; and Matisse, but neither Picasso
nor Cézanne nor Velázquez...

Was Nietzsche of the detribalized tribe? Or was he more German than
mad? And of his acolytes I'd include only Foucault who had the baldness
and the loud taste in attire so typically uncitizen, and perhaps Deleuze, for
he did sport extraordinarily long fingernails, although he gradually glad-
mouthed himself back to the closed-in compulsiveness of self-indulgent
French rhetoric; the others (Barthes, Derrida, Kristeva) remain too rooted
in a Jacobin arrogance where doubt is a cover for self-accretion, they suffer
from the blindness of brilliance, and besides, the text of itself (and for itself)
cannot be the Middle World—it is a skein, not a body.

Is one always of the Middle World? It may happen, as in the case of
Beckett who walked in order to fall down and Paul Celan who never escaped,
not even when he became a dead goose in the Seine, but one may also grow
out of it. One is not normally born there, and your children cannot inherit
uncitizenship.

How does one draw a map of MOR? Wherever its citizens are, there
the Middle World is. I don't have a complete topography because cities and
countries may change their coloring on the map. Once more, I'll not argue
the nuances. It should be pointed out that Middle Worlders, paradoxically,

have a sharpened awareness of place (topoi, locus)—as with nomads the environment may be constantly changing and you do not possess it, but it is always a potentially dangerous framework with which you must interact, and therefore they will know cloud and well and star and fire better than sedentary citizens do.

Alexandria was Middle World territory (by the way, the Middle World has nothing to do with modernity) and so was Beirut once upon a time; Sarajevo belonged, before the pigs slaughtered it to "purity"; Hong Kong was an outpost (the poet P.K. Leung wrote, in an admirable volume called *City at the End of Time*: *Ironically, Hong Kong as a colony provides an alternative space for Chinese people and culture to exist, a hybrid for one to reflect upon the problems of a "pure" and "original" state*); Paris used to be a section of MOR when it still had a proletariat, many of whom were of foreign origin, living within the walls (by the way, the Middle World has nothing to do with riches or urban sophistication); Cuba may be of the Middle World despite its best efforts at being communist; Berlin, still, although it is now becoming "normalized" as the pan-Germanic capital; Jerusalem, even though its present rulers try to stamp it with the seal of fanatic exclusivism; South Africa went through birth pains, it was close to understanding a cardinal Middle World law—that you can only survive and move forward by continuing to invent yourself—but then it became a majority-led democracy instead; New York, except when it is too close to America; I have heard tales of tolerance and center-insouciance from a town once known as Mogador, now Essaouira; Tangier, where I celebrated my twenty-first birthday (bird-day) wrapped in a burnus, was a refuge despite the closed warren of its casbah; Gorée, Zanzibar, Haiti, and the other Caribbean islands—most islands tend to be natural outcrops of MOR; Palestine most certainly—"exodus" can be a high road to the Middle World, and what is now termed the Territories (an euphemism for ghettos and Bantustans, subject to apartheid) will breed a new generation of uncitizens.

There could be areas of Middle Worldness that are socially defined, separate and specific, perhaps temporary, drifting through the surrounding waters of belonging like ice-floes ultimately melting: I'm thinking of that long middle period when mentally disturbed people are "cured" and have to learn the vocabulary and the codes of a "normal" world, where one audited fiction must now take precedence over the deviant one; and feminists who broke away from rules and values imposed by the patriarchy to re-invent their lives freed from the shackles of family and decorum, and who may do so until the bitter end of loneliness; and "rehabilitated" prisoners becoming invisible while carrying with them an inner universe of extreme humiliation where isolation bounces off steel and concrete; and societies gutted by war and self-war, which have to rebuild around the ruins of brutally destroyed "normalcy."

What are the further characteristics of a Middle World resident?

It is important to know that being of the Middle World is neither romantic nor does it imply a value. The uncitizen may well have a number of negative affinities and certainly he or she will bristle with contradictions. He will have a conflicted relationship to identity—perhaps mourning the loss of its essence while multiplying the acquisition of other facets.

Culturally such a person will be a hybrid. (*"Purity is the opposite of integrity."*—Wieseltier.) This is both a precondition and a consequence. Is the bastard more tolerant? Not sure. There could be greater understanding, yes, because he ought to have "natural access" to the different strains of his make-up. But often the hybrid is very persnickety in the itemization of grades of distinction.

The Middle World person has a vivid consciousness of being the Other, and is probably proud of it. (Jenaro Talens wrote: *Yo soy él que occupa el mismo lugar que yo*—"I am he who occupies the same space as I.")

At heart he will be a nomad and he will practice nomadic thinking, even if he doesn't move around much. The best-seasoned nomads are those who never travel.

In any given country he/she will be a Southerner.

As an artist he will practice an inventive and transformative reporting of fact, using the self ("identity") as a transient and mutating guest in his work.

He will be obliged to create concepts: the security of repeating the known is forbidden to him, and this is why fundamentalists of all stripes will abhor and wish to expectorate the very name.

He will be fascinated by the processes of metamorphosis and evolution of change when the yardstick is lost. James Joyce ended up living in MOR.

He is superstitious: all gods must be placated and survival is a question of nurtured luck.

To him culture is a matter (the matter) of food, drinking sessions, markets, street life, theaters, clubs… and he has a keen interest in clothes.

He is less attracted to conference halls and academics.

He will assiduously exercise the necessary art of being invisible among the poor but will have scant patience with bureaucrats and culturocrats. He will also have no loyalty to the state although he may sometimes pretend to in order to embarrass the authorities of the day. Patriotism is like God, a concept much too distant for useful contemplation.

He will be attached to fetishes. The chameleon and the parrot are emblems.

To him (her) the form—more correctly, the posture—is as important as the contents. He will learn the Oriental way, by mimesis. There is as much mysticism in light as there is in darkness.

Role-playing may be significant, appearances matter a lot, the personality will be split so as to cover all bases and accommodate all comers. Consciousness, even when it is centered, is multiple. Considerations of "bourgeois honesty" are secondary. When you're blind you don't know what "straight ahead" means.

Whether or not he/she is a criminal is not important; the world of thievery and honor may well be his environment of predilection—as it was for Jean Genet, a prime protagonist of Middle World uncitizenship.

He/she will inhabit the *nada* and have a lifelong intimate dialogue and affinity with death.

He will recognize likeness with other Middle Worlders and there may even be a code of sharing.

A central question remains: how do we as a species of intelligence (that is, of projecting backward and forward hypotheses of invention, the experience of memory and of imagination) and of self-reflexive fancy (by allowing these hypotheses then to define us), among other intelligent life-forms (no life without change and a measure of adaptation in the will to endure, therefore no life without intelligence)—how do we see/invent ourselves? Perhaps we are at last abutting on the outer boundaries of sequential thinking, the Cartesian folly that the mind is logical and the perceivable world outside conforms to the laws of the mind, and the Copernican angst which decided that the geometrical description of the trajectory of planets was not make-believe but true—these positions whence flowed the arid arrogances of "progress" and "conquest" with the last shudders constituted by those protagonists of the autonomy of language, of "creating and knowing by naming," who hold to the primacy of text or discourse, the deconstructionists who were so homo-infatuated they believed the outlaw mind could be in-lawed, that a flaw was but an imperfect or flubbed law. They subscribed only to the thrust for power of Nietzsche's will and autonomy of language and conveniently forgot about the breakdown. They thought that a pattern surmises control which can be subsumed in laws and that laws construct reality; they forgot to forget themselves, forgot as well that perception (through language) is itself a narrative—of necessity using all the tricks of invention (repetition, likeness, believability...) and mistaking itself as it must, for "reality." Wasn't it Ronald Reagan, that masterful deconstructionist (or destroyer?), who claimed that reality is but an illusion that can be overcome?

If, as I claim, the opposite is true, if the narrative is but a shadow of the *nada*—with all the creative potential and beauty of illusion and invention, and if we are constantly defined and undefined by the narrative of self-invention, by the ultimate joy of nothing-making—on what must we then base our moral conduct? To be of the Middle World is to be aware of the moral implications of narrative, to know and respect the knowledge that we are all part of the same nothing. It is to "know" about the power and the limits (and the fugacity) of self-invention. And that the ultimate power is non-power. The Middle World is (ideally?) where the nothingness of being and the being of nothingness are continually inflected by the ethical awareness of living in a society where you are responsible through the narrative for others, and by the sharpened imperative of non-power.

I'm leaving many stones unturned here. Perhaps just as well, because we don't necessarily know what to do about the scorpions and the spiders. Among these would be: what privileges, if any, come with the territory? Does the uncitizen define his own moral parameters? Will the emerging shared ethic be new or is the Morican but an old-fashioned humanist at bay? Is there really honor among thieves? Since moral awareness is rooted in language, what happens to the polyglot? How does the Middle Worlder use his narrative tongue? Can he still have one, or is he tongue-tied like Man Friday? Can he be a native anywhere? What are the uses of language to him? If awareness is movement, where does he think he's going—or does it matter? If past and present are one seamless whole (the white hole of becoming), if you live in the possible tense, if you think of the past as destroyed time—what happens to memory? Should anything happen to memory? If you keep on inventing and multiplying yourself—whose memory do you ultimately mix with the soil?

I'm done. But I cannot conclude without tipping a hat to a true ancestor of the Middle World, Constantin Cavafy, the Alexandrian poet of Greek extraction who died in 1933. He it was who famously wrote: "And now, what's going to happen to us without barbarians? They were, those people, a kind of solution."

Well, we know now he need not have worried, since we are still here.

In his introduction to the translation of Cavafy's poems, Edmund Keeley celebrates the uncitizen's Alexandrian myth, talking of "the virtues of historical perspicacity, of seeing things not only for what they are but what they are likely to become, including the inevitable reversals in history that finally teach one not so much the moral as the tragical sense of life... the virtues of irony..."

One should keep the soul open to those that satisfy the spirit and the body: beautiful lovers given to sensual pleasures, imaginative creations of various kinds, mixed cultures and mixed faiths, the value of both art and artifice, of spectacle, of politic theater—so that the soul may carry within it the ripening prospect of its own death, but also so that the day's work may show there's no other life worthy of celebration.

May this perspective serve to warn us against those excesses that lead to fanaticism, intolerance, self-satisfied complacency; may it find wisdom and courage to reside in a recognition of human limitations and finitude and above all the inevitable fate of all things mortal. May we learn from Cavafy's "commitment to hedonism, to political skepticism, and to honest self-awareness... (to) judgment suspended and mercy granted, through not to the viciously power hungry, or puritanically arrogant, or the blindly self-deceived."

GOING BACK HOME FROM GREECE

Well, we're nearly there, Hermippos.
Day after tomorrow, it seems—that's what the captain said.
At least we are sailing our seas,
the waters of Cyprus, Syria and Egypt,
the beloved waters of our home countries.
Why so silent? Ask your heart:
didn't you too feel happier

the farther we got from Greece?
What's the point of fooling ourselves?
That would hardly be properly Greek.

It's time we admitted the truth:
we are Greeks also—what else are we?—
but with Asiatic affections and feelings,
affections and feelings
sometimes alien to Hellenism.

It isn't right, Hermippos, for us philosophers
to be like some of our petty kings
(remember how we laughed at them
when they used to come to our lectures?)
who through their showy Hellenified exteriors,
Macedonian exteriors (naturally),
let a bit of Arabia peep out now and then,
a bit of Media they can't keep back.
And to what laughable lengths the fools went
trying to cover it up!

No, that's not all right for us.
For Greeks like us that kind of pettiness won't do.
We must not be ashamed
of the Syrian and Egyptian blood in out veins;
we should really honor it, take pride in it.

TWO BY TWO

by GUNNHILD ØYEHAUG

(from a section dedicated to Norwegian fiction, in Issue 35)

A T TEN MINUTES to one one night in November, Edel loses it. She has been standing by the window with her arms crossed since ten past twelve, alternately looking down the drive and at the watch on her wrist. A few hours earlier, she had been lying on the bed clutching a book to her chest with her eyes shut tight, feeling good, strong, and completely open. Then she got up to clear the snow, so that Alvin could drive straight into the garage without having to stop and clear the snow himself. She had wanted to *reach out* to him—that was the expression she'd used when she thought about what it was she'd wanted to do. It was a cliché, but that was okay, it was what she wanted. She imagined her own small hand reaching out and being taken by Alvin's hand, Alvin's big, strong hand. Her eyes filled with tears when she thought of their two joined hands and everything they symbolized. And clearing the snow—it dawned on her that clearing the snow symbolized that she was making room for him again. She was making room for him again after he had asked for forgiveness and said that from now on, she was the only one, there would be no others; she had let him stay in her life as Thomas's father, as someone she shared her home with, someone she refused to look in the eye at the breakfast table and whose shoes she occasionally kicked as she passed them in the hallway. So she cleared the snow, and as she shoveled she looked up at the double garage and thought that it symbolized her goal. She was clearing the way for him—she was the garage that he could come home to. Her small car was already parked on one side, and when his car was on the other side things would be as they should be. Her small car parked alongside his big car. She ran up the driveway through the uncleared snow and turned on the light and looked at her little car standing there all alone, waiting, and then cried as she cleared the rest of the driveway to the garage.

That was forty minutes ago. It is snowing hard again now, snowing so much that it looks like the snowflakes are falling together, two by two, three by three, four by four, falling through the air until they land suddenly and mutely in the snow. In only forty minutes, the driveway has been covered again. And the man that she cleared the way and made room for is not here. He should have been here forty minutes ago. The last ferry docked at twenty past eleven and it takes three quarters of an hour to drive here from the ferry—and that's being generous. In other words, he should have been here at ten past twelve, when she finished clearing the snow and stood waiting, red-cheeked, by the window, with a magnanimous, nearly loved-up look on her face.

Every minute that passed after ten past twelve pulled this look of love from her face, like a net being dragged from the water. By the thirtieth minute past twelve, when she called his mobile and heard it ringing in the bread box in the kitchen, her face was no longer remotely magnanimous. She screamed with rage, she who had felt no rage one hour earlier as she'd lain on the bed feeling good, strong, and open, before she'd decided to get up and clear the snow. At twelve-thirty there was nothing left in her that was in any way still touched by the good, light magnanimity she had felt blossom in her heart just over an hour ago, as she'd lain on the bed and read *Birthday Letters* by Ted Hughes. Ted Hughes wrote the book for his deceased wife, Sylvia Plath. In the book he expresses his love for Sylvia, who took her own life largely because she felt that this love was lacking—she believed that he did not love her, that he was unfaithful, which he was, and on 11 February 1963 she put her head in a gas oven and took her own life. In the years that followed, the English press and many others held Ted Hughes responsible and criticized him for not talking about it, for not expressing any regret, not even asking for forgiveness, nothing. He received prizes for his poetry, but people looked at him with eyes that no doubt clearly expressed what they really thought of his behavior. Edel is one of those who have held it against him. She loved Sylvia Plath and she has borne a grudge against Ted Hughes, though she has found some solace in the fact that even among famous poets there are those who share her experience. She, a small bookseller in a rural community, can see herself in a famous poet, Plath—there *are* bonds between people, she has thought; even successful poets in big cities wander around in their homes in desperation, even they rage and throw things against the wall. The fact that they have cried and felt small, small and betrayed, that they have wanted to be stones that sink to the bottom and stay there, has been a huge relief to her. And yet it was awful that Sylvia had suspected Ted and was right. Because that meant it was possible: to suspect and to be right.

But then she read *Birthday Letters*. With great resentment, she picked the book with the red poppies on the cover from the cardboard box of books that she had ordered, and with great reluctance she opened the book and read the first poem. She did not know how it happened, but as she read the book, it struck her: even though he betrayed her, he must have loved her. He *saw* her, saw all the big and small things that she went around doing and feeling—and if only she had known *that*, as she went around doing all those things that she did not think were noticed! When Edel got to the last poem, she discovered that the red poppies on the cover referred to this poem about the red poppies that Sylvia had loved and seen as a symbol of life; and this evening, as she, Edel, lay on the bed reading this last poem, she felt she was the one who saw all this for her beloved Sylvia, in a stream of warmth and the dark timbre of the voice that *saw* and *said*, that twisted and twisted down and down until finally she could barely breathe, suffocated by a pressing joy, or sadness: This Is Life, You Are Loved and You Are Betrayed, I Must Accept It, I Accept It: Life Is Good, Painful, and Awful! She thought to herself: This is *Acceptance*! The notion of *acceptance* radiated inside her like the sun suddenly staring through the clouds, forcing them open and covering the fjord like an iridescent bridal veil. This is *God*, thought Edel, and she felt like she was about to explode; she clutched the book to her breast and closed her eyes and felt completely open. She felt overwhelmed by something else, too, and had to scribble down some words on a piece of paper: *The power of literature.*

The reason that Edel let go of this good, magnanimous feeling, of the notion of "acceptance," and has now lost the plot instead, is that she suspected, but could not see, the scene that was unfolding in a house by the ferry, forty-five minutes' drive from the double garage, around the same time that she was clearing the snow from the driveway. The scene that Edel suspected but could not see looked like this: her husband, Alvin, was standing behind Susanne, who lives in the house that stands alone by the ferry, forty-five minutes' drive from the double garage. They were both naked. Susanne was bending forward and holding on to a window ledge. Alvin was standing behind her and holding her hips. Alvin thought to himself that this was not what was supposed to happen, this was not what he had intended, he should have driven straight home, he should never have stopped at Susanne's, just to say hallo, to find out if she was very sad because he had stopped coming, if she had been all right in the last six months, and to say that it was difficult, nearly impossible, just to drive by her house when he finished work, to say that he stood up on the bridge of the ferry and tried to see if he could see her every evening when she had the lights on and it was dark all around, and her house twinkled at him like a small star in the night sky, but that it could not carry on, he had a family to consider, Edel had threatened to leave him and take Thomas with her and he could not bear that, he had to sacrifice their love for Thomas, that was just the way it was, that was what he'd wanted to say, he'd wanted to take responsibility for his family, that was what he had chosen, having spent a long and painful period thinking and doubting, he could not come in and stand here like he was now, holding her by the hips and pressing his cock between her legs.

Thomas—for whom Alvin was going to sacrifice his love and not stand as he was standing now, for his sake—is asleep. He was out all afternoon selling raffle tickets in the snow and spent the whole time thinking about Noah's ark, which he'd learned about at school. He thought about giraffes and leopards. He thought about rhinoceroses and dreamed of stroking them and sitting on their backs, touching their horns. He thought about how enormous the boat must have been, as the teacher had said yes when he'd asked if it was bigger than the hotel. He wondered whether there were also two ants on board. And two lice! And now he is lying curled up like a small fetus, dreaming about crocodiles. Because there were crocodiles on board, he had asked about that. He is dreaming about a big crocodile that has laid a crocodile egg in a nest, while Edel storms through the sitting room and pounds up the stairs to the bedroom. She throws on a pair of trousers and a sweater, puts on a pair of shoes, and hurls *Birthday Letters* at the wall as hard as she can. Alvin comes all over Susanne's buttocks. In the crocodile nest, the first baby crocodile breaks through the hard shell of its egg. A rhinoceros stands for a long time looking at another rhinoceros, then suddenly walks away, out of the ark's big front door, and the rhinoceros that is left behind does not know why. Thomas shouts to Noah: Wait! Wait for the other rhinoceros! He tugs at Noah's tunic. Then he runs toward the door to bring back the rhino that has walked away. The one that was left behind falls to the ground with a great thud.

Thomas stands in the doorway with tousled hair.

"Something went bump, Mummy," he says.

"It was a book that I threw against the wall," replies Edel.

"Why did you throw it against the wall?" asks Thomas.

"I was angry," says Edel. "It was a bad book. A terrible, terrible book. Put your clothes on, Thomas, we have to go and get Daddy."

"Why?" asks Thomas.

"His car has broken down and he can't get home. Hurry up," she says, and Thomas says that he does not want to, he has to sleep! If he does not go to sleep now, the rhinoceros might leave forever!

"You can dream in the car," says Edel.

"But I might not have the same dream!" says Thomas.

"Of course you will. Come on, I'll help you get dressed," she says, and takes him firmly by the arm, her whole body shaking.

"I want to have the same dream!" whines Thomas.

Susanne is shaking. She stammers. "Alvin," she says, and turns toward him, wanting him to put his arms around her. "I love you," she whispers into his neck. "I knew that you'd come back." He holds her tight, but says nothing. "I can't say it," he says finally. "You know I have said that I can't. It would be wrong. It would build up your hopes, you know I would love to… but Thomas…" She nods and looks at him, he can see that she is not entirely happy. But she tells herself that she can cope with anything and that he must be able to see that, on her face, how big and generous she is. Maybe that will make him understand that deep down, he loves her, and that it would be impossible, impossible to leave her. She looks at him with understanding on her face.

*　　*　　*

"Bloody hell, I have to clear the snow again," shouts Edel. "Bloody, fuck, shit, *shit*!"

She drives through the village through the snowstorm, her windshield wipers racing furiously back and forth. A triangle of snow builds up under one of them; in a while she will undoubtedly have to get out and brush it off. A triangle! Naturally, a symbolic triangle had to appear right in front of her eyes! She snorts, that she could be so stupid. Oh, *Life*—right. Oh, Terrible, Oh Good, Oh Pain, it is none of that, it is pure and simple lunacy and shit. And the outside is just bodies, skeletons packaged in flesh, doing this and that and nothing makes sense. That, thinks Edel, and laughs a sad laugh aloud for herself, is what I will say at the seminar on Monday. "Muuummmmyyy," complains Thomas. She has woken him, he is lying across the backseat with his duvet over him. She let him lie down without putting the safety belt on. "Go to sleep," she says. She has been taking courses in English literature at the college in the next village and up until now has enjoyed her current one, "Symbolism in Literature." She felt that it was true that you should not scorn symbolism and simply look at it as antiquated, romantic thought, things should make sense, the expression and the content, she believed that something could stand for something else, a rose for love, an ocean for life, a cross for death, but now it just irritates her, because now she realizes that of the two lanes on the road along the fjord toward the ferry, only her side has been cleared. She immediately thinks: *Is that how it is*, is that what this means, is his path closed, will he not come back, is it only she who can reach out to him, and he cannot reach her, is his lane full of snow, is that how it is? She feels helpless, is that what this means? No, she refuses to read it that way! It is just a road, she thinks, a stupid road, without any symbolic meaning. Crap and idiocy, and on top of that: asphalt. She wished she had fuzzy dice hanging from the mirror, or an air freshener, a Little Tree, the most pointless thing she can think of, when she gets back to the village she will stop at the gas station and buy a Little Tree to remind her of this, to mark this evening when she said good-bye to symbolic thinking and to—what, what else is she going to say good-bye to? Her marriage? But she is on her way to collect him, why, why is she doing this, shouldn't she drive back home instead and lock the door, let him sleep in the garage, should she stop driving, should she just stop, why did she react in this way, it has to be the least reflective thing she has ever done, she just did it, and what should she do now, should she carry on driving? She slows down as she swings into a wide bend, she sees an orange light pulsing in the trees on the other side of the road, it must be a snowplow, she is frightened of snowplows, she comes to a near standstill and lets the snowplow sail past on the other side of the road, the snow blasting over the barrier beyond the plow and hitting the trees, and tears come to her eyes, spontaneously, *because now his lane is also being cleared.*

Alvin looks at Susanne's face. The pleading in her eyes makes him feel ashamed. He kisses her on the cheek and goes to look for his pants. "What have you been up to recently, then?" he asks, and Susanne tries to hold in her stomach as she picks up her bra from the floor. "Not much, same as always, really... no, hang on..." She has thought of something. "Give me a second," she says, and with a sparkle in her eyes she pulls on her knickers and practically runs to the CD player. Alvin thinks suddenly that there is something helpless about her body dressed only in underwear, as she bends down to put on some music, he feels like he can't breathe, he tightens the belt on his trousers and pulls on his jacket. "Susanne, I'm going to have to leave. Edel will flip if I'm not home soon, I'm sorry, Susanne," he says. But Susanne does not listen, she has put on a CD of salsa music and starts dancing in front of him. He must not go. She must get him to stay. She must get him to say something nice to her before he goes. "I've been going to salsa classes!" she says, and dances closer and closer to him, with a provocative, slightly coy look on her face. She takes him by the hands, he says "Nooooo..." then she lets go and turns her back to him, rolling her hips. She's a bit nervous, so her dancing feels contrived. Alvin is so embarrassed on her behalf that he goes over to the dancing back and puts his arms round her and says that he really *must* go now, but that she's good at dancing, and she should carry on with it. "I'm a fool, Susanne," he says. "No, you're not," she says. "You are the best person I know." He kisses her on the forehead. "I might go to Cuba soon," she says, even though it's a lie. "Well, I hope you have a good time, then," he says.

*   *   *

Edel shakes her head, she doesn't want to think about it anymore, she doesn't want to interpret things symbolically anymore. We have rejected nature, that is what we have done, thinks Edel, as she drives slowly forward on the newly cleared road and the snowstorm gradually dies down, yes, nature has been abandoned and we are to blame, we have focused on language and become complicated. We have to get back to nature, we have to stop reading books, we have to stop interpreting everything, we have to stop thinking figuratively, we have to live like animals, we have to eat food and sleep. We must renounce symbolism. We must stop thinking altogether. We must live in one simple dimension. Ah! She is happy. She feels crazy. Or perhaps she has actually been crazy up to this moment and has now regained her sanity. She has a horrible, crystal-clear feeling in her head. As if her head is two wide-open eyes with a cold wind blowing into them. She shakes her head. Your husband has fucked another woman this evening. She wants to laugh. And so we have to stop thinking symbolically! Ha ha. Jesus! she mumbles. And then she laughs again. What a thing to mumble. In fact she wants to cry. She has to pull into a bus stop and cry. Imagine, she thinks as she leans forward over the steering wheel, crying, imagine if it's not what I think, but that he's been in an accident. She looks over her shoulder at Thomas, he's asleep, lying with his face to the back of the seat, she can only see his hair sticking up from the duvet, a small fan that spreads across the pillow, and she thinks: Then he will be fatherless and I will be a single mother, and she leans over the wheel again.

Alvin cannot quite understand what has happened. He drives home along the fjord, it has stopped snowing, the branches on the trees on the mountainside are weighed down, the road is white, no one has driven here since the snowplow swept past, no tracks in the snow. The streetlights stand silently with bowed heads off into the distance, he imagines the noise that is made when the light from each streetlamp hits the roof of his car as he drives past, *bzzzzzzzzzt*, he imagines that they are X-ray beams that penetrate the roof of the car and illuminate him, so that if you were looking in from the outside you would see a skeleton sitting there holding the wheel and driving along the road. Out of the light: a man. In the light: a skeleton. On, off, on, off. In a kind of corny, gray light, you can now see his right hand with all its white bones moving like tentacles, gripping the stick shift and changing gears. And then he dresses the skeleton up in bluish-red muscles, veins, and sinews, at the very moment he remembers a picture in the anatomy book at secondary school that made a lasting impression on him: a person without skin, only muscles, veins, and sinews. Teeth without lips, eyeballs without eyelids. Sometimes it comes back to him, like when Edel was shouting and screaming and saying it was over, he could barely hear what she was saying, he just stood there staring at her, imagining her as a face without skin, only bluish-red, knotted muscles in her cheeks, over her lips and teeth. He feels hot, flushed, conspicuously flushed, and it will not have died down by the time he reaches home, he knows that, because he has done it before, he should really take a long detour when he gets to the village, but it will not be of much help, since he will get home even later and Edel will know, maybe she'll have packed the suitcase on wheels like she did the last time—the good, big, red suitcase with wheels—and then remembered that it was a gift from him and stopped right in front of the front door, opened the suitcase, and taken out all the clothes, then kicked the suitcase across the floor so that it hit the chest of drawers and lay there open like a gaping mouth, just like last time, and then run up into the attic and searched and searched until she found the old bag that she had brought her clothes in when she moved in with him, as she had last time, to make a symbolic point to herself that she was on her own again, and then woken Thomas up and gone down to the hotel; maybe he smells of perfume, he thinks, thank God he took her from behind, touching as little skin as possible from the waist up. It was really only the lower part of his stomach that had touched her hips. He pictures Susanne's salsa-rolling hips and feels sick. He stops the car in the middle of the road, gets out, and leaves the door open, walks to the edge of the road, turns around, stretches his arms out from his body, and allows himself to fall backward into the snow. It is soft. If he lies here for a while, he will cool down. He will lie here and slowly but surely erase Susanne from his mind. Because now he can feel it in his bones, it is over.

Susanne pulls on some sweatpants and opens a bottle of wine. She sits down on the sofa and tries to think that she has just had a visit from her lover and that she is a grown woman with a rich life. She managed to get him to come. He could not stop thinking about her. He could not get her out of his mind—that's how strong the power is that she is fortunate enough to possess. But she knows there's no point. She tries not to think about the desperation that drove her to dance for him. She tries not to think about the embarrassed look on his face when she wanted him to dance. She drinks the glass of wine in one slurp, swallowing only a couple of times. It tastes of alcohol. Susanne purses her lips and goes over to the phone, looks up the number of a travel agent in the directory. She just doesn't understand, she thinks, how Alvin, the best person she knows, so sensitive and observant, who has told her the strangest things about what he thinks, could just come like that and fuck her and then leave with an embarrassed, hard expression on his face. She feels it, deep down, that he will not come back. This time it's over. She hopes he has an accident. She hopes he has an accident and ends up in the fjord. She dials the number for the travel agent. He could quite possibly have an accident with all this snow. The travel agent is closed and will open again tomorrow morning at eight. She throws herself down on the floor. She wonders if she should slide her way over to the sofa, she pictures herself wriggling, exhausted and doomed, like a soldier on a muddy battle-field, over to the sofa—but she knows it isn't true, the truth is that she's lying on her back on the floor, she's looking up at the ceiling, the back of her throat is burning and the tears are running from her eyes down into her ears.

"*Please*," says Thomas. The missing rhino has not come back and Thomas is not allowed to leave the ark. Noah is so big that he nearly reaches the ceiling and he says firmly that it is not possible to go out, it has started to rain so they have to shut the door soon. Thomas tries to get to the door all the same, but the floor is heaving with baby crocodiles, so he slips and falls and doesn't make it. He notices that there is an elevator like the one at the hotel beside the door and he can see that it is on its way down, the floor numbers are showing on a panel above the door, and he thinks that maybe it is the rhinoceros, *2, 1, pling*: it is two lizards. The lizards waddle over the baby crocodiles. Edel lifts her head from the wheel. She starts the car and swings out into the road. "Bloody shit," she mumbles.

Bloody, fuck, shit, *shit*.

* * *

Alvin has made an angel in the snow, which he realizes is a great paradox, symbolically. It makes him think about Edel, it makes him want to cry, but he fails, so he sits up, pulls up his knees, and crouches huddled in his own angel. A pathetic, overly symbolic position, Edel thinks as she pulls up beside him before he has looked up. He looks up. He is not surprised to see her there. She stops the car, gets out, and stands in front of him. "What happened?" she says. He shrugs his shoulders and opens his hands. Closes them again. "This," he says. "I made an angel in the snow." "You little shit," she says, and nearly starts to laugh. She isn't reacting the way she thought she would. She had imagined the scene and it was not like this, she shouted and cried and then he fell to the ground, but now it almost feels as if she isn't here at all. The whole scene is slightly comical. "We're finished," she says, without feeling anything, and then goes back to sit in the car. Her head feels crystal clear and cold, almost light. Her feet feel light as well. "The car broke down!" he shouts, coming after her. "Bloody hell, Edel! I've been standing here for nearly an hour! And I couldn't phone you because I couldn't find my mobile! I've been sitting here waiting for help but no one came." The crystal-clear, weightless Edel smiles. "I would have liked to see that," she says. Alvin says nothing, just gets into his car, and his hands shake as he turns the key, because now it *is* over.

But the car doesn't start.

The car just manages to splutter a few times but will not start. "There you go," says Alvin. Edel says nothing. The blood is about to leave her legs and rush to her head, her cheeks. She looks at him, coughs. Nothing of what is happening now is as she'd imagined. She does not know whether it's true or not. "Get out of the way," she says, and sits down in the driver's seat of his car, it's cold, so he can't have stopped, he must have been there for a while. It is cold in the car. She turns the key, the car barely reacts. It's true. The car has broken down. She does not know what to do. She has driven along the fjord to collect him, to shout at him and leave him, and her side of the road was cleared of snow first, and then his side was cleared, it hits her, all this actually happened. It literally happened. She goes round to the boot and gets out a towrope and hands it to him. Alvin stands looking at Thomas, who is sleeping in the backseat of Edel's car, and tries to behave like someone whose car has broken down and who has been waiting in the snow for an hour. "What's he been up to today?" he asks, casually, and coughs. "He learned about Noah's ark and sold raffle tickets," answers Edel. "Come and look at him," says Alvin. Edel stands beside him and looks at Thomas. He's lying asleep with his arms stretched out above his head, along the back of the seat. In the same position that Susanne is now lying on the floor, without knowing that the painful pressure she feels in her heart is the same pressure that is in Edel's and Alvin's hearts right now, as they stand there side by side.

Edel drives the small car and tows the big car, which Alvin is steering. She refuses, she thinks, to interpret this symbolically. It's just the way things have turned out. They drive along the fjord. It's night. There are three of them. And the fact that there is a rope between the cars has no significance other than the physical fact that when a car breaks down it needs to be towed. I just don't understand this, Alvin thinks. He feels that he is being watched, as if someone is laughing at him; he said the car had broken down, and that's what happened. He got exactly what he asked for. He leans forward toward the windshield to see if he can see the stars, but is blinded by the light from the streetlamps, which stand silently with bowed heads, illuminating the cars as they pass. At regular intervals along the road you can see a skeleton, an adult, sitting at the wheel of a car, then a child's skeleton lying across the backseat, and then finally another adult skeleton sitting more or less directly behind the first. The adult skeletons have their arms in front of them, holding their steering wheels. The child skeleton is not holding anything but has his arms stretched out above his head.

You can also see a larger skeleton, standing on all fours, which has a huge horn on its snout; it is standing beside the child skeleton. A similar skeleton now appears from the left, to the surprise of the first, which lifts its head and looks at the approaching skeleton expectantly. They stand for a moment staring at each other, and then the one rhinoceros rubs up against the other. A couple of antelope skeletons wander past, and farther along a tiger skeleton and a lion skeleton can be seen, and two small cat skeletons and then dogs and a mass of small crocodile jaws that nibble the child skeleton's legs, making it laugh and wriggle. And if X-rays could also show the contours and shape of other things that were not of solid, indisputable mass, you would be able to see the outline of an enormous wooden boat, with pairs of skeletons, two by two, arranged on many levels, two skeletons for each sort of animal. A big human skeleton lifts its arm and then everyone feels the boat leave the ground and float through the air.

Translated by Kari Dickson

THE BASTARD

by NYUOL LUETH TONG

(from a section dedicated to South Sudanese fiction, in Issue 43)

MAMA TAUGHT ME better. She could give me a glare that brought me to my knees when she heard me talk about anyone without respect—especially Mabiordit. It was Mabiordit who had sheltered us when we came to Juba looking for Jal e Jal and ended up stranded, with nothing in Mama's purse but twenty pounds and a battered Nokia mobile that could receive calls but not make them.

The trip from Panagam had taken three days. Two bus tickets at two hundred pounds each were beyond our means, so we paid a local merchant fifty pounds and crouched on sacks of maize flour in the back of his rusted Honda pickup truck. The roads were still under construction, full of potholes, and so narrow that you could nearly touch the mud-thatch huts and thorny shrubs on either side. At one point we had to flatten ourselves against the flour sacks to keep from getting scratched when the truck pulled over to let a group of Land Rovers pass. They whizzed by like bullets, darkened windows shielding the faces of their drivers—government officials and

NGO directors. They left nothing but dust in their wake.

In Juba, after trekking across five hundred miles—almost the length of South Sudan—we found Jal e Jal happily married, with three children, and not in the least pleased by our presence. After exchanging pleasantries, he adjusted himself in his chair, faced us directly, and confirmed the rumor, spread by various relatives, that what he and Mama had done on the grass-covered shores of the Loll River fifteen years ago—never mind that it begot me—was *awoc*, a mistake. He wanted nothing to do with us, he said, and would be grateful if we never contacted him again. Then he rose up, fixed his blue tie, buttoned his black suit, and disappeared through the square door of the New Cush restaurant. There was nothing more to say.

All of this was fine by me. I was done waiting for my father's return from war. I wanted nothing to do with Jal e Jal—but you should've seen Mama, the grace and dignity on her face. It was heartbreaking and revolting at the same time. I wanted to slap her. What Jal e Jal deserved was a hard kick in the ass: fifteen years ago she had destroyed her marriage, disgraced her family, and deferred her dreams, all for him. Now she had discarded everything for him once again—a house built by her own hands, based on her blind brother's measurements, a world back in Panagam that she had forged from nothing—only to find that he had mutated into someone else.

Mabiordit, my dead aunt Adau's husband, was the only other person we knew in Juba. Aunt Adau had been found floating facedown in the Loll River twenty years ago, just a year into their marriage. This tragedy might have warranted an investigation if it hadn't been wartime. Air strikes and raids were a constant threat back then; death was so ubiquitous that people stopped asking how or why. Despite my suspicions about Mabiordit, we had no choice but to accept his invitation.

Mabiordit had extended it after Mama paid a woman selling mango juice five pounds to place the call to him, giving her a chance to explain our predicament. Mabiordit told Mama that he had a busy schedule; he was meeting with some important investors at the Equity Bank in downtown Juba at three o'clock. That would be our meeting point, he said. It sounded impressive; Mabiordit had been a poor militiaman during the war, whom we knew had never had any education.

We were downtown by midday, at a roadside café outside the Equity Bank. We drank over-sugared tea and ate biscuits for brunch. Then we sat on a metal bench, facing the street, and watched the city people to kill time. So this was Juba, the nation's largest and oldest city, a swirl of congestion and commotion. In places it looked like a ghost town: looking around I could see old, dilapidated brick buildings, and electric wires twisted and tangled around wooden utility poles. But the air was thick with cement dust from the construction sites that lined the streets, stirred up by workers digging foundations and expanding the thin dirt roads. This was coupled with the roar of countless motorcycles, and of the minibuses haphazardly collecting passengers. A random madness seemed to be the core energy of the city.

No wonder the littered streets, mud huts, and stick-and-plastic-bag slums were bustling with young people from rural villages. They were barefoot and penniless, but buoyant with dreams of a larger world to be part of. We had heard news of East African entrepreneurs peddling loan schemes, insurance pyramids, and housing projects, of NGOs with abundant resources and grand notions of salvation and development. The NGOs were convinced they could steer our nascent state away from corruption and nepotism, if only by holding up the warning signs:

MANY HAVE TAKEN THIS ROAD
IT DOES NOT LEAD TO FREEDOM
IT DOES NOT LEAD TO PROSPERITY
IT DOES NOT LEAD TO STABILITY
IT DOES NOT LEAD TO DEMOCRACY
JUST LOOK AT YOUR BRETHREN COUNTRIES

At four o'clock we began to look around for Mabiordit. Mama remembered him as a giant, broad-shouldered man, with crooked teeth and a flat nose and dark, rugged skin. She said that she used to like him, in her teens; he was the most courteous of the men who called on her older sister. He would come in the evening, after Mama and Aunt Adau had pounded the maize into flour, prepared the dinner, and milked the cows. He would wait in the yard, under their sterile mango tree—sometimes for two hours, sometimes in the rain—until they were done with their chores and able to sit down with him.

Aunt Adau sometimes sent Mama to keep him company while she finished her work. Unlike the other men, Mabiordit didn't treat Mama as the ten-year-old she was; he gave her the same regard he gave Aunt Adau, the object of his passions. They talked about themselves through metaphors and riddles and allusions, drawing from Dinka folklore and proverbs. He was the first man she had a crush on, Mama said, and her feelings continued even after he became her brother-in-law. It was Aunt Adau's sudden death and Jal e Jal's appearance in her life that same year that made her see the ridiculousness of her infatuation.

Mama was the only girl among the boys who marched six miles a day, and canoed in the rainy season, to St. Joseph Educational Center. The Comboni Missionaries had built the school in the early '70s, with the intention of educating leaders for the then semi-autonomous region of South Sudan. The headmaster, Father Peter—a Ugandan priest who kept the school running even during the impossible days of war—had plans for outstanding students to continue their education in Nairobi or Kampala, where they could find better schools and earn scholarships to study in Europe or even the United States.

Mama was smart; she excelled in math, English, and history, and particularly in the study of the curative plants she watered in the chapel yard. She used them to treat the sick cows and goats she tended after school, and she could recite long medical terminologies that she barely understood. She would make up theories about how to remedy the diseases that bewildered diviners and doctors both, including her father, Doctor Josephdit, whom she helped at the one-room clinic they ran at home. Everyone believed she was going to be a great doctor.

Mama's father was the premier doctor in the area, even though he had no formal training. His qualifications consisted of his wide travels around the country during the first war, his mastery of the Dinka, Nuer, Zande, and Shilluk tongues, and his indigenization of foreign herbal practices he had encountered in Panagam and beyond. Mama admired him and his profession but aspired to be a real doctor, a better one.

The other student thought to be brilliant and promising was Jal e Jal. He was a serious and reclusive boy from the swamp villages on the far side of the river, where people lived in straw huts built on thick floating islands of vegetation. Jal e Jal knew that education was what made presidents out of nobodies, and he knew that he was going to be the first person from the swamp to earn a college degree. He was going to be heard on radios and seen on TV and read about in newspapers. He would be famous. He would matter.

Mama and Jal e Jal were bonded by their big dreams. People saw them often on the banks of the Loll, reclined on the grass and reading English words out loud, words that even their teachers could not pronounce. They had no interest in the gossip circulating in Panagam, or in the latest fashions or music from Khartoum and Kampala. They found comfort in what the future had in store for them.

Before long Jal e Jal developed romantic feelings for Mama. After the break for farming season one year, he asked her to meet him at their usual study spot. On his way there he picked lilies from the river to give to her. His mother was a follower of the spirit of the Loll River, the symbol of which was the water lily, and he figured he could use the help of the spirits.

They met under the sausage tree on the riverbank, where monkeys congregated in the dry season when the streams in the forest dried up. Mama thought nothing of the meeting, so she wore her working garb, which was powdered with flour on the front. She had wild stories for Jal e Jal about the patients her father was treating—like the chief's wife, who had been having encounters with spirits that she was convinced wanted to make love to her.

After much coaxing, Mama accepted the lilies. She wanted only to put an end to what seemed to her to be a silly declaration of love from her best friend. Jal e Jal, of course, saw the whole thing from an entirely different perspective. He stepped closer to Mama, his eyes shut, reaching for a kiss. Mama took a step back, surprised. Jal e Jal thought she was teasing him, playing with him, and kept pushing and pushing until Mama found herself pressed against the large trunk of the sausage tree. Trapped, she threw a punch at him and split his lip. Then she dropped the lilies and ran away.

The next day they walked home from school together as if nothing had happened. A year after that, Josephdit married Mama off.

Her husband, the Colonel, was a family friend, and the marriage was meant to cement that friendship. Mama was sixteen at the time. The family received a number of handsome cows in bride wealth, close to two hundred heads, which were distributed among relatives and friends. The wedding was considered one of the most extravagant in Panagam since the first war.

The Colonel was a rich man in his late fifties. He had eight wives, thirty children, and a dozen grandchildren, some of whom were Mama's age. In fact, his grandson Ater—a chubby fellow who enjoyed cattle-herding and fishing and hated walking the six miles to school—was Mama's classmate at St. Joseph. There was a rumor that the Colonel had originally wanted Mama's hand for Ater, and had only changed his mind when he saw her during his visit to arrange the marriage.

Mama's feet began to bleed on her first day at the Colonel's house. The man's huge homestead consisted of ten thatched adobe huts nearly a mile away from the water pump, the market, and the forest; she had to make four trips a day to fetch water and firewood sufficient to roast meat and prepare the sorghum gruel. She also had to fill the large earthen buckets in the backyard with enough water for the men's baths in the evening, and for the baths she gave the children. When she wasn't walking to the water pump or sweeping the compound or washing clothes, she was in the kitchen. She cooked not only for the family, which was made up of nearly forty members, but also for the crowd that surrounded the Colonel.

Her husband was a vain man. He exhibited his best qualities only when he was the center of attention. When he received noteworthy guests—the district commissioner, the local commander, NGO representatives—he put on a modest cotton robe and sat on a wooden chair under the tree in the middle of the compound, surrounded by children chewing on mango or maize. The wives also dressed modestly—scarves and loose robes, long enough to reach their feet and wide enough to conceal their bodies. Anyone who passed by the homestead on such days was invited in, at the Colonel's orders, and offered some porridge to eat or some milk to drink.

When he wasn't entertaining a guest, the Colonel confined himself to his sleeping hut, away from his wives and children, and demanded absolute quiet. The children had to feign naps until the sun was iridescent above the trees in the afternoon, at which time the Colonel would wake up, take a hot shower, and walk to the market. There, he would join the chief and his council and pontificate about the war and the village for hours.

Two months after the wedding, Mama stumbled upon Jal e Jal at the water pump. She smiled and waved, but he pretended he was busy watching some women by a cluster of trees. Mama brought the water container down from her head and placed it just outside the dirt path. Jal e Jal was a mess;

he had grown a beard and a mustache, and his shirt was dyed with sweat and dirt. Where was the clean, promising future president of the republic? She walked closer to him, and could smell cow dung emanating from his clothes.

"What happened to my lilies?" She asked.

"Why?"

"I want them," she said.

"You threw them away."

"I left them with you, and now I want them back."

They met on the riverbank late at night a week later. Jal e Jal had plucked fresh water lilies for her. They decided to elope, but were captured the next day. Jal e Jal was fined seven cows and given fifty whips on his back. This would have ordinarily sufficed, but the Colonel, vain and proud as he was, wasn't satisfied. The marriage ended. All of the cows in bride wealth were retrieved. Fearing for his life, Jal e Jal joined the militia and disappeared. Josephdit denounced Mama, and the family was disgraced. Only Uncle Marial stood by her.

Around four months ago, a man selling cattle passed through Panagam and spent the night in our house. Mama made porridge and chicken soup that evening, and the traveler ate dinner with me by the fireside while Mama ate alone in the kitchen. After dinner, Mama collected the dishes in a bucket and washed them outside by moonlight. She joined us by the fire when she'd finished, bringing with her a new rug she had woven out of grass from the backyard. She unfolded it on the ground and sat down.

The guest glanced at Mama and then at me. He said nothing, but we knew he was grateful for the hospitality. After a long silence that bordered on awkwardness, Mama laughed as if she were among friends; it broke the ice. The man told us his name was Malwal, and that he was a veteran. He was from Kuacjok, five hours south of us. After the signing of the peace agreement, he had quit the army and returned home to take up his family's profession, buying and selling cattle. The work had taken him to eight of the ten states within South Sudan. He would purchase cows from villagers in remote areas, then sell them for three times as much in the larger cities around the country.

It was a lucrative business, Malwal said, but it had its dangers. A year earlier, some bandits had ambushed him in the long stretch of wilderness between Juba and Wau. They took the fifty cows he had just purchased and every pound he had saved.

"How did you escape?" I blurted out, interrupting him.

Mama gave me a look, and apologized for my poor manners. Malwal explained that an old friend of his in the army—now a captain, and a big shot in the national security community—had stumbled upon him that night and, with his heavily armed bodyguards, rescued him from the bandits. They killed two of them, and gave Malwal a ride to Juba.

This was when Mama said that Jal e Jal had been in the army, too. The guest began to ask questions. We didn't know which part of the army Jal e Jal had served in, but Mama had a very vivid description of him, which she shared excitedly. Jal e Jal was dark, she said, and his lower lip had a scar in the middle. (She didn't mention that it was her punch that had created the cut.) His laughter always came out like a storm, a burst, and often forced others to laugh.

The guest smiled, and said he knew exactly whom Mama was describing. He gave her Jal e Jal's phone number.

The man left early the next morning, while we were still sleeping. At breakfast, around ten, Mama placed the number and her Nokia on the table and watched them like she was expecting them to interact. I drank my milk and ate my corn gruel and watched her walk back and forth, in and out of the hut, stealing a glance now and then at the folded piece of paper and the overused phone on the table. I had never seen Mama that rattled.

The next day we visited the diviner to determine our chances of finding Jal e Jal in Juba. The diviner lived on the edge of Panagam, near the pasture and the cattle camp, where the Chinese in their green uniforms and orange caps were clearing shrubs and trees with huge machines for a highway that seemed to be under perpetual construction. The diviner called the highway the beast's heel. She believed the beast was slouching through the entire country, carrying the youth away to distant lands, from which they returned more foreign than the foreigners.

At the door of the diviner's shrine, we took off our sandals and crawled inside. The diviner was sitting in the back, smoke drifting across her face, curling around the ring of charms on her neck, the feathers in her cow-dung-dyed hair, the twisted horns of oxen hanging over her head. We sat on the ground against the mud wall and waited.

Suddenly, the room beamed with the diviner's voice, welcoming us. Technically it was the spirits, not the diviner, who saw the future; the spirits had something like a remote control that enabled them to fast-forward, pause, and rewind the affairs of the world whenever they wanted. They didn't directly shape what happened on earth—humans did that—but they could watch. The diviner was the interface, whose role was to convince the spirits to do so. I watched every move she made, to see how she summoned them.

The spirits disliked this kind of interruption, and usually refused such requests. Giving away information about how things would unfold in the future was a tremendous sacrifice for them; it spoiled the drama, the comedy, and the tragedy of human affairs, without which eternity would be, for the spirits, a condition of indefinite boredom and nothingness. As a result, the diviners often made things up, validating what the people who had come to them already believed.

Mama was quiet. According to the diviner, the spirits had been following us carefully. She said that Jal e Jal was being held captive under a spell cast by a beautiful and well-connected witch, and that the only way to break the spell was to go to him. Once he saw us, his childhood sweetheart and grown son, the spell would break, and he would leave his rich wife in a split second to come home with us. The diviner swore that this was true, so Mama believed it.

Mabiordit showed up in a dust-coated pickup truck. He was two hours late, and the night was creeping in beneath a horizon streaked with crimson and purple. He parked the truck on the sanded open area near the entrance of Equity Bank, where scrawny, half-naked children and elderly men and women extended their hands, begging the men in tailored suits and leather shoes for money.

He was tall, very tall, but not as muscular as Mama remembered. He recognized us, and walked over with a limp, smiling, his arms stretched out like he was coming to scoop us off our feet. I offered my hand, but he hugged me instead.

"Mony, yin ba raan ci det," he said. His breath was hot on my neck. I liked that he thought I was big and grown up. I was very skinny, true, but

I was also tall, and my hair was longer than Mama's. That gave me a little bit more height, enough to reach Mabiordit's broad shoulders. He patted me on the back and moved on to Mama, who was standing just behind me. He hugged her for about a minute, and it seemed to make Mama uncomfortable. I could see her face going blank, the joy of seeing him squeezed out by the way he wrapped his hands around her.

Mabiordit blathered on as he rumbled the truck home. He complained about the system, about how people like him, people who had fought and bled, were being passed over by young spoiled bastards with college degrees who had spent most of their lives abroad.

"Those bastards speak English through their noses," he said. "You can never trust a bastard with anything. By definition, a bastard is he who does not belong."

Both Mama and I were tired, and the heat coming through the pickup's glassless window frames didn't help. I couldn't stop watching Mama. The mask of strength and composure that she had assumed since Jal e Jal had shattered her hopes was still intact. I was bothered by it; it worried me that I couldn't see her pain.

"Home," Mabiordit said.

He stopped the car and jumped out. Home was a rectangular brick structure that looked like several classrooms stuck together. It seemed to be under construction, like the other houses I had seen during the ride. We were given the guest room: a wooden bed, two plastic chairs, a table, and a small closet. Mabiordit's wife, Aunt Achill, explained that the bathroom was the roofless brick square we saw standing in the backyard, and that each room was supplied with a flashlight. Mabiordit told Mama we could stay with them for as long as we needed.

Aunt Achill's first husband had been Mabiordit's sergeant, a great fighter who loved babies and carving toys from wood: cows and birds, figurines and deities, people making love, giving birth, dancing, shooting arrows at hyenas. He had been killed in the war fifteen years ago, leaving her with two boys, John and Deng, who were now fifteen and sixteen—the fattest boys I had ever seen. After his death, at least for Mabiordit, the war had lost its aura and larger purpose, so our host had decided to quit the army and care for the man's family.

For his generosity, we showed him gratitude and deference almost to the point of servility. Women no longer crawled for men—this tradition had died long before the war—but Mama would get on her knees whenever she served him a cup of tea or a plate of porridge.

Now that we had a place to sleep, we only had to find a way to make money and return home. All over Juba new houses, hotels, and shops were sprouting out of the bushes. I could be useful to someone, I thought; Uncle Marial had taught me a few things about digging foundations, plastering walls, and making bricks. Our house had taken around five years to build, but it was a masterpiece—oval and elegant, roofed with plaited grass, plastered with blue ash.

About a week into our stay, Mama woke up in the middle of the night. She pulled up the blanket, and woke me up in the process. She wanted to go to the bathroom.

She searched for the flashlight under the bed, and turned it on. What she saw so startled her that she almost bolted out of the room. In the far corner, in one of the plastic chairs, was Mabiordit, glowing in the beam of the flashlight. Mama composed herself and sat on the edge of the bed. I kept my head under the blanket and only heard his hoarse voice.

"Just making rounds," he said. "You know."

Mama said nothing—which meant she didn't know.

"I make rounds at night sometimes," he explained. "Making sure everyone is well."

An awkward silence suffocated the room. Those who have taken a life, or seen a life being taken and felt glad about it or thought it was right, even momentarily, could never completely be sound psychologically. This was the danger of war. It dissolved boundaries. The burden of the warrior was that he must walk with the living and also with the dead.

I stood up in the bed, almost hitting the ceiling with my head. Mama had placed the flashlight on the table face-up, so the room was lit up. Mabiordit saw me and lowered his head. Then he lifted his eyes toward me, and toward Mama.

"Better check on the boys," he said.

He rose up and walked out.

Mama kept asking me how long he had been sitting on the chair, watching us sleep. How long? And why? As was typical, her mind twisted the whole thing into something banal and innocent. Maybe he had fought with his wife—they had been arguing about almost everything since we moved in. Maybe he needed someone to talk to.

"He's sick in the head," I said.

"Don't say that," Mama said. "How can you say that?"

I grabbed the blanket and moved to the ground. I spent the rest of the night down there, gazing at the ceiling in the dark.

The next morning, all of us—Mama and I, Aunt Achill and her boys—had tea with biscuits out in the compound. The sun was hot on our bodies and drained the energy from our limbs. We had hardly slept.

Mabiordit showed up in his sleeping turban. His homemade metal armchair was waiting in the shade by the curtained window of his bedroom. Aunt Achil sent one of her sons to fetch Mabiordit's table, and the other son followed with a tray of hot tea, several stacks of bread, a bowl of sugar, and a jug of milk.

Mabiordit stationed himself between Mama and me. We gave each other surprised looks and said nothing. He poured his tea, mixed it with milk, and added three spoonfuls of sugar. He picked up the bread, half-dipped it, and swallowed it whole. He was acting as if nothing had happened, which made us feel like maybe nothing did happen, though his sitting between us was uncomfortable. His wife glared at us, especially at Mama.

Mabiordit looked at me and said, "Mony."

"Yes," I said.

"I saw you help the boys with the wall yesterday. You have an eye for balance. Standing upright depends on solid foundation. You see there?"

He pointed at the new houses with their high water domes rising up across the stretch of cleared land.

"That's what the bastards are spending the oil money on. They're building houses for themselves and for their relatives. They're building foundations for their future. And we'll not be left behind. We'll build our own. Right here. You are part of the family."

I had no idea what he was talking about. As far as I was concerned, this place was just a temporary shelter. We were going to hit the road home the moment we had enough money to afford two tickets. I knew he had come through for us; that was the only reason I was helping him and those fatties build their dream house, even after I had watched them steal cement and wood from the neighbors almost every night.

That afternoon Mabiordit came home early from work. I was sitting on the doorstep when his pickup truck came roaring up. He parked it outside the compound wall, although he usually parked inside. Walking in, he passed by me without a word or a glance.

He came out several minutes later, with his armchair, and sat in the shade of the wall, facing the field, watching John and Deng pass a soccer ball to each other. I wasn't in the mood for soccer that day. I went inside and found Mama folding our clothes. She asked me to make tea for Mabiordit, and to try to be friendly to him. I couldn't stand him, but I accepted Mama's request. She was letting go of Jal e Jal, and that was good.

I brought the tea out to Mabiordit on the same tray he had used that morning. Then I sat down again on the doorstep. In several minutes Mama joined us.

"How've you been doing?" Mabiordit said.

"Wonderful," Mama said. "Thank you."

"I'm thinking you should get a bigger room."

"Thank you," Mama said, "but that won't be necessary. This room has more space than we'll ever need."

"Mony could stay with the boys," he said. "He's a big boy."

Mama and I exchanged glances.

"A boy his age shouldn't be sleeping with his mother."

Mama said nothing. It was true; I was almost fifteen. No fifteen-year-old should share a room, let alone a bed, with his mother. The boys' room was large, but the carpet smelled like urine. John and Deng were dumb and loud. A week earlier they had fought over the blonde girl in a Bringi cigarette ad on the TV at the New Sudan Club, where we watched DVDs and music videos. Each of them claimed that she had been talking to him directly.

That night the boys were quiet. They asked me to tell them about Panagam, and life there. I told them about the Loll River, and the many hours we boys spent swimming. They fell asleep, snoring, but I stayed up thinking about Mama. Leaving her to sleep alone felt wrong.

Then I fell asleep, too, only to awake in a dream. I was back in Panagam. Mama came up from behind me, and grabbed my hand. She was wearing her butterflied nightgown. She brought out a cloth and blindfolded me with it.

I have a surprise for you, she said.

She led me by the hand through the field surrounding the house. We entered the cooking hut, and she uncovered my face. There was a tray there, with a gourd of milk and a bowl of porridge. Take it to my sleeping hut, she said. Someone is waiting there. She was blushing like a little girl.

Who? I asked.

Someone important. Go now!

Mama was so happy. I walked with the tray down a narrow path lined on the sides with palm trees. At Mama's sleeping hut, I found the door shut. I pushed it gently. In the darkness I saw the back of a man's head.

Anger possessed me. I dropped the tray and threw my whole body at the man, but he pushed me back and I fell against the wall. I woke up, then, and found myself in Juba. In Mama's room. Crouching on the dirt floor in the corner with Mabiordit standing over me.

His face had been transformed by rage into an unreal ugliness. He took a deep breath and hit the wall behind me. Then he left the room, barefoot, half-naked.

The next morning was slow. I was tired and upset, and I had no appetite. In the afternoon I decided against going out to the New Sudan Club to watch a movie with the boys. Instead I made myself a cup of tea and sat on the porch. After a while, it started to pour. I watched pebbles of rain hit the hard earth and bounce back into the sky, only to be pushed down by bigger pebbles. Soon there was a sea of rainwater before me, coursing and curving through the narrow dirt road and into the town, like the Loll River coursed through Panagam. It made the place somewhat familiar.

S & J

by ELLEN VAN NEERVEN-CURRIE

(from a section dedicated to Indigenous Australian fiction, in Issue 41)

JAYE CALLS TO stop when I'm going full-blow down the line and I press my foot down hard thinking I nicked a roo. The dust mushrooms up and at first I can't see anything. When it clears I see the bird standing in the road, pale and overdressed.

"Far out," I say.

"Pop the boot," Jaye says.

"Hold on."

"You've already stopped." She pats the radio as she gets up beside me. "And put something else on, will you? Don't want them to think we're all bogans."

Jaye walks up to the bird, smile on, arms out, and soon the bird's smiling, too, giving Jaye her backpack and following her to the car. Jaye gets in the backseat, and the girl does, too.

"Hi," she says. German accent. "Sigrid."

"Hi, Sigrid," I say. "I'm Esther."

"Es," she says. "Es and Jaye."

"Yeah," I say, starting the car up and veering back onto the road.

"I'm so glad," Sigrid says, "that I've finally met a real Aboriginal."

Through the top mirror I see she has a hand on Jaye's shoulder.

"You must tell me everything, Jaye. Tell me all about your hardship."

We pull up to the service station and Jaye steps out to refuel.

"She's very beautiful," sighs Sigrid. "Strong."

I grunt and ask where she's headed.

"Exmonth. I think that's how you say it."

"Exmouth. Like this." I show my teeth. "Well, you're in luck, because that's where we're headed, too."

"I'm very grateful, obviously," she says. "Where are you from?"

"Brissie," I say. "Brisbane. On the other side, the east coast. A little south from there, Gold Coast area, that's my country."

"Sorry?" she says. "I don't know where that is."

Jaye's walking back to the car.

"You're a nice golden color," Sigrid goes on. "You look like you're from Spain, maybe. Your parents immigrated here, yes?"

Jaye gets in. "Dinner, ladies."

She unloads her hands of raisin toast and chips and Cokes.

Jaye and I stand leaning against the car in the night air outside her grandmother's house.

"I'm really not sure, Jaye," I say.

"C'mon, sis. We can hardly toss her out, can we?"

"I thought she'd have somewhere to stay when she got here. That's what she said."

"Well, she doesn't, and she's all right, so…" Jaye straightens up and walks toward the house. "You coming, or what?"

The house is a low-set cottage off the highway, surrounded by bush. The rooms smell stale, but it's cozy. There's a fireplace. Out back the veranda is falling apart and you can barely see the washing line above the waist-high grass. Jaye's cousins have been using it as a beach house for years. Now it's her turn.

We eat on the veranda, and then Jaye digs out a bottle of vodka and a deck of mismatched cards. Sigrid teaches us a German version of Rummikub. I'm not drinking, but the night moves quickly, like a train passing stations without stopping. A large ringtail possum sits on a nearby paperbark, and Sigrid squeals when I point it out. She wants to feed it, but we have nothing besides our breakfast for tomorrow. Jaye teaches her the word for possum in Yindjibarndi, and then the name for the tree, and then the name for the one next to it, and I'm all too used to it by now and roll my eyes. When the possum skirts off I decide to do the same.

Underneath the sheets I flick around on my radio for a bit, trying to get a channel. I can still hear the clink of wine glasses and the low murmured laughter from outside. It's a hard decision, to gulp up sleep or stay awake for the morning light. I open the window and see a pink haze coming through. I like the thought of walking barefoot to the beach and out into the waves, but it would be strange to do it without Jaye.

I guess she kind of dragged me along. I didn't want to be by myself at the house all semester break. Everyone else was going back to their families, and I, the only one who lived nearby, didn't feel like sticking around. It's funny now, with the darkness and the silence, no lights, no parties, that Jaye seems more distracted. She's been on edge ever since we got here.

When we met I was a shy teen and it felt good to be going places. Doing things. She was darker than me and all the other Murris I knew, like a walking projection of what a blackfella was supposed to be. She knew language, knew them old stories. Had to say *deadly* every second sentence. Postcard blackfella.

At first I liked it. But lately she was becoming too much for me.

There are these sounds in the distance, like hooting, but it's not owls. I sit up. It's a horribly low sound. I look outside, but all I see are trees and mud and mangroves.

I pad down the hallway in my nighttime thongs. The living room is dark, but they're sitting on the couch. They're sitting too close. I go back to bed.

The droning stops. I can hear some thumping around, still, and am about to sing out "Quiet, you Brolgas" when I realize the laughter in the living room has been replaced by weighted sighs. The door to the next room opens, and the bed springs pop. I can tell they're trying to be quiet, which is worse. My chest feels tight. I pull the sheets over my head.

When I rise at eleven, the door beside mine is still shut. I put the kettle on and butter some bread and sit with my modest meal at the small, round, green table in the center of the room. School results tomorrow. Let the envelope sit in my mailbox for a week. I started well. Gone to every class and that, read the textbook in advance, even. Jaye slipped me some of her work, but she let me stay rent-free. It was fine, for a while. At what point did I start doing more of Jaye's than mine?

She's left the keys on top of the television. Longboard in hand, I cross the road and walk down the path to the beach. I drag the lead through the sand, looking for an entry point between the bucketloads of kids. For a long time I stand between surfing and not surfing.

For lunch I walk along the beach to the surf club and order some chips.

"You're not from here, hey?" the lady says.

"Yeah, how'd you know?"

The lady points to my Brisbane Broncos shirt. "First time in W.A.?"

"Yeah."

"Enjoying it?"

"Yeah."

"There's this band on here tonight. We're expecting a crowd."

"Oh, yeah—Milla Breed. My friend told me."

"This is her last show. She's going to the States."

"Good one," I say.

Sigrid is in the living room when I get back to the house, reading one of Jaye's poetry books.

"Good morning," she says.

"Hi," I say. "Where's Jaye?"

"Still in bed."

"Okay." I put the keys back. "Last night, did you hear any noises—droning noises?"

"Not at all," Sigrid says, amused.

"Right," I say.

"You and Jaye are not…"

I quickly shake my head.

"Good," she says, and smiles.

"We still going to that gig tonight?"

"Es, I'm trying to sleep, eh."

"It's four-thirty."

"You don't need to tell me the time. Hey, Sig's hungry. Can you get us a feed at the surf club? Something salty?"

At eight, the other door closed again, I pull on some jeans and the only closed-in pair of shoes I own. Flatten my hair.

When I get to the pub it looks like half the town's here, fishies and tradies. Everywhere we've been it's like a whole generation is missing. Haven't seen anyone my age since Perth, except the tourists. This last week every tourie and their dog wanted a picture with Jaye. Some wanted more than a picture. I'm always the one stuck holding the camera.

Mum used to tell me and my sisters when we were younger that being Murri wasn't a skin thing. Next to Jaye, though, that was all anyone noticed.

I think of Sigrid. Should've known.

The lady from lunchtime is at the door. I give her a fiver to get in and go to the bar to grab a drink. Milla Breed's all long black hair and long white limbs crashing on the stage. Her drummer can't keep up with her. I move a little closer when she starts a new song, trying to catch a lyric, but the words are in and out so fast you can't grab 'em. They're more utterance than words. Reminds me of the droning from last night.

She kneels, hands out to the crowd, then gets up, hands back on her guitar. She's wearing engineer boots, a denim skirt, and a black shirt. Sleeves cut off like Jaye's. Jaye likes all the grunge bands, especially the Aussie ones. She plays Breed's stuff all the time, except her third LP, which she reckons is womba. I usually stick to golden oldies, the Beatles and the Stones; Mum reckons I'm the only one she knows who likes both. But Jaye's right on this one. This bird is good at what she does.

"Hiya, Exmouth, how you doing?" she drawls.

"Show us your titties!" the big bloke in front of me screams, and I think she does but I can't see because my view is momentarily blocked.

"Get lost, dyke," one of his mates says to me when I press forward, and I tumble back onto some bird's toe and scurry to find another place to stand.

The crowd sparks as Breed plays her radio hit as a closer. She sings it differently, addressing the room between verses. Then she slows down and flicks her hair up, her gaze on mine, the blue-green of her eyes like a globe, and even though she must be forty-five, easy, I can't help but lower my own look. Her breasts prominent in the muscle shirt. I don't need to think about what Jaye would say, because I'm thinking it. Too deadly.

She waves to the crowd and floats back behind the wall. I buy a record at the bar and wait awhile to see if she's coming out again, but they've got another band up, some father-and-son act, and they're playing Cold Chisel covers and all the blokes are mumbling along as if they've forgotten about her.

As I'm walking back up to the driveway a white taxi swings in front of me. Sigrid's standing there, her hair orange in the light.

"Where you going?" I call.

"Home," she says.

I walk up closer.

"Sigrid?"

"Yeah?"

"I'm not from Spain. I'm Aboriginal."

"I know," she says. "Jaye told me."

I nod and watch her put her bags into the boot.

She turns back. "You don't look it. But you probably think I don't look German, either."

I walk inside and switch the light on. No sign of Jaye. I sit on the couch and try the remote, but the TV doesn't switch on. There's a stack of papers beside the poetry chapbooks, and I flick through a couple of *Koori Mails*. It's a while before I realize I'm waiting for her. There are a few things I want to say, and I think I will say them.

The house is still. I go through the next stack. There is Breed, on the contents page. I flick to the double-spread interview.

My stomach rises with every word. She's talking about her childhood, her family. Blue eyes on the page. By the end of it I'm so worked up I stand and think about going back to the bar. She might still be there.

Car would be faster. I open the door and walk out to it. Start the beast and drop down the driveway. In my mind I'm walking up to Breed and she looks at me and doesn't say a word, just grabs a bottle off a chair by the throat and sucks it, looking at me still. She tells me that I'll do, pulls me to her small frame, and pushes my jersey up over my head.

I stay at the foot of the road, in the driveway. I breathe heavily.

Still no sign of Jaye inside, but there is the drone again. I open the screen door and the sounds feel louder. Jaye's fluoro singlet is out there in the dark; she's in the yard with garden clippers and hasn't made a dent in the overgrowth.

"What are you doing," I say, "in the dark?"

She turns to look at me. I take a torch off the table and walk down to her. She looks at my hands and I realize I'm still carrying the paper with the interview.

"Didn't know Breed was a Koori," I say.

Jaye says nothing.

"What's up?"

"The fuck have you been?"

"What? I was at the gig; I tried to get you up for it, but—"

"I told you yonks ago I didn't want to go. The chick's sold out, eh. Going to the U.S. to be in a porno. Thought you'd left me, too, sista."

"Sigrid?" I ask pointedly.

"Sig? She's just a chick, you know. You're my best mate. I thought that was the whole deal of coming here. I was going to show you where I grew up, all them old spots, introduce you to my mob…"

"You're the one who stayed in her room all day." It's hard to believe her when she says she wants me around. I feel pretty replaceable.

Jaye's head stays down.

I sigh in defeat and put my arm around her shoulders, sweaty and acidic. She stares out into the yard.

"Why'd Sigrid go?" I ask.

"Think it was you."

"I thought it might have been those noises that scared her off. I reckon this place has ghosts."

"What, that?" Jaye's laugh mimics the drones. "It's just dingos, eh."

"We'll start tomorrow," I say. "Nice and early. Exploring."

Jaye grunts. She looks at me. "How was it, anyway?"

I'm not sure how to answer. "Not the same," I say.

At that moment the ringtail runs along the railing.

THE NEW, ABRIDGED DICTIONARY
OF ACCEPTED IDEAS
by EDWIN ROZIC AND ALEKSANDAR HEMON

(nonfiction from Issue 3)

A CENTURY OR so after Flaubert's "Dictionary of Accepted Ideas," moral and cultural relativism is rampant in the West. In this country, we have completely lost moral and intellectual control under the deluge of unacceptable ideas—anyone can say whatever she or he wants any time he or she wants to anyone she or he thinks wants to listen to him or her. We need to go back to what makes us American and find some common ground of ideas. It is time to end disagreements and begin agreements. What we offer here are the first steps toward cleansing the American mind. What we offer here is good.

America—Love it or leave it.

Arabs, The—Inscrutable. Skilled liars known for their rugs. Swarthy terrorists.

Authority—Question authority, but only in general and unless otherwise suggested.

Beggars—Call them The Homeless and don't give them money.

Believe—You have to believe in something. Things to believe in: yourself; the greatness of your country and its people; change; your own goodness; God.

Books—The great ones are tedious and irrelevant, and much too long. Never have time to read them.

Children—Human puppies. Feed them, protect them, watch Disney movies with them, prevent masturbating.

Commercials—Provide important information. Help you make an individual choice and distinguish yourself from other mindless consumers. The ones for beer are always real funny.

Constitution, The—Instant classic. The best constitution in the world—a conclusion unanimously reached after excessive studies of world constitutions, including those of Luxembourg, Sweden, Nepal, Uruguay, San Marino, Mozambique, Nepal, etc.

Creativity—Ability to deal with challenges of life and the workplace by creating new approaches. The poor are not creative, for if they were creative, they would create a way out of poverty.

Cucumber 97 percent water.

Death—Negative thinking.

Drugs—Broaden college mind. Destroy the inner city.

Earth—Always "Mother." Save it for the children.

English Language—Unspeakably intricate and hard to learn, unlike Spanish, Swahili, or Urdu, which you can figure out in a month or so.

Ethics—Part of lexical grouping. Occurs exclusively with "work" or "business."

Equality—All men are created equal, although some choose self-indulgent poverty.

Everyday Life—What happens to you every day. More important and real than that other (Every-Other-Day) life.

Facts—What reasonable thinking is based on. Some people refuse to face the facts. A fact: 99.9999 percent of the human body consists of empty space.

Free Lunch—There is no such thing as free lunch.

French, The—Impressionists. Make foreign movies. Promiscuous, particularly the women.

Gentrification—Thunder against. Point out how different things were last year when you moved to the neighborhood.

Hollywood—Capital of American immorality. Crucible of liberalism, greed, violence, and smut. Manufacturing center of instant classics.

Homosexuals—Ravenous perverts hated by God who, when befriended, help to exhibit the tolerance and sophistication of the befriender.

Human—We're all human.

Human Rights—Invented by the USA. Human rights are routinely abused in Cuba, Iraq, Iran, and other countries with whom the USA has poor trade relations.

Ideology—The rigid doctrine behind totalitarian rule. It is completely absent from the nimble-minded judgments of freedom-loving Americans.

Individualism—Praise the spirit of American individualism. Mickey Rourke is an individual.

Inner City, The—Cultureless place where whites are immediately killed.

Jews, The—The source for Jewish humor. Always stick together.

Koran—A book that explains how to blow things up.

Latin America—Not really America. Thanks to our commitment to democracy, it is now safe for Americans to imbibe multicultural cocktails on adventure vacations.

Laughter—Always uproarious except when derisive. When combined with tears, represents the limits of human emotion.

Leaders—Strong ones are the best. They make tough decisions. Everybody, dogs or people, has to have a leader.

Love—Must be directed toward one's self, because before you can love others, you must love yourself. If one loves one's self enough, one might not even need others and this makes one independent, which makes one feel good. Everyone, regardless of how dull, dumb, or evil, should love one's self.

Mountains—Where the environment is.

Negative Thinking—Responsible for everything from the demise of family values and declining productivity in the workplace to clinical depression and AIDS.

Newspapers—Necessary for job search and puppy training. The source for coupons and baseball statistics. Recyclable. Don't read, it will depress you.

Normal—The ultimate justification. As adjective, it is used to describe the appearance of mass murderers and presidential candidates. A town in the heart of Illinois.

Opera—More cultural than the theater. Always cry when attending.

Philosophy (Eastern)—Always sets you apart. Involves the inner self.

Philosophy (Western)—Tedious and turgid. Exclaim "*Everyone* is a philosopher!"

Politics—Never discuss. As in "Never discuss politics or religion." Discussing politics at a Thanksgiving dinner always fucks it up.

Positive Thinking—Better than negative thinking.

Real, The—A tourist destination. As in "I want to see the *real* Mexico."

Realism—What every real artist strives for. Americans invented realism. Good realism is always realistic.

Science—Murky activity of shadowy scientists and lab technicians. Provides evidence for groundbreaking scientific claims. An example: There is good estrogen, and there is bad estrogen.

Single—Looking for a gorgeous mate who likes challenging food, *The New Yorker*, a good sip of wine, cuddling by the fireplace, five o'clock news, our fingers intermingling on the Ferris wheel, walloping. A voluptuous soul is waiting for you to set out on the journey of self-discovery. I'll love you like the baseball loves the bat.

Slavery—Well, it was cruel and inhuman, but I had nothing to do with it and it helped the economy.

Tattoo—Hard to take off.

Travel　Express a desire to want to. Not important where. Broadens your mind. If traveling, always scorn the tourists.

Truth—When shopping, bring a friend, the truth helps.

Watermelon—98 percent water.

Work—When preceded by "hard," represents the supreme virtue. What made America great.

Yawning—Do not bother to put your hand over your mouth when yawning—there is no reason to be ashamed of your tonsils.

Yourself—You must be yourself. It is illegal to be someone else.

CONTRIBUTORS

CHRIS ADRIAN is the author of three novels including *The Children's Hospital*, which was published by McSweeney's in 2006, and a collection of short stories, *A Better Angel*. He lives in New York, where he works as a pediatric oncologist.

DANIEL ALARCÓN is a novelist, journalist, and radio producer. His novel *At Night We Walk in Circles* was published in October 2013.

JONATHAN AMES is the author of eight books, including *Wake Up, Sir!* and *The Extra Man*. He is the editor of the anthology *Sexual Metamorphosis* and is the creator of the television show *Bored to Death*. His most recent publication, the novella "You Were Never Really Here," is available as an e-book.

NICHOLSON BAKER is the author of nine novels and four works of nonfiction, including *Double Fold*, which won a National Book Critics Circle Award, and *House of Holes*, a New York Times Notable Book of the Year. His work has appeared in *The New Yorker*, *Harper's*, and the *New York Review of Books*. He lives in Maine with his family.

ARTHUR BRADFORD is the author of *Dogwalker* and *Benny's Brigade*. An O. Henry Award winner, his stories have appeared in *Esquire*, *Zoetrope*, *McSweeney's*, and *One Story*. He also the creator of the documentary series *How's Your News?* (HBO, PBS, and MTV) and most recently he directed the Emmy-nominated documentary *Six Days to Air*, about the making of South Park. He lives in Portland, Oregon, where he works with adjudicated youth.

BREYTEN BREYTENBACH was born in South Africa in the borderland between the southwestern fruit-growing region and the interior desert. He spent the first half of his life in Paradise, going to the University of Cape Town to study fine arts and literature, dropping out, leaving for Europe, bumming from boat to factory to the dark floors of artists' studios, and eventually settling in Paris where he met and married Golden Lotus. He became involved in expressions of political activism, and this led him to spend the second half of his life imprisoned in No Man's Land. Upon release he returned to the West. He has since been spending the third half of his life writing and painting and hustling between Paris, Catalonia, Dakar, Rainbow Land, and lately New York.

KEVIN BROCKMEIER is the author of seven books, including the novels *The Illumination*, *The Brief History of the Dead*, and *The Truth About Celia*; his eighth book is forthcoming in 2014. His work has been translated into seventeen languages. He lives in Little Rock, Arkansas, where he was raised.

DAN CHAON is the acclaimed author of *Among the Missing*, which was a finalist for the National Book Award, and *You Remind Me of Me*. Chaon's fiction has appeared in many journals and anthologies, including *The Best American Short Stories*, *Pushcart Prize*, and *The O. Henry Prize Stories*. He has been a finalist for the National Magazine Award in Fiction, and he was the recipient of the 2006 Academy Award in Literature from the American Academy of Arts and Letters. Chaon lives in Cleveland, Ohio, and teaches at Oberlin College, where he is the Pauline M. Delaney Professor of Creative Writing.

DANIEL G. CLOWES is a celebrated graphic novelist (*Ghost World*, *Wilson*, *David Boring*), Academy

Award–nominated screenwriter, and frequent cover artist for the *New Yorker*. He lives in Oakland, California with his wife Erika and son Charles, and their beagle Ella. A major retrospective of his work debuted at the Oakland Museum of California in 2012 and will continue on in an expanded version to the Museum of Contemporary Art in Chicago in 2013.

LYDIA DAVIS is the author, most recently, of *The Collected Stories of Lydia Davis* and the chapbook *The Cows*.

STEVE DELAHOYDE lives in Chicago, where he owns and operates the cleverly named film production company Delahoyde Projects.

RODDY DOYLE is the author of many books, including *The Commitments* and *Paddy Clarke Ha Ha Ha*. His latest novel, *The Guts*, will be published in the USA in January 2014. He lives and works in Dublin, Ireland.

JENNIFER EGAN is the author of *A Visit From the Goon Squad*, *The Keep*, *Look at Me*, *The Invisible Circus*, and the story collection *Emerald City*. Her stories have been published in *The New Yorker*, *Harper's*, *GQ*, *Zoetrope*, and *Ploughshares*, and her nonfiction appears frequently in the *New York Times Magazine*. She lives with her husband and sons in Brooklyn.

AMY FUSSELMAN is the author of *8* and *The Pharmacist's Mate*. As "Dr." Fusselman, she writes the "Family Practice" column for McSweeney's Internet Tendency. She is the editor in chief at *Ohio Edit*. Her forthcoming book is called *Savage Park*.

ANDREW SEAN GREER is the author of five works of fiction, most recently *The Impossible Lives of Greta Wells*, *The Story of a Marriage*, and *The Confessions of Max Tivoli*. He lives in San Francisco with his husband and Olive, a pug.

JENNIFER MICHAEL HECHT is the author of seven books of history, philosophy, and poetry, including the bestseller *Doubt: A History*. Her most recent works are *Who Said*, a poetry book, and *Stay: A History of Suicide and the Philosophies Against It*. Hecht has written for the *New York Times*, the *Washington Post*, the *Boston Globe*, and the *New Yorker*.

JULIE HECHT is the author of the story collections *Do the Windows Open?* and *Happy Trails to You*. She is also the author of the novel *The Unprofessionals* and *Was This Man a Genius?: Talks with Andy Kaufman*. She is the recipient of a Guggenheim Fellowship. A chapter from her next book, *May I Touch Your Hair?*, was published in the July 2013 issue of *Harper's*.

ALEKSANDAR HEMON is the author of *The Lazarus Project*, which was a finalist for the National Book Award and the National Book Critics Circle Award, and three collections of short stories.

SHEILA HETI is the author of five books, including the story collection *The Middle Stories*, published by McSweeney's, and the novel *How Should a Person Be?* She works as Interviews Editor at the *Believer*.

Before he went on television, JOHN HODGMAN was a simple writer, humorist, expert, and Former Professional Literary Agent living in New York City. In this capacity, he has served as the humor editor for the *New York Times Magazine*, frequent contributor to *This American Life*, advice columnist for *McSweeney's*, comic book reviewer for the *New York Times Book Review*, and a freelance journalist specializing in food, culture, non-wine alcohol, *Battlestar Galactica*, and most other subjects.

A.M. HOMES is the author of *May We Be Forgiven*, winner of the Women's Prize for Fiction, as well as of the memoir *The Mistress's Daughter* and the novels *This Book Will Change Your Life*, *Music for Torching*, *The End of Alice*, *In a Country of Mothers*, and *Jack*. Her books have been translated into twenty-two languages.

LAIRD HUNT is the author of five novels, including, most recently, *Kind One*, which was a finalist for a 2013 Pen/Faulkner award in fiction as well as the winner of the Anisfield-Wolf Book Award for fiction. He teaches at the University of Denver and edits the *Denver Quarterly*.

BEN JAHN's work has appeared in *ZYZZYVA*, *Fence*, *PANK*, *Five Chapters*, and the *California Prose Directory*. He received a 2010 NEA grant for fiction, and his story, "Reborn," won an NPR Three Minute Fiction contest. He lives in Richmond, California, with his girlfriend and her two kids.

ELLIE KEMPER is a writer and performer who divides her time among New York, Los Angeles, and the white sand beaches of Bora Bora.

JONATHAN LETHEM is the author of *Dissident Gardens* and eight other novels. He lives in Los Angeles and Maine.

ADAM LEVIN is the author of the novel *The Instructions* and the story collection *Hot Pink*. A winner of the New York Public Library Young Lions Fiction Award and the inaugural Indie Booksellers Choice Award, Levin lives in Chicago, where he teaches creative writing at the School of the Art Institute.

SAM LIPSYTE is the author of three novels and two short-story collections. He lives in New York City and teaches at Columbia University's School of the Arts.

CLANCY MARTIN is the author of a novel, *How to Sell*, and the forthcoming *Love, Lies and Marriage*. A Guggenheim Fellow, he is a contributing editor at *Harper's*. The story included here (also called "How to Sell") was a finalist for the National Magazine Award.

MARY MILLER Mary Miller is the author of a story collection, *Big World*, and a novel, *The Last Days of California*.

LYDIA MILLET is the author of eleven books of fiction, most recently the novel *Magnificence* (2012), a finalist for the National Book Critics' Circle and Los Angeles Times book awards. Previous novels included *My Happy Life*, which won the PEN-USA award for fiction, and *Oh Pure and Radiant Heart*, about the physicists of the Manhattan Project. Millet has also written two books for young readers, published in 2011 and 2012. She works as a staff writer and editor at the nonprofit Center for Biological Diversity, which advocates for the protection of endangered species and curbing of climate change, and lives with her children in the desert outside Tucson, Arizona.

STEVEN MILLHAUSER is the author of twelve works of fiction, including *Edwin Mullhouse: The Life and Death of an American Writer (1943-1954)*. His most recent book is *We Others: New and Selected Stories*.

JOHN MOE is the host of the public radio program *Wits* and author of the Pop Song Correspondences column on *Timothy McSweeney's Internet Tendency*. He writes, watches TV, fathers children, and husbands a wife.

KEVIN MOFFETT is the author of *Permanent Visitors* and *Further Interpretations of Real-Life Events*. *The Silent History*, a multipart narrative he wrote with Matt

Derby and Eli Horowitz, was released as an app for mobile devices in 2012 and will be published in spring 2014 by FSG.

RICK MOODY is the author of five novels (including, most recently, *The Four Fingers of Death*), three collections of stories, a memoir, and a collection of essays on listening called *On Celestial Music*. He also sings and plays in The Wingdale Community Singers, whose most recent album is *Night, Sleep, Death*.

ELLEN VAN NEERVEN-CURRIE was born in Brisbane in 1990 and is of Mununjali and Dutch descent. She is currently working on her first novel.

TOM O'DONNELL has written for *McSweeney's Internet Tendency* and the show *TripTank* on Comedy Central. His YA novel *Space Rocks!* will be published by Penguin in February of 2014.

PETER ORNER is the author of two novels, *Love and Shame and Love* and *The Second Coming of Mavala Shikongo*, and two collections, *Esther Stories* and *Last Car Over the Sagamore Bridge*, as well as the editor of two oral histories for Voice of Witness, *Underground America* and *Hope Deferred*.

GUNNHILD ØYEHAUG, born 1975 in Ørsta, Norway, lives in Bergen. She made her debut in 1998 with a collection of poetry (*Slave of the Blueberry*), and has since published a collection of short stories (*Knots*, 2004), a collection of essays (*Chair and Ecstacy*, 2006), and a novel (*Wait, Blink*, 2008). She has worked as a co-editor for the literary magazine *Kraftsentrum and Vagant*, and currently teaches creative writing at Skrivekunstakademiet in Hordaland.

TODD PRUZAN is editorial director at Ogilvy & Mather, and the co-author, with Mrs. Favell Lee Mortimer (1802–78),

of *The Clumsiest People in Europe* (2005). He helped edit the first three issues of *McSweeney's* and the first stages of its Internet Tendency.

SIMON RICH's books have been published in twelve languages. His latest is called *The Last Girlfriend on Earth*.

EDWIN ROZIC lives in Chicago, where he teaches Russians not to drop their articles. He is currently working on a screenplay which he will happily read to anyone for $8.

JOE SACCO is a cartoonist living in Portland, Oregon. He is currently working on a book about Mesopotamia.

MIKE SACKS currently works on the editorial staff of *Vanity Fair* magazine. His sequel to *And Here's the Kicker* will be released June 2014.

GEORGE SAUNDERS is the author of seven books, including *CivilWarLand in Bad Decline*, *Pastoralia*, *In Persuasion Nation*, and, most recently, *Tenth of December*. He was selected as one of the "Time 100" Most Influential people in the world. A 2006 MacArthur Fellow and the 2013 winner of the PEN/Malamud Award for the short story, he teaches in the Creative Writing Program at Syracuse University.

JENNIE ERIN SMITH is a reporter and critic specializing in animals, exploration, and natural history. Her recent work has appeared in the *Times Literary Supplement*, *The Wall Street Journal*, and the *New Yorker*. Her nonfiction book about reptile smugglers, *Stolen Wold*, was selected by the *New Yorker* and the *Washington Post* as a best book of 2011.

ZADIE SMITH is the author of several novels; her latest is *NW*.

BILL TARLIN is training for Chicago's Poetry Pentathlon. His recent e-chapbook is titled *Unstressed*.

ADRIAN TOMINE is the author of *New York Drawings*, *Scenes from an Impending Marriage*, *Shortcomings*, *Scrapbook*, *Summer Blonde*, *Sleepwalk*, and *32 Stories*. He is the creator of the ongoing comic book series *Optic Nerve*, and is a regular contributor to *The New Yorker*. He lives in Brooklyn with his wife and daughter.

NYUOL LUETH TONG was born in South Sudan. His family was forced to flee their village, becoming refugees for a decade in northern Sudan and Egypt. He occasionally writes for South Sudanese news outlets, and travels frequently around the U.S. to speak about issues both global and local. Tong is the founder and executive director of SELFSudan, a nonprofit with the mission of helping South Sudanese villagers build schools. He is currently a Reginaldo Howard Memorial Scholar at Duke University.

WELLS TOWER is the author of *Everything Ravaged, Everything Burned*, a book of short fiction.

DEB OLIN UNFERTH is the author of the memoir *Revolution*, the novel *Vacation*, and the story collection *Minor Robberies*. She has received three Pushcart Prizes, a Creative Capital Grant for Innovative Literature, and was a finalist for the National Book Critics' Circle award.

SARAH VOWELL's most recent book is *Unfamiliar Fishes*.

DAVID FOSTER WALLACE wrote the acclaimed novels *Infinite Jest*, *The Broom of the System*, and *The Pale King*, and the story collections *Oblivion*, *Brief Interviews with Hideous Men*, and *Girl With Curious Hair*. His nonfiction includes the essay collections *Both Flesh and Not*, *Consider the Lobster,* and *A Supposedly Fun Thing I'll Never Do Again*, and the full-length work *Everything and More*.

JESS WALTER is the author of eight books, most recently the novel *Beautiful Ruins* and the story collection *We Live in Water*. He has been a finalist for the National Book Award and won the Edgar Allan Poe Award.

CHRIS WARE is a regular contributor to *The New Yorker*, and was the cartoonist chosen to inaugurate the *New York Times Magazine*'s "Funny Pages" section in late 2005. He is currently at work on a long-form graphic novel, *Rusty Brown*. His most recent book, *Building Stories,* was named one of the *New York Times'* "10 Best Books of 2012," and was awarded the Lynd Ward Prize for Graphic Novel of the Year. He lives in Oak Park, Illinois with his wife, Marnie, and their daughter, Clara.

COLLEEN WERTHMANN is a writer and performer living in New York City. She can be seen in the independent film *Make Pretend* and several episodes of *Law & Order*.

LAWRENCE WESCHLER was for twenty years a staff writer at *The New Yorker* and then for twelve the director of the New York Institute for the Humanities at NYU. His *McSweeney's* pieces were eventually assembled in his *Everything that Rises: A Book of Convergences*, which won the 2007 NBCC Award for Criticism. His most recent book is *Uncanny Valley: Adventures in the Narrative*.

SEAN WILSEY is the author of *Oh the Glory of It All*, a memoir, and a forthcoming second memoir called *I Am In Love*.

INDEX OF CONTRIBUTORS FROM
McSWEENEY'S QUARTERLY CONCERN
(ISSUES 1–45)

ACKNOWLEDGMENTS

Neither this book, nor the quarterly itself, would exist without the care and occasionally terrifically long hours of several generations of McSweeney's staff and supporters, both in-office and far-flung, particularly Eli Horowitz, Jordan Bass, Laura Howard, Brian McMullen, Andrew Leland, Adam Krefman, Dan McKinley, Dave Kneebone, Andi Winnette, Michelle Quint, Ethan Nosowsky, Chelsea Hogue, Sam Riley, Sunra Thompson, Clara Sankey, Chris Ying, Dominic Luxford, Jesse Nathan, Barb Bersche, Vendela Vida, Sean Wilsey, Gabe Hudson, Daniel Handler, Juliet Litman, Angela Petrella, Heidi Meredith, Russell Quinn, Caitlin Van Dusen, Oriana Leckert, Greg Larson, Chris Monks, Em-J Staples, Meagan Day, Darren Franich, Lauren Hall, Walter Green, Rachel Khong, Jordan Karnes, Isaac Fitzgerald, Alyson Sinclair, and Daniel Gumbiner.

We are deeply grateful to the authors, artists, and designers who have allowed us to publish their work, and we remain indebted to our vast and gentle corps of interns past and present, without whom our days would be longer and our hearts colder.